# A
# BEGGAR'S
# KINGDOM

By Paullina Simons

FICTION
*Tully*
*Red Leaves*
*Eleven Hours*
*The Girl in Times Square*
*Road to Paradise*
*A Song in the Daylight*
*Lone Star*

The Bronze Horseman Series
*The Bronze Horseman*
*Tatiana and Alexander*
*The Summer Garden*
*Children of Liberty*
*Bellagrand*

The End of Forever Saga
*The Tiger Catcher*
*A Beggar's Kingdom*

NONFICTION
*Six Days in Leningrad*

COOKBOOK
*Tatiana's Table*

CHILDREN'S BOOKS
*I Love My Baby Because . . .*
*Poppet Gets Two Big Brothers*

# A
# BEGGAR'S
# KINGDOM

*The End of Forever saga*

## PAULLINA SIMONS

WILLIAM MORROW
*An Imprint of* HarperCollins*Publishers*

A BEGGAR'S KINGDOM. Copyright © 2019 by Paullina Simons. All rights reserved. Printed in the United States of America. No part of this book may be used or reproduced in any manner whatsoever without written permission except in the case of brief quotations embodied in critical articles and reviews. For information, address HarperCollins Publishers, 195 Broadway, New York, NY 10007.

HarperCollins books may be purchased for educational, business, or sales promotional use. For information, please email the Special Markets Department at SPsales@harpercollins.com.

Originally published as *A Beggar's Kingdom* in Australia in 2019 by HarperCollins Publishers Australia PTY Limited.

FIRST U.S. EDITION

Library of Congress Cataloging-in-Publication Data has been applied for.

ISBN 978-0-06-209817-7

19 20 21 22 23  LSC  10 9 8 7 6 5 4 3 2 1

*To Kevin,*
*I can do all things through you who strengthens me.*

*"Guess I was kidding myself into believing that I had a choice in this thing, huh?"*

Johnny Blaze, aka Ghost Rider

# Real Artifacts from Imaginary Places

ASHTON STOOD, HIS BLOND HAIR SPIKING OUT OF HIS baseball cap, his arms crossed, his crystal eyes incredulous, listening to Josephine trying to sweet-talk Zakiyyah into going on Peter Pan's Flight. Julian, Josephine, Ashton, and Z were in Disneyland, the last two under protest.

"Z, what's not to love?" Josephine was saying. "You fly over London with Peter Pan aboard a magical pirate ship to Neverland. Come on, let's go—look, the line's getting longer."

"Is it pretend fly?" asked Zakiyyah.

"No," replied Ashton. "It's real fly. And real London. And a real pirate ship. And definitely real Neverland."

Zakiyyah rolled her eyes. She almost gave him the finger. "Is it fast? Is it spinny? Is it dark? I don't want to be dizzy. I don't want to be scared is what I'm saying, and I don't want to be jostled."

"Would you like to be someplace else?" Ashton said.

"No, I just want to have fun."

"And Peter Pan's magical flight over London doesn't qualify?" Ashton said, and sideways to Julian added, "What kind of *fun* are we supposed to have with someone like that? I can't believe Riley agreed to let me come with you three. I'm going to have to take her to Jamaica to make it up to her."

"You have a lot of making up to do all around, especially after the crap you pulled at lunch the other week," Julian said. "So shut up and take it."

"Story of my life," Ashton said.

"What kind of fun are we supposed to have with someone like that?" Zakiyyah said to Josephine. "His idea of fun is making fun of me."

"He's not making fun of you, Z. He's teasing you."

"That's not teasing!"

"Shh, yes, it is. You're driving everybody nuts," Josephine said, and then louder to the men, "You'll have to excuse her, Z is new to this. She's never been to Disneyland."

"What kind of a human being has never been to Disneyland?" Ashton whispered to Julian.

"That's not true!" Zakiyyah said. "I went once with my cousins."

"Sitting on a bench while the kids go on rides is not going to Disneyland, Z."

Zakiyyah tutted. "Is there maybe a slow train ride?"

"How about It's a Small World?" Ashton said, addressing Zakiyyah but facing Julian and widening his eyes into saucers. "It's a slow *boat* ride."

"That might be okay. As long as the boat is not in real water. Is it in real water?"

"No," Ashton said. "The boat is in fake water."

"Is that what you mean when you say he's teasing me?" Zakiyyah said to Josephine. "You sure it's not mocking me?"

"Positive, Z. It's a world of laughter, a world of tears. Let's go on It's a Small World."

After it got dark and the toddlers had left and the crowds died down a bit, the three of them convinced Zakiyyah to go on Space Mountain. She half-agreed but balked when she saw the four-man luge they were supposed to board. Josephine would sit in front of Julian, between his legs, and that meant that Zakiyyah would have to sit in front of Ashton, between his. "Can we try a different seating arrangement?" Z said.

"Like what?" Ashton kept his voice even.

"Like maybe the girls together and the boys together."

"Jules, honey, what do you think?" Ashton asked, pitching his voice two octaves higher. "Would you like to sit between my legs, pumpkin, or do you want me between yours?"

"Z, come on," Josephine said. "Don't make that face. Ashton's right. Get in. It's one ride. You'll love it. Just…"

"Instead of you sitting in front of me," Ashton said to Zakiyyah, as cordial as could be, "would you prefer I sit in front of you?"

"You want to sit between my open legs?" Zakiyyah's disbelieving tone was not even close to cordial.

"Just making suggestions, trying to be helpful."

"Aside from other issues, I won't be able to see anything," Zakiyyah said. "You're too tall. You'll be blocking my view the whole ride."

Ashton knocked into Julian as they were about to board. "Dude," he whispered, "you haven't told her Space Mountain is a black hole with nothing to see?"

"We haven't even told her it's a roller coaster," Julian said. "You want her to go on the ride, or don't you?"

"Do you really need me to answer that?"

They climbed in, Ashton and Julian first, then the girls in front of them. Zakiyyah tried to sit forward as much as possible, but the bench was narrow and short. Her hips fitted between Ashton's splayed legs.

"Can you open your legs any wider?" she said.

"Said the bishop to the barmaid," said Ashton.

"Josephine! Your friend's friend is making inappropriate remarks to me."

"Yes, they're called jokes," Ashton said.

"They're most certainly not jokes because jokes are funny. People laugh at jokes. Did you hear anyone laughing?"

Zakiyyah sat primly, holding her purse in her lap.

Ashton shook his head, sighed. "Um, why don't you put your bag down below, maybe hold on to the grip bars."

"I'm fine just the way I am, thank you," she said. "Don't move too close."

"Not to worry."

They were off.

Zakiyyah was thrown backwards—into Ashton's chest. Her hips locked inside Ashton's legs. The purse dropped into the footwell. Seizing the handlebars, she screamed for two minutes in the cavernous dome.

When it was over, Julian helped a shaky Zakiyyah out, Josephine already on the platform, jumping and clapping. "Z! How was it? Did you love it, Z?"

"Did I love being terrified? Why didn't you tell me it was a rollercoaster in pitch black?"

They had a ride photo made of the four of them: Zakiyyah's mouth gaping open, her eyes huge, the other three exhilarated and laughing. They gave it to her as a keepsake of her first time on Space Mountain, a real artifact from an imaginary place.

"Maybe next time we can try Peter Pan," Ashton said as they were leaving the park after the fireworks.

"Who says there's going to be a next time?" said Zakiyyah.

"Thank you for making this happen," Josephine whispered to Julian in the parking lot, wrapping herself around his arm. "I know it didn't seem like it, but she had fun. Though you know what didn't help? Your Ashton pretending to be a jester. You should tell him you don't have to try so hard when you look like a knight. Is he trying to be funny like you?"

"He's both a jester and a knight without any help from me, believe me," said Julian.

Josephine kissed him without breaking stride. "You get bonus points for today," she said. "Wait until we get home."

And other days, while she walked through Limbo past the violent heretics and rowed down the River Styx in *Paradise in the*

*Park*, Julian drove around L.A. looking for new places where she might fall in love with him, like Disneyland. New places where his hands could touch her body. They strolled down Beverly and shopped for some costume jewelry, they sat at the Montage and whispered in nostalgia for the old Hotel Bel Age that overlooked the hills. He raised a glass to her in the Viper Room where not long ago someone young and beautiful died. Someone young and beautiful always died in L.A. And when the wind blew in from Laurel Canyon, she lay in his bed and drowned in his love and wished for coral trees and red gums, while Julian wished for nothing because everything had come.

But that was then.

# Part One

# The Master of the Mint

*"Gold enough stirring; choice of men, choice of hair, choice of beards, choice of legs, choice of everything."*

Thomas Dekker, *The Humors of the Patient Man and the Longing Wife*

# 1

# Fighter's Club

ASHTON WAS AFFABLE BUT SKEPTICAL. "WHY DO WE NEED TO paint the apartment ourselves?"

"Because the work of one's hands is the beginning of virtue," Julian said, dipping the roller into the tray. "Don't just stand there. Get cracking."

"Who told you such nonsense?" Ashton continued to just stand there. "And you're not listening. I meant, painting seems like a permanent improvement. Why are we painting at all? There's no way, no how we're staying in London another year, right? That's just you being insane like always, or trying to save money on the lease, or...Jules? Tell the truth. Don't baby me. I'm a grown man. I can take it. We're not staying in London until the lease runs out in a year, right? That's not why you're painting?"

"Will you grab a roller? I'm almost done with my wall."

"Answer my question!"

"Grab a roller!"

"Oh, God. What did I get myself into?"

But Julian knew: Ashton might believe a year in London was too long, but Julian knew for certain it wasn't long enough.

Twelve months to move out of his old place on Hermit Street, and calm Mrs. Pallaver who cried when he left, even though he'd been a recluse tenant who had shunned her only child.

Twelve months to decorate their new bachelor digs in Notting Hill, to paint the walls a manly blue and the bathrooms a girly pink, just for fun.

Twelve months to return to work at Nextel as if he were born to it, to wake up every morning, put on a suit, take the tube, manage people, edit copy, hold meetings, make decisions and new friends. Twelve months to hang out with Ashton like it was the good old days, twelve months to keep him from drinking every night, from making time with every pretty girl, twelve months to grow his beard halfway down his chest, to fake-flirt sometimes, twelve months to learn how to smile like he was merry and his soul was new.

Twelve months to crack the books. Where was he headed to next? It had to be sometime and somewhere after 1603. Lots of epochs to cover, lots of countries, lots of history. No time to waste.

Twelve months to memorize thousands of causes for infectious diseases of the skin: scabies, syphilis, scarlet fever, impetigo. Pressure ulcers and venous insufficiencies. Spider angiomas and facial granulomas.

Carbuncles, too. Can't forget the carbuncles.

Twelve months to learn how to fence, to ride horses, ring bells, melt wax, preserve food in jars.

Twelve months to reread Shakespeare, Milton, Marlowe, Ben Johnson. In her next incarnation, Josephine could be an actress again; he must be ready for the possibility.

Twelve months to learn how not to die in a cave, twelve months to train to dive into cave waters.

Twelve months to learn how to jump.

Twelve months to make himself better for her.

It wasn't enough time.

∞

Every Wednesday Julian took the Overground to Hoxton, past the shanty village with the graffitied tents and cucumber supports to have lunch with Devi Prak, his cook and shaman, his healer and destroyer. Julian drank tiger water—made from real tigers—received acupuncture needles, sometimes fell into a deep sleep, sometimes forgot to return to work. Eventually he started taking Wednesday afternoons off. Now that Ashton was his boss, such things were no longer considered fireable offenses.

Ashton, unchangeable and eternally the same on every continent, lived as if he didn't miss L.A. at all. He made all new friends and was constantly out partying, hiking, celebrating, seeing shows and parades. He had to make time for Julian on his calendar, they had to plan in firm pen the evenings they would spend together. He flew back to L.A. once a month to visit his girlfriend, and Riley flew in once a month to spend the weekend in London. When she came, she brought fresh flowers and organic honey, marking their flat with her girl things and girl smells, leaving her moisturizers in their pink bathroom.

And one weekend a month, Ashton would vanish, and was gone, gone, gone, Julian knew not where. Julian asked once, and Ashton said, seeing a man about a horse. When Julian prodded, Ashton said, where are you on Wednesday afternoons? Seeing a man about a horse, right? And Julian said, no, I'm seeing an acupuncturist, a Vietnamese healer, "a very nice man, quiet, unassuming. You'd like him." Julian had nothing to be ashamed of. And it was almost the whole truth.

"Uh-huh," Ashton said. "Well, then I'm also seeing a healer."

There were so few things Ashton kept from him, Julian knew better than to ask again, and didn't.

He was plenty busy himself. He took riding lessons Saturday mornings, and spelunking Saturday afternoons. He joined a boxing gym by his old haunt near Finsbury Park and sparred on Thursday and Saturday nights. He hiked every other Sunday with a group of over-friendly and unbearably active Malaysians, beautiful people but depressingly indefatigable.

He trained his body through deprivation by fasting for days, by going without anything but water. Riley would be proud of him and was, when Julian told her of his ordeals. He continued to explore London on foot, reading every plaque, absorbing every word. He didn't know if he'd be returning to London on his next Orphean adventure, but he wanted to control what he could. After work, when Ashton went out drinking, Julian would wander home, six miles from Nextel to Notting Hill, mouthing to himself the historical tidbits he found along the way, an insane vagrant in a sharp suit. In September he entered one of the London Triathlon events in the Docklands. One-mile swim, thirty-mile bike ride, six-mile run. He came in seventh. An astonished Ashton and Riley cheered for him at the finish line.

"Who *are* you?" Ashton said.

"Ashton Bennett, do not discourage him!" Riley handed Julian a towel and a water bottle.

"How is asking a simple question discouragement?"

"He's improving himself, what are you doing? That was amazing, Jules."

"Thanks, Riles."

"Maybe next year you can run the London Marathon. Wouldn't that be something?"

"Yeah, maybe." Julian stayed noncommittal. He didn't plan on being here next year. The only action was in the here and now. There was no action in the future; therefore there was no future. Devi taught him that. Devi taught him a lot. The future was all just possibility. *Maybe* was the appropriate response, the only response. Maybe.

Then again, maybe not.

"But what exactly *are* you doing?" Ashton asked. "I'm not judging. But it seems so eclectic and odd. A triathlon, fencing, boxing, spelunking. Reading history books, Shakespeare. Horseback riding."

"My resolve is not to seem the best," Julian said, "but to be the best."

"Why don't you begin being the best by shaving that nest off your face?"

"Ashton! *That's* not judging?"

"It's fine, Riles," Julian said. "He's just jealous because he's barely started shaving."

She came to Julian during the new moon, her loving face, her waving hands.

In astronomy, the new moon is the one brief moment during the month when the moon and the sun have the same ecliptical longitude. Devi was right: everything returned to the meridian, the invisible mythical line measuring time and distance. When the moon and the stars were aligned, Josephine walked toward him smiling, and sometimes Julian would catch himself smiling back. He knew she was waiting for him. He couldn't pass the time fast enough until he saw her again.

To be on the meridian was life.

The rest was waiting.

∞

A reluctant Julian was dragged back to California by Ashton to spend the holidays with his family in Simi Valley. In protest, he went as he was, heavily bearded and tightly ponytailed like an anointed priest.

Before he left London, Zakiyyah called to ask him about Josephine's crystal necklace. Josephine's mother, Ava, kept calling her about it, Z said. Could he bring it with him to L.A.? Julian lied and told her he lost it. For some reason she sounded super-skeptical when she said, are you *sure* you lost it? It's not in some obvious place—like on your nightstand or something?

It was on his nightstand.

"Please, Julian. It belonged to her family."

And now it belongs to me.

"I don't know what to tell you," Julian said.

"Who was that—Z?" Ashton said, overhearing.

"Yes, still bugging me about the stupid crystal."

"The one on your nightstand?"

"Yes, Ashton. The one on my nightstand."

Over Christmas break in Simi Valley, his parents, brothers, their wives and girlfriends, his nieces and nephews, and Riley all wanted to know when the boys would be moving back home. Not wanting to hurt his mother's feelings or get her hopes up, Julian deflected. That was him: always dampening expectations.

He cited ethics: they couldn't break their lease. He cited family: Ashton's father, after some health problems, had finally retired from the news service, turning over most of the daily operations to his son. He cited friendship: someone had to help Ashton be in charge. Ashton's livelihood once again depended on Julian.

"Someone has to be Ashton's wingman," is what he told his mother.

"Are you sure you're *my* wingman, Jules?" But Ashton backed Julian up. It was true, they weren't ready to leave England yet. "I can't navigate London without Jules," Ashton said. "Your son is insane, Mrs. C. Riley will tell you. He's like an autistic savant. His psychotic knowledge of London is both random and shockingly specific. He has no idea what the exhibits at the Tate look like, but he knows precisely when it opens and closes. He knows the hours and locations of nearly every establishment in central London. He knows where all the pubs are and all the churches, and what stores are next to each other. Though he's never been on a double-decker, he can tell you the numbers of every bus route. He can tell you what West End theatre is playing what show. He knows which comedians are doing standup. He knows where the gentleman's clubs are—though he swears, Mrs. C, that he has not been inside, and from the monastic growth on his face, I'm inclined to believe him. He can't tell you what the best vanilla shake in London tastes like, but he sure can tell you where you need to stand in line to get one—Clapham apparently."

"Explain yourself, Jules," Tristan said.

"Because he's still walking everywhere, isn't he?" Julian's mother said, shaking her head, as if suddenly understanding something she didn't want to about her fourth-born son (or as Julian liked to call it "fourth-favorite"). "Jules, I thought you were better?"

"I am, Mom."

"Then why are you still looking for that non-existent café? You're not still dreaming that awful dream, are you?"

Julian was spared an answer by his father. "Son, Ashton told us you're boxing again," Brandon Cruz said. "Please tell us it's not true." After nearly forty years in the California educational system, the senior Cruz had retired and now kept busy by trying to save Ashton's flagging store. "Your mother is very concerned. Why would you start that nonsense again after all these years?"

Once, to be in the ring was life. It's not nonsense, Dad, Julian wanted to say. It's not nonsense.

"Son, I hate to say it, but your father is right, you shouldn't be boxing, you're blind in one eye."

"I'm not blind, Mom. I'm legally blind. Big difference." He smiled a weary smile of a man being assailed.

"Still, though, why?"

"He's trying to improve himself, Mrs. Cruz," Riley chimed in with fond approval, patting Julian's back. "He's boosting his self-confidence, increasing his fitness levels—and muscle mass." She squeezed his tricep. "He is de-stressing and revitalizing himself. Staying healthy, you know? He's doing much better, honest."

"Oh, Ashton!" exclaimed Julian's mother, "it can't be easy, but you really *are* doing a wonderful job with him. Except for the hair, Riley is right, he looks much better. Thank you for watching over him." Julian's entire family bathed Ashton with affection and praise. Joanne sat him at her right hand and gifted him a tray of homemade cardamom shortbread! Ashton took the cookies, looking altruistic and put-upon.

Wordlessly, Julian watched them for a few minutes. "Tristan, bro, earlier you asked me for a London life hack?" he finally said. "I got one for you." He put down his beer and folded his hands. "If you want to display a head severed from the human body, you need to weatherproof it first. Otherwise after a few weeks, you'll have nothing but a bare skull. You want to preserve the fleshy facial features at the moment of death, the bulging eyes, the open sockets. So, what you do is, before the head starts to decompose, you partially boil it in a waxy resin called pitch—are you familiar with pitch, Trist? No? Well, it's basically rubber distilled from tar. Very effective. You waterproof the head by boiling it in tar, and then you can keep it outside on a spike to your heart's content—in all kinds of weather, even London weather. How long will it last, you ask? A good hundred years." Julian smirked. "Someone said of William Wallace's preserved head at the Great Stone Gate on London Bridge that in his actual life, he had never looked so good."

It was Ashton, his mouth full of shortbread, who broke the incredulous silence of the Cruz family at Christmas by throwing his arm around Julian, swallowing, and saying, "What Jules is *trying* to say is he's not quite ready to return to the fun and frolic of L.A. just yet."

"In London in the old days, they used to break the teeth of the bears in the baiting pits," Julian said in reply, moving out from under Ashton's arm. "They broke them to make it a more even fight when the dogs attacked the bear. They did it to prolong the fight, before the bear, even without the teeth, ripped the dogs apart."

"Settle down, Jules," said Riley, passing him her smart water. "Believe me, we got the message at the parboiled head."

"Man is more than his genes or his upbringing," Julian said, refusing the water and picking up his beer instead. "A man is a force of the living. But—he's also a servant of the dead. As such, he's an instrument of some powerful magic—since both life and death are mystical forces. The key," Julian said, "is to live in balance between the two, so as to increase your own force."

*Don't worry,* Riley whispered to a miserable-looking Joanne Cruz. *He just needs time.*

To be on the meridian, in the cave, on the river, was life.

The rest was just waiting.

∞

Finally the Ides of March and his birthday were upon him. And that meant that after a year of training and boxing and fencing, the vernal equinox was upon him.

"I wish I could bring some money with me," Julian said to Devi a few days before March 20.

"How is money going to help you?"

"If I'd had money in 1603, I would've asked her to marry me earlier. We could've left." It would've been different. "I'd just feel better if I had some options."

"Options." Devi shook his black-haired head. He was starting to get some gray in it. It was time. The man was over seventy. "Some men are never satisfied."

"Can you answer my question?"

"There's no easy way to do what you want."

"Is there a hard way?"

"No."

"Why can't I bring money with me?"

"A thousand reasons."

"Name two."

"You don't know where you're going," Devi said. "Are you going to bring every denomination of coin from every place in the world, from every century?"

Julian thought about it. "What about gold? Or diamonds?"

"You want to take *diamonds* with you." It wasn't a question.

"Something of value, yes."

"You can't. What I mean is—you literally can't," Devi said. "The diamond you talk about, where was it mined, Russia, South Africa? Was it worked on by human hands? Was it then picked up by these hands and shipped to where you could buy it? Was it bought and sold before you ever laid your paws on it, a dozen times, a hundred times? You think it's sparkly and new just for you? A thousand hearts were broken over your diamond. Bodies were killed, discarded, cuckolded, buried, unearthed. The blood of greed, envy, outrage, and love was spilled over your diamond. Where do you want to end up, Julian? With her, or not with her?"

∞

Having bought a sturdy Peak Design waterproof backpack and loaded it with every possible thing he could need that would fit, ultimately Julian decided not to bring it. Well, decided was a wrong word. He showed it to Devi, who told him he was an idiot.

"I like it very much," Devi said. "What's in it?"

"Water, batteries, flashlights—note the plural—a retractable walking pole, crampons, Cliff Bars, a first aid kit, a Mylar blanket, a Suunto unbreakable ultimate core watch, heavy-duty insulated waterproof gloves, three lighters, a Damascus steel blade, a parachute cord, carabiners, climbing hooks, and a headlamp."

"No shovel or fire extinguisher?"

"Not funny."

"What about glacier glasses?"

"Why would I need glacier glasses?"

"How do you know you're not headed into a glacier cave?" Devi paused. "Permafrost in bedrock. Ponded water that forms frozen waterfalls, ice columns, ice stalagmites." He paused again. "Sometimes the ceiling of the cave is a crystalline block filled with snow and rocks and dirt."

"You mean full of debris that freezes in the icy ceiling?"

"Yes," Devi said, his face a block of ice. "I mean full of things that freeze in opaque ice four hundred feet deep. Things you can see as you pass under them but can't get to." Devi blinked and shuddered as if coming out of a trance. "That reminds me, best bring an ice axe, too."

"You're hilarious."

"You haven't mentioned a toiletry kit, a journal, a camera, a neck warmer, and a fleece hat. I feel you're not prepared."

"I'm tired of your mocking nonsense."

"No, no, you're fine," Devi said. "Get going. When noon comes, and the blue shaft opens, just send in the backpack by itself to find her. Because there will be room for only one of you. But the bag's got everything, so it should go."

"Why can't I throw the backpack in and then jump after it?"

"I don't know why you can't. But as I recall from your story, last time you got stuck. What happens if the backpack gets stuck, and you can't get to it?"

"Why are you always such a downer? It's no to everything."

"I'm the only one in your life who said yes to you about the most important thing," Devi said, "and here you are whining that I haven't said yes to enough *other* things? No to the backpack, Julian. Yes to eternal life."

∞

"If I can't bring a backpack, can I bring a friend?" a defeated Julian asked. He would convince Ashton to go with him. He wasn't ready to part with his friend.

"I don't know. Does he love her?"

"No, but..." Julian mulled. "Maybe I can be like Nightcrawler. Anything that touches me goes with me."

"You don't impress me with your comic-book knowledge," Devi said. "I don't know who Nightcrawler is. What if there's time for only one of you to jump in? You get left behind in this world, and your friend's stuck in the Cave of Despair without you?"

"I'll go first, then."

"And abandon him trapped in a cave without you? Nice."

But isn't that what Julian was about to do, abandon Ashton, without a word, without a goodbye? Guilt pinched him inside, made his body twist. "Cave of Despair? I thought you said Q'an Doh meant Cave of Hope?"

"Despair and hope is almost the same word in your language and my language and any language," Devi said. "In French, hope is *l'espoir* and despair is *désespoir*. Literally means the loss of hope. In Italian hope is *di speranza*. And despair is *di disperazione*. In Vietnamese one is *hy vong* and the other is *tuyet vong*. With hope, without hope. It all depends on your inclination. Which way are you inclined today, Julian Cruz?"

Julian admitted that today, on the brink of another leap through time, despite the remorse over Ashton, he was inclined to hope. "In English, hope and despair are separate words."

Devi tasted his homemade kimchi, shrugged, and added to it some more sugar and vinegar. "The English borrowed the word despair from the French, who borrowed it from Latin, in which it means down from hope."

"What about the Russians? You have no idea about them, do you?"

"What do you mean?" Devi said calmly. "In Russian, despair is *otchayanyie*. And *chai* is another word for hope. All from the same source, Julian, despite your scorn."

Julian sat and watched Devi's back as the compact sturdy man continued to adjust the seasonings on his spicy cabbage. Julian had grown to love kimchi. "What does the name of the cave actually mean?"

"Q'an Doh," Devi replied, "means Red Faith."

∞

Julian wanted to bring a zip line—a cable line, two anchors, and a pulley—strong enough to hold a man.

Devi groaned for five minutes, head in hands, chanting *oms* and *lordhavemercies*, before he replied. "The anchor hook must be thrown over the precipice. Can you throw that far, and catch it on something that won't break apart when you put your two hundred pounds on it?"

"Calm down, I'm one seventy." He had gained thirty of his grief-lost pounds back.

"Okay, light heavyweight," Devi said. "Keep up the nonstop

eating before you grab that pulley. You won't beat the cave. It'll be a death slide."

"You don't know everything," Julian said irritably.

"I liked you better last year when you were a babe in the woods, desperate and ignorant. Now you're still desperate, but unfortunately you know just enough to kill yourself."

"Last year I was freezing and unprepared, thanks to you!"

"So bring the zip line if you're so smart," Devi said. "What are you asking me for? Bring a sleeping bag. An easy-to-set-up nylon tent. I'd also recommend a bowl and some cutlery. You said they didn't have forks in Elizabethan England. So BYOF— bring your own fork."

Silently, they appraised each other.

"Listen to me." Devi put down his cleaver and his cabbage. "I know what you're doing. In a way, it's admirable. But don't you understand that you must rediscover what you're made of when you go back in? The way you must discover her anew. You don't know who she is or where she'll be. You don't know if you still want her. You don't know if you believe. Nothing else will help you but the blind flight of faith before the moongate. If you make it across, you'll know you're ready. *That* is how you'll know you're a servant not just of the dead and the living, but also of yourself. Will a pole vault help you with that? Will a zip line? Will a contraption of carabiners and hooks and sliding cables bring you closer to what you must be, Julian Cruz?"

Julian's shoulders slumped. "You've been to the gym with me. You've seen me jump. No matter how fast I run and leap, I can't clear ten feet."

"And yet somehow," Devi said, "without knowing how depressingly limited you are, you still managed to fly."

The little man was so exasperating.

A pared-down Julian brought a headlamp, replacement batteries, replacement bulbs and three (count them, three) waterproof flashlights, all Industrial Light and Magic bright. He had a shoemaker braid the soft rawhide rope of his necklace tightly around the rolled-up red beret. Now her beret was a coiled leather collar at the back of his neck, under his ponytail. The crystal hung at his chest. Julian didn't want to worry about losing either of them again.

"Do you have any advice for me, wise man?" It was midnight, the day before the equinox.

"Did you say goodbye to your friend?"

Julian's body tightened before he spoke. "No. But we spent all Sunday together. We had a good day. Do you have his cell number?"

The cook shook his head. "You worry about all the wrong things, as always." Conflict wrestled on Devi's inscrutable face. "Count your days," he said.

"What does that mean?"

"Why do you always ask me to repeat the simplest things? Count your days, Julian."

"Why?"

"You wanted advice? There it is. Take it. Or leave it."

"Why?"

"You're such a procrastinator. Go get some sleep."

Julian *was* procrastinating. He was remembering being alone in the cave.

"Go catch that tiger, Wart," Devi said, his voice full of gruff affection. "In the first part of your adventure, you had to find out if you could pull the sword out of the stone. You found out you could. In the second part, hopefully you'll meet your queen of light and dark—and also learn the meaning of your lifelong friendship with the Ill-Made Knight."

"What about my last act?"

"Ah, in the last act, you might discover what power you have and what power you don't. What a valuable lesson *that* would be. After doing what he thinks is impossible, man remembers his limitations."

"Who in their right mind would want that," Julian muttered. "I hope you're right, and Gertrude Stein is wrong."

"That wisecracking old Gertrude," said the cook. "All right, let's have it. What did she say?"

"There ain't no answer. There ain't going to be an answer. There never has been an answer. *That's* the answer."

"Is it too much to hope," Devi said, "that one day you'll learn to ask better questions? You haven't asked a decent one since the one you asked my mother." *What is the sign by which you recognize the Lord?*

"I'll learn to ask better questions," Julian said, "when you and your mother start giving me better answers." *A baby in a swaddling blanket indeed!*

# 2

# Oxygen for Julian

HE TRAVELLED THROUGH A DIFFERENT SHAFT, HE TRAVELLED through a different cave, he travelled to a different life.

Noon came to zero meridian at the Royal Observatory in Greenwich, England, the sun struck the crystal in his palm, the kaleidoscope flare exploded, the blue chasm opened for Julian once more. This time he didn't get stuck. He slid without resistance, plummeted through the sightless air, skydived. He could've brought the bigger backpack, Ashton, Devi, Sweeney, an airplane. It occurred to him that if he didn't stop falling, he'd crash to the ground. Before he had a chance to ponder this, he plunged into warm water.

It was like falling into terror.

His boots never touched bottom. He panic-paddled from the ebony depths to the surface and fumbled in his cargo pocket for the headlamp. When he switched it on, he felt better; when he slipped it over his forehead he felt better still. The rocky bank was only a foot away. He swam to it, grabbed a ridge, and pulled himself out. At first unsettled by the bathwater temperature—in a cave no less—now Julian was grateful. It could've been freezing, and then where would he be. How long did the *Titanic*'s men last in the northern Atlantic?

It was hard to call any footwear waterproof when everything on him was sopping wet, his Thermoprene suit, his boots, his jacket and pants, his two shirts. Wiping his face, he shined a flashlight around the cave. This was a whole new subterranean world than the one he had encountered the first time he went in, a year earlier. He was at the edge of a black cove at the bottom of a mountainous gorge. Hundreds of ragged feet of rock flared up around him. On two sides of the inlet, the vertical slope was unscalable limestone. But on his bank and the bank opposite, the angle was more gradual, and the walls, though rocky and uneven, looked climbable. Good thing Julian had brought crampons. He attached them to the bottom of his boots, careful not to cut himself on the razor-sharp spikes. The blades scraped against the rock as he took a few steps to adjust to walking on them. It was like balancing on Poppa W's razor wire.

Feeling heavy and cumbersome, Julian wrung out his jacket, shook himself off like a dog, and checked his equipment before climbing to find the moongate. Batteries, extra lights, her stone on his chest, the beret wrapped in rawhide at the back of his neck, his Suunto watch, an impressive wrist computer with a barometer, altimeter, and heart monitor. Proud of his new gadget, Julian switched on the Suunto to check the cave temperature and his GPS coordinates. How deep was he below sea level? What direction was he facing?

The unbreakable scientifically precise timekeeper showed him noon, the coordinates of the prime meridian, the direction as north. In other words, the exact measurements of the Transit Circle as the sun hit the quartz crystal. Well, that was £400 well spent.

On all fours, Julian crawled up the rough slope to the highest elevation in the cave floor where it hit the limestone wall. The walls were solid. Feeling for the moongate with his bare hands, he walked back and forth along the wall but found no opening. On this side at least, the chamber was hermetically sealed.

Julian knew there had to be a way out because otherwise there would be no river and no Josephine, and also because he could hear running water in the distance. He scaled back down to the swimming hole and shined one of his heavy-duty, high-powered flashlights up and down the cave walls. Finally he spotted it. Across the pool, up the slope in the far corner, as if concealed from casual view, the water trickled out from a perfectly round opening in the bedrock and dribbled down into the cove below.

The only way to get to the other side was to swim across. Julian felt some relief. It wasn't long-jumping over a canyon, it was just swimming, right? When he first fell in, he had swum to the wrong side, that was all. Shame, but now he would swim to the right side.

He hesitated before he dived. Was the pool a wormhole, a shortcut between two distant points in infinite time and space? He didn't know. He didn't think so. It didn't look far, maybe thirty, forty feet. *And* the water was warm. He was a good swimmer. He came in seventh in the London Triathlon. Riley had been so proud of him. Granted he didn't enter the top-level category, but still, he had to swim an entire mile, not a few measly feet. Full of confidence, Julian jumped in, like the starting gun had gone off. He swam methodically, pacing himself, without undue exertion. The headlamp illumined only a few feet of black water in front of him. He couldn't see the other bank. No matter. A minute or two at most and he'd be there. He was glad he had listened to Devi and brought a minimum in his backpack. Fifty pounds of extra weight would've been a burden.

Julian swam and swam and swam and swam. It felt longer than forty feet. He must have gotten confused, lost his orientation. It had looked so easy—swimming forward—but for some reason forward wasn't getting him to the other side, and his headlamp with its short beam was annoyingly little help.

He swam and swam and swam and swam. Above him the cliffs loomed, ominous and oppressive like stone Titans. How could he see those, much farther away, but not see the opposite bank of a medium-sized cave pool?

Julian began to tire, to feel oppressively heavy. And when he started to feel heavy, he panicked.

And when he panicked, he started to sink.

His boots, jacket, gloves, flashlights all felt like anchors strapped to his body. Yes, the water was warm, but so what? He was being sucked into a slow warm drain.

Was he just treading water or actually moving forward? He spun around but couldn't see where he had been, nor where he was going. He was in the middle of nothing and nowhere. He stopped swimming, held his breath, listened for the trickling stream on the rocks. He heard no sound except his anxious gasps.

He didn't know what to do.

There was no going back. The only way out was through it.

Julian resumed the front stroke, in slow motion. His body was weighted down, as if concrete blocks were tied to his feet. The body refused to cooperate with staying afloat. He tried to turn onto his back for a rest, but kept sinking. When he stopped flapping his arms, he sank. Even as he swam forward, he sank. It became nearly impossible to hold his head above water.

He flung away the waterlogged gloves, the extra lamps, the batteries, the carabiners, the hooks, his non-working £400 Suunto Ultimate watch. He threw off his jacket and unstrapped and kicked off his boots with the metal crampons. He unzipped and pulled off his cargo pants. He discarded everything but his headlamp and a thin Maglite that fit into a chest pouch in his wetsuit.

And still he sank. Fear was heavier than fifty pounds of gear.

His head slipped under water. He resurfaced, opened his mouth, tried to swim. The effort required to stay afloat became greater. His breath got shorter, the time under got longer. In panicked desperation, gulping for air, Julian lowered his chin to his chest and rammed forward.

His headlamp hit something solid and immovable. Rock! The lamp cracked, slipped off his head and vanished into the deep. He grabbed on to the edge of the rock and after a few moments of gasping, pulled himself out.

For a long time he lay in the darkness getting his breath back. Had the headlamp not been on his head to absorb the blow, he would've cracked his skull open. He must've been swimming pretty fast, despite his clear perceptions to the contrary. That was quite a jolt he had received. What an ugly cheat it was, not to be able to trust your own senses.

So—four sources of light were not enough. New boots, hooks, spikes, new jacket, new pants, not enough. Extra batteries, bulbs, gloves, all of it at the bottom of the bottomless cave. After all the preparation to offer his woman a new and improved man, Julian was right back on novice course, climbing a steep uneven terrain, barefoot and without his clothes, holding a small cheap flashlight between his chattering teeth.

∞

Past the moongate, the river was shallow and flowed slowly— and in the wrong direction! It flowed back toward the black hole cove. After a curve in the cave and a shallow whirlpool, it finally turned and flowed in the direction Julian was wading, filling the barrel-shaped passage to his knees. The cylindrical walls shimmered with hallucinations, with carved etchings. Julian no longer believed his eyes. It could be a Rorschach test. He saw what he wanted to see, not what was really there. But why would he want to see illusions of writhing beasts with open groaning, screaming mouths, why would he wish to see colliding live things loving each other, fucking each other, killing each other? In many cases all three.

Before long, trouble came. It came in the form of water that rose to his legs and then to his waist. The Thermoprene suit was wet inside, and the trapped moisture kept him warm, but the water that seeped in and trickled down his ribs and back also made him itch like a motherfucker. The cave remained troublingly warm, as did the water. Weren't caves supposed to be 54°F at all times? Maybe not magic caves. He should've brought an inflatable boat. He was so tired. There was no ledge or shelf for him to rest on, no dry ground. Endlessly, relentlessly, half-blind, Julian trudged hip-deep in water, avoiding the images that filled his defective vision, of gods and men and beasts intertwined.

He should've known better than to complain about cave drawings. As soon as they vanished, the water rose to his chest. He could no longer walk in it. That meant he could no longer carry the flashlight or even hold it in his mouth. In impenetrable darkness, he swam. Either the water level kept rising or the cave narrowed, because when Julian lifted his arm for the front stroke, he hit the roof of the cave. The space between the surface of the water and the ceiling—in other words the space in which he breathed—was no longer large enough to fit his head. He had eight inches, then six, then four.

He stopped swimming, turned on the flashlight, stuck it between his teeth, and put both palms on the ceiling to rest for a bit while he looked around. He lifted his mouth to the limestone and breathed through the slit of remaining air. He couldn't stay still for long because the channel began to fill up with black rushing water. Oh—now it was rushing. It swallowed him and pitched him forward before he had a chance to put away his one light. While Julian was flung about like a rubber duck, the flashlight slipped out of his hands and swirled into the void, and Julian once again was plunged into wet spinning darkness.

What did he learn in advanced spelunking that could help him now? The first thing he remembered was decidedly unhelpful.

*Never cave alone.*

Dennis, his unruffled instructor, could not have been more plain. The only reasons to be alone in a cave were injury and emergency.

As he tumbled through the gushing current, Julian came up with a third reason. Insanity.

Cave diving was the most advanced, specialized, dangerous of all caving activities. Without training, Dennis said, no human being had the knowledge to stay alive. Only months of rigorous preparation could help you. You had to learn to control five things on which your life depended. If those five things weren't built into your muscle memory, you would die.

Not could die.

Would die.

Julian recalled precisely two things.

Number one: *respiration*.

Number two: *emotion*.

The first one was impossible, since he was fully submerged in the current, and as for the second one, check. Emotion aplenty.

You have no training for open water, he kept hearing in his head. Stop. Think. Picture the reaper. See her face. Prevent your death. *Respiration. Emotion.*

What else?

His head bobbed up for a moment, he gasped for air, was pulled under, and then driven forward. But there was air above him! There was oxygen for Julian. Sounded like a song.

Respiration!

Emotion!

Calm yourself!

Think!

Another bob.

Another gasp.

Oxygen for Julian.

He must keep his mouth closed. If he swallowed water and his lungs filled up, he wouldn't be able to continue bobbing like a buoy. He would sink. Think! Breathe! Another bob. Another gasp. Oxygen for Julian.

Trouble was, when his mouth was closed, he couldn't breathe. How could he save her when he couldn't even save himself? Josephine. Mary.

Calm yourself. Think! Breathe.

Oxygen for Julian.

All he could feel was panic for his life.

Finally, Julian found something to grab on to, a churning plank. Pulling himself on top of it, he lay down on it lengthways, grabbed the short edge with both hands, put his head down, gurgled up a lungful of water, and was asleep in seconds. No terror was so strong that it could force his eyes open.

# 3

# Silver Cross

HE WAKES UP BECAUSE HE'S BURNING. HE CAN'T TELL WHAT'S wrong with him, only that it's so hot, he wants to crawl out of his skin to cool down. The plank he drifts on is hot, the water underneath him is hot, the air is hot. Not warm like cove water, but hot like near boiling. He falls sideways into the water, and the steaming plank, scorched as a summer deck, drifts down river.

Julian can finally stand, and even though his flashlight is gone, the cave isn't completely without light. He can see.

Why is it so blisteringly hot? His body itches intensely under the Thermoprene. He unzips the suit, pulls it halfway down, stands against the wall of the cave and like an animal rubs against the rock to relieve his back. He pulls the suit down to his knees and scratches his legs, his stomach. It's better, but not great. The more he scratches, the more it itches, his skin as if crawling with a thousand mosquitoes feasting on his body.

Now that he's out of the water, Julian remembers the other three things he learned about cave diving. *Posture. Propulsion.* And *buoyancy.* How the hell do you learn buoyancy, he thinks. You either float or you don't. I know this for a fact. Idiots.

Julian is so excited to be alive even though he is fucking itchy.

No way he can zip up the suit again. He tries. As soon as the foam fabric touches his body, he's in a frenzy. Both he and suit need to dry, but as he dries, he starts to sweat, and the salt in his sweat makes his itchy body burn. What a hot mess he is. He's got to get out, get to somewhere cooler. Where is he? Where did the river bring him?

Leaving the wetsuit dangling at his waist, Julian climbs up the slope, away from the river and toward the dim flickering light. He's burning the soles of his bare feet and the palms of his hands on the hot rocks. The light that illumines a sliver of the cave is somewhere above his head. He keeps climbing to it, as if up a spiral staircase carved into the rocks, up, up, up, and round and round.

There's an overhanging wooden ledge above him. *Wooden?* He pulls himself up and GI Joes through a narrow opening, crawling out into a tight, musty space with timber rafters. It looks like a secret closet under a dormer. It's half-height, but there's a *door* in front of him! The ambient flicker that led him here is streaming through a keyhole in that door. He hears muffled voices. He peeks through the keyhole.

He sees a small section of a shimmering room lit entirely by candles placed so close together it looks like a fire. How long did it take someone to make those, Julian thinks, knowing what a thankless and tedious task it is, and just as he thinks this—he leans on the door too hard. It swings open and he falls through.

As he tumbles out, he knocks over the small table, and the stacked candles fall in a melting waxy jumble onto the floor. The rug fringe catches fire. Someone in the room squeals.

"Careful! You'll burn the house down!"

Someone else squeals. "Well, don't just sit there. Put it out!"

Julian swats the rug with his bare hands and blows at the downed candles. With potential disaster averted, his eyes adjusting to the dim remaining light, he surveys the room, still on his knees.

Before he fell into the dormered space, his plans were grand. He was prepared. He's read, he's fenced, he's cave dived, he is a daredevil, he isn't scared.

But in this room, the plans change. Between two windows there's a bed, and on this bed sit two naked women intertwined, pressing their breasts against one another and eyeing him with lanquid curiosity. The burning fireplace is behind them. He can't see the women's faces, only the contours of their naked bodies. They're like iridescent drawings. But mostly they're women's naked bodies.

"Well, hello there," one girl says. "Where did *you* come from? Did you sneak in to spy on us? That costs extra, you know." The girl has a British accent, not posh—not that he expects posh here, wherever he is. "Look at him, he's got a beard, how delicious. Maybe we won't charge him?"

"Well, that would hardly be fair," whispers the other, also in a British accent, "we charge everyone else."

"Oh, don't be a ninny, let him sample the goods. We can charge him double next time, right, handsome? Come here," the girl croons. "Come here, precious." Two pairs of female arms reach out to him. "Don't be shy," the girl says, wiggling her fingers at him, motioning him forward. "Don't be afraid of us, we won't bite."

Julian gets up off the floor, stands straight. They appraise him, their smiles widening. "Well," one girl says, "maybe bite a little." All he can see in the semi-darkness is the whites of their teeth and the length of their brown hair. He is about to ask if he should light another candle—to see them better—but they grab his hands and pull him onto the bed, onto his back, crouching around him, interested and unafraid. They stroke his beard, pat his chest, tap his shoulders and arms, examine his necklace close to their faces, rub his stomach. "Look how warm you are, how damp you are. Why are you sweating? Are you hot?" They giggle. They pull at the wetsuit. To be helpful, Julian mutely shows them how to work the front zipper.

The nubile girls get distracted by the zipper of a commercially made suit. With some chagrin Julian notes that they're more fascinated by the zipper than they are by the naked man underneath it. They unzip him past his groin, and with delight zip him up to his throat. Instead of playing with Julian, they're playing with the zipper.

The suit is damp. His skin is damp. He had just been itchy and uncomfortable. He had just been tired and thirsty. Not anymore. He's less the sum of all other parts than he is of the awakened primal hungry thing. He takes in their curves and dark nipples, their swaying white breasts, their loose hair and limbs amber in the candlelight. One has straight long brown hair, one wavy thick slightly shorter brown hair. One has larger breasts, one has larger hips. They're both rounded and soft. They're on their knees on the bed, joyfully running the polymer zipper up and down over Julian.

This is so unexpected.

Julian smiles.

"Ooh, what's this?" one girl coos.

"Do you mean the zipper?" he asks. "Or…"

"What's a zipper? No, this squishy black covering all over you. How do you squirm out of it? Oh, look, it stretches. And what's this around your neck, some kind of talisman?"

"Yes," he says, pulling the girl's hand away from it and trying to glimpse into her shadowed face. "It's some kind of talisman."

"How do we get you out of this unwieldy thing?"

"You could stop playing with the zipper and pull the suit off my feet." Julian is on his back. "Or do you want me to do it?"

"No, no, handsome, you just lie there, you've done enough, don't you think? You almost started a fire. We'll find other things for you to do."

The women get off the bed and pull off his wetsuit. He feels better now that he is naked himself. He lies on a bed of silk sheets, while two young beauties, bounteous and bare, stand at his feet, lustily appraising him. They're both delicious, both about the same height. Is one of them his? Julian hopes so. It's hard to tell in the ghostly light. They're both so beautiful, and he is so fired up.

"Are you sure we should touch him? Remember what the Baroness said? What if he carries the sickness?"

"Where are you from, sire?"

"Wales. The unknown forest."

"There you go. Wales. The unknown forest. Where's that?"

"Over yonder," Julian says. "Where there is no sickness."

"There you go. Just look at him. What sickness? I've never seen a healthier specimen of a man, have you?"

"I suppose not."

"He is so robust, so full-bodied."

"He is."

"He's the epitome of male health. Have you no interest in touching him where he's especially strong and vigorous? Then leave at once. I'll have him all to myself."

"I didn't say I had no interest in touching him."

The girls stand, admiring him, smiling. He lies, admiring them, smiling.

The room is warm and getting warmer. Everything that can stir in Julian, stirs, simmers, gets hotter. Everything that can be switched on and lit up is switched on and lit up.

"What are your names, ladies?" Please let one of them be his.

"What do you want them to be, sire?"

"Josephine," Julian says, his voice thick. He opens his arms.

"Your wish is my command," says one. "I'm Josephine."

Not to be outdone the other chimes in, "I'm Josephine, too." They crawl to him, lie next to him, one on the left, the other on the right, pressing their breasts into his ribs. What good did Julian ever do in his life to deserve this? One kisses his left cheek, one kisses the right. One kisses his lips, the other pushes her away and kisses him, too. They run their hands over his body, from his long beard to his knees. They ooh. They ahh. He puts his arms around the girls, leaves his hands in their hair, one head silky and straight, the other soft and thick. He wills himself not to close his eyes.

"What would you like, sire?" one croons in her easy sexy voice.

"What we mean to say is, what would you like *first*?" the other croons in her easy sexy voice.

"I don't know," he murmurs. He doesn't know where to start. He wants it all. "What have you got?"

A better question might be what haven't they got.

For his visual pleasure, the girls fondle each other leaning over him, playing with each other's breasts. Two sets of breasts are heaved into Julian's hands, two sets of nipples are pressed into Julian's mouth. They fight to climb on top of him and for his auditory pleasure, argue over which one gets to mount him first, a discussion Julian deeply enjoys. After a while, he informs them—again, trying to be helpful—that they can take turns or, if they wish, both get on top of him. He points to his mouth. They eagerly assent. For his tactile pleasure, they give him a lot, and finally—God, finally—all at once. They move him to the middle of the bed, throw off all the blankets and pillows, and ride him like a carousel. One mounts him, first facing him, then facing away from him. One presents herself to his mouth. They switch. They switch again. Their lack of modesty is as stunning as it is magnificent. They pull him up, both get on their hands and knees in front of him and summon him with their moans and beckoning open hips to alternate between them. A minute for me and a few seconds for her, sire. No, no, a minute for me and a few seconds for *her*, sire. Julian obliges. No one wants the bell at the end of *that* round to ring, not them, and emphatically not him.

While mortal man rejoices, refracts and rejuvenates, all the while wishing he were immortal and needed no bells and no rounds, the roses and lilies show him that downtime can also be wonderful, by intermingling with each other in ways Julian has only dreamed of. The flowers have reappeared on the earth. The girls make kissing and sucking sounds when he uses his mouth and fingers to please them, as if to guide Julian aurally to what they would like him to do to them orally.

He fights the desire to close his eyes as he is smothered under their warm abundant flesh in friction against every inflamed inch of him. With impressed murmurs, they cluck over his rigid boxer's body, they praise his drive, his short rest, his devouring lust. They kiss his lips until he can't breathe. One slides south. Aren't you something, she purrs. She kisses his stomach. Josephine, she calls to the other one. Come down here.

I'm coming, Josephine. They both kiss his stomach. Their hair, their kisses, their lips, their hands slide farther south. His hands remain on their heads, in their hair.

Four breasts bounce against him, four hands and two warm mouths caress him in tandem. They feed him and drink from him and melt in the fading fire. One scoots up to his face, holding on to the frame of the bed and lowers her hips to him. One remains down below.

I'm coming, Josephine.

They entrust him again and again with their bodies and their happiness, and he bestows them with his own gifts because he doesn't like to deny insatiable beautiful girls with lips of scarlet.

If you keep this up, next time I'll charge you double, one moaning girl murmurs.

If you keep this up, next time I'll give it to you for free, murmurs the other.

Julian can't decide which murmur he prefers.

The honeycomb hours pour forth in a treacly feast, in debauched splendor. The fire goes out. The room is lit only by faint moonlight through the open windows. It's hot, and outside is quiet except for occasional bursts of revelry on the street below. Exhausted, the girls lie in his arms during another break, ply him and themselves with house wine, and confer to him all manner of knowledge.

Julian learns he's near Whitehall Palace, in a house of pleasure named the Silver Cross. So for the second time, he's back in London. He knows the tavern fairly well. The Silver Cross, a block away from Trafalgar Square, is one of London's oldest pubs. He's drunk and eaten there a few times with Ashton. The selection of beer is first rate and the red meat is tender. Whitehall, a short stroll from Westminster, was once the residence of kings. In 1530, Henry VIII bought the white marble palace from a cardinal, lived there, died there. A fire had decimated the palace (*a* fire? or *the* fire?) and now only the Banqueting House remains, and the eponymous street. It's July, the girls inform him, which explains why it's so bloody hot, that and the fiery female flesh scorching his hands.

Before Oliver Cromwell in his Puritan zeal shuttered all of London's playhouses, pubs and houses of bawd, Charles I licensed the Silver Cross as a legal brothel and the irony is, to the present day the license has never been revoked. The king was beheaded, England became a republic, there was a civil war. There was so much else to think about besides a brothel license. For four hundred years, it had slipped everyone's mind. Julian read this on a plaque in the pub, while dining and drinking there with Ashton.

The Silver Cross is run by a woman named Baroness Tilly. She has ten high-quality girls and "ten rooms of pleasure." The house is colloquially called the Lord's Tavern after its most frequent patrons—"the Right Honorable Lords Spiritual and Temporal of the Kingdom of Great Britain, England, Scotland, and Ireland in Parliament Assembled!" the girls proclaim to him in happy unison. They do so many splendid things to him in happy unison. With the recently re-established House of Lords, the Temporal Peers have become the tavern's most generous benefactors. They have unlimited time, unlimited money and unlimited vices. The girls are top-notch, game for all sorts of debauchery (as Julian can attest), and most importantly (after the recent "epidemic of death"), clean. The girls and the rooms adhere to rules of purity not found in other similar establishments, "like that pig-pit the Haymarket, or Miss Cresswell's in Clerkenwell."

Did someone say Clerkenwell?

Yes, sire, do you know it? It's filthy.

I know it. It's not so bad. His heart pinches when he remembers Clerkenwell, the rides to Cripplegate through the brothel quarter on Turnbull Street. He wants to peer into the girl's face but can't keep his eyes open.

At the Silver Cross, the rooms are spotless, richly decorated, well furnished. "And the girls, too," Julian murmurs sleepily. His body is raw, sore, sated in all its imaginable and unimagined earthly cravings. This is his favorite room in the world.

Yes, this room is nice, the girls murmur in return, but there are a few others that have bathtubs, and in those rooms the girls can soap him, and lather him, and wash him. Would he like that, for the eager girls to soap his naked body? Look, it's almost dawn, one girl says, what's better than dawn by cocklight? Nothing, says the other, tugging on him and smiling. Nothing's better than the crowing of the cock to usher in a new day.

Julian is nearly unconscious. Yet the mention of being soaped by the caressing hands of the lush sirens in his bed calls him to attention and turns the girls once again into warm quivering masses of excited and groany giggles—

The bedroom door is thrown open. The giggling stops. In the frame stands a tall woman wearing yesterday's theatrically overdone face makeup and an outrageous pink velvet housecoat with a red fringe.

"Mallory!" she shouts. "How many times have I told you— No! Bad girl! No, no, no, no, no!"

One of the girls scrambles off the bed and searches the floor for her clothes.

"This isn't your job! Do you know what your job is?"

"Yes, Aunt Tilly."

Julian nearly cries. Don't go, Mallory! Her back is to him, but if only he could catch a glimpse of her face...

"No, I don't think you do know what your job is. And it's Baroness Tilly while you're working—and I assume this was work?"

"All my other work was done, Baroness." The girl throws a chemise over herself, a skirt, a flowy blouse, an apron. She ties up her hair. "I was finished for the day."

"You don't look as if you were finished."

"Just wanted to make some extra money, Baroness…"

"That's everybody's excuse. But you know I forbid it. Your mother, may she rest in peace, forbid it. I will not tell you again. I'm going to send you to the South of France if you don't stop this. Do you want to be sent away with your boorish benefactor? He'll be a lot stricter than me."

"No, Baroness."

"I didn't think so. Then, go do what you've been hired to do and stop the wickedness at once. Oh—and who is this man? I allowed you upstairs at the start of the night for the viewing pleasure of Lord Fabian, and here you are, at nearly dawn, with another man in your bed."

Viewing pleasure? Lord Fabian? What? Julian lifts his head off the pillows. Baroness Tilly, a broad, vulgar woman, turns her unwelcome attention to him. "I don't remember you walking past me, good sir, and I certainly don't remember you paying me. No one goes upstairs with my girls without me knowing about it. Announce yourself! Mallory, Margrave, who is this man?"

Still in bed with Julian, Margrave, a most unblushing flower a few minutes earlier, gets tongue-tied. Her brazen demeanor vanishes. She stammers.

The standing girl comes to his aid. "I believe he said he's here for the position of the keeper of the house, Baroness. Aren't you, sire? He came from the Golden Flute across the river. Madame Maud sent him."

"So why is he up here with you? Why didn't he speak to me first if Maud sent him?"

"He wandered in and got lost, he didn't see you."

"Oh, enough! There's clean-up needed in Room Four. Golden Flute indeed. I am so tired of your nonsense, Mallory, so very tired."

Mallory rushes past the hyperventilating baroness. Margrave covers Julian with a quilt. He finds it fascinating that she remains uncovered as if it's only his modesty she is concerned with.

"Margrave, don't sit there like a wanton hussy, get dressed. It's morning. What is your name, sir?"

"Julian Cruz."

"Well, Master Cruz, this is not the way I usually make the acquaintance of the keepers of my house. Did you need to sample the product before you could hawk it? I admire that. We have only the best here, sire. These are not the usual wagtails and bunters you're used to at the Golden Flute, I can assure you."

Julian doesn't need to be assured. He knows.

"Our old keeper died last month without any warning. A little warning would've been *so* helpful. It would've given me and the girls time to prepare. This is a house run nearly entirely by women and there are things we do well, wouldn't you agree, Master Cruz?"

Julian would agree.

"But there are other things we cannot do. Fix doors, patch holes, replace broken lanterns, fix the roof. We have lanterns that have not been filled with oil because Ilbert refuses to buy some, and the candles are running low, as is the soap. After the recent health problems, soap is an absolute necessity. We're quite busy here. I hope you can manage. Marg, go tell Mallory to prepare the gentleman's room, and you, sir, meet me downstairs as soon as you're attired." (Attired in what exactly, Julian wants to know.) "I'll go over the rest of the details, and we'll raise a glass. Margrave—spit spot." With that, Baroness Tilly claps her hands twice, and exits.

As soon as she's gone, Margrave jumps out of bed.

"We could've got into so much trouble," she bleats, tying the sashes of her robe. "The Baroness hates it when Mallory disobeys. Not that she does anything about it, the girl is a terror." She smiles. "But who could resist you? Even heartless Mallory couldn't. Wait here, I'll be right back with a robe. You should ask the Baroness for an advance, go buy yourself some clothes befitting a brothel keeper."

"What do they wear, tuxedoes?"

"If you like, sire. Forever naked would be my preference." Beaming, she straightens out, and Julian catches her eye. It's dawn, he can see her smiling round face. She is pretty and young and sexy. Low light, a tired mind, lust, pounding desire are all great equalizers.

But Margrave is not his girl.

# 4

# Keeper of the Brothel

THE ALE IS A COVER. ALE FOR BREAKFAST, ALE FOR DINNER, ale for supper. It's a euphemism for the other things that go on at the Silver Cross. Yet downstairs, the wood-paneled restaurant-bar appears as just that: a well-to-do tavern, patronized by connected and wealthy men (much as in the present). The ale is top-notch, Baroness Tilly tells him, the food superb.

Naked underneath a black velvet robe, Julian sits across from the Baroness, feeling ridiculous. Tilly's pink robe has been replaced by hooped petticoats and gaudy layers of sweeping silk ornamental fabrics with puffy sleeves and lace velvet collars. She wears a huge blonde wig, her eyes hastily drawn in black and her oversized mouth made ever larger by smeared red cake-paint.

The pub is narrow and tall, with flagstone floors and tables of heavy oak. It's upholstered in leather, draped with blue velvet curtains, and set with crystal and fine china. The breakfast tables are lined with white napkins.

"It's a beautiful place, wouldn't you agree," the Baroness says. After colorfully describing what's expected of him (the daily inspections of the girls before they begin work is one of Julian's more intriguing duties), she offers him a salary and only as an afterthought inquires about his experience, which he recounts to her just as colorfully—parroting her own words from minutes ago (taking extra time to detail how he imagines the inspections immediately. Where are these girls? When can he inspect them, so he can find his girl?

He and the Baroness have a sumptuous breakfast of porridge and milk, smoked herring, spiced eel pie ("caught fresh from the Thames just yesterday!") and bread and marmalade. And ale. The Baroness lingers over breakfast as if starved for some normal company, entertaining an increasingly impatient Julian with stories about the Silver Cross. A hundred years earlier, a man named Parson from Old Fish Street was paraded in shame down Parliament Street for selling the sexual services of his apparently accomplished wife. After spending years in prison, he opened the Silver Cross in revenge, and his wife became the cornerstone of his business.

Julian tells the Baroness he's read somewhere that a prostitute was murdered in the Silver Cross, and it's been haunted ever since.

"I don't know nothing about that," the Baroness says, frowning. "Where did you read that, the *Gazette*?" Grudgingly she admits that the Silver Cross has only recently reopened, having been shuttered for the better part of last year, "because of the horror that befell all London. But we've had no recent murders here, sire, I can assure you. Murder is very bad for business."

"What horror?" Julian asks and instantly regrets it when she stares at him suspiciously. He clears his throat. "I meant why stay shuttered for so long?" His eyes dart around, trying to catch the date from the newspaper lying on the next table.

"Where are you from, good sir, that you don't know about the terrible pestilence that destroyed our town?"

The unknown forest, Julian tells her. Wales. Largely spared from the plague. One of these days, Julian will meet an actual Welshman and be promptly pilloried on Cheapside.

"I thought you've just come from across the river?" She lowers her voice. "You know, that's where the Black Death took wind. From south of the river."

Julian nods. It's common knowledge—everything is worse south of the river.

"It got so *bad*," the Baroness says, "death galloped in *such* triumph through our streets that King Charlie himself had had enough. He packed up his court and fled the city! That's how we knew we was all doomed. When our own king abandoned us. His Majesty's Government didn't meet for a year."

Julian commiserates. In 1665, the plague had reduced London to a wasteland. He hopes it's a few years later, the worst behind them. He tries to make out that elusive date on the newspaper. LONDON GAZETTE, it reads. PUBLISHED BY AUTHORITY. What year does it say?

"Yes, our once lively city has become a graveyard," the Baroness goes on. "Nothing but a field of dismal misery. There was nothing open because there was no one alive." She dabs her eye. "I'll confess to you, sire, the plague has been absolutely *terrible* for business!"

"One hundred and thirty parishes in London," Julian says. "Surely there are still men left. The bells still ring."

"Oh, even more than before, because now they ring for the dead. But the dogs don't bark. Because they're also dead. Dead with all the honorable deep-pocketed gentlemen!" She sniffles.

Good God, what year is it? He squints at the *Gazette*, adjusts in his seat. "Does that say July *1666*?" he asks, something inside him falling.

"Yes," the Baroness says slowly. "Why?"

"The Silver Cross survived the fire?"

"What fire?"

"The one near Pudding Lane."

"Pudding Lane? All the way down there by the bridge, inside the wall? I wouldn't know nothing about that. I don't go down there. We always have fires in London, good sir. Too many candles."

"You'd know this fire," Julian says pensively. "There won't be a house left standing between Temple Bar and London

Bridge. Pardon me, I've been traveling so long, I've lost track of my days." Maybe he's wrong about the year. He's never been good with dates. What a failing to have when dates are of the essence. Cromwell, Puritans, beheadings, republic, Charles I, Charles II, when was the Glorious Revolution? Was the Great Fire of London before it or after? A little knowledge is an awful thing—

"It's a Tuesday. Second week in July. We just finished the beer festival for the Feast of Saints." The Baroness smiles. "*That* was very good for business."

"I'm sure." Julian shifts in his seat. "Can I get a small advance on my salary so I can buy myself a wardrobe befitting a tavern keeper? You said we needed fresh flowers. Perhaps I can take a walk to the market. Is Covent Garden open?" He wants to walk to Clerkenwell. He needs to see what's become of the life he once lived with her.

The Baroness agrees to an advance. "Usually I send Ilbert to the market, but frankly, he has appalling taste in flowers. He always manages to get the ugliest ones. When you see Mallory, remind her to lend you something to wear. And tell her Gasper is here. The girl needs to be told everything three times. He's been waiting an hour." Gasper is a skeletal man in the corner by the open door, a stinking man in rags with flies buzzing around him, his head tilted and trembling.

As Julian walks up the main stairs, he hears the Baroness berating a humpbacked imp. "Ilbert," she yells. "How many times must I tell you—it's against the law to wash the entrails of pigs in the local waters!"

"I'm not the only one that breaks the laws, madam. The alley is slippery with refuse. It's hard to carry the carcass to a less local water."

"Oh, Holy Helpers, Ilbert, you are but an arsworm! You know Scotland Yard is next door! One of them clappers saw you. He told me you was throwing coal ashes right into Parliament Street. Have you no mind, scoundrel? We're in front of the Palace of Whitehall, the residence of our king! You can't keep breaking the laws of men."

"But all the men is dead, madam. You said so yourself."

"The few that are left will stone you to death, you scoundrel! I will celebrate when that day comes. Until then, stop mouthing off to me and go sweep the stones outside, as decreed by the Commissioner for Streets and Ways. And stop hooping the barrels on the sidewalk and sawing timber on the street. I can't afford another fine because of you."

"Where would you like me to saw the timber, madam? In the palace gardens?"

"You are an annoyance and a disorder, Ilbert, in desperate need of reforming. They will dispose of you with the ashes, dust and dirt, and I shall have nothing whatsoever to say about it except hallelujah."

∞

Tucked into a dormered corner on the second floor, on the other side of the house from his favorite room, Julian's quarters are spacious and sunny. From his two open windows he can see the eastern Thames, curving toward Blackfriars, toward the direction of the slate-colored Globe, he can hear the bells of a hundred churches. His room has a four-poster bed with a heavy canopy, an intricately carved armchair, a walnut cupboard, a small table under the windows where he can eat or write, a wardrobe where he can hang his clothes once he gets some, and a washing station in the corner by the fireplace that includes not only a basin, but also a bathtub with a stone hearth. He could use a bath after last night's steamy banquet. Perhaps the girls could come and wash him as they had so kindly offered.

In the desk he finds a quill with a bottle of ink. Julian remembers Devi's instruction to count the days. Opening the bottle of ink, he dips the quill into it, pulls up the sleeve of his robe, and with the quill tip punctures the inside of his forearm, near his wrist, tapping a *dot* of ink into the wound. *One.*

When he turns around, a girl stands silently in the doorway, towels and sheets in her hands, her expression wary, her brown gaze on his arm. It's Mallory.

"I can explain," he says, putting the quill away.

"No need, sire." He can barely hear her voice.

"I'm marking the days." He steps toward her.

"Aren't we all. May I make up your room?" Her gaze is on the bed.

"Mallory..."

The girl can't look into his face. It's either shyness or embarrassment. She stares at the periphery of his ear, at a slice of his beard, at his black robe, at anything but him. When he tries to touch her, she flinches from him. Holding her by the flesh of her arm, he lifts her chin to him. His eyes meet hers.

Mallory is his girl.

Julian fills to the brim with the wine of his ravished heart. He searches her face for a flicker of familiarity, of recognition and finds himself faintly disappointed that he can't find any. She doesn't fight him or move away. In her deep brown eyes there's a hint of morning shame at the memory of their shameless night. Her full red lips are slightly parted.

"May I make up your room, sire...please?" She averts her gaze.

He watches her as she scurries and hurries in her maid's clothes, a long black skirt, a gray workman-like bodice, a black apron. That is not what she looked like last night, sumptuous and inflamed. Her hair, once so wonderfully down, is tied up and hidden in a white bonnet. She is less hourglassy than Mary was, perhaps because she toils all day and has less to eat. And whereas Mary was a newborn soul that hadn't learned to smile, this Mallory doesn't smile perhaps because there's less to smile about. Her delicate life is rough with work. She is efficient. In five minutes, the bed is made up, some ale is in a silver decanter, yellow lilies are by the open window. Julian condemns the yellow lilies but says nothing. The girl doesn't know they stand for falsehood. He'll replace them when he goes out, perhaps with red tulips for desire.

"Will that be all, sire?"

"The Baroness said you might have some clothes for me."

"Yes, pardon me. I forgot." She returns with some faded breeches, a frayed tunic, and a pair of old shoes. "If there's nothing else…"

"Oh, but there is." He reaches for her hand.

She retreats. "I'm very busy, sire. I'm not…I'm the maid, that's all I am."

"That's not all you are."

"Last night was an aberration."

"It wasn't."

"You heard the Baroness. Me, Carling, and Ivy got ten rooms to clean and the downstairs to sweep and get ready for lunch. There's only three maids cleaning, and you saw, the Baroness is already upset with me."

"I don't much care what she thinks."

"I don't have that luxury, not to care what she thinks, sire."

From the floor below, Julian hears Tilly calling Mallory's name. He tuts. "You're making me forget everything, Mallory. The Baroness said someone named Gasper is downstairs for you."

Mallory hardens.

"Who's Gasper, your father?"

"No, sire, I don't think my mother knew who my father was."

"So Gasper *could* be your father?"

"Well, I suppose so. Anything is possible."

"That's true. I know for a fact," Julian says, "that *anything* is possible."

"But since Gasper was married to my aunt, I'd say it's not very likely. He's come to collect."

"Your Aunt Tilly, the Baroness?"

"No, my mother's other sister. She's dead."

"And your mother?"

"She is also dead."

"Oh." Julian can't take his eyes off her pale, diffident, serious, beautiful face, with pursed lips and moist eyes. "Where are you from?"

"Clerkenwell."

His expression must fall, because Mallory softens. "Did *you* perhaps know my mother, sire?" Almost imperceptibly, she smiles.

"No." Circling his arm around her waist, he brings her to him. "Oh, Mallory," he whispers.

She lets him embrace her, as if it's her duty.

"Mallory! Gasper is waiting!"

Julian doesn't want to let her go.

"That's my cue, sire," she says, easing out of his arms, her breathy voice low. "Gasper's waiting."

"What's another minute? I've waited too, and longer than he has."

"Have you also come to collect, sire?"

"What? No." Julian raises her hand to his lips, kissing the inside of her wrist. "Come back tonight."

"I can't. Aunt Tilly forbids it. Besides, I'm busy tonight. Perhaps Margrave..."

"No," Julian says. "Not Margrave. *You.*"

"Believe me, I promise you, swear to you, I'm not the girl for you, sire..." She stands stiffly.

"You are." Their eyes lock. Pulling away, she hurries out, but the relieved and excited Julian is not put off by her daytime restraint. Her nighttime body is fresh in his memory and visceral in his loins. He has found her again, his garden of pomegranates, his orchard of new wine. He's elated, not afraid.

∞

It is thus that Julian becomes the landlord of a brothel. It's an excellent job, one of the best he's had, better than substitute teaching, better than working for fucking Graham. If only Ashton could see him now. No one would appreciate the multi-layered delights and ironies of Julian's new position better than Ashton. The job allows him to make money and be surrounded day and night by sexy, enthusiastic women. Nights are busy, but it's quiet during the day, and he can catch up on his sleep or read or go out for a walk to buy flowers and candles. In the mornings, Julian sends Ilbert to the butcher and the coal boy. He supervises the maids and the girls himself (of course) and selects his own roses and lilies.

Fresh flowers must be in vases in all the rooms, everything must be stripped and washed from the night before, the chamber pots emptied, the floors swept and mopped, beds made, windows opened, and rooms aired out. It's like running a naughty bed and breakfast. Once a week Julian pays off the parish constable, a solid, likable chap named Parker.

Every morning, the Baroness and Julian count the silver, mostly pennies and farthings, and a few shillings. He helps the madam separate the operational coin from the profit, and at noon leaves for King Street to deliver the bag of silver to Lord Waas, the owner of the Silver Cross.

The London of 1666 isn't quite what it was when Julian was last here in 1603. Yes, the roads have widened, and the trees have grown. But the city has been decimated by wholescale death and hasn't had time to recover. The fear of the plague is apparent in the diminished bedlam on the streets and in the caution of the people who scurry past him, covering their mouths and faces. One afternoon, Julian takes a long aching walk all the way to Clerkenwell. The Fortune Theatre has been dismantled. The brothel quarter is shuttered. The Collins Manor with its stables and grounds is gone. Five new homes have been built in its place.

But even with London thus reduced, the clatter and cry of every living thing remains unending. The blacksmiths are the loudest of all, for they make things everyone else uses in their trades, so the blacksmith's trade never stops, even at night. There are a hundred parishes within the City gates and another thirty scattered without, and every parish has a church and the belfries ring on the hour and half-hour and quarter-hour to announce the time, and the blacksmith foundries make the bells, and to make them they must test them, and every time they test them, the bells toll, and there are a hundred foundries, a hundred churches, and a million bells, over spires and doors and horses' necks, and the metal against metal rings and rings and rings, far away, nearby, nonstop, even when Julian sleeps.

Aside from the relentless tolling of the bells, the job brings Julian happiness. Not only is he in the daily proximity of his beloved, but he is surrounded by other attractive women, more playful than she, women who defer to him and flirt with him. The visiting men seek no trouble except when they're blind drunk and then a not so gentle shove from Julian into the street is enough for them to return sober and chastised the following evening.

It's boisterous at night—like Normandie, the street where Josephine used to live with Z—but with more sex and less hip hop. There's plenty to drink, and if Julian wanted to have a social life on the side, he could. Margrave (though not Mallory) has bragged to the other girls about the unrestrained bounty that is Julian. "His blood boils with such excess!" Margrave tells the other girls. "Mal and I feared there wouldn't be enough of him for the two of us, but it turns out there wasn't enough of us for the one of him! There's enough of him to board all ten of us, isn't that right, sire?" Occasionally in the late evenings, especially if it's slow, he hears the patter of their feet outside his door, their low whispers, seductive warbles, spicy pleas. One kiss, sire, one bob, sire, one bout in the bowl, sire. He's grateful the girls are often too tired if not too proud to beg. Grateful yet regretful. Now that he is landlord, the Baroness has commanded him to keep away. "They need to be fresh for the next day, Master Julian, no sense tiring them out unnecessarily."

Every single day, the Right Reverend Anselmo arrives before the evening rush and stands in the middle of the restaurant downstairs, loudly sermonizing their sins away. "Constable Parker says we must put up with him to stay open," the Baroness tells Julian. "The reverend is sent from the deanery of Whitehall to maintain something called prima facie decorum." The Baroness swears. "Royal prerogative and all that. We must be mindful of our hallowed location. If it was up to me, I'd have that eunuch Anselmo castrated again. He calls my beautiful home the shambles! Can you imagine!"

Julian doesn't have to imagine. Nightly he hears the vicar's clarion call.

"He says the devil slaughters the souls of Christian men in our humble tavern!" The Baroness spits like a man. "In infinite ways, the devil butchers men's souls at the Silver Cross, he says. Ah, yes, that Anselmo is a British treasure. He's a convert, you know. He used to be a Catholic. Now he's a reformed Puritan. And you know what they say about reformed Puritans."

"That there's nothing worse than a reformed whore," Julian says, and the Baroness howls with laughter and for weeks repeats the line to everyone she greets.

∞

One afternoon, while eating and socializing with the girls, amusing them by garbling their names, Julian makes the mistake of calling the one who's named Jeanne "Saint Joan of Arc." Immediately the banter stops. The Baroness steps forward from her table in the back corner. She hears everything. "Why would you call the Maid of Orleans *Saint* Joan?" the Baroness asks. "She was no saint."

"My mistake. Wasn't she canonized?"

"Canonized?" The Baroness doesn't laugh. "She's a rebel burned for heresy, for slaughtering the English, for impersonating a man, for saying she heard the voice of God command her to raise an army against the Crown. She was burned at the stake as a witch, not a saint."

"My mistake, Baroness." Julian must be more careful. Sometimes he forgets that beheadings and burnings aren't just facts in history, but are real blood and real hatred. But *wasn't* Joan of Arc canonized, though? Why is it, no matter how much Julian thinks he knows, it's never enough?

He tries remembering the names of the girls by height, but four of them are the same height, and he tries remembering them by age, but eight of them are under twenty, and he tries remembering them by hair color, but all ten of them are some shade between brown and black. Six of them are bosomy, eight of them are hippy, two of them have barely any breasts at all, and their clientele is limited and specific. The Baroness tells Julian that there's only one way he must rank the girls, "And that's by how much money they bring in. That's your only yardstick as the keeper of this house."

"That is not his only yardstick, Baroness," Margrave says, and the girls titter.

"Hush, Margrave. Stop wearing him like a medal."

The madam is right. Julian learns their names much faster using her method. Brynhilda, a large, buxom lass of Germanic origin, is first. The men wait hours for her. Mute Kitty is second because she's quickest. Beatrix and Millicent are sisters, work in tandem, and are three and four. Brazen Margrave is five, Ru is peppy and six, and French Catholic Severine is seven. The girl who'd been calling herself Jeanne before Julian ruined it for her, and who now must refer to herself as plain Joan, is currently underworked and number eight, boyish Allie is nine, and Greta is last. Greta is skeletal and at almost thirty has outlasted her usefulness. But her great-grandfather is rumored to be Parson, the man who founded the Silver Cross, so she's not going anywhere.

The ten bedrooms and ten girls mix and match depending on the workload. The rooms are strictly for pleasure, six on the

second floor, four on the third. The girls sleep high up on the
fourth floor, in the stifling attic rooms by the dormers, five ladies
to a cubby. The three maids, including Mallory, are segregated
down on the ground floor, in the back by the servants' kitchen.
They mix with no one.

Except for Mallory—who is the prettiest of all the girls at
the Silver Cross—the cleaning girls are desperately unattractive.
Carling is lame and Ivy is scarred. Carling and Ivy loathe Mallory,
because she's the Baroness's niece and "not nearly ugly enough."
Though she's not allowed to sit with Julian and the regulars
while they have their dinner of spiced eel and fish pies, all the
girls, the maids and the molls, resent Mallory for having too
many privileges. The main complaint about her is that she never
gets punished for the things she does wrong. Julian doesn't dare
ask what she does wrong, lest it reveal how he feels about her.

The girls don't stop complaining about one thing or another.
Nothing is so trivial that it won't cause offense. Yes, on the one
hand, Julian is surrounded by women. But on the other, Julian
is surrounded by women. They're soft and busty, flirtatious,
voluptuous, and their erotic inclinations know no bounds. But
when they're not arguing with him over the house-set price of
goods and services, they're bad-mouthing each other. They're
also not above blatant mendacity. They ascribe to each other all
manner of vice and malice, they saddle one another with the lies
of the most hideous contagious diseases. They often accuse one
another of attempted murder through poison and infection. It's
astonishing. They are beautiful but venal.

Fortunately, it's the Baroness not Julian who deals with the
bulk of their grievances. When he asks her how she sustains
herself, she laughs. "Oh, dear boy," she says. "Margrave is right
about you. You're too good a man. She says you may be of noble
blood. Eventually you'll learn how to handle the *commoners*." A
commoner is another name for prostitute. "Rule number one:
You must stop being so respectful. Do like me and pay them
absolutely no mind. I pretend to listen, for they need to complain.

It's about seniority. It's about money. It's only when they don't complain that they worry me. And by the way, do you know who *never* complains? Mallory. And she's the one who's got the most to complain about, for the other girls are simply dreadful to her. But she never disparages them in return, she never whines about the cleaning, or being overworked, and she never says a bad word to or about anyone. Or a good word, for that matter. She's my niece, and I love her like family, but frankly, she is too tame! She's the one who vexes me the most with her unspeakable silence. Oh, how she vexes me!"

# 5

# Lord Fabian

LATE ONE NIGHT JULIAN IS ASKED BY IVY THE MAID TO BRING some wine to Room Two, his favorite room. It's an odd request, for Julian is not usually in the business of fetching and carrying. He doesn't mind the chore; the evening has been passing without a crisis. He's only had to throw one man out into the street. As is his custom, Julian is formally dressed, in black silk hose and pointed-toe black leather shoes. He wears a blue velvet waistcoat with dark red buttons. His long thick hair is shiny and down, slicked back behind his ears. And he has shaved his epic beard, because wouldn't you know it—in 1666, no one has beards! He can't keep up with men's facial hair fashion. Considered most virile at the turn of the century—the longer, the better—beards are now deemed lawless and dirty.

Julian knocks. A male voice answers. The room is dim, lit by three candles and a low fire. In a chair by the unmade bed sits a big fat man in loosened silk robes. Across the room from him, by the row of candles, illuminated from the side, Mallory stands naked. The man in the chair motions Julian to bring the wine and place it on the table by his elbow. Julian sets down the decanter, takes the empty one and turns to leave. He tries not to look at Mallory.

The man grabs his arm. "What do you think of our beauty, sir?" he says, chuffing like a horse.

Julian still won't look at her. *Our?* "Beautiful." He yanks his

"Do you know who I am?"

"Nope." Julian doesn't bother faking politeness. He doesn't need to. He's in charge. His antenna is up, and so is his concern for Mallory.

"This is Lord Fabian, sire," Mallory says softly. "He is one of our most kind and generous patrons."

"I know who *you* are," the fat man says to Julian. His puffy white shirt is open. His chest is hairy, he's perspiring, sickly perfumed. "And *you* certainly know who the girl is." He sniggers, winded even from speaking.

"Lord Fabian watched us the other night, sire," Mallory says. She points to a tapestried panel on the wall. "From a hidden enclosure."

That does not endear Julian to the man. He backs away to stand between Mallory and the lord, shielding her from the man's lecherous gaze.

"You put on quite a show, young man. Well done." Fabian wipes his brow with a soiled handkerchief. "I'd like you to do it again." He pauses. "But this time while I watch comfortably from a chair instead of peeping through a hole in a wall like a burglar."

"No," Julian says.

"Pardon me?"

"You heard me. Mallory, get dressed, come with me. The Baroness is asking for you downstairs."

"No, sire," Mallory says calmly. "The Baroness knows where I am. She allows me this indulgence from time to time—because it's Lord Fabian."

"I should think she allows it," Fabian says, bristling, "all the money she's made off me."

"Yes, you have been *very* good to me, my lord."

"Come, Mallory," Julian says, reaching for her.

She pulls away from his hand. "No."

From *me* you pull away, Julian wants to say to her.

"I demand you stay," Fabian says to Julian, "or God help me, I'll have your job. And possibly your head on a spike."

Julian walks out, leaving the door open behind him.

He returns to his room and sits on the bed, contemplating his options. Before he has time to get more upset, there's a knock. It's Mallory, hastily dressed.

"Sire, may I talk to you?" She shuts the door behind her. "Why won't you help me?" She comes forward. "Is it because I refuse to come to you privately?"

"No."

"If you help me, I will agree to see you from time to time."

"No." He frowns. Is she trying to make him more upset? "I don't want you to come to me because we made a bargain, Mallory. I want you to come to me because you want to."

"I'm too busy around here to *want* to do anything, sire. But you don't seem as if you are too busy tonight to help me. So why are you saying no?"

"I'm saying no because I don't want to do it."

"You don't want to be with me?" Her voice is soft, cajoling, her brown eyes large like a baby fawn's.

"Not like this."

"I know you must think him vile, but if *you* touch me, *he* won't touch me. Don't you want that? In some way, this is to protect me."

"There must be another way."

"There isn't," Mallory says. "Not at the moment. The lord wants to perform and can't. This makes him angry, first with himself, and then with me. He says I judge him for his malady, and no matter what I try to do or say to let him know it's not true is wrong. Unfortunately, the pressure of my willing body works on him in reverse. But then *you* appeared to us, sire, to me and Margrave! Afterward, the lord told me he hadn't felt as aroused and happy in many years."

"Good for him. Nothing I enjoy more than hearing I make that man happy and aroused. But you're not one of Tilly's girls. You're a maid." Julian is trying to shut his heart to her. "Just do your job and stay away from him."

Mallory wrings her hands. "The Baroness allows me to be with him because he promised her he wouldn't really touch me. He is my only customer. Mostly all he does is look, because that's all he *can* do, and that's the truth. I only do it to make a little money on the side."

"What's it to me?"

"The other girls get paid more, and I work so much harder."

"So complain, Mallory. Speak up. The Baroness says you never say a word."

"What's there to say!" The girl takes a deep breath, and then lowers her deathless voice. "Listen to me, sire, *please*."

Julian closes his eyes, to avoid looking at her. He wants to put his hands over his ears to not hear her.

"You're an idling satyr," she purrs, reaching for him, caressing him through his silk hose. "Why waste your unused pillar of gold? Put it to use, sire. Put it to good use."

"Don't butter me up, I'm not toast. You know I don't want to be idle," Julian says after a beat. "I'm just not going up on *his* stage."

"It's your life and your stage," says Mallory. "As it is mine. Decide if you want to be in the center of it or in the wings." She takes his hand. "In the center of it, *with me*."

"No." He turns to the window. What is she doing to him?

"Please, Julian."

She calls him by his name. Next to the things she did to him when they were together, it's the ultimate seduction. Will the vixen stop at *nothing*?

"The lord said he'll give me a crown if you lie with me," Mallory says. "A *crown*, sire! A quarter of a pound. A crown for a few minutes of your time. I make a shilling a week. I have to work five back-breaking weeks to make one crown. The other smuts, with all their experience, make three pennies a customer. Even Brynhilda's tits fetch her barely six. And the lord is offering us a crown! Why can't you help me? You did it the other night."

"The other night, I did it for free." He pulls his hand away from her.

"*You* may have done it for free," Mallory returns cruelly. "But Marg and I knew he was watching us. We got paid for touching each other, and I got paid a bonus for touching you. Two extra shillings after you broke in."

"Did you split that with Margrave?"

Mallory's face is cold. "She makes plenty as it is."

Julian is astonished. "The other night...that was you performing for *him*?"

"I beg pardon, sire, I hate to be impertinent, but...are you aware where you are? Where you and I both work?"

"Quite aware, thank you. I just thought you had been performing for me. My mistake." Julian stares into his hands. *This* is Josephine's acting life. Mary Collins told her lady mother: all she wanted was to be up on a stage. Josephine told him she invented a stage everywhere she went. Well, here is what the stage looks like in 1666.

Minutes pass. He pulls up his velvet sleeve, counts the ink dots. *Seven*. A week has passed since his first night here with her. "Fine," he says. "I'll do it. But tell your lord it's a crown only if he leaves the room and spies through the hole." Julian pauses. "It's two crowns if he stays in the chair."

Mallory beams. Julian doesn't beam.

Without hesitation, Fabian agrees to two crowns. They should've asked for more, Julian thinks, as he pushes the heavy bed farther away from the man's repugnant feet, and he and Mallory undress. Julian wishes he had money he could offer her instead of the toady watching them from three floorboards away.

He and Mallory stand naked in front of each other.

Julian *really* wants to touch her.

Can he even perform in front of Lord Odious?

Why, yes, it turns out he can.

He does it by trying to forget that Fabian exists, though that's less easy than it sounds, what with the barrage of winded wheezing commands spitting forth from the man's foaming mouth as he sits in the nearby chair and directs Julian—as if Julian has no idea what to do on his own.

Why are you standing there? Kiss her. You're in a pantomime of love, Fabian says. So pantomime.

They kneel on the bed. Julian cups Mallory's face. It's not a pantomime, he whispers to his maid and his princess, as he kisses her, kisses her until her nipples harden and he hardens and everything else on her softens.

Fondle her.

Pull on her nipples until she moans.

Tug on her until she squirms.

Lay her down, pour some wine on her.

Open her, eat her pussy.

I didn't tell you to talk to her, what did you say to her?

*Do you like that, Mallory?*

*Yes, sire.*

Do not ask her what she wants or what she likes, you do what I want, you do what I like. Turn her over. Get behind her. Grab her, so she stops moving. Pull out all the way, so I can see. Now thrust all the way in. Tell her to hold on to the headboard if she needs to.

*Hold on to the headboard, Mallory.*

The orders are barked only to Julian. But Julian knows, Fabian is not barking. He is begging. He's beseeching Julian to be his proxy with the maiden. All things he cannot do himself, Fabian does through Julian. But Fabian's shallow panting is so distressing that at one point, Julian lies flat on top of Mallory, even though his instructions were expressly not to. He stops moving and covers her body with his to shield her from the fat lord's jealous gaze. Easing one arm under her, Julian slows between her hips and presses his face against her cheek, to cover her ear. *It's going to be okay. Are you okay?*

*I'm fine.* She pats his back. *It's not me he covets, sire. It's you and your able-bodied youth. He's not looking at me. He's watching you. It's*

*your strong legs he desires, and your arms that hold your weight and
hold mine. Your hard stomach. Your hard everything.*

They kiss in a prolonged moan as if they are real lovers.

*I'd like to kill him,* Julian says.

*No, no, not until we separate the fool from his money,* says
Mallory.

Julian laughs, Fabian shouts, Julian loses his rhythm, and
rhythm is so important in love.

Stand on the floor, have her kneel in front of you. Tell her
to suck your cock, but do not discharge in her mouth. So what
if the floor is hard. I want to see her on the hard floor. She is
getting two crowns from me. She can take a little discomfort in
her knees for two crowns, can't she? Because you're about to give
her more discomfort than that. Tell her to get on her hands and
knees. Yes, right on the floor.

∞

Julian is in his own bed when he hears a soft tap. Mallory steps
in, dressed in her morning clothes, gray apron, black skirt.

"Am I disturbing you, sire?" Her voice is a whisper.

"No." He sits up.

The candles have been blown out, the room is dark.
Uncertainly she closes the door behind her.

"I think the lord was pleased."

"And that is what I was aiming for. To please *him.*"

Even in the night, he sees her blushing face. "I just wanted to
say thank you for tonight."

"You're welcome."

"I'm sorry to have put you in such a spot. He's a peculiar
man, I grant you, but he *is* generous, and very little is required
of me."

"And thank *you* for that."

She stammers. "I meant to say that usually not very much is
required of me."

"What about the other night with Margrave?"

"Yes, we do that sometimes if the lord wishes it, lie together. She is my friend." Mallory bobs her head. "Well, a friend *and* an enemy."

"Where I come from, we call that a frenemy."

Mallory smiles. "What a good word. Is it Welsh? *Frenemy.* I'll remember that." She doesn't leave. She takes a step to his bedside table. In her hands is a decanter and a plate. "I brought you a piece of pie. Margrave mentioned the other day that you liked apple pie and there was hardly any left after supper. I saved you a piece and some wine if you're thirsty."

"It's after four in the morning. Leave it. I'll have it for breakfast."

She sets it by his bed.

He waits.

"I'm so tired, sire," Mallory whispers.

Julian swings open the covers.

She takes off her clothes, folds them, stacks them neatly in the corner, and climbs into bed with him. He spoons her, draws the quilt over them, and covers her with his arm.

"I'm worried about that man, Mallory," Julian said. "I can't help it. I don't know if you are safe with him."

"Oh, sire," she coos. "You are so kind-hearted. Trust me, you don't have to worry about him."

She nestles against him, milling into him a little, murmuring something sexy and inaudible. Julian starts to say something, but she is already asleep. He lies awake cradling her, running his fingers up and down her arm, remembering how much Josephine had loved falling asleep like this back in L.A., in another life. They would deplete themselves there, too, and fall into a stupor at the break of dawn. What sweet days they were before the demon that lay in wait came for them. What warm days of syrupy, salty bliss, of ocean water, of lilies and superhighways. That wasn't shadowboxing, that wasn't a shadowlife. That was real.

Or is this real?

Julian clutches the sleeping girl to him, embraces her in a brothel built into the wall of a palace that's about to crumble and be dismantled for marble. *Josephine, Mia, Mary, Mallory,* he whispers. I really believed our time had run out, even as I continued to search for you in the London of my nightmares— or is it the London of my dreams? You are my love, the heat of my heart, raising me in flames above my mundane days and dropping me naked at your feet. Where will all this lead us? Where will all this end? I wish I knew. I wish I could see the future. Because sometimes, even when we are like this, it feels to me that you and I are nothing but winged phantoms, Josephine.

# 6

# Infelice

THE FOLLOWING EVENING MALLORY'S AT HIS DOOR AGAIN. "The lord is back."

"He's here every night now?" Julian says. "Doesn't he have some government business to attend to? A bill to veto? A bishop to consecrate? A family of his own, perhaps? You'd think a man of his, um, stature had some other hobbies."

"He's a widower," Mallory says. "He works late, and to unwind he comes here to spend a little time with me. I offered him a double with me and Marg. But all he wants is you and me."

That's all I want, too. You and me. Quietly Julian sits. His body throbs for her. Though not on these terms! he pretends to justify to himself.

Even that's a lie.

To his marrow, Julian is relieved that the girl in his hands is real. That someone other than him sees Julian make love to her and says, yes! I see her. She is under him, and she is alive. Her arms are around his back. She wraps her legs around him. His hands grip her hips. She bears his weight. She lives. She is not a hallucination. She is not his imagination.

Look, I, the vile creature, see it, too.

The pearls are cast before swine, yes, but they are pearls, and they are cast.

Once again Fabian asks Julian for all sorts of things, and Julian complies. With every fevered caress, Mallory grows more vivid, Fabian more dim, and the silver piles up on the table next to the wine.

Julian almost forgets the man heavy in the chair and sees only the light moaning girl under him. After it's over and it's nearly dawn, she knocks on his door again and climbs into his bed. As he cradles her in his arms, he tries to make pillow talk in the foggy minutes before they're both unconscious. "What kind of name is Mallory? Is it derived from Mary?"

"Mother thought so," the girl replies. "She was sore mistaken. When she went to baptize me, she found out Mallory was derived not from Mary but from France."

"Did your mother love France?"

"Oh, no," Mallory says. "Hence her predicament. When she found out that my name meant suffering in French, she hated France even more."

Julian also doesn't like that her name means suffering. "Mallory is a good name."

"Thank you, sire."

"I like your name, your face, your voice. I like all of you."

"Thank you, sire."

"You can just go ahead and call me Julian." As you used to.

"Very well." Then: "Is your name derived from Caesar? Like a conquering emperor, strong in battle, virile, *constant as the northern star*?"

"I don't know about that. Maybe the constant part." He lifts his head off the pillow and leans over her to study her sleepy face. "Mallory, are you quoting *Julius Caesar* to me?"

She smiles. "I saw it in a playhouse once. Mother and I were walking past the Fortune a few years back when it was still open. They let us in for half a penny. I liked it."

"Oh, you would, Mal. You would."

She nestles into him. "*Julian*...yours is my favorite name in the whole world."

And the next night, and the next, lust and love abounding.

When Fabian is away one night, Julian falls into a panic. He cannot be without her.

"He's not here today," Mallory confirms, peeking into Julian's room. "You must be so grateful we don't have to work—*again*. Now you can *finally* get a good night's rest, be refreshed for the morning." She vanishes before she can see his wounded expression.

Half a minute goes by before she reopens the door and pokes her head in. Her face is lit with a luminous smile. "You keep saying you don't think I'm funny, sire," Mallory says. "I just wanted to prove you wrong."

∞

Julian utterly loses himself in this version of his girl. She is quiet, unassuming, agreeable. She is never painted, yet her mouth is always red; she is youthful and lovely. Her body is abundant everything. Every night Julian's carnal strings are pulled by his naked puppet master, first in front of Fabian and sometimes by themselves in the conjoined intimacy of his bed.

She is amiable and kind. This is how Julian knows the other girls are mendacious fools. They call Mallory wanton and cunning. This could not be more false. She holds his gaze, speaks truth to him with courtesy. No matter what he talks about, she listens raptly. She even tolerates his homilies on the fauna and flora of London's public gardens. She tolerates them especially well. She is endlessly fascinated by his tales of the plants and flowers that have been imported from faraway lands like China and India and planted in the royal gardens of the kings and queens. On Sunday afternoons, they walk together arm in arm through the Westminster parks like a gentleman and a lady, he in his velvet waistcoat, she in her Sunday best. "Mallory, why do you keep your eyes to the ground when we walk?" Julian asks.

"That's where the pennies and the berries are, sire." Mallory smiles as she devours his heart. She likes St. James's Park most of all, because that's where they have the most exotic foliage, and the crocodiles in the ponds and elephants grazing. Once she and Julian even saw two camels! She's amazed by this; he no less so. It's remarkable to see a crocodile in the middle of post-plague Westminster in 1666.

Mallory loves to hear about the blooming things. She listens to him as if he's reciting poetry, sonnets he had composed for her, borne of love and loss. She listens to him wax and wane about oleander and elephant ear, larkspur and lily of the valley, about golden chain and bleeding heart. She adores his stories of rosary peas and laurels, jasmine and azaleas, wild cherries, oak, and yew. Moonseed and mistletoe please her, hemlock and nightshade enchant her.

And in return, on their weekday morning trips to Covent Garden, Mallory entertains Julian with the things *she* loves. In lavish detail she recounts for him the one play she's seen besides *Julius Caesar* and tells him about her modest dream of one day being able to attend the theatre like a rich lady—which to her means any time she chooses. *He loved his wife so much, he built her a theatre so she could attend the opera any time she wanted,* echoes in Julian's overfilled heart.

"You don't wish to be on stage yourself, Mallory?"

Coquettishly she dismisses him. "I don't need to be on stage, sire. I told you, my life is my stage." She confesses that if she could be in any play, she'd like to be in *The Honest Whore,* the backdrop for Othello. She saw it five years ago at the Mermaid Theatre by Puddle Dock when she was fifteen. Her mother took her. It was subtitled *Humors of the Patient Man and the Longing Wife.* Julian and Mallory are walking back from Covent Garden, pushing a cart filled with red peonies and yellow daisies as she regales him with the colors of the play. "The Duke of Milan fakes his daughter's death so her lover Hippolito will leave her alone."

"Why does he need to fake her death?" Julian asks. "Is Hippolito very persistent?" He smiles.

"Very," she replies. "It's one of Hippolito's most endearing qualities."

"But not his only endearing quality, right?"

"By *far* not his only endearing quality." Mallory covers Julian's hand with hers as he pushes the flower cart. "The daughter's name is Infelice. Which means unhappiness." Mallory shrugs. "Almost like my name. Don't look so suddenly glum, sire. Unfortunately for Infelice, a whore named Bellafront also falls in love with Hippolito. He doesn't want to love Bellafront back, because he wishes to remain faithful to Infelice, but he cannot help himself. He falls in love with Bellafront, too."

Julian stops walking near St. Martin-in-the-Fields and waits for the church bells to stop ringing as he draws the girl to him. "Mallory, my beauty, have you considered the possibility that the new seductress and the former lover are one and the same?" He kisses her.

"That can't be. Infelice is dead."

"She is not. You said so yourself. She's hidden."

"Hidden!" As if the thought had never occurred to her.

"Yes. Bellafront is Infelice disguised."

Mallory looks thrilled and stunned by this development. "You don't say, sire. You don't say. Well, well. Was I too young when I saw the play and simply missed such a vital detail?"

"Yes, Bellafront," he says fondly, his arms around her. "I think you missed it."

Julian doesn't need to exaggerate any aspect of his present life, doesn't need to embellish any part of his existence by hyperbole. In every sense, in every way, without any help from heightened metaphor, Julian's love-soaked days here with Josephine are altogether marvelous and good.

Except...sometimes near Covent Garden, as they pass empty lanes of such dismal misery that they must put their heads down, Julian glimpses something else in Mallory. Something hidden. To comfort her, he tells her that the ruthless epidemic that took her mother and aunt is the last such epidemic England will ever have. Mallory doesn't believe him, and why should she? Seeing the world as it is, especially around the nearly abandoned Drury Lane, his words are impossible to believe. She bristles as he carries on about the need to cleanse London of the parasitic scourge. "Please, sire!" she exclaims with barely concealed scorn. "What do you think we need here, an overflowing volcano, like Pompeii? The brimstone fire of Sodom and Gomorrah?"

"Yes," Julian says. "A fire." Slightly his limbs shake. He wishes he knew the exact date of the Great Fire. It *was* in 1666, right? He's not sure of anything anymore.

"Look at the way we live," Mallory says. "Fire, no fire. What do you think a little flame will do? Drury Lane will remain the same fetid alley, riddled with the dead. And my mother will still be gone. She's the only one who ever loved me, the only one who tried to keep me from harm."

Your mother is not the only one who ever loved you, Mallory.

"What does it matter to Mother what might happen in the future? She's dead. Frankly, what you're saying is nothing but cold comfort, sire."

In the night, when they are warmer, Mallory divulges things about the Black Plague. They had suffered bouts of the pestilence before, and no one paid much mind to the initial stages of the plague. At the first sign that it was a real epidemic, not just a flu that was going around, Anna sent Mallory south to live with her sister Olivia. As everyone around her continued to die, the mother finally abandoned her house of bawd and traveled across the river to reunite with her daughter. She carried in her hands bouquets of wormwood, a most bitter smelling and tasting flower. "Mother had heard that it might protect me from harm. She made me drink a potion made from vinegar and wormwood. Oh, was it ever vile!"

"Did they paint your door?"

"With a bloody cross? Yes," Mallory says. "Death is a pale horse, but it shall not come near thee, Mother prayed over me. Then her buboes burst, and she bled to death."

Mallory shows Julian a sheet of yellowing parchment. It's from the parish of Clerkenwell. The paper is called the Bill of Mortality. Every week, the parish publishes the causes and numbers of the local dead. Anna ripped it from the priory wall as she was fleeing.

**Diseases and Casualties this Week:**

**Apoplexie** 1

**Burned in his bed by a candle** 1

**Canker** 1

**Cough** 2

**Fright** 3

**Grief** 3

**Killed by a fall from a Bellfry** 1

**Lethargy** 1

**Suddenly** 1

**Timpany** 1

**Plague** 7165

Seven thousand people dead in one parish! Out of how many? "Eight thousand," Mallory replies. Julian shudders. She leaves the list with him when she goes to start her day. "For safekeeping," she says.

Does she mean the Bill of Mortality or her?

What happened to you, Mallory? Julian asks when they lie in the hot bath together.

I don't know what you mean.

Once upon a time, you used to be in such revolt.

When was this?

When I knew you last, Julian whispers.

Who has time to revolt, sire, Mallory says, her face turned away from him. I don't have time for such frivolity.

The steam from the bath fills the room and escapes through the open window. Mallory hints she might like to escape, too. Where, he says, and she replies, what's it to you. She is smoke herself, her skin translucent crepe paper, once real, now an ashen vapor.

∞

Carling and Ivy, the cleaning girls Mallory shares the room with, have confronted her about her mysterious absences from their quarters behind the kitchen. They demand she pay them, or they'll tell the Baroness she's up to no good. Julian pays them. Blackmail doesn't sit well with him; he knows it's a temporary fix. Now that the urchins know he will pay, they'll keep raising the price. But what choice does he have? The Baroness will not take kindly to his poaching the orphaned niece entrusted into her care by her two dead sisters.

But the second reason Julian pays off Carling and Ivy is Lord Fabian. Because things have changed in Room Two, and not for the better. A week earlier, as Julian was in the final pangs of his exertions, he felt a fist strike him between the shoulder blades. It was Fabian. He'd gotten out of his chair, waddled over to the bed and hit Julian. "Stop it!" Fabian hissed. "You're hurting her. You're tormenting her."

"No, my lord," Mallory said, underneath Julian, peeking her head out, controlling her panting breath. "He's not hurting me."

"You were crying out."

"Not from pain, my lord."

After that night, Fabian stopped requesting Julian's presence in Room Two. That is why Julian pays off the hooligan maids— so Mallory can continue to share his bed.

Sometimes in the afterglow, while she lies in his arms, he tries to talk to her about a future that doesn't involve the Silver Cross or Miss Tilly's girls, or Lord Fabian, but Mallory always falls asleep, and the next morning is up and out before he wakes.

The bells ring, the children play, the ink dots on his arm multiply like summer bug bites.

He and Mallory walk along the Thames, through the parks, through green lanes. They stop for fireworks and carriage races. Whitehall Palace is open to the public. They stroll through the royal gardens, and when they're not discussing unusual plants, Julian attempts a conversation about a life that might include something for just the two of them, that might include marriage and even babies. He talks about it in fantabulous terms, in the language of dreamers not realists, not as in, let's get married, but more as in, what if we were a prince and a princess and got married and lived in a white marble palace like this one? Wouldn't that be something? Mostly Mallory nods.

The immutable tattooing makes Julian feel ridiculous. Count the days, Devi said, but a few times Julian gets on with his day without marking the days—on purpose, not on purpose.

He and Mallory still haven't talked about the future in the language of realists. He doesn't want to rush things, push things, like before in L.A. when he ruined everything with his hurry, as if he had felt on some subliminal level that Josephine was running out of time. Here in post-plague London, he wants to live with her—and does live with her—the way most people live. As if they're going to live forever.

# 7

# Dead Queen, Revisited

AT THE END OF AUGUST ONE OF THE PATRONS OF THE SILVER
Cross dies in the night.

A panting, irritated Baroness Tilly bangs on Julian's door.
She was woken up by the one-eyed Ilbert, who said the dead
man's blood dripped through the floorboards into his cubby
below. "It's the *last* thing we need," the Baroness says to Julian.
"Today is a Saturday, our busiest night of the week. Nothing
could be worse for business than death. Julian, let's hurry and
take care of it before the stench takes hold."

It's Lord Fabian.

In his velvet robes, the man lies face down on the floor. He
has collapsed, hit the iron leg of the table, and smashed his
head open. He may have bled to death, but it's hard to tell. Why
would he fall in the first place? Julian and the Baroness stand
in shock.

"His heart must've finally gave out, the poor fat bugger," the
Baroness says. She is probably right. Nothing is out of place,
except the overturned table, the silver decanter on its side, the
broken crystal glasses, and the enormous corpse.

"This is the kind of thing that closes down establishments!"
the Baroness says. "People are *so* superstitious about death. And
this is one of our best rooms. Bugger it. Bugger it all to hell."

Fabian's head is turned to the side. His eyes bulge out of their
sockets, as if he had suffocated before he died, not simply lost

consciousness after a fall and a blow to the head. The suffocation seems odd for a cardiac event. Blood spills out of his filled-up mouth. There's foam around his lips—as if he'd been gasping for breath before dying. From the disturbance around the armchair and the knocked-over table, it looks to Julian that the man could've gone into convulsions. The foul mess under his swollen body suggests a severe gastric disturbance.

To keep from retching, Julian and the Baroness breathe into their velvet sleeves. He opens the windows to let in some air. It's already miserably hot, though it's barely sunrise.

Lord Fabian is a nobleman, a temporal lord, a peer in Parliament. He is a well-known figure around London, and there's going to be an outcry if his desiccated, exsanguinated corpse is found in a brothel. Someone will get charged with murder. Not may. *Will.* Someone will get quartered. In 1666, they disembowel first and ask questions later.

While the Baroness wrings her hands, Julian looks around. Usually Fabian keeps a small purse on the table by the wine. From the black pouch, the lord pulled out shillings and half-crowns and stacked them in phallic towers for him and Mallory. It takes Julian a moment to find it, but there it is; it's fallen off the table and under the bed. At least Fabian wasn't robbed, that's something.

"These things happen, Baroness," Julian says. "The man fell and hit his head. As you said, he probably had a heart attack. Let's call for Parker. He's a reasonable chap. He'll see this for what it is, a terrible accident."

"This is the City of Westminster!" she hisses. "Good God, man, do you know *nothing*? Lords of His Majesty's Government don't drop dead in brothels."

"This one did."

"Who was the lord with, do you know?" The Baroness trembles. "Please tell me it wasn't Mallory!"

"No, madam," Julian says. "It wasn't Mallory."

"How do you *know*? How do you know for *certain*?"

Julian knows because Mallory was with him last night. He can't admit it to the Baroness. He goes on the attack instead. "Baroness, who did you assign Lord Fabian to?" he asks, turning Tilly's own words against her, since the woman is constantly bragging about how no man can walk up the stairs without her knowledge.

The whoremonger grows reticent. "I may have overlooked writing his name in my book," she confesses. And then, "Truth is, I didn't see him come in." She hesitates. "It's not unusual. He often enters the back way, to avoid being seen. He's too recognizable. But enough claptrap," she says with a forceful air. "He's not getting any fresher while we stand here shooting our mouths off. What does it matter who was with him and which way he came?"

"You asked me who was with him, madam."

"The man is dead! Isn't that what's most important? We must get him out of here before anyone else wakes up. Isn't *that* what's most important?"

Julian is tasked with removing Fabian's corpse from the premises, dumping it in a nearby canal, and cleaning up the room as if the death never happened. It's a stifling end-summer morning in Westminster, where no smell, no matter how faint, cannot be made worse by the wretched heat. A man dead and decomposing in the swelter of August is not what Julian would call a faint smell. The Baroness insists Ilbert help Julian. She calls the eel-like servant a humpbacked tomb of discretion. "Oh, and Julian," the Baroness says before she leaves, "have Carling and Ivy wash down the room. Keep my niece out of it. She and Lord Fabian were close. I don't want her getting upset. As soon as you've cleared him out, let me know, and I'll take Mal to the market while the other girls mop up."

Julian and Ilbert wrap Fabian's body in burlap and tie him up with twine. A quick-thinking Ilbert first cleans up the mess around Fabian so they can work without getting soiled themselves. He then suggests lining the burlap with pieces of flagstone from the basement to help weigh the body down during final disposal.

It takes hours, but fortunately the girls work late and sleep past noon, so the house stays quiet. Just in case, the Baroness stands guard up in the attic with a tray of biscuits and marmalade to stop the girls from wandering downstairs.

Julian and Ilbert drag the heavy, unwieldy sack down the narrow back stairs into the alley, and heave the body into a cart, the very same pushcart Julian and Mallory line with flowers each morning. Julian orders Ilbert to take the cart to a canal or an estuary as far away as possible from Whitehall and the Silver Cross. Anywhere Ilbert wishes. But far from here. Ilbert nods as if he understands things.

"What do you think happened to him, Ilbert?"

"I know nothing about nothing, sire," the tomb of discretion replies. "He could've died from many things."

"Like what?"

"I have one eye and my hump prevents me from looking anywhere but down." Ilbert's cunning expression reads as if down is where it's all at. It reminds Julian of what Mallory had once said in passing, why her gaze was always to the ground. Because that's where the pennies and the berries were, she said.

After Ilbert leaves, Julian vomits in the alley that centuries later will become Craig's Court.

He cleans himself up in the downstairs slop sink and, carrying buckets filled with vinegar and lye, goes upstairs to collect the last of the man's belongings for burning before Carling and Ivy arrive to clean. The room reeks. It will take the maids hours to rid it of the smell of human waste and death. But they must do it, the room must be ready for business by nightfall. What a great room it was, Julian laments, now ruined.

After collecting Fabian's clothes and righting the table, Julian surveys the floor for anything suspicious in case Constable Parker comes to call. Near the open window, where Fabian fell, Julian notices that one of the floorboards isn't level. A short plank seems to have gotten loose. He pops it out, aligns it straight, and is about to bang it into place with his fist when underneath, resting on the subflooring, he sees a dark brown satchel.

Alarm pounds through Julian's body.

The purse is brown leather with red velvet ribbons, stitched with gold and silver. As he lifts it out, he hears the sound of dull rolling marbles. Pulling open the strings, Julian finds inside not marbles but gold coin.

There are female voices in the corridor. Awkwardly, he stuffs the satchel down his belted breeches, a kangaroo pouch with a golden joey in it. He must calm down or he'll have a heart attack himself, drop dead with a bag of gold in his pants. He replaces the short board, bangs it in until it lies evenly with the rest of the floor and takes one last glance around to make sure nothing else looks disturbed.

His bedroom door has no lock, as most rooms do not in a brothel. He drags an oak table to barricade the door and sits down on the bed with his back to the entrance as a precaution.

Trying to be as quiet as possible, Julian pours out the clanging gold onto his bedspread. Each the size of a half-dollar, the coins are gleaming, hefty, pristine. He's never seen anything like them.

Except...

He's seen something a little bit like them. The head of the coin is the imperious, fully robed body of a queen. He recognizes the queen because in 1603, her face was on all the silver shillings and farthings and pennies he took with him to Smythe Field market to buy flowers for Mary's wedding. It's Elizabeth I. *Elizabeth Regina* is stamped on the face. On the obverse side is the royal coat of arms.

Julian is confounded and troubled. Why is there a bag of freshly minted historic coin? Why was it hidden in the floorboards at the Silver Cross? Is it Fabian's? Was he hiding sovereigns in a brothel and dropped dead? Was that why his face was on the floor, was that why he fell? Did he know he was dying and was trying to get to his money?

Julian counts it. There are 49 gold coins. He estimates each weighs about half an ounce. That's about 25 ounces of gold he's got on his bed. Breathing heavily, he sits, his hands running over the bullion. Why would a lord hide a treasure in the Silver Cross of all places? Didn't he have a home where he could stash his ill-gotten gains? Was it blackmail money on the way to another destination? Or was Fabian the destination? Was it in transit or being delivered? Did Fabian steal the money and was killed for it, or was it his money and he was killed for it? Was it even his money? Is it even real gold? The weight of his intuition heavy in his hand tells him that it is.

Julian has a million questions and zero answers.

He also has zero time to reflect and ruminate. Coincidence or not, an esteemed member of the House of Lords was killed literally over gold. Before Julian can find out if it was by chance or design, he must get the treasure out of the brothel.

But get it out to where? He has no friends in London in 1666. No Devi to consult, no Ashton to help him. He's friendly with the girls but knows no one else except Mallory, and until he finds out more, she can't be endangered in any way. If it's real gold as Julian suspects, she can't be an accomplice to a theft of this magnitude. They cut you in half for stealing pewter bowls. She can't help him anyway, she has no room of her own to hide the money. She keeps her dead mother's Bill of Mortality in his desk for safety. Can Julian hide the money in his unlocked cupboard? What about in *his* floorboards? He investigates, but his floor is assiduously nailed down.

Afraid, exhilarated, his heart thumping, Julian returns the coins to their pouch, except for two. After he changes into fresh clothes, he binds the purse inside his trunk hose, pulling a pair of belted breeches over them. He tightens another belt around all three—the hose, the breeches and the purse—to keep the coins from jingling as he walks.

Julian needs to do two things. He must find a goldsmith on Cheapside who can appraise the coin. And he must hide the money somewhere safe until the investigation into Lord Fabian's death is behind them, and then he and Mallory together can decide what to do.

Flattening out the bedspread where the weight of the coin has made a tell-tale depression, Julian throws on his coat to cover the awkward and conspicuous bulge in his groin and heads downstairs. After giving cleaning instructions to Carling and Ivy, he learns that the Baroness has taken "an extremely unhappy" Mallory and left for the afternoon. Relieved that he doesn't have to explain to the Baroness why he's wearing a coat in ninety-degree heat, Julian runs out to Parliament Street.

It's brutally hot out. It has been a nearly rainless August. Why can't it rain just once in London, just *once*! Stepping over the horse manure on the cobblestones, Julian hurries to the Strand where he hops on a hackney carriage that takes him through Temple Bar to Cheapside.

Cheapside, the queen of thoroughfares, is wide like a boulevard and sports fountains and water channels. It has dozens of taverns, merchants' mansions, luxury shops, milliners and cobblers, silversmiths and blacksmiths. Cheapside has everything, including the most venerable gold dealers in the world. Everyone in London shops on Cheapside on Saturday afternoons. The jammed congestion around St. Paul's is so bad, Julian must hop off the carriage and walk the rest of the way to Goldsmiths Row, sweating in his absurd overcoat.

The building he enters is dark inside, a grand space like a cave chamber, but no amount of dimness can hide its ostentatious wealth. It's not just the gold trinkets in the glass cases and the gold display platters on the walls. Even the crown mouldings, the door latches, and the sills on the windows are plated gold. Plated gold, right, not *cast* in gold? The candlesticks are gold, and the beveled edges of the polished oak table behind which Julian sits are trimmed in gold. The hands of all the softly chiming clocks are gold. The man across from him has a gold pocket watch laid out on the table to remind Julian of the value of time.

"How can I be of service, sire?" the elegant man says. He's impeccably dressed in gray velvet and white silk. His name is Arnold Bertie. He is in the employ of the great Earl of Lindsey who is one of the owners of the Worshipful Company of Goldsmiths.

His fingers shaking, Julian slides the gold coin across the table. "I was hoping you could tell me something about this coin."

Bertie doesn't pick it up. That's how Julian instantly knows it's not counterfeit. The gentleman, for whom gold is his livelihood, doesn't touch the coin with his hands. "Sire, *please*," he says to Julian. "Do *not* slide it across the desk. You could scratch the coin." Bertie pulls out a silk white cloth, a magnifying glass, brings forth the burning lantern, pulls closer the candlesticks, and tenderly picks up the gold piece with a white-gloved hand, laying it on the white silk. Wordlessly he examines it for no less than ten minutes. He treats the coin like a holy relic. From his drawer, he produces a scale and eases the coin onto it. "Astounding!" he cries. "Wherever did you get this?"

"It was a small token of affection from a deceased uncle."

"Oh, this is no small token, I can assure you. What you've got here is one of the most exquisite coins ever to be hammered by the Royal Mint. It's called *angel*. It's an Elizabethan fine gold sovereign. Nothing even close to it is being made today. Or for that matter is likely to be made again. It is simply too expensive to produce. It is 23-carat gold, and precisely one-half of a Troy ounce. The coin is 99% pure gold. It is a work of art. And judging by its condition, yours has never been used."

Julian doesn't know what to say.

"Are you all right, sire? You look unwell."

"I'm fine," Julian says, his voice unsteady. "Please— continue."

Bertie gazes upon the coin with reverence. "During the Elizabethan era, all our coin was hand-hammered like this one, but you can imagine how much labor that entailed, melting the gold ingots, softening them, casting them into blanks, hammering and softening them again. The hammering and annealing happened another twelve times before the edges were deemed sufficiently rounded, and that was just to make the blank, sire. Then it had to be coined in a hand-held die, coined with the precision of a master craftsman. These coins haven't been minted for over a hundred years, at least not to my knowledge. Is it the only one you've got? Such a shame. I don't suppose you'd be interested in selling this piece to us? Would you like me to see what we can give you for it today?"

"Well, I suppose there's no harm in that," Julian says evenly.

Clutching the coin inside a silk handkerchief, Bertie disappears. Julian, his nerves electrified, waits impatiently.

In a few minutes, Bertie returns. "Here's what I can offer. The Charles II guinea, weighing barely half of this coin, and not comparable to it in either quality or gold content, is worth twenty-two shillings, so a little more than one pound sterling. For this coin, I can offer you three hundred shillings."

Three hundred shillings. Julian is speechless. That's *fifteen pounds*! Mallory would have to work six years to make that. As a keeper of a brothel, Julian would have to work three.

*And there's another 48 where it came from.*

Julian knocks over the chair as he stands, dropping his hat on the floor. "I'm sorry, Bertie," he says, clutching his groin where the coins warmly reside. "I'm in a terrible rush. Simply maddening hurry. I accept your offer, if you would be so kind."

"Oh! Very good, sire. I am *delighted*. How would you like your money?"

"Three dimes, a hundred-dollar bill and eighty-seven ones," Julian mutters in a daze. "I mean—ten guineas, fifteen crowns, and twenty-five shillings."

With money in hand and coins in his crotch, he bows and backs out. Lost and breathless, Julian stands on Cheapside, trying to think, think! To the left of him is Poultry, to the right

St. Paul's. The river is up ahead, all around him is the London Wall. Where does he go? He's boxed in.

He has stolen an unconscionable amount of gold. Julian is certain he and the dead lord can't be the only ones who know about the fortune in the floorboards. For all Julian knows, Ilbert may know about it. If Fabian didn't drop dead by accident, which seems less and less likely, he was probably killed for this money. Greater men have been murdered for far less. Now the killer will be coming to get what's his, and he won't stop until Julian is dead, and all the cullies are dead, and the Silver Cross is burned to the ground.

Is this Julian's way of protecting Mallory?

Nearly fifty gold coins at fifteen pounds each. That is £735 in 1666. Motionless he stands, watching the slow carriages, the hurrying people, the cantering horses. He's euphoric, but in trouble.

It's impossibly hot out and he's wearing a long wool coat to disguise his thievery. He looks like a criminal, looks guilty and sweaty, his face red and wet. Lowering his head, Julian hurries away from Cheapside, up St. Martin's Le Grand to Cripplegate on the way to the familiar and haunted Clerkenwell. It's all he knows. In the courtyard gardens of the church of St. Giles by Cripplegate, just outside the City gates, Julian finds a bench between the side of the church and the Roman wall and drops down. He needs a prayer. But how does one pray for help in a situation like this? He needs to hide the money is what he needs to do, and then he must persuade Mallory to run away with him. He was able to persuade Josephine to marry him, almost against her will, and he was able to persuade Mary—when it was too late. This time, he must do better, try harder. That's why he's been given a second chance! Where is it safe for him to stash it? He gazes around the empty garden, the quiet alley. The stone church stands silently, its grounds wilting with heavy, end-August browning leaves, the London Wall a few yards away. The last time, Julian wanted to take Mary to Italy. This time, with

£700, they can go anywhere. They've been offered a new life. They can travel like the Pilgrims across the sea, to Massachusetts Bay Colony. But run they must; they can't stay where they are, that's for sure. He's been lulled into a false sense of immortality, he knows that now, the bathwater in the brothel too warm, the girl too addicting. Now he must act.

Julian stares into the distance a few more seconds—and then shoots up and bolts, the crowns and guineas jingling in his pocket. He knows what to do. He needs to find a mason; he needs a hammer, a chisel, a trowel, some lime-based mortar. He has figured out where to hide the money. All will be well. He will fix it. He will fix everything.

# 8

# Bellafront

GRIMY, SWEATY, PANTING, GROSS, JULIAN RETURNS LATE TO
the Silver Cross.

The Baroness is ready to send him to Newgate for his day-long absence just when she needs him most. Not only had he vanished, but he's come back with no flowers! And in his absence, a nasty fight has broken out between the girls, the constable has come by twice, inquiring about a possible death on the premises, Ilbert has been making strange noises about blackmail, and Carling and Ivy did such a poor job disinfecting the room that an early client has just stormed downstairs demanding a refund.

In the corner of the tavern, Father Anselmo stands, loudly pleading to the men present. "My fallen angels, have you already forgotten that pestilence was retribution for your wicked ways?" he cries. "It was punishment for your wrongdoing. I beseech you, good gentlemen and a lady—turn from your stinking and horrible sin of lechery! Which grows daily in this stew by your continual employment of strumpets, all to the one misguided and idle women. How long can this continue—until you're *all* dead of syphilis or the plague? A conflagration will not be enough to punish you for your sins. How long do you intend to dwell in your odious wickedness? Until there is more death? Don't you know that wanton lust, divorced from civilizing forces, leads to errors in judgment, to compromised honor, to blackmail, to murder! All the deadly sins are boiling under your roof, and you call yourselves reputable men. Repent! Repent before it's too late."

The Baroness, her face unpainted, perspiring, aggravated, folds her hands together in a frantic plea to Julian. She looks as Julian feels. "I'm going to throw myself into the River Thames if that miserable wretch doesn't shut his gob this instant!" she exclaims about Anselmo. "Where have you been all day, Julian? Why do you look as if you've been swimming in mud? Why aren't you dressed for the evening? It's Saturday night. You know how busy we get. We have no flowers, and Room Two still smells of corpse. The girls are ripping each other's hair out—and I mean that in the most literal sense. Ilbert is more insolent than ever, you're nowhere to be found, and look like a leper. Please— go change into your evening attire. Blimey, one little death, and everything's gone to pot!" The woman fans herself wildly, raising her eyes to the ceiling. "Bloody helpers, it's hot! I'm praying for a little rain and for that beastly man to lose his tongue. Is that really so much to ask, O Lord?"

Julian pats Tilly's arm. On the outside, he remains composed. "I think some of your prayers may already be answered," he says. "There was a strong east wind as I was returning. Rain is around the corner. About everything else, Baroness, don't worry. I'll take care of the constable and the girls and the smell. Give me an hour. I'll take care of it all." Calmly he starts up the stairs. "Which girls are fighting?"

"All of them. But mainly Margrave and Mallory. Tell them to stop hollering or they can leave right now and go work at the Haymarket. They beat their girls there, soundly, like gongs."

"Mallory is fighting?" Julian hurries.

On the second floor, thirteen girls are yelling in the corridor. Margrave is soaked from head to chest as she and Mallory scream at each other. Julian's first instinct is to defend Mallory, but a more careful listen tells him that Mallory is the attacker. Apparently, she threw a bucket of putrid water into Margrave's face. It's gone into the girl's eyes and nose and mouth and is burning her. Instead of apologizing, Mallory stands and shouts. Julian has never seen Mallory this red-faced and enraged.

Julian steps between the two women, separating them and pulling Mallory away. She doesn't want to hear it, not even from him. But he's had enough. He raises his voice to show the girls he means business. "Stop it, you two. Margrave, go clean yourself up. Mallory, you too, downstairs. You look a fright. You're scaring off the customers." He frowns. "What's the matter with you?" he says to her quietly. "Go." And louder, "Carling, Ivy, come with me—the rest of you, get back to work. Show's over."

The Baroness is right. Fabian's room still smells awful. Death must have seeped into the floorboards.

"We tried, sire!" Carling and Ivy cry. "We used up all the vinegar you gave us and all the lye."

Julian sighs. "Let's declare this room occupied for the rest of the night. Put a sign on the door. We'll work with nine rooms tonight, nothing we can do." The Baroness won't be happy with the loss of earnings. And tomorrow is Sunday, and all the markets will be closed. Nowhere to buy more lye. Exasperated, Julian follows the maids downstairs. He hasn't gotten himself cleaned up as he had promised the Baroness, but he needs to speak to Mallory. He finds her in the servants' kitchen, still irate. "Mallory?"

"Go away."

"Why are you upset? What has Margrave done?"

"She's a thief."

"I thought she was your friend?"

"She hates me. She's always hated me."

"What could she possibly steal from you? You have nothing. You barely have a change of clothes."

"Yes, by all means, demean me."

"I'm not demeaning you," Julian says, chastised, "I'm trying to understand."

"Please, sire, can you leave so I can do my job?" She won't look at him.

As he's about to head upstairs, he hears the Baroness sharply calling his name from the ground floor of the tavern. She's still in her pink velvet robe, but now Constable Parker stands by her side. Julian's mood worsens. He wasn't expecting to face Parker so soon. He can't deal with the constable at the moment, not least of all because he is so disheveled.

Usually Parker is delightfully apathetic. He comes every week, Julian gives him a drink, a meal, and a cut of the week's earnings. For this, Parker looks the other way if a fight breaks out, or if there's some petty theft. But tonight Parker says he can't really look the other way because there's chatter all over Westminster that a well-born man has been found dead in a brothel.

"Who says a man's been found dead?" Julian asks.

"The one-humped bloke with a shovel."

"Ilbert?" The Baroness laughs. "No, no, constable. Ilbert was born in an insane asylum. Born to a leper who died at childbirth. He is half-blind because of his mother's leprosy. It ate away his brain. He once told me," the Baroness says, "that two men died of spotted fever on Drury Lane!"

"That's probably correct, madam."

"He's never been to Drury Lane. How would he know? The other day he was whispering to Father Anselmo that English aristocrats and Members of Parliament were conducting a sado-masochistic orgy in this very house until daybreak. Don't you think I'd know if this was happening under my own roof? Orgy! What is this, the Haymarket? Besides, we don't have rooms big enough for an orgy even if we wanted one. So you see, Ilbert often makes things up, all cock and bull stories from him. Pay him no mind, constable, no mind at all."

The constable almost buys the Baroness's own cock and bull story. "Here's my pickle," Parker says. "Ilbert keeps muttering that some fat man has died. I wondered if he could've meant Lord Fabian, so I took a stroll over to the honorable gentleman's home in Belgravia, to make sure he was all right. The gentleman is widowed and childless. And wouldn't you know it, his butler informed me that Lord Fabian is missing! He hasn't been home since early Friday morning. That's never happened before, apparently. The household is frantic."

Julian and the Baroness shrug. "Maybe he's at work," the Baroness says.

"Great minds think alike, madam," Parker says. "That was my thinking. So I took a ride over to the Tower this afternoon, and guess what?"

"I can't fathom."

"The Tower?" says Julian. "Like the Tower of London?"

"Yes, sir," Parker says. "That's where the honorable gentleman works. Unfortunately, no one was there to answer my queries at the weekend. I was told to come back on Monday."

Julian and the Baroness both exhale with relief as the constable shakes Julian's hand and feigns to go. Then, almost as an aside, he asks to speak to the cleaning girl.

"Which cleaning girl? We got three."

"Ilbert mentioned that one of them was always hanging around the gentleman," Parker said. "Maybe she can tell us something—like the last time she saw him."

"I assure you, constable, he hasn't been here." The Baroness waves her little book of hours in the air. "No one goes upstairs without me knowing. No orgies. No Lord Fabian."

"Just a quick word with the girl, Baroness."

"She's my niece, constable. She's the only daughter of my youngest sister, may God rest her soul. I can vouch for Mallory on the Bible."

Parker raises his hand to assure her. "It's just routine, Baroness, please don't worry." He coughs. "Though one other small thing...Ilbert says that a week ago he saw this Mallory girl in the main kitchen, where she has no business being, crushing something with a mortar into a pestle. When he confronted her, she scraped out the pestle and hurried off."

"Probably grinding some nuts," the Baroness says. "Is that also against the law?"

"By also, do you mean grinding some nuts and *also* murder?" Parker says. "One of them is against the law, madam, yes. And Ilbert may be a more enterprising fellow than he lets on because he ran his finger through the pestle she left behind and tasted the grindings."

"And?"

"Ilbert says he damn near died. Says he was sick for *three days*. The bitter thing that touched his tongue burned a hole in it, singed his throat and gave him terrible digestive upset. He started vomiting up blood, which may be the only thing that saved him, since he believes he vomited up whatever was poisoning him."

"Poisoning?" Julian opens his hands with a chuckle. "Constable Parker, Ilbert touches his mouth and face after handling the filthiest things. Has the man *ever* had a bath? He could've eaten a spoiled pig snout, old fish, bad eggs. In any case, it clearly wasn't poison since Ilbert's still walking around, alive as all that."

"As opposed to who?" Parker says. "As opposed to an esteemed Member of Parliament, a Lord Temporal, who has vanished and can't be found?"

"Do you always assume the worst when a man can't be found for a day?"

The constable eyes Julian, then the Baroness. "Not any man. Lord Fabian. Many powerful people are going to notice the lord's conspicuous absence. Among them His Majesty Charles II, your king."

Julian and the Baroness stand motionless. Julian's leg itches with anxiety.

"I don't need to remind you both," Parker says, "that murder by poison is a heinous crime. The punishment for it is being boiled in oil. Now will you two let me talk to the girl so we can clear her of any wrongdoing?"

They look for her, but Mallory can't be found. Night is falling and the tavern is getting busy. The Baroness manages to charm

Parker into returning on Monday morning, when he can have all day with Mallory if he likes. "And perhaps the honorable Lord Fabian will turn up by then, and this confusion will be put behind us."

As soon as Parker leaves, Julian turns to the Baroness. "Ilbert's not to be trusted."

"What could Mallory have been grinding up in that pestle? Damn that girl!"

"Nuts, Baroness! But this isn't about Mallory. It's about Ilbert. You do remember, don't you, how just this morning he and I dragged Fabian's body down the stairs?"

"Shh!"

"On your orders, he helped me bind the man," Julian says. "He carted him away. Ilbert knows for a fact there's a body, for an absolute fact. What's stopping him from leading the constable right to it?"

"Why would he do that?" The madam sounds offended. "We've had a death here before, some years ago. Ilbert was exemplary. Took care of everything. He's been working for me for twelve years. He's like a loyal son."

"You're sure about that? Because if he squeals, we'll all be boiled in oil for murder and for conspiracy to conceal it. You, me, Mallory, and half your girls."

"Murder! What are you on about? The lord had a heart attack! You said so yourself."

"Who will believe you," Julian says, "when his body is found bound and dumped in a canal?"

∞

That Saturday night, from September 1 to September 2, 1666, is one of the worst Julian has at the Silver Cross. It's one crisis after another. He barely has enough time to wash and change before Room Two is demanded by a contingent of celebrants who are willing to overlook the smell. They pay handsomely for a flow of wine and meat and girls to be brought up at regular intervals throughout the night. Carling stokes the fire, Mallory lights the candles and Ivy carries the ale and the steins. But the other nine rooms also need tending. At one point, Julian is reduced to changing the enseamed sheets himself. A fight breaks out between Brynhilda and a customer over the difference between services provided and price paid. Brynhilda, twice the size of the weasely john, punches him in the face, sending him tumbling down the stairs. For this Julian must negotiate a peace and restitution. One of the girls is sick in the night, vomiting violently in the middle of working, and the Baroness herself must haggle for a reduced fee instead of a refund. The night refuses to end.

It's after five in the morning when the business of the house finally dies down, the patrons leave, the Baroness goes to bed, and an exhausted Julian locks up and returns to his room. It's dark blue outside. Dawn is near. After taking off his jacket and puffy shirt, he gets the quill and dips it in ink. How many *dots*? Six columns of seven plus one; 43 *dots* in all. His forearm burns as the quill pierces the skin. He wipes up the drop of blood and wonders how many days he's missed, four, a week, more?

A voice from a corner says, "Julian."

He drops the quill, nearly falls himself. He thought he was alone.

Mallory is crammed between the dormered wall and the side of the cupboard, huddled on the floor, her knees drawn up. How did he not see her?

"Don't scare me like that," Julian says. "What are you doing?" He scans the room. It looks as if his things have been gone through. The journal is not where he left it, the shirts have been refolded. "Why are you on the floor?"

"Shh," she says.

"What's the matter?"

She rocks back and forth.

"Is it about Margrave?"

She won't say.

He perches on the bed. Seeing her distraught makes him distraught. Outside the sun is not up yet, the air is blue-gray with a tinge of amber. The east wind is strong. On this wind, Julian can smell burning wood. What fools build fires in this crazy hot weather?

"You have to help me," she says in a low cold voice. "This is all your fault."

What is she talking about?

"Marg robbed me," Mallory says from the floor.

"Peanut, don't get offended again, but what could she take from you?"

She doesn't answer. "You have to silence Ilbert," Mallory says at last. "Do you know anyone in this town who can do it? Or can *you* do it?" She says the last part as if she doesn't expect Julian can silence a mosquito.

"What do you mean, silence him? Like tell him to shut his trap? I can do it."

"Well, perhaps before you beg him politely to quiet down, you can ask him what he's done with the lord's body."

So she knows. The Baroness tried to shield her from it, Julian didn't want to tell her, but she's found out anyway. There are no secrets in a brothel.

"Mal, I'm really sorry—"

She cuts him off. "I heard you tell the imp to take the body far from here, and instead, Ilbert threw it into a canal a few streets away, a canal with barely six inches of standing water. The body isn't even submerged. It's what some might call hiding evidence in plain sight."

Julian pales. "How do you know this?"

"Ah, it's a funny story. I know this," Mallory says, "because Ilbert told me."

"Why would Ilbert tell you that?"

"Oh, no, dear one. You misunderstand. He didn't confess to me because he wanted to get it off his skeletal chest. He told me, you see, because he wanted me to pay him to keep quiet."

"Pay him? Why would *you* pay him?"

Mallory doesn't answer. "But I can't pay him because Margrave has stolen my money."

"What money? The money we've been earning for you on the side? I thought you always keep it on your person? Isn't that what you told me? Keep your valuables on you?"

"That little game Ilbert was playing with the constable about the mortar and pestle," Mallory continues, as if Julian hasn't spoken, "that was just him letting me and the Baroness know that we'll all hang unless he gets what he wants."

"What does he want?"

"Half," Mallory says.

Julian fumbles inside his waistcoat pocket for the purse with the guineas in it. "Half of what?" he asks dully.

"Don't you get it? If Margrave didn't rob me, then Ilbert must've robbed me, in which case, he's just toying with us. Tormenting us before the slaughter. It wouldn't surprise me about him, wouldn't surprise me in the slightest."

She puts her face in her hands.

"Half of what?" Julian repeats in a whisper.

"Half a bag of fucking gold," says Mallory.

Julian stops being mild or consoling. He gets off the bed, stands in front of her. He doesn't speak because he can't speak. He tries to put together his next thought, his next word. The sun drifts up over the gray slate rooftops of Whitehall. The wind is strong and dry. It still smells of burning wood. He crouches in front of her, sinks to the floor next to her. Their feet could touch, but they don't.

"Lord Fabian hid it in the floorboards in Room Two," Mallory says. "It's not there anymore. I didn't take it. You're saying Margrave didn't take it. So if it wasn't Ilbert, who could've taken it, Julian?"

She doesn't look at him as she speaks, doesn't see the shock on his face. This can't be. It simply can't be. "Why would Fabian hide gold in the floorboards of a brothel?" Julian asks.

"It was ill-gotten gold," Mallory says. "The lord was Master of the Royal Mint up in the Tower of London. Oh, you didn't know that? Yes. That's what he was. These days they use a machine press, but a hundred years ago they hammered the coin in dies. Two years ago, I found one of those hand-made coins on him as I was undressing him. That's when he told me he was a lifelong coin collector. He said that a few years earlier, in the chaos after Cromwell fell from power, he swiped one of the discarded dies they used to cast the commemorative Elizabethan sovereigns. He said the die had been retired prematurely. It needed a little sharpening on the face side, a little etching. He said the coat of arms side was perfect. After he fixed the die, he started staying late and hammering his own coin. He told his boss, the Warden of the Mint, that he was working overtime on commemorative metal for our new king, Charles II. And he was. But he was also minting coin for himself, using the purloined die."

His body slumping, Julian waits for the rest.

"It took him over six years to mint just 49 coins! He had to be so careful. He could make barely one every seven weeks, they were so labor-intensive in the hammering and softening. He told me when he got to fifty, he would stop. The risk of getting caught siphoning off drops of liquefied bullion was becoming too great. To make the coins accurately, he had to use drops from the rare 23-carat gold ingots, not the 22-carat they use today. A month or so ago, he got to 49. He needed only one more! And now they're gone."

Julian sways. "And he is also gone."

"Yes," Mallory says without inflection. "He is also gone."

"Why would he hide them here?"

"He used to keep them at his house. I was the one who persuaded him that here was safer. And it was—much safer. The floor is nailed down in every room. I made the hiding place for the coins myself. In the lord's house, the servants were disgustingly nosy. They waited for him to come home, they undressed him, bathed him, they dusted every nook. A locked chest with a key the lord carried on his person had alerted his staff that there was something in the chest worth locking away. He didn't trust them. But he trusted me."

"Why would he trust you?" Julian says in a hoarse voice.

"He was lonely. He liked me."

Julian doesn't look at her.

"When I found that one coin on him, he was relieved!" Mallory says. "His secret had been choking him. He was dying to tell someone. He was an artist and each coin was his masterpiece. I made a proper show of being impressed. I made a place where he could hide them. Room Two has always been a special, mysterious room. It's secluded and private, and in it, the candles that fall don't catch fire, though sometimes you do hear strange noises from the closet under the dormer. Some say the room is haunted. You appeared from the closet in that room." She half-smiles.

Julian's face is a mask.

"Every time the lord minted a new coin, we would celebrate. We'd have some wine and admire it. Make a pomp of placing it together with the others. I never took a coin from him, not one. He had to know I could be trusted. That I wouldn't steal from him or betray him or blackmail him."

"Why would he trust *you*?" Julian repeats.

"You're beheaded for stealing from the king's Royal Mint. It's called treason to the realm."

"That's not what I'm asking." He takes a breath. "What were *you* getting out of it?"

"A way out."

Rigidly Julian waits for her to say more.

"We were going to leave for the South of France. For Nice or Marseilles."

"Leave as in...leave together?"

"Yes."

"Lord Fabian was the benefactor who would take you away to the South of France?"

"Yes."

"But what were you *actually* planning to do?"

"I told you I've been planning my escape, didn't I?"

Julian sits on the floor and wishes he could stop listening to her air more misdeeds through her bitter lips.

*I don't know if you are safe with him, Julian says.*

*Oh, sire, she coos. You are so kind-hearted. Trust me, you don't have to worry about him.*

As in, Fabian is not the one Julian needs to worry about. Julian had heard it all wrong.

"Everything was going perfectly," Mallory continues. "Only one more coin to cast. Seven weeks to go! So close. But then you came into our life and ruined everything. *Everything!* At first your blind desire for me allowed me to make some extra money, and gave him a little pleasure, but quickly it all went wrong. And I didn't even know how wrong until it was too late."

"How is that my fault?"

"Because you ruined it with your love!" she cries. "At first, the lord thought you and I were just for show, another night of staged ribaldry at the Silver Cross. But soon he began to suspect that you weren't putting on a show, you weren't acting—like everyone else in this godforsaken place—but that you really loved me! He thought he was using *you*, and then it dawned on him that it was the other way around, that you were using *him*! And when he suspected that I might love you back, that's when everything I've been working for since I was eighteen was destroyed."

"*Might* love me back?"

"He and I had violent words about it," says Mallory. "I told him it wasn't true. I swore to him I didn't even slightly love you."

"Ah."

"He didn't believe me. He didn't believe that when the time came, I would leave you and travel with him to Marseilles. I vowed to him I would. I begged him, I pleaded. I tried, Julian, oh how I tried to save his pitiable life! But he was so stubborn and jealous. He wouldn't listen." She wrings her hands. "The other night he came and said he was taking his coin and leaving for good because he was afraid you would kill him and lure me away."

"He was afraid *I* would kill him?"

"Yes. So you could have me all to yourself. I tried to persuade him otherwise, but it was no use. He said when he saw us together, he saw the face of love. He said he knew what it looked like because it was how he himself gazed upon me. He didn't trust me anymore and could never trust me again."

It's Julian's turn to put his head in his hands. Mallory is right. It *is* his fault. How badly Julian has misjudged another man. How badly he has misjudged his woman. Again. "Fabian was right not to trust you," Julian says. "You killed him for fifty pieces of gold."

"Forty-nine," she cries, "and do you have any idea how much they're worth?"

As it turns out, he does. "But you were with me all night. You *couldn't* have killed him." He whispers it. He *still* refuses to believe it's true. *You're not going to marry another man, are you, when you promised yourself to me, Josephine.*

"I wasn't with you all night."

"How did you do it?" Julian doesn't want to know.

"With your help." Mallory wipes her face. "A thousand ways to kill a human being. That's what you taught me. Oleander, wild cherry, rosary pea. You made it so easy. You're a very good teacher, Julian. You explained it well. I learned so much about all the wonderful plants that grow in London's parks. I pulled off the rosary pea from a bush while we were walking in the palace garden last week. Right in front of you, I dropped the pea in my apron. All it took was a little grinding and a drink of honeyed wine. He drank around eleven. I begged him not to leave until I came back to say goodbye. Then I was with you. At four in the morning when you were asleep, I checked on him." She shakes her head. "Poor lord. He became so angry when he realized he had been poisoned. He worked himself up into quite a rage. I must say, I didn't expect him to go into such violent convulsions. Flailing, foaming, hitting his head, falling down right over the spot in the floor where we kept his gold. I didn't want him to die alone. I sat with him until the end. I held his hand. I figured as soon as his body was removed, I'd get my money. No one knew it was there but me—or so I thought. But then the Baroness shepherded me out for the day, Carling and Ivy mopped up, and when I came back, the gold was gone."

Rosary pea! When they strolled through the park on Sundays, arm in arm like lovers, she was scheming to betray a man who loved her, to kill him and rob him and run off—by herself—without the other man who loved her.

She dry heaves.

Wait, no, it's Julian. He's the one who's dry heaving.

She begins to crawl to him but sees his face and stops.

"Julian," Mallory says from her hiding place, "I've never been touched or held by anyone in my whole hard life the way you hold me when you love me, and when we sleep. You gave me something I didn't know I wanted, that I didn't know was real. For that, I thank you. But the most important thing to me is not love, not even yours. It's to save my own life. It's the only one I've got, and it's what my mother kept saying she wanted for me. I do this partly to honor her."

"You poisoned a man to honor your mother," Julian says.

"It was never going to last between me and you," Mallory says. "Don't look so upset."

"I don't look upset," he says. "I *am* upset. Do you know the difference?"

"I do. But don't be. You are young, passionate, beautiful. The girls swoon over you. Pay me no mind. You'll find someone else."

"You don't love me?"

"I love you," Mallory says. "But I can't trust you."

"You can't trust *me*?"

"That's right. You sold me to the lord. What you wanted came first."

"I didn't sell you!" Julian exclaims. "I gave you what *you* wanted. I would've never done it. You begged me to help you. You wanted to make money. I gave that to you."

"And you wanted to have *me*—at any cost. Well, this is the price."

"Mallory! You killed a man who took care of you so you could get to his gold, and you're talking to me about trust?"

"What did you do for his gold?"

"I didn't kill him. I didn't betray my benefactor." Julian shudders. Little did he know that his girl was in the fourth ring of the ninth circle of hell. And he was right by her side. "Oh, Mallory." He shrinks and bends like a bow.

"You traded your body and mine," she says. "You don't think that's worse?"

"No."

"You whored yourself out, and you whored me out."

"Stop being cruel. I did it for you."

"You say for me. I say for you. So you could have what you want. Well, I did the things I did to have what *I* want." Mallory whispers this, but her words are so deadly she might as well be screaming.

Julian doesn't know what to do. To tell her or not to tell her? Who's to say his own fate will be different from the Temporal Lord's? She's already disposed of one man. What's one more?

"I saved some money, Mallory," Julian says. "You can have it. Let's go. Let's run together."

She shakes her head.

"You said you want to save your life. That's also what I want. I swear to you." Julian clenches his fist over his heart. "To save you is all I want. You're in terrible danger. You don't even know. Parker suspects you of foul play. And you know the punishment that awaits you. Please, let me protect you. You can't do it alone," he adds when he gets no reply from her.

"Is that a threat, Julian? Are you going to give me up to the constable?" There is something merciless and frightening in Mallory's expression.

Julian becomes certain if he tells her about the treasure, she will kill him. She will poison his wine, too, and form a Satan's alliance with Ilbert, and like Fabian, Julian will be tossed face down into the shallow canal by Savoy Palace.

"I'm not going to give you up," he says, struggling to his feet and pulling her up with him. "You are my country. My allegiance is to you." He fights to avoid placing a confrontational emphasis on *my*. But also—he can't form a coherent thought anymore. He will have to deal with this tomorrow. It will be here soon enough.

He makes her lie down with him in the bed and with cold scared arms holds her cold scared body, hiding his terrified face behind her. Cyril Connolly is wrong. It *is* possible to be made wretched in a brothel.

Half-dressed, they fall into a restless sleep, the sleep of guilty lovers in anguish as they choose something else over what they feel for each other.

# 9

# Bill of Mortality

A NOXIOUS COMMOTION AWAKENS THEM A FEW HOURS LATER. Sitting up against the headboard, Mallory looks like a cornered animal.

"Margrave is dying! Margrave is dying!" Julian hears as he opens the bedroom door.

Casting Mallory a long backwards glance, telling her to stay in his room and not come out, Julian runs upstairs, hoping it's hyperbole.

But Margrave does not look well. She's winded, profusely hot, abnormally thirsty, wet, and gray. He crouches in front of her low bed. No one else wants to get near her; the other girls are afraid it's pestilence (though Julian doesn't think so); most of them have cleared the room. Only the lowly and unwanted Greta remains unafraid by Margrave's side, holding her hand.

"I didn't feel well all night, sire," the girl whispers, reaching for Julian. Her swollen tongue is bleeding. She has foam around her mouth.

Julian races downstairs to the kitchen, grabs a few coals from the basket by the hearth, and shaves them down with a knife until fine powder lines the bottom of a mug. He fills the mug with a bit of ale and flies upstairs. In the ten minutes he is gone, Margrave has gotten worse. Her body is jerking. She mumbles incoherently. Greta is down on her knees. "Margrave, drink this," Julian says. "It doesn't taste great, but it will help you."

The girl takes a sip, makes a face.

"I know," he says. "It's activated charcoal. It'll absorb whatever's making you sick. It's an antidote for poison. Please, drink all of it." God help them all, is it the rosary pea?

Margrave drinks all of it. He waits with her while Greta mouths words of extreme unction from the Gospel of James. *Is any among you afflicted? Is any among you sick? The prayer of faith shall save you. The Lord shall raise you.* The hot burning wind blowing in through the open windows isn't helping. Carling and Ivy reluctantly bring wet rags and Greta wipes Margrave down while Julian paces the room, smelling the wind. A rat king of anxiety is gnawing out his guts.

Greta lays down her rags. Carling and Ivy cry.

"What?" he barks. Margrave has stopped convulsing.

From down below, he hears the Baroness holler. "Fire! There's a fire!"

Shrieking, Carling and Ivy push past Julian and plummet down the stairs. "You've done all you can for Margrave, O noble sire," Greta says. "But she is gone."

Alas it's true. Poor Margrave. Julian can't bear to return to his room, where Mallory is waiting. Instead he follows the maids downstairs to inform the Baroness of the girl's demise.

Constable Parker stands grimly at the front door. The Baroness is with him. Parker is dressed in his most formal attire, a black uniform and a tall red hat. Next to him is the High Constable of Westminster with a royal staff in his hand. Behind them are foot guards from the King's Regiment and horse guards from the Lord General's Troop. What's going on? Julian stops hurrying down the stairs.

"By the proclamation of the Honorable High Constable of the City of Westminster—" Parker reads from an unrolled parchment.

The Baroness interrupts him. "Wait, constable—where's the fire?"

"The City. Started near a bakery in Pudding Lane." Parker is thrown off his officious manner.

"Pudding Lane!" The Baroness utters a shrill cry. *"Pudding Lane?"*

"Baroness, Margrave is dead!" Ivy wails, clutching the Baroness's elbow. "She's dead, madam!"

"She's been poisoned!" Carling joins in. "For sure, she has!"

Baroness Tilly turns from the wailing girls, from the frowning constable, her gaze seeking out Julian, who stands motionless at the foot of the stairs. He wishes he could vanish before she catches his eye. "You said there wouldn't be a house left standing between Temple Bar and London Bridge after the fire at Pudding Lane...And a prostitute's been murdered..."

Julian remains silent. Walk lightly, Devi told him. Carry no stick. Do not disturb the order of the universe.

"How could you have known *any* of that?" the Baroness hisses.

Parker thinks she's addressing him. "Everybody knows it by now, madam," the constable replies. "Fire started around midnight last night. It was small at first. Can you smell it? The Mayor of London is refusing to demolish the burning buildings to help contain it. He believes it's not necessary. As if to prove him wrong, the fire's been burning uncontained for over fourteen hours." Clearing his throat, Parker raises his voice. "The fire is not why we're here, Baroness. Where's your niece? We've come to take her into custody for the murder of Lord Fabian. His body was found this morning in the Savoy Canal. We have reason to believe he's been poisoned in your very house. And did I just hear correctly that Margrave has also been poisoned?"

The Baroness pierces Julian with her glare. It's too late for regrets. In the Baroness's eyes...Julian can't put a finger on it. There's hatred, disbelief, incomprehension, and a terror of sorcery. That's how she stares at him. As if he is *the other.*

"Constable—arrest that man!" the Baroness shrieks to Parker, pointing her finger in Julian's direction. "Arrest him for the lord's murder, and for treason to the Crown! Arrest him for *witchcraft.* My niece is innocent! *He's* the one who killed Lord Fabian!"

"No, it wasn't the kind master!" Greta cries. "Mallory killed our Margrave when she threw poisoned water in her face."

The other girls squeal their assent. It was her! It was her! Our kind master is innocent of wrongdoing.

"He is sent by the devil, constable!" the Baroness yells. "He's a warlock! He carries knowledge of all the poisons right here." She taps herself violently on the head. "I can prove it. Ilbert, get over here! Where are you?"

Julian is frozen. He can't run out the front door, the constable and the palace guards are blocking the way. And what does he do about Mallory? He can't leave her. The Baroness continues to screech, flinging her pink velvet arm at him, her manicured nails shaking the air. "Don't let him get away!" She, too, is blocking the narrow entry in and out of the Silver Cross. No men can move past her to grab him. Meanwhile, the florid girls have formed a line of defense in front of him.

Tilly's high-pitched screeching mentally and physically paralyzes Julian. The High Constable bangs the floor with his heavy staff. "Out of the way, madam! Out of the way, ladies!" In one second, Julian won't have the luxury of wavering, he won't be able to move even if he wishes to.

From behind, he feels a shadow barreling down the stairs. There is a hard knock into the center of his spine, and a shove forward. "Don't just stand there—run!" Mallory says, already in front of him. "Back alley, go!"

The Baroness shouts hysterically. "Mallory, Mallory, darling, no!"

Julian and Mallory race through the kitchen, down the narrow corridor.

The back door is blocked by Ilbert, who is curved over a broom and a metal bucket.

"Move, hunchback!" Mallory yells.

"Where are you two off to?" Ilbert straightens and raises the broom as a weapon and moves nowhere.

Julian lunges past Mallory and slams into Ilbert, knocking the man down with the force of his body, broom, bucket and all. As Ilbert's spindly fingers grab at their feet, Julian and Mallory jump over him and run down the winding alley that leads to the Strand.

The entrance to the Strand is blocked by a single royal guard. The uniformed man jumps off the horse and draws his sword. "Stop right there!" he says.

"Mallory, for God's sake, move!" Why is the girl always in front of him? Does she plan to fight? Match the sword with her fists? Pushing her out of the way, Julian charges the guard.

"Julian, no! He'll kill you!"

The guard lowers his sword slightly. "Julian?" he says. "Did you just say *Julian*?"

"Don't tell him anything!" Mallory yells.

"What's it to you?" Julian says, ready to bust his way out.

"Julian what?" the guard asks, the metal blade still pointed.

"Julian Cruz—why?"

The sword is lowered for good.

Julian remains in a fighting stance. His fists are up. His guard is not lowered. He and the Mountie stare at each other. The young man in uniform wears a tall red tubular hat. Julian's certain he's never met him before. He doesn't recognize him. "Do I know you?"

"Are you related to a Julian Cruz, from Wales?" the guard asks.

Julian doesn't know how to answer that. "Yes!" Mallory answers for him, clutching the back of his tunic.

"Who are you, his grandson?"

"Yes!" Mallory says from behind. "Tell him yes."

"Yes?" Julian replies uncertainly.

The guard steps aside. He points his sword to the Strand. "Go this way, straight to Temple Bar." He speaks quickly. "Then try to get into the City through the entrance at Aldgate. It's unmanned because of the fire. Hide inside the walls. There's nowhere else for you to go. You're both wanted for the murder of the Master of the Mint. But the City is on fire, and no one will look for you there until it dies down. Don't stick around. As soon as you can, get out. Whatever you do, don't take the bridge south or any of the river crossings. You'll be stopped. Find another way out. Now go!"

Mallory doesn't have to be told twice. She grabs Julian's hand.

Slowly, Julian walks by, considering the man. "I don't understand," he says perplexed. "How do you know me?"

"I don't know *you*," the guard replies. "But I know Julian Cruz. He is my grandfather's favorite story, I heard about him many times when I was growing up. Grandfather was about to die, but a man named Julian Cruz appeared out of nowhere, like an angel of the Lord, and saved his eyes and saved his life."

"Cedric is your grandfather?" Julian says, astonished.

"How did you know my grandfather's name?" The guard is stunted by confusion. "I'm only here because of Julian Cruz. My grandfather got married, had children, had my father. He never forgot."

"Is he still alive?"

"Julian, we must go!" Mallory cries.

"Yes, alive…but for the love of God, the girl is right, run, sire! You're out of time. They're coming."

Julian shakes the royal guard's hand. "Tell my friend Cedric," he says, pointing to the impatient girl waiting on the Strand, "that is Lady Mary. *The* Lady Mary."

The man's uncomprehending eyes well up. With a trembling hand, he salutes Julian. Mallory and Julian run, bobbing and weaving through the crowd.

"Who is Cedric?" Mallory asks.

"I think a better question, especially from you," Julian says, "would be who is Lady Mary."

"Okay, who?"

Julian smiles. "Take my hand," he says. "When we get out of here, I will tell you everything."

The dry east wind carries the smell of burnt dwellings, clothes, wicker, trees, wood. It's already harder to breathe, and they're still so far from the fire. In the distance beyond Temple Bar, beyond the Roman wall, black smoke swirls.

Behind them—though not far enough behind them—the horsemen and footmen give chase, forging a path through the panicked crowd.

It's the stampede out of the fire that saves Julian and Mallory. Of all the people on the Strand, only they are headed inside the burning City. Everyone else hurries in the opposite direction. Barging past the fleeing crowd, the royal horses get spooked. The guards—in their heavy uniforms, big boots, big hats, and big swords—can run, but Julian and Mallory are faster. Hearing the fading equine cry, Julian glances behind him (or is he Orpheus and is not supposed to?). The cavalry and infantry have mercifully dropped back.

"We're okay, we'll make it," Julian says to her, panting. "We're almost at Temple Bar."

But they can't get through Temple Bar. The guard isn't letting people in, only out. "Are you crazy?" the gatekeeper says to Julian, as frantic people shove past them. "Where do you think you're going? To a river crossing? Impossible. The Thames inside the gates is cut off by the flames."

People push past, adult daughters dragging their mothers, little children hanging onto their mothers' skirts, mothers and children everywhere. As soon as the guard loses track of them, Julian pulls Mallory offside, and they inch through the gate unnoticed.

It's another five long city blocks from Temple to Aldgate with the thick hot smoke blowing in their faces. They don't run anymore, they walk, gasping to catch their breath. Julian wishes he could express to Mallory how much he doesn't want to head inside the inferno. She must feel ambivalent herself because after a few blocks, she stops walking. Her hands fall, her head hangs. She slides down to the sidewalk near Primrose Hill. "Forget it," she says dejectedly. "What's the point? Where are we going to run with nothing?"

Julian crouches in front of her.

"The entire City's on fire. Even if we make it out somehow, what then?"

He takes a hot gray breath. He doesn't want to confess. But sometimes, you must trust the one you love. Sometimes, you must trust her even if she breaks your heart with murder.

And sometimes, you must trust her even after.

"Mallory, I have the gold," Julian says. "Ilbert didn't take it. Margrave didn't take it. I took it. Now get up and let's go find a place to hide."

She stares at him for several fiery seconds. "You took *my* gold?"

"Well…" Julian draws out. "*Yours,* really?"

"It wasn't *yours!*"

"I thought it was his."

"It wasn't his anymore. He was dead. The dead own nothing."

"Semantics, I know," Julian says, "but he was dead only after you killed him."

Angrily, Mallory jumps to her feet.

"I took it for you, Mallory," Julian says. "So you and I could run from here. You know, like together."

"You stole my money to *help* me?"

"To help *us,* yes. I thought you and me…I thought there was a you and me," he says. "That was before I knew you were planning to run off, ditching me to be boiled in oil for a murder I didn't commit."

"Don't look all wounded, you thief! Why didn't you just pay off Ilbert if you had the coin? You could've saved us a lot of trouble."

"Because I don't have it. I hid it."

"Where, back at the house? Bloody hell! A lot of good that'll do us now."

"Not at the house."

"Where, then?"

"Inside the London Wall," Julian says. "Next to St. Giles Church by Cripplegate."

"What do you mean, *inside* the wall?"

"I bought a chisel and a hammer," Julian says, "popped out two Kentish ragstones, scraped out a hole in the interior bricks, hid the purse, replaced the boulders and spackled mortar around them to seal them. I'm not saying it was easy." Gouging out a space in the interior stone with an inadequately short chisel, piece by piece, chunk by chunk, took hours. It was one of the more physically grueling things Julian has ever done.

"Oh, you're a mason now, too." Mallory's anger dissipates. She eyes him with trepidation, a little amazement, a little hope.

"I'm not a mason," he says, "but I became a mason. I did what I had to do."

"O Lord, Julian! I suppose that's quick thinking on your part, but why on earth would you hide it all the way up there?"

"As opposed to where, the Baroness's bedchamber?"

"Why go all the way to Clerkenwell?"

"You're from Clerkenwell," Julian says. "Do you remember? You lived there once in a big gray mansion."

"Must be another molly you were sweet on. That's not where I lived. I lived in a ramshackle, falling-down, white-limed bordello where I slept on the floor while my mother entertained men in the bed, one of whom was my father." Mallory flings her arm to point to the London Wall just up ahead near Aldgate. "The wall circles the City for a square mile! There's the wall! *There's* the wall! And *there*, too! You could've hidden the coin close by, and we wouldn't have to cross a city on fire to get to it."

"I didn't know we'd need it so quickly," Julian says. "I had no idea, did I, that you killed Fabian and Margrave, or that you'd hang murder over both our heads. I thought we had plenty of time to decide what to do. And I didn't know there'd be a fire."

What garbage. What absolute tripe. Julian knew there'd be a fire. He just didn't know when. *He knew in part.*

"Sounds to me like you knew nothing." Mallory starts down Fleet Street. "Well, don't just stand there like Lot," she barks. "Are you coming or not?"

He catches up. "Where are we going?"

"Where are we going? Have you gone soft in the head? To Cripplegate, of course. To Clerkenwell. Just like you planned. We're not leaving my gold in a fucking wall. What if the fire destroys it?"

Julian wants to tell her that the fractured Roman wall will be the only thing left standing of old London 400 years from now, that after the Great Fire, after industrialization, expansion, demolition, after the Blitz! a piece of the wall where he hid the gold will remain. He knows this because he's seen it with his own eyes as he ambled past St. Giles through the maze of modern Barbican, searching for the café with the golden awning.

Julian points to the black plumes spreading north and west from the Thames, the vicious winds, the livid flame. "We can't get to Cripplegate," he says. "Between us and your gold is hellfire. But don't worry. We just have to stay safe for a little while longer. Safe and hidden. We'll get to it. Let's wait it out. The wall's not going anywhere, I promise you. Let's find an abandoned shop, lie low. After the fire dies down, five days tops, then we'll go get it."

"This fire is going to rage for five days?"

A breath. "Yes."

Mallory crows in disbelief. "What's going to be left of this city after a fire that rages for five days?"

"Nothing."

Julian wishes they were in the East End. Wapping, Shoreditch, Bethnal Green. The East End is a little safer because of the direction of the wind. Trouble is, the two of them are on the west side. And between east and west there's a mountain of flame. Not listening to him anymore, Mallory rushes down Fleet

Street; Julian follows close behind. Aldgate is unmanned. The gates are open. The gatekeepers have fled.

Inside the City walls, the heat and smoke are much worse. Julian knows something about out of control firestorms. In California, the Santa Ana winds are called the devil winds. Every September during the drought, they blow downhill through the mountain passes and scorch the forest using chaparral as fuel, and then obliterate the valley from San Bernardino to Santa Barbara, using homes as fuel. That's what this is, too. But instead of thorny bushes and tangled shrubs, the City of London all in a blaze is chaparral for the wildfire. It's the destruction of a civilization. Why can't his stubborn girl understand? "Mallory, please." He wipes his sweating face. He is so hot.

Without looking back at him, she hurries down Ludgate Street. She is brave because she knows he is right behind her. It's as if in the heart of her soul she knows he won't leave her side. "Is the man afraid of a little smoke?"

"Not smoke, Mallory. *Fire.* And yes," Julian says. "Afraid of *this* fire. But not for myself. For you." He tries to take her hand. She pulls away. Her legs get caught up in her skirts, she trips, rights herself, won't even let him balance her.

"I can't believe you'd hide all of it," she says. "Not leave even one little coin for the just in case."

"I sold one coin for the just in case," Julian says, showing her the crowns and shillings inside his small purse.

She snatches it out of his hands and hides it in the apron of her skirt. "For safekeeping," she says. "How much did you get for it?"

"Three hundred shillings." Julian thinks she'll be as impressed as he was.

"You got three hundred shillings for a priceless sovereign?" In disgust she shakes her head. "You were robbed. Come on, hurry. We need to get my money before you give any more of it away."

Julian is troubled as they race forward, sweat dripping off them. But Mallory's spirits have been lifted not only by the promise of a stash of gold nearby but by the actual shillings now in her possession. Things are looking up. She chatters excitedly. "Why so glum, mason? With the gold, we can get anywhere, bribe anyone, barter for anything. No guard will stand in our way. We'll buy our way out. We are set for life. We'll make it last. You'll see, we won't need much."

"Much? How about nothing?" Julian says, looking around for a conduit, a fountain, a bucket of dirty water. They need to breathe into something wet—and soon. Smoke inhalation doesn't favor survival. "Because that's what we'll have if we continue to Cripplegate. Nothing."

"You yourself were blithely headed into the City not ten minutes ago!"

"To hide you!"

"Julian," Mallory says, slowing down and turning her face to him. "There's a time to think and a time to act. If we are going to make it, you really need to learn the difference between the two. Guess which time this is. Do you remember yourself on the stairs not an hour ago? Had I not reminded you with a sharp fist to your back that the time had come to run, not ponder, you'd be in Parker's custody right now on your way to Tyburn. The Master of the Mint is dead! A prostitute is dead! And London is burning. This is no time to stand around, waxing poetic about what could've been and should've been." She takes his hand and stares deep into his face. "No one can protect us if we ourselves are not prepared, not even God. Not because he won't. But because he can't. That's what Jesus said. Carry oil in your lamps, he told us. I can't protect you if you are not ready."

"I'm not sure that by oil in your lamps Jesus meant murder," says Julian.

"You and I have a chance for a real life somewhere," Mallory says. "Someplace beyond this city. It's waiting for us, like you said. But first we must *act*. We can't simply *will* it to happen.

We have to do something for ourselves. What will you do if the wall falls and we can't find the purse? How will you feel if the guards find us hiding like leeches in some wet gulley? What are you going to say to me then? I'm sorry, O dainty duck, I tried?" Mallory pulls on him. "Let's go. To get to the wall is the most important thing."

"Are you sure it's not love over gold, Mallory?" Julian says.

"Without the gold there's nothing, not even love," she replies. "But with it, there may be both. So hurry."

It's difficult to run. With each panting breath, they swallow more smoke. They're dripping wet. He gapes at her as they do their best to hurry. "Who *are* you?" he says. "This wasn't you two days ago, a month ago."

"You are *so* wrong, dear dove." Mallory yanks on him. "This was always me. Ruthless and resolute. What did Ivy call me?"

"Wanton and cunning."

"You should've listened to her. The other Mallory you saw, you know what that was?" Stopping for a moment, the young panting woman sidles up to Julian, batting her eyelashes, rubbing against him, pitching her voice to a high shy purr. "That was an *act*, sire." She kisses him deeply on the lips and tugs on him to get going. "I told you my life was my stage. Why do men never listen when women speak?"

Julian is breathless with love and terror as she leads him deeper into the siege. "Without your life, there's nothing else, Mallory. No acting, no cunning, no gold."

She shakes her head. "Gold over everything."

Julian shakes his head, even though he knows she is right.

Because what you want most is what you have the least of.

Josephine over everything.

Hand in hand, they walk into the apocalypse.

The church at Cripplegate is a long way away through a burning city. It's nearly a mile away. In just the last few minutes, the smoke has grown higher, turned blacker, the smell of charred wood and linen has become more acrid. There's screaming near them, the neighing of frightened horses. The flames rise in the streets, and the wind carries fire like airborne tumbleweeds. They're almost at St. Paul's.

"Why couldn't you have dug a hole in the ground at St. Paul's?" Mallory says. "Would've been so much simpler."

"I didn't do that," Julian says, "because tomorrow, there isn't going to be a St. Paul's."

Mallory glances into his face to see if he's joking. "You kept yammering about it." She sounds mystified. "You wouldn't shut up about a fire cleansing our city of Black Death. How did you know it was coming? How did you know the *future*?"

"Oh, Mallory," Julian says. "I wish to God I knew the future. I don't. I know the past."

Their eyes catch for a moment. "Do you know what happens to you and me?" she asks, almost whispering, as if she wants to know, doesn't want to know.

"No," Julian says, and can't even tell if he's lying.

A vicar stands in the churchyard of St. Paul's, shouting encouragement to the fleeing people. "We have a mayor who's helpless before the conflagration!" the priest shouts. "Brothers and sisters, help yourselves! Do not be like our esteemed leader. Lord, what can I do, he cries. He says he's out of solutions, though the fire has raged for barely a day! He's like a fainting woman, and do you know why? Because his faith is faint! Do not be like Thomas Bludworth! Be unshakable! Straight is the gate and narrow is the way that leads unto life. Aldgate, Ludgate, Newgate, Bishopsgate, Cripplegate, Moorgate, Aldersgate! Seven gates out! Seven ways to save your life! Run, brothers and sisters, go find your gate!"

Julian's eyes are tearing, and it takes him a moment to recognize Reverend Anselmo from the Silver Cross. Weakened by inhaling the smoke, the holy man wobbles on the apple crate as he fortifies the misplaced with prayer. "Oh, it's you two," Anselmo says when they stop at his feet. "The whole world is looking for you."

Mallory holds on to Julian, weighing on him as she rests. "They're not looking for us here," she says.

"Yes, hide in hell," the vicar says. "That'll teach them."

"All the parish churches inside the City will soon be cinders, Reverend," Julian says. "Despite what you think of us over on Whitehall, you're safer in the Silver Cross."

"I don't go where it's safe, my son," Anselmo says. "I go where I'm needed. And today, it's here."

"You don't have any water, do you?" Julian asks. They desperately need something wet to breathe into.

"Find your narrow gate out, and you will find living water there," replies Anselmo.

"Come on, Julian," Mallory says. "No time to waste."

The wood houses crackle, timber bursting apart in venomous flames and falling in ruins. The smoke makes everything dark upon the streets, dark upon the steeples, smoke whirls like ghosts between the homes and the cathedrals.

St. Martin's Le Grand that leads to Cripplegate is impassable. The buildings have collapsed into the road. "Julian," Mallory says, "in case we get separated, tell me where in the wall you hid my purse."

"It's down the slope and straight across from the last window in the back of the nave. About three feet off the ground. The gray mortar should still be fresh. You can't miss it. But we're not going to get separated."

They walk in single file, she ahead of him. They're drenched with sweat. The fire that swirls and fills the air with black satanic smoke slows them down. Her especially. "It's not too far now," Mallory says. She's wheezing. "We're close. Soon we'll be out." She stops walking. "Just let me catch my breath for a minute."

"We don't have a minute, Mallory," Julian says, throwing his arm around her and helping her forward. "You told me so yourself. It's more true now than ever." There's no preparation for the plague. There's no preparation for the fire. Not even when you know it's coming. No oil in the lamp will protect them now.

Nothing could have prepared them for this except staying away. The hot wind fans the flames just like the Santa Anas. Who travels faster, a young determined rasping beauty under his arm or a blaze blown out of all control by a stiff dry breeze?

"Come on, just a little farther." Who says that?

It's Julian. Mallory has stopped speaking.

The smoke chokes him, shreds his throat, tears at the whites of his eyes. The plumes are heavy, a canopy of ash in the air. Mallory breaks into a coughing fit. She has pulled away from him and is staggering along the side of a building, trying to hide her face from the smoke. He barely makes her out, even though she's right next to him. He searches for her like a blind man, his hands outstretched. Mallory, Mallory, is that you? She doesn't answer.

Julian stares into his empty palm. His right fingers are tingling.

Mallory!

He can't find her. He can't see her.

People are hurrying past him, but none of them is her.

One second she was by his side, and the next...*Mallory!* His arms ache.

In the black trails, all women look like her. From the river upward, a flame tsunami rises higher and then falls. It's raining fire. It's light, but there is no sun. It's day, but it looks like night.

Julian finds her lying on the pavement, wedged into the side of a building, as if she's trying to hide. Mallory, what happened?

She is mouthing something, but he can't hear. The smoke must have paralyzed her vocal cords. He kneels on the stones by her side.

Can you get up? Julian wants to ask this. The problem is, he also can't speak. It must be the smoke. *Please* let it be the smoke. Oh God, Mallory. How far are they from Cripplegate? How far are they from the gold, from the wall? How far from each other, from salvation? So close, so close! Julian's legs, neck, chest feel as if they're being stabbed with ice picks.

Why did he let go of her hand! Or did she let go of his? She let go and fell noiselessly to the cobblestones, and the burning sky fell with her.

She holds her throat. He holds his throat. He reaches out to touch her, opens his mouth to beg her, *beg* her not to die. *I love you*, he whispers inaudibly. Please don't die before you are redeemed.

Mallory almost smiles. Pulling a crumpled piece of parchment out of her apron, she slides it into his palm. Julian tries to stand her up, but she can't, and he can't. Why did you fall? Why did you let go of my hand? Why did you run into the fire, why did I hide your gold, why did I take it? Why did you kill him and her, why?

She is gasping.

Timber is being torn to pieces. Julian's body feels as if it's being torn to pieces. The ashes of London rise in the black ugly fumes and are carried by the wind into Mallory's throat, into Julian's throat, into Mallory's soul, into Julian's soul.

He is convulsing. His throat closes. He can't yell, can't speak, can't tell her what he feels.

Reaching up, she touches his face, her eyes clearing and glazing over. *Julian* ...

Still on his knees, he tips over her.

*Go*, she whispers. Or did she say *gold*?

*Julian, go and come back for me.*

# 10

## Six Persuasions

EACH DAY MAN IS PERISHING. YET HE IS RENEWED DAY BY DAY.

Julian didn't know about the renewed part.

But about perishing? Check.

Still on his knees, covered with grime and soot, he threw up in front of Sweeney. This time he didn't get up and walk out. They had to call an ambulance and carry him down the mountain on a stretcher. He was taken to Queen Elizabeth Hospital and treated with hyperbaric oxygen. The hospital called the police because Julian had no ID, nothing but a coin, out of circulation for four hundred years, and a Bill of Mortality from 1665 clutched in his blackened fist. Julian gave the police Nextel's number, and Ashton arrived at Queen Elizabeth with Julian's ID and optimistically with a change of clothes.

But Julian wasn't going anywhere. His body has been ravaged by prolonged inhalation of carbon monoxide, he was coughing up blood and had swelling in his lungs that was causing continued oxygen deprivation. Julian scribbled his signature on a document making Ashton his health care proxy, and Ashton talked to the doctors.

"What are you talking about, smoke inhalation?" Ashton said. "Like from cigarettes?" He was standing at Julian's bedside.

Like from a fire, one doctor said. Also he has a number of burst blood vessels in his arms and legs, and Lichtenberg flowers down his back from his neck to his pelvis.

"Is that also from smoke inhalation?"

No, another doctor said. We see Lichtenberg burns after an electrocution.

Ashton refused to believe it. It was obvious they'd mixed up Julian's chart with someone else's. They brought out Julian's chart, showed Ashton there was no mistake. They pointed out that Julian had complained of being electrocuted a year earlier. Then, they had concluded, it was psychosomatic. This year they weren't so sure. This year, the symptoms were visible.

"What about the tattooed dots on his arm that weren't there the day before yesterday?" Ashton said. "Is that also from smoke inhalation? Or is it from electrocution? Or are the tattoos psychosomatic?"

The doctors had no opinion about the tattoos. Tattoos weren't a medical emergency like swollen lungs.

Julian himself was confused and on painkillers and refused to confirm or deny anything. An X-ray showed three fractured bones in each foot.

"Is that *also* fucking psychosomatic?" Ashton said, fuming at their ignorance, and at his own.

After a week, Julian was sent home with an oxygen tank to help him breathe until his lungs healed. *Oxygen for Julian.*

While Ashton was at work, Julian, his crutches against the railing, sat motionlessly on the cold rainy balcony and rocked back and forth. When you want to escape from your blinding rage, stop moving, stop speaking. All action feeds the beast. Stop feeding it.

"Dude, I *beg* you. Explain," Ashton kept asking in the evenings after work.

Which part?

"Um, the *swollen* lungs? Electrocution burns? Breeches and tunic? The broken feet, the catatonia, the tattoos? Literally a single thing. What happened to you? Where did you go?"

Smoke inhalation is from a fire.

"*What* fucking fire?"

The Great Fire of London.

At first Ashton had nothing to say. Then: "Why do you refuse to be straight with me? Why can't you reply to a serious question with a serious answer? *What* fucking fire?"

I just told you, the Great Fire of London.

Ahhhh!

You wanted me to be straight. I'm straight.

Julian stuffed the ends of the plastic tubing into his nostrils, inhaled deeply, and closed his eyes. I can't explain any better than that, Ash. We'll try again if I'm renewed.

∞

A week went by, the lungs got better, the tank had gone. Ashton and Julian still hadn't talked. Julian still hadn't returned to work.

After another week, Ashton walked into Julian's bedroom on a Saturday afternoon and surveyed the abnormal disorder inside. Julian knew his room did not look rational to a man who was used to Julian being meticulous with his belongings and who was suddenly greeted with a scene as after a ransacking or an earthquake. Hundreds of books were strewn on the bed and the floor: history, how-to, biography, travel, plays, and philosophies. Everywhere newspapers, broken pencils, open notebooks, pencil shavings, a sharpener on its side, half-empty plastic cups of water, an unmade bed, and on it, a half-naked Julian with a magnifying glass and a superbright LED lamp trained on a coffee-table tome of London paintings from the 1600s. He was trying to find a glimpse of something true somewhere, anywhere, to prove to himself she had been real. He'd been sleeping poorly, attacked by bewildering nightmares, callbacks to old visions and memories once so vivid, now half-forgotten. This time, there was no Josephine shining on the street. Instead there was terror and fire followed by a dismal icy darkness.

A pallid, unshaven Julian raised his head from the book to face Ashton grimly homing in on the chaos. Julian tried to smile.

He could tell his friend wanted to make a joke, lighten the mood, but comedy was beyond even him.

"What the fuck," Ashton said. That was as funny as he could make it.

"Don't ask."

"I feel I must, dude. I must ask. What the fuck."

"Everything's okay."

"It's two in the afternoon," Ashton said, as if that was the only thing that was wrong.

"Then what are *you* still doing home? Did you go to Valentina's, get us food like you said?"

"Don't answer my questions with questions," Ashton said. "What are you doing? What are you writing, reading, looking for? Why the magnifying glass, why the mania? What's happening? What the fuck is happening?"

Dressed in nothing but boxer briefs, Julian swung his aching feet onto the floor. He was uncontained. He was a dead leaf in the yellow river, an ailing creature, a rotting marmoset. How could he have not seen it coming? How could he have allowed it to happen. Allowed it to happen *again*.

"Why are you examining this nonsense with a microscope? Old London? What are you looking for?" Ashton picked up *A Philosophical Enquiry into the Origin of Our Ideas of the Sublime and Beautiful*. "Edmund Burke? If you're going to self-destruct, why can't you self-destruct with porn, with ribald novels from de Sade: *Erotica, Justine*?"

Julian could not explain to Ashton the inner howl of his helplessness.

"Burke wrote that all things are good that obey reason," Ashton said. "Does *anything* you're doing fit that category?"

"Did you come in just to harass me?"

"I need another reason? Put some clothes on, will you. You have a visitor."

"You're full of shit. Who?"

"I don't know *who*, but there's a *man* on the landing who says, and I quote, that he lost the piece of paper with my number but knew where I lived and you had told him to come tell me you weren't coming back. I understood not a single fucking thing of that. The individual words maybe."

"Devi?"

"I don't know, Jules. I'm guessing he's a fellow inmate, let out for an afternoon. Hurry up. It doesn't look as if he's got long before they come to take him back to the asylum. Kind of like you."

∞

A pale Devi stood at the door when Julian limped out into the living room in sweats and a pullover.

"Hello, Julian. I see you've returned—again." Devi sounded so disappointed.

"You're minimally observant."

"Returned from where?" Ashton said.

"How are you feeling?" said Devi.

"How do I look?" said Julian.

"Like a man who's been in a hundred and one fights. And lost them all."

From the kitchen, Ashton smirked. "So he knows about the boxing? Wow."

"Devi, you've met Ashton?"

"Not formally."

"Ashton, Devi. Devi, Ashton."

With wary reserve, Ashton stepped forward, and the two men shook hands, Ashton silent and blond towering over the little man silent and dark.

"Returned from where?" Ashton repeated. Neither Julian nor Devi answered. Ashton swore under his breath, grabbed his jacket and said he was going on a food run. Devi said Julian needed some plain chicken and white rice. Julian said no. Ashton said he was getting it anyway and split.

"You need food," Devi said, coming closer.

Julian sank into the sofa.

"How's your friend handling you?"

"Fine."

"You haven't told him?"

"Told him *what*."

Devi perched stiffly in the corner of the opposite sofa. "Tell *me*."

"You really need to be told? You know what happened."

"I don't."

"Is that why you didn't want me to go? Did you know all along?"

Devi stared into his crippled hands. "I'm waiting."

Julian told him.

London burned. It burned to the ground. And she along with it. *All the glory was laid to dust.*

Then they were mute.

"Come back to Quatrang with me, Julian," Devi said. "You need healing." He added, "Please."

"I've had just about enough of your healing, don't you think?"

"Very often," Devi said, "what God first helps us with is not virtue itself, but the power of trying again. And you did that. You tried again. What a noble thing that is. What a gallant effort. Don't minimize it."

"Hard to minimize it, Devi." Julian rolled up his sleeve, thrusting the inside of his forearm across the coffee table into the cook's face. "You see the ink? Forty-five *minimized* tattoos."

"Is that how many days you had?"

"No. I got sick of marking them, so I missed some. A week, maybe more."

Devi bowed his head.

"Let's not minimize it," Julian said. "Let's *maximize* it, shall we? Here on my arm is the answer to the question I asked you before the first time I went. Do you remember?"

"I remember."

"I asked you if I was going to find her young or old. And you said young. But you were wrong. Or lying. Which is it?"

Devi didn't speak.

"I asked you at what point I was going to be inserted into her life, and you told me you didn't know. Were you lying?"

"No."

"Well, now you know," Julian said. "And I know. Aren't you glad we're both so *full* of knowledge. When I find her, she's not young." Julian fell back against the cushions. "She is old. Each time she is at the end of her life." Barely able to breathe, as if his lungs were still filled with smoke, he stared at the columns of black *dots* on his arm. *Sans teeth, sans eyes, sans taste, sans everything.*

"Is that *too* much time, Julian, or not *enough*?" Devi said. "I'm not clear. Because most of us don't get even a picosecond extra."

"Oh, fuck that."

"I told you not to go," the shaman whispered.

"You didn't tell me she would die again!" Julian yelled.

"Control your temper. I told you, you couldn't change things. I told you this over and over."

"Okay, fine," Julian said through his teeth. "You told me. I hear you—finally. Loud and clear. I'm done with this bullshit. With *all* of it." He glared at Devi.

"Yes," Devi said. "By all means live out your days in bitter pity for yourself while your life passes you by." He stood up, gathering his hat into his hands and left.

∞

After Ashton came back from Valentina's with some precooked chicken and rice and found Devi gone and Julian back in his room, he banged on the bedroom door. "Food's here."

Julian sat on the sofa, Ashton across from him.

"So the man left?"

"The man left."

"They took him back?" When Julian said nothing, Ashton said, "Who was he?"

"A cook from Great Eastern Road."

"Cook. Great Eastern Road. Really. Well. Thanks for clearing *that* up." When Julian offered nothing else, Ashton pressed further. "Is he the shaman you were asking me about a year ago? Some Hmong man who summoned the dead?"

Julian half-nodded.

"Does he have anything to do with what happened to you?"

Julian half-nodded.

"Jules, I can't play twenty questions. I'm not Socrates. I'm going to start throwing shit by the next question. Talk to me. What happened to you?"

"Forget it, Ash. Honestly. It doesn't matter anymore. It's in the past." Julian clenched and unclenched his hands. "And you don't want to know."

"Like hell I don't. And it's not in the past. It's the fucking here and now. Julian, you left home in the morning and by the afternoon you were in an ICU with smoke inhalation and electrocution burns. Does that sound like the past to you?"

"If I tell you, you won't believe me."

"Try me."

For interminable minutes, Julian stared at Ashton. "Short or long?"

"Short. Elevator pitch. Two sentences."

"Devi showed me a way to go back in time to find Josephine. And I've gone twice."

"Go back, like astral projection?"

"Go back, like body and soul."

At first, Ashton was without words. "It's a terrible pitch," he said finally. "Based on that, I won't be able to produce your script, I'm afraid. It's not even remotely believable and you've left too many hanging questions. Have you got anything else? I'm serious now. *Anything* else."

"The first time I went, she died," Julian said. "And I was blasted back into my present life. It was just before you moved here. I went again a month ago. I thought I was leaving London for good. If she hadn't died, I'd still be there with her. But...here I am, so." He took a breath. "Don't look at me like that."

"Like what, Julian," Ashton said slowly. "How am I looking at you?"

"Like I'm nuts."

"*No.*"

"I leap into a wormhole," Julian said, "and float for a long time down an underground river, and when I come out on the other side, she lives."

Ashton draped himself over the couch. "Okay," he said. "I guess it's time for the long version." He shot up. "Wait!" From the kitchen he brought a bottle of Grey Goose, two glasses, some ice, and some soda water. He made the drinks, gave one to Julian, didn't clink, and gulped down half of his. "Go."

Julian spoke for a long time. Meridian, crystal, the Transit Circle, tear in the fabric of the universe, future tense, moongate, river, dead queen, Wales, Mary, Lord Falk, the Silver Cross, Mallory, Fabian, Margrave, murder, gold, the Fire. Body immolating and reforming at the speed of light. Correction: at the speed of light, *squared.*

Ashton reached over and swallowed Julian's untouched vodka.

"I know how it sounds," Julian said.

"Oh no, my friend. I don't think you do."

"Do you remember the dream I used to have of her? Where she is walking toward me, happy and smiling? Devi says it could be a vision of her and me in the future."

"Well, if Devi says...You mean in the future that Devi just finished telling you doesn't exist, or some other future?"

"Everything you're thinking of, Ash, I've thought of," said Julian. "Yet here it is. I know you don't believe me, but I'm not lying. There *is* a difference."

"Oh, a huge one. If you were lying, it would mean you were sane."

In silence the two men sat in their open sunny flat. Julian was oddly comforted by the shellshocked look on Ashton's normally placid face, as if his friend didn't know how to begin to begin to figure out how to help him. You can't help me, Ash, Julian wanted to say. You can't help a husk whose fruits have fallen and rotted on the ground.

"Explain my injuries," Julian said.

"I can't explain them," Ashton said, "but you entered a triathlon event without my knowledge. You spent a year growing a sick beard without explanation and shaved it off without explanation."

"I shaved it off because in 1666 men didn't have beards."

"Oh, *that's* why. You're boxing, caving, fencing. I can't explain any of those things. 1666. Is that when you became a *landlord in a brothel*?"

"Yes."

"You, Julian Cruz, son of a professor and a principal, were a caretaker in a house of women who got naked and had sex for money?"

"Yes."

"I'm supposed to believe this?"

"*That's* the part you find unbelievable? Not wormholes and—"

"Frankly, yes. Okay, from the top. You fell in love with a girl, but then she died."

"Yes."

"And you found a charlatan who showed you how to travel back in time to find her."

"A shaman, but yes."

"Potato, potahtoe. You traveled into this past."

"Yes."

"Not once but *twice*."

"Yes."

"And you found her, and fell in love with her again, and she with you, and both times, she died."

"Yes."

"And you were a *landlord in a brothel*?"

∞

Persuasion #1: Julian showed Ashton the list of casualties from Mallory's yellowing but intact Bill of Mortality. "Look at the paper. It's from 1665. Why is it still in such good condition?"

"That's your proof? How the hell should I know?"

"Because," Julian said, "the paper is only a year old, not four hundred years old."

Apoplexie 1
Burned in his bed by a candle 1
Canker 1
Cough 2
Fright 3
Grief 3
Killed by a fall from a Bellfry 1
Lethargy 1
Suddenly 1
Timpany 1
Plague 7165

"What's timpany?" Ashton said.

"*That's* your question?"

"How does one die suddenly?"

"That's your question?"

"How does one die of grief, I wonder."

"To paraphrase John Green," Julian said, uncle of nieces besotted with Hazel and Augustus, "slowly, and all at once."

∞

Persuasion #2: Julian took Ashton to the Silver Cross, off Craig's Court on lit-up Whitehall. It was a Friday night. They ate. They drank. They read the plaque on the wall. "THE SILVER CROSS HAS BEEN THE SITE OF A PUBLIC HOUSE SINCE THE 17TH CENTURY AND WAS EVEN THE SITE OF A LICENSED BROTHEL."

Persuasion #3: Julian tried to hand Ashton his breeches and tunic.

"You got them in a costume store," Ashton said, pulling his arms behind his back.

Persuasion #4: The Elizabethan gold coin.

"It's fake," Ashton said.

"Do you want to know how much one of these fake coins is worth today?"

"Fine, but it'll prove nothing."

Julian showed him the online collector's currency markets. An Elizabeth I gold sovereign in fairly good condition, not mint condition, was selling for £50,000. "And there were 48 more."

"So you say." Ashton fake-shrugged. "Yours isn't real. And even if it is real, so what? You found it on the street."

"I found fifty thousand quid on the street. That sounds normal to you."

"Jules, we left normal back at Tequila Cantina's when you showed me a ring for a chick whose mother you'd never met."

Persuasion #5: The pièce de résistance. Julian took Ashton to St. Giles at Cripplegate. He would unveil for his friend the ultimate proof—the gold in the wall. They went to a hardware store, purchased a hammer, a chisel, a bucket, a trowel, and some mortar.

"You know," Ashton said, pointing to the supplies in Julian's hands, "when someone is sick and you entertain him in his sickness, you become an accomplice in his disorder."

"Let's see what you say after I show you a leather purse full of ancient gold coins hidden in the London Wall."

"*After*, I'll be visiting you in jail," said Ashton, "because it's against the law to deface a historical monument. Douchebaggery most foul. Vandalism in the first degree. In Singapore you'd get fifty lashes."

Ashton kept watch on a bench by the church, while across the narrow canal, over a hanging bridge, Julian spent the afternoon walking up and down the same fifty feet, feeling the remains of the crumbling Roman wall with his hands. When he reached the end near the circular turret, he'd turn around and creep back, inch by inch searching for the Kentish ragstone spackled by an amateur mason. Sometimes Ashton was on his phone, but mostly, he sat and watched Julian.

Hours passed. Julian, exhausted and sore from walking bent at the waist, collapsed next to Ashton. "I don't understand why I can't find it. It was so easy. Down the hill, in a straight line from the nave's last window, three feet off the ground. It doesn't make sense."

"Yes, *that's* the part that doesn't make sense." Ashton shook his head. "Just for a second, step out of your skin and think about how you appear to me. Hunched over for the last two hours, pacing up and down the same stretch of wall, mumbling to yourself."

"You think I'm nuts." It wasn't a question.

"Yes, Julian. Mentally ill." Ashton wasn't smiling.

"You think I'm obsessing over a girl and you're afraid that eventually that obsession is going to drive me insane."

"Eventually? And not a girl. A *coin*."

∞

Persuasion #6: One Sunday Julian took Ashton to Greenwich. To show him the telescope, to introduce him to the guard.

"Hello, Sweeney. This is my friend, Ashton."

"Hello, Ashton," Sweeney said, turning to Julian. "And who are you?"

"The guy who threw up a few months ago," Julian said. "You had to call me an ambulance, remember?"

"I don't remember the ambulance, but so many people pass this way, mate, and I'm terrible with faces, sorry. Me memory's really the pits. One time, there was a bloke who appeared in my Transit Room nekkid! I have no idea how he got through security with his junk hanging out."

"Maybe it was so small they didn't notice," Ashton said to Sweeney, and to Julian he said, "*Naked*?!"

"Don't know *what* that guy is on about," said Julian.

He and Ashton stood for a few minutes in front of the well, the stairs, the railing, the glossy Transit Circle. They looked up at the gray sky through the retracted roof. Julian told Ashton about noon and infinite meridians and the blue halo opening to another dimension. They visited the gift shop, walked around the soaked gardens, stood on the stone plaza with the panorama of London laid out before them, today glum and obscured, the oaks heavy with rain, the river in a mist.

Ashton didn't speak on the train back home.

# 11

# Objects of Outrage

IN MAY, A MORE OR LESS HEALED JULIAN RETURNED TO
Nextel. Reuters' interest in buying the news agency intensified,
and Ashton and Julian worked long hours trying to make the
business efficient and profitable so that they could sell it. At night
they went out drinking, sometimes even with Roger and Nigel.

Working was good.

Drinking, too.

It made time pass.

Something had to.

When he felt well enough in his body to no longer ignore the
remorse in his soul, Julian went to Quatrang one morning before
work to make peace with Devi. Not wanting to go by himself, he
dragged Ashton along. "Why do we have to go see that man?
You said yourself you were done with him."

"I am," Julian said. "But I want to apologize for the way I
acted. I was rude. Plus I want to show you some things."

"Unless it's naked girls dancing, I don't want to see anything."

Devi was happy to see Julian. He said nothing when Julian
walked in, he didn't react, not smiling or even joking, but there
was something in the way he had glanced up when the door
opened that made Julian think the cook had been hoping Julian
would return.

Ashton and Devi were even less impressed with each other
on the second day of their acquaintance. They shook hands,

but they may as well have been drawing swords. Barely able to fit inside the tiny Quatrang, Ashton stood in the corner by the window, tense and uncharacteristically awkward.

"You're just in time," Devi said. "I trust you two haven't had your first meal of the day yet? I've been simmering a mohinga in a cauldron in the back. Would you like some?"

"What's a mohinga?"

"Catfish soup with banana tree stem," Devi said cheerfully. "A squeeze of lime, dried chilis, crispy onions. Very delicious. Can I bring you two a bowl?"

"For *breakfast*?"

"Of course. When else would you eat a mohinga?"

Julian shook his head. "No, thank you."

"It's the most popular breakfast dish in Burma," Devi said, sounding offended for Burma.

"Devi, how about some eggs? French toast?"

"What am I, the Waffle House?"

"I'll try this mohinga," Ashton said.

"Look at you trying to impress him," Julian said after Devi disappeared behind the curtain.

"What I'm trying to do is get out of here," Ashton said. "I'm giving this thing a half-hour. Like lunch with my old man."

"Speaking of your father," Devi said, carrying out two bowls of strong-smelling fish soup, "how is he?"

"Um, he's…fine?" Ashton squinted at Julian with a sideways glare that Julian did not return.

"He must be happy having you in London with him, working with him?"

"He's semi-retired, but…I guess."

"You and your father have had some difficulties in the past, yes? Is it better now?"

Ashton shook his head. "Whatever. Not really. Maybe a little. It doesn't matter," he said. "I don't want what I haven't got."

For a moment, the three men sat in silence, absorbing this. Julian wished he could say the same.

"Your father, does he have other children besides you?"

"What, Julian forgot to mention that part? No," Ashton said. "I was his only child, and I *still* wasn't his favorite."

"Oh, I am certain that's not true," Devi said. "He is your father. You're his only son."

"Well, that he knows of," interjected Julian.

"No, no," Ashton said. "I'm pretty sure I'm it."

Devi wouldn't let it go. "Do you spend time together? Do father and son things?"

"Father and son things? We don't fly kites if that's what you're asking. We have lunch once a week."

"Well, that counts!" Devi said. He seemed happy it was so. "He must enjoy that very much."

Ashton glanced at Julian by his side, as in what the hell.

In the uncomfortable hush that followed, Julian took the opportunity to apologize to Devi. He hoped there were no hard feelings.

"Apology not necessary," Devi said. "I'm used to it."

"I bet you are," muttered Ashton.

"I was so angry," Julian said.

"You still are," Ashton said.

Devi nodded. "Stage two of grief: anger. It's to be expected. No one should take it personally." That sounded directed at Ashton. Certainly, that's how Ashton took it because he scowled. They finished the mohinga, had kimchi and a banana cake with brandy. Gratefully Julian drank two glasses of the proffered murky tiger water. Ashton was given sake.

"So what's wrong with him?" Ashton blurted to Devi after a second helping of the banana cake. "What really happened to his body? I've never seen anything like his injuries. Smoke inhalation? Electrocution? Multiple foot fractures?"

"Possibly by traveling into another dimension," Devi said, "he had accumulated and stored a tremendous amount of energy, and on his improbable return, all of it was released as he was hurled through the physical universe at incredible speed."

"Can you just stop it," Ashton said. "Can't one of you give me a straight answer for once?"

"That wasn't straight enough for you?" Devi said. "He's lucky to be back in one piece. He's doing quite well, all things considered."

"You think *this* is doing well?"

Devi shrugged. "Your friend's predicament is not going to end here, Ashton. To truly help him, you must find a way to believe him, so he doesn't have to keep dealing with the burden of your skepticism among all the other things he has to deal with. Ease his burden, don't add to it. And, Julian, your accomplishment is not diminished just because you perceive yourself as having failed."

"I don't *perceive* myself as having failed," Julian said, jumping off the stool. "I actually *have* failed." It was time to go. "Ashton, ready? Thanks for the grub, Devi."

As they were leaving, Ashton said to Devi, "We're not trying to solve a crime here. I *am* helping him. He's not looking for a solution to his predicament. He's looking for compassion."

"He's looking for a little bit of a solution, too," Devi said.

∞

On the train to work, Ashton couldn't stop talking about Devi. "The balls on that guy! Telling me what to do with you. Did I ask for his advice?"

"He's the master of offering deeply unwanted advice," Julian said. "It's called being a shaman."

"Being a fraud more like," Ashton said. "There's something he wants from you. It's so obvious. How can you not see it? I don't know why you bought into his lies. Has he hypnotized you? What's in that gross water he keeps plying you with?"

"Tiger."

"Right, okay. What I'm saying is he totally wants you to do again whatever it is you do for him."

"I don't do it for him."

Ashton harrumphed.

"And you're wrong," Julian said. "Last time he tried to talk me out of it." Tried to talk me out of it by fearmongering, Julian thought, not meeting Ashton's eye.

"Not this time."

"He doesn't care, honest. He doesn't have a dog in this fight."

"Oh, not a dog, that swindler," Ashton said. "Maybe a tiger."

"How can he be a swindler, Ash? I fall into a starry profusion, through a sharp-fanged warp, and crawl out somewhere else in time and space, and find Josephine again. I told you about the Great Fire, about the Globe Theatre, the leper colony in the marshes near Drury Lane."

"He's drugged you. You're having visions."

"If I was going to have visions, why would I have them of her working in a brothel and murdering one of her customers? And did Devi break my feet and scorch my lungs, too?"

"He's a dangerous and powerful man," Ashton said. "He's like an assassin bug—tiny but lethal."

"Assassin bug?"

"One of the scariest insects known to mankind."

Julian groaned. "Tell you what," he said, "next time we go to Quatrang, I'll tell him in front of you that I'm not going back, so you can see he wants nothing from me. Will that make you feel better?"

"Why would there be a next time?" said Ashton.

"There isn't going to be."

"I mean, next time for Quatrang, fool."

"Oh."

As they got off at Bank, Ashton asked Julian if Devi was right. Was his skepticism a burden?

Julian admitted it was. "But it's fine, Ash, it's no longer an issue. It's in the past. And the past is done."

They strode quickly down the long length of the Bank of England's windowless marble wall, and as they turned the corner on Lothbury, Ashton said, "Then why do I keep feeling as

Faulkner did, that if the past was truly done, there would be less grief and sorrow? Seems to me that not only is the past not done, it's not even the fucking past."

Faulkner was right. There was no *was*. There was only *is*.

But Julian *was* done. To prove to his friend there was nothing to worry about, the next time they had lunch at Devi's, Julian announced he wasn't going back.

"That's fine," Devi said.

"I mean it."

"I hope so. As you know, I think that's best—for many reasons."

Julian gave Devi a shut-the-hell-up glare and Ashton an I-told-you-so one. Both men rolled their eyes.

"Sometimes, Ashton, I argue with your friend," Devi said, "because in arguing back, Julian defines for himself what he is. When I agree with him too much, it unsettles him, makes him cantankerous. Like now."

"That's not true!" That was Julian.

Ashton said nothing.

"All things being equal, Julian will always choose a fight," Devi said. "He prefers it to almost anything—inside and outside the ring. He needs combat to survive. The easy life suffocates him. The easy answer is the last thing he wants. Contact and combat is your friend's motto."

Ashton said nothing, looking upset that Devi figured out in five minutes what had taken him much longer.

"How is your father, Ashton?" Devi said. "Have you seen him this week? What did you two talk about?"

"I can't *stand* that man," Ashton said to Julian after they left.

Julian smirked. "What's with you two? He's not crazy about you either. The other week he called you a born wanderer."

"That's what I'm talking about, his insufferability," Ashton said, full of pique. "I'm not the born wanderer. That's how you know the guy's a fraud. He can't even see what's in front of him. *You're* the born wanderer."

Julian continued to see Devi but on his own. Devi cooked for Julian. Often they had cha ca, sizzling chunks of fried fish with garlic, ginger, turmeric and dill. Julian could've eaten it every day for a year, it was that good. When he told the cook what Ashton had said, Devi smiled condescendingly. "Ask your friend if he knows the meaning of the word wander. You're only a wanderer if you travel alone. When there are two of you, it's not called wandering. It's called an adventure. And you and your girl are on an extraordinary adventure."

"*Were* on an adventure."

"That's what I meant."

"And Ashton is not alone. He's with Riley."

"Tell me more about this Riley," Devi said. "Is she living here in London with him?"

Damn that Devi! "Even so, he's still not alone. I'm here with him."

"*Are* you, Julian?"

It was *really* time to go.

"When is he moving back to L.A.?" Devi asked. "I don't see the harp or the lamb with him. I see the smoke of torment. I see woe in the street."

"Can you stop it? I don't know what you're talking about. What do you see?"

"Not much. I told you, I feel things. Things that aren't good."

"How many more things that aren't good can happen to me, Devi?"

"Not to you," Devi said. "To him."

Grimly Julian stared at the shaman. Julian hated to be reminded of their conversation the previous year. *What are you prepared to give up, Julian, to live as you want?* Julian hated to have been proven wrong, hated to have failed. His blood was boiling. "Well, I'm never going back again," he said, grabbing his coat. "So we're good."

After that day, he stopped visiting Devi.

∞

Almost all Julian did until the end of the year was work and box and swim.

Except for the weekends when Ashton was away either back in L.A. or somewhere unspecified, or when Julian was at the pool or the gym, the two men hardly left each other's side. They shopped together, went to work together, drank together, sparred together, played video games together. On rainy Notting Hill weekend afternoons, they scoped the streets, checking out garage sales, open markets, art galleries, pretty girls. They rode bikes through Hyde Park and Kensington Gardens, they hiked through Holland Park, they had long liquid brunches at quaint London pubs—like the Silver Cross—and got dressed up in fitted bespoke suits to go out on Saturday nights, when the class of women they chatted up increased geometrically with the price of their silk ties from Jermyn Street. Ashton tried, you had to give him that. No matter what Devi said, Ashton did his best.

Julian, too.

"Let me ask you a question, Jules," Ashton said one night, late on the Central Line, as they were heading home thoroughly inebriated after last rounds at the Counting House.

"You're in no state to question me, especially in that tone of voice," Julian said, "and I'm certainly in no state to answer you."

"In other words, the perfect time to have a serious conversation—when we're both three sheets to the wind. Let me ask you: when you meet this girl, does she know who you are?"

"Why would she? How could she?"

"Uh-huh. But at the very least her name is Josephine, right?"

"No—because it wasn't her name," Julian said. "Her name was Mia."

"Wait, so, a derivative of the most common name in the English language?"

"She falls in love with me!"

"Don't shout, we're on the tube," Ashton said. "People will think we're drunk."

"We *are* drunk."

After they got off at Notting Hill Gate and were staggering home, Ashton resumed. "Jules, have you considered the possibility that it's just a random girl?"

"You think I'm on the receiving end of some cosmic prank? Go to hell."

"Oh, sure, I mean, what are the chances of finding a nipply, lusty, brown-haired, brown-eyed chick named Mary who falls for you?"

"I'm done listening to you."

But Ashton was on a roll. "You think you're falling in love with Josephine, but it's just some murdering broad named Mallory."

"Am I listening?"

"You hook up with her in a brothel of all places—where naturally all true love begins—and she goes all doe-eyed on you, tells you you're her one and only john, starts killing and stealing, and your first thought is—*Josephine!*"

"I'm not only not listening, I'm no longer your friend." Julian tried to speed up, but drunk Ashton was a faster and more coherent man than drunk Julian.

"Are you pissed off because you know I'm right?"

"Why are you still speaking?" Julian said. "You think I travel through time so I can hook up with a stranger? What about her feelings for me?"

Ashton's smile was from one side of the street to the other. "Jules, that's my other point. Can we get real for a sec?"

"No."

"We roomed together and lived together, lest you forgot."

"I wish I forgot."

"In our sophomore year, your bed was separated from mine by a thin sheet we hung up for fake privacy. Do you remember? Did you think this sheet was soundproof?"

"Go to hell."

"I know all about you. Plus Gwen used to brag to Riley, who would then scold me—oh, and thanks for that, too, by the way. Julian does this, and Julian does that. Fuck you, buddy." A grinning Ashton hooked his long arm around Julian's neck as they zigzagged down the sidewalk. Julian tried to get away, but Ashton wouldn't let him.

"Your point?"

"My point is," Ashton said, "that *any* girl would be happy to biblically acquaint herself with you."

"Get off me."

"During foreplay you could ask her if she's the one, and I promise you, *promise* you, by the time you get to the afterglow, she'll be chirping yes! Yes, I'm the one, Jules! Wait, no, it's me, *I'm* the one!"

Julian pushed Ashton off him. "You're ridiculous."

"But am I wrong?"

"Both ridiculous *and* wrong."

"Here's my final point," Ashton said, grabbing Julian again. "Why do you have to spelunk, box, swim, bust up your body? Why can't you find them and seduce them right here in London, in the comfort of your own home, in your tiny, woefully inadequate bed?"

"I'm moving out."

"I promise to set you up only with brown-eyed girls named Maria. I know about a dozen off the top of my head."

"I'm packing my shit as soon as we get home."

"I'm not saying love again. I'm saying…"

"Shut up."

Ashton was laughing, his arm around Julian's neck. "You've tried it your way, Jules. You've tried it your way twice. Come on, buddy. Now let's try it Ashton's way."

And Julian said okay. "I'll try it Ashton's way, said the barmaid to the bishop."

∞

Julian didn't know how his friend accomplished these things, but Ashton did set him up with an attractive brown-haired woman named Mary. They went out for a bite and a drink at her local pub and ended up at her place near the Imperial War Museum in Lambeth. When they were still at the pub, he told her he wasn't looking for anything serious, and the woman said thank God because she wasn't either.

Julian left in the middle of the night. There was no tube and he couldn't find a cab, so he had to hoof home five miles across Lambeth Bridge and around Hyde Park. The next morning when Ashton asked him how it went, Julian said, "What can I tell you, everything is worse south of the river." They both chuckled. "But on the bright side, the Imperial War Museum is near her. Let's go grab a bite and check it out."

"No, thank you. I don't do anything south of the river, especially having to do with the war."

And so it went.

Julian sparred with four different partners on four different days. He hit the speedbag five times a week with a thousand blurs of his gloved fists. He pummeled the heavy bag three times a week with five hundred blows of thunder. The bag would fall before Julian fell, and the blows reverberated through the gym, the glass in the grubby windows rattling with Julian's immense anger. He pounded the bag to cleanse his body of rage, he swam miles in the local gym pool to exhaust himself, and when that still didn't work, he slept with the women he chatted up in pubs and clubs and Franz Ferdinand concerts. They weren't all named Mary. And Ashton's theory proved not entirely correct. Not one of them, no matter how brown-haired and brown-eyed and Mary-monikered, no matter how long-limbed and white skinned, felt remotely like the Mary of Clerkenwell or the Mallory of the Silver Cross. Or the Josephine of L.A. Not one quantum particle of them felt like the girl he was eternally entangled with.

But Ashton was right: Julian had to move on. He had to try to find a way to live again. At the very least he had to have sex again.

And at the very least, that's what he did.

On Sunday mornings, Ashton would crawl out of his room to find Julian making coffee or eating leftovers, and there would be another irate woman yelling, Callie from Portobello, Candy from King's Road, a girl from the Botanist and from the Colbert. "Howling in the night, yelling in the mornings, destroying speedbags," Ashton said. "All you do is fuck and fight. Both with the same temper."

"I'm doing what you told me to, remember? You're never happy."

"When will it end? I'm going crazy from the racket, both in the middle of the night and in the mornings. I'm going to charge the noise-cancelling headphones you forced me to buy against my share of the rent. Can't you stay at their place? Are you doing this deliberately? Are you making our apartment uninhabitable so I start praying you'll go do the time warp again?" Ashton grinned at his own cleverness.

"Ash, I know it's difficult for you to believe," said Julian, "but when I'm with a girl, I hardly think of you at all. One might say never."

"Yeah, yeah."

Women left Julian nasty messages or waited by his front door to shout obscenities to his face. You never called me, you piece of shit. You said you would and you never did, and then I saw you in the pub with someone else. I know you said we weren't serious, but you could've called me. Julian was left neutral by it. Other women couldn't move the needle, they broke their mouths on his bitter stone, shattering as they came, while he kept waiting for the end-bell to ring. It never did. Rage was blacker than blindness, blacker than grief.

*Julian, go and come back for me.* Clutching the Bill of Mortality in one hand, the gold coin in the other, he kept hearing Mallory's dying voice in his head—when he wasn't dreaming of Josephine, walking toward his café table.

*Julian, come back for me.*

Why, when the new moon was invisible in the sky, did he dream of her smiling? Earth, moon, and sun all in a line, a meridian line, a wishing moon, Josephine smiling, Mallory pleading...

*Come back for me.*

And in Notting Hill, the cast-off girls had fun, then wanted more, got insulted, bellowed at him, all hawks in motion. He told them he wasn't looking for anything. And they assured him neither were they. Yet there was so much yelling. I'm serious, he would say. Please listen to me. But they had three pints, two cocktails, half a bottle of wine, and they couldn't listen. And when he told one sober woman right at the outset, even before they had ordered the wine, that he wasn't looking for anything long-term, she slapped him across the face and said, don't get ahead of yourself, buddy, who even says you'll get anywhere with me. He got somewhere with her, and now she, too, was shouting at him.

"Jules, what a mess you're making of things," Ashton said. "I think you've forgotten how to date women."

"You call what I'm doing dating?"

"That's true, this isn't quite what I had in mind when I advised you to *plug* back into your life. You've gone from a monk to a player overnight. But sooner or later, all this whatever you want to call it is going to turn into a bloodbath. You'll be sorry when one of them bashes your brains in with a cricket bat."

"How do you know that's not what I'm hoping for?" said Julian.

# 12

# A Subject of Choice

AFTER CHRISTMAS, ASHTON ASKED JULIAN TO SIGN OFF ON THE sale of the Treasure Box. Nextel was becoming too big a responsibility. There was a lot to do in London, both in work and in life. And the prop business was dying without Ashton, who sounded philosophical when he spoke about it. It couldn't continue. Back in L.A. over the holidays, he and Julian held an auction for the remainder of the props, gave away some posters and trinkets to friends, kept a few items Ashton valued, like his Bob Marley poster, and didn't renew their lease on the building. "It'll be a taco place now. They might call it Treasure Taco." Ashton grinned.

"Are you sure that instead of selling Treasure Box, you don't want to move back to L.A.?" Julian said.

"What do I have to move back for now?"

"How about for me?" Riley said two months later. It was March. She was visiting the boys for a long weekend to celebrate Julian's 36th birthday.

"But, cupcake, you're here in London with me," Ashton said. "If I go back, I'll be in L.A. without you. Come here, delicious. Give me a big smooch."

"You're impossible."

"Is that why you love me?"

"I love you in spite of it." Leaving Ashton's side, Riley draped her arm around Julian. "What about you, Jules? Ashton told me you're finally dating..."

Julian and Ashton exchanged a glance.

"...And I'm so happy about that, but when are you going to find a girl and settle down?"

"I found a girl already."

"I meant...*another* girl." Riley rolled her eyes at Ashton as if to say, can you believe this guy?

"I'm trying, Riles." Julian knocked into Riley's shoulder. "Do you know what Muhammad Ali said? That it was indeed possible for the heavyweight champion of the world to be with just one woman."

"To be fair," Ashton said, "like you, he went through a flock of women before he said that."

Julian nodded. "That's how he found her."

Riley lifted her eyes and stared at Ashton across the kitchen island. Ashton didn't return her gaze. Her voice when she spoke barely trembled. "Is that what *you're* doing, Ash? Still looking for the one?"

Biting his lip, Julian backed away.

Ashton put up his fists. "Jules, you bastard! Don't run away now. Get over here so I can kill you. Riles, baby girl, he was talking about himself! What, you didn't catch the self-aggrandizing boxing metaphor, comparing his sorry ass with the greatest boxer who ever lived? Thanks a lot, Jules. Why is it when *he* checks out of the human race, I'm the one who gets in trouble? Come here, my dear, step into my bedroom, I have something to show you."

∞

"Julian, how is he?" Riley was talking quietly, to not wake Ashton. It was her last night before she flew back home.

"He's good, look at him."

"He looks good. But I mean...how *is* he?"

Julian replied in kind. "He is...*good*?"

"Is he drinking too much?"

"No, just the right amount. He's not missing work or anything, if that's what you're asking."

"Did you see how much Grey Goose he put away tonight?"

"Yeah, he was being good for you, he barely touched the stuff."

Riley rolled her eyes. "Always with the jokes."

"He's fine, Riles. Don't worry."

She sighed.

"What's the matter?" Julian didn't really want to talk about what the matter was. He knew what the matter was. After seven years, there was still no ring on her finger. And she was thirty-four. It was occurring to her there might never be a ring on her finger.

"What's the matter? Oh, you know. Same old, same old. Nothing ever changes, Jules. All the girls keep panting for him. It's accurate to say I'm on the verge of suicide because of it."

"What girls," Julian said.

Riley patted Julian's chest. "You're a good friend. To him first, of course. But also to me. What else are you going to say?" She and Julian were spread out on the couch. They'd been watching TV when they both noticed that Ashton had fallen asleep. They turned down *Sherlock* and lounged casually, quietly chatting, both of them watching Ashton's face look more intense in sleep than it ever looked awake—as if Ashton were dreaming of armies of dragons ridden by naked nymphs. Their heads were close together in the center of the sofa, their legs hanging over the sofa arms.

"Julian, you lie," Riley said.

"Oh, yeah?" Julian half-focused on Sherlock explaining something to a skeptical Watson; Julian was trying to read the detective's lips.

"You didn't really flip for me all those years ago, did you?"

"What?" Julian looked away from the TV at Riley's pretend-casual face, regrouped, rerouted.

"Isn't that what you told Gwen when you broke up with

her?" Riley said. "That you and Ashton flipped for us, you won, and you picked her. That's a dirty lie, right?"

"Why?"

"No, no, don't do that." She sat up a little straighter, tucked her feet under herself and half-faced him. Her makeup was off, her hair was in a ponytail. She was in sweats and ready for bed. She looked, as always, flawless. "Don't answer a question with a question. Just answer. You lie, right?"

"Right."

"Are you lying?"

"When?" Julian said. He was still slouching. "Then, or now?"

"Julian!" She elbowed him, moving closer to his head.

He laughed. "What do you want from me?"

"The truth. Did you or did you not flip for me?"

"Yes," Julian said. "We did. We flipped for you."

"Is it true that you won?"

"That's also true."

Riley exhaled. Julian stopped pretend-watching *Sherlock* and carefully turned his head to her. Her expression hardly changed, it was still rather easygoing and composed, but there was something unfathomable and desolate in her brown eyes.

"I didn't quite win you," Julian said. "I picked heads and got heads."

"So it was your choice?"

"Yes."

"And you chose Gwen?"

"Yes."

"Why?"

Julian didn't know what to say. "You didn't want me to pick Gwen?"

"I'm asking why you did. Tell me. I'm not—I won't be offended or hurt. But I need to"—Riley paused—"I'm thinking about an awful lot these days, piecing my life together, trying to make sense of the forks in the road that led me here." She smiled thinly. "Trying to make heads or tails of stuff."

"What do you want to know?"

"Why did you choose Gwen and not me?"

Julian shrugged as nonchalantly as the moment allowed. "I thought you and Ashton were a better fit," he said. "Look at him." (Admittedly Ashton did not look his best at the moment: slumped on the couch, passed out, legs sprawled, arms out, head back, mouth open.) "And look at you. You're superstars. And I was a disillusioned former boxer wannabe, stuck being a nerdy writer because of circumstances outside my control. I didn't want"—Julian broke off—"I saw our future, Riley. Beyond the first few great weeks. I don't always see the future." How true that was. "But I saw it then. I didn't want you being with me and pining for him," Julian said. "I didn't want him pining for you. It would've come between me and him, and I couldn't have that. You unhappy with me, wishing for him, and him hostile to me and wishing for you."

"As if anything could ever come between you two," Riley said.

"*You* would have. We can't share the same woman."

"You are Ashton's brother from another mother," said Riley. "He and you have real love. Yes, yes, I know, you're both men and yes, you're both sexual beings who love women, but you're also men who have deep respect and trust and love for each other. Nothing can take that away."

"*That* would have."

She fell silent. They stared at Sherlock and Watson on the flatscreen. "Is this the future you imagined?" Riley asked. She sounded so sad. "When you two were the happiest single guys in Southern California?"

"Who could have ever imagined *this* future, Riley?" Julian shut his eyes.

"Don't you want to find love again, Jules?"

"I found love. I have it. It hasn't gone anywhere. It's still right here."

"So what are you doing with the other girls?"

"Passing the time. Counting the minutes. Pretending I'm still of the world."

She fell like a parachute to the ground.

"Is that what he's doing, too?"

"No, Riley," Julian said. He was a good friend—to Ashton first.

After a while she spoke again. "But what if Ashton wasn't with you that night? What if you were out with Doug or Lee instead?"

"What's your question?"

"Would you have chosen me then?"

Julian told her the truth because she asked for it. "Yes," he said.

Their eyes met for a moment, and then they both fell mute. Julian put his arm around her.

"I'm all in, Jules," Riley said, her voice low and blue. "There's nothing to be done. This is it. He is it. But if you only knew how I sometimes wish you had chosen less wisely." She leaned her head sideways, her blonde perfumed hair grazing against Julian's cheek.

When they lifted their gazes, an awake Ashton was watching them from his couch. "Riley is right—you're such a liar, Jules," Ashton said, rubbing his stubble. "Why don't you tell her the actual truth?" He struggled to a sitting position. "Why don't you tell her that you've never in your life dated or been attracted to a blonde chick."

"Shut up, I would've been his first," Riley said. "I would've seduced him."

"I'd like to see you try. Do it now. I don't mind."

"That you pretend you don't mind bothers me most of all."

"In London, he's been with no one but a phantom and one-night stands. All brunettes, by the way, even the ghost. But I'm not pretending. Go ahead. Seduce him."

"Calm down, Doctor Detroit," Julian said, getting up and giving Riley his hand to help her off the couch. "You've had too much to drink. Go to bed."

∞

After Riley flew back to L.A., Julian returned to Quatrang, for the first time in months.

"Hello, Julian," Devi said as soon as he heard the door open. "I just made some banh khot. Would you like some? Small pancakes with shrimp cooked in coconut milk and sprinkled with dried garlic flakes and ginger. And I made your favorite kimchi just fresh yesterday. Shall I get you a plate?"

They had lunch, drank tiger water, chatted about trivial things. Devi said his fishmonger had called him earlier about a fresh shipment of high-quality squid. Did Julian have a few minutes to walk to the market? Julian did, and carried the squid and the cabbage back to Great Eastern Road for Devi, and when they were back inside, after another glass of tiger water, just before Julian headed to work, he said to Devi, "I'm going back." He tried to keep his shoulders from slumping under the weight of the impossible choice he couldn't help but make.

"I know," the Hmong cook said.

Julian was nonplussed. "How could you possibly know when I myself didn't know?"

"Because it's the only imperative of your life, Julian. It's stamped on every breath your soul makes."

Julian had been furious with fate, with life, with God, with Devi—and with himself most of all. He was doing something wrong. He had to try harder. "It's my fault. I live inside her days, pretending everything will magically turn out fine."

"Yes, it's called human existence."

"Except I know what most people do not," Julian said. "I *know* she's at the end of her days. I didn't know it in L.A. And I didn't know it in Clerkenwell. But after the Silver Cross, I can no longer deny it. I can't continue to behave as I've been behaving. I have to get her out of whatever she's doing as soon as possible and get her to another place. Change her geographical location, not just the direction of her heart."

"You can try." Devi tilted his head. "But the direction of her heart first, right? You're not going to kidnap her or anything?"

"Or anything," Julian said. "Conceivably I could have more time, couldn't I? More than two months? That part is not etched in stone, is it?" He sounded desperately uncertain.

"I don't know if you've ever had even two months, to be honest," Devi said. "You could have that again. Frankly, you could have less. I don't know if the end of her life means months or hours. I don't know how this works. You're in uncharted territory. You wanted a fate beyond the fates. Here it is."

It hadn't occurred to Julian he could have even *less* time. As always, leave it to Devi to make him feel worse.

∞

On March 20, Ashton accompanied Julian to Greenwich.

"Are you sure you want to come, bud?" Julian said.

"I wouldn't miss it. What, son of Titan isn't coming?"

"He never comes. Says he can't."

"Why?"

"He won't say."

"Probably because the evilmonger has hypnotized you into believing you could ride alone down Satan's highway," said Ashton.

Julian wore a thick Thermoprene semi-dry wetsuit with a hood. On his feet were hyperstretch dive boots, on his hands Kevlar dive gloves. He brought two headlamps this time, two flashlights, and one divelight. Reluctantly he brought a grappling hook, some carabiners, and webbing. Ashton insisted. "If you're going to pretend to do it," he told Julian a week ago, "no reason not to pretend to do it right. What's the point of diving into this fake thing half-baked? That's not the kind of men we are," Ashton said. "We dive into our fake trips full-baked!"

Ashton took Julian to a hiking supply store on Holborn where he outfitted him with a light hard-shell waterproof Camelbak pack that was big enough to store Julian's flashlights, but also had room for a rappel hook, four carabiners and a thirty-foot coil of parachute cord. "Why aren't you taking my multi-tool on your fake adventure?" Ashton asked. "You haven't lost it, have you?"

"I have it. I can't bring it. Only new things. With no past life."

"Of course. My bad." Ashton made Julian buy a brand new Swiss Army multi-tool. "Fake caving is like real mountaineering, my friend," Ashton said, "except underground, and you know— fake. But still, brutal Darwinian selection must apply. Bring the least of what you can't do without. But bring it."

"Yeah," Julian said, "that's what I did last year. All of it was at the bottom of a cave pool in five seconds."

Julian forewent the heavy crampons this time, the useless Suunto watch, the extra batteries.

"Water?"

"I'm constantly wet. A blow-dryer maybe."

"Food?"

"Last thing I'm thinking of."

Finally, he was ready. Ashton forced Julian to wear a harness seat over his wetsuit in case he needed to rappel down a cliff. "If you don't need it, discard it."

"Rappel. Aren't you the optimist. Not rappel, Ashton. Fly."

"Well, you know what they say. You can fly with a harness. But you can't rappel without one."

The one adjustment Julian made was to the Camelbak. He wore it on his chest instead of on his back. He didn't want it to get stuck behind him in the shaft.

They got to the Observatory by 11:30 and stood silently at the railing around the Transit Circle. The roof was retracted. There was no sun. Sweeney had gone on his break. It was just the two of them in front of the black telescope, side by side, at zero meridian.

At 11:50 a.m. Julian took off his coat and handed it to Ashton. He pulled the Thermoprene hood over his slicked-back hair. He had no beard, and the dark wavy hair was down to his jaw. Ashton regarded him with a peculiar expression. "It's okay," Julian said. "Nothing's wrong." He smiled lightly.

"Nothing's wrong? You look ready to go deep-sea diving on top of a hill on dry land. Do you know where you're going?"

"Do any of us really know where we're going, Ash?" Julian said, Josephine's long-ago words catching in his throat. Pulling out the long rawhide rope, he laid the crystal into the palm of his hand and waited for noon. His hand was trembling.

Ashton studied the shaking hand, the stone. "Boy, Jules, that guy has really done a number on you. Is this the famous sun catcher?"

"It's the Josephine catcher."

Ashton continued to stare at the stone. "Did you know that dilithium crystals power the U.S.S. *Enterprise*?"

"Dilithium is imaginary. This is an actual quartz crystal. This is what mountains are made of."

"Yes, so completely different," Ashton said. "Did you know that the kyber crystal powers the lightsaber?"

Fondly Julian gazed at his friend. "Yes, I know. Because the living crystal has intense focused energy."

"The kyber crystal is also imaginary, Jules."

"In four minutes, Ashton, you'll know that the crystal in my hand is a superweapon."

11:56.

"Is it going to be like magic?" All things considered, Ashton was in pretty good humor. Julian knew why. Because his friend didn't believe.

Ashton didn't believe *yet*.

*"There's a magic deeper still which we do not know,"* Julian said, quoting Devi quoting C.S. Lewis. "I really can't say how it's going to be for you."

"Jules?"

"Yes, Ash?"

"In your best-case scenario, if this shebang works, you're vanishing and you aren't coming back?" Ashton looked nothing but skeptical.

"I'm not coming back." Julian couldn't look at his friend as he said it. What was the worst-case scenario? What could he live with? What could he bear?

"Look at me, Jules."

Reluctantly Julian met his friend's probing gaze. In Ashton's pale blue eyes was disbelief, unbelief, nonbelief for the undertaking, that was there first, but underneath was something else. A sudden stinging realization that even if the cave was fake, Julian, at least theoretically, was fully prepared to abandon everything real for it, including the man in front of him. That was Julian's best-case scenario. Leaving Ashton behind forever. And now his friend knew it.

Julian turned his eyes away, to the footwell beneath the telescope.

11:58.

Wordlessly, he gave Ashton a one-armed hug.

Ashton patted Julian's back. He didn't say a word.

Julian's palm was flat, the crystal shimmering. He took a breath. "Ash, can you promise me something?"

"I haven't done enough?"

"If I'm gone for good, please go back to L.A. Marry Riley. She loves you. She needs to be your wife. She needs to have your babies."

Ashton's ice blue eyes trickled, like melting kyber crystals. "One crisis at a time, brother," he said quietly. "I guess we better hope you don't come back, eh, so you don't ever have to worry about it."

Julian couldn't worry about it even now. He pushed Ashton an arm's length away so nothing else would touch him but her crystal and hopped over the railing.

11:59.

Mia, Mary, Mallory!

Most of his days, Julian lived and couldn't tell if he was real and alive, or not at all. Except for 11:59 on March 20. He was real and alive now. His heart was pounding at two hundred beats a minute. The kingdom was about to open again. The eternity was full of the beggar's cries.

Julian didn't want to relive the dread ride on the black river. He would not confess the terror he felt in the swirling madness of a million unfulfilled desires.

He was doing it for her.

*Julian, go and come back for me.*

12:00.

# Part Two

# In the Fields of St. Giles

*"O, you shall be exposed, my lord, to dangers,*
*As infinite as imminent!*
*But I'll be true…*
*Will you be true?"*

Cressida to Troilus,
William Shakespeare, *Troilus* and *Cressida* Act IV, Scene 4

# 13

## Rappel

FIRST WAS THE LABYRINTH, A NARROW MAZE OF FISSURES and dead ends, nowhere, nowhere, nowhere, walking and aching for miles in his dive boots on the uneven cave floor. The boots ripped. Thermoprene wasn't meant for serrated-edge ground.

Julian moved through crevices—treacherous, utterly infuriating. The height of the walls was ten feet, but the width was between three feet and *eighteen inches*! It was so narrow in places that Julian had to creep sideways as if on a window ledge, his back against the wall. The hard-shell pack on his chest made him too bulky. He had to take it off and carry it in his hands. Often these crevices ended abruptly in a hill of stones, and he had to double back and head into a different fissure, climbing over boulders, searching for a one-man slot that might lead the way out. The claustrophobia of the maze was matched by his stifling frustration.

And because nothing is so bad that it can't be made worse, he tripped over his shredded boots and dropped the backpack. Julian tried desperately to catch it. It careened off a stone, teetered for a moment on a ledge, and then slipped through a crevice and disappeared before Julian could grab the strap. He cursed wildly for five minutes before he resigned himself to the backpack's loss and resumed his trek. Like he always said, you can't overprepare, and in the end, it won't matter. Why was it still so hard to accept how many things were out of his control.

When he finally climbed over a rocky protrusion and walked out onto a mesa above a cave chamber, he wished he were back in the suffocating web of stone. The high plateau where he stood over a canyon was covered with cones, limestone deposits, rocks and cave matter. These prevented him from walking, much less running and leaping. The growths were three-dimensional etchings rising from the ground, appearing to him as writhing monsters, as grisly beasts. In the beam of his headlamp, their shadows, tall and self-important, reflected off the cave walls.

He stood at the rim of a miniature Grand Canyon, if the Grand Canyon were contained in a closed space the size of two airplane hangars, one on top of another, and instead of the sun and birds and evergreens and the sky, there was nothing but rutted darkness. The things that looked like birds and trees were stone. It was the Grand Canyon without any of the grandeur and with all the peril.

A thousand feet below him, the river he needed to get to carved through the canyon floor, emerging from one end of the cave and meandering into the other. The perfectly round moongate rose over the river's right exit. The waters flowed through the moongate. There was no jumping over this chasm. To get to the bottom, Julian had to rappel the steep canyon wall with a useless harness and without rope or an anchor because all the rope and anchors were inside his lost backpack.

Watch out for falling mountains, like in Topanga, Ashton told Julian. No danger of that here. The only thing that would be tumbling off these cliffs was his sorry ass.

Julian had no choice. He scaled down a thousand feet, hugging the canyon wall.

Dripping water had hollowed out holes in the vertical rock, like jug handles. The surface was jagged, uneven. It took him infinite time, using the rule of three. Three limbs always attached to the wall—two legs, one arm, two arms, one leg—finding a step or a ridge to hold on to. His headlamp illuminated the rock four inches from his face, and nothing else.

Why couldn't Julian have crampons to help with his descent today, when he could most use them? Instead of cleats, he had torn slippery Thermoprene on his feet.

One misstep, one mishandling, one ridge not wide enough for his gloved hand, one stony lump not large enough for his barely clad foot and down he'd go, careening against the stone with her crystal and beret.

To navigate down the canyon wall, he needed a cord and spikes, he needed an anchor, a hook, belays, carabiners.

But Julian didn't have those things. He had nothing.

He crept down the ravine harnessed to nothing but his red faith.

∞

He reached the bottom by falling the last ten feet. He landed roughly and lay on his back on the pebbly shore, gathering himself. His headlamp was dimming. No wonder. He must have been glued to the wall like a salamander for a hundred thousand hours. It was a good thing he'd brought another headlamp and stuffed it inside his wetsuit.

The enormous canyon above him was a live ominous presence he couldn't see but strongly felt. It pressed down on his chest. He rested for barely a few breaths. He had to hurry. She was waiting.

Wading into the river waist-deep, Julian chugged down handfuls of cold cave water, hoping it wasn't the water of forgetfulness, and swam through the moongate, looking for something to grab onto and float. He felt better in the water, invigorated even, after the physical and mental stress of his interminable free-climb descent. He had made it over the bright black chasm. Now the river would take him to her. Very soon he would see her face. If only he could tell her from the start how much he had missed her, having lived a lonely year without her. And though Julian was relieved he had made it, he was frightened of what lay ahead. It had been such a worrying supernatural effort to get to the river. Almost as if he was being kept from her.

He had no trouble finding something to drift on. The river was filled with crap. Julian had his pick of garbage. He grabbed onto a small door and found a narrow board to use for an oar. Balancing in the middle of the panel, he sat cross-legged and paddled through the rubble.

What was going on with this river? Like a tsunami had swept through and washed a demolished city into the water. Was he hallucinating? In the beam of his waning headlamp, the river looked filled with human things. Fragments of chairs, segments of walls, washboards, empty buckets. The flowing debris got trapped in the bends as if under the starlings of London Bridge, piling up higher and higher, narrowing the river and increasing the pressure of its current. Paddling became impossible. Julian threw away the oar but didn't lie down. The flow was too strong. He'd get thrown off if he relaxed his body.

Were there other humans on it? He called out. Only his voice echoed back. Were the humans dead, except for him? Did they run to the river and die, leaving their things and bodies behind? Or was the river where they lived, amid the junk, wet with life?

And what was more frightening?

The descent down the cliffs took a lot out of Julian. He didn't have a moment to recover before being hurled into the junkyard flood. He had to be at full attention. There was no floating, no drifting, no sleeping. He turned off his light to conserve it, saved the other one for the just in case, and swirled in the darkness. He kept getting knocked into impassable hard things and navigating out of piers built up from refuse.

Where was he headed that this was what he had to overcome to get there?

Josephine, I will follow you to the end of forever. Julian tried to close his eyes for a moment. But where are you taking me?

After what felt like years, he was tossed from his useless carriage into shallow water.

# 14

## Gin Lane

JULIAN REALIZES HE CAN SEE THE CONTOURS OF THE CAVE, even without the headlamp. Light is coming from elsewhere. Thank God, because he couldn't have taken much more. Before he starts forward, he unbuckles and throws off the harness. That Ashton and his adorable desire to control what couldn't be controlled.

To climb out, Julian moves boulders and trellises out of his way. There's a musty unpleasant smell around him, and mud underneath his feet. At least he hopes it's mud. The light filters in through a small break in an exterior wall, a hole mostly plugged up by a giant object blocking Julian's way out. He pushes at the object with his gloved hand. It's mushy, it gives way, yet doesn't give way. He takes off his glove and tries again. It's pliant but won't budge. He pushes on it with one hand, then two. If he didn't know better, he'd say it feels like a woman's generous rear end, but that's silly. He's not crawling back in time past a woman's ass.

He taps on the squishy bottom. He knocks on it as if it's a door, waiting to be opened. He slaps it. As a last resort, he pinches the thick skin under the loose fabric. There's a yelp, a curse, motion and commotion.

Now we're getting somewhere.

"Yowse!" a female voice shrieks. "A rat just bit me arse!" The enormous shape shifts barely an inch. Julian pinches the flesh once more, but harder. Finally, there's significant movement. He shoves away the stool and squeezes past.

A large woman with a bloated face stands staring at him in wobbly confusion, her dim eyes widening. "Why are you pinching me arse, scoundrel?" she says in a thick common tongue.

England again. Is he *never* leaving England?

Rather, is *Josephine* never leaving England?

"Why are you touching me delicate parts? I'll have you arrested for lewd acts of wanton disregard for me human flesh! Constable!"

No constable comes.

Julian, still on his knees, looks around. The woman isn't the only squalid thing here. Able-bodied men and boys in shabby frock coats loiter on the cobblestones. A few women in stiff excessive crinolines lean against the buildings.

It's fetid and damp. He sees seven streets like spokes, crisscrossing the square. Julian stops paying attention to the chirping woman.

Fuck.

He realizes where he is. Not only is Josephine never leaving England, she seems to be never leaving London. And what a London this is. He has followed her into Seven Dials, the maze of streets between Covent Garden and Soho, followed her into the Seven Dials not of today but of yesterday.

O London! Why, you magnificent city, why? All your marble palaces and gilded gardens, your broom-swept streets and river embankments, you could've spit her out anywhere. Why, of all places, here?

Seven Dials is the heart of the rookery of St. Giles in the Fields, one of the worst slums in London. Julian doesn't need to learn the year. He knows. It's sometime after the Great Fire and before 1845 when the city tore down half the rookery to transect it with Oxford Street, hoping that the new shopping boulevard might reduce the numbers of shiftless vagrants. The ooze of primordial morass seeps over the cobblestones, the foul fumes rise in the air. From every graveyard lane to every decrepit dwelling, it's clear to Julian that 1845 is still the far-away future.

Rookery: a collective noun for a breeding ground for animals.

Rookery: a place where birds are confined, noisy birds like ravens.

Rookery: a colony of penguins.

Rookery: St. Giles in the Fields.

Kneeling at Seven Dials, Julian prays to St. Giles, the patron saint of cripples and lepers. He can see the church's pale white spire needled above its parish. In 1603 he took Mary past that church rising over Drury Lane. They rode their wagon through fields of flowers, reciting Shakespeare. Fields of asphodel surrounded the church then. Marshland and open ditches surround the parish now. And within: hovels and gin shops. Not even brothels, that's too precious and quaint. Sex for sale straight up on the undrained streets.

Seven Dials. Again the number seven, a number that has subsumed him.

Seven times for her soul.

Seven sins, seven ages of Josephine.

Seven weeks for him to save her.

And how can he save her here? She might not have seven days to live here.

Seven is nothing but a foul metaphor for his existence. And hers. Because a 7 looks like the gallows.

The square is dissected by three streets plus one for bad luck. The roads that divide Seven Dials are impossibly narrow, in all epochs, past and present. One small car can barely fit between the sidewalks. There are no cars or sidewalks in the slum today. The cobblestones are glued together with the mortar of muck. The plaques on the corners read Great Earl, Little Earl, Great Lion, Little Lion, Great St. Andrew, Little St. Andrew—and Queen Street. The famous Doric pillar that stands in the middle of the square and acts as a sundial is missing.

Is this going to be Julian's fate? A circus with seven gates, seven spokes, seven streets, seven threads, all leading to the same dead end?

It is so ordinary that he should be on his knees in a crowded public place that no one even notices him except the heavy woman on the low stool. The mangy court is mobbed, yet no one's moving. The crowd is drinking, squabbling, singing—and it's not even night. From the patch of sky, Julian guesses it's early afternoon.

After a heavy sigh, he rises to his feet. He feels unhinged—as if anyone could tell. He decides to spout some nonsense himself. "Ladies! Gentlemen!" Julian calls out. "What year is it, I beg of you!"

The heavy woman barks, "Are you dull in the head, boy? It's 1775."

"Oh, 1775!" Julian exclaims. "Splendid! Then my time machine worked!"

"Good on yer, mate!" a wily young man rejoins, traipsing by with a basket full of plums. "What's a time machine? Keep up the good work. In that spiffing suit, you can go anywhere."

"Don't you worry, ladies and gentlemen!" Julian shouts, enunciating every word like a carnival barker. "It's hard to believe, but I promise you, your Seven Dials will soon be a unique retail and leisure destination!"

People respond by laughing. They don't stop drinking. Loosely they collect around him to listen. They were bored in the middle of their day, and suddenly a sideshow. "Seven Dials will be home to over 120 quality shops! Home to five West End theatres! Home to two luxury hotels!"

They guffaw. The undersized plum seller, a slim costermonger in a shabby frock, offers him a sip of brew to keep him going. Julian is thirsty; he gulps it down. It's strong, not like that weak tea of an ale that Krea used to make. "Hotel Covent Garden will be just a few steps away on Monmouth Street!" he yells, wiping his mouth. "You'll be able to get a two-bedroom suite with a terrace overlooking this beautiful city for a special bargain price of only 867 pound sterling!"

When Julian spews to the vagabonds that a hotel a few steps down from where they spend their aimless days will cost nearly 900 pounds, which is a sum they've never heard of, much less made as a total sum of all sporadic labor in their lifetimes, they still howl—but less cheerfully. They suspect he's mocking them.

"I'm not mocking you, good people, not at all. I'm telling you this to raise your spirits," Julian continues, undaunted by their hostility. "Fret not!"

"All right, mate, pipe down," the diminutive costermonger says. "How about you gimme a farthing for the liquor you took from me."

"Shut yer pie hole, Monk!" the heavy woman on the stool screeches. "He's a nice boy! He touched me parts like I was a lady!" Toothlessly she grins at Julian. "I'm Agatha, pleased to meet ya."

"Pleased to meet you, too, my dear Agatha," Julian shouts. "Where's your sundial pillar? The most famous Doric pillar in the middle of your resplendent square, what's happened to it?"

"Demolished two years ago," a breathy voice replies by Julian's arm, and before he turns his head, he knows it's her. His rantings have brought her to him. Well done, Julian Cruz. Now you can stop. Underneath the devil-may-care vaudeville, he is despondent. Look where she has led him.

He lowers his gaze on a petite creature in sexless rags, militant of face, short of hair, unsmiling, and soft as a pair of bolt cutters. Her pale, open, wide-boned features, her large mistrusting eyes, her pursed lips are smudged with the slum. His eyes watering, Julian stares deeply into her face. His happiness and misery must be on full display and must be incongruous, because the girl, a dirty thin scavenger, glares back at him, perplexed and defiant.

"Why did they demolish it?" he asks her quietly. The fight has gone out of him. He wants to press her to his chest.

"The city wanted to stop cracks and crooks like you from staging it as their meeting place," she replies, leaving his side and walking over to Agatha. "Has he been bothering you, Mum? Wanna get up, stretch yer legs?"

Agatha is her mother!

He should've known. All the mothers' names begin with A. Ava. Aurora. Anna. Now Agatha.

"Bothering me? No. He pawed me with his male hands!" Agatha says. "Last time I was manhandled like that was when your dear papa and me fadoodled, may he rest in peace, the cheating no-good drunken dead bastard."

Someone grabs Julian's sleeve. It's grubby Monk, with black teeth and in black rags, solicitously offering Julian more brew. Another man steps forward, this one over six feet tall. He's wearing a suit but his hair is unwashed and uncombed. "Why were you staring at our Miri over there?" the giant demands like the Grand Inquisitor except more dour. "Do you know her?"

*Our* Miri?

"Calm yourself, Mortimer," Miri returns. "He don't know me."

"Are you sure about that?" Julian mines her face for a blink of recognition. He doesn't need much, just a trace.

She blinks all right—with insurrection. She is uncommonly wary of him. "Did someone cloy your peck?" Ah. Now Julian understands. She thinks he suspects her of pickpocketing him. "Wasn't me, mate, I promise you," she says. "I don't go near the likes of you. You got the wrong girl."

Julian shakes his head, but before he can speak, Agatha shouts, "Miryam! Don't be rude to our kind gentleman, or he'll clump yer. Where are yer manners?"

Miryam, sea of bitterness, sea of sorrow. That's what her name means. Julian lowers his head to look for his bearings on the cobblestones. The tall man and the small kid continue to flank him, curious but also guarded. They both smell awful. Mortimer is in his twenties, but Monk can't be any older than twelve or thirteen.

"What's that yer wearing?" Monk pulls the stretchy Thermoprene of the wetsuit.

It's not quite the nubile beauty queens pawing at his suit at the Silver Cross. Already what a disappointment this new world is. "I told you, it's a time-travel suit," Julian replies, pulling away. "Don't rip it. Or I won't be able to go back."

"He's right, Monk, best not touch him," Miryam says, gesturing to Monk to step away.

Instantly obeying her, Mortimer, who wasn't even near Julian, steps away, but Monk just laughs. "Jasper, get over here!" he shouts to a bull-necked, curly-haired teenager peddling some home brew from a large glass bottle. "Did you hear? Jack here's wearing a traveling suit!"

"Oh!" Jasper says, affably rushing toward them. "Traveling suit from where?"

"He says from the future."

"Brilliant!" Jasper is remarkably sanguine about time travel. "Let's introduce him to my Flora, Monk. Flora is a fortune-teller most accomplished. You got any money, Jack, for a quick fortune? Flora will lap you up like milk, won't she, Miri?"

"Don't know, don't care." Miri lowers the dress hem that rode up above her mother's scabbed knees. Agatha's meaty legs are covered with unhealed sores. It could be syphilis. It could be impetigo. It could be anything.

Jasper and Mortimer are brothers. "Mort, smile," Jasper says. "I made three farthings selling brew this morning."

"Why should I smile because you made three farthings?" says Mortimer. "I'll smile when they're still in yer pocket come sundown."

Jasper ignores his brother. "Jack, have you met Monk the dwarf?"

"I'm not a friggin' dwarf!" Monk yells. Jasper and Monk tussle; Julian can't tell if it's play.

He pulls his hands behind his back. Julian is a boxer, and his hands are weapons. He's a fighter who keeps his guns hidden and his fists unclenched. He hides his menace with fake solemnity. But he won't shake their hands. He's afraid they'll know who he is by the strength of his grip.

While the hullaballoo continues, Julian reaches for Miri's hand. He doesn't mind that she should know who he is. Gasping in surprise at being touched, she tries to yank her arm away. "Miri," he whispers. "It's *me*." He peers into her face.

She's baffled. In this version of herself she barely comes up to his clavicles. Mallory's mother in Clerkenwell's brothels had obviously fed her baby better than Agatha has fed Miri, who looks permanently hungry, her face angular, the cheekbones gaunt, the jaw set sharply against her paper-thin skin.

He holds on to her another moment.

"You got the wrong girl, mister, I promise," she mutters in confusion and turns to her complaining mother.

"I'm hot," Agatha says. "I'm sweating. My legs itch like demons. And I'm hungry. Did you bring me something to eat, child?"

"Don't scratch, Mum, you'll open yer sores again," the girl says, unbuttoning her mother's cardigan. "I got to get the papers out. When I'm done and paid, I'll bring you something. And I fed you this morning."

"That was hours ago, luv. All you give me was bacon rashers."

"And bread, Mum. And jam. And a tomato."

"Hungry I am, is all," Agatha says, patting Miri's small hip. Julian watches the mother touch the daughter, noting Agatha's scabrous arm.

"Miri, be a dear and brush me hair," Agatha says, winking at Julian in response to his stare. "I want to look me best for our newcomer."

Dear God. Julian backs away. He's got to go. He needs to see if his money is still in the wall. Will he find it in 1775? Here's his problem: to try, he needs masonry supplies. And to get masonry supplies, he needs money. Yet no one is offering him a job in St. Giles, probably because there are no jobs to be had.

And even if he does get the sovereigns out of the wall, he can't step inside Goldsmiths on Cheapside to meet a coin trader in a body-hugging, nothing left to the imagination wetsuit. Eyeing Miri's chums, Julian sees other complications ahead, large and small, dwarfish and tall, but right now he's got to borrow some clothes from them. You must be dressed the part, or no one will buy what you're selling.

Julian addresses the tall man. "Mortimer, I have a proposition for you. Do you have a suit, hat, and shoes I can borrow? Maybe a cloak, too?"

"I don't hear proposition," Mortimer says. "I hear begging."

"I'll return them tonight."

"And I have a bridge I can sell yer. No."

"Your clothes and two shillings."

Mortimer shakes his head.

"Two *shillings*?" Monk squeals. "Take it, Mort, take it!" Mortimer and Monk turn to Miri for her approval.

"Forget Mortimer," she says gruffly to Julian. "For two shillings, I'll get you something. But no boots."

"I need something for my feet."

"Let's take him to Cleon, Miri," Monk says. "He'll have boots."

"Maybe Cleon has work for him, too," Mortimer says with a sly gleam.

"Stop it, Mort," Miri says. "He can't work with Cleon, you can see he's not a tosher. You'll kill him, and I'll never get my promised shillings. No."

"What's a tosher?" Julian whispers to Monk, but before he can answer, Miri shouts, perhaps even at Julian.

"What are you standing around for? Step on it! I don't got all day. Some of us have work to do."

The men spring to attention and follow her slavishly across the square to Lyon Street. Julian catches up with her. She's out front like a sergeant. "Your mother needs medicine for her legs," Julian says. His Thermoprene boots are torn and his bare feet touch the stones. His *bare feet* are touching these cobblestones. He won't think about it.

"Oh, you're a doctor, too, are you?" Miri snaps.

"A doctor?" Jasper perks up. Though Julian denies his medical pedigree, no one listens. "Mort, did you hear? Jack's a doctor. Let's take him to Aunt Hazel's."

"He said he's *not* a doctor," Miri says. So *she* is listening.

"It's our aunt," Jasper explains. "She can't get out of bed."

"If I had me a bed to sleep in," Miri says, "I wouldn't get out of no bed neither."

Astrologers and alchemists abound as Julian and his new companions turn the corner on Monmouth Street, which centuries later will become Shaftesbury Avenue. Also everywhere: pickpockets, prostitutes, street sweepers, and street sellers. The children, like Julian, are barefoot. The women wear rags, and the fronts of many of their dresses are open, exposing their hanging breasts. Their faces are covered with sores. Empty bottles of gin lie on the street. Up above, Julian spots a man hanging by a rope on one of the balconies. "That's Owen the Barber," Monk says.

"That *was* Owen the Barber," Miri corrects. "No one wants a cut or a shave, how's he to make money, he's in the wrong trade." Below swinging Owen, two men and a child are stuffing a half-naked woman into a coffin. Julian assumes she is dead, though nothing is a given. "That's old June," Miri says unsentimentally. "She's finally had enuf."

June doesn't look old to Julian. She looks thirty.

A man chases a young boy with a mallet. Apparently the boy stole his bottle of gin.

"Kilman Distillery is on the next street over," Monk explains to Julian, without any ironic emphasis on the word *Kilman*. "In the afternoons everybody goes a little crazy on Gin Lane."

"Could it be because the gin's mixed with turpentine?" Mortimer says with distaste.

Miri marches ahead, skipping over a dog and his owner, who are lying on the ground, faces to the stones, gnawing on the same denuded meat bone. She weaves past carts of rotting apples and buckets of slop, past men wolf-calling in her direction.

Between King Street and Drury Lane, they duck into an unnamed alley and Julian follows through a passage so tight he must walk it sideways. These inner tenements are hidden from the street. A sign with an arrow pointing down into the decrepit darkness reads: DRUNK FOR A PENNY. DEAD DRUNK FOR TWO. CLEAN STRAW FOR NOTHING.

They cross an interior square called Neal's Yard and approach a canal that smells worse than anything Julian has ever smelled. A rope bridge hangs over it, and one at a time, they walk across. Julian is the only one who holds on to the ropes for fear of losing his balance and falling in. Miri and the three men sprint down the swaying bridge like cats. In the next tenement they descend a long flight of stairs into the gin cellar.

There is an open sewer in the middle of a large windowless room, maybe twenty feet wide. People sit around the pit on benches and on the ground, chatting and drinking. Their clothes hang drying on lines. Julian wishes he could hold on to something.

"I can see by his deathly pallor our traveler has never been to the cellars of St. Giles," Monk says, with great amusement. "But clearly you've heard of them, Jack."

"Oh, yes," says Julian.

"The pit's here on purpose. It's not 'cause we dirty. It's to keep the barnyard constables away from our treasures. It's like a castle moat." Monk laughs and jumps over the pit. Miri, Mortimer, and Jasper are already on the other side. Only Julian is left. Julian—who flew over a black chasm in a sightless cave, much wider than this puddle of raw sewage—can't get his legs to obey him. If he falls into the pit, he's dead. He won't recover.

Somehow he leaps across. They laugh at him, even Miri.

Especially Miri.

I just leaped over a cesspool for you, Josephine, Julian thinks. Impressed yet?

In one of the open rooms a level below the drains, a woman lies moaning on a fleabag mattress on the floor. It's Aunt Hazel. The woman seems fine, if a little frail, and if you discount the part where she lives below a sewer in a room with no windows. Jasper hitches up his aunt's skirt to expose her blue veiny calves. "Can you help her, Jack? She's our only living relative."

The woman speaks. "Well, no, Jasper. There's also yer no-good uncle on Jacob's Island. He's got all yer new cousins by them scags he fiddles." She looks up at Julian expectantly. "What's wrong with me legs?"

Julian knows that claiming ignorance is not an option. Miri is watching. He must fake wisdom. He needs Miri to trust him enough to help her mother. He strokes his chin, eyeing the bulging veins. "Madam, you have a leg swelling, but tell me, has it been accompanied by a ringing in your ears?"

"Oh yes!"

"Any unusual thirst?"

"Very much so. Have you got some gin to quench it?"

"All in good time. Joint pain?"

"Every minute! Only gin will cure it."

"What about occasional mania? Bursts of activity followed by energy depletion?"

"Not recently, but otherwise yes, me whole life."

Julian continues to stroke his chin and finally makes his prognosis. "You, madam, have a wraith deficiency!"

Mortimer, Jasper, and the aunt nod vigorously. Miri eyes him with half-amusement, half-skepticism. "Yes," the woman cries, "that's what it must be! What's the cure? Gin?"

"Chickweed," Julian replies. "And sunlight. Thirty minutes a day."

"Sunlight? No, thank you. And I ain't got no chickweed."

"You'll need to get some. Apply the chickweed directly to your legs. If you can heat up the plant, even better. You can get it at any apothecary. I can pick some up for you, if you like." Julian fakes a stern voice. "But I can't pick up sunlight for you, madam. That you must get for yourself. Agreed?"

Aunt Hazel nods gratefully.

"Don't thank me yet," Julian says to the two softened brothers. "Let's see if your aunt gets better." He glances at Miri, hoping she's impressed.

Turns out not only is she not impressed, but she's vanished.

∞

Two corridors, four rooms and another cesspit later, Julian is lost, but the boys have finally arrived at Cleon's door. If the men decide to turn on him, Julian's a goner. If they thought there was anything on him to rob, they could kill him and dump him into the black hole of sewage, and no one would be any the wiser.

While Mortimer steps inside the room to wake up Cleon, Monk, and Jasper advance on Julian in the hall to interrogate him some more. Julian forces his hands to stay behind his back.

"So who is you, really?"

"Where's you really from?"

"I told you, gentlemen."

"They ain't got normal clothes in the future?"

"They do. The suit is for swimming."

"Where could you possibly be swimming—the Thames?"

"Maybe that's where Fulko should go to hide, Monk," Jasper says. "The future."

Julian is about to ask who Fulko is, but Miri returns with a fine dark suit for him, a billycock hat, and a long black silk cloak. Where would she get attire as high-quality as this? "Two shillings, you promised," Miri says. She has changed her clothes. She's put on a long gray skirt with no petticoat and an embroidered, patched-up, cropped blue jacket. It could be the nicest thing she owns. Her man's cap has been replaced by a white bonnet. She has brushed her short straight hair, she has washed her face. Julian can't tell which is the disguise: the cleaned-up young woman in front of him or the one before, in rags.

"What d'you think of me fine idea, Miri?" Jasper asks. "After we spring Fulko from Newgate, your husband-to-be should go and hide in the future with Jack."

"Only if I get to go with him," Miri casually replies. She's hard to excite with all this talk of a *future* she hasn't seen and doesn't believe in.

"Who's him in that sentence?" Julian says. "Me? Or your husband-to-be?" He grimaces at his own words and leans against the wall for support. She has a fiancé? Not again. Can't she ever, just once, come to him not in a brothel or encumbered by Lord Falks and Fario Rimas? One single time. "What's he in for?"

Monk gets vague, refuses to answer. "Robbin', mostly."

"Lift that, draw that," Jasper concurs. "But now he's facing the chats." Chats are gallows.

"Could he be facing the chats, Jasper," Miri says, "because a man died while Fulko was fleecing him?"

"The mark had a bad heart," Monk cries. "That's not Fulko's fault!"

"Tell that to the judge, Monk," Jasper says. "Unless you and Miri do something, your brother is gon be hanged at Tyburn a fortnight past the summer solstice."

The Fulko character is Monk's brother? Oh, the tangle of these men and the girl.

"He won't hang," Monk says fiercely. "By all the stars in the heavens, he won't hang."

"There's a bloody code in the Old Bailey." Miri stares into her shoes. "You know that, Monk. A hanging for a death."

Better than before, Julian thinks, when it was being boiled in oil for a death.

"He did it for you, Miri!" an aggrieved Monk cries. The mood in the corridor shifts. A minute ago they were joking. Now it's a good thing no one's carrying knives. Julian drops the clothes she has given him on the ground to free his hands. He can't tell where this is going.

"I didn't tell him to kill no man," Miri says. "Robbin' is one thing. But killing is wrong."

So in this incarnation, she is against wanton murder. Good to know.

"You told him you wanted to get hitched. He was saving for your nuptials!"

"By saving you mean robbin'?"

"You said you was gonner get him out, Miri," Monk says in a threatening voice. "You said."

"Okay, Monk." That's Julian. "Why don't we calm down." One more exchange like the last one, and Julian is going to have to come between Monk and Miri. Nice way to make new friends.

"You know what Pastor Wyatt told us to do," Miri says. She is not intimidated by this Monk fellow. She doesn't seem to be intimidated by much. "We need to cobble together four pound to pay off the magistrate. We both have to do it, not just me. You two pound, me two pound."

"I know that's what he said, I ain't stupid," says Monk.

"How close are you to your two pound?"

"Within a couple of farthings," Monk says. Four farthings make a penny. "You?"

Miri shakes her head. "Real money, Monk, not your counterfeit bullshit."

"That's right, real money, Miri. You?"

"Yeah." The girl doesn't look at him. "Me too, Monk. Within a couple of farthings."

False coining is a betrayal of the realm. In 1666, Constable Parker had five people hanged in Westminster for counterfeiting. Julian wonders what the punishment is these days.

"Miri works as a pure finder, Jack," Monk suddenly says, with a cruel gleam.

"Monk!" She shakes her head.

"What? I'm just telling Jack how you make your money to get your fiancé out. Miri picks up dog mess off the streets and sells it to tanners who use it to cure leather. Don't pay very much, does it, Miri?"

Julian's mouth twists with pity. He can't look at her.

"Cleon!" Miri yells, banging at the closed door. "Let's go! I can't wait all day."

"Jack, you need money?" Monk asks. "Go work for Cleon. He's been looking for a new helper since Basil died in a sluice." The suddenly pious urchins cross themselves.

"Sluice?"

"Yeah, poor fucker got caught in a sewer sluice when the water level rose too fast. The tidal wave of sludge shattered him to smithereens. We couldn't find most of him."

"We looked," Jasper says.

"Oh, we looked so thorough. We found a foot."

"And a hand. Don't forget the hand."

"Not a whole hand," Monk says.

"Almost. It was only missing those two small fingers."

When Julian refrains from the reaction that Monk was clearly looking for, Monk elaborates. "Cleon is a sewer hunter, a scavenger. Been down there seventy years, looking for this or that. What do you say, you wanna go work for him?"

Julian says nothing. What an actor he is! Josephine's got nothing on him. He waters the shantytown version of Josephine with his fertile gaze. The flower reacts poorly. She shrivels.

Blessedly Mortimer sticks his head out and motions them in.

# 15

# Cleon the Sewer Hunter

CLEON IS AN UNFRIENDLY, LEATHER-SKINNED OLD MAN, WHO sits on the low bed, glowering at Julian. He wears dirty canvas trousers and a long overcoat. His worker's apron with a dozen pockets hangs on a hook by the bed. His huge hands are permanently darkened by his profession. He's got no time for nonsense. He has no men's shoes either. Coldly he assesses Julian's wetsuit. "Thermoprene, you say? Will it keep me dry?"

"Warm, mainly."

"What do I care about warm," says Cleon, standing up and touching the suit. He is Julian's height, but thinner. The suit will be too big on him. He offers Julian a farthing for it.

Julian asks for a straight trade instead. Wetsuit for shoes. "I don't want your boots, Cleon," he says. "I need shoes. I can't wear boots with breeches and hose. What am I, a stablehand?"

Cleon is unmoved by Julian's keen sense of fashion. "You scoundrel," he says to Mortimer. "You woke me up for a jester who doesn't want to sell the only thing he's got?"

How is Cleon still alive after going into the sewers every night for seven decades? "When were you born?" Julian asks him, trying to keep the longing out of his voice. He wants Cleon to be a hundred and ten. Maybe he's seen some things, remembered things from the Great Fire.

"In 1695," Cleon says. "What's it to you?"

He's eighty! Cleon is a roach, built to survive the sub-earth's pathogens. His immune system has been toughened by the gutters of London. He's become impervious to infection, viruses, bacteria, parasites, and tumors.

"London has four hundred sewers," Cleon tells Julian. "And I been through them all. You want a job? I got a spot open since Basil hit that little snag. It's man's work, though, and frankly you look like a white-gloved pansy." Before Julian can disagree, Cleon continues. "You know how many miles of tunnels me and my men navigate? Twelve thousand. We go into the sewers at low tide and wander under cover of night collecting things that fall through the gutter grates. Metal, cutlery, coins, jewelry."

Julian gets an idea. "In the dark?"

"We carry torches. Lanterns."

Julian smiles. He *does* have something to barter with, after all. He shows Cleon his two headlamps, one with a still-fresh battery. "Have you seen one of these?" he asks innocently, knowing well that no one has seen them because they don't yet exist. He demonstrates by strapping it to his forehead and flicking on the switch. Cleon gasps. The lamp burns bright. It takes a lot to impress the sewer hunter. He's seen it all. But not this.

Miri doesn't gasp. She's resistant to headlamps.

"It's like your torch, Cleon," Julian says, "but you strap it to your head. And the light is cold. Nice, huh?" He sees by Cleon's face that it's the greatest thing the ancient hunter has ever seen. Cleon will give him all the treasures in his room for it. He will sell Julian a human being for the lamp. "The cold light is called LED. Light-emitting diode. Do you want to try?" Julian fits and adjusts the strap around Cleon's head and teaches him how to turn the lamp on. Cleon switches it on and off, on and off. Julian puts his hand over the switch. "Stop. Turn it on only when you're using it, or the battery will drain."

"What's a battery? How much do you want for it?"

"I want shoes with buckles and six shillings," Julian quickly says; six shillings for the masonry supplies. What a surprise, turns out that Cleon does have a pair of shoes, right under his bed. He gives Julian another two shillings for the wetsuit, eight shillings in all. Julian is pleased. Not bad for a day's work, and he didn't even have to go into the sewers. He goes out into the corridor to change. The breeches on the suit Miri brought for him are too short, as are the shirt sleeves. The waistcoat is too tight, and the felt hat too small. Cleon's shoes are old and smell like a run-over skunk. But who is Julian to be so picky. He's nothing but a beggar.

He returns to the room, handing the wetsuit to Cleon.

"It's from the *future*, Cleon," Jasper says proudly, as if the wetsuit was his to give.

"I don't doubt it one bit," Cleon says, cradling the headlamp to his chest. "Where else would he get something magical like this?"

"I got to go, toshers," Miri says. "You can stay and wax about the future. In the present, I got a war to peddle."

"Wait," Julian says, "I have to go, too. I'll follow you out. I won't find my way without you."

"Monk'll show you."

"I don't trust him."

"As well you shouldn't, mate," Monk says, with a mock bow. "You shouldn't trust none of us. We'll rob yer blind and throw you in the sewer."

∞

Julian and Miri walk without speaking. She runs ahead of him on to Monmouth Street and heads to Piccadilly. "Why are you following me?"

"I'm not, really. I'm walking in the same direction as you." Julian pauses. "I'm trying to be chivalrous."

"Can you be chivalrous from across the street?"

He can't tell if she's joking. "Aren't you going to ask me what my name is?"

"I would," Miri says, "but here's the thing. I don't give a toss."

She slips into a joint and emerges five minutes later with a bound stack of the *London Chronicle*. The date reads May 20–24, 1775. Lexington and Concord have already fallen to the Americans a month earlier in April. The front page doesn't mention it. The front page reads as if the battles that began the American Revolution have not yet been fought, much less fought and lost. What's that all about? "Have you heard the news about Lexington and Concord?" he asks her.

"Oh, you're still here."

"Yes. Can I carry those for you?"

"Why, so you can steal 'em? No."

At the intersection of Monmouth and Piccadilly, Miri jumps on top of a beer crate and starts yelling. "A great empire and little minds go ill together!" she proclaims. "The great Edmund Burke said so himself. America's rebels are about to fall. Read all about it! The Crown calls them a mob of merchants. But is that what they are? Read all about it! The Crown says the rebels' military cause is hopeless. But *is* it hopeless? Read all about it! They've run out of gunpowder, rifles, clothing, and food. Can they still fight? The *Chronicle* will tell you! What is the rebels' aim? It's all right here! They have *never* governed themselves. Do they *really* think they can win? Put a penny in this bucket, gentlemen, and find out!"

As always, Julian is captivated by her, impressed by her bravado, theatrically barking to indifferent businessmen and gentlemen of leisure. But despite her great gifts, business is slow. The Londoners are as suspicious of Miri as she is of Julian. They don't like a pauper girl shouting at them in the middle of their city. After fifteen minutes, barely a dozen pennies line the bottom of her bucket. Didn't she say she needs two pounds to spring her lover from prison? That's four hundred and eighty pennies. Julian may soon be able to give her the money she needs, but is that a smart move? Does he really want to be grappling with another fiancé? How many days between now and Fulko's hanging? Maybe it's better to let the halls of justice do the dirty work for him.

The crossroads that will one day become Piccadilly Circus is narrow, uneven, poorly cobbled. Miri has not picked a great spot to sell her newspapers. There are no sidewalks, and the people treat her as a nuisance. Just as Julian thinks that she's in danger of coming to blows with someone, an annoyed wiseacre in a well-made suit shoves her off her crate. The people hurrying by cheer. She swears.

Julian does more than swear. Taking a step forward, he bodychecks the man. The man loses his balance and falls. Julian stands over him. He's barely taken his hands out of his pockets. "What the hell did you do that for?" the man yells, scrambling to his feet. His tailored suit has mud all over it.

"I could ask you the same question, mate," Julian says. "What are you doing shoving young ladies off crates?"

"That's not a lady!"

Julian grabs him by the jacket collar. "You're a true gent," he says, shoving him away. "Move along. But if it's trouble you want," he adds, his fists up, "come get it."

Cursing, the man slips away into the crowd. Julian turns to Miri. She's almost smiling. "What did you do *that* for?" she says, but breathier. "I get knocked off me crate a dozen times a day."

"Not while I'm with you," Julian says. "But look what the gent kindly left behind." He opens his palm to show her the man's small coin purse.

"You fleeced him?" She sounds thrilled but incredulous.

"Let's say I relieved him of his monetary burden." Julian smiles.

Miri keeps herself from smiling. "I wouldn't go around knocking men to the ground and mugging them," she says. "That's what Fulko did and look where it got him." They count the coins. Two crowns. *Two crowns—that's what Fabian gave Mallory to lie down with Julian.* "Two crowns," she says excitedly, as he watches her face for a blink of old memory, of new meaning, of anything.

"Yes, a half-pound," he says slowly. "A few more of these and you'll have your share for Fulko."

Miri chews her lip. She wants to take the purse. "What do you want for it?" she says. "I ain't foining with you, if that's what yer thinking."

"Did I ask you to foin with me?" Julian is crestfallen to be so misunderstood. *Though one time you asked me to foin with you for two crowns.*

Leaving the purse with him and grabbing her papers, Miri walks quickly. "How am I gonner sell my papers at Piccadilly tomorrow? I liked that spot. Can you hurry? Yer crawling like yer headed to confession. The bloke will come back and bring a charlie with him."

She returns the unsold papers to the *Chronicle* office and keeps six pence for the two dozen papers she sold. Julian needs to leave her but doesn't want to. Masonry supplies, the wall, goldsmiths, men's clothing shop, apothecary for her mother, a meal, a bath. If he gives Miri the man's stolen purse, he's afraid he won't have an excuse to seek her out when he returns to St. Giles. What if he doesn't find her again in that tangled warren? He is so lost in thought about the girl that he doesn't hear the actual girl address him. "Monk keeps calling you Jack," she says. "You got a real name?"

"Julian Cruz." He roams her face for recognition.

"Julian Cruz," she repeats, eyeing him cautiously. His name off her lips jolts his loins. He can't call her exceedingly good-humored, but at least she no longer stares at him as if she's about to stick him with a shiv.

"Let me help you again tomorrow, Miri."

"You think you helped me today? Ha. You made it so I can't go back to my favorite spot to sell my papers, yes, you've helped me marvelous much."

"We'll go somewhere else. You bark, I'll be security. Every good barker needs security."

"Yer going to provide security?" With great doubt she looks him over. "You nearly needed smellin' salts earlier because of a little stench. Some security you'll be against actual fists."

"I got actual fists, too, don't I?"

"What you got is no sense."

Julian's hazel eye catches her brown eye just long enough for a beat of a heart to pass from his chest into hers. He extends his hand with the purse in it. "Go ahead, take it," he says. He forces out a smile. "I'll come back to return your suit. Where can I find you?"

She doesn't smile back as she grabs the pouch. "You ain't got to come back at all now. Consider us square."

"No, I'll come back."

"No, you don't got to."

"I do. I promised chickweed to Hazel. And your mother..."

"Leave my mother alone," she says. Julian's face must show his misery, because she adds, "If you see me mum, or Monk, or the others, don't tell them about the money. They'll steal it off me when I sleep." And off his fallen face, she says, "Everything, everywhere is for the demon drink. Nothing left for nothing else."

"Not even two quid for Fulko?"

"Nothing," Miri repeats. "But if he hangs, mark my words, I'll be the only one they'll blame, as if I'm the only one with the power to save him."

"Aren't you?" Julian whispers.

Miri runs.

# 16

# Agatha

JULIAN CAN'T EXPLAIN WHY HE DIDN'T FIND THE SPACKLED stones in the London Wall when he was with Ashton. He barely has to search for them in 1775. And that's despite the passage into the City at Cripplegate having been dismantled and replaced with a wide road, and the church at Cripplegate having been thrown into such disrepair that it's been shut down for supposed renovations. Despite the changes in infrastructure, Julian finds his unmarked gray boulders three feet off the ground in less than five minutes.

It's another matter to retrieve the leather purse from the wall. It takes hours. Julian gets muddy and grubby, sweating with the labor of chiseling out and removing the heavy exterior stone. The purse is dusty and the leather is cracked in places but otherwise it's aged reasonably well over the last hundred years. Inside, the money is pristine. He is so relieved. It means he won't have to sleep in the rookery. Though it does mean he won't sleep in the rookery with Miri. Well, he'll have to find another way to get close to her. He's not planning to stay with her in St. Giles. The endgame is to get her out of the rat sewer as soon as he can.

Julian shakes with indecision about how many of his remaining 47 coins to take. Getting money out of the wall is a time-consuming and dangerous task. The risk of getting noticed and caught is great. But it's also a risk carrying gold into a place like St. Giles. Fabian was killed for this money in the past; Julian can certainly be killed for this money in the present. Miri's gang will slice him open if they suspect he has even two guineas. Look at the way Monk has been patting his wetsuit, searching for a pocket.

But here's the thing. It's not his gold. It's hers. To protect what's hers, Julian takes only four coins to start. He will come back for the rest when the time comes. The wet mortar gets all over his trousers and shoes and sleeves as he trowels around the stone to seal it. When he is done, he chisels a small cross in the soft cement, like a Hansel and Gretel crumb, and, cleaning himself up as best he can, heads to Cheapside.

Many of the bullion traders' businesses have been destroyed in the Great Fire, and though Cheapside has been rebuilt, the old ostentation is gone. The dealer shops are as elegant as before, but there are no more gold candlesticks or gold frames on the wall behind Lord Asquith, the gentleman who sits at the walnut desk across from Julian. What does remain is the abounding white-gloved reverence for his Elizabethan treasure. "Wherever did you get this, sire?" Asquith asks, in the tone of someone inspecting the fine details of a beautiful woman. "And are you sure you want to trade it? It must have some sentimental value."

"It does," Julian says. "But it's gold. It's meant to be spent. I'm not making a wedding band out of it, am I?"

"Quite right. Do you have a number in mind?" Asquith coughs. "There are fifty-two goldsmiths around here in a space of a mile, and I realize you could've gone elsewhere, so I appreciate your honoring us with your business. Tell me a number, and I will try to match it."

Julian hasn't thought of a number. He can barely remember what he got last time. Mallory told him he was undersold. "Five hundred shillings," he says.

The speed with which Lord Asquith hands Julian a velvet pouch with twenty-five pounds sterling tells Julian he has once again grossly undervalued the coin's worth. Mallory would not be happy with him. He thanks Asquith and walks down the street to find another dealer. Instead of asking Julian for a number, the second man offers Julian a number: one hundred pounds for his freshly minted sovereign. That bastard Asquith! Never mind. It's Julian's fault. As in the rookery, so at the goldsmiths, a fool will soon be parted from his money.

With £125 in his pocket and another two gold sovereigns for the just in case, Julian takes a carriage to the Sir Paul Pindar's Head Tavern in Bishopsgate, past Finsbury Fields. Julian's heart aches when he glimpses the field where he once strolled with Mary.

Ambassadors to England used to stay at the Pindar Mansion, but by 1775, it has been subdivided into a ward for paupers. Downstairs it remains a tavern. Julian has a large meal of mutton and potatoes and washes it down with two pewter tankards of strong ale. For a shilling, he rents the best room at the inn. After bathing, he sleeps so long that when he wakes up, he fears two precious weeks have flown by.

But no, it's the next morning, May 21, 1775. Below the Silver Cross dots on his left forearm, Julian begins a new column of hope and hopelessness by tattooing his first rookery speck with a quill full of ink. He is not going to miss marking a single day this time. He plans for success, won't settle for anything less, but once and for all, he is going to know whether he and Josephine are free or enslaved to a demon.

At Birkin's tailors on Bond Street Julian buys himself a fine wool suit, gold-buckle shoes, a white linen shirt, silk hose, and a fine felt hat. But when he catches his reflection in the mirror, he reconsiders. He looks somewhere between pompous and dashing. He looks like a man a girl like Miri will rob, not a man she will ever trust, or love.

He keeps the dandy threads, but purchases a second suit, well made but more modest, a subdued narrow waistcoat, a matching vest, an off-white shirt and hose. And simple shoes with pewter buckles. He keeps the fancy hat because he likes it.

Thus outfitted, on a sunny May morning, Julian strolls a few city blocks to Grosvenor Square. In a tall white-granite townhouse on one of the corners of the exquisitely landscaped park, he finds three large impeccable rooms for rent on the top floor. Julian pays upfront until the end of May. It only costs him a pound. On second thought, in an act of rebellion and bravery, he pays through for another hundred days—until the end of the summer.

The rooms have a balcony and come fully furnished. Breakfast and supper are served downstairs in the dining room, and afternoon tea can be brought up to the rooms, "if the sire so desires."

Hiding his two remaining gold coins in the feathers of the goosedown mattress, he drapes the cloak Miri had given him over his shoulders and heads to the apothecary.

∞

Julian returns to Seven Dials laden with ointments and a hot breakfast for Agatha. In the alleys behind the narrow houses where they pitch their buckets of waste and old water, the gloop runs through the streets, mixing and melting with mud, and steams up in the morning sun. He finds Agatha in her chair, watching the quiet but misty square.

"I didn't recognize you in yer new clothes!" Agatha says, smiling happily. "Don't you look smart."

Julian suspects he's still overdressed. If Miri can't learn to trust him, he'll have a bear of a time getting near her, he thinks, perching next to the lumbering and receptive Agatha as he serves her breakfast. This early in the morning, Seven Dials is empty. The business of the rookery has not yet begun. Agatha is up, she tells him, because she's waiting for the parish priest to arrive with her daily relief. If she's not up and about, the pastor knows she's stayed up too late the night before doing things she's not supposed to, and then she doesn't get her allowance. "Consider this me job," Agatha says to Julian, sunny as all that.

While the woman scarfs the bacon and bread with grateful gusto, Julian mixes coconut oil with frankincense and honey into a greasy salve. He cuts up a roll of gauze and folds it over itself several times, to thicken it. Dipping the cotton into the sticky potion, he sits on the ground by Agatha's feet and rubs the salve into the lesions on her legs. He's doing it for Miri. If anyone asks, that's Julian's answer to everything. He is doing it for the girl.

"So where's your daughter today?" he asks Agatha in his most casual tone.

"Prob'ly sleeping. She works all night. We won't see her till noon."

Does Julian dare ask? "Doing what?"

"Oh, this and that," Agatha replies, to confirm Julian's worst fears. "I keep telling her, no one else works so hard, why should she? Julian, it's nice of yer to help me, real nice." The mother sits without protest and allows Julian, a young man she barely knows, to treat the sores on her legs. She is starved for a sympathetic ear, for a genuine human connection. While Julian tends to her, Agatha distracts him with the details of all the petty miseries that have plagued her since youth. She floods him with rambling tales about her life, the life of every person she's ever met, and every small and grand injustice she has ever borne.

Julian learns that Lena, near St. Clement, sells apples as she waits for her parish relief and acts "holier than thou," but everyone hates her because she's had three bastard children by three different men and has been using the children to raise her relief to nearly "a full shilling a day!" which is unheard of. Now as punishment, Lena is apprenticed to the parish and must sell pamphlets about Judgment Day for half a penny each. "Work is part of her penance," Agatha says. "As work often is. But does she sell them? No. She gives Miri a farthing to do it. And Miri does it! What does my poor Miri have to atone for? She's a perfect child. I'd rather collect my lousy threepence and not have to be put through the wringer of a fake job, don't you agree?"

Julian learns that Miri is twenty-three. Mortimer, the old man of their merry band, is twenty-seven, Jasper is twenty, and so is Monk.

"Monk is *twenty*?" That's shocking.

"I agree, his feeble-mindedness makes him seem young," says Agatha. "His brother Fulko is Miri's age. You want to talk about feeble-minded. *That* boy doesn't have the sense God gave a gnat. He just charms and tricks his way out of things. Which is prob'ly how he got Miri to fall for him. But he ain't charming his way out of a killing."

Miri *fell* for Fulko? Julian mentions that she and Monk are raising money to get Fulko's sentence commuted.

"Oh, sure," Agatha says dryly. "They been raising this money since Christmas. I do hope Fulko is not holding his breath. And commuted to what exactly, transportation? Blimey. It's a slow death, also he don't want to leave the country. *I* didn't. You look surprised. But them bastards threatened me with transportation, too."

"Transportation to where?"

"Where d'you think? Those damn penal colonies, the Americas. Miri was one at the time. Can you imagine? A littl'un on a boat for months! In the middle of the open sea! I told them I'd rather hang at Tyburn. They said that could be arranged. I got out of it by pleading the belly."

"Pleading the what?"

"Pleading the belly. You know." Agatha points to her bulging stomach. "Showed 'em I was preggers so they'd go easy on me. Worked like a charm. Usually does. The baby didn't make it, but she served her purpose, got her mum out of transportation and sprung early from Bridewell."

"Where was Miri?"

"The orphanage, where else? I don't like to brag about it, but truth is, I've had some trouble with the law meself. Me husband was no good, and I had to make a living somehow. I was *ruined* by marriage, Julian," Agatha says, as if divulging great confidences. "I had to steal to keep Miri from starving. I admit to some occasional disorderly behavior. Some begging. But you beg too often, they flog you till your back's bloody, you beg after that, they hang you. Well, they didn't hang me, but those fuckers did send me to Bridewell, that unholy pit of sexual corruption, and took me Miri away. They called me a common nightwalker!" Years later, Agatha still broils from the insult. "I wasn't no common nightwalker! I wasn't like that Priscilla over there, putting on airs, do you see her? Like she's goin' to catch a customer this early in the morning. Oh, look! There's my friend, Repentance Hedges. Repentance, come here, meet Julian! When did *you* get out, girl?" And to Julian, Agatha mutters from the side of her mouth, "Repentance is fifty-two and spent thirty years in and out of prison. The parish keeps collecting for her damn kids, slothful and soused to the one. Monk and Fulko are two of them. I keep reminding Miri, Repentance will soon be her mother by law. If that don't get you to change your mind about marrying a no-good nobody, nothing will. Just look at that woman!" Agatha speaks from the bottomless pool of her indignation. "Repentance's been engaged in lewd behavior for as long as I've known her. But nowadays she has a hard time attracting customers, not being in the first blush of youth and all. Repentance, how are you? Yer looking good, girl." Agatha clicks her tongue in disapproval.

Repentance approaches, her old striped petticoat dragging on the ground. "Who's your most kind friend, Agatha?" She smiles invitingly at Julian.

Agatha stops smiling. "Move along, the kind man ain't got no pennies for you."

Repentance continues to smile. She looks older than fifty-two. It doesn't help that some of her teeth are missing. Her skin is ashen white, a sign of mercury poisoning. Mercury is taken to treat syphilis. "He *looks* like he's got money. He's wearing money. Look at his felt hat, Agatha. And his cufflinks! Hello, good sir, would you like a little bit of company? Not a lot, just ever so little."

"That's where all my money is," Julian says, rising to his feet. "In my felt hat and my cufflinks."

"I don't need much," Repentance says. "Tuppence for a quick shag will do. Standing up, just over there."

As politely as he is able, Julian declines.

Repentance bristles. "You going to insult a woman's honor by refusing to occupy her?"

Julian is saved by Pastor Wyatt, who arrives on the scene just in time with relief and prayers. Repentance vanishes. Wyatt is a goodly and serious priest, bald with small penetrating eyes. After examining the medicated gauze on Agatha's legs and laying a sign of the cross on both her and Julian, he places tuppence into her fist. "If you listen to the Lord, Agatha, he will heal you. Stay away from the drink, and everything else will be made better."

After the pastor departs, Agatha smiles a gap-toothed grin at Julian. She appears in better spirits with money in her hand. "Do you know what I could use right now? A dram of that very good rum Elvar is selling on the corner of Queen Street. It's exactly a penny. Would you be a dear?" She tries to stuff the coin into Julian's fist, but because he is ambulatory and she's not, she can't reach him.

"Agatha," Julian says, "like the pastor, I must advise you against rum. It will interact poorly with the ointment on your legs. Rum will make you vomit, is that what you want? It'll make you go off bacon."

"Go off bacon? Damnation!" Agatha loves her rashers. But she also loves her gin. Gin and bacon are her two great loves. Reprieve comes in the shape of avian Hazel, who emerges in the square, sidestepping gingerly as if she's just learned to walk. When she sees her old friend, Agatha forgets about rum for a moment. "Hazel, is that you?" she shouts. "What are you doing up and about?"

Julian praises Hazel for following his advice and getting some fresh air. He gives the woman the chickweed he's bought for her. "Just chew the leaves, Hazel. Every day. And put some on your legs. You'll feel better in no time."

"This nice man told me I have a wraith deficiency!" Hazel informs Agatha as if Julian has given her a diploma.

"Yeah? Look what he gave *me*. Bandages!" Agatha shows Hazel the gauze around her injured legs. "He told me I might have *impetigo!*"

"Might? I *have* a wraith deficiency!"

As they squabble, Julian takes the opportunity to slip away. Reeling from his morning with Agatha, he stumbles through the rookery, searching for Miri. The girl could've sailed to America with her mother when she was a baby. She could've gotten out.

Miri was such a good girl when she was little, Julian keeps hearing Agatha say. Agatha would visit her at the orphanage from time to time. "She'd put on these little acts. She'd get up on a box and perform silly things she'd heard on the streets." Agatha's bloated face dissolved in the memory. "With her elbows out and hands on her hips, she'd yell, Akimbo, akimbo! To this day I don't know what it meant."

"It means elbows out and hands on your hips," Julian said.

"She'd recite a little parable called the Lump of Ice and Crystal. Begotten in a muddy puddle, a lump of ice resented the crystal's clarity, so it started praying to the sun. The sun heard the ice's prayer and began to shine." Agatha smiled, her eyes glistening. "I remember it like it was yesterday. She was such a good happy girl, never envious, never wanting more than she had. Always smiling. You wouldn't know it now from looking at her, but she was beautiful, too."

Julian knows it. A good happy girl always smiling.

"They threw Miri out of the orphanage when she was eleven. She'd locked a constable in one of the rooms and beat the daylights out of him with his own stick. Damn near killed him. Said he tried to touch her. How she escaped death for that, I'll never know."

Julian searches for Miri among the wretched.

Everything could've been completely different.

He finds her off Long Acre, in one of the narrow alleys between two tenements. She's waiting her turn in line for the spout valve. For a few minutes each morning, the city turns on the water, to wash the refuse from the streets into the sewer grates.

It's Miri's turn at the open valve. Julian watches her as she, bent at the waist as if taking a consecrating bow to the standpipe, runs her hands under the water and washes her face and neck. She gargles. She is quick, efficient, impassive. Before she straightens, she notices a spot on her old shoes. She sticks the shoe under the water until the spot comes off. Then she straightens out, turns, and sees Julian.

His pity for her, his desperation, his bitter tenderness, his excruciating helplessness must be so plain on his tormented face that when Miri catches his expression, she reacts like anyone half-sane would. Realizing that there are things in the universe she doesn't understand and doesn't want to, and for which there is no good or rational explanation, Miri flees. She runs from him as fast as her old clean shoes will carry her.

# 17

# Midsummer Night's Dream

Two days later, Julian is having a late drink at the Lamb and Flag near Covent Garden, drowning his wordless angst in a tankard of ale, maybe three. He likes the Lamb and Flag. In the late afternoons they host bare-knuckle fights in the back garden, the rookery version of happy hour. It's quite entertaining. Brutal but entertaining.

Tonight, there's laughter in the pub garden, raucous men getting drunk, nearly coming to blows. He hears a woman's voice behind him. "Hey, handsome," the voice purrs. "Would ya like some company?"

Julian spins around.

It's Miri.

It's not the Miri he knows, the waif of Neal's Yard. It's a different Miri. She stands close to him in a blonde wig, wearing a frozen come-hither smile and a starched white dress sewn with blue flowers. The dress has a swing to it, a hula-hoop crinoline, a tight corset, and a low neckline that exposes the tops of her young white breasts nearly to the nipples, the breasts in full pushed-up display to entice what she had clearly hoped was a different man drinking alone, looking for company. Over her blonde wig is a white bonnet. Silk ribbons hold up her fake yellow hair. Her face is scrubbed, there's red on her cheeks and lips, and her eyes are lined in black crayon. The smile that wasn't meant for him is flirty and sexy. She's got an air mystery to her, and erotic history. Julian is Miri's accidental mark tonight.

"Hello, Miri," he says.

Never has Julian wiped a smile faster off a woman's face.

Irritated and embarrassed, she backs away, but not far enough. The two of them are hemmed in on a dark warm night in Covent Garden.

"What are you selling tonight?" Julian asks. "War, or something else?"

"Leave me alone."

"But you just asked if I'd like some company," Julian says, standing up. "I do—very much. And I'm willing to pay handsomely for it. What's your usual rate? I'll triple it."

"Leave me alone."

"A shilling, Miri? A guinea? A quid?"

She whirls from him and insinuates herself beside another inebriated dupe. A minute later she leaves on the mark's arm. Julian follows, hoping he is sober enough not to pick a fight with the chap until he sees where this is going. With all deliberate speed, Miri lures the gentleman into St. Giles. The guy needs to be pretty desperate to follow her there, Julian thinks, pacing them; either that, or desperately ignorant. Kind of like him. The idiot doesn't balk at his surroundings, not even when she leads him through Seven Dials. Nothing tips him off. Julian can hear Miri purring to the man in her purry voice. She flatters and cajoles him into an alley, down the stairs, and into the St. Giles dining hall in the cellar. She promises the mark some beer, and even dancing. "We're not Puritans," Miri tells him. "We have music. We know how to have fun."

The man wraps his drunken arm around her delicate hip. "All in good time," she says, easing out of his hands. "Why don't we start with a meal and some songs, and we'll see where we end up."

Oh, the royal treatment the legless gentleman gets in the crowded rookery mess hall. Julian finds a spot in the corner and silently watches. The hall is a long room with a burning fireplace, a sink, a water tap, and a half-naked woman playing a fiddle. Only one of her breasts is out. Like a king, Miri's guest of honor is placed at the head of a long table and stuffed with food and lubed with drink. The rookery table is laden. It's a feast in a castle. There's steak with onions, mutton pork chops, fried potatoes, sausage, cheese, and dessert of pudding pie, home-brewed gin, and a snuff of tobacco. Young topless women dance on his table. Though keeping most of her clothes on, Miri is one of those women. Julian watches her two-step and spin, hooking her arms with another girl, clicking her stacked heels, flushed and sweating, her bodice unbuttoned, her half-covered breasts bouncing up and down. If he didn't know it was all an elaborate con, from the expression on her face he'd think she was happy.

And then the mark passes out in his plate.

The topless woman continues to play the fiddle, but the dancing on the table ceases cold. Miri jumps down. Mortimer and Monk strip the man of everything not attached to his skin. They clean him like a fish. They take his silk purse, his leather billfold, his coat, his boots, his hat. They take all his clothes and his cloak (so *that's* where Miri gets the clothes she gave to Julian). The boys are good enough to leave the chap his linen drawers. Mortimer motions Julian over for an assist. He and Mortimer grab the man by the arms and legs, carry him upstairs and outside, throw him into a handcart—like Lord Fabian, but alive, so a modest improvement—and wheel him back to Covent Garden, dumping him in an alley next to the long-closed Lamb and Flag. It's four in the morning.

"Well done, mate," Mortimer says to Julian as they head back. "I have a hard time loading them up and carting them by myself. Monk's no help. And me brother is usually, um, disabled well before midnight. I used to do this with Fulko, but you know…" Mortimer trails off, but he might as well draw a noose around the ellipsis.

"How often do you do this?" Julian asks.

"Most nights. Except Sundays. Too quiet. Especially Easter Sunday, it's dead out here at Easter. But Christmas is very good. Everybody's pockets are full at Christmas. That's when Fulko got caught."

"Miri does this every night?" Julian is upset. Her time grows shorter with every new thing he learns about her.

"Yes, but what's it to you? She wants to. No one's forcing her. I tell her to be more careful, but she don't listen to nobody. Everyone helps out. Miri, Flora, Hazel when she could walk, our mother. Miri's mother. We use different women, go to different pubs, mark different men. You don't want to accidentally grab a man you've already fleeced, but it rarely happens." Mortimer snickers. "Usually they're too ashamed to return to the same pub." He's quite talkative tonight, as if he and Julian are partners in crime, as if Julian can be trusted.

The dining hall has been cleaned up and the busty fiddler has left. Jasper is passed out on the floor by the slop sink. Sitting at one of the tables, Monk and Miri count their loot. Miri's blonde wig lies next to her. They divide the ten shillings three ways, three shillings each. Monk does not offer Julian the extra shilling for helping.

"Why did you follow me?" Miri challenges Julian in front of the others.

"Because what you were doing did not look safe."

"What's it to you?"

"I told you, Jack," Mortimer says smugly.

"She's right, don't worry about her, Jack," Monk says. "Our Miri can take care of herself."

"But, Miri, Jack is right, too," Mortimer says, defending Julian's defending. "The drunk ones can get violent real quick. One of them broke Miri's jaw once, remember, Miri?"

"No, Mort, I forgot."

In the silence that follows, blood rushes to Julian's face. But his anger isn't directed at the drunk man. It's directed at Miri—for constantly putting herself in harm's way, where a broken jaw, or worse, is inevitable. How can she not sense her life hangs in the balance?

"I don't need no friggin' protection," Miri says. "Not from you, Mort, not from him"—she gestures unkindly to Julian—"not from nobody." She rolls her share of the coin into a small purse and sticks the purse inside her breasts. She has thrown a shawl over her exposed flesh. Show is over, business is closed, she's covered up again.

"Same time tomorrow night, Jack?" Mortimer says to Julian. "Miri, what time you starting out tomorrow?"

"Probably after midnight. Got things to do before. But I told you—we don't need *his* help."

"Maybe not you," Mortimer says, "but I need it."

"Where you sleeping tonight, mate?" Monk asks Julian. "It's fourpence a night at Dyott House or Mother Dowling's. Only threepence if you can stomach the cellar without retching." Monk chuckles. "Tuppence if you don't mind sharing your cellar room with others. Or you can be like Jasper and Miri and sleep for free on the floor of the kitchen."

"I'm good," Julian says, paling as he imagines Miri on the floor near pits of refuse.

"You got to sleep somewhere." Monk narrows his eyes. "Where does a well-dressed man like you sleep?"

To earn their confidence (hers mostly) Julian forgoes his warm bath and white bed and opts for fourpence at Dyott House. By the time he wakes on a fleabag unmade mattress a few hours later, he no longer needs to worry about dressing down. He looks and smells as if he is thoroughly from St. Giles.

Walking home through Covent Garden, Julian sees the robbed man from the night before, hatless, shoeless and sobered-up, shouting at a constable on Long Acre, pointing to Little Owl Street. The policeman impatiently explains that there aren't enough days left in eternity to search the foul alleys of the rookery to find the cadgers who had taken the man's pocket watch, gold cufflinks, and wedding ring. "If you can recognize the dance hall where the molly shook you down," the constable says to the irate man, "where you passed out, if you can point me in the general direction of this fine dining establishment, I'll be more than glad to oblige you by arresting the scofflaws."

Julian hears the man describe Miri to the constable, the blonde Miri of the flowing dress and swelling breasts, of sweet breath and a voice that melts ice. The man calls her a disorderly whore. Julian wants to brawl with him. Miri is not disorderly! She is chaste and buxom, streetwalking at night, keeping her virtue as best she can while she endangers her future by continuing to plunder well-to-do drunks. Not him, but other well-to-do drunks. She thinks he is not worthy of being plundered by her.

That evening, Miri takes the long way around the rookery to Drury Lane, to the Theatre Royal, zigzagging through the back streets and alleys to make sure she's not being followed. How long is Julian going to hide in the shadows before he can approach the woman as a man? She is dressed sharply differently from the night before. She is in clean, conservative clothes, in a long straight skirt and covered up to the neck in a prim bodice. Her hair is neat inside a dark bonnet. Her plain shoes are spotless. After buying a ticket at the box office, she disappears inside.

It's a warm and humid late May night in London and the theatre doors have been left ajar to ventilate the auditorium. *A Midsummer Night's Dream* is playing. Richard Garrick—the owner of the Theatre Royal and its legendary lead actor for the last thirty years—is retiring, the marquee says, and these performances are his last. Julian stands by the open doors, listening in. *I am sick when I look not on you*, Garrick says and Julian repeats, searching for the back of her head in the packed gallery.

He has learned a new meaning of survival of the fittest. If nothing abounds but dirt, those who survive eat dirt.

Except for Miri. Sometimes in this dirt she plants roses.

# 18

# The Ride of Paul Revere

EVERYTHING STINKS, EVERY MINUTE OF EVERY DAY. IT STINKS when Julian sleeps and when he is awake. It stinks when he eats and bathes and when he dreams of love. Gin ferments and leaches into the pores of the skin of the people who drink it, gin mixes with grease and sweat and urine, gin mixes with unwashed hair, with decomposing mutton, with blood both clotted and flowing, gin mixes with dirt and sulfur from the fire pits, with rancid cheese and old milk, with every sour excretion in the human body and itself is excreted in greater quantities than the body can metabolize. Everything stinks, and everyone. The priests, the paupers, the men, the women, the horses, the rivers, the food stalls, the goldsmiths. Everything is covered with a thick layer of black soot from the coal-burning chimneys. The soot is never wiped off, and the manure is never cleaned up. That's not a rookery thing. That's an eighteenth-century big city thing. Gin is the rookery thing, the stench of gin mixed with dying bodies and rat kings.

And Julian walks in this stink, a solitary nocturnal man, dreaming of lavender love with his beloved.

∞

You know who is not dreaming of lavender love? His beloved. The next time Julian has an opportunity to whisper in her ear, he offers her what her drunk marks in pubs offer her: money. From him, she balks.

"I don't want anything from you," Julian says, trying to placate her.

"Good, we're even, 'cause I don't want nothing from you," says Miri.

"I mean, nothing in return. I don't want you to get me drunk, and I don't want you to touch me."

"So what *do* you want, then?"

"Nothing. Come for a walk with me."

"I walk all fuggin' day long."

"Come to the park with me."

"Why? Smuts go in parks. No."

"Come for a carriage ride with me."

"To where? No!"

"For a meal with me in another tavern?"

"I eat plenty right here, and *no*."

Come for anything with me, Miri, Julian wants to say. Come however you want. Just come.

After she rejects him, Miri trusts him even less. In her world Julian is the ultimate crook, the consummate swindler, because in her world, nothing is given for nothing. Everything is a barter, everything is a trade. Somehow, with his offer of money for nothing, Julian has managed to make things worse. He wants to explain to her but can't that he's a drowning man, grasping at anything to pull himself and her out. Well done, Jules, as Ashton would say. Well fucking done.

Once upon a time she was born into a noble life of milk baths and servants and afterward reborn into the Silver Cross, a life of toil and prostitution, and in that life she killed a man in cold blood for a few pieces of gold and a woman out of vengeance. And now she is here, a closed-up con artist in a wasteland of decay and despair. Her suffering is getting worse, the older her soul grows. Is this how she atones for betraying the one who put his trust in her, by having trust scraped from

her soul until not a shred is left? How can a shuttered heart be
changed?

∞

On the other hand, her friends and her mother grow fonder
by the day of the man she keeps refusing. Agatha adores him,
which makes Miri only more cross. Even Mortimer, that tough
nut, has cracked, now that he's got someone to help carry the
half-naked marks out of the rookery. Monk shows his affection
by constantly mocking Julian's delicate sensibilities. "Look there,
Jack, the St. Giles blackbirds are beggin' drunk again," Monk
says. "This don't please you? Has the neighborhood really gone
downhill?"

"Tell me you don't find the stench of half-open shallow
burial grounds objectionable?" Julian says. "It can't just be me."

"Oh, it's just you, Jack," Monk says. "Repentance—that's me
and Fulko's mum—used to work at Smithfields. She says the
regular normal smells, like you was just mentionin', in Smithfields
was combined with damp waste from the cattlemarket and
rotting carcasses from the shambles. What a pungent brew that
was! Mum says she returned to St. Giles for the clean air." Monk
laughs, slapping Julian on the back. "And what's the moral of
that story? Cheer up, it can always be worse."

Hazel is out and about. Agatha's legs heal. Days pass with the
regularity of the tolling bells, quiet mornings, loud afternoons,
busy nights.

*Dot 8.*

*Dot 10.*

Everything is the same, day after day, but it can all change
any minute, any second. The police can come; during her next
trick, she can get beaten. She can get sick, raped, killed. Julian
fears she may not make it out of *dot 11* of the life she leads.

Sure enough, on *dot 13*, the man she chooses to plunder
nearly plunders her, right on King Street. He pulls her down

to the pavement and mauls her. It takes a quick-thinking Julian to break cover and stagger between them, pretending to be drunk himself. Even that's not enough. He must grab the man by the scruff of the neck and throw him face down onto the cobblestones. Only when the man is unconscious does he let go of Miri's ripped skirts. Once free, she jumps up and runs, saying to Julian, "Why are you *always* around," by way of thanks.

Dot 15.

On *dot 16*, Julian finally meets the famous Flora, Jasper's disorderly fortune-teller. Holding Flora tenderly by the hand, Jasper points out Julian to her, as if the fortune-teller can't divine for herself which face is new in their common circle.

Miri might not make much eye contact with Julian, but the same can't be said for Flora. She's a tipsy cheerful creature with way too much lipstick and way too much cleavage. Invading his personal space and revealing her bare ankles to entice him, she inches up to him with a flounce in her excessive skirts, shaking her elaborately pinned rats-tails red hair at him, and giving him her best gin-soaked smile, never mind that it's barely midday. "Hullo, there," she says, extending her hand. "Jasper's told me so much about you. Where you actually from?"

You'd think she would know the answer to that, being a fortune-teller and all, but whatever. "From Wales. From the unknown forest."

"I've never seen a forest," Jasper says. "They have that in the future?"

Flora's dress is held together by pins and ribbons. It looks good only from a distance—as does Flora. Up close, the young woman's "disorderly" living is stamped around her eyes and her blemished skin. You know who doesn't think Flora looks good only from afar? Jasper. He is smitten with her.

A smiling Flora whistles as she paws Julian's chest and shoulders. "This one's a keeper."

"Tell me something I don't know," Agatha says from her chair, crankily pulling on Julian to get him away from Flora.

"Agatha, Jasper, let go of me, and let me do my job," Flora says. "Blimey, the two of you." Flora caresses Julian's knuckly hands, looking into his square palms. "He's come from a long way away!" she proclaims.

"Long way like Wales?" Julian says.

"Farther!"

Cynically Julian considers her while the young woman runs through a litany of generic claims: Julian's heart is full of strong emotion. He has many difficult decisions to make that cause him anxiety. He's got secrets that weigh heavy upon him. He must work on his friendships. He's in conflict with the truth.

About whom could those things not be said?

"But is he from the *future*, Flora, darling?" Jasper asks adoringly. "That's the only thing we wants to know."

"Jasper, why would anyone from the future come *here*?" Flora says. "They can go anywhere. Why would they want to glance in on your miserable lot? Of course he's not from the future."

Jasper takes Flora's hand. "*My* lot's not so miserable."

"Aha!" Monk says, sticking a finger into Julian's chest. "Flora says you ain't from the future. Lies and damnations! I knew it! She's a soothsayer, and yer a cadger most cunning."

Desolately Julian glances around Seven Dials. There's been no sighting of Miri this morning, not a glimpse. The *dots* are beginning to weigh on him. They're beginning to press him into the ground. One *dot,* one heaping shovel full of dirt. And he's got 16. He sighs. "Would you like me to prove to you I'm from the future, Monk?"

There's tepid applause. The curious and the idle at Seven Dials would like a freakshow.

"What's today's date, June 4?" Julian winces. *So much time has passed.* "Listen to me, gentle men and gentle ladies," Julian says. "The battles of Lexington and Concord have been fought and lost. Paul Revere has taken his midnight ride. He has warned the colonials that the British were coming. He has told them to take up arms, and they did. And the Redcoats lost."

Everyone ridicules Julian, including the great and powerful seer named Flora. A dozen grimy faces frown at him, a dozen boozy voices argue with him.

"We'll ask Miri when she returns," Mortimer says. "She hawks them papers, she'll tell us if it's true, she's smart. She taught herself how to read."

They laugh at Julian. Ridicule suits them, adds a gloss to their collective disposition. "What about after Lexington?" Monk asks. "Bet you don't know *that*. What's going to happen between the Crown and the Colonies?"

"The Colonies will declare their independence," Julian says.

A gassy upheaval follows his words, a mini revolution in Seven Dials. Never! When?

"July 4, 1776."

"That's rather specific, Jack," Monk says, after a small silence. The crowd laughs nervously. "And what about after that?"

"England will lose the war," says Julian. "England will lose America."

The crowd grows less amused. They stop taunting. No one likes talk of their country losing wars, not the rich or the poor.

"Nothing in the spirit world tells me this is true," Flora says.

"Maybe you should find different spirits to listen to, Flora," says Julian.

A frowning Mortimer, his hat askew, wags his finger from above. "Don't let the wrong ear hear you say those things, Jack. That's treason talk."

The crowd grimly assents.

"Yes, Mortimer, you know what else is treason?" Julian says. "Counterfeiting. It's punishable by death. *You* should be more careful."

"Witchcraft is worse," Mortimer rejoins.

They stop mocking when Miri runs across the square, holding up a copy of the *London Chronicle*. They stop making all sounds.

"We lost Concord!" she yells. "We lost Lexington *and* Concord!"

Everyone turns and stares at Julian with incomprehension.

Miri reads from the paper. "The king's troops are in full retreat! The provincials are in possession of Concord!"

"There's a simple explanation," Flora says. "He saw the paper already. He read it earlier this morning."

"It's hot off the press," Miri says. "Feel the page. It's warm. What did he read earlier this morning?" She doesn't understand the fearful wariness with which everyone suddenly regards Julian. But to be fair, Miri's been staring at him like that from the start.

It takes Julian longer than it should to understand why there's been such a delay in receiving the news. But that's how long the information must take to cross the Atlantic—*seven* weeks.

"It's a lucky guess," Flora says dismissively. "Nothing but dumb luck. He had a 50-50 chance of getting the winning side right."

One day Julian needs to explain to Flora the fortune-teller the difference between prophecy and probability. It's a big one. *She must die* or *she might die.*

Agatha pulls Julian down to sit by her side. "My dear boy," she says kindly and quietly. "A word to the wise. It was funny what you was saying when we all thought you was joking. But now—for your own sake—stop speaking. Lie low and hope people forget what you told them today. Otherwise someone will get nervous and open their trap. Like Mortimer—he's always snitching on others to take attention off hisself. And then yer going to be stoned in the pillory for being a warlock. And worse."

"Worse than a warlock?"

"Worse than the pillory. Better to be a murderer than a soothsayer." Agatha is serious. "They might hang you for killing, but they burn you for witchcraft."

As if that's on Julian's radar of immediate concerns. He rises, scanning the square for Miri. That impossible girl. She's vanished again! It would be almost funny if it wasn't happening to him. Here Julian is—living 300 years in the past, in eighteenth-century

London, on the one hand having found her, on the other—still searching for her, as ever.

"You keep seeking out my child," Agatha says. "Why?" Her eyes blink in weary compassion. "Sit down, my dear, take the weight off yer feet. Sit. A word to the wise there, too. I don't like to meddle in what's not my business, oh, I gossip about it, I gossip most wicked, Lord have mercy on me. But no frisson between a man and a woman can ever end in anything but misery. Especially not between you and *that* woman."

"I don't know what you're talking about," Julian says.

"Julian, you been good to me," says Agatha. "You healed my legs. Even our pastor can't believe it. So I tell you this. Them boys over there, they love Fulko, their brother, their friend, but Miri is their mother. They'll get by without Fulko. But they can't live without Miri."

"Join the club," Julian mutters.

"Stay away from her," Agatha says. "It'll come to no good."

Is there anything Julian wants to hear less? Why does the mother keep telling him to stay away from her daughter? "But how does *Miri* feel about marrying Fulko?"

"It's marriage," says Agatha. "He's a *man*. How *can* one feel about such a thing? Soul-wrenching resignation, of course, is what she feels."

"That's not what I'm asking," Julian says, struggling with his words. "I mean...does she *love* him?"

Agatha doesn't reply. When Julian glances at her, there is sharp pity on her face. "Oh, Julian," she says. "You poor soul."

They sit side by side, an infirm woman and an able-bodied man, watching four cripples in slings shuffle by, blood-soaked rags on their feet.

"In your daughter is the answer to my sorrow and the burden I carry," Julian finally says to Agatha. "The burden I'm enslaved by."

"That is terrible and most peculiar," Agatha says, pale of face. "I don't think she knows this."

"Oh," Julian says, "she knows. She doesn't care. But she knows."

∞

Later that afternoon, Julian finally catches up with Miri on Queen Street, where she is walking without companions and they can speak semi-privately on a public street. The conversation with the mother, instead of dissuading Julian, has given him new purpose. He is fed up with waiting, with following, with silence, with unwanted protection, with improving nothing. Of course Miri does not yet know of his intentions and as usual hurries when she hears him calling her name from behind. Most women would stop. She speeds up. Julian has to run around and stand in her way to keep her from walking. He hasn't had many women frown at him with such suspicion. Natch, *any* women.

"Can you move out of my way," she says. "What do you want?"

Isn't that the question for the ages.

"I want you to stop robbing men, Miri, for one."

"That and two pennies will get you a tuppence. What the devil do you care what I do?"

"You'll get caught. You'll get hurt. The court may show you mercy. But a drunk robbed man won't. Do you remember what happened the other day?"

"Look at you, Mr. Deliverance." Miri tries to get around him. "Yes, I remember what happened. You think I couldn't have got him off me myself?"

"No, I don't think you could've."

"So what? Even if I couldn't, what do *you* care? And who even says I wanted him off me? Did you ever think of that? Maybe I wanted to foin with him right there on the pavement. Maybe that's exactly what I wanted." Defiantly she snubs her nose at him.

Don't you remember Lord Fabian? Don't you remember the Great Fire? "Why do you keep putting yourself in harm's way?"

"Frankly, the only thing I see in my way is you." Miri steps, Julian steps, she goes one way, he goes one way, too. "For your information," she says, "I been making my own way since I was eleven, living by my wits, doing just fine. Twelve years I somehow managed without you, and now suddenly some fast-talking cadger is going to come between me and my mark?"

"What's going to happen to your mother if you get hurt or arrested?" says Julian. "She can't live on threepence a day."

"What do *you* care? Who do you think's been taking care of her all these years before you crawled out of hell?"

"If something happens to you, she'll be on her own. Fine, don't stay safe for yourself. But do it for your mother."

"And how do you think I'm going to make money?" Miri says. "You saw what the newspapers pay. Pennies. Monk told you what pure finding pays. Pennies."

"I told you, I'll give you money," Julian says. "Like that purse I gave you, the one you told no one about, I gave you that, didn't I? I'll give you more. It'll be our little secret. I will hire you."

"I knew it!" she exclaims. "Pray tell, hire me to do *what*?"

"Hire you not to rob people who can assault you, or have you arrested and hanged."

"And?"

"That's it."

Miri shoves him. "I don't want a farthing of your fugging money. Let me pass."

"It's not my money," Julian says. "It's your money."

She reels in confusion.

"You already died for it once," he says. "You paid for that blood money with your life. Please, Miri. Don't die again, because you won't take it from me. Let me help you."

"I don't know what you're *talking* about," she says, panting. "You're a madman. Let me through."

"You may not have much time," says Julian, because he doesn't know what else to say.

"Much time for what?"

"Let me take you to the theatre. You like the theatre, don't you?"

Miri is baffled and anxious, yet the word theatre makes her blink, stammer, waver. "How did you—how do you—"

"*Troilus and Cressida* is playing. We'll get the best seats, we'll take a carriage…"

"Why would we take a carriage, the theatre is five steps away." Miri takes a breath, composes herself. "If it's my money, like you say, just give it to me."

"I can't."

"I bet you bloody can't!"

"You know better than I do that my blood and yours will run into the sewer drains for that money," says Julian. "I beg you to believe me, Miri. You're in terrible danger."

"Look at *you*," she says, her low voice scathing. "Come to steer me in the right direction, have you? Come to save me by leading me into your own hovel of bawd, into your own stew of debauchery?"

"Why do you keep saying that? I told you it's not what I want."

"Really? Your interest in me is all pure, is it, all innocent?"

"It's not all pure," Julian admits. "But it is holy."

"Oh!" she exclaims. "Of course! Everyone else's lust is swineherd lust, but yours is holy!"

"Stop being deliberately blind to me," he says, raising his voice, "intentionally deaf to the things I'm telling you. Decide if you want to submit or triumph, Miri. Decide for yourself."

"Submit to you?" Fed up with him physically stopping her from walking away, Miri goes to strike him. He jerks his chin out of the way.

"Submit to your fate or triumph over it," says Julian.

"Oh, dear Lord! What do you *want*?"

"Nothing but you."

She slaps him across the face. He doesn't move away from her hand that time. Maybe he doesn't want to.

"I go with *no* man," Miri says. "Especially a dodger I don't know."

"By no man, do you mean you go with *every* man?" Julian says. "What about the drunks you lure to the cellars? Don't you understand—one of them could be the death of you."

"Yes, *you*." She goes to strike him again, but he blocks her, grabbing and lowering her arm. He doesn't let go. "Listen to Paul Revere, Miri! Take up arms and save your life."

"I don't know Paul fugging Revere," Miri says through her teeth, "and I don't know *you*."

"You *know* me," Julian says. He circles his arms around her for a moment, pressing her tiny frame to his chest. He is desperate; he knows how he must seem to her.

Breathless, she struggles away, punching him with her little fists. She is so small, so tough, so fragile.

"There's nothing you can do to me, Miri, that will make me leave your side," Julian says. "Accept it. Nothing. You can't even *die* to escape me."

"What are you talking about?" She shoves him in the chest. The more he stands and takes it, the more feral she gets. "I'm marrying Fulko, or did you forget?"

"No, you're not. The gallows are waiting for him."

"We'll tie that noose when we get to it," she says, heaving. "But I'm not walking out on him because you make eyes at me from across the street. You've put Monk and Jasper under your spell, you've put Flora under your spell, you've put me mum under your spell, half of Seven Dials under your spell! You're not putting me under your spell."

"No?" Julian says. Again he draws her to him.

She wrenches away.

But not *right* away.

"What's wrong with you?" she cries.

He lets her go, watching her disappear down the street, his heart aching with an unending ache. On the outside she is brittle, hiding in a turtle shell because on the inside she's like blown-out glass. One tap and she will shatter. Her vulnerability batters his senses. He is doing all the wrong things because he can't think straight. He is going to ruin everything.

Or is it already ruined?

*Dot 18.*

*Dot 19.*

Julian hates her gang for needing her, hates her mother for not saving her, hates Fulko, whom he's never met, for failing to protect her, hates Flora the fortune-teller for being a phony and not telling her to run like the wind. But most of all, with a steadfast hate, Julian hates the quill—as if it's the pen's fault that directed by a human hand, it can make a mark in the arm of a man to remind him how much time has passed.

Or how much time is left.

*Dot 20.*

Julian desperately searches for another way to lift her soul to him. He needs to do something instead of waltzing alone, dancing his solitary tango before the looming drowning, do something other than throw himself into a canal in Kensington, all grime and misery and bereft of imagination.

# 19

# Bucket of Blood

THERE IS A MOMENT IN THE MORNINGS—WHEN JULIAN IS still in his warm bed, in his light room, as the days stretch out long and hard in front of him and long and hard behind him, when senseless acts of depravity abound and a purple haze of gin rises from all human endeavor—when he struggles to get up and out. He has lost the will to get out of bed. He could sleep in instead. Have breakfast. Go for a walk. Read in the library, the fire lit, a tumbler of whisky in his hand. Mark the day, don't mark the day. It doesn't matter. Like petals of a daisy, the days will fall, and her life will fade. This is not like Julian, to feel so despondent. He's been such a go-getter lately. This is how he felt in L.A. after she died. The sickness in his soul rose up and crushed against his skin. Like a flood tide in a sluice, the grief filled up all the available space inside him.

That's what it feels like now.

Julian forces himself out of bed, into a bath, into clothes, downstairs, out. He reminds himself—dully—that as long as there's life, there's hope. He forces himself forward, toward an impossible future in which she still walks, possible and alive, yet so far away from him.

∞

God works in mysterious ways. Because just as Julian turns the corner on Monmouth Street heading into the rookery, he gets jumped from behind by a gang of hoodlums. Someone hits him across the back with a metal object. Two guys grab his arms, and a hand slithers into his coat pocket.

Julian is not in the mood to be mugged. Roughly he yanks out his arms, elbowing someone's nose, someone's jaw, and spins around to face his attackers. There are four of them. They are scrawny, they stink, and they look like Monk. Only one of them looks meaty enough to give Julian any trouble, and he's the one wielding the pipe. One whimpering fool holds his bloody nose, but another continues to tug at Julian's pockets. Julian slaps him on the head to check his distance and when that doesn't do it, he jabs him in the face. The wailing boy retreats.

From behind, Julian again feels a hand in his coat. He shoves the thug away without even turning around to face him. "What do you want, money? Here." Reaching into his pocket, he pulls out some change and pitches it onto the cobblestones. Three of the four boys instantly forget Julian as they drop to their knees—bloody nose, sore jaw forgotten—squealing and cursing and beating on each other to get to the pennies. Only the bloke with the raised pipe remains standing, though he takes a cautious step back.

Julian nods. "You *should* step back. You should *run*. That would be the smart thing to do. Let's see if you're smart."

The guy charges. Julian doesn't step out of his way. He lunges forward instead. Turning his left shoulder, he slams into the guy, catching the pipe with his right and yanking it out of the guy's hands. The tramp staggers back and dumbly stares into his empty hand and then with panic at Julian, as if the latter removed the pipe from him not by force but by black magic.

"You learned a valuable lesson today, mate," Julian says. "You're not very smart. You're also a crap fighter. What are you doing robbing people?"

"Don't hurt me, Monk made me do it!" the guy squeals. He whistles to his partners, who scramble to their feet, and all four of them hightail it down the street, leaving Julian alone and puzzled.

*Monk* made him do it?

But Monk likes him. Monk is his friend. Why would Monk make him do it?

∞

"Miri made me do it!" Monk cries when Julian confronts him in Seven Dials. Miri is not there to defend herself. But Jasper and Mortimer nod vigorously. "She did, she did," Jasper slurs. "She made him do it." Jasper is plucky but drunk.

"Why would Miri tell you to send your goons to rob me and beat me?" Julian says incredulously. "Does she want you to hang? Do you know what you get for highway robbery? Death. Corporal fear and threat of one's life, and all that."

"She said you got money, lots of it! She said you were an easy mark!"

"She said *I* was an easy mark?"

"I didn't want to do it, Jack! She told me to."

"You always do what the girl tells you?"

"You wasn't harmed," Mortimer says, "so what are you on about?"

"I wasn't harmed because I fought back," Julian says. "But what if I couldn't?" Did Miri really tell Monk he was an easy mark?

"I'm not mad, Jack," Monk says, adjusting the missing buttons on his oversized waistcoat.

"*You're* not mad?"

"That's correct, I bear you no ill-will," Monk says, circling Julian. "Just the opposite." There's a fire in Monk's gaze. "I watched you in that skirmish," he says, eyes darting with excitement. "You know how to fight!"

"So?" Julian is wary.

"What do you think, Mortimer?" Monk says. "Should we try to make some money off his fists?"

Julian frowns.

"Ever hear of the Bucket of Blood, Jack?"

Julian's heard some of the patrons at the Lamb and Flag refer to their pub as a bucket of blood because of the fights that take place there. Is that what Monk means?

"He's ideal, Mort! He looks so clean and pasty." Monk skips around Julian. "What do you say, Jack, will you help us with a little hustle to buy freedom for me brother?"

"You want me to fight for money?"

"We want you to pretend you can't, and *then* fight for money."

At first Julian refuses.

"Fine, Jack," Monk says, "have it your way, but you know, Miri looks at you like yer dirt. She told me to fleece you. She thinks yer a weasel. You sure you don't want to prove her wrong?"

"Flora don't think yer a weasel, she likes you. She'll come and watch," Jasper pipes in, slurring his words. "Me girl loves a good fight."

"*Everybody* loves a good fight," Monk says. "Even Miri."

Mortimer suddenly changes his mind about Julian fighting. "The man wants to be on his way, Monk, let him be on his way! Why make him fight if he don't want to?"

"I'll do it," says Julian.

Monk hoots. While Mortimer stands ill-disposed and Jasper rolls in the dirt, Monk goes to work on Julian, shining his shoes, dusting him off, straightening his collar.

Agatha sides with cranky Mortimer. "Don't do it, Julian," she says. "Yer going to get knocked on yer noggin' and who's gonna bring me breakfast then?" She reaches for him. "It's rough over there at the Lamb and Flag. You can get hurt good and proper."

Julian knows. He's been diverting himself in the late afternoons watching their bloody brawls. But it's rough in here, too. It's fucking rough everywhere.

"Miri, Miri!" Monk yells, waving like the possessed across Seven Dials at Miri walking toward them from Earl Street with

Flora by her side. Julian stuffs his hands in his pockets and looks away. He's got some words for her he needs to keep inside.

"Miryam, help!" Agatha cries. "Crazy Monk is getting our poor Julian ready for the slaughter at the Lamb and Flag!"

Miri gives Julian a once-over. If he was unsure about fighting before, he's one hundred percent sure about it now. The expression in her eyes would make Monk fight Ali. Julian has never seen a girl more incredulous—and more skeptical. Ancient damnation, as Monk would say.

"No, Monk," Miri says. "It's worse than him going down into the sewers with Cleon."

"But he wants to do it!"

"He's feeble-minded and got no sense," says Miri. "I don't give a toss about him, but you'll be sprung for his murder. I won't have you on the chats for him, Monk. He's not worth it. It's illegal, every which way to Tyburn, to conspire to kill a weakling and to bet on his death in the process. So no, Monk."

Julian interrupts. The little boys Miri runs around with might need a mother, but Julian does not. He already has one. "It's touching you being all concerned for my welfare," he says to Miri, "but where was that noble worry when you ordered Monk to hire thugs to rob me?"

"Monk! You told him?"

"*They* told him!" Monk cries. "And he came for me. What was I meant to do?"

"I don't know, Monk—lie!" says an exasperated Miri.

"Listen," Julian says to them, "I didn't want to go down in the sewers, but I'll do this for you. After all," he adds, "we're trying to raise money for a good cause. We're trying to get Miri's future husband out of jail. That's worth my getting clobbered over, isn't it?" He glares at Miri. She looks away.

"Damn straight, it is," Monk says. "Wait, what? No, you can't get clobbered. All me money is going on you *not* getting clobbered. It's the only way we make money. I thought you understood."

"I do, Monk," Julian says. "I was making a joke. I thought *you* understood."

"Oh," Monk says, as if unsure what a joke is. "Ha ha."

Miri won't look at Julian. She turns to her mother. Julian's temper continues to rumble while his body engages in an ultimate hustle: making himself look like a bourgeois milksop who's never raised a hand to a dog, much less a human being. Clearly, from Miri's reaction, he's been doing a bang-up job of looking like a wimp so far. Since Topanga, everywhere he's gone, Julian has been nothing but Ralph Dibny, the intellectual dweeb in a suit. A teacher, a writer, a gardener, a brothel keeper, an apothecary.

Well, no more.

Now he will be what he is in the true of his heart—a fighter.

He turns away from them long enough to slip the rawhide rope that holds his crystal and beret over his head and to drop them into a pocket deep in his breeches. He doesn't want anyone to notice the crystal; they might think it's worth something, and if he gets knocked out, they'll steal it off him. He can't fight with it on. But he also can't fight without it on his body. What if he gets beaten lifeless?

His so-called friends pool their meager resources to see how much they can bet. With Agatha's threepence and the change in their pockets, they scrape up a shilling. Julian doesn't know how this can be. Miri is clearly not contributing from the purse he had given her with the two crowns in it. What about the rest of them? They roll drunks every night who jingle with shillings and cufflinks. Where's all that money?

Julian asks, but no one will admit to anything. The money's gone, that's all anyone knows. And frankly, Flora looks like the kind of girl who spends it as fast as she makes it, and she doesn't make it that fast.

"He's got money," Miri says, pointing at Julian. "He bragged to me the other day how he's got lots."

They turn to Julian, expecting him to solve their financial dilemma. Julian shakes his head as he digs into his coat pockets. How is it that one way or another, the con men—and women—not only manage to separate the fool from his money but somehow get the fool to agree to get himself beat up in the process. He counts his coins. Thirty-two shillings. Monk's pupils dilate as if he's watching a naked woman dance.

In a gaggle, they start toward Covent Garden with Monk hyperactively and repetitively explaining the hustle to Julian. He must look like a country gentleman, having a stroll down the Strand after supper at the Savoy Palace, who decides to try his luck in a fight. He can't ever admit that he knows Monk and the rest. Julian agrees and then stipulates his own rules. "We have only one chance to make money off this shindig," he says, "and that's before they see me fight. The second time around—if there is a second time—you'll be lucky to get a farthing on a shilling, and I'm not fighting for you for halfpennies. I've seen how they bludgeon each other over at the Lamb and Flag. They bring beefy criminals into that pit. When it ends, someone's always getting dragged out feet first. You understand why I don't want that to be me, right?"

"Can you take a bare-knuckle punch, though?" Monk asks. Miri makes a scoffing sound. Julian wants to take a punch from Monk right then and there to prove to her he can.

"You don't seem so sure." Monk is anxious. "I don't want Miri to be right—I don't want to hang if you lose yer miserable life."

"Miri's always right," says Miri.

"Miri is not always right," Julian counters, adding to Monk, "You worry about your end, and I'll worry about mine. Oh, and one more thing—whatever we win, I get back the money I put in, which is thirty-two shillings, plus half the winnings."

Monk rebels like a proud Colonial.

"Then I'm not doing it," Julian says. "Half, Monk. I'm putting in *all* the capital and taking *all* the risk. I'm gambling everything and stand to lose everything." Involuntarily Julian shudders when he says this. "Are *you* in danger of getting maimed? No.

So consider my half of the pot your punishment for trying to rob me. Drive up the odds if you can, and we'll see what we see."

Monk has no choice but to agree.

In Covent Garden, in a crook of a claustrophobic alley named Rose Street stands the Lamb and Flag, and at sunset behind the pub in the beer garden, when the parish constables are changing shifts and every decent human being is out having supper, the crowd gathers gaily for the daily blood-letting. All the tables and chairs have been pushed to the side. The mob surrounds the garden which is now a fighting pit. Everyone stands, tankard in hand, screaming and cheering. The spectators are geographically separated from the cluster of gamblers.

Julian instructs Monk to go to Red Corner and deal with Big Legs, and not to Black Corner that's manned by Little Legs. Julian has seen that dude at work. Little Legs is nasty and greedy, plus he's a swindler. He gives exorbitantly long odds and then counts on the drunk gamblers' poor math skills by paying out the wrong amounts. Big Legs gives shorter odds but pays what he owes. "Don't get greedy, Monk," Julian says. "Go to Big Legs."

"But Little Legs is my friend," Monk says in feeble protest.

"Of *course* he is. Why am I not surprised that you'd be friends with a ruthless felon like Little Legs, Monk?"

"We was card sharpers together. Made some good money on Old Nob back in the day." Old Nob is cribbage.

"Did you hear what I said to you or are you deaf? Go to Big Legs."

In his fine suit, Julian pushes his way to the front. Meanwhile in the pit, the smaller man gets his nose broken. The crowd cheers raucously. Julian has seen the big guy before. He is the cock of the game. His name is Mr. "Smackdown" Brown. Julian has yet to see him lose a fight. A heavyweight. Well over six feet, probably 220. A brute who thinks force alone will tip the scales, and he's not wrong, force goes a long way. Aside from that, Brown's got another handicap. Like Julian, he can't see well out of one of his eyes. Brown barely has to compensate for this since all the men here fight right-handed, so all the blows come to the left side of his face and body. Julian is counting on that to be Brown's downfall. Because to adjust for his own lopsided vision, the right-handed Julian had long ago trained himself to fight southpaw. He can't see perfectly out of his left eye, but he can dominate with either hand. This afternoon, he will fight left-handed. He judges that no one in this crowd, in London, in 1775, has ever seen a man throw a left uppercut or a left cross. He hopes they don't think him a warlock; that, coupled with Lexington and Concord, could be his undoing.

"Who's *next*?" the emcee yells, a whittled man, tinier than Monk. They call him Mr. Tall.

When no one else volunteers, Jasper shoves Julian forward. Julian takes off his black felt hat and throws it in the ring. The crowd takes one look at him—polished shoes, frock coat, clean face, quiet manner—and roars with laughter. Julian doesn't take it personally. The hefty man he's about to fight is naked from the waist up and missing some teeth. Everyone can evaluate him upfront. Julian, on the other hand, has all his teeth and wears silk hose. No one notices his broken and re-set nose—a tell, if ever there was one.

Mr. Tall asks him if he's fighting of his own free will. Julian nods. He's asked to pick a fighting name. He calls himself Mr. Concord, for the battle across the Atlantic that's already been won or lost, depending on your perspective. In his other life, when he was a prizefighter, training for the World Middleweight title, he was Julian "the Hammer" Cruz, to honor his mother's Norse heritage as well as to draw attention to the force of his fists. Here he'll be just plain Mr. Concord.

The betting begins. The shouting, the frenzied calling of odds, the writing down of amounts with wax crayons on torn bits of paper continues for ten or fifteen minutes. Mr. Concord stands calmly in the fighting pit, hiding his hands in his coat pockets, his eyes straight ahead. He doesn't meet Brown's gaze. Sometimes fighters can tell when they're being hustled.

Something in the ice of their opponents' eyes. Julian doesn't want to take any chances.

Finally, the betting's done. Now Julian can undress. He hopes Monk has locked in good odds. He takes off his coat, the same coat Miri had given him his first day in the rookery. Thirty shillings at 20 to 1 odds will win the gang thirty pounds. That's a lot of money. Monk would have to steal two solid gold watches and face death to make that kind of money. Julian unbuttons his fine cloth olive green waistcoat. He unbuttons his spotless white shirt and pulls off his cufflinks. He knows that in a moment, Mr. Tall, Big Legs, Little Legs, possibly even the dense and toothless Mr. Brown, are going to know a hustle when they see it. In a moment, when Julian removes the rest of his costume, Miri will know who he is. It's time to reveal himself to the skittish and unseeing Miryam.

And when Julian stands shirtless and motionless before them in the warm June evening, wearing only his shoes and breeches, they see it. A thrilled hush rolls through the crowd. They thought they were about to witness a mutilation. But when they catch sight of Julian's lean, strongly muscled boxer's body, when they catch sight of his powerful arms and chest, they realize they're going to witness something better. They're going to see an actual fight. Julian won't look into Mr. Brown's face to check if the giant realizes it, too. Julian's hands remain in his pockets. He has never fought in a circus like this, and he's fought in some real dives in the Mojave. If only Ashton could see him now. He would go ballistic. Thrilled but ballistic. Ashton was never one for unbalanced fights. Not good for the fighters, not good for the audience, he used to say. But Julian wants to make it good for this audience. After all, Miri is watching.

Standing in the center of the pit, in a sonorous voice, Mr. Tall reads the Prize Ring rules of 1743 to the crowd that knows them by heart, reciting the rules loudly and drunkenly along with the emcee. "There's no time limit! There's no head-butting! There's no biting! There's no kicking, kneeing, holding, or throwing! There is no other weapons of any kind! There's no hitting below the belt! There's no hitting the fighter when he is down! When the fighter is down for a count of thirty (*thirty!*), the fight is called, and the man standing is declared the victor!"

The crowd cheers.

"Mr. Brown, Mr. Concord, do you understand these rules?"

Mr. Brown and Mr. Concord nod.

"Then step in. When I ring my bell, the fight will begin."

How long has it been since Julian has heard a ringing of the bell, signaling the start of a real fight? Fourteen years. How he has missed it. Julian, who until now has kept his hands in his pockets, takes them out, steps into the center of the pit, and raises his fists to his chest, leading with his right, rearing with his left. The strongest hand is always at the back. The crowd howls with laughter. "What are you doing keeping your right arm forward, imbecile?" he hears someone shout. "You gonner get clobbered!"

Mr. Brown is used to fighters backing away from him, so he doesn't know what to do about Julian, who, as soon as the bell rings, charges like a battering ram and hits Smackdown Brown with a straight right, and before the man can turn or sway, follows with a left hook to the jaw. Because he's blind in one eye, Brown doesn't see it. His head snapping back, the man staggers, loses his balance and falls. The crowd goes wild. There is screaming, jumping, hooting, hollering.

Julian stands to the side and waits for Mr. Brown to get up. It takes the colossus until the count of twenty to recover. He doesn't move or respond to the first ten. But get back up he does, and with his face and ears livid, becomes a Madrid bull, head down, chin at his chest. And like a matador, Julian steps out of Brown's way, letting the force of the man's big body propel him into the crowd. The laughter makes Brown all the angrier because now he's being humiliated.

Mr. Brown is strong and game and enraged, but he's also untrained. He is a truck without a driver, barreling down the highway. He doesn't pace himself and doesn't protect his face, especially on the right. He's not used to protecting anything, and this is his downfall. A man who hasn't learned to protect himself—the cardinal rule of all fighting—will not last long in combat. Brown keeps his fists chest-level, leaving Julian to pound his unprotected gut, his solar plexus and ribs, and to slap the top of his constantly bowed head. Julian hits Brown from left and right, from down and sideways, he dances around him, feinting away from most return contact. At one point, Brown tries to land a dozen punches, and every one of them misses as Julian ducks and bobs like a street jester away from balls pitched at his head. Wildly Brown flails. Every few swings, he glances Julian's head and arms. For every blow he lands, Smackdown gets back five, but you gotta give it to the big guy, he keeps lunging. Brown's entire strategy is offense: one mighty punch, the opponent laid out. He doesn't know what to do with someone who's toying with him, who bobs and sways and slips, who ducks right and hits left, jabbing and short righting him. Julian spins Brown around, disorients him, and then hits him with a combination cross that nearly knocks him down for the second time.

The bell doesn't ring again because there is only one round. During a match, all time stops in the ring. Without the bell, a boxer can't tell if a minute has passed or an hour. You fight until you fall. Julian knows how long the fight lasts only by the condition of the man in front of him. Much too soon, a bloodied, confused Brown begins to wobble. Has Julian given the crowd their money's worth? From their roar, it seems that he has. Has he given himself some seldom-found joy, especially these days? Regretfully, he supposes so. Julian hits Brown with four straight rights in a row and follows with a left uppercut. Brown flaps sideways and swings on his way to the ground. He connects on that last punch, clocking Julian pretty good, breaking his lip. Mr. Smackdown Brown hits the dirt, shudders once, and is still.

You can't say that about the crowd. They remain in a frenzy for ten minutes, nearly in bare-knuckled combat themselves, as Big Legs and Little Legs pay out on the unlikely David downing

Goliath. Wiping the blood from his mouth, Julian stands basking in the applause for a few moments. Mr. Tall grabs Julian's fist and raises it in the air. Julian glimpses Miri's disbelieving face deep in the crowd. He throws on his white shirt, buttons up, grabs the rest of his clothes and hurries through the slapping, congratulating, shrieking crowd to wait for his gang on the corner of Long Acre and Church Lane, as agreed. Even from blocks away, he can still hear them shouting on Rose Street.

When he is finally by himself, Julian smiles. To defeat another man in a fierce contest of nothing but fist and will is something. The memories of Julian's joyous days and bitter years roar past him in a heady, fast-moving carnival barge. How much he had once. How much he has lost. It takes him a while to calm down.

Monk is beside himself, as is Jasper, and Flora, and even Mortimer. Miri says nothing, hiding near Flora's shoulder. Julian doesn't challenge her or address her, though he would like to, would like to come up to her and quietly ask if she still thinks of him as feckless Dibny. But Julian has learned long ago that no one likes a sore winner. In victory, as in defeat, there must be nothing but grace. He wanted to show her what he could be, and that he has done. How she reacts remains to be seen.

The odds were 20 to 1. Julian can tell that Monk wishes he knew math better, like Little Legs, so he can cheat Julian out of his half of the money. You'd think Monk would be happy getting fifteen quid, more money than he's ever seen at one time in his life, but no. "There's only one of you but six of us, mate," Monk grumbles. "I don't know why you have to take half."

"Because that was the deal, Monk."

"I know, but still. We need it more than you do."

"That wasn't the deal, Monk."

Monk can't stay upset for long. He's too happy to have some real money in his pocket.

"I tell you what," Julian says, refocusing the little man. "I'll feed us tonight. Food and drink are on me. Which way to Pottage

Island? Onward! I'll buy the meat and mead and then it's back to the castle, and you lost boys can eat, drink and be merry, and continue to live by plunder."

"That's us!" Monk cries. "The plundering lost boys!"

What a celebration they have, what a drunken debauched feast of mutton and wine. The naked girl with the fiddle outdoes herself. This time both her breasts are out. Julian concludes that London is not what one might kindly call a sober town. Gin and respectability do not hand in hand together go. But gin and topless girls go together very well.

Hours into the night, from his corner at the long communal table, Julian overhears Jasper trying to woo Flora with tall tales of himself as a different man in the unattainable future. "Please, darling, don't be mad at me. I know I had a bit to drink again, but we was celebratin'. It's not going to be like this all the time. Look, we got us some money, finally, and after this, I'm going to get a real job. Truly I am, why won't you believe me, my tartlet? I'm going to rent us those nice two rooms yer always eyeing above Lou's. *Why* do we need two rooms? Well, one for you and me, and one for the baby, of course. And you won't have to work anymore, Flora, I'll do all the work. I don't want no girl of mine to work. If you want to tell fortunes on the side, that's okay, but no more strenuous labor for you, my blossom. I *know* I have to stop the gin, Flora, don't you think I know that? I will stop—*tomorrow*. We'll get married—*tomorrow*. And rent those rooms—*tomorrow*. And have that baby you wanted—*tomorrow*. Don't worry, Flora. Everything will be good—*tomorrow*."

The only one in the hall who remains as quiet as Flora is Miri. She has danced and eaten and drunk, and now sits on the bench a few places away from Julian. At least she is at his table. After Julian has had enough gin, he sidles up to her. "I was going to offer you my winnings," he says in his rumbly baritone. "I only took my half of the pot to give to you. But I remembered just in time how upset you get when I offer you money, even though I keep telling you there are no strings attached."

"Are there *any* strings attached?" Miri says, studying the table.

Beat. "No."

"None?" Her gaze rises and meets his dilated gaze. "How's your lip?"

It must look pretty bad if she's asking. She has raised her eyes and his hopes. "Fine."

"So where'd you learn to fight like that?"

"Once upon a time I used to be a boxer. A prizefighter. Once upon a time I was a contender." Julian smiles.

Miri doesn't quite smile back, but she almost smirks from the side of her mouth. "I mean, where did you learn to fight with your left? No one fights with their left."

"*I* do," Julian says. "I learned when I was forced to. You'd be surprised how many things you learn to do because you're forced to." Be alone. Fall into wormholes. Help girls dress as boys. Prepare murdered bodies for shallow graves. Purloin gold. Dive head first into fires. Fight Goliath. Stay patient though your heart screams in panic.

"You don't have to tell *me* about it," says Miri.

Julian palms his empty glass. "I came from a family of teachers. They used nothing but words to resolve their conflicts. Every dinner-table argument was gray. Nothing was black and white. Nothing was ever settled, and no one ever won. A physical fight, on the other hand, is so cathartic. No words are necessary." He smiles. "And there is always a winner."

"Do you like that?"

"I like the winning, yes. Your life force is literally in your hands. Swift justice, certain victory, raising my arms above my head like I'm some kind of hero."

Miri asks him to show her.

Raising his arms above his head, Julian pumps his swollen fists through the air.

"You're some kind of hero," she says, her eyes softening. Or is the softening only his gin-soaked imagination? "I saw your reflexes against that guy. He swung at you a hundred times yet couldn't land a punch."

"He didn't try very hard."

"So how come I connected with your jaw the other day? And you didn't even get mad."

He mines her face. What is he going to tell her? That he let her hit him? He doesn't know what to say.

"So what else do you like besides a fight?"

Julian struggles to focus. That could almost be flirtatious, right?

"Many things." He leans toward her. She leans away, slightly. His sore and swollen hand reaches for her skirt. This bare-knuckle fighting is for chumps. He wishes his hands had at least been taped.

She rises from the bench, away from his hand. "I meant… would you like some gin and water?"

Julian struggles to focus. "Since one of your jobs is fleecing drunken men, Miri, reluctantly I'll have to say no."

She inclines toward his head. Her breath tickles his ear. "You don't want to be fleeced by me, Julian?" For half a moment, her deepening eyes half-hooded, she fixes into his face. Miri has called him by name. It's like the hammer of Thor in his gut.

"Bring me gin only," Julian says. "Leave the water."

# 20

# The Advocate

THE FOLLOWING MORNING ONLY JULIAN IS HUNGOVER. HIS
crew is as fresh and clear-headed as if they've just enjoyed
a royal slumber. Sober—and wealthy!—having danced and
drunk the night away, they begin by having a kingly breakfast
and making feverish, grandiose plans; plans that unfortunately
include their new best friend, the lackluster Julian. Now that
he's proven to them he can do anything—travel through time,
predict the future, knock out giants—anything but be well in his
liquor, they entrust him with going to the Old Bailey—London's
central criminal court for over 1500 years—to haggle with the
magistrate over Fulko's fate.

A few days later, with his lip almost healed, Julian sets
off—with half of the prize money in his pocket as a potential
bribe. Neither Jasper, nor Mortimer, nor Monk, Fulko's ever-
loving brother, are willing to part with their loot to bail out their
own. Julian is dressed in his Sunday best, a scarlet waistcoat,
embroidered in gold, a ruffled white shirt, nankeen buff-colored
breeches, and Miri's black silk cloak.

Being a superstitious lot, his new friends don't accompany
him to the courthouse. They wait in the rookery where they're
more comfortable—and safer. Monk tells Julian that he hasn't
left the rookery of his own accord since 1770. "Last time I set
foot in the Old Bailey," Monk says with a sniffle, "I thought I was
coming in for a small infraction of pilfery of a hat and a pewter

mug and maybe a cufflink or two, and it was seven months on the hulks before I saw the spire of our beautiful St. Giles in the Fields again." He crosses himself.

∞

Julian heads down Holborn to the Old Bailey. Up on Ludgate Hill, the rebuilt and stunningly familiar enormous white marble dome of post-Great-Fire St. Paul's shines in the sparkling morning. The courthouse is just outside the London Wall, and the adjacent Newgate prison is just inside. Past, present, and future, the Old Bailey has only one main courtroom. The rest of the massive building contains spaces for wheeling and dealing before getting into that courtroom.

Julian waits a long time in the cavernous reception chamber for someone to call Fulko's name. Finally, he is shown into one of the small rooms and left there to chafe for another hour until the unapologetic magistrate arrives.

The magistrate is an elderly phlegmatic gentleman by the name of Colin Ford, in an ill-fitting, rumpled suit. Ford looks like he was ready to retire twenty years ago. He is slumped, dogged, and resistant to animation except for the teeth bared in a frozen smile; that is his resting "I've seen it all before" face.

Colin Ford has no patience for Fulko Gib, or for Julian's half-hearted entreaties on the prisoner's behalf. Julian suspects he might not be the best man for the job. He told the lost boys as much. No one listened. They thought they stood a better chance with Julian. "You pulverized Smackdown Brown," Monk said. "You're not afraid of a little magistrate, are you?"

Yet in some ways Colin Ford *is* more intimidating. For one, he is not afraid of Julian's fists. Ford holds Fulko's papers on the table in front of him without referring to them once. He appears to know the case history by heart. "I'm not entirely certain what you are here to accomplish, Mr. Cruz—as Mr. Gib's advocate, as you call yourself. Do you wish to arrange a visit with the prisoner, to say goodbye?"

Julian is mealy-mouthed but acts most sincere in stating he has a different purpose. "The purpose of computing his sentence." Celebrating with the crew these last few days has been terrible on his English. "I mean commuting."

"Commuting his sentence." Colin Ford folds his hands. "Where are you from, sir? Not from London, clearly, but from where? Do they have laws in your country? Do you know how laws work?"

Mumble, mumble. Colin Ford is sharper than Julian anticipated. A small bribe looks unlikely to solve the matter. Julian sits up straighter, pays attention. Something else is being required from him—like his active presence in the living moment.

"After Master Gib killed a man in the course of separating him from the gold watch, worth eight pounds," Colin Ford says, "he compounded his crime by immediately taking the watch to Lou's Pawnshop, a known destination of stolen goods. But even Lou had the sense to say that he would not give Fulko money for the watch until he produced the gentleman who had given it to him. Needless to say, Fulko could not produce this gentleman on account of the gentleman's being dead. So he produced Little Legs instead. Are you familiar with Little Legs? Yes, I see by your expression that you are.

"This occurred just after Christmas," Ford continues. "The wheels of justice have not turned swiftly. Master Gib was indicted, evidence was collected, witnesses were produced, facts were presented. He stood in the dock and was tried before a jury and a judge. He was convicted. As the law requires, he was given three months to appeal. That period has expired. He's not awaiting trial. He has been sentenced to death. No more advocacy is required."

"It's your last sentence that I would like to discuss with you, Mr. Ford."

"The time for negotiating has passed. The time has come for a hanging. Oh, and by the by, would you like to know what Master Gib said in his own defense? That he was as innocent as a child unborn. His words, not mine. That was his entire summation: I am as innocent as a child unborn." Colin Ford sits back as if he's made an irrefutable case.

"Well, he didn't have money for a more robust defense," Julian says. "But we have money now."

"But he's been convicted. The defense part is over, robust or otherwise."

"Perhaps he can appeal."

"Are you hard of hearing, Mr. Cruz? Or have I been unclear? The period for appeal closed on the 15th of April."

"Are you going to let a few days stand in the way of a man's life, Mr. Ford? A few arbitrary days, against a human soul?"

*Dot 22.*

"It's not arbitrary. It's the *law*."

Julian shrugs as if to say law, schmaw.

"Master Fulko is incurable," Colin Ford says. "As are many of his ilk. The man has lost all respect for the court and its punishments. There is no remorse. There's no terror in his heart for any fate that awaits him, there is only defiance. I'm afraid no accommodation can be made for a man like that. The Honorable John Jenkins has had enough. Fulko Gib is sentenced to hang a fortnight from June 22, and hang he shall, by the neck, until he is dead."

Julian must think fast. "What about clemency? There must be something I can offer you in return for some clemency for the young man."

Ford clasps his hands. He is tired, looks tired, talks tired, but his eyes burn bright with life, with knowledge, with opinion. "I have no need of your gifts, sir. But please—do let's talk about clemency. In one of his previous *twenty-six* indictments, Master Gib was charged with treacherously and feloniously counterfeiting silver coinage in contravention of the realm. He was also found guilty of forging a thousand pounds' worth of bank notes. Both are capital crimes. Somehow he escaped death by sweet-talking the bailiff into leaving open one of the side gates in the yard during a torrential rain. The bailiff claimed the bolt had slipped out of the lock. That was clemency, was it not? Gib fled, hid in the rookery—really just another form of prison— and did not resurface for four years."

Julian must think faster than that! Soon his time with the magistrate will be over and he will have accomplished nothing. He decides to use some of what Agatha has taught him. To move the needle in his favor, Julian pleads the belly.

He tells Colin Ford that Fulko's fiancée is with child. She has no means of support other than her future husband. If Ford doesn't help Fulko, his bride and baby will become another pair of paupers who are doled out a pittance from collections in the poorest parish in London.

"I am well aware of the penury of St. Giles in the Fields," Ford says. "We have corralled our poor into one paddock, at some distance away from the regular folk, to conceal their suffering. No one wants to look at dissolute people in decay, it hurts our sensibilities. There's nothing to be done about it. The poor will always be with us. We must muddle through as best we can— together. Our problem is that unfortunately we can't forget about St. Giles. There's too much crime steaming up from that boiling sea. Of course, because of it, we all remain gainfully employed, which is more than I can say for the members of that parish—a hidden half-city of masterless men, idle and unapprenticed, who make their living through crime, petty and grand—men who can work, but prefer not to." Colin Ford clears the phlegm from his throat. "What I'm saying with all due respect for the parish and its situation is that Master Gib is not a means of support for a woman with child. I'm not entirely certain that scoundrel can support his own neck on a gallows rope."

"And yet, he's the father of the young woman's baby," Julian says. "Please consider a commutation. I will pay you any sum you require. Perhaps Judge Jenkins can commute his sentence to transportation?"

"What's the difference between transportation and a hanging?" Colin Ford asks. "The wife and child are on their own either way. Or is your plan to send his wife and baby to America with him?"

Julian becomes enlivened. "Why not?" Possibilities spring up he hadn't seen before. There's a way to get Miri out of London! "Yes, absolutely, put him and his wife and child on the boat and send them far away. Rid your country of his nuisance. He'll be America's problem. Exile him." Julian breathes out. "While there's still time. While you still can." What Julian knows that the judges and the barristers and the magistrates do not yet know is that the American option is five minutes away from being eliminated. Once war begins in earnest, once the Royal army is unable to dispatch with the Rebels as planned, the "transportation" of British criminals across the Atlantic is going to come to a permanent halt.

"She's with child, you say?" Colin Ford cleans his glasses with his handkerchief. "And what reason does this woman have to suspect Fulko Gib is the father? Perhaps she has him mixed up with someone else. I've seen that happen." Ford pauses for emphasis. "Many times."

Julian assures the magistrate this is not one of those times.

Ford doesn't say yes, he doesn't say no. He takes a pinch of snuff from a tobacco box in his desk. "What's *your* interest in this?" he asks Julian.

"I'm the young lady's cousin," Julian replies. "I care deeply about her well-being. Her mother and my mother are sisters."

"Who is her mother?"

"You don't know her, I'm sure."

"I know everyone. Been doing this job a few years. Who is it?"

"Agatha."

"Agatha Bromley?" Ford nods. "I know her well. And I know her daughter, Miryam Bromley. I haven't seen her for some time. I was hoping she had gotten out. She was always too good for that life. At eleven, she was brought to me for nearly killing a constable. After what she told me about the man, I'd say he was lucky to escape with his life. At fourteen she was brought to me again, this time for grand larceny. Miryam was charged with breaking into a home and taking two satin pillowcases, two blankets, and, most remarkably, an entire feather mattress. She also took linen sheets, two pillows, a linen nightgown, and one bound and printed copy of the Holy Bible."

Julian tries hard not to clench his fists in front of the magistrate. He doesn't want the unflappable man to see how tense and unhappy the words are making him.

"Miryam told me she took those things," Colin Ford continues, "so her ailing mother could have a place where she might rest comfortably, a proper bed with pillows and blankets. She took the Bible, she said, so she could learn how to read so she could read to her mother. Both times, I didn't brand the girl, or beat her, or imprison her. I let her go. That was clemency, was it not?" Ford shakes his head. "I can't believe that bright young lady has got herself embroiled with a no-good ruffian like Fulko. I must have been wrong about her."

"You weren't wrong about her," Julian says.

The magistrate leans forward. "Are you sure you want to force her hand in marriage to that thieving vagrant? A marriage to a man who assaults men and women alike, who can't hold a job and has zero desire to. A man who has not spent a single sober free day on earth since he was ten years old. That parish, sir, is raised on gin."

Julian fights the impulse to hang his head.

"Is it your opinion that by arranging this journey to America, you will be saving the troubled young lady from the rookery?"

Julian barely nods.

"It will mean her marrying that man and then being sent away—while pregnant—on a treacherous passage to an unfamiliar colony, a colony that's having some difficulties. I ask you again, is there no better way?"

"There isn't." There must be a better way. Julian just can't think of one.

After a contemplation, Colin Ford speaks. "Very well. Bring the young woman to me. Let me talk to her. Let her plead her own belly to me. Then I'll decide if I can help you. Oh, and you said you were willing to pay for her way across?"

"You mean for the commutation of Fulko's sentence, don't you, Mr. Ford?"

"That's what I meant. How much might that sum be?"

"Whatever it costs," Julian says.

Colin Ford's eyes flare. He sits up a little more alertly, speaks with slightly more enthusiasm. "Bring her to me tomorrow. I must be in court by 10 a.m. Bring her to me at nine. They're usually not up and about in the rookery until well past noon. If she comes to me early, I will know she's taking this plan seriously. Oh, and I almost forgot—has her mother finally passed away?"

"No. Why do you ask?"

"I ask," Colin Ford says nasally, "because the Miryam Bromley I know would not sail so much as across the Thames and leave her mother behind. Her mother is the only family the girl has, your, um, connections to her notwithstanding. And her mother is most certainly not well enough to survive a voyage across an ocean."

Julian is mute.

Colin Ford smirks. "Quite a pickle, isn't it, sir? I'll see you tomorrow."

∞

Julian reveals no details of the conversation with the magistrate to his anxiously waiting Bloods and Crips. He says obliquely that there may be hope, that he must return in the morning and must bring Miri with him. No one is happy with this, least of all Miri. Julian declines any mention of joint transportation to perilous lands unknown and phantoms unborn. He keeps repeating that

Colin Ford has asked to see her first thing in the morning and leaves it at that.

Miri says she can't go and won't go, adding, "looking like this." She points to her tattered dress.

Julian offers to take her shopping for a more presentable outfit.

"Where to?" Miri says gruffly. "Covent Garden? They've got nothing good there. I've had enough of Monmouth finery, thanks marvelous much."

"I was thinking Bond Street."

Jasper and Monk ooh and ahh, Mortimer stays sullen and quiet, but surprising everyone, Julian most of all, Miri agrees!

While she's off, putting on her cleanest dress and scrubbing her hands and face to look presentable for Bond Street, Julian sits with Agatha. From the stalls he has brought her some bread with warm bacon and apple cider, though Agatha keeps insisting on rum. As she eats, Julian probes into the mother's aversion to travel.

"Travel where?" says Agatha.

"Anywhere, really."

"Like the park?"

"Farther."

"Stratford?"

"Farther."

"I don't know nothing farther than Stratford. Not bloody Scotland?"

"Not Scotland. What about America?"

Agatha laughs fondly. "Oh, you are daft," she says. "So, so daft."

Julian presses. He would accompany her, of course. He would buy her a passage on a big boat, with a first-class cabin. She'd be well fed and safe. There might even be a dram or two of gin. It would take six weeks to cross the ocean.

"What about Miri?"

Julian says she will go, too—on a different boat.

"Oh, my Julian," says Agatha, shaking her head.

He persists. The three of them could stay in Maine until the war is over. Everything would be okay after that.

"Why would I ever want to sail the ocean?" Agatha says. "I don't even want to get on a boat across the Thames to visit my syphilitic cousin Eunice."

Julian begins to tell her about a house near the water in a small rocky town where she can walk and buy flowers and fish, and about her daughter staying alive, but the alive daughter returns, ready for her shopping trip. Agatha pats Julian's head as he rises to his feet. The look on Agatha's face as she watches Miri walk away tells Julian there is nothing the mother doesn't already know about a desperate desire for salvaged children.

# 21

## *Troilus and Cressida*

INSIDE WHITE'S THE MILLINER'S, A LARGE DRESS SHOP ON Bond Street, Miri is intimidated. She doesn't speak, lest the well-dressed saleswomen hear her common dialect. Gingerly she walks around, afraid to touch the displayed clothing. After much silent browsing, she decides on a long lilac skirt, with a white lace hoopless petticoat, and a cropped pale yellow taffeta jacket, stitched with maroon ribbons. It comes with a matching silk bonnet lined with ostrich feathers. For her feet, she selects pointed-toe ivory shoes with gold buckles and stacked heels. Julian buys her embroidered white gloves and pearly beads for her throat. The shop ladies fuss over her, complimenting her on her alabaster skin and her shiny black hair. What about her soft red lips, Julian wants to say. And her melting chocolate eyes. You forgot about those.

Miri walks out of the shop, her tiny slender frame shaking with joy. She twirls her walking stick umbrella, her old clothes in a tightly wrapped bundle in her hand. "How do I look? Unrecognizable?"

"I'd know you anywhere," Julian says.

She scans up and down Bond Street. "Well, where to now? I can't go back to St. Giles looking like this."

"Like what, a princess?"

Miri attempts a non-reaction. "I'd never willingly go to the Old Bailey, visit some magistrate. But if I must go, I need to look my best, that is all. I'm doing it for Fulko," she declares, all serious.

"Of course you are." Julian is all serious back. "Would you like to take a carriage ride?"

"I still don't know what you mean by that. Carriage ride to where?"

"Nowhere. I said ride, not journey."

"Why would we hire a carriage if we ain't going nowhere?"

"Let's ride around London in an open carriage. It's a beautiful day."

"For what reason?"

"For no other reason than to ride," says Julian.

In vain Miri tries to hide how badly she would like this. The gap between her daily life and a carriage ride is vaster than the black chasm Julian leaps over in the Cave of Desperate Hope.

He offers her his hand to help her up into the cab, and though Miri is agile and doesn't need the help, she takes his hand anyway. They ride to the pastures at Hyde Park. They ride around Green Park, past Buckingham Palace, and down Pall Mall.

Before re-entering the Strand, she asks the driver to stop. She doesn't want to go back to the bloody Strand, she says. "It's like my backyard. I'd like to see something new."

"What about a ride through the City, to London Bridge, to St. Paul's?"

She shakes her head. "I've never liked it over there," she says. "I don't know why."

Julian directs the driver to take them down to the river and along the Thames to Westminster, past the Houses of Parliament. Westminster Bridge is there, built twenty-five years earlier, but there is no Clock Tower or Big Ben rising over it. Julian's eye can't get used to it. The mind's eye keeps supplying what's missing in real life. He keeps looking up to see the time, as they pass by the House of Commons.

They hop off to get some bread and sausage at a food stall and with an ale and a pastry, find a bench near the House of Lords. Julian wants to tease her a little, ask her if the House of Lords brings back any memories. But it will just confuse and irritate her, and hasn't he done enough of that? He keeps quiet, while she barely touches her food because she doesn't want to spill crumbs on her new skirt.

"You must be quite rich to let us ride so long," Miri says.

"Not me," he says. "You're rich."

It confuses and irritates her.

After the intimate break by the river, another carriage takes them back to her neighborhood. Motionlessly they stand in the congested clacking crossroads of the Strand and St. Martin's Lane. Julian can tell Miri wants to say something. She certainly makes no move to cross the street.

"What is it?" he asks.

"Nothing, nothing."

"Are you ready to go back?"

She chews her lip.

"Or…would you like to see that play I was telling you about? Drury Lane is showing *Troilus and Cressida*."

"When?"

"Now."

For a good minute, Miri stands mute. "What's it about?" she finally says. And then she smiles. Her face warms, flushes, becomes even more beautiful.

Julian smiles back. "I need to bark it up like one of your newspapers? Fine. It's set during the Trojan War. Troilus is Paris's brother and he falls in love with Cressida, the daughter of a Trojan noble. Troy is fighting a losing battle with the Greeks for its survival, but not Troilus. All he wants is to be with Cressida."

"Do you have tickets?"

"We will in five minutes."

"It's a shilling. And you spent all yer money ridin' around London for no reason."

"Not for no reason," Julian says, "and it's more than a shilling for box seats. Let's hurry. It's first come, first served." Even the luxury boxes are unnumbered. Julian wishes he could say the same for their days.

They hurry. She raises her silk skirts above the manure.

At the ticket office on Catherine Street, Julian buys two box seats, the best in the house. Seat purchases are divided by class, but Julian knows that money speaks louder than class. He offers the ticket seller twenty shillings a seat instead of the usual five, and not a minute later, they're in the most expensive box right by the side of the stage. A chandelier of three hundred wax candles hovers over the proscenium. Every night those candles need to be manually replaced with new ones. For the rest of his days, Julian will live in full appreciation of the chandlery arts.

Miri can't hide her excitement. "You spent two *pound* on these seats? As God is my witness, you've lost your mind." Her thrilled demeanor denies her words. "When I save up a shilling, I buy a ticket in the back gallery. I stand the entire play."

Her hands in a knot in her lap, Miri doesn't breathe through the first act, doesn't speak during the intermission, and doesn't breathe through the second. After it's over, she cries. Miri, who's seen it all, endured all, cries. "That's the saddest play I ever saw," she says, even though *Troilus and Cressida* is a comedy. *"Tear my bright hair and break my heart, I will not go from Troy.* But why did Cressida betray Troilus if she loved him? How could she do that? You don't betray the one you love. Why did she have to go with that awful Greek? And Troilus who loved her so much, how could he be so cruel and compare the body she gave him to leftover scraps from the table? Oh, it's just awful—they lost their city and the love between them was destroyed. Why did you take me to this—wait—why are you waving down a carriage?"

"Well," Julian says, "I was thinking we could go have some supper and talk about the play."

"Supper where? Neal's Yard?"

"How about a dining room on Grosvenor Square?"

She stands in the middle of the street. "Sounds far."

"It is far."

The carriage doesn't come right away, and Julian and Miri walk for a bit, past St. James's Park, as familiar to him as skin and heat. Oh, how they wore out the paths of that park with their lovers' strolls, waxing poetic about which wild berries could kill a grown man. In 1775, in the silence of his overflowing heart, Julian offers Miri his arm, and in silence she takes it. It's nearing the summer solstice, and the days are long on the 51st parallel. During the gloaming, the sun sets slow in the sky, and the city burns orange flame forever.

"I don't know if I'm using the right word," Miri says, "but for some reason, this feels familiar to me, walking here." She doesn't say walking here *with you*. "And yet I know I never been down this way in my life."

"You are right," Julian says. "Some things are hard to explain."

In the crystal dining room of the corner townhouse on Grosvenor Square, Miri sips red wine out of crystal goblets while a man in a black suit delivers her lamb and roast potatoes and fine Stilton cheese. All her life Miri has eaten with her hands, and Julian can see it's an effort for her to pick up a knife and fork. She asks if she can eat the Yorkshire pudding with her hands. "Probably not," says Julian. "Not when it's dripping with gravy." In the corner of the candle-lit, white-walled dining room, a quartet of strings—a cello, a viola and two violins—plays Bach's mournful fugues.

The normally terse Miri doesn't stop talking. As if perhaps even her terseness has been a disguise. She talks about the ladies' shops and how nice they smelled inside, full of perfumed atomizers. She talks about the carriage and how nice it was not to walk but be driven. Holding her wine goblet like a beer stein, she talks about *Troilus and Cressida*.

"That was not a very good comedy," she says. "The lovers are separated the minute they come together. What's so funny about that?"

Julian cannot disagree.

"That Shakespeare didn't take Troilus's heart seriously is what bothers me most of all," Miri continues. "Troilus the ever-faithful is betrayed by that dreadful girl."

"Nonetheless, she never stops being the subject of his heart."

"Yes, but the good Cressida is only in his mind! She doesn't exist. And the real, wanton Cressida is not worthy."

"She is," Julian says. "The war between his faith in the idealized Cressida and his knowledge of the true Cressida might resolve into a truce of enduring love."

"That's not the play we saw. Shakespeare forgot the difference between a comedy and a tragedy," Miri says. "Comedies have a happy ending. Did that seem like a happy ending to you? Now, *A Midsummer Night's Dream*, that's a much better comedy. I saw that the other week"—she rolls her eyes—"but I suppose you already know that, pacing fifty steps behind me as you do."

Julian smiles. "You don't like to cry?"

"Who does? Who wants to see a play about love being fickle and fleeting?"

"I don't know, the theatre tonight was packed to the rafters."

"People have no sense." Miri smiles lightly. "Why, did *you* like it very much? I suppose you would. You like the point of it—that love turns men into weaklings. Men who do not love go and fight instead. Like Achilles. But men who love write poetry and wail under the windows of their beloveds, like Troilus and Romeo."

She's teasing him. He could cry. "Sometimes men who love still fight. *Tear my bright hair and break my heart, I will not go from Troy,*" Julian whispers.

They linger in the dining room. Julian doesn't want this watershed day to end, a day not quite like all the others. A man in a black suit keeps coming over and refilling Miri's wine. He removes her dirty plate from the table and brings her a clean one. Another man places a dessert menu in front of her. He nods his head when she orders a pudding with vanilla sauce and raspberries, and says, "Very good, miss."

Julian watches her, trying not to frighten the horses by his staring, by his open adoration of her lovely, serious, deeply affected face. She is so grown-up, yet longs to be a child, a child she never got to be.

"I have an idea," Julian says. "Do you want to hear?"

"I'm not sure," Miri replies, her eyes twinkling faintly. "By the expression on your face, I'd say no."

"We have to be up and out so early tomorrow," he says. "Instead of going back, why don't you stay upstairs with me? I have three rooms on the top floor. You could have the bed. I'll sleep on the sofa. You could get a good night's rest." Instead of looking for trouble. Instead of picking the pockets of drunks. Instead of undressing men and carting them into alleys.

"You have three rooms, why? There's only one of you."

Slowly Miri walks with him up the stairs, woozy from the wine, holding on to the railing, as if she can't quite believe she's agreed to enter a man's apartment. Inside his high-ceilinged rooms, she is composed but stunned, walking around, touching the chairs. The ceilings are white. The walls are pale blue. There are ten-foot windows.

"This must cost you a fortune," she says. "We have fourteen ladies staying in one room, not near half as nice."

"The ladies or the room?"

And Miri laughs.

That's a first.

In the third room with the sinks and the dressing tables and a tub, she turns on the faucet and is amazed when water spurts out. She asks if he's ever had a bath in the tub. Every day he doesn't sleep in the rookery, he tells her. Miri's face is full of longing as she stares down into the white porcelain, but she can't bring herself to ask if she can have a bath, and he doesn't want to scare her away by offering to draw her one. They remain silent.

She touches the sideboards, the drapes. From the windows, they can see the heavy trees in the square and beyond it silhouettes of buildings against the night sky. The air is cool but not cold. She stands out on the balcony for a few minutes. "What is this called?"

"It's called a balcony." Julian nearly breaks down. Do you remember how you asked me this, Miri, under the stars of somebody else's life, and I told you it was a Juliet balcony?

"What's the matter with your voice?"

"Nothing." He clears his throat.

"What do you do on this balcony?"

"You can sit, watch the park."

"Why?"

"For beauty. For pleasure. To listen to the sounds of the city."

"What sounds? It's so quiet." Miri doesn't know quiet, and it shows. She's nervous around it. She likes it, but it sets her on edge.

"There's nothing like the largest city in the world, asleep and silent."

"London is the largest city in the world?"

"By far."

"Larger even than Paris?"

"By far."

"How do you know that?"

He shrugs. "How do you know about *A Midsummer Night's Dream*?"

"Because I saw it."

"That's how you know most things. You see them." Though not all things.

She can't seem to relax. It's as if she wants something from him and can't say what. He pours her a glass of red wine, pulls two chairs outside, and they sit listening to the trees. It begins to drizzle.

"The world is full of beauty," he says softly, "don't you agree?"

Miri shrugs. "Sometimes yes. Mostly no. Oh, there's beauty in the theatre," she says. "That's where I see it most often. That's why I spend my precious money on it. But otherwise, I've seen things in my life that are decidedly not beautiful. I don't always look. But I can't help but see."

Julian asks what things, though he doesn't want to know. He senses she wants to tell him, as if to explain why she has been so difficult, so uneasy, and he will listen, but he doesn't want to hear it. He can only imagine what she's seen, what she knows.

"Sometimes what I see doesn't look like beauty," Miri says. "Sometimes I see things that in their mass, shape, activity, unending debauchery, flagrant pain, oozing dark things, limbs that look like they're being broken, bodies that look like they're being busted open, the screaming that goes on that some think is some kind of sexual abandon, but I regard as terror, sometimes those things look more like satanic rituals to me than acts of beauty, to be perfectly honest."

Julian listens, nods. He can't explain to her with words that what she has seen is not what it is. What she has seen has been degraded, subjugated to its basest component, often removed even from its primal physical pleasure. There is no pleasure in what Flora feels in the alleys behind Neal's Yard. He wants to tell Miri it's not always like that. That sometimes it can also be an act of beauty.

"I will admit that Fulko is not the best of men," Miri continues. "Yes, he can be idle and stupid, but he is polite to me and he's not rife with disease, and that's something."

"Polite and not rife with disease, what more can one wish for in a husband."

"You jest," Miri says, "but Fulko's grandfather was a Puritan, and his mother, Repentance, is a Puritan's daughter. Yes, she went the dissolute way, but she taught Fulko and Monk to respect women. Fulko and I have a union of the mind. He never beats me. Or does anything to me, really. He barely touches me."

"Is that what you want, Miri—to be barely touched?"

She doesn't know how to answer him. So she doesn't answer him. She won't look at him.

"A union of the mind is good," Julian quickly says. He's not going to argue her out of her lifelong opinion arrived at in the worst way—through punishing experience. He needs to get her to forget what she is living for, by showing her what he is living for. Just not tonight.

Julian helps her take off the yellow jacket and unhook the lilac skirt and then steps into the drawing room to allow her to settle in. He hears her fight sleep a long time, pacing in the bedroom, reluctant and timid to lie down in his bed. Julian knows the intolerable fact about her—that she sleeps on the floor of a dark room behind the galley where she drags her drunken marks. That is her bedroom. That is her home.

After the pacing stops, Julian lets half an hour go by before checking on her.

Miri is asleep in his bed. Lovingly and carefully, she has laid out her new clothes on the back of a chair, climbed deep into the center of the mattress, and covered herself to the neck in the goosedown.

Julian sits next to her, caressing her hair. Miri, I may not be *your* dream, he whispers. But you are mine. From the beginning, this was so. Since I first met you, against all reason, you were everything I ever wanted. Was everyone right, was my love for you unrequited? Am I unanswered, dissolved, disappearing, undesired?

Am I requited, Miri?

*Mea pulchra puella.* Will we be friends? You are beautiful, but will you soon be dead, like all the rest? I can't bear it. I refuse to believe it.

The mystery of human existence is that even here, in this disaster of a ramshackle life, Julian still lives his days with her forward, not backward. He lives as everyone does—as they can, aware perhaps of the timer, but never in a countdown. Each morning brings a new possibility of life beating on, full of plays and pastries and carriage rides, full of yellow silk jackets on slender brides. Each new day Julian continues to open his eyes and feel hope. Despite having marked his trembling arm with another despised *dot* of ink, everything seems as if it could work out. Julian, next to Miri asleep in his bed, halfway across time and ocean, sees her death side by side with her life, with her beauty.

But he sees her life and her beauty first.

# 22

# Grosvenor Park

EARLY THE NEXT MORNING THEY TAKE A CARRIAGE TO THE halls of justice.

"Miri, I have to tell you something," Julian says to her when they're on the wide steps headed to the Old Bailey's double doors. He stops her from walking. "Don't be upset with me, please. I didn't know what to do. As you'll see in a minute, the magistrate has no soft spot for your fiancé. Everything I suggested, he shot down. I was out of ideas. So I may have told the man a little white fib, which you should know about before you go in there, in case he asks. I feel he might ask."

"What fib?" Miri says. She was in such a good mood this morning. Now the expression in her eyes turns guarded again, and cold.

"Um, I may have told the magistrate that you were carrying Fulko's baby," Julian says.

"Why would you have told him a thing like that?" she exclaims.

"I'm sorry. He trapped me. I didn't know what else to say. Your mother told me pleading the belly worked for her, so I took a chance. Look, tell Colin Ford that I was wrong. Tell him I'm a man and don't know anything about such things. That I misunderstood. The thing is, when I told him that, that's when he finally relented and said he'd see what he could do for Fulko."

Miri shakes her head in disgust as they continue up the steps

Miri shakes her head in disgust as they continue up the steps into the courthouse. "You clearly don't know *anything* about how these baby things work," she says. "What, you didn't read all about it in your books about the booming population of London? Have you heard of something called time and opportunity? I really hope you haven't made things worse with your damnable lies."

Julian also hopes this.

Colin Ford comes into the room where they've been waiting without speaking and sits across from Miri behind his desk. Julian remains standing in the farthest corner.

"Miryam Bromley, how are you, young lady? Do you remember me?"

"No, sire." She looks into her lap.

"I haven't laid eyes on you in nine years, since you were brought to me for stealing a mattress for your mother. Do you remember me now? How *is* your mother?"

"She is well, sire, thank you."

"How's the mattress?"

Miri doesn't answer.

Colin Ford takes in Miri's new sharp outfit, all yellow and lilac, her crisp collar, her spotless pointy shoes, her clean hands and face, her silk bonnet, her graceful demeanor. He studies her, once or twice lifting his saturated gaze to Julian. "Miss Bromley, tell me, how long have you been with Master Fulko?"

"A few years, sire, I can't be sure. We been friends since we was—since we were—kids. Then we fell in together. I was twenty-one maybe."

"And how long has he been in jail?"

"Which time, sire?"

"This time, Miss Bromley."

"Possibly since Advent."

"So about six months you'd say?"

Belatedly Julian sees where this is heading. Damn. This is unfortunate. Miri is right. Julian has no idea about how these baby things work.

"Yes, sire," says Miri, casting Julian a condemning glance.

"And how many times, would you say, in total, have you been to visit your fiancé at Newgate in the last six months?"

"Twice, I think."

"Twice. I see." Colin levels a stare at Julian. "I doubt you had a chance to be alone with him, so would you say then, that you are at least six months pregnant?"

"Yes, sire," Miri says faintly.

Ford takes in Miri's narrow waist, her flat stomach. "You're looking quite well for someone who's having a child in a few months if I may be so forward as to notice."

"Thank you, sire."

"Are you aware that the father of your child is scheduled for execution next month?"

"Yes, sire."

"Is it your wish not to have him executed?"

"Yes, sire."

"Are you asking me to commute his sentence?"

"Yes, sire."

"Your cousin here, Mr. Cruz, has asked me to commute his sentence to transportation. Is that in accordance with your wishes as well, Miss Bromley?"

"Yes, sire."

"He would be shipped to America, if we can get him on a transport, for a term of no less than seven years. Is that something you would prefer for Master Fulko, instead of a hanging?"

"Yes, sire." Miri suddenly sounds unsure.

"I see. And you yourself are willing and ready to marry him immediately and to accompany him on the transport ship to the Americas as his wife and the mother of his unborn child? Mr. Cruz here told me you would be ready to leave at a moment's notice."

In confusion, Miri glances back at Julian.

"That is why you're here, isn't it, Miss Bromley?" Colin Ford says. "To plead the belly for yourself and for your future husband and to agree to leave the country with him on a convict ship?"

Miri sits without reacting. She doesn't turn to Julian, she doesn't look away from Colin Ford's gaze. Her hands remain folded on her lap. She doesn't twitch. After a few silent moments, she speaks. "Yes, sire," Miri says.

Ford emits an impressed snort. It's quiet in the small room while he collects himself.

"Very good, Miss Bromley. That is admirable. Quite admirable indeed. And what about your mother?"

Julian interrupts. "I will take care of Miryam's mother," he says. "I will arrange for her passage."

Colin Ford leaves his gaze on Julian. "Miss Bromley, may I make a suggestion?"

Miri sits.

"Let Fulko Gib meet his fate head on, so to speak, and you remain in London, with your mother, and get on with your life."

"I would agree to that," Miri says, "if by Fulko's fate you mean transportation and not a hanging. I would need your assurance."

"Assurance?" Ford shakes his head. "No."

"Then yes, I will go with him to the penal colonies as his wife."

"Well, hold on. I meant, I can try. That's all I can promise you."

Miri takes out the bag of silver she's brought with her, Julian's share of the Lamb and Flag money. "There's fifteen pounds here," she says. "For Fulko." She lays the purse on Ford's desk. He looks at it. He doesn't touch it.

Julian steps forward. "Put your money away, Miss Bromley," he says. "Magistrate, allow me to offer you something more as our thanks for saving Miss Bromley's future husband from the gallows." Julian slides the large and gleaming Elizabethan coin across the table. The goldsmiths on Cheapside would not be happy with him for so mistreating the precious sovereign.

Both Colin Ford and Miri are mute, staring at it. She, because she doesn't know what it is.

And he, because he does.

"Consider it done," Colin Ford says, reaching for the gold.

Julian slams his palm over the coin, startling both the magistrate and the girl. "Transportation for Fulko Gib in return for the gold," Julian says. "Not execution. Do we have your word?"

"My solemn word. In three weeks' time I will release Fulko Gib to Pastor Wyatt so he can say goodbye to his family and to Miss Bromley before he sails." His nominal smile stretched over his prominent teeth, Colin Ford reaches again for the coin.

Julian lifts his hand. The gold vanishes from the table.

∞

Ahead of Julian, Miri hurries down Ludgate Hill. He runs to catch up with her. "Please don't be upset with me," he says. "Look, everything worked out."

She swirls to him. Stinging hurt is in her eyes. "You haggled with that man to put me on a ship with Fulko and send me off to the Americas? You wanted me to marry Fulko so I could go with him as his *wife*?"

"To save you," Julian says feebly.

"You agreed to have me marry another man to *save* me? To go thousands of miles away from London"—she doesn't say *away from you*—"to *save* me?"

Julian hangs his head. How can he explain what cannot be explained?

On Fleet Street she speeds up again, trying to outpace him. "I'm starting to believe you about one thing, though," she says. "You *must* be from another world. But as for the rest—I knew you were a fake, and I was right."

"I'm not a fake," Julian says.

"You tell me some cock and bull story about how you care for me, and then you push me to marry another! You care for me so much you want me to leave the country on a convict ship!"

"Please don't be upset with me, Miri," Julian says. Yes, he may be going about it all wrong. He doesn't know how to do it right. *I'd rather you marry him and live* is what Julian wants to say and can't. "But you're not going with him anymore," is what he says, in a tone that suggests he doesn't consider that good news. "We worked it out, no reason to be upset."

"Some suitor you are," Miri says. "What full-blooded man would do this? What man who liked a young lady would agree to this? Why did you buy me a silk jacket, a new hat? Why did you feed me, take me to a play? Why torture me before you pimp me out?"

Julian stops her from walking; he takes her into his arms. "Nothing will change if I can't find a way to save you," he says, his voice falling in his throat. "Don't you understand? *Nothing* will change."

"Save me for what? Save me from what? What are you talking about?" Miri struggles to free herself from him. He lets her. "You understand *nothing*! about women."

When he tries to follow her, she scolds him not to. "Leave me alone," she says. "Why can't you just leave me alone."

Julian stops walking, and she runs off, toward Temple Bar.

Imagine that. Julian has been cast out of St. Giles. He is not worthy to be in the rookery with Miri.

∞

He wanders the city the rest of the day—past London Bridge, all houses and shops demolished to widen the passage for carts and horses, past Blackfriars Bridge, brand new, six years new, past Westminster Bridge, still looking for that Clock Tower. It is late and he is exhausted by the time he returns to Grosvenor Square. As he enters the iron gate of the townhouse, his path lit by oil lamps, he hears Miri's voice behind him, from across the street inside the park. Not addressing him. Addressing someone else.

"No, sir. No, sir. *No*, sir."

Julian runs across the road. "Low women are not welcome in Grosvenor Park," Julian hears a man say. Miri is pinned against an aspen. A growling man in a posh frock mauls her yellow silk jacket. "It's a private garden. Why are you wandering around here if this is not what you want?"

Julian doesn't wait to evaluate the situation. He punches the man in the back of the head and shoves him away. The man staggers but puts up his fists. "I was here first," he says. "Go get your own."

"This is my own," Julian says, and uppercuts him. The man falls. Julian grabs Miri's hand, and they hurry out of the park.

"I was waiting for you," she says. "But a constable come and told me women of dubious character couldn't wait over by the light. So I waited in the dark. The man thought I was offering him something."

Julian runs his hand over her face. "*Are* you of dubious character, Miri?" He wants to smile.

"Obviously so, since my fella's in prison and I'm here cavorting with you." She shows Julian the short, pointed shiv clutched in her fist. "It's good you come when you did."

"Well, certainly for him."

They embrace a long time once they're inside the apartment, and the door is locked. Her small black head is under his chin. "We were waiting for you," she says, lifting her face to him. "Everybody wanted to thank you for Fulko. Mortimer even bought a pig in your honor. Why didn't you come? You always come back. No matter what I say to you, you always come back."

His palms around her face, Julian kisses her long and true. He kisses her until they're both out of breath.

"Could I have some wine, please?" she whispers hoarsely. "It was nice to sit out on the balcony like we did last night. Maybe we can do that again?"

They sit out on the balcony, their chairs touching. Miri tries to hold the glass with just one hand. Her other hand she leaves inside Julian's paw.

"How did they like your clothes?" he asks.

She chuckles. "Me own mum didn't recognize me. Barely glanced at me as I walked by. I said to her, Mum, how many children do you have? Then she wailed. That man bought you them beautiful clothes, she said. You can't go into Neal's Yard in those. They'll get ruined like everything's ruined."

Julian gazes at her as she talks.

"What was that you give the magistrate?" she asks.

"A gold coin."

"How much is it worth?"

"The last one went for a hundred pounds."

"A hundred pounds for one little coin?" She is stunned.

"It's half an ounce of pure gold."

She whistles. "The magistrate better deliver Fulko to us in a chariot for that kind of money. You got any more of those coins?"

He smiles. "Who wants to know? Monk? Or you?"

"Is the answer different depending?" The quiet night is warm. Her expression is impenetrable. Julian has no idea what's inside her.

"Why did you tell me mum you was going to put her on a boat, too?" Miri says. "What is it with you, putting everyone on boats, shipping us off to America? Mum told everyone in Seven Dials. He's going to put me on a boat, first class. I told her you was just joking. Mortimer went mental. He said you wanted to take me away from them from the beginning."

"He's not wrong."

Miri points behind them into the luxury rooms and forward into the green square. "But why go anywhere? Look how nice it is here."

But where does it last? "It's nice in Maine," Julian says. "There's beauty there."

Miri waves her hand to London under the stars. "There's beauty here, too," she says. "I never seen it before. But I see it now."

They finish their wine.

And finally, timidly, not looking at him, stumbling over her words, Miri asks Julian if she can have a bath. She's never had one. Julian finds it hard to believe, but she says it's true. She's been washing her body at a sink or a bucket or a standpipe in the street.

"Not even when you were at the orphanage?" he asks, as they get up to go inside.

Miri rolls her eyes. "You *should* ship Mum off to Maine," she says, "so she stops blabbing with her big mouth."

While she mills about, Julian fills the tub. They wait for the coals underneath to get hot, for the water to heat up. Julian throws some water onto the coals. Hissing steam rises like fog, misting up the room. For extra warmth and a dazzling shimmer, he lights a dozen jar candles on the tables around the basin and the window sill.

He stands. She stands.

"It's ready for you," he says.

"Can you step out? So I can get undressed and get in?"

"Don't you need my help with the hooks in the back of the skirt?"

Miri lets him unhook her. "Why do women wear silly clothes that fasten in the back?" she asks.

"Perhaps so men can undress them," replies Julian, undoing her buttons, unlacing the lilac ribbons. Then he steps out. From the drawing room, he listens as she finishes taking off her clothes and lowers herself into the water. There is an audible inhale and after that, silence. Only her deep, contented breathing is heard through the apartment. While he waits, he draws the drapes on the open balcony doors.

"Julian."

"Yes, Miri?"

"*Will you walk in, my lord,*" Miri says, quoting Cressida.

He walks in. She shimmers in the candlelight, covered up to the neck with water and soap bubbles.

"Can you wash my hair?" she asks, her voice foaming wet. "But I don't want to be touched."

"I have to touch you to wash your hair."

"You know what I mean." Her face is flushed pink.

"Okay, Miri. Just your hair."

Julian takes off his waistcoat, his white shirt with the big puffy sleeves, his shoes, his hose, his crystal necklace. Shirtless he sits on a low stool behind her, wearing only his breeches. He is bubbling and foaming, too, and he's not even in the water.

"The water's hot," she says.

"Is it *too* hot?"

"I didn't say that." Her voice is barely above a whisper, her head tilted against the porcelain.

"Sit up, Miri."

She sits up, her wet bare back to him. He lathers her head. His two gnarly, fighting, yearning, rough hands knead and caress her scalp with rhythmic fingers, with slow open circles of love and desire.

She grips the edges of the tub.

"It is nice?" Julian's voice is low.

"It's nice," she says. "My hair must be clean by now."

"It's important to be thorough. Okay, now dunk and rinse."

He waits, watching the outlines of her bare body gleam under the opaque surface.

"Now what?" she says, rinsed off, her hair slicked back, settling against the porcelain.

"If you lean forward, I can scrub your back."

"How dirty is my back," she murmurs. But she leans forward. "I still don't want to be touched." She barely whispers it.

"Okay," Julian says, lathering his hands. "I'll wash your back without touching you." In measured rings, his soapy palms and thumbs caress her from her neck to the small of her back. Rhythm is the basis of speech, of rhetoric, of logic. Rhythm is the underpinning of melody, and melody is infused with harmony, and harmony is love. That's where music comes from. Two voices, two souls, two hearts in synchrony, in union, as one.

And something else, too.

Rhythm is the footing of the act of love.

Julian wants to tell her this.

Julian wants to show her this.

Miri speaks first. "I like this bath thing." The exhale that leaves her throat sounds almost like a moan. He leaves his palms flat against her bare back, his thumbs circling her. "It's soothing."

Julian moves the bench to the side of the tub.

"What are you doing?" she asks.

"Let me wash your arms and hands."

Leaning back, she lifts her right arm out of the water. This time she doesn't say she doesn't want to be touched. She doesn't say anything.

He soaps her, caressing her from the shoulder to the fingertips and back again. His slippery hand intertwines with hers in the warm suds.

"You might want to turn to me," he says. "So I could wash your other arm."

His bare chest is above the porcelain rim. She turns her face and gazes at him, her brown eyes replaced by dilated black pupils. "Do you like the fighting?" she asks, reaching out and stroking his bicep.

"I do," he confesses. "Rather, I used to quite like it. Once upon a time, it's all there was."

"So tell me something..." she whispers. "How can your fighting hands be so rough and do what you did to that man, yet touch me so tender?"

"You know how, Miri," Julian replies. *"Because love turns men into weaklings."*

"I understand *nothing*," she says, arching her back, lifting her breasts out of the water.

"Yes," he says, "because mystery is incomplete knowledge. He cups her wet breasts, fondles them with his unsteady hands.

"I have a feeling," she says, moaning, holding on to the bathtub, "that even if I had knowledge, some things would remain a mystery."

He leans in. She is wet, her lips are wet.

*"Will you walk in, my lord?"*

Groaning, he kisses her. His soapy palms rub rings against her dark nipples until she can't take it and he can't take it.

"Can you touch me," Miri whispers, her head tipping back, grabbing the edge of the tub. She opens her legs slightly. *"Touch me with your fighting hands...but soft, Julian, okay, be gentle, please...be kind."*

He slips his hand between her legs. "Like this?" he whispers, caressing her.

Miri doesn't speak at first. *Yes, like that.*

His left arm goes around her to keep her from sinking under. "Like this, Miri?"

*Yes.* She is shuddering.

"Do you like that?" Julian whispers.

She cannot speak. Leaning over her, he kisses her open moaning mouth like it's the last hour before Revelation. His fingers continue to bring paradise to her body.

A sleepless night of rapture follows for Miri and Julian, the windows open, the curtains blowing, full of sounds of sleeping London and awake lovers.

Finally, oh God, finally, Julian drinks from the rivers of Babylon and the delta of the gods. Finally her small hips are in his grasping hands and she bears his weight above her. Finally they beat to the rhythm of common time. No patch of damp, starved for affection Miri remains unravished by Julian's burning lips.

My love, I found you again, he whispers. And this time I have truly earned you.

Come, Julian, come closer, my gentle fighting knight, don't be afraid, I won't break, do unto me as you wish, O God, walk in, walk in. She was a lump of ice but the sun had heard her prayer and began to shine. Now she has melted away. The woman she is for the outside world is not the woman in bed with him. There is no protective shell around her anymore. Only Julian is around her.

My desire is boundless, he whispers into her overcome mouth, overcome himself, my act is limitless, my will infinite, my love unconfined.

You were right, my lord, she whispers, stretched out on the rack of his bed. Your desire for me was not all innocent. But it was holy.

And he has his own whispers as he cocoons her in his arms. Do you remember me, Miri?

She's been devoured, emptied, filled, comforted. Am I supposed to? And what do you mean, you found me *again*?

Is there a trace of anything old you feel for me?

No, my angel. You are altogether marvelous and new. Her sleepy hands caress him. What are these tattooed names, these dots on your arm? In the moonlight, she lifts his left arm, studies the inside of it. They're not birthmarks. Are they deliberate? Who is Mary, who is Mallory, who is Mia? Why is her name the smallest of the three? Did you like her the least?

I knew her the least, he says, pulling his arm away, hiding it behind his back like sin. Could you have opened your mouth and said my name, Julian asks, when you first met me?

When I first met you, Miri says, you were odd and worrying. You wore a stretched suit and said things that made no sense. You still do that. You looked at me strangely, too deeply. You stared at me with pain in your eyes. You do see how that can unsettle any girl, not just me, how that can make any girl uneasy? You looked at me like I broke your heart, yet I didn't know you at all.

In bed she gazes at him, waiting for him to say she is wrong, and he offers her nothing except his overflowing face.

See, you're still looking at me that way.

He blinks her ghost away from his eyes. Why did you ask Monk to send in the clowns to foist me?

Because I was afraid of you.

Why?

Because *this* is what I feared, Miri says. I was afraid of my dishonor. I didn't need more trouble in my life. I'm already tangled up to my throat.

Julian lies holding her soft small body in his hands.

Do you think I have flagrantly flung myself at you?

Um, no, Miri, I would not say that is what you did.

I tried to be circumspect.

You succeeded admirably.

I suppose there's no harm in telling you the truth *now*, Miri whispers. Don't judge me, promise? The first day we met, I sneaked away to change because I didn't want you to see me the way I was, so grubby. I wanted you to see me with a clean face, in a skirt and blouse. Even though I was wary and full of misgivings, I still wanted to look my best for you. I suppose what I mean to say is that I wanted to look worthy of the way you looked at me.

My eyes look on you, Miri, Julian says, but it's my heart that sees you.

They kiss, pressed breast to breast.

I couldn't stay away, Miri says. Do you know when I knew it was hopeless to resist? At the Lamb and Flag.

Julian allows himself a small smile. Sometimes when we seek to conquer love, we must use all our weapons.

When you let yourself be provoked by Monk into an illegal brawl to get back at me, she continues. You stood there mad because I tried to rob you, challenging me, shirtless in your velvet breeches, perspiring, panting, all brawn and grit, your blood and the other bloke's blood spilled over your face and chest, and I knew then that you were...what's the word I'm looking for?

Irresistible?

Mine, Miri whispers, her hands enfolding him in the blue dark. Did you love me the first moment you saw me?

I loved you way before then, says Julian.

In a box of bliss with her, he almost forgets the scourge outside.

He decorates the room where they lie together with bouquets of asphodels he buys in Covent Garden.

Asphodels, the immortal flowers grown in Elysian Fields, in the Isles of the Blessed.

Branched asphodels.

Summer asphodels.

White or rimmed lichen asphodels.

Wild onion, too.

Poison to sheep.

Fatal to mice.

Heal sickness in pigs.

Asphodels bloom after winter rains, on dry grasslands and rocky sands.

Bog asphodel, the wedding flower he left planted in the earth in distant Clerkenwell.

Asphodel, the forever flower.

Like onionweed they grow.

*Will you walk in, my lord, walk in.*

∞

*Dot 29, 31, 39...*

Day for night returns to Julian's life.

Because almost every night, no matter how inflamed the love in their white bed, no matter how many times Miri pleads for Prospero to wield his magical staff, in the end, she changes into her old clothes and says dejectedly, "I must go back." She doesn't want Mortimer or Monk to grow suspicious and wicked in the brief weeks left before Fulko sails for the new world and Miri and Julian can live as they wish.

They walk arm in arm through nighttime London, disengaging only when they reach the end of Piccadilly. Sometimes when it rains they flag down a carriage and let the horses pull them down the cobblestones, while inside the cab Julian kisses her hands and begs her not to leave him.

*Dot 40.*

Every night when they return to the rookery, they're welcomed like Odysseus and Penelope, with drums and meat. There's always a resplendent feast on the rotted table, plenty of ale and gin in the mugs, and dancing revelry until dawn.

The charade in front of Miri's three "children"—Jasper, Mortimer, and Monk—entails elaborate schemes and lies and sleights of dress and separate entries into St. Giles. She quits her job as a pure finder, stops selling the *Chronicle* and the *Gazette*, so she and Julian can spend their days together, pretending day is night. If her boys looked closer, they'd be able to tell their Miri is not the same girl. A hum doesn't leave her throat. She skips when she walks through St. Giles.

Miri *skips* when she walks through St. Giles.

Perhaps Mortimer can tell the difference. The more cheerful she becomes, the grimmer he grows. A silent giant with a titanic envy, Mortimer sits in the corner of the dining hall in the cellar and like a black crow watches her dancing on the tables and telling jokes in her clean lace dresses.

Julian and Miri are careful not to touch while they're in St. Giles, but they don't glance behind them as they embrace on the steps of the church of St. Martin-in-the-Fields, ambling to Charing Cross on their way to their rooms, twirling their umbrellas, chatting about Brighton and Torquay, where they might go, where they might live.

She wants to learn to waltz like a lady, she wants to take piano lessons. She wants to learn how to act.

She crawls to him in their bed—when morning is sunset and afternoon is dusk—to sleep as one. She's so hot when she sleeps, like she's *burning*, and this torments Julian and makes him sleepless. He tries to unravel himself from her, to creep away, but in her dreams she finds him and cocoons him inside her hot limbs. Julian lies awake as if he's in a never-ending great fire.

He lavishes her with gifts: candy from confectioners' shops, drinking chocolate, his own body. He takes her for strolls near

Westminster, where the river is not overrun with criminal gangs, he buys her a folio of *A Midsummer Night's Dream*, so they can run lines together, and she can pretend to be a star. *O, I am out of breath in this fond chase! The more my prayer, the lesser is my grace.* She jumps up on the table in the drawing room to recite her monologues. Laughing, Miri stands naked in the candlelight to illumine herself, a beacon to the meridian line between what is and what might never be.

Sometimes in bed Miri weeps into his chest.

Tangled, they lie in abandon. Where did you come from? she murmurs.

I crawled down a canyon wall for you, swam miles under the earth for you.

You make it sound almost romantic. Where are you really from, my lord?

The caves. The tunnels.

Like where Cleon goes?

Something like that.

*Like where Cleon goes.*

Julian sits upright. Cleon!

Miri has given him an idea.

Hurry, he says to her, get dressed, let's go talk to Cleon.

*Dot 43.*

In the maze of St. Giles, in his room, Cleon eyes them both with hostility.

"What are you asking me? Have I seen *what* in the tunnels? A way out? You go out the way you come in, mate. But in reverse. Is that what yer asking?"

Julian wishes he had another headlamp to trade. He wants something else from the surly man. Something mystical. "Have you ever seen anything, anything at all," Julian asks, "in the miles of underground you've scoured for seventy years, that made you doubt your reality? Have you ever seen something you could point to and say, this is not the usual thing I find?"

"Like me?" pipes in the newly sunny Miri. Julian kisses her hand, his focus trained on the sewer hunter.

Cleon won't bite. But his eyes deepen. He steps away from Julian. "What are you looking for?"

Julian mines the man's leathery face. "The mystery of the seven stars?" he says. "A lake where Satan and martyrs swim? Maybe a golden seal that opens at dawn, where blessed and cursed creatures dwell under the earth? Mountains? A mighty wind? A meandering river? A spot where men die in the black waters of a wormwood pool? Or perhaps, just the opposite. A place where men—and women—leap over the bitter waters and live."

Both Miri and Cleon gape at Julian, troubled and darkened.

Undeterred, Julian waits.

"There's a foot tunnel under the Thames," Cleon says at last, "that connects Greenwich with the Isle of Dogs. It was started to be built and then abandoned. It's nearly impossible to find. It appears only at certain times of the year, during the newest moon and the lowest tide. Blink and you will miss it."

Julian can barely breathe. He knows there's something there in the shape of things Cleon is telling him. He feels it. The Isle of Dogs is directly across the river from Greenwich. The Isle of Dogs lies on the Prime Meridian. A coincidence? No such thing.

"You go every night under the city of souls for seventy years, you see some things," Cleon says. "You see some things you don't want to see."

Standing close to Julian, Miri nudges him. I told you, she whispers.

Julian holds her hand. "What did you see, Cleon? What happened in that foot tunnel?"

"A man got swallowed up into the blackness," Cleon says. "He went looking for trouble. Like you want to. And he found it. One minute he was there. The next he wasn't."

"Did he ever come back?"

"I never seen him again."

"When was that?"

"In 1710."

Julian tries to stay calm. "What time of year was it?"

"I don't know! There are no seasons in the tunnels."

"Come on, Cleon."

"September." Cleon speaks with reluctance.

"Like the September equinox maybe?"

"I don't know what that is. What difference does it make?"

"Who was the man?"

Cleon doesn't want to tell him. "It was me dad, if you really must know."

Julian stares at the motionless sewer hunter. "Where's your mother?"

"Died in 1700."

Julian exhales. "Your father searched for your mother for ten years, and then *vanished*?" Julian lets Miri yank on him. She doesn't like this. She wants to go.

"He was deranged," Cleon said. "He was made mad by grief. People like that do all sorts of things normal people don't do."

"Oh my God, Cleon," Julian says, "is *that* why you've been underground for seven decades? Have you been trying to find your father?"

"I'm a sewer hunter." Cleon is grim. "It's me job. It's what me father did before me. It's what I do."

"Can you show us the foot tunnel?"

"Who is *us*?" Miri cries. "Not me."

"Never!" Cleon says. He shoves Julian toward the door. "Get out. You want to go there, you go on yer own. I won't take you."

"We can't find it on our own, Cleon. Show us where it is—please."

"Who's this *we*, Julian? I don't go down there," Miri says. "I *won't* go down there. I heard a story that in the sewers, a pregnant sow gave birth to a litter of pups who multiplied like roaches and now feed on offal and whatever still walks below."

"That's nothing but an old wives' tale, you silly creature," Cleon says, banging his long pole on the ground. "But woe to them that fall into the bottomless pit of serpents. Only sorcery opens it." He glares at Julian with fear and hatred. "Don't tell me it's true what they're all whispering about you. That you're a left-handed warlock." The old man shakes his head. "Leave me alone, and get out of here. What are you fooling with this stuff for? You don't need it. She is here with you. There's nothing but battle and torment on that footpath you're trying to find." He slams the door and locks it behind them.

∞

Julian is flattened by his failure with Cleon. It doesn't help that July is months from September. By the time he will need the foot tunnel, it will either be unnecessary or too late. And Miri is a sentient human being. She has her own will. She can't be put in a burlap sack like a minted sovereign and hidden behind a brick in the wall. She can't be knocked out and carried over his shoulder to the Isle of Dogs. She has followed his slow seduction this far, into his bed, onto his body. Why isn't that enough?

The tiny gargantuan marks on his arm tell Julian why.

*Dot 44.*

*Dot 45.*

Misunderstanding his wordless anxiety, Miri eats pudding and pleads with him. It's another few days until Fulko is gone to America and our worries are over. I know you don't want to hide. I know you want more. You will have it. Why the tunnels, convict ships, marriage to someone else? Why are your measures to win my heart so drastic? You've won it. Rejoice.

In new dresses, with ribbons in her hair and perfume that smells like hyacinth, Miri has been transformed into a gleaming philosophical woman. There are no more shivs, no more fleecings. She doesn't need a convict ship or a first-class passage to a mythical place called Maine or a September sewer passage to the infinite meridian, into a breach wide enough for them both. She needs a few precious days of status quo. Fulko will soon return to St. Giles. There will be a church service to bless his journey. There will be a banquet in his honor. His mother Repentance will receive an extra donation because she'll be losing a son. They will bid him farewell, and Fulko will be off to the seas. And Miri and Julian will be free.

∞

From the pocket of his breeches, Julian pulls out two gold bands. Look what I made for us, he whispers, on his knees by the bed, holding the rings in the palm of his hand. I took my last sovereign to the goldsmiths on Cheapside. I had it melted down and cast into two rings. As soon as Fulko leaves, I want us to be married. Will you marry me, Miri?

Tears trickle down her face. What a waste of a precious sovereign, she says. She slips the smaller band on her finger. How did you know what size to make for me?

I have watched your hands for so long, he says, I've cast it from memory.

They wear the rings in bed, raising their arms above their heads to the skies, staring at the gold, dimly sparkling in the sapphire night. Julian must gird himself to look past the rows of black *dots* lining the inside of his arm.

I want to believe you so much, Julian, Miri says. But what about your fears for me? You keep telling me I'm in terrible danger.

I've stopped telling you that, haven't I. His voice is a whisper.

Will marriage or Maine make me safe?

Julian doesn't reply.

Miri lowers her arm. He lowers his. The rings come off. He drops them into his pocket, touches the crystal at his heart, and lies down next to her in heavy silence.

Tell me the truth—do you still feel that I'm not safe?

Not when we're here, he replies. But when you leave these rooms? Yes.

Do you know what me mum tells me every night when I come back to St. Giles? Miri says. She tells me to forget her and follow you. Even to the tunnels under the Isle of Dogs, Mum? I ask. Even there, she says. She has no future, she says, but I still have mine.

In their white and blue room, Julian's silence is a tomb.

Do I, Julian? Miri whispers. *Do* I have a future?

Julian can't answer her in Grosvenor Square where everything smells like lilac and lavender, where the honking boats on the distant Thames and the clops of the blacks and bays on the London streets lay a soundtrack to their fleeting lifelong love affair.

# 23

# Bowl of St. Giles

SOMETIMES THE WORLD SHINES AT DAWN, LEAFY TREES against the shimmering river, the light of azure rising with pink and gold. The water is a gleaming mirror, there's no wind, there is no sound. St. Paul's, the Savoy Palace, Blackfriars, St. Magnus are all reflected in the Thames. The sky is a painting. The world is a painting. There's an unruffled promise of another day.

And sometimes, there isn't.

As Julian and Miri approach Seven Dials, they're animated and brisk, debating whether to pay a visit to Pastor Wyatt to ask about the exact date of Fulko's impending furlough. At Monmouth Street and Hog Lane, Julian squints at a figure of a corpulent woman, hobbling on the stones, weakly waving a walking stick. Look, Julian says. That almost looks like your mother.

Miri laughs. Agatha has not walked outside Seven Dials in five years.

It *is* Agatha. "Miri, Miri!" she cries. There's commotion behind her.

"What is it, Mum?" They run up. "What are you doing out? Julian, see if you can find her a stool, she's going to fall."

"No! *Run*." Agatha clutches her daughter. "They're coming for you."

Growing cold, Julian looks around the street. A bizarre energy slices the air, molecules of venom swirling.

"Fulko's been hanged!" Agatha hisses, wheezing.

"What? That's impossible!" cries Miri.

"And Monk's out for your blood. Run, Miri!"

Julian doesn't listen any further. He pulls Miri as fast as he can down Hog Lane.

But it's too late. Hell has been emptied out. Its minions are in the streets.

A dozen boys from the hood surround them, thieves and vagrants, blackbirds, Gaelic drunks. They've all obviously been promised a dram of rum to stop Miri and Julian from getting away. Another dozen men rush forward from Earl Street, Mortimer out front.

"Where was you, Miri?" Mortimer asks in a lethal timbre, his limbs twitching. "Yesterday, you didn't show up all day. Maybe if you was here, you'd know yer groom drank a bowl of ale in St. Giles on his way to Tyburn for his execution."

"Mort, there has to be some mistake! It can't be."

The hoodlums keep trying to grab Julian's hands. He elbows one guy in the face, strikes another.

"And you should've thought twice before you took another man's wife," Mortimer says to Julian. "Now you will pay."

"She's not his wife," Julian says. The thugs keep trying to restrain him and he keeps jabbing them to hurt them. The street grows crowded with screamers and thieves.

"Tell that to the judge," Mortimer says. "And to Monk, whose brother is dead."

A human chain of hooligans shouts from Monmouth Street all the way to Neal's Yard where Monk is. "We got 'em, Monk! They're here, they're here."

"Mort, what happened?" Miri asks, amid the angry ruckus.

"Monk went to Pastor Wyatt to ask about Fulko," Mortimer tells her, towering above all, eyes darting up and down the street. "We hadn't heard a thing about his release, so the pastor went to inquire at the Old Bailey. He couldn't find a Colin Ford, the man you claimed you spoke to. Then he learned that Colin Ford retired a fortnight ago."

"Retired?"

"Yes. Without leaving behind any paperwork for a commutation for Fulko like you promised. As Fulko was sentenced, so he was hanged, yesterday, precisely at noon. And you would've known that, Miri, had you been here, and not with *him*." Mortimer spits in Julian's direction.

Miri is in shock. She's also anxious for her mother. Propped against a building, Agatha is being held back by two of her friends from the neighborhood.

"Leave my mum alone!" Miri yells.

"Leave my daughter alone!" Agatha yells from the other side of the street.

Accompanied by Pastor Wyatt, Monk appears on Earl Street, running to where Julian and Miri stand lassoed. There's frenzy in the air. Next to the priest are four constables. That Monk doesn't care he's in such proximity to the authorities from whom he's been on the lam his entire life speaks to his turmoil. He is also stuporously drunk, as is Jasper.

"Here they are, pastor!" Mortimer says, grabbing Miri, whom he is supposed to love, by the collar. Before Julian can intercede, little Miri rips away and kicks Mortimer hard in the knee with the stacked heel of her shoe. Howling in pain, a hobbled Mortimer drops to the ground.

Miri is crying. She tries and fails to break through the mob, to make her way to Monk and Jasper, who are tottering from the gin. Julian remains shoulder to shoulder by Miri's side, shielding her body from grasping hands. "Monk," Miri cries, "I'm so sorry! We give that man money. I promise you, we give that man money for Fulko."

Monk wails, unable to form coherent words.

Back on his feet, Mortimer limps toward Miri. "You say you give him money," he says. "All we have is your word. You gave Fulko your word, too."

"Don't speak to me, traitor," Miri says to Mortimer.

"You told us you pled the belly," Mortimer says. "Is the belly because of *him*?" He stabs at Julian with his finger. "Did you go begging for Fulko's life full of another man's seed?"

"No! It was just a lie to help Fulko!" Miri stretches out her hand to her drunk friend. "Monk, please believe me!"

"Coining is a crime punishable by death," one of the constables says to Miri. "Mortimer showed us some of the fake silver you been making. Is that what you give the magistrate? No wonder he didn't help you."

"Them aren't mine! Mortimer, what have you done?"

Mortimer averts his gaze. While Julian and Miri were welded together, Fulko was hanged. In Mortimer's eyes, that justifies everything he says and does.

Miri grabs desperately at Julian. *Is this it?* she whispers. *Is this what you saw for me?*

"I thought you was on our side, Miri." Monk slurs his words, as if he can't quite get them past his throat.

"Monk, what are you talking about? Colin Ford deceived us!"

"Who is Colin Ford to me? But you owe me," Monk says. "You owed me brother, and you betrayed him."

"Betrayed us all," Mortimer adds.

"Shut the fuck up, Mort!" yells Miri. "I did everything I could, Monk! It wasn't my fault!"

"That man lured you away from us with his black magic," says Mortimer, pointing at Julian with hate in his eyes.

"You were right about him, Mort!" Monk sobs. "I should've listened."

"Monk, what are you talking about?" Miri cries. "You and I are family."

"No," Monk says. "Me brother was me family. Yer nothing to me now. You chose that man over us." Monk spits in Julian's direction. "You chose him over me brother." Monk's face is distorted by grief and spite. "Arrest them, constable! They killed me brother! They're coiners and thieves! They're witches and warlocks!"

Julian grabs Miri's hand. Mortimer throws himself across their path. Julian hits Mortimer, lays him out. Two other men grab Miri. In the melee, Julian and Miri are separated. She fights. He fights. No one can hold Julian, but very soon they hold Miri.

When he sees that she's in their clutches, Julian stops struggling. He and Miri are thrown to the ground, and their hands and feet are bound with rope. He tries to catch her eye, but her head is turned away. She is searching for her mother, yelling in the direction of Agatha's piercing sobs. "It's okay, Mum," she keeps calling out, "it's okay, Mum..."

In two prison transports, Julian and Miri are carted to Newgate. In the vibrating wagon, on the floor next to two other tied-up men, Julian hears the receding sound of the clopping horses pulling the second wagon, the Doppler effect of hope and love and all that's good in the world, carrying away the receding Miri.

∞

At Newgate, in a concrete cell, Julian has days to count and recount the *46 dots* on his arm.

On the morning of what would be *dot 49*, he is taken to the courtroom at the Old Bailey, where there's no barrister defending him. Julian stands in the dock, and one by one, the people he knew from the rookery step up into the witness box and describe in florid and unembellished detail the things Julian has told them. They tell the judge how he knew before anyone else about the defeat in Lexington and Concord. One by one, they accuse him of allegiance to the Rebels. They describe how he appeared on the scene out of nowhere, as if by magic, in a strange suit made of Lord knows what, and how he told them he was from the future and had invented a time machine. How he put magic potions on the legs of an invalid and healed her unhealable sores and told another woman to chew on magic grass and made her walk for the first time in years.

Miri is brought in.

He is a warlock, the witnesses declare, and she is a witch who consorts with warlocks. She has pled the belly to the magistrate. Her unborn child is the devil's spawn. Ten men come forward to say she robbed them and took their clothes. A constable says they found counterfeit coin on the cellar floor where Miri sleeps. Eleven men step up to claim Julian punched a man with his left hand with intent to kill him. That the man lived is dumb luck, but they accuse Julian of attempted murder.

The judge is the Honorable John Jenkins, the one Colin Ford promised he would speak to after snatching Julian's gold. "Either you're telling the truth," Jenkins says to Julian, "and are guilty of witchcraft, or you are lying to simple folk, using false words to threaten, cajole, confuse and endanger the decent people of this city. You live idly and assault the true and good subjects of the realm. You have no papers, which is also against the law. You cannot prove by any method who you are or where you're from. Have you anything to say in your defense?"

Julian has nothing to say in his defense. He says only one thing. "Punish me as you see fit, your honor. But the young woman by my side is innocent of any wrongdoing."

Miri speaks. The magistrate, Colin Ford, she says, took a gold sovereign from them, promising to commute Fulko Gib's sentence.

A gold sovereign? Where did this so-called sovereign come from, you?

Miri says nothing. All eyes turn to Julian.

"Speak up," the judge says to him. "Where would you or your consort get a sovereign coin from?"

Julian says nothing. He wants to tell them that he acquired the coin from Lord Fabian, Master of the Mint back in 1666, long deceased, but fears it won't serve his cause. He wishes he still had the fourth and last coin, to prove to them he is telling the truth, but he sold it to make the wedding rings for him and Miri.

"There are four things wrong with your malicious lie," Judge Jenkins tells Miri. "One, we've just established. You are not the kind of people to be in possession of a priceless coin. Two, the magistrate has taken his retirement, so he's not here to defend himself. Three, what you're accusing the honorable Colin Ford of is accepting bribery. It is a crime against the realm to offer a bribe to a high officer of the law and for him to accept one. And four, even if you did have such a coin, and Colin Ford were here to defend himself, and he did accept this bribe, the magistrate has no power of clemency."

"He took our money with the promise that you would help us, sire," Miri says. "He told us that *you* had such power."

Judge Jenkins stares at Miri for a long time.

He sentences them first to the pillory and then Julian to two years hard labor and Miri to two years in a workhouse. "You're both getting off lightly," Jenkins tells them. "Especially, you," he says to Julian, "for you have no defense for the crimes you've committed. By all rights, the girl should be hanged for coining and thievery, and you, sir, should be burned at the stake for witchcraft. Here's your clemency—you're escaping with your wretched lives. Be grateful."

In two separate wagons, Miri and Julian are pulled to Charing Cross, not far from the statue of the executed Charles I, to be set upon the pillory for public abuse and humiliation during the busiest hour of lunchtime. The pillory is part of the underbelly of the mercantile pageantry of London's shopping avenues. The pickpockets and petty criminals get pelted and harassed in full view of the people they have rolled.

Side by side, the shackled Julian and Miri stand on a round platform, surrounded by beggars and balladmongers, while the new magistrate named Brian Hanney—a young, stringy man with a promising career of apathy ahead of him—nasally drones out the proclamation of their guilt. Julian is condemned for inciting a riot by his loud anti-Royalist assertions. They're both guilty of perjury, slander, fraud, robbery, vagrancy, and bribery

of an appointed court official. The pelting is to begin in precisely
one minute, Brian Hanney announces, and to last precisely one
hour. Before Julian can utter a word of complaint, an excitable
youth lobs a soft tomato at the stage, which misses Julian and
hits the magistrate, squelching him in the neck.

Oh, it's not a youth. It's Jasper. He's armed with a basket of
rotting fruit. Monk stands next to him. Miri stares at Monk with
heartbreak and condemnation. Unable to bear her gaze, he hides
behind Jasper's back.

"I said in precisely one minute!" Brian Hanney yells, wiping
the red juice off his white collar. "Or you will be next, whoever
dares throw early!"

While the magistrate attempts to control the crowd, a
manacled Julian creeps toward Miri. He can't touch her arm or
take her hand. He does the only thing he can. He presses his
forehead against her head. "Listen to me," he says. "Look up,
look at me."

Her body trembling, she looks up.

"Don't be afraid, Miri," he says to her. "You're going to be
okay. I promise you. It's going to be all right. Don't be afraid."

They're dragged apart. Julian's head and hands are fitted
through holes in a wide wooden board nailed to a thick post.
The framework of the pillory looks a lot like the cross. It's hard
not to be afraid. All around them is the terrible sound of a mob
crazed by blood lust. Verbal assault is hurled at their heads. The
magistrate swings his arm to signal the start of the pelting and
quickly jumps off the stage.

Julian and Miri's bodies are exposed to the circling crowd,
from back to front. The drunks pummel them with apple cores,
tomatoes, potatoes, gin bottles, stones, old bones, pieces of wood.

Wait, gin bottles? Stones?

Most of it misses Julian. The tomatoes don't miss. Other
things don't miss. "Stop throwin'," someone yells. "Look, the
woman's hurt. Stop throwin'." Julian's legs go weak. *Miri.* His
hands prickle from anxiety. He feels woozy as if he's about to

pass out. He turns his head to look at her, to see if she's all right, but there's a wooden post between them, blocking his view. He can feel her fear, but he can't see her. The noise of the crowd is like machine-gun fire. No words of love can be heard above its din. *Miri?* Can you hear me? Julian barely hears his own voice. His body is in agony. His slack legs won't hold him. He's being held up only by his drooping head, by his flaccid arms through the holes.

She doesn't answer. *Miri!* he yells again or thinks he yells. The noise of the crowd dims. Through his faltering sight, Julian can see Monk and Jasper, the basket of tomatoes falling from their hands, tomatoes rolling like her red beret had once rolled. The men race to the magistrate, yelling, pulling on him, shouting, pointing.

Never mind, Julian hears someone say. Throw what you can at the bloke, quick, before they call it off early. They always call it off early when someone dies, it's so unfair.

A stone makes landing, the sharp end hitting the side of Julian's head. Blood drips onto the wooden platform.

Don't be afraid, Miri, Julian wants to say. You will live again.

# 24

# Quatrang

EVERYTHING I DO IS WRONG. WHAT I FEEL IS RIGHT IS WRONG. I fight, I don't fight, we hide, we walk in plain sight, I give away your money, I cover up your sins, I gamble with your life, I say the right things, keep bad words to myself, I give you myself, I help you find your best self.

And still it's wrong.

I'm sorry, Miri.

In the pillory pose, a convulsing Julian pitched forward. Ashton grabbed him, shock and incomprehension on his face. Julian was wearing breeches, hose, funny shoes. He had on a waistcoat, a puffy shirt. Julian stank and was stained with tomato juice. Behind them, Sweeney yelled for help. Ashton's bewildered expression told Julian that Ashton was seeing things that could not be attributed merely to Julian's psychosis.

"Jules, my God, you're bleeding." Ashton pressed the palm of his hand against Julian's head wound. The blood ran down Ashton's wrist, down Julian's face and neck.

I was stoned in the pillory, Julian said, in the middle of a medical emergency and unable to explain further. An ambulance took him to Queen Elizabeth. The bleeding was stopped, the head was stitched up, antibiotics were administered. X-rays showed multiple splinter-like fractures in his hands and feet. The doctors counted a half-dozen separate fractures in each foot, a half-dozen in each hand. Julian displayed marks of electrocution, the profuse violet flowers swelling like burns over his torso and arms and legs. The doctor asked where the injuries had come from this time. Ashton said *don't ask*, but Julian replied, "I was stoned in a pillory."

"I told you not to ask," Ashton said.

Julian turned his face away from his friend, and from the acid memory of being catapulted through her death.

Everything I do is wrong.

The doctor and Ashton continued discussing things. Julian implored Ashton to stop speaking. Leave it. You know there's nothing they can do.

Yes, they might think it's black magic, Ashton said.

No, they'll fire Sweeney and replace him with a real guard. They'll forbid me entry to the Transit Circle. I won't be able to go back.

Go back? Are you *insane*? Have you *seen* yourself? Of course you won't be able to go *back*.

Please, Ashton.

You mean, if I continue to speak to the doctor, you might stop doing the thing that's killing you?

Please, Ashton.

"If there's one word that describes you, it's *relentless*," Ashton said after the doctor left, without answers. "You wouldn't think it by looking at you. That's why your whole life, you've been underestimated. They laughed when you told them you'd be a boxer. They laughed until they watched you fight. When you went missing, they said you'd never be found. They said you were dead. Then they said you'd never come out of the coma. They said you'd never fully recover. Your brain would never function again like it used to. You wouldn't make any money working for yourself, being Mr. Know-it-All. They said you'd go broke. When you met her, they said you didn't love her. When she died, they said you'd get over it. And then *I* said, no how, no way did you travel through time." Ashton fell silent. "Honest to God, I don't know what's going on with you,

Julian." He stared out the window. "I don't know who you are anymore."

"Yes, you do."

"I really don't," Ashton said. "It's not like before, in the desert. That time you walked off and vanished when I wasn't looking. Yes, *something* happened, but I wasn't paying attention, and afterward, even you couldn't tell me what it was. This time, I didn't walk off. I was looking. You never left my side. You stepped over the railing and were maybe a foot away from me, but you never left my side or my sight. There was a flash of light, like a flare from a mirror pointing into the sun. I blinked."

"You didn't blink," Julian said. "You were blinded."

"I *blinked*," Ashton repeated. "And you pitched forward. That's all. Nothing else happened. A flare. And a pitch. I thought you tripped. I grabbed you."

"I wasn't in Thermoprene anymore."

"That's the least of it. Nor did you stink or have broken feet or bleed from a head wound, or wear breeches. Or carry gold rings in your pockets. Nor were you electrocuted. I know all this. Except I also know that you never left my sight."

"Except when you blinked."

"I fucking *blinked*! I didn't space out, or faint, or step away. I *blinked*. You do know the definition of the word blink, don't you?" Ashton said. "To quickly shut and open one's eyes."

"Who are you going to believe, me or your lying eyes?"

"One hundred percent my lying eyes."

"Time is relative, Ash," Julian said. "It's just coordinates. Like latitude and longitude. Time is just direction. And most of the time that direction is forward." He closed his eyes.

There was no denying it, no pretending anymore, no wishing it away: 49 days is what she had. What he had. What they had together.

Los Angeles, from their first word at Book Soup to Fario Rima on Normandie Avenue, 49 days.

Clerkenwell, from her first wail in the garden to Falk's hands around her throat, 49 days.

The Silver Cross, from the great bed to the Great Fire, 49 days.

St. Giles in the Fields, from Seven Dials to the stones at Charing Cross, 49 days.

It was the loudest, most implacable, merciless, pitiless truth of Julian's life. It was an unending scream—49 fucking fucking days.

Gravity bends to *my* will, not the other way around. But my will is not enough. I am a Möbius strip of light and shadow. I am nothing but a quantum particle entangled with your immortal soul and spiraling through infinite meridians toward you—and away from you. I am a devastated supplicant, begging, pleading for a redress to your blight, stretching out my hand to the window, the sun, the heavens. Oh, Miri. Our bodies are like mercury, like quicksilver. They're torn apart but not disintegrated. They wait for someone to come and collect the pieces, like you waited for me, and still I failed you. Sometimes poverty hides inside a goddess, and sometimes the goddess hides inside poverty. You were royalty walking through that rookery. I knew it, and still I lost you.

∞

After weeks of uneasy convalescence, they went to Quatrang, Julian limping on his healing feet. Ashton insisted. I want to hear what the little wise man has to say, Ashton said, his teeth snapped shut like a portcullis.

Devi's place was shut like a portcullis. The rolling steel shutter was padlocked into the hook in the concrete. Julian rapped his knuckles on the window of the Vietnamese joint next door.

"Sometimes he leave like that without notice," the harried owner said. "I think his mother die."

"That's not it, Shinko," the man's agitated wife said, stepping forward, dishrags in her hands. "He gone over a month."

"Over a *month*? How long have I been home?"

"It's May," Ashton said.

Julian reeled against the steel shutter. Time had ceased to exist as he had ceased to exist. *May?*

"He is"—the woman waved her rag through the air, still talking about Devi—"over in mountain, looking for his son."

"*What* mountain?" said Julian.

"*What* son?" said Ashton.

"I not know what mountain. He go look for him. Son missing."

"Also his mother die," said Shinko.

"How long does it take to bury mother! But to find son?" Wife of Shinko started yelling at Shinko in Vietnamese. They skulked off.

Julian stood dumbly. So did Ashton.

∞

Weeks later, Devi returned, late May, early June. The boys returned, too.

"You're back," Devi said to Julian. He looked a decade older.

"*You're* back," Julian said to Devi. He looked a decade older, too.

Ashton grabbed Devi by the arms.

Julian pulled Ashton off. *Dude, stop it, what's wrong with you?* Devi didn't even fight back.

"Leave him alone," Ashton said to Devi, ripping his arm away from Julian. He looked so angry. Julian wasn't used to it. "Why are you doing this to him? What voodoo wand are you waving over him?"

"Why does everyone blame poor voodoo for everything?" Devi muttered, unperturbed by the violence.

"You're going to kill him, don't you understand?"

"Like you, I keep telling him not to go."

"Bullshit. You're a devil worshipper," Ashton said. "You say white, but you mean black."

*Ash, come on, man,* Julian thought, but didn't say.

Devi straightened his shirt. "It's fine, Julian. Your friend is worried about you. I understand."

"You understand *nothing*. I looked up the meaning of *Quatrang*."

"It means *white crow*. Why is this upsetting?"

Again Julian had to come between his friend and his shaman, pushing Ashton to one corner, keeping a lackluster Devi away in the other.

"*White crow* means a rare thing," Devi said. "Something unique and unseen."

"*White crow* means a malevolent omen," Ashton said. "A sign of bad things to come. It also means a Trojan horse. Something that at first seems great but turns out to be a disaster. Which do you think is more applicable in Julian's case, your definition or mine?"

They both swirled to Julian for his opinion.

Julian said nothing. He turned to Devi. "Did you find your son? Shinko's wife said you were looking for him. What mountains?"

"My mother d-d-d-died," Devi stuttered, after a long pause. Even Ashton looked thrown by Devi's sudden speech impediment. "I brought her b-body back home to Vietnam to b-bury her. I s-s-s-stayed a few extra days." Devi dusted himself off, flattened his black shirt. When he spoke again, the stammer was gone, and he was back to his old self, even a little energized. He stared at Ashton coldly. "What do we think of a man who, instead of putting a roof over his house, yells at the wind and rain for making him wet?"

"You are most certainly *not* the wind and rain," Ashton said.

"First fight the wrong that's in *you*," Devi said. "Because it's impossible to change the weather."

Julian had to separate Ashton from Devi. "Ashton, stop it!" What was going on with these two!

Walking unafraid, Devi strode past Ashton to the back of the counter to grab his black apron. "What did Thomas Aquinas write?" the Hmong cook asked, tying the apron strings. "For those who believe in God, no explanation for miracles is necessary. For those who don't, no explanation is possible."

"Fuck you," Ashton said. "I believe in God. And miracles. It's you I don't believe in. And just to be clear—what you've brought him is not miracles but the fucking apocalypse."

# 25

# Karmadon

"DEVI, WHY DO YOU KEEP DOING THAT? DON'T PROVOKE HIM," Julian said to Devi a few days later, when he returned to Quatrang alone. "This is hard for him. He has no idea what's happening. His eyes showed him one thing, yet everything he thinks he knows keeps telling him another. Just imagine what that must be like. Have some compassion. Not just for me. For him, too."

"He is worse than doubting Thomas," Devi said. "Even when he sees with his own eyes, he refuses to believe."

"You're surprised by this? You yourself have no idea what's going on."

Devi drew the acupuncture needles on Julian's body along the lines of the meridian, fed Julian chicken marinated in garlic, lemon, and brown sugar, gave Julian tiger water and a little fermented sickly-sweet coconut milk to drink. "You and your friend should go take a walk," Devi said.

"Where to, or are you insulting me?"

"To Big Ben, the most famous mechanical clock ever built. Go there for an hour after a new moon and observe how many people gather around, holding talismans of the dead, trying to step through the swings of the 700-pound pendulum, between the tick and the tock. They're all trying to do what you have done."

"How is that going to help Ashton—to see other people's pain? He doesn't even want to see mine."

"Maybe it will help *you*," Devi said. "To stand witness to people who would take your 49 days in one chime of the clock over what they have now, which is *nothing*."

"They're deluded," Julian said grimly. "They don't know what they're asking for."

"So walk away, Julian," said Devi. "Walk away, do something else."

"I can't." Julian's body hung off his soul like an oversized coat. "You know I can't."

Devi told Julian about a woman who every year jumped into a vortex in a river. "Not the Thames. The River Vistula in Poland in a small town called Kazimierz Dolny. It's not even close to zero meridian." She jumped into the Vistula, Devi said, because she had heard from a mystic that by a river of life you could get back to the ones you loved.

"Like you're trying to get back to your son?"

"I wish to discuss it—not at all."

"You told me you *had* a son. Yet the woman next door said you were searching for a missing child. Is your son alive or not?"

"I don't want to talk about it."

"Is Ashton right about you? Do you want something from me?"

"Have I asked you for anything?" Devi said, after the most imperceptible of pauses. "Have I in any way reaped your formidable spiritual strength for myself?"

"What are you talking about, I'm not strong," Julian said. Everything I do is wrong. "I'm *nothing*."

Julian returned to Devi the following day, the following week, the following month.

"What if it's me?" he said to the shaman, lying on the table, riddled with needles. "What if I'm the reason she dies? She kisses me and dies. She touches me and dies. She joins the skillions of her other selves who laughed and loved me and then died with their unrealized dreams unspent in their pockets. What else can I do, Devi? What can I do that I haven't already done? Go but keep away from her? Stay away until I know she makes it without me over the 49 days, and then..."

"Are you at the bargaining stage, Julian? Are you negotiating with the Almighty?"

"Trying to haggle with somebody," Julian said. "What else can I do? *Not go?*" He said it in the smallest voice.

"Yes," Devi said, in his smallest voice. "But then for absolute certain nothing will change. It will be what it is. The next stage will be depression. And finally, acceptance."

Ignoring him, Julian plowed on. "How do you know she didn't live to a ripe old age without ever meeting me?"

"You're right, I *don't* know."

"How do you know *I'm* not the catalyst in her untimely death? That if she hadn't met me in Book Soup, she wouldn't still be singing, emceeing, dancing on boardwalks, living."

Neither one spoke.

"Where's your warrior spirit, Julian?" Devi said, quiet, quiet.

"Shackled to her in the pillory."

Julian would never accept her death, never.

Another month passed. Another moon rose. Julian returned to Quatrang. "Last night," he said to Devi, "I dreamed of her again." Shining and smiling and new, walking toward him in another life.

Devi extended his hand with the glass of tiger water.

∞

Barely healed, Julian redoubled his fight against the second law of the ordered universe, the law that governed matter: He struggled away from chaos and toward perfection.

He attempted to make himself a better man.

He'd been trying to reinvent *her*, redeem *her*, to perfect *her* soul, but what if what he needed to do was reinvent himself, to improve his own? She wasn't being granted a reprieve not because she wasn't worthy, but because *he* wasn't worthy. Aside from ceasing the casual sexual encounters and increasing his time at the gym, Julian started going to church. On Sundays, while Ashton slumbered, he rose at 7:30 and took a cab to Quatrang, and he and Devi walked together to St. Monica's in Hoxton Square for the 9:30 mass. In earnest he started reading theological writers: Aquinas, C.S. Lewis, Dostoyevsky, even Kierkegaard. He started reading the Bible.

"Jules, why are you reading the Bible?" Ashton asked. "Are you looking for a loophole?"

"Sidesplitting. The Comedy Cellar in Leicester Square has open mike night on Mondays. That's where you should be. You and Devi."

"Never lump me in with him. Or I'll stop joking entirely." Ashton always had a lot to say about what Devi had to say. Julian's friend and his shaman fought each other through Julian. "He thinks it's the *Almighty* you're bargaining with?" Ashton laughed. "He didn't say you were going *against* God, against God's will? Imagine that."

How Julian regretted being the conduit through which their sharpened spears passed.

"You think your shaman is an agent of *God*?" Ashton continued. "You're hilarious. *You* should be at the Comedy Cellar. Think again. Devi's name says it all. Devi, Devil. Leave the last L off for satanic ruses. I'd say by the results alone, I'm right. You were the one who summoned the dark force. He didn't come to you. You sought him out. And now you've waged your soul to the scatterer of lies. I don't know about this girl of yours, but I know about you. You're being damned and refuse to see it. Just think about it—who keeps sending you into hell? Who keeps shattering your body? Who are you in a vicious battle with for your own soul? Why the *hell* would you ever think it's God, Jules?"

∞

In July, Julian's father died.

Julian flew back home.

This is what civilized people did, even fake people. Returned for funerals.

He decided not to rent a car. Ashton was already in L.A., and he had rented a car for the two of them. Julian took a cab from LAX to West Hollywood. He wanted to walk around Sunset, see his old haunts.

Joanne Cruz, née Osment, his mother, passed him on Cahuenga.

She walked right by him.

She didn't recognize him.

He stopped, watched her walk by, debated what to do.

Mom? he said.

She startled, turned around.

Julian! She hurried back to him. Oh, son. She burst into tears. She embraced him.

His own mother.

I'm so sorry, my love, she said, your father died, my eyes are going bad.

But Julian knew the truth. *His own mother didn't recognize him.*

∞

In early August, his cell phone rang. It was a 718 area code. Julian knew only one person in that area code. Cautiously he answered.

"Let me do it," a grumbly female voice said. It was Ava McKenzie. "You're doing it all wrong."

He was doing it all wrong! It was the same voice that had been hounding him since his return. Now it was calling him long distance to torment him. "Who is this?" Julian said.

"Ava McKenzie, your almost mother-in-law," the voice replied. "Give me the crystal. Next time, *I* go, not you."

"Hello, Ava, how are you? Are you well?" Julian said, stunned and troubled. "Sorry, um, our connection is bad, I couldn't hear what you just said." His hands shaking, Julian dropped the phone, and hung up. How could Ava possibly know anything about anything?

When he asked Ashton about it, a casually shrugging Ashton couldn't explain it either.

Couldn't, or didn't want to?

Julian left it, but the unsettled feeling didn't leave him.

∞

On a Sunday morning in September, Riley, who was spending a long weekend with the boys, declared she was headed to church with Julian. Ashton laughed at them from the comfort of his warm bed.

After the service, Riley met Devi.

Polite as always, Devi shook Riley's hand. He tried to stay neutral while she charmed him. They chatted about the break in the rain and the pleasantly dry sidewalks. Devi recommended a park, perhaps St. James's (though Julian would've liked to go anywhere but there), and Riley nodded, saying that for some reason she craved a vanilla shake. "I usually stay away from sweets. I'm more of a bean sprout girl myself." The best shakes were on the other side of town, Mr. Useless-Know-it-All chimed in, in Clapham. Devi said there was no good reason to go all the way across the river for a vanilla shake. There were some adequate shake places near the Bethnal Green Sunday market, which also had some bean sprouts if Riley was interested. And because she was Riley, she said she wanted to go there immediately and asked Devi to join them. "I won't take no for an answer," Riley said, smiling down at him. She was five-eleven without heels and he was five-six in shoes.

Surprising everyone, maybe even himself, Devi thanked her with a bow and accepted! They walked a mile to the market, which sold its fruits and vegetables for £1 a bowl, and for two hours Julian doggedly traipsed behind, carrying Devi's mangoes and limes as Devi and Riley sauntered through the stalls, munching on grapes and discussing the health benefits of garlic and honey. Riley bought a vanilla shake, and so did Devi. When it was time to say goodbye, he kissed her hand, and she hugged him, his head fitting under her chin.

"I love him," Riley said, as she and Julian headed up Great Eastern Road to Old Street station. "And I think he loves me."

"Who doesn't?" Julian said. "And was that the goal? To get a lonely seventy-year-old man to fall in love with you?"

"He looks pretty good for seventy," said Riley.

"Calm yourself. It's B day. You don't cavort with seventy-year-old faith healers on B days."

*"Au contraire, mon ami,"* said Riley. "Clearly, I do."

At Paddington they switched to the Piccadilly Line and took a train to Green Park, slightly better than St. James's, fewer memories.

"Devi is *such* a nice man," Riley said, sitting close to Julian on the tube. "I don't know why Ashton doesn't like him. But he's sad, too. Devi, not Ashton."

"He just lost his mother."

Riley shook her head. "Sadder than that. Like permanently sad. You should talk to him."

"I never stop talking to him."

"Ugh, not about *you*, you self-involved lout. About *him*."

In Green Park, wandering, gazing at ducks, listening to mothers berating their children, Riley said she was thinking about the sermon that morning and about what the priest had said— *that her body was bought at a price.* "You know what I'd like to buy for myself, perhaps even with my body?" Riley said. "Freedom."

Freedom from what, Julian wanted to ask, from Ashton? Riley, her blonde head bobbing, her face altered by circumstance, continued without prodding. "For me, I want freedom from fear," she said. "For you, I want freedom from grief. You've been knocked down, Jules, and even with the help of your delightful shaman, you can't get up."

Because it's brand new, Julian wanted to say. Every year, the love is brand new. The death, too. But the truth was, Riley was right; he didn't know how he could continue to live like this.

"For both of us," Riley said, "I want freedom from those who enslave us. Freedom from pain. Freedom from joy, from desire, from hate. I want freedom from love," Riley said, her brown eyes with no tears left, staring straight ahead.

"Sounds like you want freedom from life," said Julian.

Riley, her beautiful face distorted, didn't reply.

∞

"Why do you keep looking at me?" Devi said a week after Riley had gone back home.

"I'm not allowed to look at you?"

"You're looking at me an unacceptable amount," the cook said. "Stop harassing me. Why can't you be like your friend's girlfriend?"

"She was nice, wasn't she?"

"You're foolish," Devi said. "She cares about fresh produce, that's what's important. She was elegant and circumspect. I liked that, too. She wasn't idly curious—like some people."

"I'm not idly curious," Julian said. "I'm purposefully curious. What mountain did you go to?"

"The Mountain of Purgatory."

"Seriously."

"I don't want to talk about it. You spend half of each year telling me to mind my business. Follow your own advice."

"Is Ashton right? Are you using me for some nefarious purpose?"

"Even a stopped clock is right twice a day," Devi said.

"Come on," Julian said. "I thought we were friends."

"We are not friends."

"We're not friends?"

Devi blinked. Julian seized his chance. "You told me you *had* a son. Why did Shinko's wife say your son was *missing*?"

"Are the dead not missing?" Devi said. "Is that what *you* of all people maintain? Done with your pho?" Devi yanked the bowl away even though Julian was still eating. "Time to go back to work, my friend."

"You just said we weren't friends."

Over the next few visits, Julian tried in other ways. "Would you like me to go to the Islington Farmers' Market for you on Sunday after church?"

"No."

Julian chewed his lip in thought. "Would you like me to go *with* you? I can help you carry the cabbage back. Cabbage is *so* heavy."

"You can come with me if you like, be Sisyphus if you like, but I still won't tell you."

The Islington Farmers' Market was enormous and crowded. They browsed through the produce stalls. "Did you go into the caves looking for your son?" Julian asked. "Like Cleon looks for his father in the tunnels?"

"I can't talk to you, I'm buying bok choy," Devi said. "But are you really comparing me to your sewer hunter?"

"Cleon told me there's a tunnel under the Thames, smack on the prime meridian, where his father vanished in 1710. Is he right?"

"Well, you met Cleon in 1775, and the foot tunnel from Greenwich to the Isle of Dogs wasn't built until 1902, so you tell me if he's right. Here, hold the bean sprouts. I'm going to buy some garlic."

Julian carried the sprouts and the bok choy. "He said it was begun and then abandoned."

"In other words, no foot tunnel? Take my garlic."

"His father found the passage on the *fall* equinox, not the spring one like me, is that possible?"

"*Definitely* not. Look what you're doing, you're dropping my garlic on the ground."

With their purchases they took a cab to Kingsland Road. Devi needed some fish sauce from a Vietnamese grocer. "I'm carrying three cabbage heads for you, five live lobsters, five pounds of shrimp, and half a pig," Julian said. "Why won't you tell me?"

"Because I don't want to," said Devi. "But I do need to sit for a bit. I'm not as young as I used to be."

"Who is?" said Julian, looking around for a place to rest.

Devi motioned him to St. Leonard's. They dipped through the gate into the oak-covered courtyard and found a secluded bench.

And there, Devi told him.

∞

Twenty young photographers went into the red cleft in a town called Karmadon in the Caucasus Mountains. The light wasn't good. They waited. But when the light still wasn't good by seven in the evening, they decided to wrap for the night. They were packing away their cameras and water bottles when a block of ice half a mile wide broke off the top of Khoka Mountain, more than two miles above their heads, twelve thousand feet above sea level. The frozen mass dropped from the sky, the ice careening down the steep mountain at more than sixty miles an hour, picking up rock and trees and carrying them down, too, into the cleft. In less than two minutes it had reached the bottom of the gorge. It buried two villages under hundreds of feet of ice and stone, buried one hundred and twenty-seven people, twenty of them still packing up their cameras and water bottles.

"One of those photographers was my son."

Julian bowed his head, his hands clenched around the plastic handles of the shopping bags between his feet. So Devi knew. Devi knew everything.

Devi closed his shop and traveled east. He didn't cook back then. He performed acupuncture and sold candles and incense.

The search party looked for three months. Devi stayed for two years. Only seventeen people would eventually be found. Devi's son was not one of them. Geologists called the Karmadon slide an extraordinary event of historical proportions. They said it would take twelve years for the ice in the canyon to melt. And maybe when the ice melted, they would find Devi's son.

So every few years Devi went back to Karmadon to see if the ice had melted.

Julian didn't want to ask.

No, Devi said. The ice has not melted.

When his son went missing, an intermittent stutter found him. The mud and stone slid down twelve thousand feet and crushed itself into the red cleft that was Devi's voice box. "The Karmadon tremor in my throat," Devi said, "is what's left of my son."

"How old was he?"

"Almost thirty. He was the son of a man who was the son of men who were catchers of tigers, but he didn't want to learn the ancient rites. When we came to London, all he wanted was to be a real boy. And for twenty years that's what he was. Twenty years mucking about in the red and white home colors of Arsenal, twenty years of mediocre grades and weekend-long pub crawls." Devi broke off to collect himself.

Julian stared at the shopping bags. "Is that why you became a shaman, to find him?"

"I tried." Devi folded his hands. "Unlike your Josephine, my son proved resistant to my efforts. His soul was new. There was nowhere for me to go."

"But you said you did try, though?"

"I did try," Devi repeated quietly.

Pensively, Julian half-turned to Devi. "So Ashton *was* right," he said. "From the start he suspected you wanted something from me."

The expression of lofty disdain returned to Devi's face. "If by right, you mean completely wrong, then yes."

"Are you trying to get me to do what you couldn't do?"

"And what would that be, Julian?"

"Is that why you got all excited when you learned that Josephine's soul was old?"

"What gave my excitement away, my indifferent attitude, my laconic nature?"

"Did you hope that one of her iterations would be during a time when I could send you a message?"

"Ah, see, messages are tricky things," Devi said. "Like premonitions of the future, messages obey laws of unintended consequences. They can be—and many times are—misinterpreted, often with catastrophic results. Partial knowledge isn't helpful. Don't open your mouth to argue. Has your partial knowledge helped you in the slightest? Precisely. My son had been traveling around the globe with his friends. They'd gone to New Zealand, Singapore, Japan, Nepal. The Caucasus was their last stop before home. He didn't listen to my advice. What can a father tell a son anyway, be careful, watch out, don't be reckless? I told him all those things. I saw danger everywhere. Not in ice slides, obviously. I didn't tell him to watch out for falling mountains. But everywhere else. And before he went traveling, he did go to a fortune-teller. Not to me or his grandmother but to a tarot card reader in Covent Garden, so, you know, completely foolproof. He asked her if his trip was going to be a success. He drew only one card—the Magician. That was enough for him. The Magician is the one who bridges the gap between the divine and the mundane, between heaven and earth. The woman told him his trip was going to be a transformative one."

"She wasn't wrong," Julian said quietly.

"Yet, *so* unhelpful."

Julian stayed with Devi the rest of that Sunday. After they returned to Quatrang, Devi showed Julian how to use a cleaver to shred cabbage. Julian was awkward and terrible. He nearly chopped off two of his fingers. "So I can be like you," Julian said, making a joke about it. "Everyone will think we're related."

The Vietnamese man dispassionately regarded the Norwegian-Mexican man. "Oh, yes," he said, "that's what they will think."

Devi taught Julian how to season the cabbage to make kimchi, how to roll the rice paper around the vegetables. They ate together, they drank together. Now it was deep Sunday night, and they were alone together.

"Are you an enchanter, Devi? Ashton thinks you're a sorcerer. If you are, you're not a very good one."

"Not a very good one what?"

"Either."

"I showed you a way in, that's all," Devi said. "The rest has been up to you. Maybe you're the sorcerer, did your friend think of that?"

"Could there be another way in?" Julian asked. "Or another way out—"

"No."

Julian became more alert. "No what?"

"Neither."

"Why are you being so short with me?"

"I'm always short with you. I must be careful of what I say. You tend to twist my words."

Julian sat up straighter on the stool. "Can I go in through the other equinox, in September?"

"*Definitely* not. Why would you want to?"

"I don't know. Maybe if I go in through the other equinox, I'll come out at a different point. Or there will be another way out. Maybe I can bring her back with me, hide her from death."

"God, Julian, what power do you think you've been given?"

"Um, the power to hide her from death?"

Devi looked despairing.

"Why do you keep returning to Karmadon, then?" Julian exclaimed.

"Not to *save* him, you fool. To *bury* him." Devi stared at his severed-by-frostbite fingers.

Julian was too agitated to be empathetic. "Be honest with me, did you disarm me with your mysticism so you could use my life in some way? Are you Prospero?"

Devi gazed upon Julian with exasperation, affection, wonder, exhaustion. "Have I been able to help you as you wish? Certainly your bad-tempered friend doesn't think so."

"Ashton is not bad-tempered. He is literally the most cheerful soul around. You bring out the worst in him. He thinks you're a wolf, and I'm the sheep. The sheep aren't told what their purpose is. They're led into the meadow, they're sheared, and then they are slaughtered."

Devi took hold of Julian's wrist, pressing hard on his pulsing radial artery to quiet him. "Calm down. If you're a sheep, then you're a sheep who has leapt where others could not leap. You're grasping at the wrong things. Believe me, if I had the power to bring about a storm to part the seas, as you suggest, I would've brought the storm to part the seas when you could've done me the most good. If I could've brought you to a time when you could warn me or give me a chance to save my son—which has been the strongest and most unfulfilled desire of my life—I would've done it. Your cranky friend once said something that stuck with me. He said he did not want what he didn't have. That's when I realized I was wrong about him. He's a better man than me, and he's a better man than you."

"I could've told you that."

"There is a lot you could've told me and didn't, and there is a lot you can't tell me because you don't know yourself." Devi pushed Julian off the stool and to the door. "The truth is hidden from you, Julian, like light from the blind and the insane. You can't imagine the scope of your ignorance, just as a blind man can't imagine darkness—until he can see." They were at the door. "Can't you *see* that you're being given a chance to make a tempest out of your love for her?" Devi said. "Drop by drop, your love has been falling upon her soul. One of these blessed days, maybe it will be enough."

"And maybe it won't," Julian said as he left Quatrang.

# 26

# Best Shakes in London

ALL SORTS OF THINGS HAPPENED IN LONDON ON SUNDAY afternoons around the solstices and equinoxes. It was a Sunday, third week in September, around the autumnal equinox. Lost in his own head, Julian was out by himself after mass, he didn't quite know where, maybe Sloane Square, the White Tower, or Mayfair. On one of the streets crowded with shops and early evening tourists, could've been Poultry or Jubilee, he was almost sure it wasn't Bloomsbury or Gloucester Road, he sighted the black curly-haired mane and the petite generous frame of a black woman who looked a surprising lot like Zakiyyah Job.

It was incongruous, like time travel.

Julian blinked, came to, looked around. Where the hell was he? Oh, yeah, on Bedford Road. In Clapham. Walking past the palm trees in the front garden of a yellow stucco pub called the Falcon. Down the block, by the clapboard façade of a burger and shake place called Red Dog South, that's where she stood, the waiting woman.

Julian ducked into the street garden at the Falcon and hid under a black umbrella between a palm tree and a picnic table. That couldn't be *Zakiyyah*! He was imagining things.

Chestnut trees grew wild on Clapham Common, Victorian mansions lined the streets. There was a Holy Trinity Georgian church and a Venn Street Food Market every weekend. Nearby was a place called *Rookery* Road. Caffè Nero on Clapham

High Street sported golden awnings and had floor-to-ceiling windows, and even tables outside. Perhaps that's why Julian was in Clapham. Examining Caffè Nero's awnings. Why else would he find himself here?

But at the moment, he was hiding outside the Falcon, studying a young black woman with a surplus of wild curls, standing half-perched against a short wooden fence. She was in profile to Julian, in phone pose, sipping a vanilla shake, occasionally raising her eyes to Red Dog's door. Red Dog was famous for its vanilla shakes. Many people traveled from miles around to buy one. Many said they were the best in London.

The door to the joint opened, and out walked Ashton, carrying a paper bag and another shake. He smiled at the woman. The woman beamed back. Ashton was unshaven and dressed super casual in jeans and a T-shirt. She was in a summer dress. He walked up to her, and she straightened out, lifting her head to him. He said something. She laughed. His arm slipped around the small of her back. He pulled her to him, her large breasts flattening against his chest. Her head tipped up, his head tipped sideways, he leaned in and kissed her.

Ashton didn't kiss the woman as if they had just met. The hand on her back, pressing her to him, her arms apart holding her drink, his mouth licking the vanilla from her lips, Ashton kissed her as if they had been together long enough for him to know how he felt, and how she felt.

Julian was not one hundred percent certain the black girl was Zakiyyah. But he was one hundred percent certain that the tall blond guy with the shake, gazing down on the beauty queen as if she hung the moon, was Ashton.

∞

Julian watched them run across the street and into the chestnut trees of the Common. He sank down at a picnic table under a palm and ordered a much-needed beer. After downing the pint, he pulled out his phone and called Zakiyyah. She picked up on the second ring.

"Julian?"

"Hey, Z."

Hey, Z? Pretty friendly for months between conversations.

There was silence, barely audible whispering. Sounded like *ask if everything's okay.*

"Uh, is everything okay?" she said.

"Yes, it's great. Just calling to say hi. Haven't spoken to you in a few months. How have you been?"

"I've been…well. Thank you for asking. How have *you* been?"

"I have also," Julian said, "been well."

"Really?"

"Yes. Why? What have you heard? Have you heard otherwise?"

"Um, no."

More whispers.

"Are you sure you're all right?"

"Oh, yes. Funny thing, though, you'll never guess who called me last week."

Silence on the other end.

"Mia's mother, Ava," Julian continued. "From Brooklyn. And she said some odd things to me. Quite peculiar."

"Well, she's an odd duck, Julian. I've been telling you this. I really want to hear all about it, but now, uh, is not a good time."

"No?"

There was a police siren on Clapham High Street, quick high-decibel blares rushing by. He waited for the cop car to pass before he spoke again.

"Where is that siren coming from?" Zakiyyah said.

"The London Metropolitan Police siren?" said Julian. "Probably on my end, Zakiyyah, no?"

"Yes. Um, our connection is excellent."

∞

Ashton didn't come home that Sunday night, and wasn't at work Monday.

Is that where he'd been vanishing all this time, to Clapham with *Zakiyyah*? Julian couldn't process it, couldn't believe it. After work he went to the gym, sparred with three different partners, killed the speed bag, slaughtered the punching bag, came home late and exhausted, waited up for as long as he could, and then fell asleep on the couch.

He was stiff when Ashton finally came home after two in the morning, looking disheveled and not sober. His tie was askew, his shirt unbuttoned.

"As they say, you're in your cups, Ash."

"Who says this?" He threw off his black leather jacket, his shoes, threw down his keys and wallet and fell onto the couch across from Julian. "What are you doing up?"

"I wasn't up," Julian said. "I was sleeping. Until you woke me."

Ashton closed his eyes. "I had too much to drink," he said. "And if I say this, then believe me, it was too much."

"Where've you been?"

"Bankside with Nigel. They have some late-closing pubs there. I can't keep up with him. Man, can that guy put it away."

Julian went into the kitchen to get a drink of water. Tripping over his feet, Ashton followed. Standing over the island, they didn't speak until Julian said, "You'll never guess who I saw yesterday at Red Dog."

Ashton palmed his water. "Go to bed, Jules." He didn't look up. "I told you, one crisis at a time. You got plenty of your own shit to worry about."

"You're not going to ask me who I saw?"

"Why?" Ashton said. "You know I know."

Julian stood quietly. The apartment was dark. Only the light above the stove was on, that, and the faint cold glow from the streetlight.

"What the hell were you doing in Clapham?" Ashton said. "Who goes there?"

"Me. I go everywhere."

"Clapham?"

"*You* went to Clapham."

"To hide from you!"

"You told me you don't do south of the river."

"It was to hide from you!"

They fell silent.

"How long has it been going on?" Julian asked.

"What, Clapham?"

"No, Ashton. Not Clapham. The whole damn thing."

Ashton was quiet. "A long time. Since before I left L.A."

A stunned exhale escaped Julian. "You hid this from me for *four* years?"

"With remarkably little effort. Like hid in plain sight."

"Why didn't you just tell me?"

"Didn't want to put you in an awkward spot, my man," Ashton said. "I know how close you are with Riley. Plus I was a little afraid you'd slip, frankly. Sorry, dude. I didn't mean to go behind your back."

"*My* back?"

"See, that's another reason I didn't tell you. You can be such a judgmental bastard."

Julian didn't know what to say. Sometimes your friends fucked up. It wasn't your job to condemn or forgive them. Your job was to catch them when they fell. It was your only job.

"Is that why you moved to London? You told everybody it was to help me. But was it to hide your own hot mess?"

"First of all, after watching you suffer smoke inhalation from the Great Fire and get stitches in your head from being stoned in the pillory, I fear you may be beyond help." Bleary-eyed but intense, Ashton stared at Julian. "And second of all, it's not my hot mess. But third of all, even if it was, so what? Your own hot mess has followed *you* to London. Why can't I be just like you, walk like you, talk like you?" Ashton smiled, wobbling slightly.

Julian took a breath. "How are you juggling this?"

"You know how. Riley comes once a month. We have a great time. Z comes once a month. We have a great time. If it's one thing I know and can do is show my girls a great time. Every two months I fly back home. A few days with Riley, a few days with Z. Everybody's happy."

"Are they?"

"Yes." Ashton smiled. "And I'm happy. And now that you know, it'll be easier. Certainly cheaper. The fucking Windmill in Clapham is costing me nearly seven hundred quid a weekend."

"Easier? Me lying to Riley when she comes here—*next* week—will be easier?"

"Not lying. Saying nothing. You're good at that," Ashton said. "You've been saying nothing most of your adult life."

Julian said nothing.

"Why did you blab about my shit to Zakiyyah?" Julian asked. "She went and told Ava. Who now wants to come to London, God help me, to fix things. Why did you do it?"

"Why?" Ashton said. "Because what's going on with you is so unprecedented, so unbelievable, so upsetting, so extraordinary that it demands to be gnawed over. How do you think I could've kept it to myself?"

"I don't know, Ashton, the way I keep things to *my*self. I swear to God, if that woman sets one foot in London..."

"What are you gonna do, tough guy, hm?" Ashton gulped down his water. They retreated to their couches, slumping across from each other.

"I thought you hated Z," Julian said, cracking his knuckles in confusion.

"Less than I thought, it turns out."

"And she's okay with this, flying out here once a month? I thought she had a job she couldn't get away from?"

"Oh, she's quit that a while ago. Works for herself now, consulting. Still does the same thing, travels around training teachers in art therapy, but on her own time. It's better."

"Oh, I'm sure—for you."

"The other day I was thinking about it," Ashton said, "and it occurred to me that I see Z about as many days a year as you say you see Mia."

"I don't say I see her. I actually see her."

"Okay, fine. Except you see her all at once, and I spread my trysts around. But over twelve months, the sum of our days with our women is about the same."

"Your math is for shit," Julian said. "First of all, you need to double that number by Riley, and two, let's see, oh, yeah—your women still live."

"They live, but they grumble."

"You're giving them a lot to grumble about."

Ashton sighed. "I like love, Jules," he said, "you know I do. But I like life more. Love makes life so serious. Do you know what I wish sometimes? It's perverse, I know, but sometimes, I actually wish I could have what you have. There's no fighting, no drudgery, no everydayness, nothing but *falling in love*. Nothing but magic. Every minute is a thrill, you're both with your best foot forward, you haven't said the three dreaded words yet, you're pursuing and romancing and seducing and laughing and playing and drinking and eating and traveling and fucking and having the most amazing time. Right before everything turns to shit, you know what I mean?"

"No," Julian said.

They looked at each other full in the face.

"You do," Ashton said. "You know what I mean."

Ashton didn't understand that all Julian wanted was what Ashton was rejecting. All he wanted was the easy intimacy of old love. "Tell me," Julian said, "what happens when you get your weekends screwed up? You're juggling fireballs, and one weekend both your fireballs drop into your lap?"

Ashton waved around his phone. "Will never happen. Infallible smartphone."

"Pride before a fall, my man," said Julian. "Phones can break." Like hearts.

They draped over their dueling sofas. It was the dead of night.

"Ash, I don't get it," Julian said. "If you want to be with Zakiyyah, why don't you just break up with Riley and be with her?"

Ashton stared at the ceiling. "The other day I was having my weekly meal with dear old dad, and do you know what he said to me? I want you to know, Ashton, ho-ho-ho, I loved your mother. I loved her very much. But she was driving me mental. I couldn't live with her. I said to him, thanks, Pops, appreciate it. Thanks for teaching your only son what love looks like—abandonment." Ashton took a pained breath, slowly sobering up. "I adore Zakiyyah," he said, his glazed eyes closing. "But you know I can't stomach the bond. Plus I can't leave you."

"For God's sake, Ashton, make your own life right," Julian said. "Leave me. Move back to L.A. Go with Z."

"Also," Ashton continued, "Riley allows me to keep myself at a slight distance."

"You mean, a slight distance of five thousand miles?"

"Precisely. I'm afraid if I become uncoupled from Riley, inevitable conflict will follow. Why can't I move back to L.A.? Why can't we be together all the time? Why can't we get married? I love Z too much to allow her to drive me mental. So I hide her to protect her, but to protect me, too. I keep Riley close," Ashton said, "so I can keep Z, who I want to be closest to, a little farther."

Julian rubbed his temples. He opened his mouth to tell Ashton that he was not being fair to two women, whose best years were flying by while they wasted their time on him. He opened his mouth to ask Ashton what would happen to both Riley and Zakiyyah when he found himself another girl to entertain in Clapham Junction. Then he closed his mouth. "Dude," was all Julian said.

"I know," Ashton said. "Everything you're thinking of, I know."

"Do you still love Riley?"

"I do," Ashton said.

Julian breathed out. Could he help it if he felt envy?

No. He could only help how he acted, what he said. So he acted remote and said nothing. But what Julian blackly felt was: here is Ashton, who can walk out of their white apartment into a pristine street, meet Z or Riley at the tube station, and never leave their side. Instead, the love of Ashton's life was kept deliberately at a distance, down the street on the Circle Line, riding round and round because Ashton didn't want her to get off until the third weekend in October.

"What a jam-packed life you lead," Julian said. "You're so lucky." Devi's face flashed in front of him. When he would complain to Devi about the rank injustice of his brief joyful days followed by a year of sorrow, Devi would say to him, *you are so lucky,* with the same shade of black envy Julian's tone was colored with now.

How little Julian understood the men closest to him.

"I guess I *am* pretty lucky," Ashton said, his face relaxing into his worn-out casual killer smile. Mr. Fantastic. Mr. Razzle-Dazzle. Pressed but stained wool trousers, wrinkled white shirt, four-day-old stubble, bushy dark blond like his eyebrows. Beer-soaked liquid blue eyes. Couldn't last two seconds without everybody around him loving him.

"Is this how you want to continue to live?" Julian asked. "Getting drunk with Nigel and lying to two women? It is just two, isn't it?"

"Look at you, ringmaster, asking that question," said Ashton. "*My* life is superb."

"Have you thought about what would happen if one of them got pregnant?"

"Oh, I have—and impossible." Ashton made a scissor motion through the air. "Taking no chances with that accidental baby bullshit."

Julian sat up. Suddenly he wasn't remote. Suddenly he could not say nothing. Something in his chest dropped. "You're— you're joking, right? *Please,* tell me you're joking."

"Why would I joke about that? You know I can't have a baby." Ashton's head fell back on the couch. "I'm a baby myself. The original lost boy."

"Oh, Ashton..." Julian slumped forward, his head over his knees. Why did he feel so knocked out as if something devastating had happened? Not all actions in your life were irreversible like this. He felt dread. It felt like death. Like standing on Normandie.

"Aside from other things," Ashton said, "it's entrapment. It's how my mother trapped my father, with the unlucky accident that was *moi*. And how did that work out? She was making him nuts, you heard. So when I'm six, Dad splits and keeps getting paternity tests through my twenties, hoping I'm not his, while stuck with me, Mom rides the heroin highway another six years, conveniently ODing at the table in our dining room where I can find her when I come home from school."

Julian couldn't speak. When he tried to say something, his throat closed up like it was bleeding fire.

"Do they know?"

Ashton shook his head. "It doesn't come up, except when they ask if I want kids, to which I say no, which is not a lie."

"But also not the truth. When did you do this?"

Ashton waved to the past. "Years ago. Right after you left for London. When I first hooked up with Z. I saw nothing but problems ahead. God forbid they both got pregnant at the same time. What a mess that would've been."

"Why didn't you talk to me first?"

"I don't know if you recall, but you weren't available, dude." Beat. "You haven't been available for a while."

"Oh, Ashton. Why did you do it?" Overcome, Julian covered his face. He couldn't sit up. He couldn't bear to look at his friend. "Didn't you think of the future?"

"Why are you taking it so personally? You and I weren't planning to have kids, were we? And I thought of nothing else *but* the future. The rest of my life, to be exact."

Julian wanted to cry. Ashton, did you forget the plans we once made? We'd build two houses in the hills next to each other, like Marlon Brando and Jack Nicholson, one for you and one for me—you being Brando and me being Jack of course—and in between the houses there'd be a pool and a patio where our kids and wives could swim and grill and shout for us to leave the football and the boxing on TV and come join the family. Our L.A. revels were never more steeped in the sun and the sea, swelling with the righteousness and joy of the whole universe, than when you and I dreamed that dream, of a life that will never be. Did you forget?

Ashton sat up, his eyes on Julian across the coffee table. The expression on his face told Julian that Ashton had not forgotten. "Whatever it is you're half-remembering," Ashton said quietly, "that dream's been cold and dead a long time, brother."

Julian groaned. "Okay, but this isn't about me. It's not about us, or our stupid pie-in-the-sky plans. They weren't even plans. It was just drunken banter." It was physically painful for him to speak. "But one of your women might have eventually liked to get knocked up by you. Have a baby Ashton."

Ashton struggled up, looking wiped out. "And you wonder why my foot's always propping open the door," he said, stumbling down the hall to his room.

We all fuck up and need to be forgiven, thought Julian, unable to get up. We beg to be forgiven, even when we fuck everything up, absolutely fucking everything. Bent in half, heads bowed, we limp forward, scarred, sterile, undeserving and unworthy, toward the mystery of bright grace.

# 27

# Refugees

BEAUTIFUL AND SMILING, ONE WOMAN WALTZED IN WITH her weekend bag.

Beautiful and smiling, the other woman waltzed in with her weekend bag.

As a third wheel, Julian leaned over the island with one chatty couple eating Thai food out of plastic containers.

As a third wheel, Julian leaned over the island with the other chatty couple eating sushi out of plastic containers.

The action was the same, yet in one case, Julian's eyes remained averted. He owed nothing to Zakiyyah, but Ashton was right, it was impossible for Julian to interact with Riley with the same ease he used to, casually ironic and lightly affectionate. He couldn't and wouldn't let his friend down, but he also couldn't look Riley in the face. He continued pretending as best he could, but their camaraderie had ceased. The few Sundays when he took her to see Devi, and she and the cook strolled through Brick Lane Market, arm in arm, chatting about produce and incense, Julian trudged behind them, counting his lucky stars. He didn't want to be left alone with Riley. No more strolls through Green Park, no more heart to hearts for them.

He kept busy with work, with Devi, with horseback riding, with boxing. There was square dancing in the rec hall at St. Monica's on Saturdays. Devi had asked him to attend. It was widow night.

widow night. Julian got paired up with a nice seventy-year-old woman with cataracts. She could really move, though.

Some weekend nights, one couple tangled on the couch.

Two weekends later, the other couple tangled on the couch.

In the mornings, the door to Ashton's bedroom was closed. There was giggling, rough-housing, open laughing. Occasionally at night Julian would need to put on headphones, to give himself a break from their intimacy.

And occasionally he wouldn't.

Zakiyyah was louder.

The woman was a juggernaut in many ways. She was a laughing, clucking, wiping, fixing, baking, tea-making, straightening, back-rubbing force of nature. She ironed Ashton's previously pressed white shirts that had lain in the closet too long and stocked their medicine cabinet with Neosporin and Band-Aids ("What does she think happens around here that we need a year's supply of bandages?" Julian asked). She threw away their leftovers and bought fresh fruit, and put pink flowers in vases on window sills and lit up the candy apple scented candles all over the apartment as if it was 1603, and electricity and tea hadn't been discovered yet.

She'd been in a minor car wreck back in L.A. that may or may not have been her fault. Rule number one, Ashton told her, is never say sorry to another driver after an accident. Ashton's second rule, he said with a grin, is never say sorry, period.

"Oh, *another* one of your rules?" Zakiyyah said. "Do you follow that one half as well as your two-minute sex rule?" He tackled her, tickling her. Squealing, she tickled him back. They both fell off the couch.

Smiling appropriately, Julian studied them as they rough-housed. For fear of saying the wrong thing, he frequently would spend hours in their company saying nothing at all.

Riley often asked why he spaced out so often.

Zakiyyah did not. She and Julian didn't have that kind of a relationship, where she could ask him things. He couldn't reconcile the Zakiyyah he'd been superficially acquainted with—the prim, scholarly, school-marmy human being—with the luminescent, gentle, radiant creature who flew into their apartment like the good fairy Glinda, dazzled them for four days with her crazy hair, her commercial-grade smile and sweet tea and company, and flew out, leaving everything fragrant and emptier.

"I thought you couldn't stand him," Julian said to her one Friday night.

"Oh, I absolutely couldn't," Zakiyyah cheerfully admitted. "Until I could. Who could resist him? Look at him. He's so cute." He was asleep on the sofa, his head in Zakiyyah's lap. She stroked his head, his cheek, fondly rubbed his shoulder. "What are you asking, Julian?" Zakiyyah said with warm eyes and a moist smile. "When I knew? Maybe when he made another one of his stupid jokes that finally broke me. Or maybe when he barged into my house uninvited, sat himself down at my table, and told me that his friendship with you was the most important relationship of his life. You were his only family, he said, and he would do anything to help you."

"That's how he seduced you?" Julian said. "That Ashton. He's a real keeper. How do you know it wasn't posturing? Using me as an excuse to get you into bed? You think he's above that?"

Zakiyyah laughed. "Oh, Julian, why are you so funny?"

"Z, it's literally the oldest trick in the book," Julian said. "What woman can resist a man, any man, but especially *that* man after he tells her he's all alone in the world?"

"That's not why he said it!"

"Did you go to bed with him?"

"Yes, but—"

"I rest my case."

Zakiyyah shook Ashton awake. "Ash, wake up!" Leaning over him, she tickled him with her curls and kissed his cheek. "Ash! Are you awake? Who's right, me or Jules? He thinks you didn't mean the things you said to me that time in my apartment, that you only said them to get me into bed."

"Why does one of you have to be wrong?" Ashton said, rubbing his eyes. "Why couldn't I have meant them *and* said them to get you into bed?"

"Ashton!"

"Ashton!" Julian mimicked Zakiyyah's high-pitched squeal.

"Jules, do you really want to know why she slept with me?" Ashton said. "Because she finally laughed at one of my jokes, and realized I was amazingly funny as well as adorable." Turning his head, he gazed up sleepily at Zakiyyah. "Do you remember the joke, Ziggy?"

Adoringly she nodded, gazing back. "Two men are golfing," she said, "and one of them stops for a funeral procession crossing their path. His friend compliments him for being so respectful to funerals, and the man says, Well, it's the least I can do, we were married for forty years."

Zakiyyah laughed and laughed, leaning over Ashton in a deep embrace, nuzzling him into her abundant breasts, kissing him.

Every space he was in, Ashton made better by his presence.

∞

Ashton and Zakiyyah sat draped around each other on the couch opposite Julian, watching TV but mostly chatting. Zakiyyah was telling Julian some small stories about Mia, about her standing on a crate on Rockaway pier in the summers while the buskers played, reciting *by heart* nearly the entire narrative poem of *Venus and Adonis*, and fuming that no one threw money into her hat, no one except her mother, who had come and listened to her for the entire afternoon.

Her mother?

"Yes, why? Mia was incredibly close to her mother. After her dad died, it was just the two of them, and they had an unbreakable bond. The closest mother–daughter bond I've ever seen. Mia could do no wrong in her mother's eyes. Even her theatre obsession didn't derail them, no matter what Mia told you about it."

"You mean the three of them, right? She had a sister, too," Julian said. "A sister who died of leukemia."

Widening his eyes at Julian, as if signaling him to stop, Ashton took Zakiyyah's hand.

"That wasn't Mia," Zakiyyah said quietly. "It was my sister who died of leukemia. Azubah. Mia was an only child."

Ancient damnation! as Monk would say. Even *that* wasn't true?

"Next thing you'll tell me," Zakiyyah said, "is she told you we both wanted to be actors. She loved to tell that one."

"Even *that* wasn't true?"

"*Especially* that," said Zakiyyah. "I went out west solely to help her, to take care of her. She was so flighty. She couldn't cook, or drive, or keep track of her money."

"She could cook," Julian said. "She made shame toast."

"Like I said," said Zakiyyah. "Her mother had begged me. Who could've known that L.A. was going to give her the heebie-jeebies and after a few months, she'd bail on me and move back. Do I seem like an actress to you, Jules? I mean, honestly. Just look at me. Everything I feel is on my face." She kissed Ashton.

Julian's astonished gaze was to the ceiling. Was anything true? Was anything real?

Turned out yes. Some things were both—true and real.

∞

Early one Saturday morning, on a second weekend in March, Julian, Ashton, and Riley were hanging out at the apartment, having Friday night Thai for breakfast and debating where to go that night for Julian's birthday, when the doorbell rang.

Julian walked to the intercom, and Ashton said, "Jules, did you forget it's broken?" The night before, Ashton had to go down for the Thai. "The man, I swear, remembers nothing. Your turn," he said to Julian, waving at the door with a pair of chopsticks full of cold sesame noodles he was sharing with Riley. "I went last night. *And* I paid. Off you trot, as they say in our adopted country." He and Riley were canoodling over the guide to the weekend in the *Standard*, deciding whether to go to the fair at Hampstead Heath or the artwalk in Kensington. Or would Riley prefer a browse through Portobello Market?

Riley chuckled. "Why, because I'm your Portobello Belle?"

"That you are, baby, and I got one for you," said Ashton, leaning forward to kiss her, sesame sauce lips and all.

Julian bounded down three flights of stairs and opened the glass front door. On the stoop with her weekend bag stood Zakiyyah.

"Hey, Jules," she said with a smile.

Julian didn't smile.

"Z..." he said. They hugged awkwardly like two trees. "Um..." He tried to remember the maze of Ashton's schedule. Weren't second weekends usually Riley's weekends? "He asked me to come this weekend instead," Zakiyyah said, noticing Julian's confusion. "He said next week was your birthday and you had plans."

Ashton could not continue to live as he'd been living, that was clear now. "Uh...did you text him today, Z?"

"No, my flight got in at 6 a.m., I thought he'd be sleeping, plus I forgot to turn my roaming on, I have to call the phone company as soon as I get upstairs."

Julian couldn't even text Ashton himself, one, because he'd left his phone on his bed, and two, because Ashton's infallible smartphone that was never wrong was lying on the black granite island right next to the sesame noodles he was sucking barely dressed out of Riley's mouth.

Zakiyyah looked so pretty. Despite the tedious multi-stop travel from L.A. to New York to London, she was flushed, her dark face dewy and fresh. Piled on top of her head, her black curls were swept up in a fancy twist with a red satin ribbon.

Her smile had been so wide just a moment earlier. She was a nice woman. Julian had changed his mind about her. She was a beautiful girl, inside and out. No wonder Mia had adored her. No wonder Ashton adored her. Julian had gotten to know her. They played cards and board games, they went out drinking, had breakfast together, yakked into the night. Julian didn't know what to do.

"Z, if I asked you to wait right here," he said, "for just one minute, would you find me reprehensible?"

She furrowed. "I don't want to do that."

Was Julian the only one whose legs were weak?

"Why are you acting weird?" Zakiyyah said. "Can you help me with my bag or, barring that, move out of the way?"

"Riley is upstairs," Julian said. "Your boyfriend screwed up who had custody of him this weekend."

Zakiyyah was motionless.

For a minute, there was nothing.

There was nothing but silence.

"That's *impossible*," Zakiyyah said. "He deliberately asked me to switch for this weekend. He said your birthday was next weekend."

"He got mixed up. My birthday is today. You know it is. It's the Ides of March."

"Happy birthday."

"Thanks."

Zakiyyah's eyes welled up. She stared down at the bag by her feet, at the purse in her hands, at her waterproof boots. She flattened out the folds of her easy-wear gray dress, twirled a button on her overcoat. Julian once heard Ashton tell her it was his favorite dress. Except for the wet blackening of her eyes, she remained impassive.

"I'm an idiot, right?" she said.

"No."

"I'm a fool."

"No."

"You think I should run and not look back?"

"Yes, that is what I think. I'm sorry."

"But, Julian, look at me!" Zakiyyah cried, no longer impassive. "Don't you know that I *love* him?" It wasn't a question. It was a fiery yawp.

"I know." It wasn't unique to Zakiyyah or Riley, or Julian. It was what it was. Everyone loved him.

"I can't live without him."

Funny how glib those words sounded to Julian after five years, two continents and three life-sucking, soul-consuming travels, after all the devastating injuries to his body and heart. You *think* you can't live without someone, and then you do.

You *know* you can't live without someone.

And then you do.

It was as if Zakiyyah had read his mind. "You call what you do living?" she said. *"Please."* Grabbing her bag, she moved Julian out of the way with the flat of her hand, pushed past him into the vestibule and started up the stairs.

He followed her. "Where are you going, Z?"

"Where do you think?"

Julian raced around Zakiyyah and took her elbow to stop her. She yanked away. He had to block her from taking another step. He took her by both arms.

"Let go of me."

"Zakiyyah, listen to me," he said. "I know you're upset."

"Thanks for telling me how I feel, genius."

"Okay, you're talking, not listening. Listen, Z. Because you're upset and not thinking clearly, you're acting on impulse. You want to confront him, is that it? To expose him once and for all?"

"That's right."

"Okay, go for it," Julian said, "but know what you're about to do. You think you'll cause a scene—and you will—but the only one who will be walking back down these stairs and going home is you. Riley will not leave him over this. Riley will *never* leave him. And he will never leave her."

"Bullshit." Zakiyyah moved to go around him. "She will—after she learns the truth. Get out of my way."

"Never, Z. Do you know why? Because she already knows the truth. And she gives him a pass for it. She never causes the kind of scene you're about to cause. She never humiliates him, as you're about to. *Never.* She knows what he is, and she looks the other way. For this, he stays with her. Because he trusts her. Ashton hates confrontation, as you must know, otherwise you wouldn't be so gung ho to hurt him now. What do you think will happen when you get upstairs? You think you're going to give him an ultimatum? Make him choose? Either her or me, Ashton? You know he will never say sorry. You'll fight. Riley might cry, you will definitely cry. When he won't give you a straight answer, you'll storm out. But he won't follow you. Because he'll know you are not the girl for him. Do you know how he'll know? Because of what you're about to do. You'll say choose, Ashton, her or me, and he will give you his answer. He will choose her. So, if you want to never see him again," Julian said, "by all means, take the stairs two at a time. Use the next twenty minutes well, because that's all you'll have. Twenty minutes to shout and say goodbye—but say goodbye to him for good."

Zakiyyah's lips trembled, her shoulders, hands and knees trembled.

"If you want to keep him in your life, turn around, Z."

"He told me he *loved* me."

"How long has he been telling you this?"

"Over four years."

Julian nodded. "He will love you less in twenty minutes. He made a stupid but honest mistake in his schedule. For this you want to wreck his life."

"I don't want to wreck it. I want him to live it."

Julian bowed his head. "*That* fight might be worth having. Just not now."

"What do you think I should *do*, Julian? *Nothing?*"

"Z, you've been coming to London in secret for years, you've been staying with us for months. Ashton's been out, been asleep, been in the shower. You haven't once asked me what you should do. Why start now?"

Tears flowed down her cheeks.

"Please, Julian, what should I do?" Zakiyyah whispered.

The bag was down. The purse was down. They sat side by side on the stairs. Julian took her hand in his. "It's hard to accept that the person we love will not change," he said, his voice breaking. "Not in this life. And possibly not in any other. Our love is so strong that we think it can change things. It can change the world, can beat back death, can change the man we love." Or woman. "Because our love has changed *us.*"

"Yes," said Zakiyyah.

"It's not enough."

"You don't believe that. You of all people."

"I do," Julian said. "Me of all people."

"Tell me the truth. Do *you* think he will ever change?"

For a few moments, Julian sat without answering her.

He and Ashton were the Faces once. They were the chosen ones. They had floated through their charmed GenX twenties in a heated pool of girls and fun. Everything good was placed on a buffet in front of them. Here, feast, Life said. What's not yet yours is waiting to be yours. The meal is served, the parade is on, the sails are in the air, and the girls are pretty. Taste and see.

Of late, Julian had been waiting to become philosophical about his crushed dreams, his wasted life.

He was still waiting.

What was the point of falling in love if you stayed exactly as you were?

That was Zakiyyah's fateful question.

That was Julian's fateful question.

"No, I don't," Julian said. "Ashton will never change."

"You don't know!" she cried. "You don't know anything. Look what you've done with *your* life."

"Why is everyone attacking *me*? What does Ashton have to do with what I've done with my life?"

"He's only in London because of you!"

"Are you sure about that?"

Zakiyyah frowned as if she didn't understand and didn't want to.

"Are you sure he's not here because he's been trying to hide *you*?"

She grit her teeth. "He would never have moved here if it wasn't for you."

"Ashton is not my fault." God!

"Well, whose fault is he? You've lied and protected him his whole adult life!"

"Because he is my *friend*," Julian said, "not because he is my *fault*."

"He *said* he loved me!"

"He does. But he *says* it because he knows you want to hear it."

Zakiyyah exhaled like the balloon of her heart had popped. The air leaving her lungs in a grieving hiss, she stood up, staring intensely at Julian still drooped on the stairs. She glanced up to one more landing, one more flight, to the open door of the apartment beckoning her, the open door beyond which was Ashton, his handsome face, his harmless ways, his pure, delighted sparkling smile despite his damaged life. Grace, and smile. Endure it, and smile. Grit your teeth, and smile. Break your heart, and smile. Who wouldn't want to be around someone like Ashton? He was everyone's favorite person. Until now he brought joy to everyone who knew him. The terrible struggle shrank Zakiyyah's frame, inverted her shoulders, hunched her back, made her less beautiful.

"I will never love again like I love him," she said hoarsely, barely getting the words out. "There will never be another man for me in my life, never."

"I know," Julian said. "But like from black tar heroin, you

can turn your back and walk away cold turkey, go through withdrawal and find yourself another man."

"That man is upstairs."

Julian shook his head. "Accept him or leave him, Z."

With hope in her voice, she said, "How do I accept him? Turn around, go home, come back next weekend, like nothing's happened?"

"Correct."

"Can I do that?"

"I don't know. Only you know what you can and can't do." From his own experience, Julian would say human beings were capable of a lot.

"Mia was completely wrong for you, and you didn't care."

"I cared. But she died before I could act. She left me no choice. But *you* still have a choice, Z."

"You think *I* have a choice?" Zakiyyah laughed coldly. "Could you have left Mia?"

"No."

"No matter what?"

"No matter what."

"And she was faithless, too, and lied to you, said things to you that were untrue."

"Her heart was true."

"Like Ashton's?"

"Yes. Like his is true."

"She was living with another man, Julian! For three years, she was engaged to *another* man, and you didn't care! But you're telling *me* to care."

"No. I'm telling you to decide what you can and can't live with and then act accordingly."

"Is that what you do?"

"Absolutely," Julian said. "That is what I do. I can't live without Mia. So I act accordingly."

It was a cold waterfall, standing on the stairs watching a gorgeous girl, her ebony face streaked with tears, rend her robes in turmoil, looking up, looking down, in a suspended moment in time, a still frame in the middle of her gusty ride, trying to decide what the story of her life would be, how the poetry of her days would play out. Could it continue even with the ugly, could it reform without beauty, would it break apart? In front of Julian on the painted stairs, Zakiyyah set fire to herself, laid siege to her desire, to the vanishing dream of a life which had in it one man and one man only. In that waterless minute Zakiyyah had to imagine a different life than the one she'd been living: wandering around London, riding the Circle Line in rings of hope and sorrow, in an endless yellow loop of longing and enchantment, waiting for Ashton to become the man he would never be.

It was as if Zakiyyah too was in a rowboat on the black river of lament, and the cyclone had swallowed her.

"Can I do it?" she whispered. "Turn around, walk away, and know that I will never see him again? Never touch him again? It's like death. I can't. I can't!" Her fists were clenched so violently, her nails dug in, broke her skin, made her bleed. Small red droplets fell on the gray stairs.

Life ground down to cold slow motion in front of Julian, and then stopped.

∞

Soon Julian wasn't on the stairs anymore with a crying woman, but in the cave of faith, leaping across the blackest sea, traveling down a calm unruffled river, clutching the crystal, his other life fading and receding, Zakiyyah, Riley, Devi, even Ashton. Only his own dark future lay ahead of him. Everything else was fog and forgotten. How could he know how Zakiyyah would choose when he didn't know how he himself would choose?

Zakiyyah had mangled Leonard Cohen, grabbing Julian's hand on the stairs. *To love each heart will come*, she said, but *like a refugee*. Julian wanted to tell her that sometimes not even then, but her heart was broken enough.

# Part Three

# Lady of the Camellias

*"Oh, I would give ten years of my life to weep at her feet for an hour."*

Alexandre Dumas, *La Dame aux Camélias*

# 28

# Airy's Transit Circle

To get to the light, Julian climbs a familiar-looking iron staircase, narrow like a ladder. When he pops open the grate and climbs out, he finds himself back in the Transit Room inside the Royal Observatory.

"Ashton?" he calls out. How could it not work! Julian had been drifting down the river for so long. But it's unmistakable: though the window to the courtyard and the roof are closed, the familiar telescope is in front of him, and the black stairs flank it. Ashton is nowhere to be found. Neither is Sweeney.

Nope, that's not true. There's Sweeney. First the shuffling of torpid footsteps, and here comes the heavy man, huffing and panting. He's dressed more formally than a minute ago. He wears a funny hat.

"Sweeney," a crushed Julian says. "It's you."

"Who else would it be," Sweeney says. "I'm the caretaker, I'm always here. And who might you be?"

"It's me, Sweeney. Where's Ashton?"

"Who's Ashton? And who the bloody crickets are *you*?"

Before Julian can answer, a gray-haired, dapper man in his fifties—wearing no less than a frock coat and top hat—enters the Transit Room. "Mr. Sweeney!" the man exclaims. "Did you see the sun flare just now? I was nearly blinded. That was the largest one yet. Do you have my pen? I must record it in my notebook—" He spots Julian and stops speaking. Turning sharply, he glares at the caretaker. "Mr. Sweeney! I thought I had made it abundantly clear. There are to be no visitors at my Observatory before noon, and certainly not at *any* time near my telescope."

"It *is* noon, Mr. Airy."

Mr. Airy! Could this be George Airy, Britain's most famous Astronomer Royal? George Airy not only invented Julian's mystical telescope but presided over the reorganization of the Observatory during the period that just happened to coincide (or correlate?) with Britain's unmatched navigational prowess. Under Airy's watch, Britain became the most powerful empire the world had ever known, largely due to the expertise of its navy.

The cranky genius has big gray sideburns and a bulbous nose. He is dressed impeccably in tails, like a prince dressed by others. If there's a daytime ball somewhere, George Airy is ready to attend it. He carries a stack of papers under one arm and a cane in the other. He already has a significant stoop.

Once a relieved Julian realizes the vortex has worked, he relaxes. To stop upsetting the great man, he takes a few steps away from the precious telescope. No protective railing has been built around the Transit Circle (not yet anyway; leave it to Julian to alert George Airy to the necessity of a fence!).

"Yes, it is noon at *this* precise moment, Mr. Sweeney," George Airy says, "noon on Thursday, August 3, 1854"—(look at that; Julian didn't even have to ask! Well, he's come to the right place to know the correct time, and to the right man, for that matter)— "But the question before us is not what time it is *now*, but what time was it when the good gentleman got here? That's assuming he did not materialize at my telescope spontaneously—during the sun flare perhaps? We are assuming that, are we not, Mr. Sweeney?"

Sweeney stammers in shame.

Setting down his cane, the astronomer pulls out his gold pocket watch and studies it intently. "To arrive here at noon, the gentleman would've had to walk through the gate down at the foot of the garden by 11:55 or 11:56 if he's a fast walker and a tireless climber. That sounds like before noon to me, Mr. Sweeney, does it not?"

"I didn't let him in through the gate, sir. It wasn't me. I come back and here he was."

"Come back from where, good sir?"

A flushed Sweeney has no response, as if he can't admit what he was up to.

Julian had suspected he might head into 19th century London. 1603, 1666, 1775. Now 1854. London, always London. He tried to prepare for it. While Ashton was busy loving not one but two women, Julian read *War and Peace* to learn about Austerlitz and Waterloo, *Pride and Prejudice* to familiarize himself with the manners of early 19th century England, *Jane Eyre* to absorb how women were treated, and most of Dickens to familiarize himself with all life. He even read Karl Marx when he couldn't get to sleep. *"Everything in existence is worth being destroyed,"* Marx wrote, a true modern prince of darkness. Julian thought the economist identified most strongly with Mephistopheles in *Faust*, which Julian also read.

Yet here Julian is, wedged into a dinky year he can recall nothing about, a year after the European unrest but before the coming of electricity. Gas lamps abound in 1854. The railroad is running. What else? Any epidemics, any wars?

While Julian's thoughts are thus occupied, George Airy makes a noise of exasperation. So far, the scientist has barely glanced Julian's way—as if Julian is superfluous to his mounting irritation. "It's Mirabelle, isn't it?" the astronomer says. "She is always to blame. She was supposed to be here at noon to mark the angle of the sun. Was she here? No. And she always forgets to lock the gate, no matter how many times I remind her." Critically Airy looks upon Sweeney. "Is the widow Pye the reason you weren't at your post?"

"I—I—I don't know what you mean, Mr. Airy, sir," Sweeney stammers.

"My niece can hardly be expected to follow the rules," George Airy says haughtily. "After all, she *is* a woman. Her career as an astronomer is limited by virtue of her sex and her general inattention to detail. But we men must adhere most strictly to the procedures I've spent two decades setting before us. Otherwise the world is going to dissolve into chaos. It's headed that way already, Mr. Sweeney, what with the damn French daring to take credit for spotting the irregularities in the motion of Uranus. The irregularities that led them to posit that there might be a new, massive body, a planet they wish to call Neptune! The insolence of the French never ceases to gall me. Did they forget that the only reason they noticed the planetary anomalies in the first place is because of the data *I* provided for them? I supplied them with the very particulars they now use to belittle me with! Without me, there would *be* no data! And therefore, there would be no discoveries of planets, large or otherwise!" George Airy gathers steam, pointing in Julian's direction. "Or the chaos might be this *dummerer*, this odd mute gentleman in the room with us. How did he get inside my Transit Room? Who is he? As you see, Mr. Sweeney—except for my square of the observable universe—*everything* is sheer disorder. I beg of you, do not let our small bastion fall into anarchy. We men must hold steadfast."

"Yes, sir."

"Do not open the gate before noon. Ah-ah—no more defending the indefensible. Please go and get Mirabelle for me. I must speak to her *immediately*."

A voice sounds. "No need to get me, Uncle George. I'm here."

Julian grabs at the non-existent black railing. He teeters out of balance. A tall, statuesque woman appears at the far end of the Transit Room, framed by the white casing of the interior door. She is dressed in a navy-blue linen skirt and a maroon jacket. Her white collar is at her neck, her sleeves have no frills, no embellishments. She wears no jewelry. Her dark hair is braided and twisted into two large pouffes at her ears—a Victorian Princess Leia. But inside the sensible dress is the most stunning rendition of Josephine Julian has ever seen. She *is* a princess, a painting, a beauty queen. *Mirabelle*. Miri but with belle there, too.

From across the room, Mirabelle casts her polite gaze on Julian. He stands as straight as he can, the wetsuit clinging to his strong frame, his wavy hair damp, the dark stubble on his pale face grown messy by an infinity of sunless days, his deep-set kaleidoscope eyes—green blue brown—reflecting off her shine. He can't help himself. The relief and happiness must be plain on his face, in his incongruous half-smile. Pulled down to his Adam's apple, the small round bulb of the headlamp pulses the last of its white LED light. Julian knows what he looks like; the question is, what does Mirabelle see? He lowers his gaze, feeling awkward and self-conscious.

A second girl jams in under her elbow. Short and dark-haired, she is embellished with all the baubles the tall girl lacks. She's heavy with jewelry and ribbons, with gold pins and pink beads.

"Hello, Mirabelle, hello, Filippa," says Airy. "Nice of you to finally join us."

"I came as soon as I heard my name, Uncle," says Mirabelle. If only Julian could have such an effect on her. He is glad her gaze is not on him anymore. He feels like the gawky speechless kid at recess all those years ago.

"We did nothing wrong, Mr. Airy," Filippa says, holding on to Mirabelle's arm while smiling flirtatiously at Julian.

"I'm talking to my niece right now, Filippa, not you. Mirabelle, why weren't you at the Transit Circle at noon? Without a careful observation of planetary trajectories, our work here cannot be successful."

"Yesterday you told me not to touch the telescope, Uncle, because it needed recalibrating," says Mirabelle.

"Ah, yes." Airy proceeds without pause. "I shall attend to that summarily. But also—I've told you time and again, the gate to the Royal Observatory is to stay latched until noon."

"It was. As far as I know it's still latched."

"Do you see this gentleman in the room with us?"

"Yes, Uncle George. He is difficult to miss."

The floor, Julian! The floor is very interesting.

"How did he get here if the gate was locked?"

"And I would know this how? Perhaps you should ask him."

"Why, oh why, can't women follow the most basic rules!" George Airy exclaims.

"I *can* follow the most basic rules," the young woman says calmly. "Shall we take a walk down to the gate so you can see the status of the latch for yourself?"

"What you're saying cannot be, Mirabelle," the irate astronomer replies, "for there's a gentleman in this room who had no way of getting here except by that gate. As you yourself confirmed, we all see the gentleman, do we not? He's not a mirage, is he?"

"No, Mr. Airy, he's *definitely* not a mirage," says Filippa. Mirabelle elbows her friend.

"Can you explain him to me, Mirabelle?"

"I cannot. I shall not endeavor to explain any man."

"So if you didn't let him in, how in the name of Dickens did he get here? And more important, why?"

All eyes turn to Julian, even hers.

Mirabelle is composed, white-necked, white-faced, spotlessly clean and coiffed. She is an elongated statue of the animated fiery girl who fought to survive the alleys of St. Giles. That girl lived. This woman exists. Though she is exquisite, Julian can't tell if she has ever strolled through a garden of pleasure, or even desired to. She is elegant, yet slightly forlorn. Something blackens the pastel edges of her beauty.

"Answer me, child," George Airy says. "You know how precious time is, especially mine."

"Everyone's time is precious, Uncle George."

Silently, Julian concurs.

"Then answer my simple query. Who *is* he?"

Mirabelle's voice is mellifluous and carries far despite its softness, despite its breathiness. She always sounds like herself.

There's never any mistaking it. The present voice carries farther than most, because of her height. It's got a wry, dry tinge to it, a slight I-know-things-better-than-you air. "He looks like a seminarian to me, Uncle," Mirabelle says. "A man of the cloth. Look at his clerical collar." She points to the headlamp. "He must be looking for our Charles Spurgeon, the Prince of Preachers, isn't that right, sir?"

Julian fights to stay as composed as she is. She is helping him out, rescuing him. Why?

"He's looking for Spurgeon in *my* observatory?" Airy casts Julian a skeptical unwelcome gaze. But the astronomer must detect something unscientific in the invisible dynamic between the stranger and his niece—sense some new energy that has charged the stale particles in the room—because his high-handed demeanor softens. He wrinkles his prominent brow. "You're far afield of the New Park Chapel," Airy says, finally addressing Julian. "We're in Greenwich, sir, and the chapel is in Southwark. You're in the wrong part of town."

"He is lost," says Mirabelle.

"I'm not lost," Julian says. His voice is hoarse. "I'm found." Those are the first words in his new life.

"Where did you come from, good sir?"

"Bangor." Julian chose Bangor because it was, then as now, one of the smallest towns in Britain. "It's a cathedral city in Wales, near the Menai Strait…"

"I know where Bangor is," George Airy says. "It's 4 degrees of longitude west of here, 4.1 degrees to be precise."

"Yes, sir."

Woe to him who thinks he can outsmart a scientist.

"What is that you're wearing?" Airy asks. "Is that some type of Welsh attire? We've never seen it in London."

"We certainly haven't," Filippa says, her chest heaving out of her flouncy ruching.

"We wear this in the mines and seas of Wales," Julian says. "It's a wetsuit made to protect me from the elements when I travel." He snaps the Thermoprene to show them. "It's windproof and water-resistant."

Filippa looks impressed.

A prickly, angular woman in her forties pushes through between the girls. She's panting and fretful. She's got a severe hairdo and her lace collar is so tight it appears to be choking her throat. "I beg your pardon, Mr. Airy, sir, for all the commotion," she says, her voice a steel string. What have my girls done now? I take my eyes off them for a second and—Mirabelle, Filippa, explain yourselves!"

"Where have you been, Mummy?" Filippa asks. "Talking to Mr. Sweeney again?"

Filippa's mother raises her hackles like a porcupine. "Do not be cheeky, my darling. Mr. Sweeney and I may have discussed the weather for a few minutes, a few seconds…"

George Airy gives Sweeney a condemning glance. Sweeney doesn't know where to look.

Amid the recriminations, Mirabelle glides forward. The spot where Julian stood a blink ago with a grim and fearful Ashton is now inhabited by his light and fearless Eurydice. Ashton had gripped his forearm. "Don't do this again," Ashton said. "I beg you. Nothing good's going to come of it."

Unlike Ashton, Mirabelle says nothing. Nor does she touch him.

Julian turns to the Astronomer Royal. "You're George Airy, aren't you? You're famous at Bangor College, you know. The head of our Literature Department has heard that you've developed special lenses for astigmatism. They're revolutionary. The department chairman asked me to speak to you while I'm in London to evaluate this new technology. We have several professors, myself included, in dire need of better optometric equipment."

"Mummy, he's a professor!" Filippa squeals.

George Airy nearly squeals himself. "You're a professor?" And close on its heels: "They heard about my lenses all the way in Bangor?" The peacock tries not to open his tail. "Well, I'm delighted, though I'm not sure how this can be. I did give a pair to my sister, Mirabelle's mother. She taught piano at the London Conservatory. Aubrey Taylor. Perhaps you've heard of her?"

"I'm afraid not," Julian says. "But don't the lenses have the same curved aperture technology you used to build this Transit Circle? With the aperture width of eight inches and a focal length of over eleven feet, I believe your telescope is the most accurate in the world, isn't it?"

George Airy sputters. "How did you—how did—how—"

"I must have read about your lenses in an academic paper."

After that, Julian can say no wrong and do no wrong.

The astronomer cannot look more flattered, more gratified. "Well, I am pleased indeed. I only developed the lenses to correct my own poor vision," Airy says, "and yet look how beneficial the technology has been to my country. You're a professor, you say? Of mathematics, I hope?" The astronomer smiles. "*I* used to be a professor of mathematics. And then a professor of astronomy. I quite enjoyed my time at Cambridge." Airy attempts to become businesslike again, tap-tapping his parchment as if formulating a plan. "Mirabelle, dear girl, I have a wonderful idea. Why don't you accompany this fine young man to Charles Spurgeon and make a proper introduction. We can't just send him on his way. That would be terribly inhospitable. And Charles is so fond of you."

"I have so much to do, Uncle..."

"So what's one more thing? Introduce Charles to...what is your name, dear sir?"

"Julian Cruz."

"Julian Cruz," George Airy repeats. "*That's* Welsh?"

"Yes," Julian replies without inflection. "Iolyn Corse is the proper way to say it."

"Julian Cruz!" says Filippa.

Julian waits, his quiet gaze on the face of the only girl in the world, as ever searching for a blink of retention, recognition, memory. With his whole being, he is yearning to see a trace of himself. Mirabelle doesn't acknowledge him, but neither does she look away. Only her mouth moves, imperceptibly, inaudibly repeating his name so no one will hear.

Filippa's mother gives her daughter a shove, and the small girl lurches forward. "I'm Filippa Pye." The girl extends her hand to Julian. "Pleased to make your acquaintance. This is my mother, Prunella Pye."

"Pleasure is all mine," Prunella Pye pants, hooking Julian's hand with her clammy, bony fingers.

George Airy drags his niece forward, in front of Filippa. "And this is my niece, Mirabelle Taylor."

Julian tilts his head. "Pleasure to meet you, Miss Taylor," he says. She doesn't extend her hand, and he will not presume to impose his paw on her. Besides, his paw is shaking.

Lightly Mirabelle smiles. "Julian Cruz," she echoes. "So, then, you're *not* Charles Spurgeon's father? Our esteemed pastor has been waiting for his father to visit from Colchester. But we fear the man is ill and may not be coming."

The priest's *father*! Julian must look worse than he thinks. "Father?" He can't help it. Pride gets the better of him. "How old do I look?"

"Oh, not especially old, I suppose." Mirabelle's dark eyes flicker ever so slightly. "Our darling reverend has just turned twenty."

Julian's eyes flicker back.

Filippa swings around Mirabelle, planting herself in front of her. It's the Conga line. "We'll all take you to Mr. Spurgeon, sir," she chirps.

"Oh, no need to bother yourself, Pippa," George Airy says. "You and your mother do too much already. Don't you have a ball to prepare for? That ball isn't going to throw itself, you know."

"It's no bother at all, Mr. Airy," Filippa says. "In fact, there's really no need for Miri to come with *us*." (Julian flinches when he hears the princess called by her rookery name.) "We all know how busy Mirabelle is these days. Why, she still hasn't finished sorting your documents."

"Oh, *that* trifle," Airy says in the tone of a man who cares not a whit for organization, not one whit.

"But, sir," cries Filippa, "you said she must work harder to transcribe your notes and separate your correspondence! And she got your ledger entries wrong this morning." Filippa looks up at Julian. "Mr. Airy invented a new system of accounting called double-entry, Mr. Cruz. But math is confusing for Mirabelle, entering the same information twice into the debit and credit columns. She makes many errors."

"Really, Filippa, you worry yourself over nothing," George Airy says. "I will check over the numbers myself. Double-entry accounting is one of my greatest joys." Airy's rounded nose reddens. "Mirabelle, it's settled then? You will take this man to Charles Spurgeon and not disappoint me?"

"As you wish, Uncle," Mirabelle says. "I don't like to disappoint anyone."

Filippa persists. "But what about labeling your boxes, Mr. Airy?"

"Mr. Sweeney will label them." Airy takes a shallow bow, kisses his niece on the cheek and rushes off with his cane and his papers.

"What boxes?" stammers Sweeney.

"Oh, it's not hard, Mr. Sweeney," Mirabelle says dryly. "Remember last month when you helped me label Uncle George's empty boxes, *'empty'*? Do that, just more of it." Mirabelle turns to Julian. "Order is the ruling feature of my uncle's life."

Filippa steps between them. "Mirabelle," the girl says, "but what about your appointment at the *Institute* at three o'clock? Have you forgotten all about Florence and the Institute?"

"Hush now," Mirabelle says. "It's barely noon. Plenty of time for everything."

Stepping away from the women, Julian switches off the headlamp and removes it from his neck. He's got to sort himself out. He's mired in a bog. He needs his money. And if it's no longer there, he needs to find a prizefighting ring and earn some money. If he's ever going to present himself to her, and that's not a given, he needs to present himself to her as a strong smart man, not a crestfallen pauper in a wetsuit.

His arrogance and desperation in St. Giles didn't serve Miri's salvation or his own. He's been given another chance by the angels or demons. Will he take it? *Can* he do it this time before he runs out of time? Devi didn't think so. But Julian has made it his life's business to refuse to accept implacable facts.

He tips his proverbial hat. "Perhaps I can meet with Mr. Spurgeon another day, ladies."

"No, you can't leave!" Filippa cries.

Julian can't explain to Filippa and her mother that he is not fit to walk alongside *that* woman. Mirabelle must notice his self-conscious embarrassed hesitation. "I see that in your travels, you have misplaced your coat, Mr. Cruz." She turns to the caretaker. "Mr. Sweeney, would you please be so kind as to lend Mr. Cruz your cloak? Yes, Mr. Sweeney, the cloak you're wearing, that one. Right off your shoulders."

A grumbling Sweeney hands it over.

Julian can't help but smile. "Some things never change, do they, Sweeney?" he says, throwing the black cape over his shoulders, covering his ridiculous wetsuit, and feeling better. "You're still giving me your coat."

"Whatever do you mean," Sweeney says. "I never give you my coat in my life." The portly gentleman looks discomfited. "Keep the coat. Consider it almsgiving."

"Oh, that is *so* kind of you, Mr. Sweeney!" Prunella says with undue exuberance.

Filippa pulls on her mother's arm. "I hope *Mrs.* Sweeney will be as delighted as you to hear that her husband has given his coat away," she says.

Prunella yanks out her arm and fluffs up her sleeve. "Mind your own business, my impertinent darling," the bony woman says, heading for the door. "You forget yourself. Unlike you, your widowed mother does *not* need a chaperone."

Filippa hurries after her. They all walk out into the courtyard on top of the hill. The August air is muggy and still. Before they turn their backs to it, Julian catches a long glimpse of the Thames in the distance below them, meandering through hazy London as far as the eye can see.

Mirabelle leads the way to the carriage, waiting for them behind Flamsteed House. Prunella and Filippa trail behind. Since he and Mirabelle are walking without speaking, with astonishing clarity Julian can hear Prunella's shrill voice scolding Filippa. "It's just good manners, Pippa. This man is a professor, highly educated. He's from Wales. He may be a nonconformist. They are serious thinkers over there, the Welsh nonconformists. Practical, temperate, hard-working. In many ways, they mirror the Puritans. They are utterly unimpressed by flamboyant displays from their women, by physical contact, really, of *any* kind." Julian keeps his eyes in front of him, lest he accidentally catch Mirabelle's inquisitive gaze, wanting to know if what Prunella is saying is in any way true, and God *forbid* she sees in Julian's eyes how untrue it is.

"This man needs a serious, unsensual demeanor from his young lady," Prunella continues. "So adjust your behavior, dear heart." *Now* Prunella lowers her voice, but on the empty road between the trees, the only thing that's heard is her irritable alto. "Before it's too late for you, like it's too late for our Mirabelle."

"Are you *sure* it's too late for her, Mummy?" Filippa says, the anxiety sharp in her voice.

Julian and Mirabelle both pretend they're deaf. Her face expressionless, Mirabelle ties the ribbon ends of her white bonnet under her chin.

Julian clears his throat. "I heard your uncle mention there was a sun flare today, Miss Taylor," he says. "Do they occur frequently?" First order of business between them: mystical phenomena.

"Not *too* frequently," Mirabelle replies. "We keep a record of all anomalous events at the Observatory. If you wish, you can ask my uncle to let you take a look at the data."

"Going back how far?" What is Julian hoping for? That somehow George Airy kept records on sun flares going back two hundred years? *Come on, Julian, shape up.*

"Since 1834. The year he became Astronomer Royal."

Julian nods, trying to verbalize the second order of business between them. "Your uncle mentioned that your mother teaches piano. Do you play?"

"My mother is a good teacher," Mirabelle replies, "but I'm a poor student, I'm afraid. I play, but I don't have the flair for it."

"Do you prefer the spoken word?"

"Why, yes. Yes, I do, Mr. Cruz. How did you know?"

"Lucky guess."

"I used to have *quite* a flair for the dramatic," Mirabelle says wistfully. "But not anymore. Nowadays I occasionally read poetry."

Do you stand on a crate over Rockaway Bay, Mirabelle? Julian wants to ask. "What kind of poetry?" he asks. "Shakespeare's *Venus and Adonis* perhaps?"

"Why, yes, Mr. Cruz!"

The look on her face is less calm, slightly incredulous.

Julian smiles.

Overhearing, Filippa catches up to them. "Mirabelle used to sing and dance like a carnival performer. She liked the applause, didn't you, Miri?"

"A little too much, if you ask me," Prunella intones from behind.

"I did not," says Mirabelle. "Not too much. Just enough."

"And if there was no chance for applause," Filippa says, "then you could just throw money at her."

"Filippa is joking."

"I would find that highly entertaining, Miss Taylor," says Julian. "Seeing you sing and dance, I mean."

"Which would *you* do, Mr. Cruz," Filippa asks with a glint, "applaud or throw money?"

"I would do both."

Mirabelle stares at her shoes, suppressing her own glint.

During the twenty-minute ride to New Park Chapel, Filippa info dumps on Julian. She has been endowed with a biblical propensity for small talk. There is something desperate in her ceaseless verbal patter, as she sits by Julian's elbow, her smile pasted on, her mouth in motion.

Across from them, an unruffled Mirabelle sits next to Prunella, both women watching Filippa besiege Julian, one with detached amusement, one with public dismay.

Filippa tells him where they live (in Sydenham, Kent), how long she and Mirabelle have been friends (since childhood), and how many jobs and separate responsibilities Mirabelle has at the moment (eight).

"What do *you* do, Filippa?" Julian asks, to be polite.

The girl takes the question as a strong sign of his interest in her. She unfurls. "Oh, don't worry, as little as possible, Mr. Cruz! I make pudding, I darn stockings, and I embroider bags. Mummy and I are also organizing a ball." In the next breath, Filippa invites Julian to the ball, "as *my* honored guest of course."

The dance is at the end of August. Julian protests. He says he doesn't know if he'll be in London then, but Filippa refuses to take no for an answer.

Julian steals a glance at Mirabelle.

"Mirabelle probably won't attend," Filippa says, catching him looking. "She said she was busy. She's—"

Mirabelle interrupts. "I don't remember saying I was busy, Pippa."

"You did. Doctor Snow asked if you would honor him by attending and you said you were too busy."

Mirabelle allows herself a small roll of the eye.

"Who is Doctor Snow?" asks Julian. Does she have a suitor? Well, why wouldn't she? Look at her.

"The esteemed John Snow, the famous scientist. Have you heard of him?"

"Oh, I've heard of *a* Jon Snow," Julian says. "Mine might be a different man. What does yours do?"

"He invented something called chloroform to give to our Queen Victoria to ease her burden when she was being delivered of her infant," Mirabelle says.

"He has also been consumed with discovering what causes cholera," Filippa says. "Our soldiers are having a terrible time with the sickness."

"Cholera? Soldiers?" Julian says, falling back against the seat. "You're not helping John Snow with that, are you, Miss Taylor?"

"Of course she is!" Filippa says, with a gossipy scrunch of her nose.

"Oh, look, we've arrived," Mirabelle cuts in, calling out to the carriage driver, "Barney, stop here, please, where there are no puddles. Are you ready, Ju—um, Mr. Cruz?"

"I'd stay away from cholera research," Julian says to her, staring at the flowing waters of the Thames. "Cholera is quite infectious."

# 29

# The Prince of Preachers

Julian hears the women whispering in front of him as they walk to the vestry.

"Pippa, stop yammering," Mirabelle says, "assailing that poor man with every silly thing that pops into your brain."

"It's called enchanting him with conversation, not that you'd know anything about it."

"Don't listen to me, listen to your mother, Pips. Men do not like chattering chicks. It makes them anxious."

"Is that why you've been like a tomb? Do you suppose he finds your sullenness attractive?"

"I don't care about that, Pippa, you know I don't. I'm trying to help *you* out. As a friend. Fine, do as you please. But don't talk about *me*. Talk about the weather and the ball, or whatever else you think might interest him. But not *me*. Unless you keep talking about me because you think *I* interest him. Then by all means, keep going." Boom. Filippa is made mute. Mirabelle spins around, casting Julian a small apologetic smile. "This way, Mr. Cruz. And please, when you meet him, don't be intimidated by our reverend. He'll seem brash at the outset, but really he's the most gentle, most devout soul."

In Spurgeon's chaotic, dark wood, book-lined study, the women settle in as they wait for him.

"I don't know if Charles will be to your taste, Mr. Cruz, you being from Wales," Prunella says, as if she has any idea what

Julian's taste might be. "Some have criticized our pastor for his evangelical eloquence." She takes off her bonnet. "Some chide him for his manner of preaching. He likes to call it plain talk for working men and women. But some—no one in this room, of course, but others—denounce him as nothing more than a fire eater at Astley's Circus."

"But not *women*, Mrs. Pye," Mirabelle says. "Women find him quite attractive."

Prunella makes a face of distaste just like the one Mortimer used to make about gin laced with turpentine.

Mirabelle shows Julian a large basket overflowing with hand-sewn slippers. "The women know he is unmarried, and they keep sending him their slippers as a token of their interest." She smiles. "He's also deluged with requests for locks of his hair." Mirabelle permits herself half a blink in the direction of Julian's own thick wavy mane.

"It's shocking Charles has any hair left," Prunella says with a judgmental huff. "He keeps accommodating the brazen creatures. One of these days, he'll accommodate one of them right into marriage!"

While they have a few minutes, Mirabelle fills Julian in on a few details about the preacher. Spurgeon has an impressive résumé. He arrived in London a year earlier, in 1853, when he was just nineteen. He walked into the New Park Street Chapel, took the pulpit without invitation, and began speaking. His first sermons, underpinned by the Puritan teachings from his childhood, were attended by only a few hundred people, but now, merely a year later, two thousand people crush into the nave to hear him. The ministry is in the process of renting out the nearby Surrey Music Hall which holds 10,000 souls. They're worried it still won't be enough space.

"Mirabelle!" a loud, happy voice roars from behind them.

Charles Spurgeon is quite a presence. He wears a clerical collar, monochrome gray trousers, and a waistcoat. He sports tremendous sideburns that make him look older than twenty.

Perhaps that's the intention. He is not tall but appears tall. He has a strong broad face and big hands. The most commanding thing about him, however, even in the private setting of his outstanding study, is his voice. As Mirabelle's *sotto voce* cannot be extinguished, traveling with her from body to body, Charles Spurgeon's booming bass is a character unto itself.

Julian knows why—because the voice carries in from the soul.

Enthusiastically Spurgeon pumps Julian's hand, bids him to sit (Julian nearly falls down) in an armchair next to Mirabelle and offers him a glass of warm ale, which Julian drinks as if he hasn't had a drink in days. Upon seeing this, Spurgeon commands his wan, bloodless assistant named Nora to wobble forward with a carafe of ale and leave it by Julian's side with a glass. Two pints of ale drunk quickly on an empty stomach test Julian's tolerance. His head starts to swim. He decides to speak minimally for fear of sounding like an idiot. He thinks he hears Spurgeon say that *"sloth and silence are fool's virtues."* Julian hopes the man is not referring to him.

Spurgeon listens as Mirabelle explains that George Airy himself had asked her to make this introduction. "George himself!" Spurgeon exclaims, stroking his chin, regarding both Mirabelle and Julian. "Well, that is most curious, perhaps even a little mysterious. Why do you think George did that, Mirabelle?"

"My uncle is an enigma, Charles."

"Indeed, he is. Don't get me wrong, Mr. Cruz—may I call you Julian?—I am extremely well disposed toward the great George Airy, both of us kindred spirits arising from Colchester, but he is not exactly what I would call forthcoming with the personal warmth, especially toward strangers." Boisterously Spurgeon laughs.

"Mr. Cruz is a professor in Bangor!" Filippa chimes in. She is in a chair by the fireplace. Prunella stands starchily behind her daughter.

"Delightful!" Spurgeon says. "A professor of what?"

"Literature," Julian says. He tells the reverend he's in London to do some research on Charles Dickens.

"Professor of literature, you say? How wonderful! Mirabelle, did you hear that?"

"Of course, Charles. I'm sitting right next to Mr. Cruz. I cannot help but hear."

"Bangor, Wales? It's one of the smallest cathedral towns in all of Britain, you know." (That'll teach Julian to think he can outsmart a scientist *and* a reverend.) "Is the seminarian college part of Bangor Cathedral? Oh, most delightful! Are you a nonconformist, then?"

How does Julian answer, yes, no? He's read about the battles between the religious orders, but clearly not carefully enough.

"It's no business of mine," Spurgeon goes on. "But the majority in Wales are dissenters from the Anglican Church…"

"Then I'm one."

"…But it does prevent them from holding university degrees since the university exists primarily to churn out Anglican ministers."

"I misspoke—I'm not one," Julian says. Every damn word is a landmine.

"Oh, shame," says Spurgeon. "Because I *am* one." He laughs. "Yes, absolutely! In my heart, I believe we're all protestants in some form. We're always questioning one thing or another. I myself was taken into the Baptist Union and now preach the Calvinist doctrine of grace. Of course you are familiar with it?"

Julian mumbles incoherently. He is a little bit familiar with it. Last thing he needs is to start debating theology with a Baptist minister. He doesn't want to be exposed as a Catholic in front of Mirabelle.

"I overwhelm you, Mr. Cruz, I see that. *Here comes the orator with his flood of words and his drop of reason* is what you're thinking, aren't you?" Spurgeon slaps Julian good-naturedly on the shoulder but won't go and sit down. "I apologize for my forward demeanor, but I'm afraid it's the only one I've got. Some call me the fire eater of Astley's Circus to try to insult me. Little do they know that there's *nothing* I find more complimentary!"

"Mr. Cruz is coming to my ball at the end of the summer!" Filippa interjects.

"Well, I don't know about that..." Julian begins to say.

There's a twinkle in Spurgeon's eye as he leans back against his desk, arms folded. "Pippa, have you informed the good gentleman that it's a fundraising ball, so he's not caught off guard?"

"I was about to tell him, pastor. It's a fundraising ball for—"

"Charles," Mirabelle interrupts, "during his pilgrimage to us, Mr. Cruz has not only mislaid his spectacles and his cloak, but he has also misplaced his purse. Is there any way you could advance him—"

Julian has been trying to figure out a way to ask Charles for a small loan without sounding as if he is homeless and jobless and penniless, in other words without sounding exactly like what he is. And the rescue once again comes from Mirabelle, of all people.

Spurgeon walks behind his desk and pulls out a wooden box. "What is the sum you require?"

Julian is stumped. How much does it cost in 1854 to buy masonry supplies, to rent a room, to buy a suit? How much does it cost to become the man the gracious, beautiful young woman next to him might love?

Spurgeon counts what's in the box. "I have two pounds, eight shillings here," he says, extending his hand full of coin.

Is that the price? Julian mutters a thank you, casting a sideways glance at Mirabelle, as if to say with his gaze what he can't with his words, which is, forgive me for my calumnious indigence, my love. I'm not always like this, so unworthy of you.

But Mirabelle's entirely uncondemning face doesn't look as if she considers him unworthy. There is no pity in her gentle face.

Perhaps it's Julian's inability to look neutrally at the young woman that prompts Spurgeon to home in on him and Mirabelle as they sit primly in front of him. He appraises them with sober judgment. "So your uncle asked you to bring this man to me, did he?" His eyes rest on Mirabelle as his mind attempts to make sense of things. "How curious." He addresses Julian. "Did I hear Mirabelle say you've misplaced your spectacles? No man can do a lick of work without a pair. Nora! Go into my cabinet at once and fetch me a pair of spectacles for Mr. Cruz. Yes, Nora, the ones Mr. Airy designed for me, the black and gold framed ones for this fine gentleman."

When the glasses are brought and Julian adjusts them on his face, Charles stuffs a book into his hands. *The Collected Sermons of Charles Spurgeon.* Julian smiles. "I hear this is a very good book, reverend."

"Oh, you've heard correctly, it's *excellent!*"

"This is by far not all of Charles's wisdom," Mirabelle says. "It contains barely 50 of his sermons. Charles has preached more than 600 times in the twelve months he's been with us."

"When you put it like that, you make me sound verbose, Mirabelle." Spurgeon laughs at himself. "Have you told Julian what you do for me?"

"I haven't had the chance."

"In her spare time, Mirabelle diligently prepares my sermons for publication for the weekly penny press at the British Museum. She is a fine editor. She's got a keen eye for detail. It's one of her many talents."

Mirabelle has *spare* time? As in time to spare? That *is* good to know.

"How long are you in town, Mr. Cruz?"

Julian hesitates to answer.

Spurgeon becomes animated. "Mirabelle, are you thinking what I am thinking?"

"I certainly hope not, Charles."

"Ha! You've always been a witty girl, Mirabelle." Spurgeon turns to Julian. "It just so happens that Mirabelle's assistant, the second proofreader, Mr. Newington, has taken ill. In his absence,

Mirabelle and Mr. Patmore have been unable to keep up with the demands of my voluminous transcriptions."

Julian doesn't know where Charles is headed with this.

"Would you consider helping Mirabelle prepare my sermons for publication until Mr. Newington returns? We need someone with proofreading skills, good handwriting, meticulous attention to detail. Knowledge of English is helpful but not required." Spurgeon smiles. "Love of the Lord helpful but not required. What do you say, good sir?"

"Yes, Mr. Cruz, what do you say?" Mirabelle twinkles. "Do you love the Lord and know English?"

"Don't let Mirabelle put you off with her teasing," Spurgeon says. "It's just her way. She means no harm by it. You'll be doing her and me a great service if you accept."

"Please don't pressure him, Charles," says Mirabelle.

"Your sudden and welcome appearance in our midst is clearly God's will to lessen Mirabelle's burden," Charles says. "Mirabelle, admit it, it's remarkable. As always, blessings to the merciful God who has *elected* to help us, don't you agree?"

Mirabelle makes no sound. And by the fireplace, a chuffing Filippa and Prunella Pye do not sound as if *they* agree. They curdle like milk. Julian also doesn't agree. "I'm afraid my time is accounted for while I'm in London," he says. "But thank you for the offer."

"It's only for a few weeks. Coventry Patmore will be glad to pay you."

"It's not about the money, reverend..."

"Please call me Charles. What is it, then? Really, I wouldn't press the matter, but Mr. Newington's vascular malformation and your nearly simultaneous appearance on our shores I cannot take as mere coincidence. You must feel it, too, no, that you were sent to help us?"

Julian hedges, wavers.

"What's there to think about?" Charles says. "There is no tomorrow. The Lord's work begins today."

"Never have truer words been said, pastor," says Julian.

"Charles."

"Charles. But I have urgent business that can't be put off."

"Fine, take a day to think about it," Charles says. "Why don't you come tonight to Vine Cottage in Sydenham for supper with me, Mirabelle, and her family? I will introduce you to her parents who are dear friends of mine. I will ask them to host you while you're working with their daughter. It's the least they can do."

"I don't think I'll be able to do it..." A wordless stammer proceeds from Julian's throat. Filippa jumps in.

"You heard him—he doesn't want to do it, reverend!"

And Prunella: "Charles, do you *really* think it's a good idea?"

"Of course I do, Prunella, otherwise I wouldn't have suggested it."

"There's no reason or need for Mr. Cruz to work with Mirabelle," Filippa cries.

"I disagree, Pippa," says Spurgeon. "I've just explained to you the reason and the need."

"Filippa is right," Prunella says from behind her daughter's chair. "Seems downright inhospitable to put a visiting professor to work."

"Nonsense. The man can speak for himself and tell me if I've overstepped my bounds. Julian, have I overstepped them, sir?"

"Not yet," says Julian.

Spurgeon roars. "Not yet, he says! Oh marvelous, simply marvelous! Which means, I may overstep them imminently!"

Prunella: "There is certainly no reason for him to stay at Vine Cottage..."

"Mr. Cruz has traveled too far to be put up at an inn like a common Puritan trader," says Spurgeon. "Mirabelle's parents are the most *welcoming* sort. Aren't they, Mirabelle? They sponsored me when I first came to London and didn't know a soul. I lived with the Taylors nearly a year. We had a good time, Mirabelle, didn't we?"

"We did, Charles."

"Mirabelle is a fine equestrian, Julian. Have you ever ridden a horse? She can show you how. She is as excellent a teacher as I am a pastor."

"Surely the professor has better things to do than ride smelly horses with Mirabelle!" says Filippa.

"*Do* you have better things to do, Mr. Cruz?"

"I'm not sure I—"

"Reverend!" Prunella Pye sputters forward. "It is *most* inappropriate. Maybe this is how they do things in Colchester. But here in London, a gentleman of unknown origins cannot gallivant with an unmarried woman, to-ing and fro-ing as if he's a reprobate and she's a harlot. It's just not done!"

Spurgeon casts his gaze on the man and woman in front of him. "Are you a reprobate, Mr. Cruz?" he asks. "Mirabelle, are you a harlot?"

Julian keeps silent. Mirabelle keeps silent.

"You see, Prunella, they both strongly deny it," Spurgeon says. "Mr. Cruz is a man of God. It is obvious that you and Filippa see his goodness. You are certainly acting as if you do. Otherwise why invite him to a ball? The man has nothing but love in his heart." Spurgeon smiles. "Fine—I will vouch for him myself. Will *that* put you at ease, Prunella, dear?"

"It's just not how it's done, reverend," Prunella doggedly repeats, casting a glance at Filippa as if to say, I'm doing all I can, dear heart. "You are putting a tremendous burden on Jack and Aubrey," the woman continues. "Mirabelle's father is not in the best of health. Neither is her mother. I told Aubrey when it happened—having a child at 44 was unbecoming. Did she listen to me? She called Mirabelle a miracle, and you *are* a wonderful girl, dear, don't get me *wrong*, but with *all* the things a woman of nearly 45 giving birth implies, I'd call that not a miracle but a *disgrace*. And here is *precisely* what it leads to."

"What does it imply?" Spurgeon asks.

"What does it lead to?" Mirabelle asks.

"Never mind that," the stiff woman says. "Pastor, Mirabelle's fine work on your sermons doesn't require an accompanying scandal, does it?"

"Well, it doesn't *require* it, Prunella, but it certainly benefits from it." Spurgeon bursts with laughter. "Oh, please don't make that face. I'm joking."

"This is *hardly* the time for hilarity."

"If you only knew, Prunella, how much humor I suppress, you'd grant me this small indulgence. Stop fretting. Our pilgrim is a paragon of virtue."

"Is he ordained?"

"Am *I* ordained?" Spurgeon's warm demeanor cools slightly. "Come now, ladies. We have entered into the second half of the nineteenth century. A revolution is coming. A revolution in science, in dress, in the arts—and in thought. Let's rise to the modern times, shall we?"

"All the more important, then, to behave impeccably during a revolution," Prunella says, "with no stain on one's honor."

Mirabelle stands up and faces the older woman. "Whose honor is stained, dear Mrs. Pye?" She pauses. "Because *my* honor is entirely intact."

Prunella turns red, becomes agitated. "I have no idea what you could possibly be alluding to…"

"Now, now, ladies." Spurgeon makes a peacemaking motion with his hands, and begins to usher them out. "Why don't we continue this delightful conversation tonight over supper at Vine Cottage with Mirabelle's parents?"

As everyone's leaving, Julian asks for a word with Spurgeon in private and when they're alone, he turns to the pastor and says, "Charles, I'm sorry, I can't."

"Julian, no, *please* don't disappoint us."

"Who is us?"

"I've vouched for you to Madame Pye."

"You don't want me to disappoint Prunella?"

"Listen," Spurgeon says, "that Pye woman has friends all over London, high places—and low. Many of them come to my church. I'm still establishing myself in this city. I have much at stake."

"That's exactly my point—why invite trouble?"

"*Am* I inviting trouble?"

"I mean trouble with Prunella. Why provoke her?"

"Julian, forget about her for a moment. I will tell you the truth, we could really use the help." He pauses. "With Mirabelle."

Julian and Spurgeon exchange a wordless moment. "Miss Taylor needs help?"

"Very much, dear sir."

Julian sighs.

"Our Mirabelle is a precious flower," Charles says. "No harm can come to her. That is paramount. That is the only imperative that is guiding her parents, her uncle, all her friends—and me."

And me. "No harm can come to her." Julian agrees as he shakes the reverend's bearlike hand. What he doesn't say is no harm *will* come to her. "Let me think about it, all right?"

"Don't overthink it, good man," Spurgeon says. "It's only temporary."

"Everything is temporary," says Julian.

Spurgeon slaps him on the back. "You're a man after my own heart, Julian. That is precisely what I preach. Everything is temporary. No one listens. Our sorrows are like ourselves—mortal. There are no immortal sorrows for immortal souls."

"Sometimes there are, pastor," Julian says, still damp from crossing the Acheron, the half-empty river of grief. "Sometimes there are."

"The sorrows come, but they also go. They cannot make an abode in our souls."

"Sometimes, they can." Julian lowers his head. They have.

"I thought we were in agreement? You just said…"

"I can't promise anything. I must resolve certain things…"

"Well, you've come to the right place to resolve dilemmas of being and of conscience. How can I help?"

Julian stares into Spurgeon's kind, firmly-convinced-of-his-own-righteousness expression. If only the pastor knew what Julian knows. How narrow the path is. How there are no options, no twists, no widening of the way. The path is as straight as a ruler can make it.

One way is her death. In 49 days.

And he has yet to find another way.

He wants to ask a question of the reverend, yet can't. What if you knew, *knew*, with as near certainty as you knew anything, that the woman you loved most in the world was going to die, and even worse, that unlike the parable of the oil and the lamp, indeed you knew the day and the hour? What would you do?

"My sermon tomorrow will be about the things we're speaking about now."

Julian doubts that very much. "What things are those?"

"Wayward children, grieving parents. How to combat the bitterness of the soul with love," Spurgeon replies. "God is too good to be unkind and too wise to be mistaken. When we cannot trace his hand, Julian, we must trust his heart."

∞

Outside, the three women are waiting for him. Filippa resumes her babble, but Julian is distracted by a dozen things, not least of which is the utter absence of the Globe Theatre. *So goes the glory of the earth.* It should be visible from the chapel, but instead there's nothing but tenements near the river. Julian nods, pretending to listen. It had burned down centuries ago, hadn't it, and was never rebuilt. Oh my God. Filippa is inviting him to her house for afternoon tea when he's done with his errands. Theirs is a teetotaling house, she tells him, but she's sure her mother will find him something to imbibe if he wishes, and there's definitely going to be drink at the ball, but it's a black tie affair, does he have dress tails, because if he doesn't, there's a very good tailor at John Piggot on Milk Street they could recommend, they can even take him there...

The hole in the earth where the Globe once proudly stood hollows out Bankside in the distance behind Mirabelle. She is framed against the swiftly flowing Thames, a graceful, quiet princess against the immense phantom theatre where she once cried loudly and he consoled her. *Maybe we can stay and see* All's Well That Ends Well. *I'll take us another way into the city. Just wear your girl clothes next time.* Julian can barely remain upright. In a gust, his heartache squalls from his eyes to hers. A perplexed Mirabelle blinks, frowns. Julian doesn't know what to do. Oh, that he would have his request, that God would grant him the impossible thing he longs for. Mumbling something unintelligible to the women, Julian turns and hurries away from them down the empty street, wild eyes to the ground.

# 30

# Sovereign Election

JULIAN'S HEART AND SOUL ARE IN A CIVIL WAR. HE NEEDS TO be with her, yet he wants to save her. Are they one and the same? Are they in violent opposition?

In his other life, he had vowed to Devi that this time would be different. *He* was going to be different, and maybe then, with his own change, he would effect a change in her. Yet now that he's here, all he wants is what he has always wanted. Damn his plans, his careful strategies for salvation. Will it kill her if he's near her, or will it save her? Is the cat alive or dead, the box open or closed, is she real or a dream, Mia or Josephine, a particle or a wave, and if she is dead either way, what is he?

What is he with her?

What is he without her?

Is love the organizing force?

Or is it death?

Can he vanish into Victorian London, stay away from her for a month and a half? With trepidation, Julian counts the days. September 20, 1854, is the eyeless 49th day. A shiver runs through his body. September 20 is the day of the autumnal equinox. Cleon told him that a foot tunnel under the Thames can open on September 20. Is it a coincidence that her uncle, George Airy, the inventor of time, saw a flare at his observatory the precise moment that Julian appeared at the telescope? Julian no longer believes in coincidence.

First time, coincidence; second time, happenstance; third time, enemy action.

And this is the fourth.

Firmly Julian resolves that he will write Mirabelle a letter, explaining that he was called back to Bangor and will return promptly on September 21. And then, slowly, he reconsiders.

What if he stays away and she dies anyway?

Julian will have wasted everything. His hope, his chance, his miracle, his life, her life. Wasted his manhood, and her womanhood. All of it squandered, because he chose to do *nothing*. Why even cross the meridian? He could've stayed home and done nothing.

As Ashton would say, good fucking point.

The diffuse layer of coal ashes covers all, even the particles of air. Julian stumbles alone through London, in dim black fog, struggling with the direction of his own existence. He buys some masonry supplies, finds the newly renovated St. Giles by Cripplegate, carves out his leather satchel from the crumbling London wall. Why oh why does he locate the marked gray stone in five seconds in 1854 but after a million minutes of searching still can't find it in modern-day London? He retrieves two shiny coins from the dusty pouch, leaving 41 behind, and exchanges one of them for more money than he knows what to do with—*three hundred pounds*.

He's worried about carrying that much cash on his person. He's worried about carrying one shilling on his person. The teeming Victorian streets are dirty with swindlers and thieves. The wayward mob presses him on all sides while he carries three hundred pounds, plus one extra Fabian coin, plus *two*—golden—rings! hanging on a leather rope down from his neck next to her crystal.

London is recognizable, yet new. Its ranks have swelled to millions. It has bloomed with stone and glass. Horatio Nelson has fought Napoleon and died in battle, and his statue now stands in its rightful place atop his column in Trafalgar Square.

Piccadilly has been remade into a proper square and renamed a Circus; London Bridge has been demolished and rebuilt in a new spot. New bridges have popped up as if by magic all across the Thames. A blink ago with Miri, there were three. Now there are a dozen more, most notably Waterloo, the best bridge in London, with the best views.

The Strand has been widened, dirt alleys have nearly disappeared, buildings have been refaced, everything's paved. Horse-drawn carriages and omnibuses abound in the tens of thousands. So does manure, by the tons of thousands. Gas streetlights stand every thirty feet. The profuse stink of horse dung mixes with the tepid vapor rising from the Thames, the air reeking of dead fish, black coal, and sweat from the unwashed pickpockets looking for Julian's gold. As ever, London remains a magnificent pungent brew of great and small human endeavor and all its by-products. Julian walks but is lost, looks but can't see, listens but can't hear.

More restaurants, more pubs, more parks, more shops, more, more, more. There is Harrods and Fortnum and Mason, beautiful stores even in 1854. F&M is only a block away from Jermyn Street, where Julian heads to acquire some respectable clothing. In his new frock coat, he rides where nostalgia carries him, to Grosvenor Square. The war with America lost, the American ambassadors now live on Grosvenor Square, in the white marble house where he once lived with Miri.

A block away on Brook Street, there is construction and renovation at Mivart's Hotel, but Virginia Claridge, the hotel's new owner, assures Julian that she and her husband are still open for business. He rents a comfortable suite on the top floor, and Virginia promises that if he should ever return, the expanded hotel will be worth the trip. "For the moment, we're calling our place 'Claridge's, late Mivart's,'" Virginia tells Julian, "because Mivart's is still so well-known, but it's a little cumbersome to pronounce."

"You might consider changing it to plain Claridge's," Julian says.

An excited Virginia agrees that sounds much better.

Julian celebrates his first night in Victorian London by marking the middle of his forearm—above Mia, above Mary, above Mallory, above Miri—injecting his skin with a new *dot* of ink and pain. Dante is right. It's only *dot 1* and *already his desire and his will are being turned like a wheel by the love which moves the sun and the other stars.*

Julian wishes he could stay away from her.

He just can't.

∞

On Friday morning Julian lets the hotel's livery driver take him back to New Park Church. The ostensible reason is to return Spurgeon's money and Sweeney's cloak. But a part of him hopes to run into her. He's dressed and groomed like a gentleman, in a tailored gray coat, contrasting black trousers and a top hat. She might not even recognize him. He has pulled back his unruly hair and shaved, leaving the sideburns untouched to grow with the times.

At New Park, Spurgeon is preaching, and the crowds spill into the street and down the sidewalks as they hang on to his words. All the doors to the chapel are open. Still outside, Julian can hear the pastor's booming loquacious voice. He catches part of Spurgeon's homily as he makes his way to the vestry, glancing around for Mirabelle. *"The way to do a great deal is to keep on doing a little,"* he hears Spurgeon say. *"The way to do nothing at all is to be continually resolving that you will do everything."*

Julian likes that. He must remember that. In the corridor he stops and listens in earnest, swayed by the force and common sense of Spurgeon's oratory.

*"If I had never joined a Church until I had found one that was perfect, I should never have joined one at all. And the moment I did join it, if I had found one, I should have spoiled it, for it would not have been a perfect Church after I had become a member of it. Still, imperfect*

*as it is, it is the dearest place on earth to us.*" Without a microphone, the man manages to amplify his voice into every crevice of the chapel and holds bound the breast of every person who hears him, including the uneasy Julian.

"*Do I need to say more about the difficulties of true love, the truest love there is?*"

Julian doesn't think Spurgeon does.

"*Every person here knows that the hardships require supreme Grace to master them.*"

Does Julian know this?

"*And where does that Grace come from, brothers and sisters? Oh, we all know from where. We have seen it with our eyes, and with our faith. Love's is not an easy road and Love's shall not be a tinsel crown.*"

Julian leans against the wall, lowering his head.

When he looks up, whom should he lock gazes with but Mirabelle, who is standing in the door of Spurgeon's study. Has she stood there the entire time watching Julian wilt and bend under the weight of the great task before him, has she seen how unfortified he feels, how lacking in that very strength beyond his own that Spurgeon is extolling? How even a tinsel crown seems too much to ask for these days.

The pastor just told him: *Love covers all wounds by keeping silent. Love is mute under injury.* To acknowledge the pervasive sense of being wronged feels shameful to Julian, as if he fears offending not only God, but Mirabelle, too. How dare he feel wronged when his love stands across from him in all her glory? With extreme effort, an effort that feels bestowed to him by Grace, for he did not have the strength even a moment earlier, Julian masters himself and locates his game face. He forces out a smile. There's a life on the line. It's no time to be weak.

*God on high, hear my prayer. Don't give me an easier life.* Julian takes a tentative step toward Mirabelle. *Make me a stronger man.*

He clears his throat, takes off his hat, and bows his head. "Hello, Miss Taylor."

"Hello, Mr. Cruz." Approvingly she regards his new attire, but good manners dictate that she say nothing.

"I've come to repay Mr. Spurgeon. And to return Mr. Sweeney's coat." He hands her the cloak.

"That's very kind of you. Right this way. You will have to wait a little longer to see Charles," she says. "He is merely getting his breath back before the next sermon."

"He preaches twice on Fridays?"

"Yes, and herein lie our publishing difficulties." Smiling, Mirabelle leads him inside the library, where she takes out the money box into which Julian places five pounds. "That's more than…"

"Alms to the church."

"Thank you."

"You were saying?"

"I was? Oh, yes. He's only supposed to preach once a week, but some weeks, we hear from him as often as five times."

"And you edit and prepare every sermon?" Julian asks, his breath catching in his throat. Mirabelle is especially beautiful today. She's more decorated than yesterday. There is blue velvet trim around her sleeves and hem, a white lace collar, and silk ribbons in her intricately braided brown hair. Love blooms like late spring in Mirabelle. Julian can't look directly at her, afraid she will see how beguiled he is by her lucent shine, by the loving details of her Painter, by the softness of her mouth, and the burning gleam in her half-lidded eyes, which she tries not to raise, as if concealing from Julian her own fire within. There they stand, Julian staring at a spot near her neck, and Mirabelle staring at the lapels on his frock coat.

"Yes, I edit them, with Mr. Patmore and Mr. Newington—who, as you are aware, is ill."

"With vein insomnia, I presume?"

Delicately Mirabelle chuckles. "I don't know what that is, but…" She assesses him. "I like the sound of it. Did you make that up?"

"Yes."

"Ah." There is a twinkle in her eye. "And what would the symptoms of this vein insomnia be, pray tell?"

Julian keeps a straight face. "Well, there would be delusions accompanied by knee knocking, and occasionally some temporary blindness."

Thoughtfully she nods. "I see. And the cause?"

"Too much ale."

"And the cure—or is that obvious?"

They smile. Julian relaxes. Mirabelle, too. In their newfound amity, he is able to look at her when she speaks to him. "We waited for you last night," she says. "Prunella and Pippa were disappointed by your absence. Even my uncle dropped by for a visit, hoping to catch you, and he never leaves the Observatory before the work is done."

"I assume the work is never done?"

"Correct," Mirabelle says. "By the way, I told him about your interest in sun flares. He was pleased by your curiosity. He wishes to discuss the flares with you. He said you are welcome to visit the Observatory any time you like and analyze the data in his notebooks. You have made quite an impression on my uncle, and he is not an easy man to impress."

"Thank him for me," Julian stammers. "I do apologize for not appearing last night…my business—um—took longer than I expected." He trips over his lies. He lowers his gaze, steps back. "In fact, I must return to it. But I'm glad I ran into you, Miss Taylor, I wanted to let you know…"

"I'm glad you ran into me, too, Mr. Cruz."

"What I meant to say," Julian continues hastily, "is I will have to—perhaps—I have been called away, you see—back to Bangor—I'm not—another time—but thank you…" He retreats from the room, hat in hand, bowing, not wanting to turn his back on her—and bumps into Charles Spurgeon.

"Julian!" Spurgeon bellows. "My good man! You've returned!

Oh, what a delight to see you. Isn't it, Mirabelle? He's like the prodigal son!"

"Yes, Charles." She stands watching the two men, the 20-year-old and the 37-year-old. Yet somehow it's Julian who feels comforted by Spurgeon's paternal patting. The pastor is distressingly animated. He has Nora bring in wine and bread and cheese despite protestations by both Julian and Mirabelle. He inquires (interrogates?) why Julian did not visit Vine Cottage yesterday and asks Julian's "learned" opinion on the sermon he's just heard.

"Mirabelle, why don't you take Julian and today's manuscript pages into one of the empty offices in the rectory. You two might as well get started. The pages are messy, I know, I'm sorry about that. I have made too many corrections. Trying to get every word perfect. It is my great downfall. Always striving for that unattainable perfection in my writing. My sermons are a work in progress, Julian—much like our souls."

Julian shudders. Charles doesn't notice.

"You two can begin copying out a clean version right here at the rectory. Have you got enough parchment, Mirabelle? I will get you more, and, Julian, you can borrow my pen and ink."

Mutely but vigorously, Julian shakes his head.

"What Mr. Cruz is trying to say is that he can't, Charles," says Mirabelle. "He is busy. He has been called away. Anyway, I can't either, I promised Betsy I'd attend to that Arts Council matter...and I must be at the Institute later."

There is a firming of the facial muscles of the affable and effusive Charles Spurgeon in response to Mirabelle. He says nothing in reply, won't even look at her. But she says the word *Institute* and the pastor's features harden. He turns to Julian. "You agreed to help us, sir," he says without a smile.

"I didn't quite do that, Charles..." Arguing with a priest!

"Mirabelle is counting on you. Aren't you, Mirabelle?"

"Charles, come now. If Mr. Cruz says he can't, he can't."

"But you've returned to us! Why else would you be here this morning if it wasn't to say you would help us?"

It certainly would seem that way to a casual observer. What other reason would Julian have to be loitering around Spurgeon's study? Julian sees that he hasn't thought this through. Too late now for careful planning. And how bad would it be, really, to work by her side? He's not going to be chasing her through the rookery. It will just be work. Work only. They'll be professionals—though not Silver Cross professionals. Dressed professionals, proper in all ways, a gentleman and a lady. Mr. Cruz. Miss Taylor. Nothing but good manners. Plus, she'll be constantly surrounded by other people. Actual chaperones, not half-naked masters of the mint, the opposite of a chaperone. There won't be a minute of privacy, a moment to get into any trouble, a second for alchemy. She probably has six or seven people around her 24/7, Prunella and Filippa leading the charge. How could she not? Look at her.

Like a slender orchid Mirabelle stands, smiling and serene.

A trapped Julian manages a half-nod.

"Excellent!" Charles booms. "It's settled, then. I will forgo this afternoon's sermon and accompany you to Vine Cottage myself. I might as well introduce this man to your parents, Mirabelle. You come along, too, my dear. I don't want to bring Julian to your house without you by my side. As Madame Pye might say, it wouldn't be *proper*."

"All right," Mirabelle says, "but not right now, Charles. Maybe this evening. I told you, I have Betsy and then this afternoon…"

"Yes, yes, I know. The *Institute*." There's a chill in Charles's voice.

∞

From the start, things don't go as Julian expected. For one, he and Mirabelle ride alone in one carriage. No chaperone there, except for Barnabus, whose back is turned. Like a stuttering mule, Julian asks if he should ride with Spurgeon instead, and the pastor stares back blankly. "Why? Ride with Mirabelle, of course. It will give you a chance to get to know one another. You should become comfortable; after all, you'll be working together in such proximity."

Just what Julian wants to hear.

In the carriage, sitting across from him, Mirabelle makes mild small talk and then clears her throat. Julian doesn't like throat clearings. They often signal something untoward. "Before heading to Vine Cottage, Mr. Cruz, I do need to run that errand. Would you mind accompanying me?"

"Of course not."

"It's a little bit delicate, I'm afraid. I may require some assistance."

"I'm yours, Miss Taylor," Julian says. "I mean—I meant—anything I can do to help." God!

"Thank you. Have you ever heard of the Crystal Palace?"

"Of course." The Great Exhibition was held at the Crystal Palace in 1851, the very first World Fair. "Hyde Park, I believe?" Look at him, angling for a stroll in the park already! But a solemn stroll, right? Solemn and unsmiling.

"That was then," Mirabelle says, as if *then* was so last century, not three years ago. "The Exhibition Hall has been relocated to Sydenham, where I live. It took two years to erect it at our local park. It came in six months behind schedule and millions of pounds over budget."

"That's how it always is." Did she just say *erect*? Oh, what's wrong with him. Julian stares out the carriage window. It's pretty outside, hilly and forested. Sydenham, Kent, is considered posh country dwelling, even though it's only a few miles south of the river. Centuries earlier, Sydenham began as a small settlement in the woods where animals grazed. Then its residents discovered that its spring waters contained healing properties and the upmarket population swelled and has been swelling ever since. But still, the crowds in Sydenham are thin, not like London.

"The new Crystal Palace opened to great fanfare two months ago, and at first it was wonderful."

"Uh-oh."

"Yes, unfortunately, uh-oh. We were forced to shut down despite the sell-out crowds. Here's where the matter gets delicate, Mr. Cruz." Mirabelle speaks slowly and chooses her words carefully. She looks into her gloves, not at his face. "Our female visitors couldn't help but notice and take exception to—how shall I put this—the *nakedness* of the male statues lining the transept. Of course no one complained about the nude female statues in the hall, not the women, and most certainly not the men..."

"Most certainly."

"But the male Italian forms of the Greek and Roman gods being displayed rather prominently, on pedestals, no less, caused a public outcry."

His face straight, Julian listens, watching her straight face. Is it his imagination or does something mischievous gleam in those chocolate eyes of hers as she speaks?

"I, being a senior member of the Arts Council, was tasked with covering up the offending parts of the male, um, anatomy with papier mâché leaves, which I had to make myself for eighty sets of, um—" Mirabelle covers her mouth.

"This is what being good at your job as a senior member of the Arts Council gets you, Miss Taylor," Julian says. "Being tasked with *large* responsibilities." There is definitely something mischievous in his eyes as he speaks, but she doesn't know this, because she's not looking at him.

She blinks as if she can't figure out if he is being cheeky. "Yes, you are quite right," she says slowly. "It took me over two weeks to accomplish the job..."

"Well, there was a *lot* to do, and it's important to be thorough."

"Yes...anyway, once the offending parts were camouflaged, the Crystal Palace reopened."

"Congratulations."

"And yet..."

"Ah. The story continues?"

"The story always continues." She sighs theatrically. "When the hall reopened, our attendance dropped by forty percent."

Julian laughs. "And what is the lesson in that story, Miss Taylor?"

"I—uh—I don't know, Mr. Cruz."

"As with all art, never hide the parts people want to see."

"I suppose so." Mirabelle maintains a modest expression. "After a hastily convened emergency meeting, our treasurer declared that the operating costs for the Exhibition Hall would put us out of business by the year's end if we did not take immediate and drastic measures to address the prickly issue of low attendance."

*Prickly* issue? "It's important to tackle *big* problems head on," Julian says. "How did you *raise* the attendance numbers?"

"Oh, I haven't raised them yet. But I have been instructed by the Council to remove the papier mâché leaves I had just spent days gluing on and return the statues to their original, uncovered, condition."

"Well, I am a *firm* believer in doing whatever it takes, Miss Taylor," Julian says. "Is this where you require my assistance?"

She nods.

Julian tries not to smile.

She doesn't look at him.

The enormously long glass-walled Exhibition Hall is spread out over several acres on a hill in a landscaped, newly renamed Crystal Palace Park. Barnabus lets them off at the foot of the entrance, and they make their winding way up to the palace. Julian gets to walk with her in a park, after all.

It's a Friday and lunchtime, but there's hardly anyone inside the mammoth building. The sun shines down through the thousand skylights. They walk through the ornate exhibit halls, filled with baroque furniture, life-size stuffed elephants, sewing machines and threshers. Julian wishes he could spend a week in this fascinating place, but right now they have a job to do.

The task before Mirabelle is not as easy as 1-2-3. The papier mâché leaves cannot just be ripped off. "I've done too good a job of gluing them on," she says, trying to remove one dry and failing. Now they won't come off without an equal and opposite effort of water and a brush to remove the residue.

Julian didn't know there would be comedy today. As he always said, you have to know what your life is—comedy or tragedy. Lucky him that today is one and not the other.

Maintaining decorum is not easy during a job like this, but Julian and Mirabelle make a go of it. They find a short ladder and fill a bucket with warm water. He carries the ladder and the bucket, and she carries the scrub-brush. He holds the ladder steady, she climbs up to a statue of Chronos, the god of time, and begins to soak off the papier mâché and scrub the glue off the Grecian penis and testicles. Then on to Dionysus, and Tartarus, and next, and next. Julian's job is to hold the ladder. But that can't be his only job. He watches her work for a while, and then points. "Miss Taylor, you missed a spot of papier mâché. Right there, below. You can't see it from where you are, but from where I stand, it's quite visible. You must lean down and scrub harder."

"Mr. Cruz…"

"A little more elbow grease, Miss Taylor, and I'm sure you'll get it."

She scrubs. "Is it all gone?"

Julian pretends to look. "There's still some left. Look closer. Don't tell me you don't see it."

"Mr. Cruz…"

"Just apply yourself, Miss Taylor. It's not that *hard*."

After a motionless moment, Mirabelle dips the brush into the water and turns to the statue. "Fine," she says. "I will apply myself. But if you would please be so kind as to hold on to me while I work, I would be grateful. I would hate to put too much pressure on the brush and lose my footing. I can be so accident-prone."

"Hold on to you…?"

"Yes, just hold my leg firmly with your hand."

Julian looks around the empty hall. Is the unaccompanied maiden really asking him to touch her in public? Carefully, he puts his hand on Mirabelle's stacked silver buckle shoe.

"No, Mr. Cruz, that won't do. That won't do at all. One hand on the ladder, one hand on my leg."

She continues with her endeavor without returning his gawp. "You're not doing as I requested."

He puts his hand on her ankle.

"Higher."

He raises it to her calf.

"Higher."

Gingerly he holds the back of her knee.

"Mr. Cruz."

What's happening. "Higher than your *knee*?" He tries not to inflect his voice.

"Yes, Mr. Cruz. Higher than my knee. And firmer. I don't want to fall and break my leg at this eleventh hour."

Julian's head is level with her hips. He doesn't know what to do. Slowly he slides his hand upward to her thigh.

"Mr. Cruz!" exclaims Mirabelle, as loudly as possible. "That is *much* too high, sir, that's so impertinent of you!"

His hand flies off. He stammers out an apology.

Wiping her brow, she hops down from the ladder, and takes a step to him. "Did you think your earlier linguistic ribaldry went unnoticed? This is me paying you back in kind." Her smile is ear to ear.

For two more hours, they amble through the transept.

It's late afternoon by the time they're done. Tired and hot, they stroll downhill to the waiting carriage, chatting about the original Great Exhibition and all the diamonds and flowers and locomotives that were displayed there. Julian tells Mirabelle about Karl Marx's sour reaction to man's inventions, and she smirks. "Oh, for certain, he turned up his nose at the powered tractor," she says. "But what did he think of the mass-produced ice cream? The ice-cream machine was the biggest hit at the Exhibition."

"What did *you* think of it?"

"It was my favorite thing," she says. "They don't have one here in Sydenham, unfortunately. There's one near Astley's Circus in Westminster, but I'm not allowed to go there. Mummy says it's seedy near Whitehall." She smiles.

"We should ask Barnabus to drive us there. I can come with you, so you won't have to worry about the seedy part."

"When? Right now?" Putting her hand on her heart, she chuckles. "Oh, Mr. Cruz. We can't. We are woefully short on time today. I'm so sorry. Would that we could drive across the river to get an ice cream, but unfortunately the male genitalia took up all our time."

Julian laughs. And she laughs, too.

It takes them not enough minutes to arrive at her house.

"Look at that," Mirabelle says, pointing out the window. "They're waiting for us at the door." It's true, Charles and an elderly man and woman stand on the porch, waving at their carriage. "Everyone is uncommonly interested in you, Mr. Cruz."

"Perhaps it's my Welsh provenance."

"Yes, perhaps."

How does Julian help her? That's really the question. How does he not do everything wrong like last time? "I can't stay," he says. "I really can't stay." Last time he stayed she was ripped from him like skin off ice. And the time before. And the time before that...

"Perhaps just for supper?"

"Very well, then. Just for supper."

As Julian gives her his arm to help her out of the carriage, Mirabelle leans on him a moment. Her eyes peruse him, while his peruse the air to the right of her shoulder.

"Mr. Cruz, may I ask you a question?"

"Of course, Miss Taylor." He will not face the woman who's addressing him, *the* woman. For shame, Julian!

"Do you...*know* me?" she asks. "I'm not sure why I ask, it's just...for some reason you seem, how shall I put this, quite familiar with me."

"Familiar *with* you?"

She chuckles. "No, no. You haven't been in any way improper. I was joking around earlier. I mean *with* me. As if—I don't even know how to say it—as if perhaps you've mistaken me for someone else? Someone you once knew?"

Julian doesn't know how to formulate a Victorian response to so forward a question. "I haven't mistaken you for someone else," he says. "But it's true, I do feel as if I know you." In the sunlight, Julian rotates his body to hers. His gaze rises. He stares into her face. "But tell me," he says quietly, "do you feel as if you know *me*?"

Now it's Mirabelle who turns red and looks away. "No, sir." She nearly stammers. "Maybe a very little bit. But mostly I don't think so. How could I? I shouldn't think so at all. Shall we?" Composing herself, she adjusts her bonnet, holds tight her purse, and they start toward the house.

# 31

# The Love Story of George and Ricky

VINE COTTAGE WHERE MIRABELLE LIVES MIGHT SOUND LIKE a hut with vines growing over it, but it's named ironically. It's a white stone, large-windowed, vine-covered manse in the middle of a park-sized parcel of private land with lawns and woods and streams abounding, with cricket grounds and stables and hill retreats. The house sits just inside the fence off Taylor's Lane, as if the road is named after Mirabelle. The front yard is a botanical garden of well-tended, multi-colored rose bushes.

Julian's first indication that no one is upset that the two of them have arrived so much later than expected is when Charles bellows across the roses, "Back so soon?" Mirabelle is greeted at the door by Aubrey and John Taylor who look too old to be the parents of a twentysomething woman. They look seventy. Frail, white-haired John in particular seems to be in poor health. Aubrey is a solid, kindly, white-haired woman who insists that Julian call her by her given name and not Mrs. Anything—not very Victorian of her.

"We've heard so much about you." Aubrey drags him inside the house. "Where are your bags?"

"At Mivart's. He can't stay, Mummy," Mirabelle says. "Only for supper."

They revolt. "Mivart's on Brook Street? Gracious me," Aubrey says. "We will not hear of it. We practically have a hotel here, all these guest rooms and no one to enjoy them except us three. You will honor us by staying with us. Why spend your hard-earned money on frivolous nonsense?"

It's not his hard-earned money. "I really can't stay," Julian says. "I'll be glad to help Charles and Mirabelle with the sermons, but..."

"No, no, no," Spurgeon says. "The matter is settled. Barnabus! Prepare the carriage. You and I are riding to Mivart's at once and retrieving Mr. Cruz's belongings." He vanishes before Julian has a chance either to protest (what are they going to think when they see how few things he has?) or say thank you. Julian doesn't know what was going to come out of his mouth, and now will never know. The cat is both dead and alive.

"Julian, you've met my brother, George Airy?" Aubrey says, as the astronomer appears in the front hall with papers under one arm and a walking stick in the other.

"Hello, Mr. Cruz, a pleasure to see you again," Airy says. "You were delayed? Because it took you over four hours to make a trip that usually takes forty minutes."

Mirabelle intervenes. "We went to the Crystal Palace, Uncle George. To attend to that matter I told you about."

"Oh yes." Airy is neutral. "One removal of a papier mâché leaf from a sculpted genital takes how long?"

"About one minute per a set of genitals. Sometimes it required extra effort if I used too much glue." Julian stands by her side. They do not glance at each other as she speaks.

"Yes," Airy says. "And there are eighty statues in the transept. That's eighty minutes. And you've been gone four hours."

"Are you counting the time it takes to get down from the ladder and walk to each one and refill the water bucket as needed?"

George Airy nods. "You've always tried to be an efficient girl, Mirabelle. I'm sure you didn't mean to dilly-dally."

"I don't think I did dilly-dally." She turns to Julian, in her family hall, in front of her uncle, the Astronomer Royal of all of Great Britain and Scotland and Ireland, and says, "What do you say, Mr. Cruz? In your opinion, did I dilly-dally?"

"No, Miss Taylor, I did not see any dillying—or dallying," says Julian. "You were industrious and efficient. I don't believe anyone could've done the job faster or worked harder than you."

"Thank you, Mr. Cruz. I suppose I was the right woman for the job. It was an *enormous* undertaking, though, don't you agree?"

"Yes, Miss Taylor." He will not repeat the word *enormous*, no matter how much she is daring him to. They're in her house!

"Well, no use standing around like giraffes," Airy says. "Mr. Cruz probably would like to rest after all that exertion you put him through."

"Oh, I'm fine, sir," Julian says. "Miss Taylor did most of the work."

"I did, Uncle George. He just carried my water."

"Oh, I'm sure he did, child. I'm sure he did."

∞

Julian is shepherded upstairs to the best room, a spacious chamber with a balcony overlooking the expansive grounds that stretch into the sloping hills. In the room there's a four-poster bed, a couch, a dresser and washbasin, a walnut credenza, and wide low-backed mahogany chairs. It's possibly the nicest room he's ever stayed in. The effusive welcome Julian has received is above and beyond any normal welcome given by decent people to a stranger who's arrived with their only daughter hours late and without a suitcase. It's baffling.

He is brought a tray with tea and biscuits, given clean towels, hot water, new candles, a quire of parchment, pen and ink, slippers in case his feet get cold, and a cashmere-lined silk bathrobe. For a few bewildered minutes Julian sits out on the balcony with a cup of tea, nibbles on a digestive, and digests what's been happening as he stares out onto a glen framed with a wood, fields of flowers, and riding trails. There are gardens and low stone walls and gazebos for relaxation. In the far distance there's a lake. On the nearby pond glide black and white swans.

They had such a good afternoon together. They had fun. There is nothing Julian wants less than to leave. He starts berating himself for his irrationality. What's the point of leaving her house and staying somewhere else? How far would he really go, anyway? He'd be watching her from a local inn or from a hired carriage. He'd be following her, pacing behind her, secreting himself in the bushes, biding his time, silently brooding. Just as he did in the rookery. Well, been there, done that. Time for something else. Why not relax about it, stay at her house, as he wishes, as they all wish, and watch over her from two doors down the hall? Seems so much more practical. And more convenient. *And* it's safer for her. If she gets into any trouble, Julian will be here to intervene. Really, Julian concludes, his staying at Vine Cottage is for *her* protection!

There's a soft knock. Mirabelle peeks in. "Are they treating you well?" She smiles as she approaches the balcony. "Are you enjoying the view?"

"Yes, it's beautiful here."

"Isn't it? I'm blessed to grow up in a place like this."

"Yes." He is too full up to say more. Last time he felt such pity. This time he feels only relief. Why do they both feel like pain?

"Mummy sent me in to ask if you'd like anything else— anything at all, is how she put it. I said, Mummy, I'm not his maid. She told me it was just good manners."

"You and your family could not be treating me any better, Miss Taylor."

"Mummy would like me to show you the rest of the house. We have a few minutes before supper. Uncle George informed me we have forty-seven minutes before Charles and Barney return and drinks are served. Would you like to change first—perhaps into that cashmere bathrobe? I apologize, I forgot to tell my family you're not seventy-two."

"Perhaps, like you, they think I'm Charles Spurgeon's father."

"I still don't understand why my small joke piqued you, Mr. Cruz."

"I was not piqued, Miss Taylor."

"Ah."

At Vine Cottage, the rooms are light-colored with neat clean lines. Instead of stone or wood floors, hand-knotted carpets from the Ottoman Empire cover the parquet nearly wall to wall. The house is delicately Victorian, all cream ceramic candlesticks and brightly colored curtains. Mirabelle is especially proud of the gas supply that's been recently piped in to Vine Cottage. She says it's changed their life.

"And what a good life you have here," Julian says, incapable of hiding his happiness that this is so. He thanks God that her soul doesn't remember the rookery of St. Giles at all.

But there is something unsettling about the otherwise ideal home, something that's been bothering Julian since the moment he walked in. It's almost like an unwelcome pressure of the intrusive metronome when you're first learning the piano.

Ah, yes! The metaphor has led him to the truth. It's the ticking clocks. In every room in the house there's a longcase clock, a dozen pendulums swinging to and fro, tick, tick, tick... anvils to the heart. The clocks themselves are a metaphor for the actual truth. Merciless time waits for no one.

They have supper in the dining room, around a table lit with candles and set with china under a bronzed gasolier with glass shades. Except for the clock in the corner, hammering every quarter hour, it's homey and comforting. Mirabelle has been placed by his side. It spares him the need to hide what he feels every time he looks at her, and yet allows him to be bolstered by her proximity. He eats with his left hand, so his right can remain near her elbow.

They're served herring and boiled potatoes, marinated eels, cabbage and some liver with onions, everything dripping with hot butter. There's ale and gin and wine, and for dessert, bread pudding soaked in brandy. Spurgeon is a boisterous conversationalist, and not above an occasional ribald remark himself. Everyone's regard for Mirabelle is apparent. But the attention is trained on Julian— dare he say, single-mindedly? They want to know whether his family came from the coal mines, whether he is the first one of his generation to attend university, what he thinks of living close to the sea, whether he is permanently stationed in Bangor or would he consider a relocation if a suitable position became available in, say, London. He answers their questions as best he can, making up the details of Bangor College, inventing one of the courses he teaches (The Comedies of Shakespeare) and foolishly mentioning his unfinished research into Thomas Aquinas. It's a good thing he stipulates *unfinished*. Charles Spurgeon, clearly somewhat of an expert on Aquinas, launches into a monologue on the differences between the Thomian and the Calvinist philosophy on Christ, which allows Julian to shut up and finish the pickled herring on his plate.

"I simply don't understand why Aquinas rebels against sovereign election, do you, Julian?" Spurgeon says. "To me it's one of the most welcome truths in the whole of Revelation. How can your heart not dance with joy to know that the Lord has chosen you to love him?"

Julian swallows the fish. He is of a different opinion on the subject, though he doesn't want to argue in front of Mirabelle. But since at its heart, the disagreement is about Mirabelle, he cannot keep silent. "How can love, any love, but especially God's love, be received by compulsion?" Julian asks Spurgeon. "Can love compelled even be called love? If grace is a gift, as in something that's given freely, one must be free to receive it, yes. But then one must also be free to reject it."

"What fool would reject God's grace?" Spurgeon says. "A fool who's not worthy of it, that's who. No, the human being does not obtain grace by freedom. It obtains freedom by grace. Do you disagree?"

"Respectfully, yes. I prefer persuasion rather than compulsion." Julian smiles to soften his words. But there is another thing, too, that Julian agrees with even less, especially given the life he's been living. Rather, another thing that he wants to be true least of all. "If you obtain grace through no act of your own," he says, "doesn't that also mean that you might not obtain grace through no act of your own?"

"Of course it does!"

"But doesn't that mean that no matter what you do, you could be condemned from the start?" Julian says. "No matter what you do, how you act, how hard you try, there is nothing you can do to achieve a different end for yourself? No matter how you live your days, the end will be the same?" Julian shakes his head. He'd rather have his weak will, a thread of hope, and oil in his lamp. He'd rather have anything than a foreordained future.

*48 dots to go.*

He is rescued from further argument by Lena the housekeeper, who enters to whisper to Aubrey that there are people at the door. Aubrey throws a frantic glance at Spurgeon, who says he'll take care of it and leaves the table. The remaining voices die down as everyone strains to hear what the pastor is saying to the visitors and who they might be that they are not welcome at the convivial get-together at the Taylors' on a Friday evening.

"Is that Pippa's voice I hear, Mum?" Mirabelle asks. "And her mother's? You don't want to invite them in?" She lowers her voice. "What have they done?"

"Nothing, my darling. I'm in the middle of a little spat with dear Prunella."

"Ooh, I like spats. What about?"

"Nothing important." Aubrey folds and refolds her napkin. "I would just as soon not see her at the moment. It'll iron itself out. A few days. Possibly a week."

Turning her head, Mirabelle widens her eyes at Julian as if to say she has no idea what kind of espionage her mother is up to.

George Airy, who is indifferent to gossip, studies his pocket watch. "It will take me 38 minutes to get home," he says. "If I ask Barnabus to hurry, perhaps 32. I must dash. Tomorrow morning I'm leaving for your neck of the woods, Julian, for Wales. Before I go, would you care to have a cigar with me outside?"

In the garden, the astronomer lights two cigars. The men puff silently, leaning over the railing, smelling the moist greenery of the fresh night air.

There is great comfort in knowing Airy won't be long in getting to his point. The man is on the clock.

"What exciting thing is happening in Wales?" Julian asks. The sky is especially beautiful tonight, lit with a billion stars. George Airy is not impressed. He doesn't look up.

"I'm close to final revisions on my formula to measure the mean density of the earth," Airy replies. "I've been working on it on and off for over twenty years! At last I've found a mine deep enough to prove my hypothesis. In Wales, of course, where you have the deepest mines, but you must know that. It's 1,256 feet deep to be exact."

"Twenty years?" That seems inordinately long to devote to a single endeavor.

Airy shrugs. "I'm a servant of the Admiralty first and foremost. They don't care a whit about the mean density of the earth. They do care about the declination of the planets. *On comes the star,*" George Airy says with a smile, finally looking up at the sky, *"without haste and without rest until it reaches the gleaming threads of my eyepiece.* All that's left to do is measure its position with the utmost accuracy. But in the mines, something else is required of me. I like that. That's why I've kept at it. I believe I've had a breakthrough at last." With a cigar in his mouth, Airy produces from his pocket a small metal ball fastened to a string, a portable pendulum. He swings it in front of Julian, back and forth. "I'm about to prove," he says, "that the pendulum swings faster at the bottom of the mine than it does on the surface of the earth. Which means that the gravitational pull on the pendulum is greater the closer we get to the earth's core. I've efund a mine deep enough where I can finally measure by how much. And the difference between the movement of the pendulum between the two locations is going to be part of my formula. Isn't that exciting?"

"It is," Julian says. "And it has tremendous implications for the future." He pauses, thinking of himself, and of time dilation and his own space-time curve that's affected by one Mirabelle Taylor as if she is the gravitational constant pulling at Julian's core, even when his time beats faster or not at all. "This research flows from your pendulum work on the Clock Tower? That should be finished any time now?"

"Yes!" Airy exclaims, eyeing Julian with approval. "You know quite a lot about my work, Julian, I am most heartened by this. Yes, everything I do keeps coming back to time and gravity. I don't yet know how the two are connected."

"I would say inextricably," Julian says. In twenty-five years Albert Einstein will be born.

"All I know is that the best clockmakers in Britain said a pendulum clock accurate to within one second could not be built. Do you know who finally said it could and then designed it?" Airy chuckles. "Besides me, that is. Two lawyers! It's true. One of them is my good friend Edmund Beckett, and the other is Mirabelle's father, John Taylor. Clock-making is his hobby. He's a cantankerous fellow but an expert horologist."

"Perhaps it's the study of time that's been making him cantankerous," Julian says.

"You are most correct. The entire period he's been a horologist, he's been in a foul mood. But we needed someone like him—he wouldn't take no for an answer. Mirabelle inherits that quality, I'm afraid. You wouldn't think it from looking at her, but she is a willful girl. Anyway, I showed John and Edmund why an *escapement* must be part of any turret timekeeper, and that has made all the difference in the accuracy of the Great Clock they've designed for Westminster. Do you know what a gravity escapement is, Julian?"

Julian knows about escapements of all kinds. "It's what allows the extra energy that causes over-winding and inaccuracy to flow out of the swinging pendulum," he says.

"You *are* a clever man. Yes. The Great Clock of Westminster will have a three-legged gravity escapement."

Mirabelle's father helped build the Great Clock. Julian is reeling.

*Go take a gander at Big Ben. Go stand there for an hour after a new moon, and see how many people gather around you, holding talismans of the dead, trying to step through the swings of the 700-pound pendulum, between the tick and the tock. You will see them trying to do what you have done.*

"But I didn't call you out here to talk about time, my boy," Airy says. "Even though if you and I had a little more of it, we could have ourselves quite a discussion. Instead I wanted to tell you about a spring long ago when I met the most beautiful girl. Yes, once upon a time I was young and fell in love, too. It feels like yesterday."

Fell in love, *too*?

The man nods, puffing on his cigar. "I knew after two days that I wanted to marry her. So I proposed."

"Two whole days?"

"I knew what I knew. Richarda was going to be my wife. Her father, however, had other ideas."

Julian chuckles.

"You laugh, and others did also. Her father. My friends. My parents. My sister Aubrey, God bless her. But I was not to be dissuaded from what I knew was an incontrovertible truth. I didn't have a position or any income to support a family. So I went to work on those things. I received my degree from Cambridge. I became a professor. It took six years, yes, that's right, Julian, *six years*, but her father finally gave us his blessing.

We were married in 1830 and here I am, twenty-four years later, telling you about my wife and the mother of my six children."

Julian inclines his head in respect—and confusion.

"What is the moral of my story?" Airy says. "That you are in much better shape than I was. For one, Mirabelle's father will not stand in your way, I promise you. You will not have to wait six years."

Julian blinks. "What?"

"You won't have to wait six weeks."

*Six* weeks? "What?"

"Second, you're already a professor."

"Sir—uh—you misunderstand..."

"Oh, I don't think so," says Airy. "Observation is my life's work. Well, observation and keeping records, but observation first, since something must be observed before it can be recorded. Something must already exist, Julian, before it can be written about."

"Yes, sir, but—"

"I would not have noticed it if it didn't already exist. You were nearly invisible to me in the Observatory until Mirabelle stepped into the room."

Julian bows his head. Wow.

"Mirabelle is a lovely girl," George Airy continues. "Well, I don't have to tell *you*. She may not be in the first flush of youth, being nearly twenty-six, but don't let that stop you. Do what your heart tells you." The stooped man raises two fingers in the air. "Two days is what it took for me."

"Sir..."

"My advice? I wouldn't wait too long to make my intentions clear."

"Why?"

"I just wouldn't, that's all," George Airy says cryptically as he shakes Julian's hand. "Whatever we do in life, we ought to do it well, don't you agree? We ought to do it the best we can. And most expeditiously."

"I agree, but…"

"Tell Mirabelle what I told my Ricky after knowing her but two days."

Julian is afraid to ask.

"I told her, my dear, *your fate is sealed*." George Airy smiles. "Cheerio, Julian. Go. Mirabelle is waiting for you."

# 32

# Pathétique

JULIAN IS BOTH ENTHRALLED AND IN TURMOIL. THEY TAKE their tea and gooseberry jam in the drawing room, where they listen to Mirabelle play the grand piano, a Steinweg no less, the German version of a Steinway. Despite her earlier protestations, she plays beautifully. She plays Mozart's "Requiem" and Bach's Partita in E Minor. She plays Beethoven's "Pathétique," one of Julian's favorites.

He has walked in on her contented life, he thinks as she plays, he has found her purposeful and needed, beautiful and young. Why can't he leave her be? There's no pity for her here, the pity is only for himself. She isn't Miri. She isn't Mallory. She isn't Mary with Lord Falk to contend with. Everything is enchanted in Mirabelle's perfect world. She is busy. She is comely. She is loved. She can continue to transcribe the sermons of a pastor, help a genius astronomer, play music. She can sing, ride horses, be adored. She is so safe.

All he must do is *nothing*.

Julian can hardly tear his eyes away from her. But when he catches sight of her mother's expression, Aubrey's face for some reason looks like his. Worship stained with wretched desperation. This is worrying, and after the piano music, the conversation steers in a direction that Mirabelle herself finds worrying.

"Mirabelle is my life, Julian," Aubrey says. "She is the reason I get up in the morning."

"Thanks for that, woman," says John Taylor, her husband and the father of her only child. A smiling Mirabelle goes to sit by her father, putting an affectionate arm over the man's shoulders.

Aubrey waves them off. "You know what I mean, John." She continues to Julian, "She is most precious to me because I had her so late in life. We had given up, John and I, hadn't we, darling?"

"Woman, *please*. This man does not care one whit when you gave birth."

"It's true, Mummy," Mirabelle says. "He really doesn't."

"We thought the blessings of parenthood would be denied us," Aubrey goes on. "And then—it was like John was Abraham and I was Sarah!" The mother blows her nose. "But if you were going to have just one child, what a one to have."

"Mummy, please! Father, stop her."

"You know nothing can stop your mother once she gets going," John says. "She is an internal combustion engine without a switch."

"Or a clock without an escapement," says Julian.

"Indeed!" John Taylor nods approvingly at Julian.

Aubrey complains to Julian that between the Arts Council, the Observatory, Mirabelle's duties for Spurgeon, her work with Coventry Patmore, her hours at the Hospital for Sick Children and at some vague place called the Institute, her daughter is neglecting her leisure time.

Mirabelle is not amused. "Mummy," she says, "is it possible for anyone, anyone at all, to talk about anything else but me when guests are present?"

"No, angel. And Julian is hardly a guest. He is going to be your co-worker. We need to acclimate him to your schedule. He has to know what he will face come Monday morning."

"He's only agreed to help me prepare the sermons for publication, Mummy, not be shackled to me like we're on a railroad gang."

Spurgeon smiles fondly at Mirabelle. "Our Mirabelle works as I do, Julian. Nonstop. As if she's running out of time."

"Charles, *please!*" Aubrey and Mirabelle and John Taylor and Julian all exclaim. The clock in the drawing room strikes the eleventh hour.

"I'm just being jovial," Spurgeon says to them. "Of course, she's not running out of time. Julian, why are *you* chiming in? Why do you look unwell suddenly?"

"It was the liver, Mummy," says Mirabelle. "No Welshman likes liver. I told you and you didn't listen."

"Charles does have a point, though, darling," Aubrey says. "You've all but abandoned your horses, your stables, your flowers, your reading and your fishing. Your sewing work is thrown in the corner and your piano playing is rusty. You're neglecting being young, my child."

"When did Charles make this point, but more important, Mr. Cruz cares a fig about this why?"

"The girl is correct, Aubrey," John Taylor says. "You've gone on *interminably*. Trust me—your harangue is not having the effect that you think it is."

"Hush, now," Aubrey says. "I was merely prefacing my next question to Julian. Do you know how to ride? Maybe you'd like to go riding with Mirabelle tomorrow morning at dawn? We have a docile gray mare for you, so light she's almost white, a beautiful horse."

Julian doesn't answer.

Perhaps seeing his reluctance, Mirabelle answers for him. "College professors do not ride horses. Mummy, Charles, leave the poor man alone!"

Meanwhile Julian is battling with himself. Why couldn't they go riding? They're not riding naked, are they? It's just a friendly canter. He's being given a chance to be her friend. He's being given a chance not to fail, but to succeed!

What a remarkable thing man is, Julian thinks, digging his nails into his palms. He can talk himself into anything. Deny every single thing that came before so he can have what he wants.

"If Miss Taylor doesn't mind accompanying me, I would like that," Julian says.

"I don't mind, Mr. Cruz."

The parents and Charles Spurgeon beam.

Julian doesn't beam.

∞

At dawn the next morning, Mirabelle, sharply dressed in maroon velvet breeches and tall riding boots, knocks on his bedroom door. She wears a short black cropped jacket and a tall black hat fastened under her chin. It's quite similar to what Julian is wearing, except his breeches aren't velvet and his black jacket is neither fitted nor cropped. He wears no white lace around his throat. But their hats are nearly identical, and this makes them smile as they acknowledge it. They walk along the narrow path to the stables. Laughter is better than the tightening of his heart as Julian remembers Mary, forever ago, who is now, in every sense, irretrievable.

He can't help himself. "This is so familiar, isn't it, Miss Taylor?"

"I don't know what you mean. Which part?"

All Julian can do is shake his head.

"It seems natural for us to go riding," Mirabelle goes on, "but otherwise what do you mean by familiar?"

"I'm not sure what I mean." Shut up, Julian.

The Saturday morning riding lessons while Ashton sleeps and the rainy days back in Clerkenwell being taught by Cedric finally pay off. Julian saddles and dresses his own horse, he mounts it—more or less assuredly—and rides alongside her. Mirabelle is a beautiful rider. It comes *naturally* to her. Well, it should. She learned to ride at Collins Manor, when she was a noble lady and her father was a knight in the Elizabethan realm.

Side by side, Julian and Mirabelle ride in the open country. What a time to be out with her in the cool blue dawn. It's utterly quiet. Most of Sydenham hasn't woken yet. The soft sopping hills surround them as they amble through the trails on their graceful steeds. Julian is well aware how they look. A treasure for a painter and his watercolors, black and maroon, riders on horseback, a man and a woman, once and future lovers, etched against the misty horizon on ashen mares.

*And I looked, and beheld a pale horse: and his name that sat upon him was Death, and Hell followed with him.*

That wipes the softened smile off Julian's face, mutes him, and in a dumbshow they ride the rest of the way to the lake, where they dismount and let their horses drink, tying them to a weeping willow.

"Would you like to take a walk in the hills, Mr. Cruz?" She glances at his boots. "You'll get muddy, but…"

"Lead the way, Miss Taylor."

After strolling for a few minutes up a foot path that winds around the lake, Mirabelle grimaces apologetically. "I hope you can forgive my parents for their exuberance."

"There is nothing to forgive."

"They had me so late in life. That's one of the reasons they're so overwrought."

*One* of the reasons? As if there are others?

"Did I say *they*? I meant Mummy."

"Well," Julian says, "over-protectiveness is a mother's prerogative. My own mother had six of us, me and my brothers. I would often wake up in the middle of the night to find her in a chair in my bedroom staring at me. Not sleeping, mind you. Staring."

"Oh, that's precious. How old were you?"

"Eighteen." They both laugh. "She'd say, I'm making sure you're still breathing. You were out so late, or you had another fight…"

"Another fight?"

Come on, Julian. "Youthful indiscretions."

"It's the qualifier before the word *fight* that intrigues me."

She slows down and stops walking. "I just realized around the lake is at least three miles, and we've already been out so long. Perhaps we should start back. Before they worry."

Reluctantly they turn around. After a few minutes of walking downhill, Julian clears his throat. "I have a question about your parents, Miss Taylor. If they're as *overwrought* as you say, may I ask why they allow you to be out with me without a chaperone?"

"What do you mean, Mr. Cruz?"

"You don't know what I mean?"

Stretching her arms to the sky, Mirabelle twists her back languorously to crack it. "Well, Uncle George cares nothing for social norms. That's Filippa's mother's purview." She smirks. "My uncle is governed by one thing only: a ruling desire for order. The thing that too often makes him consumed with filing his correspondence instead of understanding its contents." Affection softens her already softened face.

"That's the prerogative of genius," Julian says. "To be as eccentric as he needs to be. But I don't mean him. What about your parents, what about Charles Spurgeon? An unattached woman allowed to ride alone at dawn with an unfamiliar man?"

"But you just said we were *so* familiar." She's teasing him.

He returns her smile. "I would say not just *allowed* but encouraged."

"You're right. Frankly, I'm as baffled as you are. Should we ask them upon our return?"

"You do agree it's out of the norm, then?"

Mirabelle shrugs. "It's a sad state of affairs, frankly, as far as I'm concerned. It seems that my family has finally made uneasy peace with the fact that any imminent danger to my honor has passed."

"They can't possibly..." Is *that* what's happening? "Has it passed?"

"Oh, *quite*, Mr. Cruz. I'm *twenty-five*. There's a point in every woman's life when a chaperone is simply no longer required."

"I didn't realize you were at that point, Miss Taylor." Julian doesn't look at her, doesn't catch her eye.

"Obviously I am," Mirabelle says with a hearty laugh.

Intently he studies the dirt path under their feet.

"Charles likes you and trusts you," Mirabelle says. "To my mother that speaks volumes."

But volumes about what?

"Are you intimating by your non-response that Charles's trust is misplaced?" she asks.

"No, no," Julian hurries to say. "Of course not."

"Again, I don't know if I should take that as a compliment or an insult, Mr. Cruz."

And Julian gets flustered! Like a school girl! My God, what's wrong with him.

They return to their horses. Yes, okay, he is hopeless, Julian thinks as he unties his mare. But it can't *be* hopeless. He needs to keep his hands off her. Not forever. Just until the end of September.

Apparently, he can't even do that for the next five minutes.

"Would you help me mount my horse, please?" Mirabelle asks. "My arms are sore from riding, and I'm having trouble lifting my foot into the stirrup." She holds on to the saddle. Julian comes up behind her. "Just give me a slight lift, Mr. Cruz." Glancing back at him, she smiles. "It's good practice for Pippa's ball. If you're still planning to attend, that is, and haven't been called back to Bangor."

If Julian were to touch her like this at the dance—lifting her by her hips from behind—he'd be thrown into the dungeons. His thoughts must be plain on his face, and yet for all her decorum, Mirabelle doesn't look away from him, nor does she blush while she is alone with him under the willows. "Don't worry so much," she says in a subdued breathy purr. "Our pastor has vouched for you. That's a recommendation that might as well come from Lord Jesus himself. With Charles's blessing, Mummy and Father would let you inside my bedroom if you wished."

Hopeless!

Spurgeon may trust him, but Julian doesn't trust his own hands to lift her.

"I jump and you lift," she says, blushing.

*Finally* she blushes.

Julian manages to place his hands on her hips, manages to lift her.

"You are quite strong," Mirabelle says, grabbing the reins. "Why does a professor of literature have such strong hands? Is it from all that fighting the professor had done when he was young?"

Julian can't answer her. He can't even make a joke about it. *All the better to lift you with, my dear.* Her beauty has stolen the humor from him. The horses begin a slow walk back to the stables. The man and woman ride in silence. How will Julian ever attain the capacity to deny himself the most sublime thing ever offered man? It is not in his skill set. He doesn't know how he will do it. To save her, to save her.

You'd think upon their return there would be a reprimand for being out so long. But no. There's only clucking regard. "Look at you two. You look so flushed. You must be famished." Aubrey embraces her daughter. "I've prepared a meal for you in the kitchen. But next time you two go riding, you should bring a picnic basket. That way you could have a lovely meal by the water. Mirabelle, did you show Julian the lake?"

"Yes, Mummy."

"Did he like it?"

"He's standing right here, I permit you to ask him yourself."

"Did you show him the beautiful view from the hills around the lake?"

"He's in front of you, Mummy. Ask him."

"Did you show him the boat? You didn't, did you? We have a small boat, Julian. Perhaps you two can go rowing. Mirabelle is a very good rower."

"And a beautiful rider. Your daughter seems to do many things well."

The mother dissolves like sugar in hot pride. "She does, doesn't she?" Once again there's that expression. Love steeped in anguish.

In the kitchen, Julian and Mirabelle devour the cold roast beef with biscuits, downing some ale with it, even Mirabelle, but not before clinking her stein to his. When they look up, John and Aubrey are standing at the kitchen door, watching them.

"Mummy, Father, for the love of God, I beg you—go away."

"Take your time, child," John says. "But allow yourself a few minutes to rest and to change. Doctor Snow is coming for supper."

"John Snow?" Julian says.

"He's a family friend," Mirabelle says. "He often visits on Saturdays." She leans in. "Don't be jealous of him."

Julian stammers. "I won't—I'm not—why—"

"I'm joking." She laughs.

And Julian: "Should I be?"

Mirabelle shakes her head happily. "He did ask me to marry him a few months ago, if you must know."

"Is there anyone who hasn't asked you to marry him, Miss Taylor?"

"Yes, I suppose there is, Mr. Cruz." She lifts her eyes to him. They exchange a pregnant glance. Julian is first to look away.

"I declined Doctor Snow's offer," Mirabelle says. "I knew he didn't want to marry me."

"Why ever not?"

"Thank you marvelous much for that! Because John Snow is a scientist."

As if being one somehow precludes the other.

Mirabelle may be right about John Snow. He is immune to her charms. The man is a grave, humorless, utterly bald gentleman, a few years older than Julian. His black eyes are ringed with exhaustion.

Before supper is served, they sit in upholstered yellow chairs in the parlor, drink wine and eat canapes. Snow holds the plate of food and the glass of wine but doesn't eat or drink. He is a decent but deeply distracted man. Though he is next to Mirabelle, he doesn't sit especially close, as if he is grateful for the whalebone hoops under her blue lace dress that force him to keep his distance. Snow is immune even to her sincere interest in his life's work, which is a tell-tale sign that a man does not love a woman, as far as Julian is concerned. When they discuss medicine and infection, Mirabelle seems as fascinated in micro-organisms as she is in Bach's partitas and the irresistible grace in Spurgeon's sermons, yet John Snow could not care less. "Doctor Snow is the preeminent authority on infectious diseases," Mirabelle tells Julian in a proud sisterly tone.

"Cholera and the Crimea are the two *banes* of our current existence!" John Snow exclaims in clipped Northern English, somewhat more forcefully than the casual parlor room conversation calls for.

Before Julian can open his mouth to ask a reasonable follow-up question ("What the hell does Crimea have to do with *anything*?"), Mirabelle and her parents jump up. Fussing, they grab the drink and the canapes from the scientist's hands, and loudly call to the kitchen, inquiring about the status of supper.

"John is close to making a revolutionary discovery of the causes of cholera," Mirabelle says when everyone settles down again.

"Mirabelle is too kind," Snow says. "I'm afraid I'm far from a breakthrough. The identity of the last organism has been eluding me. This summer we've had sporadic but intense flare-ups of the dreaded disease all over London, and I've realized that I'm no closer to a solution, and even worse, I'm beginning to feel as if I'm running out of time."

"Everyone is running out of time," Mirabelle's father, the amateur horologist, says grimly, to the beats of the ticking clock.

"Pipe down, Jack," says Aubrey, casting him a reproving glare.

"A real epidemic may be brewing," John Snow tells Julian. The current medical consensus on cholera is that it's transmitted through the air, but Snow doesn't think so. For three years he has strongly believed it transmits through physical contact, but lately he has distanced himself from his own theory. "I'm deadlocked at the moment," Snow says, dejected.

Julian tries to recall what he's read about *this* John Snow. He has surveyed so many topics, tried to commit so much to memory up and down the 19th century, that he can't vouch for the accuracy of his information. For some reason, Julian feels that John Snow *is* short on time. He doesn't know why and can't recall the details, but it lies on his heart heavy as truth. Is this what Devi felt years ago when he used to talk about Ashton? Some uncertain evil, a malign circle?

Julian tilts forward under the weight of his conscience. If he directs John Snow to the correct answer, he will not be heeding one of Devi's strongest admonitions. He will not be walking lightly through the past. But to say nothing at all *feels* wrong.

What does it mean to be human, to be good, to be moral, to be all three at once? It means that flawed beings often must choose between two flawed options. What should Julian do? Stay silent and let death reign, or speak and break the laws of design, which may lead to unintended consequences?

Time is ticking. Julian must act.

"At Bangor," he says carefully, oh so carefully, "my fellow academics in the field of medicine have been studying the pathogens in dysentery, which I know is not cholera, being both viral and bacterial, but nonetheless, I think they were testing the spread of dysentery by water."

The doctor, Mirabelle, her parents all stare at him. Charles is not here, or he'd be staring at Julian, too.

"It's a different disease," Snow says. "With a different pathology."

"Of course. I'm just saying, it could be a possibility."

"What possibility?" John Snow sits up stiff and straight like a closed door that's about to be kicked open.

Julian pauses and then says, "That the water may be contaminated."

"In dysentery?"

"In cholera."

"What water?"

"All water," Julian replies. "Water you drink and cook with and bathe with."

John Snow doesn't move, doesn't blink, hardly breathes, as if he's listening to the gears in his head churning and turning.

"No, it can't be," he finally says.

Julian shrugs. "You know better than me, Doctor Snow. I'm not a scientist."

Snow jumps up. The door has been kicked open. "It can't be! Do you know why? Because a city of three million people cannot have contaminated water running into its homes! You are talking plague, Mr. Cruz."

The Taylors look up at the doctor, baffled, as if they've never seen him so agitated.

"You're right." Julian inhales. "Improved sanitation is first. But after that, it will get better."

"No, no, no, no, no. It can't be." The scientist scurries out of the parlor into the hall, to fetch his hat and umbrella.

Mirabelle widens her eyes at Julian. "Were you trying to get rid of him? Well done," she whispers as they follow the doctor out.

"Aubrey, Jack, excuse me, please," he says to Mirabelle's parents. "I won't be able to stay for supper. I must return to my laboratory." He bids everyone a rushed goodnight. "Please pray with me that there's no truth to Mr. Cruz's awful suggestion."

"I thought he was praying for a breakthrough?" Julian says to Mirabelle with a shake of his head.

∞

Later that night, after supper and a breathless stroll with Mirabelle under the linden trees down the nearby Langdon Lane, Julian witnesses a first crack in the foundation. From his room upstairs, he hears the rising voices of the three Taylors down in the parlor room. There's entreaty, denial, even gruff imprecation from Mirabelle's normally impassive father. The balcony and the patio doors are flung open into the summer night and Julian can hear some of their hot words in the muggy air.

Aubrey: "It's unconscionable!"

John: "What must you put your mother through!"

Aubrey: "Why do you insist on this?"

John: "And what about…"

Julian doesn't hear what about, but he hears Mirabelle's voice.

"He's not a pawn, Mummy. Leave him alone! Don't you *dare* burden him."

Who is this *him* she's talking about? Julian? Is he the pawn? Julian walks out onto the balcony and leans over the railing to hear better.

Aubrey: "Charles says that he will be glad to speak to…" Mumble, mumble.

Mirabelle: "No, Charles must not. And to what purpose? This isn't a game, Mummy. We're not children. I gave my word! I'm not going to break my word."

Aubrey says something about her brother George Airy already having talked to someone, followed by an exclamation and the sound of glass breaking.

Mirabelle: "I cannot believe you! Oh, how you infuriate me sometimes!"

Aubrey: "We infuriate *you*?"

John: "Leave her alone, Aubrey. It's useless."

Aubrey: "What do you think you're doing to *us*?"

Mirabelle: "This isn't about you! I already did what you want. It's about me and what I want! Why can't you understand?"

Julian hears footsteps as Mirabelle runs through the house and outside. He steps back from the railing and hides by the blowing curtain. Below on the patio, he hears her sobbing.

He's flummoxed. Why are they fighting? Why is she crying? What could she possibly want that's breaking their hearts?

# 33

## *Five Minutes in China*, in Three Volumes

EVERYTHING IN JULIAN'S LIFE IS THE DEEPEST MYSTERY.

Trying in vain to stay away from her, instead he trails her like a lover.

He picks up the platonic crumbs that remain when the divine is denied him and carries her water. He needs to believe that this time will be different. And why not? She is different. And by keeping himself away, Julian is different, too.

They start their day at dawn with a horseback ride. They end it at nearly midnight in the dining room scarfing down their cold beef and pork pie.

With George away in Wales, Julian and Mirabelle sidestep the Observatory and head straight for New Park Street Chapel to pick up Spurgeon's marked-up and corrected sermons and head to the British Museum, across town. They pass the time in the long carriage ride across congested London by inventing names of new diseases, making up titles of fake books, and by debating the pros and cons of a new elixir on the market called heroin.

Mirabelle is as solemn a masterpiece as Julian has ever encountered. His breath is perpetually short when she is within his inhale. He says solemn, but he means only in the emotion that she swirls in him, which is as profound a longing as he's ever had for her. Because in her purest form, the masterpiece not only breathtaking, and open, and friendly and trusting, but aflame with humor. There is a constant twinkle in her eye, a wry smile at her perfect mouth. The masterpiece likes to tease. She likes to discuss serious things with a light touch, and she likes to be made to laugh.

"I think Barnabus may have arachnid herpes," Mirabelle says of their driver before they've crossed the river. She likes the game of making up diseases that Julian had started.

"How can you tell?" says Julian, squinting and rubbing his chin. "Because of his swollen ankles?"

"Yes, but now that you've mentioned swollen ankles, I realize I've misdiagnosed him. It's not arachnid herpes. He's got thorny tongue." Mirabelle laughs even before Julian can laugh.

"Thorny tongue? How did you come by this crack diagnosis?"

"Because he also can't pay attention and he's got stiff elbows—two sure signs of the malady."

"Barney," Julian calls through the half-open front window to the oblivious driver. "Miss Taylor and I are in a quandary. What do you think you've got, arachnid herpes or thorny tongue?"

"What?" Barnabus says. "I can't hear you. Did you say horny tongue?"

"Oh, he's deaf, too? I take it back," Mirabelle says. "It must be rooster warts." She peals with laughter.

As they're crossing the Thames at Waterloo, they invent some book titles.

"Giants and Swindlers."

"Turtles Without Faith."

"Swampy Rebels."

"Fish in Stockades."

Charles Dickens apparently has made up some book titles to emboss on the spines of fake books that furnish the nearly empty library of his new home, and this delights Mirabelle, to invent titles like the great Dickens.

They switch topics one more time after they've crossed the Strand by the Savoy Palace.

"I don't know *what* you could possibly have against heroin, Mr. Cruz. It's stronger than opium from which it's made."

"That's what I have against it, Miss Taylor."

"But opium is called God's own medicine! How can you be against it? Among all the remedies which it has pleased the Almighty to give to man to relieve his sufferings, none is so effective as opium. And heroin, produced in a laboratory with modern scientific methods, is stronger! So, it's even better. It treats coughing, pain, insomnia, digestive ailments, and hysteria."

Julian tries to list some of the disadvantages of this miracle restorative. He is met with Mirabelle's trenchant skepticism.

"What disadvantages?"

"Let's see. Ferocious addiction. Diminished respiration, a slowed heart, agonizing withdrawals. Sweating. Vomiting. Death."

"Piffle!"

The hour passes much too soon.

The grand British Museum, recently rebuilt from a mansion called Montague House, stands off Great Russell Street. Nearby, the newly constructed Oxford Street has cut a swathe through the rookery of St. Giles, severing its main arteries. There's now a shopping quarter where the heart of the slum used to be. When Julian asks Mirabelle if she's ever been to St. Giles, hoping she will say no, she pauses a moment before replying. "There's a man in St. Giles I call Magpie Smith," she says, "who lives under the stairs with his dog. You can't give him any alms because he'll spend it on drink, but you can bring him some dinner. Usually he shares it with his mangy cur."

"And do you," Julian asks, "bring him some dinner?"

"Not anymore." She smiles regretfully. "Mummy found out I was visiting him and tattled on me to Father. Now they blame me for Father's heart incident."

"Magpie Smith must miss you."

"He's comforting himself with gin, I'm sure. You sound as if you've been inside St. Giles, Mr. Cruz. It's much better than it was, you know. Maybe we can go there sometime, and you could meet my indigent friend. My parents might not mind if you're by my side. Perhaps we can bring him some heroin and see which one of us he agrees with about the elixir's merits."

"He won't be able to give you his learned opinion, Miss Taylor," says Julian, "because he'll be dead of an overdose."

Coventry Patmore, the supernumerary at the Museum, is a skeletal man with sunken eyes and receding messy hair. He appears noiselessly out of the shadows of the research department on the second floor and speaks to Mirabelle in a tone so hushed, even Mirabelle can barely hear him. "Often, I'm reduced to guessing what he needs me to do," she whispers to Julian. Being a supernumerary must be back-breaking work, because the man looks as if he's on his last legs. Coventry sets up Mirabelle and Julian with pens and parchment in a small enclave deep in the poetry stacks ("because in his other life, Coventry fancies himself a poet," says Mirabelle) and they begin. Their job is to transcribe Spurgeon's marked-up and nearly illegible sermons onto a clean parchment, proofreading and editing the words as they go, and the polished text will then be checked by Patmore before it's typeset onto printing plates.

"Make your queries quietly, Mr. Cruz," Mirabelle says, "or you'll upset Coventry."

"I have a query, Miss Taylor."

"Already? But we haven't opened…"

"If you're Coventry's assistant, does that make you the supernumerary's supernumerary?"

She giggles.

Julian's eyes are merry. "But since I'm *your* assistant, does that make me the supernumerary's supernumerary's supernumerary?"

She laughs.

Coventry Patmore springs up at her elbow. "Missssssssss Taylor! Have you forgotten where you are?"

"I beg your pardon, Coventry." She covers her mouth. "Mr. Cruz was being untoward, and I couldn't help myself."

"Do better, Miss Taylor. And instruct Mr. Cruz to be toward."

"Coventry, wait!" Lowering her voice, Mirabelle whispers to Julian, "He is a funny man. Watch." Clearing her throat and getting up, she approaches the supernumerary. "Have you heard that Thomas Robert Eeles has got hold of some new Charles Dickens titles and is planning to publish them?"

"Oh, that scavenging bookbinder!" Patmore exclaims. "How would he get his hands on them? *We* publish Dickens!"

"He met Mr. Dickens in a tavern. But don't despair, Coventry. A friend of mine who was there and witnessed the encounter managed to purloin this coveted list." Mirabelle opens a torn piece of blank parchment and pretends to study it intently. "We can make Mr. Dickens an offer for some of his new books if you like."

"Let's make him an offer for all of them."

"Reserve judgment, Coventry, until you hear the titles. Here's one." Mirabelle pretends to read. "*Five Minutes in China*, in three volumes."

Patmore frowns.

"Here's another. *A Catalogue of Statues of the Duke of Wellington.* No, let's have Thomas Robert take that one, that doesn't sound very interesting. What about *Drowsy's Recollections of Nothing*, in four volumes?"

"Miss Taylor…"

"No, here's one we should publish, though it's not Dickens. *Edmund Burke on the Sublime and Beautiful*, in six volumes!"

Once he understands he's being pranked, Coventry Patmore turns to concrete. "Are you quite finished, Miss Taylor?"

She leans forward and kisses him on the cheek. "I am, Mr. Patmore."

Julian and Mirabelle sit next to each other at a wooden table between imposing bookshelves. Reluctantly Julian wears the gold-frame spectacles Spurgeon had gifted him. He wishes he didn't need them, but without them he can't read a word of the pastor's script. Wearing glasses makes him look and feel like a teacher, not a boxer, makes him feel as if he is standing next to a blackboard, not shirtless and brawny in the ring. Wearing glasses makes him feel like Ralph Dibny.

The only good thing he can say about it is that Mirabelle doesn't seem to mind. She smiles at him just the same.

The work is painfully slow. Every few minutes they stop transcribing to discuss usage and punctuation. Sometimes even with the eyewear, Julian can't decipher Spurgeon's angry corrections of Nora's first-draft transcription. Nora transcribes Charles's sermons as if she is either new to Baptist teachings or new to the English language.

Mirabelle has a soft spot for Coventry. Mirabelle, Julian realizes, has a soft spot for everybody. (Even him?) "Coventry has a wife and four children, that's why he never stops working. Is it any wonder he's so stooped? Emily, his wife, has recently had another child, the poor thing. Even with help, she can barely cope with the three she's got. I like babies, so I offer to take him to the park some afternoons. Would you like to join me when we're finished here?"

"*If* we're finished here."

"Here's the thing you must learn, Mr. Cruz, if you haven't learned it already. You're never finished perfecting words, never. Only the Word of the Lord is finished. Everything else is in perpetual need of improvement. I, for one, have many other things to do today than sit here and figure out if Nora meant to write "divine" or "sublime.""

"Either is fine. What else is on your plate today, Miss Taylor?"

"Taking the boy to the park, for one."

"And then?"

"Can we get back to work, please? The baby is waiting."

For hours they sit lit by two gas lamps, hunched over the parchment in the musty enclave, their heads together. Her fragrant perfumed hair is near him. Her glowing skin is a hand's caress away. The sleeve of her jacket, underneath which lies her blouse, underneath which lies her bare skin, touches the sleeve of his coat, underneath which there's a white shirt-sleeve, underneath which lies his bare skin. Who can pay attention to the semi-colons and exclamation marks when their naked bodies are three types of fabric away from pressing together? Silk on linen, silk on wool. Her coral lips are an exclamation mark, her warm breath an ellipsis.

The sermon they're working on is called "My Love and I a Mystery."

Julian fears it's going to take longer than Mirabelle intends, for not only can they not agree on the correct words in the body of the text, they can't even agree on the proper punctuation for the sermon's title. Should it have a colon, a comma, an equal sign or an em-dash? There are only two of them in the poetry stacks and they are of four minds on the subject.

"A colon is not exclusive enough. As if it's the beginning of a list," Mirabelle says. "As if my love and I could be a mystery, but could be other things, too, like a play or an outing."

"A comma is not restrictive enough," Julian says. "An appositive comma means you could delete what comes after it, and the meaning of the title would hardly be changed. And yet the word *mystery* is the point."

"An equal sign is absurd," Mirabelle says. "I see that's what Nora put down. That's how we know it's the wrong punctuation. Because Nora chose it. What is this thing called love, a formula in John Snow's lab?"

"By virtue of elimination, then, the em-dash it is," says Julian.

"My Love and I: A Mystery."

"My Love and I, a Mystery."

"My Love and I=A Mystery."

"My Love and I—a Mystery."

The Patmores live a few blocks from the Museum, just past Grey Gardens. Emily Patmore, a female version of Coventry but less cheerful, thrusts the bonny child into Mirabelle's arms and tearfully flees up the stairs.

"What a relief," says Mirabelle. "Mrs. Patmore is calm today. I never know what to expect."

With the baby in the pram, they head to the park.

The afternoon sun is strong, and in her long light-blue skirt, peach jacket, and layers of lace, Mirabelle gets warm.

"Would you like me to push the pram, Miss Taylor?"

"Oh, yes, Mr. Cruz, thank you for offering. Would you mind if I take your arm?"

"Of course not, Miss Taylor."

On a weekday afternoon in London, they stroll arm in arm under the elms in the green town square, pushing a pram with a baby, while all around them lunchtime London buzzes with shouting children and clopping horses. Taking the boy out of his carriage, Mirabelle plays with him on the grass, while Julian sits on a park bench, watching them. Her light skirt is discolored after she rises.

"Best not to roll on the ground," he says. "I should've mentioned it earlier. The enzymes and chlorophyll in grass act like a dye. They stain your clothes black."

"I could've used the advice ten minutes ago, Mr. Cruz. Well, you were too busy gazing at the child to offer it. You do seem to know a number of these tidy bromides. Have you considered publishing a handy book yourself? *Cruz's Compendium of Clever Creations*." She smiles. "I could edit it for you."

"I would enjoy that very much. Perhaps after our other work is done."

"Remember what I told you? Our work is never done. That's what Charles keeps telling us. Like the work on our souls."

Again a silent shiver passes through Julian.

They rest on a bench next to each other. Mirabelle holds the baby in her lap. The child is plump and happy, grinning up at Julian.

"Would you like to hold the baby, Mr. Cruz?"

Julian takes the baby. His name is Jacob.

Mirabelle watches the man and the boy with warmth in her eyes. "You're sure-handed with him," she says. "You're familiar with babies—to use your favorite word? Familiar, that is, not babies."

"Thank you for the clarification. Yes, I have three older brothers, all married. I have many nieces and nephews." Julian is awash with guilt. His brothers, his mother, his family, Ashton abandoned by him as he chases the butterfly in his dream.

"Do you imagine someday becoming a father, Mr. Cruz? Having a child of your own?"

"Once in a while." It's painful for Julian to speak of it. He can't get her to stay alive for two months. What's the use of talking about other impossible things. "Do *you*, Miss Taylor?"

"Not really." Regret alters the features of her face. "My life and work has taken me in a different direction, I'm afraid. I don't mind. Everyone has their own path in life, even women. It's like Charles said. A modern revolution is coming. I'm hoping this means more independence for women. I like the idea of being at the vanguard of it."

Two ladies strolling by smile benevolently. "What a lovely baby you two have," one of them says. "God bless. What a beautiful young family."

Before Julian can protest, Mirabelle speaks up. "Thank you," she says. And into his stare adds, "*That* is how two unattached people sit together in a public park. By having an infant as their chaperone."

"Indeed, a tried and true method." Brandon would always tell Julian that his present children prevented him and his wife from having future children. *Babies: the best contraceptive available*, Brandon would say.

You know what else is a good contraceptive? Involuntary, unwanted, unwelcome, abiding, loathsome abstinence.

After parting with Jacob, Julian and Mirabelle return to the Museum. In the early evening, Barnabus takes them to Upper Harley Street, to a square granite building that reads "The Institute for the Care of Sick Gentlewomen in Distressed Circumstances." Finally, the *Institute*! Mirabelle asks Julian and Barnabus to wait and disappears inside. She's gone for hours.

"What's she doing there, Barney?"

"It's Mr. Hunter to you," Barnabus says, "and why don't you ask her yourself, what, the cat got your tongue? You two never stop yammering."

"Watch out, Barney, because rooster warts and thorny tongues don't heal themselves."

"What? I can't hear you."

As Julian waits for her, he negotiates with himself his impossible choices.

He can always scram if he thinks biblical proximity is just around the next ride through the meadow. To protect her from his roving hands (his roving everything), he can leave at any time if he feels there's a danger of imminent skin-on-skin intimacy. Otherwise, if he can manage to contain himself, he won't have to leave and they can stay friends, remain good friends until the threat to her life passes. And maybe after that, she can choose to love him back.

Here's Julian's daily challenge, however:

"What are your intentions, Julian?" Aubrey keeps asking every time Mirabelle is out of earshot.

"Aubrey, stop tyrannizing the man," John Taylor says. "He will make his intentions clear if he wishes to."

But Spurgeon is at it, too. "It's time, Julian. Time to announce your intentions toward our Mirabelle."

And the following evening, Aubrey, as if on a relay, despite her husband's warnings, says apologetically, "I hope you can overlook her being headstrong. She gets it from her father. She is not easily dissuaded from what she wants."

"I have yet to encounter any stubbornness from her, Aubrey," Julian says to reassure the mother.

The father sits up. The mother sits up. "What do you mean by *that*?" Aubrey Taylor says. "Are you implying that Mirabelle has put up no resistance?"

Oh, did that ever come out wrong. "I only meant she's been nothing but agreeable."

"In *all* areas?"

"Aubrey!" John exclaims. "Leave the man alone!"

"Just so you understand," Aubrey says quietly, "we're fine with her being agreeable. We would just like to know your intentions."

Julian's silence is his reply. They're nowhere near September 20 yet.

Maybe the fewer of his intentions, the longer her life.

"I'm fond of your daughter, Aubrey…"

"How fond?"

"Aubrey!"

"Hush, John! How fond, Julian?"

"Very. But I must wait." How can Julian explain to this gray, earnest woman why he must wait?

"Forgive me for being so bold," Aubrey says, "but are you promised to another?"

"Of course not."

"Then why wait?" Aubrey asks impatiently. "Why not make your intentions clear? I hope you know that both John and I would fully approve this union, should you desire it."

"Aubrey, please," John says, his face in his hands.

Julian doesn't say it, but he thinks it. *Aubrey, please.*

And here is another daily, hourly, minutely complication: Mirabelle herself.

The girl is trouble. It's as if she doesn't care about the length of her days at all. It's as if she wants Julian to fail. She is constantly assaulting his senses with her smell and the swell of her breasts in her demure yet fitted corsets. The neckline has dropped. The hemline has risen. From dawn to dusk, her lips look dipped in cherry juice.

Mirabelle is a proper young woman and well-raised. But because of that, she is the most dangerous, for she finds trails not in one epic open seduction—which in some ways would be easier to defend against—but in a hundred shiny, bobbly lures that add up to an utterly ensnared Julian. *John 21.* Truly he is a fish that cannot get away. He is wrapped head to toe in the silk threads of his very own virtuous nymph.

She waits for him to open the carriage door and then leans on his arm as she gets in. She takes his arm as she gets out. She asks for his help carrying the manuscripts and pushing the pram and when it gets too hot, she rests her hand on top of his as they stroll with baby Jacob. When he carries the boy on his shoulders, she stands in front of him and adjusts the boy's little shoes. She stands so close, Julian can smell her hair and her breath, he can see the fine lines and small pores on her face. He doesn't but he could kiss her smiling lips.

He doesn't but he could.

He could lean down and press his mouth into the cleavage of her breasts.

He doesn't, but he could.

In the late evenings, on the way back to Sydenham, the conversation drifts. Mirabelle is tired after a long day. Often she falls asleep. Her head bobs forward. One pitch from the horse and she could go flying. Chivalrously, Julian switches seats to be next to her. As if reading his mind through her dreams, Mirabelle lists sideways and drops her head on his shoulder. He puts his arm around her. Like this they ride to Vine Cottage. Mirabelle wakes just before arrival.

One night, she wakes unhappily.

"Oh, Mr. Cruz," she says, moving away (but not too far away). "I just had the most peculiar dream." She rubs her eyes. "In it you were half-man, half-ghost."

Without you I cannot live at all, Mirabelle. Sometimes I think you're half-woman, half-ghost. Julian could kiss her right now in the darkened carriage. How he wants to. His body trembles with yearning. "What was I doing in your dream?"

"Diving into the Thames. Looking for a way out."

That halts his impure longings. *Diving into the Thames?* He moves away. "A way out of what?"

"You wouldn't say. But you kept begging me to come with you. I was arguing with you in my dream, too, Mr. Cruz." Faintly Mirabelle smiles. "Except in the dream I kept calling you by your given name. I kept saying I'm wearing silk and satin, Julian, I'm not jumping into a river."

"It doesn't sound as though I was very persuasive."

"You weren't. You didn't ask me to disrobe, for one." She chuckles. "Even in my dreams, you didn't ask me to disrobe."

"What kind of slapdash dreams are these," Julian mutters. He can barely look at her.

"My sentiments exactly. And then you said you wanted to give me something I didn't have."

Julian's heart skips two beats, three. "Like what?" He is almost inaudible.

"You said, *a future.*"

He tries to keep his voice steady. "I don't know how I feel about the dream me."

"Me neither," Mirabelle says. "I asked you how long I had."

Julian stops looking at her.

"And you said, *you have less than one silver moon.*"

His head is deeply lowered.

"Mr. Cruz?"

"Yes, Miss Taylor?"

"Isn't that an odd thing to say?"

"The whole dream is odd. I'm going to give this dream Julian a good talking to. Explain to him what's what."

"I wish you would. Here we are. Oh, and Mr. Cruz?"

"Yes, Miss Taylor?"

"You may call me Mirabelle."

"Yes, Miss Taylor. And you may call me Julian."

"Yes, Mr. Cruz."

Together they make not love, but happiness.

And then, late one Friday summer night as they stroll down Langton Lane, they hear from behind them a pitched, distressing voice. "Mirabelle?!" the voice calls. "Is that *you*?"

Just before Mirabelle turns around, her eyes fix on Julian, and in them there is sadness and disappointment and farewell, wordlessly expressing what she can't articulate—that the simple beauty of the brief untroubled days they have spent together is about to vanish with the wind.

"Filippa," Mirabelle says, pulling her arm away from Julian and turning around to greet her friend. "Mrs. Pye. Good evening, ladies. Fancy running into you here. You remember Mr. Julian Cruz?"

# 34

# The Sublime and Beautiful

THE NEXT AFTERNOON, PRUNELLA ARRIVES AT VINE COTTAGE without her daughter. She and Aubrey have tea in the parlor room, while Julian and Mirabelle, barely back from fishing, pretend to retreat to their rooms. Instead they perch on the stairs and listen to the two women, their faces wedged between the slats.

"Aubrey, *dahrling*," Prunella begins by saying, "you know I'm the *last* woman in London to point out impropriety to you whom I adore and whom I generally find faultless in matters of etiquette, but I'm afraid you're not seeing things clearly. The tongues are wagging, Aubrey, there's *no* question."

*Horny tongues*, Mirabelle whispers to Julian, and they both nearly blow their cover.

"Whose tongues, Prunella?" says Aubrey. "And wagging about what, precisely?"

"About *what*?" Prunella snorts. "About the unseemly situation you've got going on under your nose. Your *very* nose. About the improper way you're *parading* your only child without heed or care on the arm of a man who is *not* her husband, a man whom you barely know."

"I find nothing wrong with him, Prunella. In fact, I find him thoroughly charming. John agrees. Julian has asked John to teach him how to make a pendulum clock. Could the man have said anything dearer to my husband, I ask you?"

"This is not about your husband's silly hobby, Aubrey. It's about your daughter's reputation. How can you be so cavalier with it, my sweet? It's the only one she's got, and you're allowing her to walk down Langton Lane at night without a chaperone!"

"Why do they need a chaperone, Prunella, when your concerned gaze follows them around? I couldn't feel more at ease if I were keeping an eye on the child myself."

"Aubrey, as they were walking, Mr. Cruz made some offhand remark..."

"About what?"

"I don't know, we weren't close enough to hear."

"Ah."

"But your daughter laughed *out loud*, so much so that her bonnet fell off! Have you ever? Unmarried women are not even allowed to *speak* to men unless it's in the presence of a chaperone, and your dear girl *laughed out loud*! And then she laid her hand on his arm, Aubrey, as if to say, oh my, Mr. Cruz, you are *such* a witty man. And he bent and picked up the bonnet she had dropped and set it on her head and tied the ribbons under her chin."

"He did *what*?"

"It's scandalous. Yet you are barely aware what your own daughter is up to."

"Do go on, Prunella. What happened next?"

"He tied it under her chin, his male fingers touching her *naked* throat! She lifted her *naked* throat to him, Aubrey! He stood half a step away. And she gazed at him the entire time he was tying the bonnet."

Mirabelle's mother lowers her voice. "You don't know the *half* of it, Prunella. Sometimes when they return home in the evening, I see them getting out from the same side of the carriage. As if they had been sitting next to each other!"

"Aubrey, *no*!"

"And do you know that every morning they go out riding together at dawn before work? Sometimes they stay out for as long as *two* hours. And at the weekend, well, I don't have to tell *you*. You and Filippa have stopped by to visit. They're never home. They're out nearly all day. Why, just this afternoon, they returned from fishing, and they were both wet! I said what happened, did it rain? They said no. Apparently my daughter, the clumsy antelope that she is, fell into the lake and he gallantly jumped in to rescue her—Prunella, what's wrong, you've gone positively *white*!"

"Aubrey, in a minute I shall require smelling salts. How can you be so blasé? Virtue is the only thing a woman has to lose. Everything else is vice. Have you *any* idea what could be happening on their little dawn rides in the glade, *any* idea at all?"

"I can't imagine," Aubrey says, dry as parchment.

"It's a catastrophe! For all you know, her virtue may already be gone."

Aubrey laughs. "Oh, Prunella, I'm just joking with you. Calm down, my dear. I know what a catastrophe is. Believe me, that's not it."

"What would you call it, dear girl? What would *you* call it?"

"I don't know, salvation?"

"Salvation, bah. Well, she is not saving *herself*, that's abundantly clear."

"That's not what I mean. Not saved," says Mirabelle's mother, "but *safe*."

Julian and Mirabelle have been barely able to suppress their laughter, but suddenly Julian can find nothing to laugh about, and to his troubled dismay, neither can Mirabelle.

∞

Later that Saturday night, Prunella and Filippa join them for supper. Charles Spurgeon comes, and George Airy, too, having returned from Wales. The evening animates with stories of mines and measures of the earth's density. George Airy asks Julian if he's found anything strange in his notebooks recording the unusual phenomena at the Observatory.

"Yes," Julian says. He's had a chance to go through them. According to Airy's records going back to 1834, the occasions of unexplained flares have occurred around the same four periods each year—the two solstices and two equinoxes. The solstices have produced the weakest phenomena, the equinoxes the strongest. The March equinox bursts are the most sustained and most visible. For some reason the September equinox flares don't happen at noon but at various times throughout the day. None of the anomalies seem to be dependent on weather or temperature. They occur in rain or shine.

"What does all that tell you?" Airy asks.

"That something peculiar happens on these four dates," Julian replies. "Something that's outside what can be explained by astronomy or earth science."

"Nothing is outside it," the learned man says.

"Oh, come now, George," Spurgeon says. "Surely, something is outside it?" Charles proceeds to tell the story of when he was a boy of ten, and a priest spoke to him of a vision he'd had of Charles preaching to a great multitude of people. Charles was stunned by this, as he had been a child severely hampered by shyness. "But the power of this positive suggestion transformed me," Spurgeon says. "It was an anomaly in every sense of the word. Who knows if what the priest had seen was true. But the mere suggestion that this was even *possible* made the thing itself come true."

"On the equinox," Julian says, "a portal opens in the balance between earth and heaven. A portal that allows mystery to flow out."

"Julian is right," Spurgeon says. "The sun flare is merely an observable reflection of some real but invisible mystery. George, don't tell me nothing like that has happened to you."

"Only when I met my wife," George Airy replies, exchanging a look with Julian.

"I hope someday to meet a woman who makes me feel like that," Charles says.

"Speaking of which," Filippa says, "do you know who's coming to our ball, pastor? Susannah Thompson, the daughter of Abner Thompson, the local ribbon-maker. You remember her, don't you? She and Mirabelle used to be close."

"We still are," Mirabelle says. "She's a wonderful girl, Charles. And she is quite taken with you."

"Ah, yes." Spurgeon looks down into his port, suddenly uncomfortable. "Well, I look forward to seeing her there."

"You're coming to our soiree, too, Mr. Cruz, aren't you?" Filippa asks Julian from across the table, her eyes darting from Mirabelle to him as they sit next to each other, palming their drinks. "It's a week from tonight. It's for an excellent cause. It's to raise money for the hospital in Scutari."

"Scutari?" Julian repeats absentmindedly.

"Yes, the Scutari Hospital in Constantinople," Filippa says. "For Florence and Mirabelle and their team of nurses. Charles, what are you going to do in a few weeks when Mirabelle is gone? Mummy and I don't know how you'll manage without her."

A hush falls over the table. Julian stops tapping his glass, stops being absentminded. He looks up, glances at the anxious, weary faces, turns to his left and peers at Mirabelle. He feels as if he's misheard, skipped a word or two in the discussion and is now struggling to catch up. "Where is Mirabelle going?"

Aubrey jumps up, knocking over her wine glass, and asks if anyone would like more sardines and artichokes.

"To Constantinople, of course," Filippa replies. "To tend to British soldiers in the Crimean War. Miri, you didn't tell him? How could you not tell him? You haven't stopped talking about it for months. I'm sorry to be the first with the news, Mr. Cruz," Filippa adds. "You and Mirabelle are so friendly and I hear you've been spending so much time together. I was sure she would've told you."

George Airy shakes his head. Charles Spurgeon folds his hands. John Taylor stiffens his spine, but it's Aubrey's face that affects Julian most of all. She looks so angry. "Hush, Pippa! Why are you always sticking your nose where it doesn't belong!"

"And where's that, Mrs. Taylor?" Filippa says. "I was just making conversation."

At the eye of the storm sits Mirabelle, her hands in her lap, her shoulders squared. She doesn't smile, she doesn't frown. She says nothing. Certainly, she doesn't look at Julian.

"Yes," Charles says, in a resigned voice. "I'm afraid it's true. Mirabelle and Florence are traveling to Paris and from there, they and their twenty nursing companions are taking the train across Europe to Turkey."

"Your friend is Florence *Nightingale*?" Julian says to Mirabelle. "The lady with the lamp?"

"I've never heard her called that, but yes," she replies.

"When do you leave? Wait, don't tell me"—Julian knows the answer even before she speaks—"is it September 20?"

"Yes—how—how did you know?"

"Lucky guess." He cannot look at her.

"I kept telling you, Julian," George Airy says, "in our material world, time is of the utmost essence."

Julian keels like a bottomed-out boat, lists as if he's been shot in his side.

"Are you all right, Mr. Cruz?" Filippa asks cheerily. "You've gone all pale."

Trying to steady himself, Julian pushes away his chair and rises from the table. "Will you excuse me, please," he says. "I'm feeling a bit under the weather."

Upstairs he keeps his balcony doors closed so he doesn't hear their voices down below.

He barely sleeps that night.

Crimea. September 20. Leaving. Halfway across the world.

Crimea is a bloodbath. And worse, the wounded soldiers are housed in deplorable infested conditions.

Leaving.

Does he let her go or does he try to stop her? As if he even can. Her parents couldn't. Charles Spurgeon couldn't. Her work couldn't. John Snow's proposal of marriage couldn't. Julian wonders how Snow is progressing in his cholera research. The British soldiers in the Crimea could use his help. They're about to fall from the disease. Not some of them. All of them.

Does he go with her? As if he even can. He has no papers, no documents, no identity, no correct sex. He is not a nurse or a woman.

Does he disappear as he first wanted to, vanish until September 20, leave her to her fate? To show how much he cares, does he turn his back on her? To show his love, does he abandon her? Not forever, like Ashton's father abandoned Ashton's mother, just for a little while.

Does he talk to her, persuade her?

And persuade her to do what exactly, leave or stay? Is London Mirabelle's destiny, or is it Scutari? Is she safe if she doesn't meet him at Coffee Plus Food, if she finds a ship to Italy, if she doesn't walk into the Great Fire, if she sails to the Americas? Which way doom, which way salvation?

Superficially London seems safer. But only on the surface. London is a cauldron of death, Julian knows that. London has never been safe.

Does he confess, tell her everything? Can a woman live knowing the date of her own death? Julian knows it, and he can barely live. What does he do as a sentient being to keep her from her fate? London or Scutari? Which way is human, which way is moral, which way is good? And is his choice different because the heart of his heart beats for her? Does love make the choice possible—or impossible?

War?

Or peace?

To ask for her hand, or to wait until after September 20?

And what if, just like before, there is no *after* September 20?

Oh God! Help me. Help me.

To save her does he do nothing—or everything?

Julian finally understands. This is why the soothsayers are in the eighth circle of hell, only one ring above the traitors. As punishment for the dark arts, the divinators must walk forever backwards, their heads twisting around to see where they're going, their tears falling down their backs as they cry. They use forbidden means to reveal what man is not supposed to know.

Julian finally understands. Foreknowledge—even paltry, impoverished, feeble—takes away his free will. It takes away his power to act, to do, to seek, to feel.

Foreknowledge takes away the life man desperately craves.

As it has taken away Julian's.

Even with his gift of partial sight, even having lived through what he has lived through, Julian cannot act. He can't reach for her hand, can't touch her face, can't kiss her. Nor can he stay away, can't turn his back on her, can't wait it out. He can't let her go, and he can't come near her. Which way does she bend to be safe, away from the wind or with it?

And the worst thing of all, the most dreadful, most unbearable thing of all: Does it even matter?

Will anything matter in the fate of her mortal life?

What if there is no fate beyond the fates? What if there never was, and never will be, what if that's the truth Julian refuses to learn?

He wishes for terrible ignorance.

Terrible knowledge is worse.

Julian spends a shivering night walking backwards, his head twisting around to see which way he is headed, tears falling down his back as he cries.

∞

Sunday morning, polite but silent with one another, he and Mirabelle head to church to hear Charles Spurgeon. In the back they stand, listening to his roar. "No sooner is Love born than she finds herself at *war*," the pastor cries. "*Everything* is against her! The world is *full* of envy, hate, and ill-will. The seed of the serpent is at *war* with *all* that is kind and tender and self-sacrificing, for these three are all marks of a *woman's* seed. The dark prince of the power of *nothing* leads the way, and the fallen spirits eagerly follow him, like bloodhounds behind their leader. These evil spirits create dissension and malice and oppression among women and men. What a *battle* is yours, you, the soldier of Love! What a crusade against *hate* and evil! Do not shrink from the fray. As a lily among thorns, so is *Love* among the sons of men. Cannon to the right of you. Cannon to the left. Yes, horse and hero fall. But *you* arise from the jaws of death and the mouth of hell. So, *forward* the light brigades, forward. *When* does your glory fade? *Never*." Julian and Mirabelle don't look at each other.

After the sermon, they approach Spurgeon in the vestry. He studies them with sad, sober eyes. Even his considerable oratorical gifts fail him. "We all told you it was time to make a decision," he whispers to Julian after Mirabelle has boarded the carriage. "You refused to listen."

"I didn't refuse," Julian says. "But what if you knew things that made that decision impossible? What then?"

"What could you possibly know?"

"Things I wish to God I didn't."

Back at Vine Cottage, they saddle their horses and ride out quietly to the lake, Mirabelle sitting side-saddle, still in her voluminous Sunday dress, falling in tulle and chiffon layers around the mare. She asks Julian to go on a boat ride. It's warm and sunny and the air is still. She sits in front of him, her light blue skirts billowing, a wide-brim hat covering her loosely bound coffee-colored hair. He tries not to look at her as he rows.

"Are you upset with me, Mr. Cruz?"

"No."

"But you're not speaking to me."

"I'm contemplating the universe." He forces out a grimace. "I'm concentrating on rowing."

She chews her lip. "I apologize for not saying anything to you about Paris."

"Do you mean the Crimean War, Miss Taylor? Because that's really the important part, I feel."

"Yes. That's what I meant."

"The less said about it, the better."

"I want to explain why I didn't tell you."

"I know why," Julian says. "You didn't want me to talk you out of it. Filippa was quite clear. Everyone's been trying to talk you out of it for months. And you're sick of it." His gaze is fixed on a line of weeping willows to the left of her head. "I know *I* would be. Once I set my mind to do something, the last thing I want is a stream of naysayers. You didn't want me to be one of them. You preferred not to sully our friendship. That's fine. You don't owe me an explanation." Will you just listen to him. He's become a stoic, an ascetic fatalist.

Mirabelle sits watching him row. The muscles in his face are constricted. He pants slightly from the exertion in his arms and chest.

"We were friends," she says. "We *are* friends. I should have told you."

Now it's his turn to twist his lip. He fights with himself to stay quiet.

A silent moment goes by. Julian's life goes by.

"One thing though..." How quickly he loses that battle. It's a knockout in the first. "Were you *ever* planning to tell me? Or were you just going to hop on a train on September 20 and be *off*? Perhaps you were planning to leave me a note? Or have your mother speak to me on your behalf? She's been talking to me on your behalf for weeks."

"Not on *my* behalf, most certainly." Mirabelle leans back. "But that's more like it, Mr. Cruz. For a minute there, I thought you weren't human."

"Whatever I am," Julian says, "I'd still like an answer to my question. The more beautiful the woman, the more honest she should be, don't you think?"

Briefly Mirabelle loses her composure. "I apologize. I was going to tell you—of course I was. I was waiting for—for the right time."

"Ah. Before or after September 20?"

"Mr. Cruz, pardon me for asking, but do you have an interest in my comings and goings besides an academic one?" She falters. "Despite several entreaties, you have not made your intentions clear to my pastor or to my parents, or frankly even to me."

"*Really*," Julian says. "You feel as if I haven't made my intentions clear—even to you?"

For a weighty moment, their eyes catch. She looks away in shame. "What I mean is, you have been very *proper*," she says quietly.

"You would've liked me to be *less* proper?"

"Perhaps…slightly less proper, yes."

"To what end?"

"I don't know what you mean."

"My impropriety, would it have a point? Would it be to keep you in London? Or…" Julian levels his locked and loaded gaze on her. "Are you interested in impropriety strictly for its own sake?"

The blunt question agitates Mirabelle. She twitches, folds and refolds her body, fiddles with her skirts, her lace, her nails. Either she doesn't have an answer, or she doesn't want to say. Which means that Julian's question hit the point too directly on the head. Is that why she's been presenting her open lips to him? Because she wanted a fleeting *improper* interlude before her real life began? "Mr. Cruz…look, there's nothing to be done about it now. I promised Florence."

"It's a very good thing, then, that I haven't been improper with you, Miss Taylor," Julian says, furiously rowing, "because

I might have erroneously construed your allowing me to be improper with you as a promise to me, a promise you obviously never intended to keep."

"Couldn't keep, not didn't intend to."

"Same difference."

"No, it isn't."

"It is, Mirabelle!"

She sucks in her breath—either from his raised voice or from her name on his lips, both a first.

"Why are we talking about this pointless thing?" Julian says, forcing himself to lower his voice. "What's there to say about it? You gave your word to Florence, and in a few weeks, you're leaving for the front. You didn't tell me, but now I know, and you said you were sorry, and I accepted your apology. It's done. Let's change the subject."

Her arms stretch out to him in supplication. "Please listen to me," she says. "Can you stop rowing?"

"No, I want to get back."

"Please. I want to tell you something."

Reluctantly Julian raises the dripping oars out of the water. The gliding boat slows to a stop. He and Mirabelle bob in the middle of the summer lake. Looking into the bottom of the boat at her feet, he sits in the middle seat, leaning slightly forward, still clenching the oars, his elbows on his knees. She sits across from him, her hands clenched in her lap.

"When I was younger I wanted to be on the stage," Mirabelle says. "That's all I ever wanted." She watches his face for a reaction. "That doesn't surprise you?"

"Not in the slightest. You are theatrical down to your fingertips."

"I am not!" she exclaims and then sighs. "Well, fine. But my parents, my friends, our pastor all told me it was madness. No young lady with a hope of marrying well could *ever* be in such a profession."

"Perhaps you should've settled for marrying badly."

"That's what *I* told them! They wouldn't listen. My father was an esteemed solicitor and clock-maker. My mother was a respected music teacher. You know what it took for them to have me. In the end, no matter what I wanted, I couldn't dishonor them." Disappointment distorts Mirabelle's comely face. "The last time I took the stage, seven years ago, I was the Lady of the Camellias. Oh, I was excellent. You should've seen me. Now they've set it to music, made an opera out of it."

"Yes. Verdi composed it. *La Traviata.*" That was the opera that once upon a time Julian wanted to see in New York with Gwen instead of *The Invention of Love.* Placido Domingo was Armand. On the lake with Mirabelle, in Sydenham, Kent, in 1854, Julian remembers it.

"But even before Verdi," she says, "Dumas's story was *grand*! So tragic, full of shattering love. I received three curtain calls." She smiles at the memory, then becomes bleak again. "I wasn't allowed to be what I wanted to be. Prunella told my mother my performances were overtly sexual. She said that continuing to be on stage would infect me with a bothersome carnal appetite."

Julian peers at her through his half-hooded eyes.

Mirabelle blushes at his gaze. "The theatre wasn't serious enough. It wasn't worthy. Well, fine. They wanted serious, I would give them serious. I said I would attend university. They had nearly the same reaction to that as they had to my desire for the stage. My mother told me I would be disparaged as a bluestocking. My father told me women could not attend university. It made women unmanageable. He said I was already plenty unmanageable. And Prunella told me that too much study could have a harmful effect on my ovaries. If I went to university, even if later I did manage to snare a foolhardy sop, I might never be able to give him children. They suggested music instead, singing, drawing. Needlepoint. Perhaps some light gardening. They wanted me married, birthing babies, and sewing. I wasn't having that nonsense. We all know how that's turning out for Emily Patmore."

So now Julian knows: Mirabelle lives but not to her satisfaction. That expression on her face when he first met her was of a woman trapped, afraid that life was passing her by, and affecting an air of indifference to her own imprisonment.

"Was that your only choice?" he asks. "Marriage or war?"

"No. First I studied to become a novitiate. But I stopped short of taking my vows when I began working at the Arts Council and for my uncle at the Observatory and transcribing the sermons at New Park Street Chapel for the previous pastor. Then I met Coventry Patmore and helped him with his printing publications for the Museum, and so on and so forth. And through the Patmores, I began work at the Hospital for Sick Children, and through the hospital I met John Snow and helped him with some of his projects, and through him, I met Florence Nightingale. Thus began my nursing work with her at the Institute. You see, it all flowed from one to the other, the way life does outside the theatre."

"From this you got Crimea?"

"Florence needs help. You have no idea how few women are willing to train as nurses to go with her abroad."

"I have some idea, because most women aren't mad."

"I'm not mad, Mr. Cruz. Our soldiers need care, and I had nothing to keep me here. Have nothing," she corrected herself. "Why would I not answer the call? I know Mummy is upset with me."

"Everyone's upset with you," Julian says. Mirabelle is careless with everyone's love because she couldn't live how she wanted. "Are you going to the front to punish your mother?"

"Of course not, why would I want to punish my mother?"

"Okay," he says in a clipped voice, his mouth twisting. "Is there anything else?"

She watches him. "You know, after I stopped performing," she says softly, "I used to pray on rainy days for some other frisson to dust me with its magic. But it never happened." She breaks off.

"Wounded and sick men are your idea of a frisson?" says Julian. Instead of healthy, hearty men?

"I'll come back, Mr. Cruz," she says. "I'm not going to the Crimea for the rest of my life."

"You make it sound as if the rest of your life is infinite time." Julian winces. "Do you remember the question you asked me in your dream?" Leaning on the oars, he droops like a sack of weeds. "Do you remember my answer?"

*You have less than one silver moon.*

"It was just a dream. I don't put much stock in that."

"But what if it wasn't?" he says. "The war is going to last a few years. There will be a siege. There will be blood. What do you think happens to nurses when they treat infected patients year in and year out?"

Mirabelle tilts her head to gaze at Julian with sympathy. Is it sympathy? He's not looking at her closely enough to divine.

"People can get sick anywhere," she says. "You don't think people get sick in London?"

And just like that, she has cut to the crux of Julian's struggle. People can die anywhere. Los Angeles. London. Crimea.

"I'm either fated to live or fated not to," Mirabelle says. "It's in God's hands, not mine. I have nothing to do with it."

"But why deliberately put yourself in harm's way?" Julian clenches his hands over the oars. He'd like to clench his hands over his ears. The lake shimmers around her. He can't make her understand what he doesn't understand himself—which way, which road, which path, which word, which act. Is there a right way? But if there isn't, what is the fucking meaning of all life.

"Your family has been using me," he says. "That's why they've allowed me to be alone with you, to ride your horses and row your boats. They're so desperate to have you stay, they've thrown their baby out with the bathwater. They've tried Charles, they've tried John Snow, others maybe. I'm their last resort. They would rather have you be publicly seduced by a Welsh pilgrim than get on that bloody train on September 20. Doesn't that mean something to you, their desperation?" Dejectedly he lifts the oars and begins to row.

She raises her eyes. "Is it only *their* desperation?"

He stares back at her, full of love and woe. His arms are shaking even while he exerts force on the paddles.

"What about the other part of my dream?" she asks. "You have nothing to say about it? That you implored me to jump in a river?"

"Don't be a skeptic, Miss Taylor," Julian says. "There *is* a passageway under the Thames. The zero meridian transects the Royal Observatory, and it transects the river, too, to the Isle of Dogs and beyond. The meridian circles the globe and rises into the stars."

"So what? And I'm not a skeptic."

"Maybe instead of going to the Crimea on September 20, you should come to the river with me."

"So you *are* asking me to jump in the river!" She laughs.

"Yes, because I'm a romantic," Julian says. "I can't help but wish, I can't help but hope." He takes a breath. "The tunnel comes to a dead end at a floodgate, a gate that controls the flow of water." That is what Cleon told him. "I heard that the gate can open on September 20, perhaps during the sun flare at the Transit Circle."

"Like a parting of the seas?"

"Like a path to the deepest channel of the Thames. We have about a minute before the floodgate closes. Maybe on the other side is..." Julian broke off. On the other side was what? A place where the waters didn't turn to blood, where the fish weren't slain, where there was no more darkness, or hailstones, or flames. What was on the other side if they crossed hand in hand and stayed steadfast?

"What's on the other side?" she asks.

"Your life."

"Under a *river*?" She is not persuaded. "In a raging current?"

"In the headwaters of your new self."

She shakes her head. "That sounds romantic to you?"

"Better than war." Julian stops rowing, reaches into his shirt, slips the rawhide rope over his head and places the entire necklace with the crystal, the rolled-up beret, and the two gold rings into her hands. "On the equinox, the crystal creates a flare when the sun hits it," he says. "Come with me on September 20, and the mystery will be revealed to you, too."

"You mean, it's already been revealed to you?"

"Yes."

"Just once?"

Julian doesn't know how to answer her. "I keep being given a second chance," is what he says at last.

*And not just me, Mirabelle.*

*But our time is running out.*

She glides the tips of her fingers over the crystal. "It's giving me a slight shock," she says, drawing her hand away. "I don't like it. What are these gold bands?"

"Many years ago, I had them made," he says. Eighty years ago. "I carry them with me." He shields his eyes so she can't look inside him. "There's a beret, too. Would you like to see it? Here." Carefully he unspools the soft hat from the rawhide wrapping, smooths it out, and hands it to her. He has taken good care of the beret over the years. It's wrinkled, but not torn. She touches it uncertainly, examining the faded black stains on the leather. The intuition worries her forehead.

"It looks like blood," she says. "It feels like blood."

Julian doesn't argue.

"Whose blood is it?"

When he says nothing, she drops the beret as if she's burned by it.

His faith is like open water.

"I will repeat what I said in my dream," Mirabelle says. "I'm not diving into the Thames with you, *Julian*. On September 20, I'm taking a train to Dover and a boat to Calais. I'm going to France. And then to the Crimea." She pauses. "Unless...there is something you'd like to ask me. That doesn't include jumping into sewers." She waits. "*Is* there something you'd like to ask me?"

Julian is going to bite his lip to blood. "No," he replies through his distorted mouth. He picks up the beret and rolls it back up into its thin red line, twining it with the rawhide rope.

"So, what are we talking about, then?" She is visibly disheartened.

"I want you to make the choice—to go or not to go—without my influence." He slips the necklace over his head and inside his shirt.

"But why?" Mirabelle exclaims. "We are influenced every day by a million things. Why would an informed choice be against my best interest? If your intentions are honorable, I must know that. And if they are dishonorable, shouldn't I know that also?"

"Do you mean to suggest *I* have a choice in the quality of my intentions?" Julian says, striving for flippancy, but doesn't answer the underlying question because he is made mute by the Gordian knot that constricts his windpipe.

And she doesn't respond to his teasing, as she normally might. "Answer me, Mr. Cruz."

What can Julian say but, "At the moment, I have no intentions, Miss Taylor."

She exhales. He picks up the oars, and they stop speaking.

When they reach shore, she barely accepts his hand to help her out of the boat, nearly falling before she rights herself and storms to the horses.

"You don't want to take a walk around the lake?" Julian asks.

"I most certainly do not."

He has upset her. "Come on. It's a beautiful day. Let's…"

"Let's ready the horses and head back, shall we?" She swirls to him. "But just so you understand—this is the last time you and I will be alone together."

He bows his head. Hasn't he been punished enough?

"This is the last time you will speak to me without someone else present."

"Why are you being cruel?"

"Oh, listen to you, black pot!" she says. "This isn't *my* doing. But now that you know I'm scheduled to depart the country in a few weeks, and now that you know why my family has been performing cartwheels in front of you—up to and including allowing you to be alone with me to motivate you—how do you think they'll react when they realize you're fully aware of what's at stake and still choose to do *nothing*? You will be fortunate if the Metropolitan Police are not called to guard me from you."

"One word from you…"

"Why would I give that word?" she cries. "To what purpose?" She pauses to compose herself. "Anyway, that's one reason. And the second reason, even if I did deign to give a *word* as you glibly suggest, now that Prunella and Filippa know you're staying with us at Vine Cottage, they will perpetrate a full-scale assault to prevent you from spending a minute alone with me. I guarantee they're already at the house waiting for us to return. Prunella's imperative is to find Pippa a husband. Nothing can or must or will stand in her way. The women will not tolerate our friendship or our professional relationship. They will accompany us on each of our daily labors, from the Observatory to the Institute. They will ride in our carriage. They will sit with us in the Museum stacks. We will never be alone again. I know that Pippa is counting the days until September 20 when I am gone, and she can have you to herself." She watches Julian watching her. "So help me untie the horses, Mr. Cruz, and square your shoulders from the onslaught that awaits us."

∞

The horses remain tied up. They continue to graze near the abundant willow under which the picnic blanket and basket have been spread out. Julian asks Mirabelle if she is hungry, and she says no. She collects daisies in the wet bog near the shore, makes a bouquet of them with some laurel and lilies. He paces the shoreline, thinking but not thinking, feeling but not feeling.

They are in a secluded cove of bush and tree, the lake lapping at their feet, the gently sloping hills around them, the birds chirping, not another soul in sight.

Holding her flowers, she steps in front of his pacing path.

"I don't understand," Mirabelle says. "On the one hand, sometimes you seem to be quite taken with me. And other times, you're as distant as the moon. And sometimes, like now, it's both at the same time."

He can hear her breath rising and falling in her chest.

"Mr. Cruz…do you plan to answer me?"

But Julian is all about studying the pebbled sand.

"Will you please look at me."

Julian shakes his head.

"Are you really not prepared to do *anything* to have me stay?"

"You mean there is something I can do to have you stay?" But he won't raise his eyes to her! "You just told me there was nothing I could do. That you gave your word. You were going no matter what."

"I suppose I wouldn't mind having a true choice to make," she says shyly.

The lake smells of backwater, overripe green, overripe red. It's a warm August day. September is nearly here.

"All I'm asking is that you wait to make any decisions about the Crimea until after September 20," Julian says. "That's all. Just wait one more day."

"And then?"

And then I will ask you everything. What you want of me, *anything* you want from me, I will do for you and give you. Yes will be my only answer. "I'm asking you to wait." *Wait one more day.*

"Why?"

"I can't tell you. And you don't want to know. But you need to trust me."

"Do you want me to go to Scutari?"

Julian cannot say.

"Do you want me to stay in London?"

Julian cannot say.

"Is there anything you want from me now?"

Julian won't move his head, won't look up, won't even breathe, for the breath will give him away.

"Why is it so hard to ask for my hand!" she exclaims.

"Not before September 21." How absurd he is! How foolish, how idiotic, how spellbound.

He descends onto the trunk of a tree that has fallen in the water. She perches near him. Taking the bouquet out of her hands and setting it between them, Julian presses his mouth into the center of her soft white palms, kissing one and then the other. "Mirabelle..." he whispers, lowering his forehead into her hands.

"*Julian*...can you please look at me?"

He shakes his head, but she has electrified him with those three little syllables and her magnetizing proximity, sitting too close in her flowing dress, her curled hair falling down, her riding boots against his dusty own.

"Come on. Look at me."

With difficulty he raises his eyes to her.

"Don't you want to kiss me?" she whispers.

He nearly groans. "There's nothing I want more." How can one heart hold so much love next to so much fear? "But I'm afraid if I kiss you, you will die."

She cocks her head. "Are you speaking metaphorically?"

"No."

"Will your kiss be so overpowering that it will cause me to cease breathing?" She mines his fallen face for clues, for humor.

"No."

"Well, what say you, O Julian Cruz of Bangor?" says Mirabelle. "Is your kiss worth it?"

Beat. Blink. One shallow breath. "No."

They stare at each other. He doesn't look away. And neither does she.

She remains pensive. "Color me intrigued," she says, her hands in his.

"Don't get on that train. Just wait."

"How can a girl live out her life without at least half-endeavoring to uncover the truth about this magic kiss of yours?"

"You're not listening to me. Do not endeavor, by half or any other way."

"It's just a kiss, Mr. Cruz, just a kiss..." she whispers, tugging on his hands, inclining her body to him, her head tilting, her mouth parting.

Julian leans forward and kisses her. Passion and heartbreak are in his open kiss.

A flushed breathless Mirabelle wrenches herself away from him and stands up.

"Where are you going?" Julian says, also standing up, raising his pleading hands.

"I'd like to go swimming," she announces. "The water might cool me off."

Julian doesn't think it will. "Did you bring a swimming suit?"

"I don't know about Wales, Mr. Cruz, but here in London, the swimming suit is a dress. It comes down to my knees and buttons to my chin. It has long sleeves. And a belt. It comes with a cap. And I must wear pantaloons under it. I might as well jump into the water in the dress I'm wearing." She takes a step toward him.

And he a step back. He can't kill her with his love again. No matter how desperately he wants to. "Miss Taylor," he says, not trusting his voice. It's thick like it's gained weight. "*Please*—let's untie the horses and leave."

"Oh, the horses are untied, Mr. Cruz. The horses are galloping."

"No, let's ride back home. Would you like me to help you into the saddle?"

"What I'd like," says Mirabelle, "is for you to help me out of my dress."

"No. I beg you."

"No?"

"No..." Julian whispers. There isn't a man in London, past, present, and future, who means it less. She stands in front of him stunning, ephemeral. Inside her perfect body is her heart, is her soul, is paradise. But Julian can't touch her until she is loosed from hell, until she's been freed to flee to another dimension, a dimension in which she will live, and only then will earth be divine. Because she will be on it.

She takes off her bonnet and pulls the pins and ribbons from her wavy hair. The dark tresses fall down below her shoulders.

"Don't do that," he says hoarsely.

"Do what?" She starts to unbutton her sleeves.

"That," he says. *"Please."* His hands are up in surrender.

"I don't know what you mean," she says, untying her bodice. "Summer is going to be over soon. I would like to take a dip in my lake before spending the winter in the Crimea. Is that wrong?" She kicks off her boots. "Would you like to come in with me, cool off? You seem quite warm yourself."

All of him is on fire.

She half-turns her back to him. "Could you help me unlace my dress?"

He doesn't move.

"You won't help me? Fine," she says. "I'll do it myself." Little by little she loosens the strands that hold the crinoline to her body. Finally, she steps out of the whalebone rings, leaving the dress and petticoat like a tent by the tree, and stands in a long ivory silk chemise, draping down to her ankles. Underneath the silk, she is naked. A distraught Julian backs away. There she is. Open your eyes and behold. And cast your lot into her pot.

"If you saw me compromised," Mirabelle says, "like a shining knight might at the sight of his imprisoned princess, would you turn your eyes from me?"

"No," he says. "I would not." He is about to forget every single thing he ever knew and fled and feared. Death has never seemed farther away.

She slips the chemise off one shoulder, then the other, and stands topless, watching his face. Pulling the silk fabric down, she wriggles it past her hips. The chemise falls to the sand. She stands before him naked, exquisitely beautiful, her pale smooth skin shimmering in sunlight, her soft pink nipples hardening, her high breasts heaving with her breath.

It's hopeless now, truly hopeless.

"I have never been touched by anyone," Mirabelle says. "I have never been with anyone."

Julian nearly cries.

"I have immortal longings in me," she says. "I am fire and air."

He and the dying girl have crossed the border into an undiscovered country, where they will perish together.

In one stride, he is by her side. He wraps his arms around her bare body before he kisses her. Why should there be a trace in *her* soul that remembers the agony of her death when there isn't even a clarion bell in *his*, which has lived through it, grieved through it and knows? He rips off his tunic, waistcoat, shirt and presses her soft breasts into his bare chest, his lips opening her lips. Finally her skin is on his skin. They sink to their knees onto the blanket, their lips, their bodies together.

Her hands rise up to touch his arms. "Mr. Cruz...I didn't realize you needed to be so muscled to be a professor of literature."

"My studies are surprisingly rigorous, Miss Taylor."

Why should her body prickle from pain when he touches her? Why should her heart spasm from the wrenching memory of the love she felt for him just before she was shot, suffocated, burned, stoned, why should *she* be in terror when he himself feels nothing but hunger?

"You think I've been happy?" She offers her white throat to his ravenous mouth, moans. "I haven't been happy. I've been in dire want of joy, of a dream, of a brush with fire. How could you not have seen it?" She arches her back, offers her white breasts to him, moans.

"I saw it." He throws off his boots and breeches and stands naked before her.

"I don't want a mere brush with fire," she whispers on her knees, looking up at him, reaching for him, her arms trembling. "I want it to go right through me."

"As you wish," he says, kneeling in front of her, his palms on her back.

"Would you turn your body from the body of your swooning princess?" She is held up by his arms. Her hands are on him.

"No," he says, lowering her to lie down on the blanket. "I would not." He bends to her breasts.

"Your hands, would you avert them?" She can barely get the words out through her rousing sighs.

"No." He grips her waist above her hips.

"What about your lips? Would you avert them?"

"No." He presses his mouth against her white stomach.

"What else would you keep from me?"

His body is over her. "Nothing."

"Will you devour me?"

"Yes."

"Overpower me?"

"Yes."

"But gently at first," she whispers. "Please. As gently as you are able."

"Yes."

"Julian...?"

"Yes, Mirabelle?"

"But only at first."

"Yes, Mirabelle."

Her moaning is like the song of the swallows before the summer's end.

It's too late now for other kinds of salvation.

Her softened body sublimates, melts in his hands, surrounding him, under him, under his mouth.

Soon there will be nothing left of her.

There is already almost nothing left of him.

*So kiss. Kiss until you forget your names, until the stars stop blazing down on dragons and horror shows, on black magic carnivals and comets of doom, on pistons in motion and cellar saloons. Kiss until dawn dissolves the earth.*

Her long arms wrap around him, her legs wrap around him. "You're cruel is what you are," she says, lying in his arms. Her hands caress him, fondle him. "Cruel and unfair. You say you have foreknowledge of forbidden things. You say my dream was a premonition. I ask all the more—then why would you keep yourself from me if you know this is all I will ever have? *Especially* if you know that. Why would you deny me just once in my life to know this? To know *you*?"

He has built them a barricade with her whalebone petticoat to hide her from sunless Hades. He has laid her inside it and himself inside her, under the willows and the sky, he has lowered himself again and again into the fields of asphodel, into the immortal flower.

"We should go back." He cannot believe it is he who says this. He is just trying to protect what's his, to keep them a secret, to hide them from the world. "Or soon they'll send out a search party. You don't want them to find us here *in flagrante delicto*, do you?"

"What if I do," she says. "Either way, I won't be able to hide this from them. It'll be on my face every time I look at you. One glance, and everyone will know what you did to me. What I wanted you to do to me." She gazes at him. They lie embraced.

"No, they won't. You'll act as if you don't know me. You'll act as if it never happened."

"But I *do* know you. It *has* happened. How do I hide that?"

"You *act*," Julian says.

It must be late afternoon. They've been missing all day.

Mirabelle, you are the source of all my joy—and all my misery. Bliss and sorrow are the headwaters of the brief eternity I spend with you.

"I love you," is what he says, and she cries.

# 35

# My Love and I—a Mystery

THERE'S NOT A GIRL MORE BEAUTIFUL THAN HIS GIRL THE
night of the dance at Sydenham Hill Manor.

Perhaps none more beautiful in all of England.

Perhaps none more beautiful in all the world.

They have spent an intoxicating week hiding their
drunkenness from the adults, like two kids who have discovered
beer and are giggling each time they steal one from the fridge.
And they keep stealing and stealing, even though the adults
have cottoned on and have started keeping the liquor in locked
cabinets. Well, Mirabelle has discovered the taste of beer. Roused
to something she had not fully imagined or understood, she has
been crawling into his bed every night and keeping him awake
until break of dawn. *Julian, are you asleep? Julian…Ju-li-an…are
you asleep?*

During the day, she was right, it has become impossible for
them to get a minute alone together. Filippa and Prunella trail
them everywhere. In the carriage, in the parks, in the stacks,
even getting ice cream at Astley's Circus, the two Pye women
loiter at their side. It's excruciating. He and Mirabelle cannot
glance at each other without Filippa glaring at them, without
Prunella interrupting them, distracting them. They are reduced
to speaking to each other through the words of Spurgeon's
complex, elaborate sermon, "My Love and I—a Mystery," which
they're almost finished transcribing.

"How do we overcome the venom and vitality of the evil that rages upon us?" Julian reads aloud to Mirabelle, and she writes it down, sentence by sentence, phrase by phrase, word by word. "My love—tell me, how *do* we overcome it?"

"We overcome it by patience.

"We overcome it by faith.

"We overcome it by hope.

"We overcome it by perseverance."

"Hang on, Mr. Cruz," Mirabelle says, "slow down. Don't be so hasty. Let me get the last of your words down. You said perseverance?" Beat. "Not *drive*?"

"Yes, Miss Taylor. Not drive."

"All right, I am ready for more. Please resume. Mr. Cruz, did you hear me? I am ready for more."

"Yes, Miss Taylor, I lost my place for a second. Here we go. We resolve to love.

"We will not be irritated into unkindness.

"We will not be perverted from generous, all-forgiving affection."

"Wait, Mr. Cruz, slow down, let me catch up…all-forgiving… *affection*, got it."

"We set our helm toward the port of love, and toward it we steer—come what may."

"Come…what…may…very well, Mr. Cruz. Should we say helm, or *rudder*?"

"Rudder is a fine word. Use it if you wish, Miss Taylor."

"I think I shall. I think I shall use *rudder*."

She doesn't lift her eyes from the parchment. And he doesn't lift his gaze from her head.

But at night, after everyone is asleep, Mirabelle, silent like a tigress, crawls into his bed and falls into his arms, charging him with her happiness, exhorting him to keep her quiet, two commands as mutually exclusive as can be.

I can't take my eyes off you, Mirabelle. Even in darkness.

Shh. Match my silence. Don't do anything to me that will make me exhale too loudly—like that, don't do that!

Yes, Mirabelle.

Caress me softly, don't stop, but don't caress me anywhere that will make me cry out—like there. Oh, God, Julian, or there. Or especially *there*…

Yes, Mirabelle.

Kiss me but do not kiss me with exultation. No exultation, I said!

Yes, Mirabelle.

Love me but without exultation, Julian.

Yes, Mirabelle.

I said without!

Oh. I thought you said with.

Now you've done it. Put your hand over my mouth. Throw the blankets over us. You're impossible, you're not following any of my instructions. Wait, wait! Let me turn over and press my face into the pillows, so no one can hear how flagrantly you're disobeying me.

Yes, Mirabelle.

And slow down.

Yes, Mirabelle.

At the ball, her shiny hair is half-up, half-down, partly braided and loosely curled, and her mulberry dress is not so appallingly large as to prevent him from standing close to her. She wears a sparkling headband that looks like a diadem, a crown for royalty. She smells of violets and wine. Her lips are the color of violets and wine. Her dress is fluted gathered silk and satin with gold embroidery. The puff sleeves are off her shoulders. The neckline is low. Her skin is alabaster, from her forehead to her white breasts.

The unworthy Julian stands next to her, barely able to breathe.

All around them are twinkling lights and clinking crystal. Everyone's face is dressed up with a smile. (Everyone's but John

Snow's, who looks as if he's come into contact with some awful, hateful thing.)

The ballroom and the adjacent, equally loud dining hall are decorated with white roses and pink peonies. There's china on the tables, long tapered candles, sparkling chandeliers, and in the corner a band. A piano, a cello, two violins, a bassoon. The evening is warm and the wall of French doors to the stone patio are flung open. A breeze cools the guests in their splendid frocks as the butlers pass around hot canapes and stemmed crystal glasses of Veuve Clicquot rosé champagne.

"The French, God bless them, are still trying to find a way to rid the champagne of its delicate bubbles," a chuckling Mirabelle tells Julian, clinking glasses with him. "But we British adore the bubbles." She smiles.

"Stop smiling at me," Julian says, unable not to smile in return.

"You don't want me to smile at you?"

"I'm begging you, behave yourself."

"Tell me, my love," she says, leaning decorously to his ear, "do you think the rosé champagne will be *more* delicious or less delicious if you poured it over my body and kissed it off me?" Chortling, she glides away.

Because he is technically not Mirabelle's guest but Filippa's, Julian must leave Mirabelle's side. With Filippa dragging him hither and yon, he is introduced to the other patrons, as if he is her escort. As if he belongs to her.

Julian is well received in his black trousers, gray tail coat and white cravat. He has shaved his whole face, though most of the other men sprout thick, bushy sideburns. Mirabelle prefers him clean-shaven, so that's that. His longish dark hair is brushed back and left down his neck, while other men's hair is short (or in the case of John Snow, non-existent). Because of the contrast, he stands out, he commands attention.

The waitstaff uses Baker's Peels—trays with long handles— to bring the ladies their food and drink, because they cannot reach them otherwise over the eight-foot-in-diameter petticoats.

Before the dancing can begin, several people dressed for a lecture give wordy speeches on the importance of Florence Nightingale's nursing work abroad while the genteel women stand and chafe in their enormous crinolines, and the men drink and check their pocket watches.

Julian has a few minutes with John Snow. The man does not look well. Snow's shiny bald head conveys his anxiety. He is constantly wiping it with his handkerchief. The hand that holds the wine glass is unsteady.

"I haven't seen you since our evening at the Taylors', doctor," Julian says. "How's it going? Any luck?"

"By luck, do you mean are people dying?" The man is in a mood. "You think you had a hard time convincing *me*?" Snow continues. "The Board of Health minister has refused to shut down the water pump on Broad Street I told him was responsible for the most recent outbreak of cholera—600 new cases just last month! He says my evidence is circumstantial. I told him you have 500 men in the city prison living in vile conditions and none of them is sick, yet here on your streets, 600 people contracted one disease, and that is circumstantial? He says, what would you have me *do*, Doctor Snow? Perhaps pump all the water out of the *Thames* and replace it with new water?" Snow tuts in disgust. "We're doomed. Do yourself a favor, Julian, drink only wine or boiled water."

"On it, believe me," Julian says.

"I told the minister that death is coming into his home, death in the form of dirty water. Did he listen?"

"Because it's impossible to comprehend," Julian says. "To fix it will require replumbing the largest city in the world."

"How about if we start small, I told him," Snow says, "start with closing off the one blasted pump in Soho that's causing most of the contamination."

"You'll get there," Julian says. "Be grateful cholera is not spread by body-to-body contact."

"What do you mean? How do you know? Is this from your dysentery study?"

"It's all about the water, John," Julian says, touching his finger to his temple in a hat-tip. "Let's go, the dancing is about to begin."

Wiping his bald dome, John Snow crawls to the dancing line as if dancing is cholera itself.

Julian hopes he won't make a fool of himself on the floor. What does he know of this kind of dancing? The men gather on one side, the ladies on the other, like the boys and girls at a wedding before "Paradise by the Dashboard Light." The first man in the line steps forward, extends his hand to the lady, and they waltz, at a tempo too allegro for Julian's inexperience. Up and down the ballroom, while the rest stand and applaud. The next pair steps forward. They dance, and then switch partners. And so on. Julian is around seventeenth. On the other side, his dazzling wine-colored bride awaits.

Before he can dance with her, Julian must dance with Filippa. "Are you enjoying yourself, Mr. Cruz?"

"Very much, Filippa. Thank you for inviting me."

"Oh, it's my pleasure *entirely*!"

Julian glimpses John Snow dancing with Mirabelle. She's patting him consolingly. He must be telling her about the contaminated pump.

Soon it's Julian's turn.

Finally, finally! he has her in his arms. His left hand slides around her waist. Her right hand rests on his chest. Her shoulders are rounded, white, bare. He wants to lean forward and kiss them. He threads his fingers through hers as they dance.

"You can't look at me like that, Mr. Cruz." She pants slightly.

"Like what, Miss Taylor?" He's panting, too.

Round and round they glide, swaying to the sound of violins.

"Like you're about to kiss me..."

"Maybe you should try being less beautiful."

"Wait, you didn't let me finish." She lowers her voice to the barest whisper. "Like you're about to kiss me—and not for the *first* time."

"Please—stop speaking, Miss Taylor, or I shall dishonor us both."

She giggles rapturously. "Do you know what Charles just told me?"

"No," Julian says. "What did he tell you, my love?"

"He said that in order to find a good father for her children, a woman first must know good from evil. And that is no *small* feat."

"Well, he's right about that."

"He told me I chose well."

"The pastor is very wise."

"He doesn't even know how well."

"Mirabelle, shh!"

Julian has two minutes with her on the dance floor. His face must show the torture of living under time flying, because Mirabelle pats him consolingly, too, and says, "Don't worry so much. It's all still ahead of us."

He stares at her as if he wants to drink her.

They waltz the rest of their eternal minute in silence, their hearts overflowing.

∞

Perspiring and hot, Julian steps outside to get some air. Spurgeon follows him out.

"I see you've been dancing quite a lot with a certain ribbon-maker's daughter, Charles." Julian is teasing.

"And you've been dancing quite a lot with a certain piano teacher's daughter, Julian."

"I'm being polite."

"Me too."

The men smile. Behind them the music blares.

"Julian, is it true?" Charles asks. "Aubrey told me that Mirabelle might not be going with Florence to Paris after all?"

Julian stays composed. "Officially she's made no decision yet."

"I don't have to tell you that Aubrey and John are ecstatic. You have no idea how desperately they didn't want her to go."

"Oh, I had some idea."

"They credit you with helping her to change her mind."

Perhaps Julian has helped her slightly, by using some of his powers of persuasion. "It's her decision, Charles. She's a strong, independent woman. She's got her own mind, as you know."

Charles hesitates. "Have *you* made your decision yet?"

"Not officially."

"Why haven't you asked for her hand, Julian? What are you waiting for? The Taylors will throw you a party that will make this one look like sedate afternoon tea at teetotaling Prunella's. Half of London will come."

"I'm not making any plans." Until September 21.

Spurgeon studies Julian's flushed, impenetrable face.

"Does it feel right," Charles asks, "to keep away from her?"

Julian admits it does not. It has felt ugly and wrong. And he hasn't kept away from her. If only.

"I can see you're still struggling with something," Spurgeon says. "But how can the struggle for love mean you are kept apart? It flies in the face of everything we know about love. Love is a *bond*. A bond unites human beings, binds them together. In the ultimate bond, they're bound together so utterly, they become as one. One flesh, one heart, one soul, one love. How can the *opposite* of that also be love? It's almost as if you're serving two masters. As if your house is divided."

Julian tilts his head in assent. "Indeed, my house may be divided," he says.

"Love is light," Spurgeon says. "The rest is darkness. You fight against the darkness, that's the answer. Isn't that what you've been doing your whole life? It's what I preach from dawn to dusk. You don't give in to it. You fill the day with what joy you can, with what light you can. Look, I must go inside. I, for one, firmly believe we shouldn't keep our girls waiting." A smiling Spurgeon pumps Julian's hand. "Live as if you have infinite time,

Julian. The way our Lord lived, though He knew the Cross was drawing near. Live as if both gardens dwell inside you, side by side, Eden and Gethsemane."

After Spurgeon leaves, Julian stands by the railing, gulping the night air, still slightly out of breath. He glances back inside the ballroom. A purple whirl of Mirabelle floats by in a fluid loop.

Down below him, in the depth of the garden, he hears quickening hissing voices. Julian recognizes them. It's Filippa and her mother. Julian's attention is diverted from the gauzy lights to the acrid darkness where the young woman stands and speaks.

She is complaining stridently to Prunella.

"Why does she *always* get her way, Mummy? You know she's doing it on purpose, she doesn't even *care* about him! She doesn't even *want* him. She just wants *me* not to have him. It's so unfair! Sometimes I hate her, I really do. I know it's not ladylike to say, but what she is doing is so unkind!"

"Darling, please don't be cross, you'll get wrinkles in your lovely cheeks, don't make that face, the frown won't leave your forehead. I know you're upset, have you tried telling her how you feel?"

"Of course I've told her! You don't even want him, I keep saying."

"And what does she say?"

"She says she can't help it if a man is interested in her."

"Did you ask her to put in a good word for you?"

"Yes, and do you think she has done so? The other night, when he left the room, and I complained about her forward behavior, she actually had the gall to say to me that nothing she could say to a man could make him stop loving one woman and love another. She actually used the word *love*, Mummy! Now do you see why I'm so cross? And she was so infuriatingly calm about it, too."

"And what did you say in reply?"

"I accused her of enticing him."

"And what did she say?"

"She said, well, Pippa, dahrrrling"—Filippa affects a posh breathy tone to mock Mirabelle—"I can hardly help whom he's interested in, can I? And then, listen to this—*then*! she said, Pips, have you tried being more interesting? The cheek!"

"Peanut, she's teasing you. She's not doing anything to entice him. Come now. All you have to do is wait her out. You know that. Just a few weeks to go, and she's gone! *Gone!* To the Crimea. With any luck, she'll get some horrible disease and come back all wasted and disfigured." Even as she says it, Prunella coughs uncomfortably. "Look at the things you're making me say. I would never forgive myself if something were to happen to that poor girl in Turkey."

"Mummy, you understand *nothing*, you see *nothing*, you're blind! *Blind!* Listen to me! Don't you *see* what's happening here? I greatly fear that Mirabelle may go back on her vaunted word and not go with Florence to Scutari."

"That's impossible! I know Mirabelle. That girl will not change her mind over some man."

"Not some man, Mummy. *The* man."

"No, no, no."

"Don't tell me you haven't seen how all of them have been working day and night, those industrious damned little dervishes, to prevent her from leaving England! All of them, Mrs. Taylor, Mr. Taylor, Charles Spurgeon, Coventry Patmore, his histrionic wife, who keeps throwing them her stupid infant to coddle, and even Mr. Airy, who's so enamored of him, he's practically ready to wed him himself!"

"Oh, Pippa, what are you saying! You're imagining things. For years they've been trying to get Mirabelle to marry John Snow, and after that, even Charles, and none of it has worked. And Doctor Snow is a *wonderful* man. If she turns her nose up at him, she will turn her nose up at anybody."

"Mummy, that's because John Snow is a *scientist*! Don't you know anything? They're not interested in women."

"But a professor and a seminarian like Julian is?"

Filippa scoffs. "Some seminarian. Do you see the way he looks at her? Did you see the way he held her as they danced? Mummy, he placed his *entire* hand on her back and drew her to him, flush to him, with his palm *flat* and all his fingers spread out! Mummy, no man of God lays his hand against a woman's back like that. He drew her to him like she belonged to him and he to her! He was intimate with her on the dance floor. And she let him! She was flushed, and her lips were parted. She stared right into his mouth as they talked. They were kindling in the middle of the ballroom, about to go up in flames, please don't *tell* me you didn't see it! *Everyone* saw it. I'm *humiliated*, mortified. He came here to dance with *me*, not her. Mummy, I'm dreading that he is going to ask her to marry him! And she is going to say yes and stay in this bloody country and have his babies, and all our plans will be ruined, and I'll *never* get married!" Filippa whimpers.

"No, he isn't! No, they won't!" Prunella starts to hyperventilate herself.

"She is in *love* with him, Mummy. This awful night has proved it to me beyond any doubt. It's the worst day of my life. How I regret inviting him. There will be no Florence, no Paris, no front, no war. There *will* be a wedding, though! Hers. Five minutes ago, she insisted she *never* wanted to get married, and now she's going to be a bride, and I'm going to die an old maid!"

Both women wail.

"Darling, *please* calm down, someone will hear you! Shh, darling. No, I *don't* believe it. It's your imagination. You're driving yourself *mad*. That's not our Mirabelle. She's too serious a girl."

"She wanted to be an *actress*, Mummy! In her heart of hearts, she's a courtesan, a dilettante, she wants all the fake stars to shine on her, she wants all the grand gestures, the operatic proclamations! While all *I* want is a *husband*!"

"He hasn't swayed her," Prunella says. "She's not interested in marriage, I promise you. For a while there, Pippa, I suspected she wasn't interested in *men*. Otherwise she would've married John Snow. Don't *worry*, darling."

"You have to do *something*, Mummy! You simply *must*."

"What would you like Mummy to do? Would you like me to speak to Mr. Cruz?"

"Dear Lord, *yes*, humiliate me further."

"So what would you like me to do? Filippa…what is that *look* on your face? Ouch, don't yank on me!"

Filippa lowers her voice to an inaudible whisper.

A raptly listening Julian strains to hear, strains to see. What *is* that look on Filippa's face? What is she saying to her mother? The two women are on the lawn below his balcony near the landscaped bushes. He can't see their expressions in the night. He can barely make out the tail ends of their words.

Filippa's voice rises. "…And in three weeks, rejected and heartbroken, she will leave for the front as planned, and we will pick up the pieces."

"You are *mad*, darling! You've gone mad! We *can't*!"

"Do you have a better solution, Mummy? My way everybody gets what they want. Your way, I die barren and alone."

Aubrey Taylor takes Julian's arm. He flinches.

"Oh! I'm so sorry, my dear boy, I didn't mean to startle you." She embraces him. "Come inside. It's about to rain. What are you doing here all by yourself? Mirabelle's waiting for you. Come, my dearest." Aubrey smiles.

Julian peers one last time into the darkness. What *was* on Filippa's face? What suggestion did she make that even her own mother recoiled?

# 36

# Foolish Mervyn and
# Crazy-eyed Sly

TWO DAYS LATER, FILIPPA ASKS JULIAN TO WALK HER HOME.
She has stayed too late at Vine Cottage, playing cards and charades
with him and Mirabelle. Anything not to let them have a moment
alone, though this evening they actually had fun. With debatable
results, Julian has taught the girls poker. John and Aubrey had gone
to bed, Barnabus went home, and the horses were in the stables.
Mirabelle asked if Filippa wanted to stay over, but thankfully
she declined. She had brought no clothes, she said, and she and
Prunella had an early appointment in the morning. "You don't
mind, do you, Julian? My house is less than a mile away." Julian
doesn't mind, but he'd like to hurry. Mirabelle will be waiting.

On the way to her house, Pippa chatters about the Christmas
holidays coming up and the Christmas ball she and her mother
are planning. Julian pays superficial attention. Christmas is
four months away. It might as well be in another century. He is
thinking about the next two hours with Mirabelle.

At her door, she thanks him for walking her home. "You are
too kind, Mr. Cruz," she says, extending her hand. "I'll see you
tomorrow. Probably in the afternoon, as Mummy and I have that
appointment."

"It's my pleasure, Pippa. See you tomorrow. Good night
now."

As he's rushing back, Julian stumbles across a covered wagon whose back wheel has come off. The accident occurred on a secluded part of Sydenham Hill Road between two cottages. The horse stands stoically, while two men, cursing and scolding each other, try to get the wheel back on. The gas lamps have long been turned off, and the gibbous moon is their only illumination. Julian is hoping to inch by unnoticed, but the men spot him and immediately advance on him for help. They smell homeless. Their clothes are mismatched loose-fitting suits. They remind Julian a little of his old friends from the rookery. One is young but hairless and nearly toothless, with a lazy eye, and the other is older, hairier, toothier, with two gleaming eyes.

"Thanks a lot, mate," the hairy bloke says. "I'm Mervyn."

"And I'm Sly," the bald chap says. "Mum calls me Sylvester, but all me friends call me Sly."

"This man doesn't give a toss what yer friends call you, crazy-eyed Sly! Shut yer mouth and let him help. If only you'd tightened the wheel nuts like I told you, instead of drinking that sixth pint, we wouldn't be in this shithole now."

"I did tighten it and you never said nothing!"

"All right," Julian says with a reluctant sigh, approaching the wagon. He doesn't want her to be asleep when he returns. "Let's see what we got here." He crouches to take a look. The hub and the nut that fasten the wheel to the axle have fallen off and are somewhere in the mud. "There's your problem right there. Your hub and nut are missing."

"We know *that*," Sly says with a wail.

"Have you looked for them?"

"Yep, but it's dark, how are we supposed to find a little nut?"

"Well, I don't know what to tell you," Julian says.

"You don't have a nut on yer?" The men stand over him, fidgeting.

"No, I don't carry wheel nuts in my pocket." Julian straightens out. "Excuse me." They're standing too close, assaulting his nose with their stink. He steps away from the men and the wagon.

"Come back in the morning and look for it. Or go to a livery stable and see if you can get another pair."

"They be all closed for the night," Mervyn says, scanning up and down the road.

"Can't leave the horse in the middle of the street, mate," Sly says, one of his eyes darting up and down Julian.

"Okay. So go find it. Have a good night."

"Can *you* help us find it?" says Sly, circling to Julian's side. He points to his eye that faces the wrong direction. "Me eye's not so good. It's not crazy, it just tracks where it wants." Toothlessly he grins. "Like me."

"Me eyes are good," Mervyn says, in front of Julian, "but I'm in me cups. Can't see bloody nothing. Help us, mate, will yer?"

There is something amiss. The drifters are too jittery to be drunk. And Mervyn's black eyes are too fixed on Julian. "Sorry, can't help you. Good night. And good luck."

"Wait, I think it's over there!" Mervyn points to a spot in the road. "I see something glistening. Can you go take a look?"

"No," says Julian.

"Come on, go look."

"Fuck you."

Sly brandishes a knife, Mervyn picks up a large stick from the ground. Almost like it was lying there waiting for Mervyn to fetch it.

"You don't want no trouble," Sly says, coming closer, his weapon shining.

"We should've got him when he was crouching," Mervyn says.

"Just get in the wagon," Sly says, "and there won't be no trouble."

"You want me in the fucking wagon?" Julian says. "Come and take me."

Sly lunges with the knife, Julian throws up his arm to block him and the knife pierces his forearm. Julian slugs Sly in the face and yanks the knife out of his arm. Mervyn swings his stick.

Julian sees it a second too late. It's heavier than it looks, and it's dense like a bat. It knocks the knife out of his hand, and before Julian can turn, Mervyn swings the stick again. The attack is so unexpected, and, like crazy-eyed Sly, Julian can't see well out of his left eye, especially at night. The second hit connects sharply with his left shoulder, glances off his neck and slams into his jaw. Julian totters. He nearly falls. Mervyn raises the stick again, but this time Julian ducks and Merv misses. From the side, Sly barrels into Julian. The boy is bloodied, but he's clearly done some fighting, because he's fast and deceptively strong, and is a good fifteen years younger than Julian. Indiscriminately Mervyn keeps whacking both Julian and Sly with the stick while they brawl, half-wrestling, half-punching. Sly is clumsy, all fists and kicks, flailing at Julian from all directions. The clash lasts barely a quarter of a minute, until another left hook finally knocks Sly into the mud.

A dazed Julian wipes his bleeding face, grips his bleeding arm. What the hell just happened? How odd this is, how excessive, beyond all norm. Is he being robbed? And where's Mervyn?

His legs are kicked out from under him from behind. Sly is on his feet. Before Julian can jump up, Sly kicks him hard enough to break his ribs. The center of Julian's body is set on fire. He groans, falters—and before he can move, a burlap sack is thrown over his head. Julian thrashes and flails around. The men can't get control of him, shouting above him. With the sack still over his head, he is bashed until he stops moving. The last blow of the stick connects with his head. Just before he passes out, Julian thinks that he is probably not going to make it back to Vine Cottage before Mirabelle falls asleep.

∞

He comes to an indeterminate time later. The sack is off his head.

He's lying on the rough cement floor of a putrid cellar room with bars on the only small window up near the ceiling. His body is sore as if he's been pounded by a meat hammer. His ribs burn, the knife wound in his arm throbs, his jaw is aching, as is his shoulder. The knuckles on his hands are swollen, and there's caked blood on his face. He has a concussion. It's not as bad as the one that nearly killed him, but it's bad enough. His vision is blurry. He can't count down from a hundred. There's a stained, reeking mattress on the floor in the corner. Julian crawls to it and spends he doesn't know how long falling in and out of consciousness.

Time passes. It's hard to tell how much. An hour? Half a day? A week?

Every once in a while, he hears the metal hatch in the bottom of the door slide sideways. The door doesn't open. A small plate with bread and a mug of water is pushed through, and the flap is closed.

"Wait!" Julian half-yells, finally. He struggles off the mattress and crawls to the door. "Wait!"

The footsteps recede down the hall. Julian hears their muffled words.

"Did he move?"

"You heard him yell, didn't yer?"

"Thank Christ. I thought you fucking killed him, swinging that sledgehammer."

"He wouldn't stop fighting, I thought he'd wake the whole bloody town. Christ, where did he learn to fight like that? They didn't tell us there'd be resistance. You should ask for more money, Merv."

"We'll be lucky we get anything at all after you tried to cut his throat with that knife of yours, you idiot. I told you, Sly, we need him more or less unharmed. They said."

"Well, he *is* one of those. Less unharmed." They horselaugh.

Julian keeps yelling through the thick door for someone else to hear him, keeps yelling up into the window.

He yells until he's hoarse, until he loses his voice.

At first he is furious. Mute but furious. But soon he grows desperate, as another night follows day, and another—and another.

There is a hole in the floor for him to relieve himself. The gash on his arm gets infected. He pours water on it to clean it, but it doesn't get better. The wound is red and inflamed at the edges. The condition of his body consumes Julian's blank hours. Better that than to be consumed by the helplessness he feels, by the sickening wrong done to him. He didn't expect it. Well, who would? He would rather think about his damaged body than about the damage out there, about the disaster left behind in the wake of his disappearance. My God, what must poor Mirabelle think? What must her parents think, Charles, George Airy? Walking home, and just vanishing. No note, no goodbye, no word to anyone. Mirabelle, I'm sorry, my love. I'm so sorry. I didn't see it, the malice. I couldn't fight it well enough. I was too shocked. I thought I could beat them.

*I didn't know I had to kill them.*

So this is what Prunella and Filippa plotted in the garden while other people danced and laughed. Oh, the charade Filippa played with him. Can you walk me home, Julian, it's not far, and it's so late. All that pretend laughing, learning poker, throwing them both off their guard with her high spirits. Filippa wanted to cause Mirabelle harm, and she succeeded. She and Prunella wanted to hurt Mirabelle so much, they risked killing Julian, risked maiming him. They threatened his life to break her heart.

Julian had been set up, exposed, ambushed. Did they think he wouldn't figure out their conspiracy until Mirabelle left for Paris? And that afterward, he would somehow fall into Filippa's arms to be comforted while Mirabelle traveled desolate and abandoned to Scutari?

The monumental injustice of it drips bile into his throat.

It takes him several concussed days to conclude he is wrong. The attack on him was too vicious to allow for a possibility of a rapprochement. It's as if Filippa realized in the few days that had passed since the dance that Julian would never be hers. The assault was vengeance on him for not loving Filippa, it was payback to Mirabelle for being loved. If I can't have what I want, the venomous girl said, and her mother agreed and helped her, then no one will have what they want.

And it's not over. There's no saying Julian won't be killed. The infection in the gash in his arm isn't going away.

That means that for Filippa and her mother, a man's death was a fair price to pay. They assessed the cost, the risk, the danger, and decided it was worth it, as long as Mirabelle didn't get what she wanted.

Julian has never hated anyone more in his life.

Not Fario Rima, not Lord Falk, not Fabian, not poor, pathetic Fulko.

All the rough fights he's had, all the times he has battled and boxed, won and lost, none of them made him feel the way he feels now. It's the first time in his life that Julian wants to kill another human being. Kill them with his bare hands.

Julian has plenty of time for his hatred to animate and harden him, to make him colder and crueler. He's got nothing but time.

He counts the days by the plates that pile up. The flies enjoy the remains of his bread and the hole in his floor. The days are long and empty, and his ribs hurt nonstop. There's too much time to think, to change your mind, to believe one thing, to stop believing.

Is Julian irrelevant? No one wants to feel this about himself, but every once in a while, it must be true. Perhaps Julian is one of the irrelevant few. Hollow is his belief, dull and faded his faith.

No man can think this about himself and stay sane. If Julian truly believed he was irrelevant, and that Mirabelle would be better off without him, then why search the world for her, why do anything? Why live?

He thinks back to the things Charles Spurgeon had told him. Anyone's life can be cut short, anyone's. The depth of your life's meaning doesn't depend on how long or short it is. It cannot depend on it.

That is so true.

Another true thing: now that Julian has been wrenched from Mirabelle, how clarifying his path has become! How fast the scales have fallen from his eyes. Separation is the opposite of love. Without each other, he is no good and she is no good. There is no protection for her when he is not by her side, and there was no protection for him. Because he wasn't safe, now she is not safe; he feels the evil omen inside every wound that throbs on his body. Oh, Mirabelle. What have I done?

What have I done *again*.

The darkness has divided them. Charles was right. But Julian has to find a way to fight against it. Charles was right about that, too.

Groaning with every step, with every deep breath, Julian slowly manages to drag his fleabag mattress under the small window. He rolls it up and stands on tip toes to glimpse what's outside. Where is he? There is a stone wall in a narrow alley. All day he watches for people, hoping someone will pass by, one measly human being!

No one comes. He could be anywhere. From the bit of sky above the back of the building, he thinks he's facing east. Facing Sydenham, where Mirabelle might be.

The days drag, and then they fly. Each morning and night when he hears the hatch open, Julian falls to the floor and yells to be let out. They laugh at him, foolish Mervyn and crazy-eyed Sly. They're outside his locked door, they can afford to be brave.

"I'm injured," he shouts. "My arm is infected. If you don't get me a doctor, my arm will gangrene. And then I will die. Is that what you want?" They don't reply, but the next morning, there's a bottle of iodine on his tray and some rolled gauze. There's also a bottle of Smith's Glyco-heroin. Why does Julian feel grateful to his captors? Is he insane?

He pours the iodine into his wound, gritting his teeth through the sting, and bandages his arm. The heroin is in liquid form and bitter, bitter, bitter on his tongue like an alkaloid. He doesn't know the dosage. He's never taken it, by any method.

Shuddering, he swallows down a gulp with some water. *"Heroin,"* the bottle reads, *"scientifically compounded, scientifically conceived, simply stands on its merits before the profession, ready to prove its efficacy to all who are interested in the art of medication."*

It's true.

In a half-hour, all of Julian's problems have been solved. He stops caring about his arm, his rib, his head, his shoulder, his jaw. He stops caring about everything. He cannot adequately explain the absolute neutralizing of his pain. Klonopin was a placebo, a baby aspirin, compared to the soul-balm that is heroin. Everything that was bad has gone away. Everything that hurt has gone away. All worry, all frenzy is gone. All fury has vanished. Everything will be fine, Julian thinks, laid out on the mattress, staring up at the ceiling with a benevolent smile. This is exactly what's needed. For her to have any chance of survival, I *do* need to stay away from her. I need to stay right here. This imprisonment is the universe sending me a sign. Thank you, O wise universe. I'll be here, and she'll be there, and everything will turn out fine. It feels good for everything to finally feel so right.

In the middle of the night Julian bolts up, sick in his body and soul. He's sweating and aching. Even with the iodine, his wound continues to fester. His broken rib is a crippling injury. But nothing hurts like his heart hurts. He has never felt worse or more terrible or more scared. He will die, he is convinced, and then she will die and she will never know how much he loved her and how hard he tried to get to her.

A small voice in his head says, well, Jules, let's get real here, how hard are you trying? Yelling into the door and sucking down liquid heroin I know might *seem* like trying, but is it *really*?

Julian can't stand another second of being alone with himself. He swallows another bitter ugly gulp, this time without the water.

And another.

And another.

And each time, after thirty minutes, everything becomes wonderful in his world, on a wretched mattress in a cage, beaten and humiliated. There is nothing to worry about. It's all going to work out, just the way it's supposed to.

He doesn't know how many days pass like this. When he opens his eyes one afternoon, naked with soul-sickness, Julian thinks, I can drink what's left of the bottle right now. This second I can tip the rest into my throat, lie down, and never feel this bad again. There is nothing I can do to save her, I know that now, so what's the point. I can't even save myself.

Before he can do it, or talk himself into it, Julian crawls to the gutter drain, opens the bottle and pours out the rest of the heroin into the hole in the concrete, tears rolling down his face from the effort and regret.

When Mervyn and Sly come to trade him food for his empty plates, Julian lies on the floor and begs them. "Whatever you want, I'll pay," he says. "Whatever you're getting, I'll double it. I'll triple it." Mervyn and Sly scoff. They don't believe he has any money. "I have money," Julian says. "Name your price."

"Yeah, sure," they sneer. "How about five quid?"

"Done," Julian says.

"How about ten?"

"Done," Julian says.

Oh, how they laugh.

"Fifty?"

"Done."

They roll in the corridor. "Why don't you give us a hundred pound, mate, and then we'll let you out."

"Done," Julian says. "Let me out and I'll give you a hundred pounds."

He can hear their laughter echo off the walls long after they leave.

With no heroin to heal him and no money to bribe them with, Julian steeps and boils inside his murderous hatred until his mind clears enough for him to remember some of the prison-break movies he's seen. With the help of movie magic, Julian devises a new plan and with grim determination proceeds to execute it. He is going to need some grim determination. It's going to be brutal.

He stops the nonsense of yelling and beating at the door when he hears them coming. The first part of his plan consists of making no sound at all. With his legs tucked under him, he sits on the floor against the wall to the left of the door where they can't see him even if they peeked through the hatch. To see him, they'd have to open the door—which is what Julian is counting on.

Mervyn and Sly come, they slide in the plate of bread and the mug of water, they wait a moment. "Hey, you," Sly says. "Your breakfast's 'ere." Julian stays silent. They leave, their footsteps receding. "What d'you think," Sly asks Mervyn. "He's sleeping in the corner on the floor or something? Because he's not on his bed."

"Suppose so."

Why didn't Julian think of this sooner? After he's sure they're gone, he covers up the little window with his jacket, so if they decided to walk down the alley, and peek inside the cell, they couldn't do it. It physically hurts him to reach up and cover his one bit of gray light, to remain in darkness, but better that than indefinite darkness.

He stays silent, as if he's already dead, and waits for his next meal.

It comes.

He doesn't touch it.

And the next.

He doesn't touch it.

"Fine," Mervyn says, "you want to play games, we can play, too. Eat, don't eat, what do we care."

They stop bringing him any new bread or water, but they keep checking on him to see if he's touched what's there.

They malinger at the door, whispering, trying to look in. After they leave, he drinks only the water, a small sip from each mug.

It's agonizing to remain on the floor in one position and do nothing but lie in wait, but Julian feels he's close, he feels they'll break soon.

On the fifth morning they come earlier than usual. It's still dark outside. They're worried about his lack of activity. He's either vanished using black magic, or he's dead. He hears their muffled voices, the bolt sliding sideways. The hatch is left open, and Julian can hear their heavy breathing, their anxious whispering. They throw in another hunk of bread.

"Sly, what are we going to do? It's been nearly a week and he hasn't touched his food."

"I see that, Merv. I ain't completely blind. Maybe he's sick."

"A week sick?"

"It's still early. Let's come back in a few hours, check on him then."

And in a few hours they are back. Julian can hear them on their knees, peering in.

"Can you see him?"

"No, I can't see him, Sly. If I could see him, I'd tell you, don't you think?"

"So where is he?"

"I don't fucking know, do I?"

"Did he escape?"

"How? Through what, the shit drain?"

"Smell it, does it smell like a dead body?"

"It stinks to high heaven."

"But does it smell like a body, Sly?"

"How the fuck should I know! Call for him. The dead don't answer."

"Hey!" Mervyn yells. "Hey, you! *You!* Wake up. Wake up!"

Julian holds his breath, standing flush against the wall. The morons don't even know his name. He squeezes a metal plate and a pewter water goblet in his tense hands. They've kept him in captivity for weeks, and they don't even know his fucking name. Bastards.

How many weeks has it been? Two, three? He can't bear to think about it. He lost a week to heroin, a week to the concussion. He could've lost longer to both. It's hard to tell.

Finally, Julian hears the key turning, the lock popping, metal against metal, the big door hesitantly creaking open. Thank you. He clenches his fists around the makeshift weapons.

"You go first."

"No, you go first."

"I can't take it. If he's dead we won't get the rest of our money. I've been counting on it. Go and look."

"Oh, for fuck's sake!"

Julian wants Sly to be first. He's faster. He needs to be disabled. The door swings out into the corridor, and Sly takes a tentative step in. It's too tentative. Sly's body is barely inside the frame. He carries a stick with him and a set of keys. Here, Julian is helped by the nerves of the impatient, foolish Mervyn who is so eager to see if Julian has kicked the bucket. Merv shoves Sly forward. That's all Julian needs. Sly turns his head to the left, sees Julian, very much alive, standing mute and grim against the wall, opens his mouth to scream, but it's too late. Julian slams the edge of the plate into Sly's head and kicks him as hard as he can in his knee. By the way Sly screams and falls, clutching his leg, Julian is sure the knee is shattered. Mervyn doesn't even try to fight. It's flight all the way for foolish Mervyn. In slow motion, he turns to run, but shock has paralyzed him, immobilized him just long enough for Julian to smash the pewter mug into his face, not once, not twice, but over and over. Julian sees nothing but red as Mervyn falls onto the concrete floor in the corridor.

Julian wastes no time asking questions. He drags Mervyn by his ankles inside the cell, leaving a snail-like trail of blood on the floor, and as the hobbled bald Sly twists in pain, Julian grabs the keys that have fallen out of Sly's hands. Mervyn is making only the smallest of sounds.

"You two are such fucking idiots," Julian says. "Enjoy your stale bread. But I'd ration your water if I were you. Because this is it. There ain't no more, and there's no more coming."

"Please don't, mate, please don't! We treated you good!" Sly cries.

"Fuck you."

"We was going to let you go tomorrow, honest!"

"Fuck you."

Sly grabs for Julian's leg. Julian stomps on Sly's wrist, kicks him again as hard as he can in his broken knee, and limps out.

They were going to let him go tomorrow? Why tomorrow? What day is tomorrow?

And more important—what day is today?

Julian stumbles down the putrid cellar corridor, holding his arm and his throbbing ribs, hurrying, almost running. At the end of the hall, he drops the cell keys in the corner and hobbles up the stairs.

∞

It takes him a few minutes to adjust to the blinding daylight. Where is he?

Oh, look where he is. Jacob's Island. The capital of cholera, the Venice of drains, a rookery to equal St. Giles in the Fields. He's been kept in a drunk tank of some lowly tavern called the Goat and Compasses, a perversion, Julian thinks, of the phrase *"And God encompasses all."* He's read about this place. It's a cantina for smugglers, villains, and pirates who sell the bodies that sometimes wash up from the nearby Thames.

He looks around to see if he can find a carriage. He has no money. He had gone to walk Filippa home with only a few shillings in his pocket and the grifters took even that from him before they threw him inside the bunker. He is lucky they missed his crystal. In the fight, it got tangled around his neck and slipped to the back.

He smells awful, the sourest man on the street, a sham deaf mute. Groaning with every step, Julian lowers his head and walks, as fast as his injuries will allow him, walks seven long miles from Jacob's Island to Sydenham. He stops a man to ask for today's date.

It's September 20, 1854. After he learns that, Julian almost can't walk any farther. Noon of the autumnal equinox has come and gone. The flare has flared, the floodgate has flooded, the portal has opened or not. Julian will never know.

Here's what he does know. His body is stinging. He stares into his shaking hands. He thought he was reacting to being in motion for the first time in weeks. But that's not it.

He has answers to so many questions he no longer wants any answers to.

Hurry, Julian, hurry.

By the time he gets to Taylor's Lane and bangs on the black door of Vine Cottage, it's early evening. He is humbled, bloodied, broken, filthy, grimy. He is a wretch.

The door is flung open by a distraught, ungroomed Aubrey. "Oh, Julian!" she cries. "Where have you been? What happened to you?" She pulls him inside, oblivious to the state of his body, as if she doesn't see it, as if it's the least important thing.

In the parlor room, sitting with a pallid John Taylor, are Prunella and Filippa. They jump up at the sight of Julian. They look shocked to see him.

"Oh, my word, Mr. Cruz!" Prunella says. "Where have you been?"

"Yes," Filippa exclaims, "we were so worried about you."

Julian trembles from the effort to control his emotion, from the scathing words that threaten to tear apart his mouth, he trembles from the forces that are about to break apart his body.

"Where is she?"

Her father cries. Her mother cries.

"Has she left?"

"She hasn't left," Filippa says, frustration in her voice. "She's upstairs. She's *sick*."

"Where have you *been*, Julian?" Aubrey asks with a condemning look on her face. "Mirabelle was asking and asking for you."

"Leave him alone, Aubrey," John says. "God, look at him."

Julian turns to Prunella and Filippa. "You did me dirty," he says to the women. His fists would clench if they could. "You did Mirabelle dirty."

"Dear boy," says Prunella, "we don't know what you're talking about."

"The men you hired to kidnap and nearly kill me are going to squeal like pigs when someone finds them, half dead and starving, locked up in the cell you paid them to lock me up in. Oh, the things they will tell the police. You better hope they die before they're found. Of course then, their deaths too will be on your heads."

"I don't know what this man is talking about, Aubrey, John!" Prunella cries, white with fear. "He's delirious."

Julian is not delirious. He is growing numb.

Mirabelle is upstairs in her room. Aubrey follows behind him. "I don't know where she went last week, she wouldn't tell me, but a day after she came back, she was like this. John Snow says it's cholera."

Julian is hoarse with anguish.

"Don't go near her, my boy. She could be contagious."

"She's not contagious. Why didn't she go with Florence to Paris as planned?" he asks before he opens the door. He is having trouble with the handle. His fingers can't grip it. Why didn't she go! She'd be safe now, at least temporarily. Why didn't she go like she was supposed to…

"She was waiting for you. She refused to believe you'd disappear for good without a word to her. She said you told her to wait until September 21. She wouldn't leave until you came back." Aubrey sobs.

How does Julian continue to stand? "You should've made her go, Aubrey."

"But I didn't want her to go!" Aubrey cries. "I wanted her to be safe. That's all I ever wanted."

"Me too," says Julian, opening the door to Mirabelle's room. He nearly falls.

Mirabelle is blue.

Her arms, her long frail neck, her lips are darkened by sickness. She lies in bed, facing the ceiling. When he walks in, she barely turns her head to the door. Her eyes blink slowly. Her lips move.

"I knew you'd come back," she whispers. "Mummy, water. But boiled water. Like John said."

Julian brings her the water. He sits on the bed and, holding her head soaked from fever, brings the glass to her mouth, watching her drink.

Go, beloved Mummy, Mirabelle says to Aubrey. I'm fine now. Everything is all right now. He's come back like I knew he would. "What day is it?"

"September 20." Weakly he takes her hand.

Mirabelle stares at him for an interminable moment. "How did you know?" she whispers.

"What?"

"How did you *know* that today would be the day that I die?"

"You're not going to…shh. How did you get sick?"

"I went to visit Magpie Smith, to ask if he saw you. I was looking everywhere for you, searching for weeks. I refused to accept you would up and leave me."

"Not of my own free will," says Julian.

"I sat with him, we had some gin and water. I was wrong to stay away. It's always wrong to stay away."

"Oh, Mirabelle."

She is stained with spotted fever. It's turning her blue, draining life from her. Julian is broken with the struggle of his own bloodied days. His hands are shaking, getting weaker. He drops the glass. It falls on the carpet, spills, rolls.

Forget the water, come closer, she whispers. He leans forward.

No. *Closer*, Julian.

Carefully, he lies down in her bed, on his side next to her, and with tremendous effort swings his arm around her body. The needles of destruction are piercing him.

I knew something happened to you. You couldn't have left me.

Never.

I should've jumped in the water, like you wanted me to.

Stop, Mirabelle, you'll be okay, just…

Don't despair, she whispers. I had joy. The happiest I've ever been was the silver moon I spent with you.

Julian wants to die.

Their breathing becomes labored. They struggle for oxygen. They're retreating from life. Julian can't feel his legs, can't smell her, or himself. His hearing grows dim. His sight blurs. With all the strength he has, he holds her to him. Mirabelle, why did you lie for me? When you first saw me at the Transit Circle, you say you didn't recognize me, yet you covered for me with your uncle, why?

"Because," Mirabelle says, with her remaining breath, "you looked at me as no one had ever looked at me. It was confounding, unfathomable, enthralling." She cups her weak hand over Julian's dirty bearded cheek. "You looked at me with all the love there was in this world." She brings her face to his. Her mouth touches him like an exhale. *Come then*, she whispers, *take the last warmth from my lips.*

# 37

# The Valley of Dry Bones

"THE HAND OF GOD WAS UPON ME. HE SET ME IN THE MIDDLE of the valley of dry bones. He asked me, can these bones live? And I said: Only God can know."

"You want to know if these bones can live?" the doctor said to Julian sunk in the hospital bed. "Let's go from the top, shall we? You've got a tail end of a nasty concussion and a cracked tooth. You've got torn ligaments in your left shoulder. You have an elbow out of joint, fractures in the capitate bones of both hands, and in the proximal phalanges of both middle fingers. You've got unhealed fractures of your sixth and ninth rib on the right side. A piece has chipped off your left patella. You have one, two, three, four, five, six fractures in the metatarsals and cuboid bones of each foot, some of them clean through. You have electrical burns all over your body as if you've been struck by lightning, and internal bleeding in your wrists and left thigh. Your heart is arrhythmic. I wish I didn't have to mention a seven-centimeter knife wound in your forearm that's gone septic, your general state of malnutrition and dehydration, traces of heroin in your blood, oh and also the *Vibrio cholerae* bacterium floating there, too, for good measure. We've had only one case of cholera in England in the last five years, besides you. Are you going to tell us what *really* happened?"

Instead of answering, Julian threw up in the bucket by the side of his bed.

These bones could barely live.

He was removed from his life, first physically and then metaphysically, as if he were still in the care of foolish Mervyn and crazy-eyed Sly. He wasn't quarantined while he was hooked up to an IV in the hospital, but neither did the doctors and nurses rush to spend a *lot* of time by his side. Devi and Ashton came to visit him on separate days like divorced parents, wearing masks and bringing him tiger water (Devi) and oatmeal cookies (Ashton).

Three weeks later back home, things weren't much better. Julian was on antibiotics, in a leg cast, and on three kinds of pain meds. He couldn't use crutches because of his upper body injuries, and his fractured feet made it excruciating for him to walk even to the kitchen.

And on top of it, Ashton was not himself. Like Julian, Ashton was mute.

"You're not talking to me now?"

"What's there to say?" Ashton said, without a smile, without lightness, as grim as Julian had ever seen him. "That you're sick, that you're nuts? That you're teaching me the true meaning of hell? That you're giving me the strongest clue of the suffering that awaits me after death? What is there to say that I haven't said? I'm out of words."

"How is...?" Julian broke off. He wanted to ask about Zakiyyah, but it was as if he'd been lobotomized. He couldn't remember how that situation had resolved itself. He wanted to ask how Riley was, but again, didn't that depend on whether Zakiyyah had made a scene or vanished into thin air? Julian decided to say nothing, taking one more unsteady step in detaching himself from his life. He figured if Ashton wanted to tell him, Ashton would tell him.

∞

When he could hobble on one crutch, Julian took a cab to the British Library on Euston Road. He searched for the names of the nurses who traveled to the Balkans with Florence Nightingale. There were two dozen altogether. He knew their shape. He knew what they looked like. And so much was written about Florence herself. But microfiche as he might, Julian could not find a mention of a willowy beauty named Mirabelle Taylor who planned to travel with Florence to the wartime hospital in Scutari.

He learned other things. The Crystal Palace in Sydenham continued to draw crowds for another eighty years, until it was destroyed by a fire in 1936, and was never rebuilt. Charles Spurgeon married Suzanna Thompson and continued to preach nonstop another thirty-five years until his death at fifty-seven. A century later Spurgeon had sold over three hundred million copies of his sermons. He had become the world's most widely read preacher, and there were more works written by him than by any other English-speaking author.

George Airy refused the knighthood twice because he couldn't afford the fees, he said. Finally in 1872, he accepted the honor. Third time was the charm. George's wife Ricky died in 1875. Sir George was ninety when he died himself, in 1892, three weeks before the much younger but less hearty Charles Spurgeon.

Airy preserved every single document he had ever received or had made a personal mark on. His journals, notebooks, brochures, scraps of speeches, notes for others, old checkbooks, bills, accounting ledgers, and all his personal correspondence were kept at the National Archives.

Because of John Snow's discovery of the causes of cholera, London's sanitation systems were gradually rebuilt, and by 1880, clean running water was piped through the city, and cholera was nearly eradicated. The rest of the world would soon follow. Snow's contribution to public health could not be overestimated. He died of a stroke in 1858, four years after Julian knew him. He was forty-five.

Edmund Beckett and George Airy completed the design of the Great Clock by the end of 1854, and since the Clock Tower wasn't finished being built until 1859, they had five years to perfect the gravity escapement, so that when it was finally installed, Big Ben became not only the most famous but one of the most accurate clocks in the world.

∞

Late one night from outside his room, breaking through the dumbshow of sleep and pain, Julian thought he heard an unlikely thing—a fight between Ashton and Riley that bordered on violence. Riley's guttural, anguished yawps were followed by Ashton's uncharacteristically defensive hums, rising to anger, falling to guilt. Stop it, calm down. Please, or someone's going to call the cops, stop it, Riley.

It wasn't bordering on violence anymore. Riley, Jesus, what's wrong with you! Sounds of a gasping struggle, chairs being knocked over, Riley, stop it!

Julian threw a pillow over his head and tried to sleep, but couldn't. Dragging his legs behind him, supporting himself on his one good elbow, he crawled across the room and sat with his back against the door and his head hung forward, listening.

How could you *do* it, Riley kept repeating in the midst of profound sobbing, flinging herself on Ashton. Did I mean *nothing* to you? Did you feel *nothing* for me? I must have meant *nothing*, for if I had meant *anything*, you would've *never* done it. How could you *do* it.

Ashton defending, cajoling, comforting, Ashton saying he was *sorry* (!), Ashton saying he didn't think of her.

It's true. You thought *nothing* of me.

I didn't do it to hurt you.

Hurt me? How could you not know it would *kill* me.

They could be talking about so many things, Julian thought. Any number of things.

No, Ashton said. He didn't know it would. He didn't know she felt this way. He thought she was a busy career girl, that she was happy in her life.

But the career is a temporary thing, Riley cried. But what you've done, that's as permanent as it gets. There's *nothing* you could've done to me that could hurt me more, she said, her racked words muffled by a towel into which she continued to cry. There is no worse thing you could've done to me. And you didn't even *talk* to me first. I loved you! I love you still. All I ever wanted was to be with you. And for you to want to be only with me. I met you when I was twenty-seven. I was so *young*! And here I am, eight years later, I'm nowhere, you're nowhere, we're nowhere, and *now* because of you, we will never be anywhere. How could you not respect me enough, love me enough, care enough to give *me* this choice.

Because I knew you'd try to talk me out of it, Ashton said, dejected and low.

Yes!

He didn't want to be talked out of it, he said.

But it's not just *you*! It's *me* too. You were brave enough to do it behind my back, brave enough to choose for yourself, why weren't you brave enough to let me choose, too? To let me know the *truth* and choose to stay with you—or not. No, you kept it from me because you *knew* how I'd feel.

I didn't want to upset you, it's true.

Upset me. You've *killed* me. You must know that. You must know what you've done.

Riley, can I tell you about my life?

I know about your life. I've heard all about it, I'm sick to death of it. What about my life?

Then you know why I couldn't have a baby. My dad did it, too. Right after my mother had me, he did it.

Oh, how proud he must be of you, a son following in his father's footsteps! I don't care about him. But you took the choice from *me*. You weren't alone in this. What about me? Did you *once* think about me?

Ashton tried other words. If I was sterile, if we couldn't have children, this is how it would be. Same as this. We could adopt, if you want.

Riley almost laughed. Except she was crying. But you weren't sterile. How could you do it. You didn't just take our phantom baby's life away from me. You took *my* life away from me. You've made me into a phantom too. Had you told me, I could've left you. I would have left you. I could've gotten over you. I could have loved someone else.

You still can, Ashton said.

I spent eight years with you! That's my sunk cost. That's my sunk life. Eight years of me sunk into a dead-end you.

Curled into a fetus, Julian fell asleep on the floor by the door to the sound of Riley's wretched sobbing, Ashton's helpless voice having long faded.

She left for Heathrow early the following morning without saying goodbye.

When Julian texted her a week later, she wrote *don't ever contact me again. You knew about it, you knew everything, and all these years you looked me in the face and lied. You are not my friend. You are nothing.* When he tried to respond, she had blocked him.

# 38

## Ghost Rider

JULIAN DIDN'T LIKE THE WAY ASHTON WAS BEHAVING TOWARD him.

They were constantly arguing. It was so unlike them. But the more Julian regained his strength, the more belligerent Ashton became. He was upset Julian had started boxing again, going to the gym, working out, running. He was upset Julian wasn't fully committed to Nextel, that he didn't like any of the girls Ashton kept trying to fix him up with, upset with how he left his ridiculous books all over the apartment. But especially, *especially*, Ashton condemned how much time Julian continued to spend with Devi.

"What's *wrong* with you?" Julian exclaimed one night, after they'd been at each other's throats about the stupidest bullshit. "What do you care how often I have lunch with him? You go out with Nigel four fucking nights a week, do you hear a peep from me?"

"Nigel is a hard drinker but a good man," Ashton said, over Julian's objection. "You on the other hand have sold your soul to the satanic shaman, and your bargain with him has no exit."

"And your bargain with Nigel does? You've never said no to him, never! Look, I'm sick to death of talking about this with you."

"Your greatest pain is nothing but amusement to that man," Ashton said. "He led you to the blue hole and fed you to the tiger as a ritual sacrifice. You think you can save her, and he cackles as a ritual sacrifice. You think you can save her, and he cackles because he knows you can't, but keeps pushing you to have at it until you die."

"He doesn't think I can save her! What are you talking about? You know he keeps telling me I can't."

"At the end of every trip, you're ripped apart, and she is ripped apart. Your body is giving up on you. And he just laughs and laughs."

"He's not laughing! He's the only one trying to help me."

"Fuck you! I don't see him here with you, watching you unable to walk on your fucked up feet, yet hitting the gym every morning in preparation for more torture. He's not watching you die day by day."

"What about *you*, my friend?" Julian said, flinging his arm out to half their kitchen counter, overflowing with liquor bottles.

"You know what, worry about yourself," Ashton said, "and I'll worry about myself. Is my body breaking apart, literally disintegrating before your eyes?"

"Yes!"

"Fuck off. This isn't about me. He keeps squawking, you're blessed, you're lucky, yet the opposite is true. Who else does that, tells you something is good when it's actually the fucking worst? Only the devil. And him. You're killing yourself in front of me, and you wonder why I'm pissed."

"Again—talking about yourself much, Ashton?"

"Fuck you! I'm never going to Greenwich with you again. Count me out."

"Did I ask you to go with me even once?"

"Yes, because I've been doing it for me."

"Go to hell."

"I'm already there, buddy. What, you can't see me? I'm right next to you."

"Shut up! What the fuck is wrong with you?"

∞

Things changed. Their camaraderie left them. It was replaced by a dour silence, a pervasive rumbling anger. Their every interaction was bloodied by hostility. Once they were brothers, for twenty years as casual and profoundly close as two unrelated men could be. But now Ashton was acting as if Julian had betrayed him.

"What is *wrong* with you!" was how their arguments usually ended, with Julian yelling this open question into Ashton's closed face. "What the fuck is wrong with you?"

And then one night, Ashton told him. "You want to know what's wrong with me? I've been duped. And I don't like being played for a fool."

"Who duped you, me?"

"Yes, you. I always knew you wore a costume to reinvent yourself, hell, I helped you pick it out. I helped you put it on. Mr. Know-it-All, Mr. Substitute Teacher, botanist on the side, night class professor, Silent Partner. But now I see my own delusions, and who likes to come face to face with those? Now I know—I only saw what I wanted to see, not what was really there. I thought that under the disguise of a hapless nerd, you were the friendly neighborhood Spider-Man, or, at the very worst, Deadpool. If only!" Ashton stood stone cold, his arms flung down. "But I've finally come to realize what you really are. You're fucking Johnny Blaze. You are Ghost Rider. You've been deceived by the devil during your agony of grief. Oh, sure, you've been given inhuman endurance and the ability to travel between dimensions, and maybe even some power of regeneration, but in return, you've traded away your only life. And fuck knows what else. I can tell by your face there's a lot you know that you're not telling me. You're doing the devil's bidding, Julian, because you've allowed your soul to merge with a demonic force. And for that, what did you get? Fucking nothing. But you've doomed yourself to ride the night—a ghost in both worlds, *this* world and the *other*, over and over, ever and ever, forever." Taking a breath, Ashton ran his hand through his hair. He looked so sick, so fed up, so busted. "Since I met you, you've been my ride or die. But

I don't want to be on your fucking flaming motorcycle anymore. I want out."

Julian gasped at the hurt of it, at the stinging truth of it. "You want out? Who's keeping you? You don't know where the door is? You don't know where Heathrow is?"

"And what are you going to do if I split?"

"You think *this* is helping me?"

"Fuck you!"

"Fuck you! What, you want to drive *me* away, too? Then keep going, Ashton, you're doing *great*."

Ashton flung his glass to the floor and stepped toward Julian. For a black moment, they clenched their fists, they nearly came to blows.

Words of anger and even hate can set things in motion in the human soul that cannot be undone. Julian knew this, had bitterly learned this. He unclenched his fists, took a deep breath, lowered his head, and backed off. Literally, backed out of the kitchen, raising his hands to placate, to surrender. After that night, he stopped asking Ashton what was wrong with him.

They didn't speak for days, then in monosyllables for weeks, and after that, talked only about the most impersonal shit. Will you pick up some beer. Did you pay the rent. That was their truce. They talked, but about nothing. Ashton went out without Julian, didn't invite him to come along, and Julian wouldn't have gone even if asked. In the mornings, Julian left before Ashton woke up, to go to the gym before work. At work, they remained professional, though without their usual banter, and after work, one man went one way and one another. By the time Ashton came home, Julian was in his room. On the weekends, Julian was at the gym or with Devi.

Except one Sunday night when Ashton was still on the couch with the TV on when Julian returned late from Quatrang.

"What are you doing?" Julian said. The TV was on so quiet, Ashton couldn't have possibly heard it.

"Nothing, what are you doing?" Ashton didn't turn his head.

Julian perched on the arm of the couch and stared at the screen for a few seconds and at Ashton's glazed face.

"Well, I'm going to bed," Julian said.

"Do you know *anything*, you fucking idiot," Ashton said. "I don't want to leave. What I want"—he covered his face—"is for you to stop leaving."

Julian sank into the couch. "Ash…what are you talking about? I'm right here." They lay across from each other, old and wiped out.

"I don't see you right here. I see the Penance Stare you keep trying to shame me with. Don't you know I'm like the Punisher? I'm immune to your stare because I have no regrets." Ashton inhaled. "I don't see you right here. I see your broken body that you've super-glued together and are now putting through the meat grinder again. I don't see you doing anything that looks remotely like life. I see you training to go back into your gloomy portal—another skeleton ride of damnation and suffering. My God. Can't you see what's happening to you—you're losing the momentum of your entire material being."

"Are you talking about me or you?" Julian got defensive again, raised his voice. Why did Ashton keep provoking him like this? "I'm not losing my fucking momentum. I have one life. This is it. There's only one river that runs through the present and the past, and I'm on it, paddling. I'm trying to find her, I'm still trying to save her."

"That's right," Ashton said. "There is nothing else, certainly not here with me. But it's not there with her either. Because there is no there there."

There is a there there, Julian thought defiantly, turning his head away. But Ashton wasn't totally wrong. There was no there here.

∞

A prime minister survived a vote of no confidence, and then was ousted by the electorate. A president was re-elected, and then

lost his majority because half the policies he was proposing were
hated by half the electorate. Gas prices went up. Then they went
down. A film won an Oscar for best picture that many thought
should not have won. Someone got nominated who shouldn't
have, and someone didn't get nominated who should have.
Interest rates went down, savings rates went down, mortgage
rates went down, the price of butter went up, beer up, cigarettes
up, taxes up, cars became lighter, more efficient, and more
dangerous, then heavier, less efficient and less dangerous. It was
cold, then hot, then windy, then not. In L.A. it was seventy-three.
Except that one time when it rained, and that other time when
the wildfires came. In London it rained and was 45°F in the
winter and rained and was 54°F in the summer, same numbers,
transposed. Someone shot up a burger joint, someone got real
offended. There was desecration of tombstones, or perhaps just
vandalism. Insurance rates went up, healthcare services went
downhill. A business closed, another took its place. There were
protests on college campuses. There was too much free speech,
and not enough, too many hammer and sickle flags and not
enough, too many babies and not enough, too many babies of
the wrong color and not enough. There was too much diversity,
too much rage—and not enough. There were too many guns, too
many murders, too many arrests, too many people in prisons,
too much crime, too much pollution, too much abortion by all
the wrong people. Your favorite show got cancelled, your favorite
singer hadn't released an album in years, or released one just a
month ago and it was underwhelming, or it was his best work
yet. The computer in your hand got smaller, lighter, thinner,
blacker, waterproof. It was a black box. Your life should've been
made of what the computer in your hands was made of. What
profit had a man of all his labor which he took under the sun?
That which was crooked could not be made straight. That which
was wanting could not be numbered. Your closest friend still
made all the wrong choices, but now he made them drunk, and
the girl you loved still died, and nothing you did made any

difference, all that maddening outrage at your own irrelevance, and nothing ever changed and on and on and on and on and on and on and on.

"My advice," Devi said to Julian when he heard his bitter lament, "when you fall into despair like this, is to remember *she* doesn't have that luxury. In abandoning yourself, you abandon her. And not just her—but the one you call your friend. How has *he* been? Have you asked how he has been, have you even thought to care? Your despair turns a cold Judas back on you all."

∞

Julian tried to get more involved, tried to care. It wasn't easy. The quantity of his available effort for others was a pound less than what any human being required, even one as low maintenance as Ashton.

"Have you heard from Riley?"

"I don't want to talk about Riley."

"Okay. Have you heard from Z?"

"I don't want to talk about Z."

"With me or with anyone?"

"You specifically."

"Right now or ever?"

"Ever."

But a few days later, Ashton threw at Julian a print-out of the email Zakiyyah had written him.

It was brutal.

*Mr. Razzle-Dazzle,*

*Stop calling me. Stop texting me. Leave me alone. Here's your solo, and hers, and mine. I'm sure it still won't be enough.*

*For you, nothing is ever enough.*

*Your hunger for love is so great and the hole so unfilled that everything gets swallowed up inside it.*

*And yet on the edges of that black hole, you dance, drink,
laugh, as if that's everything. In order to appear capable of
love, you seduce us all with your great boundless self. You act
the part. You charm, sweep off feet, romance, make come, make
weep. Oh—anything for applause. But when the real thing is
before you, you flee, because intimacy, real intimacy, terrifies
you. Yes, yes, I know—you love it when I watch you from the
front row. As long as I don't get up on stage with you.*

*So sorry. You should've told me the razzle-dazzle was
only there to hide your emptiness. You shouldn't have left me
to figure it out for myself.*

*But finally I'm on my way. I'm off the stage, Ashton. I've
given up on us. I've given up on you. You were my biggest
mistake.*

*Don't worry—I'm sure you'll have no trouble filling
your Theatre of Longing with other hearts to break.*

*Zakiyyah*

Julian folded and refolded the piece of paper, and tried to give it
back to Ashton, who wouldn't take it. "She's being deliberately
awful, she doesn't mean it. She's just mad, Ash. It'll pass."

"Yes, she does, and no, it won't," Ashton said. Julian had
never heard his friend sound so despairing.

Julian's was not the only inconsolable heart playing to an
empty house.

# 39

## A Mother

JUST WHEN JULIAN THOUGHT THINGS COULDN'T GET WORSE, one Saturday morning in July, when he and Ashton were still in their rooms, nursing substantial hangovers, their elderly neighbor banged on the door. "Someone's downstairs ringing your broken bell and swearing," she said. "I'm going to start swearing myself. Either fix your bloody bell or tell her to pipe down before I call the police."

It was Ashton's turn to traipse downstairs. He came back carrying a black suitcase. Behind him walked a huffing, stern, gray-haired Ava McKenzie. Julian used all his will to suppress a stunned groan.

"How long did you intend to leave me standing there?" Ava said to Julian by way of hello. "Is that any way to treat your almost mother-in-law?" She was dressed like a cross-country traveler, in khaki everything, including a khaki hat. Her hair had gone completely white. She had lost a tremendous amount of weight, was almost unrecognizable, but otherwise looked remarkably spry.

Her mouth was especially spry.

Both grown men, barely dressed and dumbfounded, stared at her. It was Ashton who spoke first. "Did *she* send you here?"

"I don't know who you mean," Ava said like she knew exactly.

"Tell her we don't need anything. We're fine."

While Ashton was speaking, Julian ducked away and hid the rawhide necklace with the crystal deep in the bowels of his room. He was sure Ava had come to steal it. When he came back out, she was by the island and Ashton was handing her some water in a dusty glass. Appalled, she turned to the sink to scrub it. "First of all, you don't look fine," she said to them. "Both of you were out too late last night, drinking and carousing. You look like you need a scolding and a curfew. You have not been taking care of yourselves. Ashton, you especially. You are supposed to be watching over him, but clearly in your condition, that's not possible—just look at him."

"Um, what condition is that?" said Ashton.

"I don't need anyone to take care of me," Julian grumbled—to which Ashton and Ava both scoffed!

"Has he had a piece of fruit all year?" Ava said. "I don't know how you two get up for work every morning. How you haven't been fired is a miracle."

"I can't fire myself," Ashton said. "Though sometimes I'd like to."

"And we do get up for work every morning," Julian said defensively.

"Except for the two months a year you take some me-time, right?" Ashton said.

Great, Julian thought. Now Ashton was on Ava's side.

Ashton and Ava sat on the stools at the island. Julian remained standing. "Actually, I'm in the process of selling the business," Ashton said. "I'm thinking of moving back to L.A."

"You *are*?" That was Julian.

"Yes," Ashton said. "Where have *you* been that you don't know that? Wait—don't tell me."

"You definitely need to do *something*, young man," Ava said to Ashton. "You're a mess. All the more reason for me to be here. If you leave, who's going to take care of him?" Ava was speaking as if Julian weren't standing right there. He was afraid to sit down and accord the scene any normalcy. "I told you," Ava continued, "I'm not here just for you, Ashton Bennett. I'm here for him. Not everything revolves around you."

"There it is," Ashton said. "And you say she didn't send you."

"You know who sent me? God. The way He sent Julian back in time to help my child."

"Oh, no." Ashton groaned. "Not you, too, Brutus. I can't take it. God, you say?"

"As opposed to who?" said Ava.

Julian wanted to groan himself. Why did Ava look like she knew way more than he wanted her to?

"I know enough to be here," Ava added, though no one was asking. "And you'll fill me in on the rest. We have time before next March for you to tell me everything. Look, are we going to natter incessantly, or are you going to show me your famous Portobello Market?"

"You've been here all of five minutes," Julian said. "Are you sure you don't want to rest first, freshen up?" Beat. "Let us help you find a hotel room?"

"How can I rest? I bet there's nothing in your fridge." Unceremoniously she appraised the refrigerator's contents—old butter and thirty bottles of beer—before clucking, nodding, and slamming the fridge door.

"Market's closing in an hour," Ashton said.

"Then it's even more imperative we stop standing around like pods of salt. Let's go get something for dinner."

Julian exchanged a glance with Ashton. "Who's been talking to you?" Julian asked.

Ava calmly adjusted the hat on her head and folded her hands. "I see. You need to know the chain of events that brought me here before you deign to take me to the market to buy food so I can make you something to eat," she said. "Fine. Riley said the last time she was here, neither of you looked well. She was concerned. So she called Zakiyyah, who happened to be in Brooklyn visiting her mother, and Z came to see me. We had a long talk. So here I am."

Julian didn't know where to look. "*Riley* called *Zakiyyah*?" he said quietly. Ashton said nothing at all.

Ava gave Ashton a condemning glance before she picked up her square purse. "Zakiyyah is a saint. So is Riley. How you're still in one piece, I'll never know. None of my business. I have a job to do. Let's go."

Julian stretched his mouth over his teeth. "How long do you think you can stay, Mrs. McKenzie?"

"Why so formal, Julian? I'm not your second-grade teacher. Ava will be fine. How long can I stay? Until you go back in March, that's how long. Let's see what we can do to make you stick the landing this time, eh?"

"I'm living in an insane asylum," Ashton said. "I wonder if it's contagious. Never mind. Look—it's nice of you to drop in, Ava, but we don't have a third bedroom."

"I don't need a bedroom," Ava said. "The couch will do. Can we walk and talk? Oh, and where can I exchange my money? The rates at the airport were extortionate."

On the way to Portobello Road, walking briskly between the two men, so briskly, in fact, that Julian was having trouble keeping up, Ava wondered if "the boys" could find her a small place near them, "just a studio, nothing fancy. I can rent month to month, and then we'll see. Of course, I'll need a spare key to your place. I can't be standing on the street, banging the door like this morning."

She didn't ask "the boys" what they liked to eat or drink, nor did she ask them for money. She bought bread, vegetables, chicken, flour, butter, sugar. She bought tea and coffee and wine and club soda. She bought jam and pastries. They carried the bags for her, as she marched through the Portobello stalls, haggling for onions and lemons.

Back home, she washed her hands, sneered at their lack of a suitable apron, and spent the rest of the afternoon wiping down their kitchen, throwing away old bottles and junk mail, deboning and lemon-marinating a chicken and putting it on to bake over rice and grilled onions. She asked them to set the table and when she saw their hesitation said, "Please, *please* don't tell me that you eat on the couch or stand over the island like zebras. For shame, both of you. Set the table immediately, please." She asked them if they had candlesticks, any clean silverware or clean plates. She asked them if they had any spare sheets, because if not, she would have to go buy some. "Are stores open in London tomorrow? There used to be a time when nothing was open on Sunday, when the only thing you could do on Sunday was go to church." She wondered if she should buy a small cot to put in the corner of their living room by the balcony window, and maybe a privacy partition, "with some birds painted on it."

Over dinner, Ava kept the conversation going nearly single-handedly by asking Ashton a hundred questions about the news agency, and his former store in L.A., and whether he had a car, and whether he was planning on going out tonight, "since it was Saturday night and all," barely waiting for his answers. She asked where the nearest Catholic church was so she could go to mass in the morning, and then finally addressed Julian. "So where is this Devi person? Why isn't he having dinner with you boys?"

Was there anything Ava didn't know? Julian wondered in disbelief. Who told her about Devi?

"Riley told me." Ava answered his unvoiced question. "I decided to call her myself after Z and I spoke. I wanted to get her opinion on things. She's a nice woman. She has good manners. But don't change the subject, Julian, I know you're a master of evading questions, just like my poor child was, God keep her. Answer me—why isn't Devi here?" She looked accusingly at Ashton. "It's your fault, isn't it? Riley said you're very hard on him. Why don't you like him?"

"Why don't I like him?" Ashton said. "Let's see. Oh, yeah, I know—because he is the father of demons."

She wagged her finger. "That's not a nice way to talk about people who are helping your friend."

"He's not helping him," Ashton said. "He is trying to kill him. A fine but important distinction."

"Is he always this dramatic?" Ava asked Julian.

Ashton glared at Julian from across the table. "Good thing Ava wasn't here three months ago, when half the bones in your body were broken and you had *cholera*."

"Cholera is eminently treatable," Ava said dismissively. "This isn't 1850. And bones heal."

"What about lungs swollen from smoke inhalation? Do they heal?"

"Is the man breathing, or is he not?" barked Ava. Both she and Ashton scowled at Julian, who didn't know if he should prove Ava or Ashton right by breathing too much or too little. "I rest my case," she said.

"People used to treat me with kid gloves," Julian said. "Julian this and Julian that. What can I get you, what can I do. Now it's almost the reverse. What happened to the pity?"

"And where has pity gotten you?" Ava said. "Now we're trying a different approach. Tough love is what you need, Julian. This Devi of yours, does he still go to church? Riley said he did."

Julian and Ashton shook their incredulous heads.

"What? Riley told me a lot." Critically she tutted in Ashton's direction. "Too much, if you ask me. Frankly, both Z and Riley have told me more about you, young man, than I care to know."

With that Ashton got up and said he had to be going. "Since it's Saturday night and all. Have fun, you two, storming the castle."

The next morning, Julian took Ava to St. Monica's. Before they left, she knocked on Ashton's half-open door. "Young man, are you coming to St. Monica's with us? Both Z and Riley told me that you are a baptized Catholic."

"Yes, and haven't been to church since the baptism." Ashton turned to the wall, throwing the blankets over his head.

Ava got dressed up. She put on a skirt and blouse, fussed up her hair, did her makeup, and even clipped on some earrings.

"What?" she said when she noticed Julian surreptitiously eyeing her attire. "You've never heard of Sunday best?"

Julian and Ava sat in the back pew. She was quiet except for the part where every five seconds she kept whispering, "So where is this Devi of yours?"

"All in good time," Julian said. "God first, then Devi."

Ava rolled her eyes. "Don't teach *me* how to live, young man," she said.

After the service, they met up with Devi in the narthex. "Devi," Julian said, "this is Ava. Ava, Devi. Ava is Mia's mother," he added, as if it was necessary. "She's come for a visit." A short visit, he hoped.

Devi shook the woman's hand. Silently they appraised each other. "How long are you staying?" was Devi's first question to her.

"As long as I need to," Ava said. "Those two are a mess."

"Don't I know it."

"So why aren't you with them more? You need to keep an eye on them."

"Julian and I have lunch every Wednesday. And we spend Sundays together."

"Lunch once a week," Ava said. "You call that looking after?"

"And Sunday. Also Ashton—"

"Ashton, Ashton." Ava dismissed the name, the thought, the sentiment. "You're an adult, Devi. You cannot let *him* decide what's best. You've seen the fallout from some of his decisions, have you not?"

Devi stammered, and Julian nearly laughed out loud. But then Ava turned her schoolteacher gaze on him. "Julian, Devi needs more from you, too," she said. "Devi, why don't you join us for dinner tonight? I don't care what Ashton wants. I don't care what Ashton says. He will behave himself, I promise you. I'm making a roast. Do you eat meat? Is there anything open on Sunday where I can get a roast beef? A butcher, maybe, a Sunday market?"

"Yes, there are two wonderful markets," Devi said, "one with mostly fruits and vegetables and one, a little farther away, that has everything."

Ava smiled. "That's not even a choice, is it? Let's go." She waved goodbye to Julian. "You might as well go back home. Ashton needs you. You two should go for a bike ride. It's a beautiful summer day."

"Who's going to carry your bags?" Julian asked.

"Devi, you allow him to talk to you like that?" said Ava. "What are we, invalids? Devi and I will carry them. If we get tired, we'll take a cab. Now which way? Tell me about yourself, Devi. Is it true what Riley told me, that you own a restaurant?"

"It's true. More of a lunch place, really."

"What kind of food do you make? If it's something that Riley eats, I don't know if I'd like it. That girl eats some strange things."

"I can make anything you want."

"Like lasagna?"

Devi turned back to glance at Julian standing motionless behind them. Both men smiled. "So Ava's a comedian like you?"

"Oh, I'm much funnier," Ava said. "Julian is earnest but unfortunately nearly completely humorless. I was going to be his mother-in-law. Did you know that?"

"Of course."

"But then my daughter died. But of course you know *that*."

"Yes."

"Do you have any children, Devi?"

"I did, Ava. Like you, I once did."

"A daughter?"

"A son."

Julian stood and watched them walk through leafy Hoxton Square until they disappeared from view.

∞

Julian told Ava she wouldn't be able to afford Notting Hill.

"Don't tell me what I can and can't afford," Ava said. "Just point me in the right direction, and I'll take care of the rest."

"How long is your visa for?"

"You're *very* interested in my comings and goings, I see. Why do I need a visa? I'm a dual citizen. But thank you for your admirable interest in British immigration law."

A few days later when Julian and Ashton came home from work to a hot meal and a set table, Ava informed them that she found a place to stay. "Devi helped me. He is such a nice man. He went with me to look."

Devi had gone with Julian too to help him find this apartment. "Where is the place?"

"Close." Ava beamed. "Right downstairs."

"Downstairs where?"

"Downstairs on the first floor. A small studio in the back became available. A writer had been renting it for many years, but she moved. It has wonderful spiritual energy. In some ways it's even better than your place. It's smaller, but it's got a deck where I can sit and have my morning coffee, if it ever stops raining. I even have use of a garden. I can have a barbecue, and you can't." She smiled. "Maybe I'll invite you over to *my* place."

Julian couldn't figure out how she could afford it. Wasn't she retired?

"I have to say, you two are insatiably nosy. What do you care how I can afford it? I'm independently wealthy, does that satisfy you? All that money I saved when my poor daughter, may God have mercy on her soul, decided not to get an education is now burning a hole in my pocket. Help me get the cans of tomatoes from the top cupboard, will you? I'm prepping sauce for tomorrow. Whose idea was it to put the cans this high? What if they fall on your head; then where will you be?" She stared pointedly at Julian, who in turn stared pointedly at Ashton.

"So you spilled your guts to Zakiyyah," Julian whispered, "and she bullhorned it to the world. Thanks a lot, man."

"Not to worry," Ashton said. "Now you can keep all your secrets."

Ava moved in to the studio downstairs, bought some furniture, a coffee maker, a washing machine. She forced Julian and Ashton to buy a juice extractor and a blender. Every morning before they left for work she made them smoothies and a bag of trail mix. Every night when they returned home, she had dinner waiting for them. She bought blankets for their couch, which seemed like a nothing thing until they watched TV covered by a blanket. Ashton said he had never felt so comfortable. "Why didn't we ever think of this, Julian? We're idiots."

"You never had one," Ava said, "because a blanket is too cozy and too homey. It would've made it too nice for the girls. And you didn't want to make it too nice for them. You were a wild thing. You didn't want them to think you could be domesticated."

"So you're a psychologist now, too?" Ashton said.

"I'm many things, my boy. First of which is a mother. Take your feet off the coffee table. And use a coaster, for God's sake."

Ashton needn't have worried about blankets and domestication. Because the girls were gone.

Zakiyyah was gone as if she had never existed.

And Riley had stopped visiting. She and Ashton still talked on the phone and emailed each other. But after months had passed, Julian realized she had never returned to London after that April fight. It took him a while to realize this. As always, he was too wrapped up in himself to notice other people, or how much time actually passed between events. He was boxing nonstop, training, running, and learning new combat skills. He left for two weeks for Berkshire, to train at an immersive Krav Maga camp and then continued the instruction at an elite academy in Kensington. Krav Maga was the lethal self-defense method practiced by Israeli forces. No Mervyn or Sly would ever ambush Julian again.

He was too busy to notice Riley hadn't been around because he had Ava not just feeding him and nagging him but buying him history books and old *National Geographics* on every parcel of time in London between 1880 and 1980, and then grilling him like a Krav Maga instructor for the mind. Like a true former teacher, Ava taught a class in Notting Hill five nights a week on how to beat the impossible odds of traveling through time to save a doomed child by learning all you could about the *Titanic* and the Suez Canal crisis.

Julian sat with Ashton on the couch, not moving, staring at American football on low, as they listened to Devi and Ava in the kitchen bicker over whose steeping method made better tea, and how lamb was best prepared, and who, though neither the English nor the Vietnamese were known for their desserts, made tastier sweets. They squabbled like this every evening they were together.

Heatedly and repeatedly, Ava and Devi debated whether a positive outcome was possible for Julian and Mia. Ever the romantic, Ava believed it was. One Sunday evening, she got so upset with Devi's realist stubbornness, she declared that she would go into the caves instead of Julian. "I'll show you how it's done," Ava said. "You have to be firm. My girl has no sense. She doesn't know the danger coming for her. But you do, Julian. Therefore, you can't leave it to chance. You can't leave it to her. You've left it to chance before, you've left it in her hands before, and where did that get you? No, it's settled. This time, I'll go."

"What a good idea," Ashton said. "Yes, Ava, you go."

"Ashton is joking."

"No, I'm not."

"I'm not either," said Ava.

It took time for Julian and Devi to talk her out of it, while Ashton tried to stay out of it.

"Fine, then," Ava said. "Julian and I will go together."

"Ava, you can't go period, no matter what Ashton says," Julian said. "On the other side, the girl already has a mother."

"So? On the other side, the girl frequently has a lover, too." Ava crossed her arms. "Even on this side."

"Yes," Julian said slowly. "A girl can have more than one lover. But she can only have one mother."

"Fine, I'll pretend to be someone else. Why not? *You* pretend to be someone else. Though why you picked Wales as your background, I have no idea. Why didn't you say Scotland instead? Scotland is such a nice place. Or northwest England. That's where my family's from. The coast is so beautiful there."

With difficulty Julian and Devi finally dissuaded Ava from interdimensional travel by reminding her that she was nearly 75, and that the conditions in the cave were harsh and often involved Herculean-level trials and superhuman stamina.

"How hard could it be?" Ava said, pointing at Julian. "*You* made it."

All the while a mute Ashton sat on the couch, watching them argue. The expression on his face could best be described as weary disgust, like he was watching seemingly normal human beings noisily drink camel urine—and not for the first time.

In October, with his father's approval, Ashton finalized the sale of 51% control of Nextel to Reuters. He got paid off and his role at the company became largely ceremonial, "like the French president," he said. Ironically, Reuters turned around and sold 100% of the business to their French affiliate AFX. A Frenchman named Pierre Dugard came to oversee Nextel's day-to-day operations. The place changed name, got more corporate, less loose, less fun. In December, Ashton took what he called a leave of absence, though Julian suspected it was a permanent leave. Ashton said he was flying to L.A. for Christmas, "to take care of some things." That's when Julian realized he hadn't seen Riley since April, since the argument Julian wished he had imagined. He and Ashton had never discussed that fight, as if either of them could.

"I'm glad he is reconciling with Riley," Ava said after Ashton left. "That poor boy. I thought he'd never get over Zakiyyah. He took that hard. Julian, did you know that when he was twelve, he came home from school and found his *mother* dead from a heroin overdose?"

"Yes, Ava."

"Well, that's just terrible. Terrible! How come you never told me?"

"Why would I?"

"Devi, did you know that?"

"I do now."

"That poor beautiful boy. Is he close to his dad at least?"

"Not very," said Julian.

"Yes, he is," said Devi. "He is now. They have dinner often."

"Practically never."

"Once a week," said Devi.

"Like I said," said Julian.

"I hope this thing with Riley works out," Ava said. "I love Z, of course, but Riley's a nice girl. Devi and I didn't know how to help Ashton, did we, Devi. He's been so depressed."

"I hope he doesn't come back," Devi said.

"That's not very nice, Devi!"

"I mean that kindly."

"Ashton's been depressed?" said Julian.

Oh, Julian, said Ava.

Oh, Julian, said Devi.

He thought back to the last eight months. All Julian could scrape up in his memory was Ashton's cough and cries. A drunk Ashton sometimes disgraced himself with hollow musings. Bottles of Belvedere clinking together, lined up on their kitchen window, the widow from Brooklyn pleading, don't do that, love, don't fall asleep in your empty bottles as she covered him on the couch late at night and he mumbled thank you, patting the hand that patted him.

Feeling guilty for his lack of awareness, Julian kept calling Ashton, texting him. Ashton texted back as if nothing was wrong.

His texts became sporadic. Then they stopped.

Julian spent Christmas with Devi and Ava, who had trimmed a tree, and strung up lights and fought over the menu, finally deciding to cook both a ham and sizzling pork with chili soy sauce. Julian didn't speak to Ashton on Christmas. That must have been a first.

When they finally connected a few days before New Year's, Ashton apologized, said he was out of signal, was doing some stuff, everything was all right, he'd tell Julian all about it when he saw him again.

"When's that going to be?"

"I don't know. Couple of weeks. Why, you miss me?"

Julian didn't want to admit it. But yeah.

Ashton didn't return to London until early February, just in time for the Super Bowl. He seemed in good spirits as always, but even Julian had to admit his friend had lost some of his former shine. Ashton looked malnourished. Ava clucked over him, fed him, made him cookies, brought him tea, and even put marshmallows in his hot chocolate, though Ashton hated marshmallows. "What kind of a man doesn't like marshmallows?" Ava said. "You will eat them, young man. You will eat them, and you will like them."

Ashton ate them and liked them. And when he fell asleep on the couch, Ava covered him with a blanket and he mumbled thank you and patted her hand and she leaned down and kissed his head before she went downstairs.

# 40

# Two Weddings

FOR OVER A MONTH, ASHTON DIDN'T WANT TO TALK ABOUT anything serious. He kept going out drinking, having fun, dragging Julian out with him, though Julian, in preparation for March 20, was training like Tom Brady for the Super Bowl. He went out with his friend a few times, deliberately drinking less (as if anyone could drink more), and then hailing a cab for the two of them. Invariably Ava was waiting up for them in their apartment. She didn't like it when they went out drinking. She worried. She called them both disgraceful. "Were you going to keep drinking like this if you married my daughter?" Ava said to Julian. "And you, young man, look at you, for shame!" For some reason Ashton liked it when Ava yelled at him for doing wrong. He kept promising her he'd do better next time.

As Julian had suspected, Ashton didn't return to work. The sabbatical was too long. "I'm enjoying my life way too much to work. You should quit, too, Julian. You should take the payout they're offering, it's a lot of dough. Take it, and let's go traveling. Let's go to China, or New Zealand, or Tahiti. I've always wanted to go to Tahiti. I realize besides America and England, I've never been anywhere."

"Maybe before Tahiti, you should start with Paris," Ava said. "Take Riley."

And Ashton agreed! "But not Riley—I'll take Julian."

"No, you can't make any plans with Julian," Ava said. "With any luck, he won't be coming back this time."

Bottomlessly Ashton stared at Ava, before turning and speaking to Julian. "As I was saying—Paris in the spring?"

Julian stared down Ava and said, "Sure, Ash, absolutely. When do you want to go?" and he and Ashton started making plans to go to France when the weather got warmer.

After a month had passed, sometime in March, Ashton finally told Julian about Riley.

She had been suffering from gastrointestinal upsets, Ashton said, neurological problems like unexplained ticks and respiratory troubles. Sudden onset asthma, she called it. She became offended that her doctors were downplaying her symptoms. They said it was psychosomatic. But she didn't think so. She took such good care of herself, yet kept coming down with colds, sore throats, odd rashes that wouldn't go away. She gave up her apartment and moved back home with her parents, where she started sleeping in the backyard on her mother's patio. She stopped drinking bottled water because the plastic was carcinogenic and started collecting rainwater in barrels and drinking that instead.

"You're joking, right?"

Ashton said nothing.

"Rainwater in California? I think dehydration might be her problem."

"It wasn't dehydration. Riley diagnosed herself and concluded that overstimulation from continuous electrical charges was causing the worst of her symptoms. So she quit Whole Foods."

Julian's heart thumped with worry. It didn't help that Ashton was reporting all this as if it had nothing to do with him, in a level voice of a neutral third party. "Riley quit Whole Foods?"

"Yes. She gave up her yoga studio, her online health food business, sold her car, donated her phone, her computer, her iPads, her Kindles, her blow-dryers, her televisions. Everything."

Julian sat up on his couch. Ashton lay down on his. Julian peered into his friend's face. Ashton covered his eyes.

"Ashton?"

"You wanted to know what I was doing between Christmas and New Year's?" he said. "I was driving Riley to her new residence—a wellness compound in the middle of Arizona. That's where she'll be living from now on."

"Where?"

"In the middle of Arizona. Near a town called Snowflake."

For a few moments, Julian was too stunned to speak. "Riley sold her earthly belongings," he said, "and moved to a place in Arizona called *Snowflake*?"

"She told me that my aftershave and deodorant made her vomit," Ashton said. "She told me I sent her body into crisis. She literally vomited in front of me to show me how I was making her feel. And how apparently I've been making her feel for years."

"Ashton..."

"She's lost like thirty pounds. She's probably a hundred pounds now. The doctors told her she was anorexic. She said she wasn't anorexic, she was being poisoned by the chemical fumes from the paint on the walls of her family home. She insisted that was the problem. Her father is driving out to visit her next week. He's bringing his construction crew. He's building her a house in Snowflake, an unpainted one-room log cabin."

"Why you didn't try to..."

"No one's allowed to say anything, or offer the remotest opinion, especially me. She feels mocked, misdiagnosed, hurt by the ridicule. Her father is building her a cottage so she doesn't feel ridiculed, what's so difficult to understand about that? She is staying with this other woman at the moment. The woman is in a wheelchair—a manual one of course—because she says her nerves had short-circuited from the electrical onslaught and paralyzed her."

"How long has she been in a wheelchair?"

"Twelve years."

"Oh my God."

"Riley told me that was next for her," Ashton said, "if she didn't save herself and get out. She says once her father builds her a hut, she'll be happier. She might even write me letters. But in lead-free pencil only, because pen ink has chemical dyes."

"Write you letters."

"Stop repeating everything I say."

"I don't believe what you're telling me."

"She no longer talks on the phone or watches TV or listens to the radio," Ashton said. "There is no electricity in Snowflake. Do you believe that?"

"How do they wash their hands?"

"You don't need electricity to wash your hands, time traveler, you should know that better than anyone."

"You need an electrical pilot to light the gas to heat the water tank."

"They don't heat their water. They have a well."

"In *Arizona*? Is it a drywell?" Julian was blackly unamused by his mordant wit.

"She told me she was tired of being emotionally dark," Ashton said, "of living every day with migraines and nausea and the flu."

"Is she better in Snowflake?"

"Hard to say. She says she likes being among other sick people who, like her, have retreated into the middle of nowhere to find peace. She says that must be how the pilgrims felt when they sailed here."

"The pilgrims did not come to find peace," Julian said. "They came to build a civilization."

"Potato, potahtoe."

"And those other people, have they lived in Snowflake a long time, like the wheelchair lady?"

"Yes," Ashton said. "Sometimes they still need to enter a nearby psychiatric facility because they have mental breakdowns, even in Snowflake, and need therapy and meds. Their leader,

Deborah, was just returning from such a place as I was delivering Riley into her care."

"How long had Deborah been away at the psychiatric facility?"

"Two years," Ashton replied.

"Ashton!"

"Why are you yelling at me?"

"Are you nuts? Why would you take Riley to a place like that?" Julian held his tongue from the next question on his lips. *What's wrong with you?*

"I'm no longer allowed input into Riley's emotional well-being," Ashton said in a flat voice. "She wanted to go. She needed to go. She told me what I needed to do was validate her environmental illness by taking her there. So I validated her environmental illness. What choice did I have?"

"Clearly it's a cry for help."

"She says no."

"I mean—a cry to you."

"What am I going to do? I can't move to Snowflake with her. Her dad would have to build me my own one-room house because I can't stay in Riley's. I make her vomit, or did you not hear that part?"

Julian swallowed the bitter air in his mouth, trying to hide his naked worry. "What about you moving back home?" he said carefully. "You mentioned you were thinking about it. Maybe what Riley needs is a steady dose of Ashton, and she'll feel better."

Ashton shook his head. "She took her beehive with her," he said. "So she could continue to perform apitherapy on herself, continue to be regularly stung by bees to rid herself of chemical impurities and body electro-toxicity. How is my moving back going to help her with that?"

"Come on, man, she needs you."

"She moved to Snowflake to get away from me, from everything having to do with me and her life with me. Her beautiful hair fell out in the back of her head. She is half bald. Do you know why? Because she kept sleeping on a bag of ice. She used the bag of ice as a *pillow*, Julian, because she couldn't stand thinking about me when she went to bed at night. She said thinking about me inflamed the lining of her dura mater."

"Ashton…"

"It's not *all* my fault, mind you, so that's a relief. She told her parents it was their fault, too, because she could smell the odor of the chicken slaughter plant down the road from their house, and it's been slowly killing her since childhood."

"There's a chicken slaughter plant near Riley's house?" Julian had been to Riley's parents' house in Pasadena many times. He didn't remember any such thing.

Ashton nodded. "Seventy-four miles away in Bakersfield. She says Pasadena is downwind from Bakersfield, where they use harsh chemicals to clean the abattoirs. In Snowflake, on the other hand, there is nothing for hundreds of miles. Not even ink pens to write to me with."

"Have you talked to her parents?"

"Last week. They had just returned from visiting her."

"She's been in Arizona two months. Have her symptoms improved?"

"No." Ashton studied his hands. "Her mother says a doctor in Phoenix suggested she cut gluten from her diet, so she cut gluten from her diet. Before you ask, it's too early to tell. Though the scalp-burning sensation is apparently better."

"Gluten makes your scalp burn?"

"Gluten and me, apparently." Ashton turned his head. Miserably, he and Julian stared at each other. Neither one could think of the next thing to say. Julian pitched back and covered his face.

"It's because of what I've put her through," Ashton finally said. "If she hadn't been with me, she might've remained herself."

"She could've left you at any time, Ash. It was her choice to stay. At any time, she could've found someone else."

"Like Z."

Like Z, Julian wanted to echo and didn't.

"It's like I always say," Ashton said. "If you love them more than they love you, it's bad. But if they love you more than you love them, it's even worse. Speaking of which, I forgot to tell you—Z got married."

Julian wanted to walk across, cover Ashton with a blanket, pat him, comfort him, do something, anything but lie there impotently. Ashton's face was blank. He was staring up at the ceiling.

Liquid silence fell like water drops from the loose faucet.

"I'm sorry, Ash."

"Yeah. Some music teacher from Salinas."

"Fuck. Why so fast?"

"You're a fine one to speak, buying a ring after a week and proposing after three."

"Yeah, and how did that turn out?" Julian said. "Everybody told me it wouldn't last. I should've listened."

Ashton almost smiled at that.

"What's her hurry anyway?"

"You know how it is. Clock ticking, blah blah. Everybody wants a baby. Gwen's about to pop out her second. Did I ever tell you the last words my mother spoke to me the day she knew she would die?"

"Ashton, yes but—don't. This isn't that."

"I was late for school," Ashton went on. "And she said, *run along, my love.*"

Julian groaned.

"Mom said run along. Z said run along. Riley said run along. And now even you are telling me to run along back to L.A."

"That's not what I'm saying. You know I don't want you to go."

"Yeah, yeah," Ashton said. "Run along, Ash, my only friend."

They stopped speaking. Julian didn't know what to say, what to do.

Ashton hopped off the couch. "I'm going to bed. Gonna get a drink first. You want something?" At the island, Ashton poured the Belvedere into his throat straight from the bottle.

"It's going to be okay," Julian said.

"Yes, Mr. Know-it-All. The good will end happily and the bad unhappily," said Ashton. "That's what *fiction* means." He wiped his mouth. "In real life, everybody's getting all fucked up. No point in talking about it now. One wedding too late. Whatever." He brightened. "There's another wedding coming up, though. Nigel's brother Simon is getting married up in York next weekend. You in?"

"Am I invited?"

"Who cares. Come. We can celebrate your birthday there."

"I'm not crashing a wedding."

"It's Nigel. It's fine."

"It's Nigel's brother and it's not fine." The wedding was a week before the March equinox. Julian couldn't go. He had a lot to do to get ready.

"You know, the only moment in my life I regret, the only moment I wish I could change, the part that needs a rewrite," Ashton said, still holding the bottle, "was back in L.A., five years ago. I knew how I felt about Z, but instead of breaking up with Riley like you broke up with Gwen, I let it ride. Instead of letting Riley have a chance at another life, I let it ride and ride because I didn't want to abandon her like my dad ditched my mom. I didn't know the future and was shit scared of making the wrong choice. And Riley rode my indecision all the way to Snowflake, and Z rode my indecision all the way to the altar with another man."

On the outside Ashton was dressed to slay, his hair spiked and trimmed, his face with just the right amount of stubble, his gray suit dazzling, his white shirt spotless, his tie Gucci. Only his crystal blue persuasion eyes revealed the rampant anarchy inside.

"Hey, I'm sparring tomorrow before work," Julian said. "Want to come spar with me, be my partner?"

"Always." Ashton smiled. "But seriously, don't change the subject, come to York with us. Nigel's driving. You've never been to York."

"Nigel driving is supposed to make me want to go or want to never go? I'm not sure."

"Funny."

"Stay here instead, Ash. It's my birthday weekend."

"You have a birthday every year, but how many weddings is Nigel's poor schmuck brother going to have? Two, three tops?" Ashton laughed. "Plus I already said yes."

"If you stay, we can go to that fancy new pub on Lancaster Road. You said you wanted to check it out. We'll go for my birthday, drink, talk about the good old days."

"You want to trade war stories about college, when everything was still ahead of us?" Ashton said, tipping back the last of the Belvedere. "To live like a crazy man is not enough for you? You have to talk about it, too?" He lined up the empty vodka bottle on the window sill next to the other bottles. "In the immortal words of both Samuel Beckett and Woody Allen, Julian, life's too fucking short to talk about life."

∞

Julian met Ashton the first day of orientation in his freshman year at UCLA. He was eighteen. His family was crowded into the small dorm room with him. His dad and oldest brother, Brandon, were putting together his bookshelf, Rowan was thumbtacking his posters to the walls, and his mom was making his bed. Tristan and Harlan were perched on Ashton's bed playing their Game Boys with six-year-old Dalton. Everyone stood at attention when Ashton entered, a tall, skinny, hyper kid with an irrepressible grin and a mophead of blond hair.

"Are you Julian's roommate?" Dalton asked.

"Yeah," Ashton said, looking around the room. "Which one of you is Julian?"

Timidly Julian stepped forward. He had been helping his dad and brother with the shelf, and now put down the hammer and bumped Ashton's extended fist. "Hey," he said. He was guarded. He had never lived with anyone but his brothers, was barely friends with anyone but his brothers.

"I'm Ashton." The kid smiled.

Ashton's side of the room was pretty barren. The Cruzes had been talking about it, Joanne Cruz especially, being a mom and all. There wasn't anything anywhere except a framed signed poster of Bob Marley, inscribed with *"Money can't buy life."* Tristan asked Ashton the question everyone was thinking: "Your folks already split?"

"Yeah," Ashton said with a laugh, "you could say my folks already split. You could definitely say that."

After everyone had left, Ashton said, "Nice fam you got there," falling on the bed and casually crossing his arms behind his head. "You got five brothers? Wow. Lucky. I'm an only child. And both Mom and Pops thought even that was too many."

Julian chuckled because he thought Ashton was joking. And to pretend he was joking, Ashton made a joke. "When I was a kid, we had a sandbox in our backyard that was filled with quicksand," he said, grinning. "I was an only child...*eventually.*"

Julian laughed. To imitate Ashton, Julian fell on his bed, too, trying to casually cross his arms behind his head. "Sometimes all I want is to be an only child." Julian said it, but he didn't mean it. Being an only child seemed like hell to him. Not a metaphorical hell. Actual hell. He hated being alone, probably because growing up he wasn't alone for a second.

"Yeah, we always want what we haven't got," Ashton said. "I'm trying to work on that. I want to be the guy who doesn't want what he hasn't got. Hey, Thunderpussy is playing at the Viper Room on Sunset." He grinned. "Wanna go? I can get us in. I know a guy."

"Some other time maybe. I got another thing going on."

"Another thing like a...date?" Ashton's smile was big.

Julian squinted, debating whether to reveal himself or not. "Actually...like a fight."

"A fight?" Ashton's smile got even bigger. He jumped off the bed. "So what are you lying around for? Let's go see what you got, buddy." He grabbed his jacket. "How many Germans does it take to screw in a lightbulb?" he said to Julian as they were walking out.

"I'm Norwegian not German," Julian said, "but I'll bite, how many?"

"One," Ashton said. "They're efficient, and not very funny."

Ashton forewent Thunderpussy, ducked out on his other friends, and went with Julian to the UCLA sports center to watch him battle a bigger opponent. Bigger, but not tougher. From that first freshman day, Ashton was at the ringside of every fight Julian had, first as an amateur for the university, training for the Olympics, and then without helmets and face guards as a pro, in dusty desert dives all over Death Valley, from Sacramento to Brawley below the Salton Sea. He was part of Julian's entourage in every ring, next to Mancini, his trainer, and Lopez, Mancini's son. Harlan and Tristan would drive hours from Simi Valley, lying to their unsuspecting parents, to come watch their brother fight.

"Stop hiding your brilliance in secret dumps in the Mojave," Ashton said at the start of their senior year. "Time for the big leagues, baby. It's all you want. It's what you deserve. Stop hiding from your family, stop being ashamed. Show the world what you got, bro, because what you got is dope. You can throw a punch, but even more important, you can take a punch. You're superfast, you got killer reflexes, and you're not afraid." Ashton banged on Julian's chest. "Instead of a heart," he said, "inside you is a boxing glove. You need a true title fight. And that's exactly what I'm going to get you, and what we're going to work and train for. And then we'll invite your family so they can finally see you for what you really are—a fighter."

Julian fought better and better guys all during his last year in college. Right before graduation in May, Ashton set up a pre-championship match. Julian had three months to train for the all-important bout in August. The winner would face the legendary Bernard Hopkins for the World Middleweight title. This was as big as it got. Julian was up against the undefeated Marcus "Deathblow" Hill. "Undefeated so *far*," Ashton and Julian yelled with dramatic high-fives.

But between Julian and Deathblow lay Topanga. The fight never took place. Julian was in a coma. And Marcus Hill died in a car crash while awaiting sentencing for killing his girlfriend.

# Part Four

# *Tragame Tierra*

*"Earth, swallow me whole."*

**A Spanish saying**

# 41

# The Plains of Lethe

FOR A LONG TIME JULIAN WALKED ON THE FIVE RIVERS THAT encircled Hades. He walked down the river of hate and the river of fire. He walked down the river of sorrow and the river of lament, and he walked down the river of forgetting, but not long enough. He didn't swim or row a boat because all the rivers were sheathed in ice. The dead arrived at the barren wasteland called the Plains of Lethe, nothing but a wilderness of desolation and despair. In Dante, Lethe is an earthly paradise atop the Mountain of Purgatory. The River of Lethe flows down to hell and freezes into ice around Satan. Julian had merged with a demonic force and was now forced to travel into the mouth of hell. To break the spell that hung over his life, he might have to engage Satan himself in hand-to-hand combat. Or he might have to smash the crystal of souls, as Ashton had suggested. For a moment, Julian doubled over.

He had seven weeks to wander the streets of her frozen world.

Would she recognize him, would she know his face?

He barely recognized himself.

Love did that.

Death, too.

The worst has happened. All dreams must go. Great God! What *was* this awful place? He was in a glacier cave, enormous and deathly still. He walked and walked but never got anywhere.

Julian gave his heart to know wisdom, yet all he knew was madness and folly. She died, and he was never heard from again. His little life went on without him. It barely even noticed he was gone.

And then it broke apart.

He vanished once more into the blue ether, pretending to search for her in the unknown universe but really he vanished to hide.

It was so cold, the tears turned to ice on his face.

∞

The cave is an underground corridor a continent long, an ocean wide. Ice spears hang down instead of stalactites. Julian walks for so long he forgets where he's going, he almost forgets where he's been. Though not quite. Eventually, the cavern opens into an endless field. He finds a gulley by the side of the road, falls into it, throws grass and leaves over himself for warmth and drops into a restless anguished sleep. In his oblivion he sees black lightless streets and immovable trees. He moans and stirs, trying to wake up. Where is that ice bag Riley used for a pillow so she would stop thinking about Ashton at night.

You and I, we leaned on our elbows across from each other in our eternal amity. But now I'm alone in a ditch. Woe to him who is alone when he falls, but if two are together then they have heat, for how can one be warm alone? Julian is so cold. All go into one place, searching for unattainable salvation, all are of the dust and to dust they return.

∞

Eventually he crawls out. Around him are wet flat fields. There's a chill wind from the south. The day wanes. Or not. It's gray out, as if the sun never shines. There are no rolling hills, no vivid green grass. Where is he?

For many hours Julian walks down the dirt road before he acknowledges he might not be in London. To be honest, it doesn't even look like England. This kind of flatness is new to him. Yet there is an unmistakable sharp smell of salt water assaulting his nose, stinging his eyes.

When he finally spots a lonely farm, set back from the road, he's sure the door will be opened by her. There's nothing else around. He tries to imagine what she will look like. All he sees is forever-ago Josephine behind the wheel of a speeding car.

The woman who opens the door is not her, at least Julian doesn't think so. She is a wide, tall, hard-looking woman with a dark unwelcoming face and black hair. In the poor light she looks as if she has swirling tattoos around her chin.

"Who are you?" she says and before he can answer adds, "Do you come in peace?"

"Yes," he says, trying to peek behind her broad frame for a flash of a daughter. Indeed, a younger woman sits on the couch. "Is that your daughter?"

The woman is shoved away from the door by a tall grim man who holds a walking stick in his hands—a walking stick with a sharpened tip that makes it look like a spear. "Who wants to know about my daughter?" he says. "What do you want with her, whiteman? Do you wish to marry her? You must work first."

"Manaia, leave him alone," the woman says, pushing the man aside. "We have no work for you. We hire our own. Go to town if you want work. Or to Bluff if you know how to fish."

"Ask him what he wants with our daughter, Aroha." Both the man and the woman stand at the door. Julian thinks they could be Hawaiian, both tattooed, him more, tall and broad, both severe. Julian wants to look around but will not take his eye off the man with a spike in his hands.

"If you're a traveler, where are your things?" Aroha says. "You carry nothing with you? That's not good. That's a concern to every person, native or not, who meets you. Why you wear a black suit like you're the undertaker?"

Aroha is right. Julian has nothing with him. He wears a suit, black tie, white shirt, black shoes. On his neck is the headlamp. Don't leave home without it. Sometimes the road is dark, and you can't see where you're going.

"It's an Armani," Julian says of his suit. "It's timeless in any age." Why are they provoking him with their take-no-prisoners glares? Well, he has his Penance Stare in return. He doesn't know which of them itches for a fight more, him or them. A minute ago, Julian was walking bent as if without a spine, and now look. He stands straighter. What he doesn't have is a wetsuit, or special boots, or grappling hooks. Besides his hands, he has no weapons, certainly no finely honed spear like the Polynesian gentleman. Over his hands Julian wears fine leather gloves, not waterproof thick Thinsulate, not boxing gloves.

He steps back. He hasn't even clenched his fists. "I'll be on my way, then. What town is this?"

"Underwood that way."

"What's after Underwood?" There doesn't look to be anything to Underwood.

"Invercargill. Just keep walking south. Where you coming from, Dunedin?"

"Yeah, that's it."

*Dunedin?* Did Julian bring a map of the world with him? Has he memorized all the snow-capped palaces, the solemn temples, the great globe itself? Is he in Scotland? Dunedin sounds vaguely Scottish.

"How far is Edinburgh from here?" he asks.

"I don't know where that is." The woman slams the door, but not before she says, "Watch your back, whiteman. Your back, your front. It's not safe for you here, wandering about as you are, with nothing in your hands, setting folks on edge."

Invercargill, wherever that is, is a long way to walk under hulking gray skies after a lifetime in the ice cave. Nothing comes his way down the road, no car, no horse.

It's not so much cold as brutally windy. Julian has not planned for this weather. By his outfit he'd say he hasn't planned for much of anything. He picks up the pace to keep warm. The sky turns to granite, then slate, then black. He switches on his headlamp and walks on.

He's heard the name Dunedin before, he's almost sure of it.

He doubles over, struggling to get his breath back before his mind can catch up with the segue of seemingly unrelated thoughts that lead him to the answer of where Dunedin might be, where Invercargill might be. Robert Falcon Scott sailed for Antarctica from Port Chalmers, and in the documentary he saw with Ashton when they first moved to Notting Hill, the narrator talked about a whisky distillery near Port Chalmers that produced Scotch almost as good as Scotland itself. It was called the Dunedin Distillery. The explorers bought whisky to take on the *Terra Nova* on their last voyage to the South Pole. Port Chalmers was in New Zealand, way down on South Island.

Julian stops walking. Is he in *New Zealand*?

So that family weren't Hawaiian. They were Maori. What little he knows of the Maori troubles him. They're fierce warriors.

Remembering the documentary about Robert Scott doubles Julian over again, as if bowing before the merciless God. Groaning, he presses his fists into his stomach until the agony passes and he can breathe again. He resumes walking, but slower.

A sign tells him he's entering Invercargill, New Zealand, settled by the Presbyterian Church of Scotland in 1853, population 12,782, coordinates 46S, 168E.

Longitude 168° east? Another dozen degrees and he'd be on the opposite side of zero meridian. Does the International Date Line also open up to the infinities of souls in the middle of the Southern Ocean? Since Julian is all the way here, he doesn't doubt it.

He finds himself on Clyde Street, an exceptionally wide boulevard that runs from the outskirts to town center. It's wide like an airport runway or the Interstate. A few hundred feet in the distance, a tavern glows. Soon he'll be in the warmth. Julian tries to walk faster.

From the pub a figure strolls out, lights a cigarette, turns, and stares up the road. The shape is bundled up but small and rounded like a woman. As she sees him approaching, she continues to smoke, watching him for a few moments.

And then the cigarette *falls* from her hands.

The woman scrambles and vanishes inside the tavern called the Yarrow. A minute later, a tall thin man walks out calmly into the road and turns his head in Julian's direction.

Julian blows into his palms. He's astonishingly cold. He can't feel his face. It's the blasted wind. It's shocking.

The man is in his sixties, with dark skin, black hair, black eyes. He also has curly-cue tattoos on his face, but faded, and only along the jawline. He lights a cigarette himself and smokes, exhaling vapor into the swirling air and watching Julian.

"Hey," Julian says, switching off his headlamp. "Place open for business?"

"Do you come in peace?" the man asks.

Must be an ancient greeting. Julian confirms that indeed he does.

"My name is Kiritopa," the man says. He gestures toward the tavern. "She's been waiting for you."

Julian takes a step back and scans the road for perhaps another tavern. "I don't know who *she* is. But *she* must be mistaking me for someone else."

"I don't think so," says the Maori. "A man will come out of the darkness, she's been telling us for years, dressed in black and he will wear light." He points to Julian's headlamp and throws out his cigarette. "Come in," he says, "but a word of warning. She's not as calm as I am. Are you ready?"

"No," Julian says, following the man inside. "I'm most certainly not ready."

"Yeah," the man says, not even glancing at Julian. "You don't look ready."

Inside is dark, candlelit, and *very* warm. There's a fireplace in the far corner. The place is empty. Either it's late or it's a Monday and business is light.

"She'll be out when she gets herself together. Meantime, what can I get you? You've come a long way?"

"Just Underwood," Julian replies, trying to deny their theories about him. "How about a beer?"

"You're six years too late," Kiritopa says. "No liquor sales in Southland since 1905."

So it's 1911. "A pub without beer?" Julian fights the urge to double over his knees. "What do you serve, tea?"

"Tea, yes. Apple cider."

"Apple cider will do," Julian says. "Put some whisky in it, will you?"

Kiritopa returns with a tall steaming mug. "I did put some moonshine in it for you," he says quietly. "The Kahurangis over in Bluff make the best. But don't tell no one."

"Who am I going to tell."

"Maybe your friends in Underwood?"

"Mum's the word." Julian downs the hot cider with the moonshine in it in three long, desperate gulps. The homemade liquor is Krazy Glue strong.

"The strongest moonshine in Southland," Kiritopa says with a hint of pride.

"Your place?" Julian asks, looking around the homey tavern.

"Hers technically. But we're in it together." Kiritopa doesn't look nearly as upset to see him as the woman did. Perhaps it's his phlegmatic disposition. But it's something else, too. Slight relief maybe? Like, finally, the next part of this man's life can begin. He seems ready for whatever that is. "Next time someone asks if you come in peace," Kiritopa says, "reply with *kia ora*. It means have life, be well."

The Yarrow is uncommonly warm. The burning fire doesn't explain the pervasive heat throughout the entire restaurant, with no cold spots and no drafts.

Kiritopa tells Julian the Yarrow was built directly over a hot spring. The steam heats the entire building, even the upstairs. And downstairs, in the cellar, the geyser shoots hot water into the grottos. "You can have a bath if you want. Get warm. Get clean." Kiritopa says it as if Julian needs to.

"Where is she?" he asks the Maori man, who stands by the side of his table, observing him, but not sitting down and not volunteering more information.

"Who?" Kiritopa asks quietly.

Julian rubs his face. "The woman who saw me outside, I suppose," he says. "We'll start with her."

As soon as Kiritopa leaves, Julian falls asleep in the warmth, his elbows resting on the table, his head in his hands.

"I'm Agnes," he hears a crusty voice say through the fog in his head. He opens his eyes, jerks his body upright. The small white round woman stands in front of him, her weathered face blotchy red as if she'd been crying. Her black hair is half-gray.

Julian is exhausted and can't fathom the expression in the woman's eyes. Fear and sadness and relief and grim satisfaction. But mostly fear.

"I'm Julian," he says. "Agnes what?"

"Does it matter? Agnes Patmore if you must know." She rolls her Rs quite strongly. It almost sounds like a foreign accent. Must be the Scottish dialect.

Now Julian is awake. Nothing focuses the mind like an anxious female face and the name *Patmore*. "Did you say *Patmore*?"

"Why, do you know someone named Patmore?" she asks, crestfallen.

He shrugs. "I might've known someone named Patmore. Not from here, though."

"From where, London?"

"Yes."

"Who, Coventry?"

"*What?* You knew the supernumerary at the British Museum?"

"What are you looking around my tavern for? He's ten years dead. And not a supernumerary. A poet first. Coventry was a fine poet. I married his son."

Julian sits back down. He feels unmoored by the unexpected anchoring. "Kiritopa is Coventry's son?"

"No, Kiritopa is Kiritopa. He's the son of a Maori chief. His family came to the Otago Peninsula five hundred years ago. He comes from one of the first men. I married Jacob Patmore."

"*Jacob* Patmore?"

"Why," she says, and in her voice, as in Julian's, is also exhaustion, hers the bone weariness of a sentry having been on the watchtower too long. "Don't tell me you know Jacob, too."

The woman in front of him married Jacob Patmore, the little boy Julian used to play with in Grey Gardens with Mirabelle. It's a coincidence. It simply can't be the same person.

"We were married in 1880," she says. "We were twenty-seven."

So it can be the same person—and is. Because nothing is a coincidence. "Jacob, Emily Patmore's son?"

"Yes. Did you know her, too?" Agnes's voice is low. "She wasn't a well woman, my mother by law. Didn't want me to marry her son. Told me I'd be the death of him. Can you imagine your mother by law saying that?" She doesn't take her probing eyes off Julian.

"Is Jacob still alive?" Wouldn't that be something. But what's Agnes Patmore doing in Invercargill?

Agnes shakes her head. "He died during our passage here." She tuts. "I hate that my husband is dead, but I *really* hate that his mother was right."

"Did you"—Julian doesn't look up—"did you have any children?"

Agnes is darkly quiet. She sinks into the chair across from him. "You know I did," she says. "Otherwise you wouldn't be here."

Julian breathes in and out to keep his voice steady. "I don't know what you're talking about. I'm just passing through."

"Passing through on the way to where, Antarctica, the Ross Sea?"

They don't speak for a few minutes.

"I hate that you're here," she says. "Know that, before I say anything else."

Julian is not thrilled to be here himself. "You can stop right there," he says, "and tell me nothing."

"A long time ago," Agnes says in a dull voice, sitting stiffly, "during a summer week in Blackpool, on the boardwalk by the sea, passing by Cocker's Aviary with my baby swaddled in her blanket, thinking my life was good and I was happy, a gypsy from Benin stopped me on the pier and ruined my life. Her name was Fulani. She started waving her hands in front of me and muttering foreign words."

"Foreign words like *halakar*?" Julian says, bowing his head. They speak Hausa from Mali to Benin.

"I don't know about that, what does it mean?"

"You don't want to know." *Halakar*. Annihilation.

"She was in black rags and she scared me, and she scared my husband."

"I bet."

"She followed us all the way to Mooky the Clown, and that's a long way, if you know the Blackpool boardwalk."

"I don't."

"My Jacob, the mildest of men, nearly beat her to get her away from us. She refused to leave my side. She told me to come back and find her. I would have never come back, I was so superstitious then—still am—but she whispered, *your baby is in mortal danger. You want to save her life or no?* What was I going to do?"

Julian and Agnes inhale painfully. Julian scans the empty tavern. Kiritopa sits in the far corner watching them. A native girl mops the floor. "Please," he says, "give me a drink before I hear the rest."

Agnes motions to Kiritopa. They don't speak until he returns with a full stein. "I've dispensed with the cider for you this time," the Maori says to Julian. "But drink it slow. It will knock you out if you're not used to it." He glances at Agnes. "Are you all right, Mother?" he asks, and only after she nods does he leave.

Julian forces himself not to drink it all in one gulp. He doesn't like the way the woman is studying him. And he doesn't want to hear the rest of her story. He doesn't want to hear it because he knows what she is going to tell him. Agnes will have heard a prophecy, ruinously incomplete, which has determined the crooked course of her crooked life, and the life of her only child.

"The next day, by myself, I went looking for the woman on the boardwalk. I was determined to know what she knew. Gypsies have the gift of sight."

"Partial sight," Julian says. It's worse than blindness.

"Hers was pretty full. When I found her, she told me my baby had a deep red aura. She said that a red light around a baby was a terrible omen. She'd only seen babies with red auras a few times in her life. When you move toward the source of light, all things including human souls appear blue. But when you move away from light, they turn red. The redder the red, the farther from the light. And my baby, she said, was the reddest she'd ever seen."

Julian says nothing.

"You got nothing to say?"

"I got nothing to say." The first time he saw Josephine at the Cherry Lane Theatre in New York, she was bathed in blood red footlights. *I'm dead then, good, she said to him and swiveled her hips,* and now he was here.

"Do you want to save her or not?"

Julian keeps himself from shuddering, almost. "Are you asking me or telling me what the witch said to you?"

"Both."

Julian says nothing.

"You don't believe her?"

"I wouldn't believe her if I were *you*," Julian says.

"You are lying to me. Why?"

"Listen to me, Mrs. Patmore..."

"Let me finish." Agnes's lip trembles. "The gypsy Fulani said to me"—Agnes fights her tears—"*death knows her by her name.*"

Julian sinks into his seat. Where is that tiger water to strengthen his bones? He brings the cup of moonshine to his lips instead and with all his will fights the desire to gulp it down. He takes two hard swallows.

"So I changed her name and ran," Agnes says. "And brought her here."

"How has it been?" Julian stares into his half-empty cup.

"I haven't finished telling you the rest."

"Just tell me how it's been."

"She's still alive, so all right, I suppose, until a year ago. Last spring I made a mistake. A man had come walking down the road, and I thought he was you. He also came out of the darkness wearing black. I said to him, are you the one, and he said yes, he was the one. I brought him in, but he turned out to be..."

"Not the one?"

"He wasn't good. He scared the whole town, scared my child, scared us bad."

"Who was he?"

"I don't know. It doesn't matter."

"Probably matters to him."

"He became obsessed with her."

"What happened to him?"

"He vanished," Agnes says, leveling her burning gaze on Julian. "Like he was never here."

Julian feels pale, watered down, even though his throat is on fire from the moonshine. "You don't know. Maybe he was the man you're looking for."

"I'm not looking for the man. The man is looking for her." Agnes lowers her voice again. She's nearly whispering. "The gypsy said *he will walk through the ice desert for forty days trying to find her*."

"Who did she say was coming?"

"The *one*."

Julian was hoping the mother would say the one who will save her. But that's not what the gypsy told Agnes. Julian may be the one. But he isn't the one who will save her.

"I'm not the one," he says. "Believe me."

"I *don't* believe you," she says. "Look how upset you're making me. I've never felt this way before. In my bones, I know it's you. But also"—Agnes leans forward—"if I needed more proof, Fulani said the proof was on your arm. She said you carry a map to her life and death. Show me your arm, pilgrim." She reaches for him.

He yanks away. "Don't touch me."

"I thought so." Tears roll down Agnes's face. "I don't need to see it. By your face I know the truth. Through your eyes I know you."

They don't speak while he finishes his drink. Julian is swimming in moonshine. "Where is she?"

"*Wait.*" Agnes grabs his arm. There's hatred and terror in her eyes. "The gypsy said you'd bring *light*, but you'd also bring *death*. Because death follows you to her. It's how death finds her. By *you*."

Julian's worst fears are being realized, one by one. It's not only the girl who's in danger. It's him, too. Oh, the fucking soothsayers. He falls back against the chair, while Agnes composes herself.

"You have a plan?" she asks. "I did my part. I kept her safe until you found her. Now what are you going to do?"

Julian is afraid a word will give him away. Why did he have to admit he knew Jacob Patmore! Where is he going to go now? He is penniless. He is so far from mercy. He wants to ask what month it is, what day it is, but doesn't want his ignorance to expose him further.

"What I'd like to do," he says, "is ask you for some food and be on my way."

"On your way to where? You got money to pay for the food and the shine? I didn't think so." She stands up. "You don't need money. You are where you need to be."

"Tomorrow I'll find work and repay you."

"You can work here. We got plenty for you to do." Agnes glances toward the kitchen. "I'll let you meet her. Don't be put off. She's lived her days with me like this. That can't have been easy. She doesn't believe me or doesn't want to. Amounts to the same thing. You know how the young can be. They think they will live forever."

"Yes," Julian says. "I was young once."

"She's hard. It's my fault. She'll come around eventually."

"Like the emperor penguin perhaps? By coercion?"

"If need be," Agnes says. "As long as the baby chick lives. That's all you should care about. How you get there is your problem. She is pig-headed. She could use some coercion."

"Great."

"Listen, boy," Agnes says, leaning to him. "You think I'm happy you're here? I'm wretched. Now that you're here, I know her death is near, too. But the witch was sure you were the only one who could lead her out. She said when you showed up, to let her go. She has only one narrow path to salvation—with you." Agnes spits on the floor of her restaurant before she heads to the kitchen.

∞

Julian sits palming his empty mug of shine. In a few minutes he feels a dark shape approach and stand silently by his table. He doesn't want to lift his eyes. He's only going to see her for the first time once. He takes a deep breath. "Hello," he says, raising his gaze, his heart rending.

The hostile baby chick stands in front of him.

And he thought the mother penguin was unwelcoming. The young woman's square face is hard of jaw—like his—and free of makeup, the pale skin on her large forehead wind-beaten. Her bright brown eyes glare at him defiantly. She is as plain and cold as the land he just walked through. She wears a long brown dress cinched at the waist and a black apron. If her hair is long, Julian can't tell; it's pulled back from her face and hidden under a black cap. She hides her body under ill-made, ill-fitting clothes, too long in the hem and sleeves, too loose in the hips and chest.

She is Mirabelle's shadow. She is less tall and less long and less shining than Mirabelle, for who could be more shining. But she's still tallish, still longish, still dimly shining. She looks impolite, not genteel, she has grown up in a town and a climate where people work all day in the harsh wind and have become weathered and hardened and silent. Her once delicate hands are knuckled and calloused. But she's got two magnetizing features that are visible to Julian, traits she can't hide, that draw him near. She's got a vivid, sharply drawn, abundant mouth and insolent wildfire eyes.

At the moment, the eyes are glaring at Julian as if he's Bluebeard.

In her face he searches for what he had once found in Mirabelle. It's not there. But his problem is not just the lack in her. His problem is the absence of what she must find in him. There is nothing for her to react to. Julian's eyes that had once gazed on Mirabelle with adoration now stare at this young woman in a pall, as if they're seeping blood from their unsurvivable wounds.

"Hello," she finally replies. "Cold out there." Her usually soft breathy voice is hoarse in Invercargill, deep and croaky, as if the wind has calloused her voice box. She's got a Scottish accent, trilling her Rs, *cold ut therrrrrr*. "What can I get you," she says.

"How about a menu?"

"Corrnish pasty, fish pie, fish and chips, shepherrrd's pie with lamb, maybe a mutton chop, and brread and butterr pudding."

Julian watches her standing at his table in her soiled apron.

"What?" she says. It's as if she's looking at him through snow goggles, her eyes blinded by cornea burn from the cold. She doesn't see him. In another life, her eyes shined for him. Not here. In another life, his eyes shined for her.

Still, they don't look away from each other, facing straight on, his eyes up, her eyes down, appraising, searching, contemplating.

"What's your name?"

"She didn't tell you?"

"What's your name?" Julian repeats.

She sighs. "Seamaisiona."

He sits. He doesn't know what she said.

"You didn't get that?" she says. "Want me to spell it for you?"

"Yes."

"*Shay*-ma, *shay*-na." She enunciates slowly. "It's like Mother wanted to punish me for the rest of my miserable life. She said to me Jesus told her it would be all right if she changed my name. I said to her, not Jesus, Mother, Fulani the witch."

"What was it before?"

"Mary-Margaret."

Julian twitches. She ignores him.

"Mother switched it like she switched hemispheres and oceans," she continues. "I told her, Mother, couldn't you just leave me Mary, that'd be like hiding in plain sight. Everyone's named Mary in our bloody Scottish town." She pauses. "What's the matter—you don't think I look like a Seamaisiona?"

"I do," Julian says. "The first thing I thought when I saw you is that girl looks like a Seamaisiona."

She almost laughs. She doesn't seem like the type who laughs easily. Her throaty chortle surprises even her.

"What do your friends call you, Mary-Margaret Patmore?"

"Shae."

"Is that what you want me to call you?"

"It don't matter what you call me. Are we done? Can I go get your food now?"

He takes her hand before she walks away. She doesn't pull away, just stares into his face. "You don't want to do that," she says quietly, her expression darkening.

Julian lets go.

Everywhere I've been—where I've made no effort, but even with her, where I've made all the effort—what a cold wake I leave behind, Julian thinks, finishing the last of the moonshine, thirsting for more. It's as if nothing I do matters. Nothing matters at all.

On the lower level of the tavern's basement, they've built a public bathhouse, but in the corner, there is a private room, and in this room, there's a grotto in the earth that twice a day fills up with steaming hot water. The water is soothing, delirium-inducing, like the homemade hooch. Julian undresses and immerses himself in the heat, to get away from the ice and the girl and his memories.

I've been used, banished, sent away. I'm a pauper. In another life, you could have been someone else's bride, and he would swear to you he'd never leave you, just like me. Go ruin someone else. Count me with the dead. Flood him with daisies and monologues, with chains and fiction and dust, cover him with your mocking laugh. Riley was right. I want to be free. Of love, of you, of longing, of wanting, of feeling, of leaping, of being deceived, of grieving. I want to be free of everything.

Julian has had too much drink and is slumped in the water when he hears Kiritopa's voice and feels the man's strong hands pulling him out. "Pilgrim, keep one eye open, even at night," Kiritopa says, handing Julian a towel. "I don't know if Agnes is right about the girl, but I know about you. You're not safe."

# 42

# Masha at the Cherry Lane

JULIAN AND AGNES WALK QUICKLY DOWN CLYDE STREET. Julian wishes he had a coat or some money to buy one. It's windy and cold. The Armani may be timeless, but the thin wool is no protection for Antipodean winds. He keeps his hands in his pockets. Like always, he hides the hands that perform the senseless work of his life.

"Do you see how she disobeys me?" Agnes is angry. She's almost running. "I told her not to leave the house unless you were with her. Next time she disobeys, punish her. You have my full permission to do with her as you will." They're headed to the Civic Theatre on Tay Street where Shae is rehearsing in Chekhov's *Three Sisters*.

Of *course*, she's rehearsing in *Three Sisters*. What else would it be. Julian doubles over and runs to catch up with Agnes.

"You'll see, she's very good," Agnes says. "Correction—she's an obstinate insubordinate woman, but she is a very good actress. Her gifts need to be displayed on a real stage, not in Invercargill."

"Where would this be?" Julian says. "Don't tell me—London."

"Not London. Why would I ever let her go back there? New York."

"Ah, New York," Julian says. "And how does Shayma-Shayna feel about New York?"

"Like she feels about everything that's not her idea. She

"Like she feels about everything that's not her idea. She hates it. But who cares?"

The Civic Theatre is a large ornate building, built only a few years earlier, in 1905. Agnes marches down the aisle to the front of the enormous darkened auditorium and demands Shae come speak to her at once. Julian stands nearby, doggedly examining his feet.

"Shae, was I not clear?"

"About what, Mother?"

Agnes slaps her daughter across the face. "Don't get mouthy with me. I told you—you don't leave the house unless he is with you. Not down the street, not to see Huhana—*especially* not her—not to rehearse, not to Bluff. Or Dunedin. *Nowhere.*"

"Does he come with me to the baths, too, Mother? To my bed?"

Agnes slaps her daughter again. Shae stands and takes it. The disrespect in her eyes doesn't fade.

"Wherever you go, he goes with you. Is that clear?"

"Like a bell." Ice is in Shae's voice.

"Apologize to him right now."

"Agnes, she doesn't have to..."

Agnes silences him with a withering glance. Good thing he's not closer, or she'd slap him, too. "Right now, Shae."

Shae takes two steps to Julian. They don't look at each other. "I apologize."

"It's fine."

"Tell him it won't happen again," says Agnes.

"It won't happen again," Shae says through her teeth.

"It's fine."

"It's not fine, Julian. It's bad manners. Don't let her off the hook like that. What are you standing around for?" Agnes barks to her daughter. "Go rehearse. I want Julian to see what you can do."

Shae swirls and returns to the stage.

As they make their way to the back of the theatre where they can talk without bothering the actors, Julian suggests to Agnes that maybe this "stick" approach might not be the best way to endear him to Shae.

"You think anything is going to endear you to her? You think you've got a carrot you can dangle in front of her instead?" Agnes snickers. "Try it, my boy. Be my guest. See how far you get."

They take two empty seats in the back and Julian listens, unwillingly and mostly silently, as Agnes regales him with a fever dream about her daughter's survival. What Julian would like to do is sit closer to the stage so he can hear Shae read Chekhov. Preferably the third row, as he did at the Cherry Lane. But Agnes has big plans and won't stop until Julian has heard her out.

Her plot includes a world famous inventor named Ernest Godward and his ship.

"Has he invented a time machine?" Julian asks. "Because that might help."

"The egg beater," Agnes says. "It beats eggs in three minutes for cakes, not like before when it took fifteen."

"The egg beater," Julian repeats.

"He invented the spiral hairpin for women, a curler for our hair. It's amazing. Shae uses it every night she's performing. Before you scoff again, he sold this invention for twenty *thousand* pounds."

"You're right, with an egg beater and a hair curler, we've got this thing licked." Twenty grand *is* a lot of money in 1911. Might as well be a million pounds. Once Julian had money. Forty-one Fabian coins. Even that has been taken from him. *Because money can't buy life.* He folds over his knees in the seat.

"What's wrong with you?"

"Nothing." He straightens out. "What do Godward and his brilliant egg beaters have to do with your daughter? Is she marrying him?"

"Not him, you fool—you," Agnes says. "Godward is already married. Not that that has ever stopped her, unfortunately.

Godward is leaving behind a wife and ten children and sailing to New York in October. Invercargill is too small for a genius like him. And I want Shae and you to get married and go with him."

"Shae and I are going to get married." It's not a question, or even a declaration. It's an echo.

"Of course."

"How does she feel about this?"

"I told you—no one cares how she feels. It's for her own good."

"She is going to marry me for her own good," Julian says slowly.

"Stop repeating what I say. Yes. It's for her protection."

Godward sails in October. It's mid-August now. The trip to New York will take four months. What a planner Agnes is, what a schemer. Julian is about to tell the mother a few things he knows about strategies and marriages and how many times 49 days goes into two months if by land and four if by sea, but he's interrupted by someone warm and breathy, smelling of many strong things, not all of them unpleasant, who stands behind Julian and Agnes and throws her arms around both their shoulders. The woman's blonde hair tickles the side of his face.

"Agnes, my love, good morning to you," says a happy alto voice. "And who is *this* delectable creature you've got sitting by your side?" Julian turns his head to find himself inches away from the vivacious face of a young Maori woman, with bleached hair and bleached eyebrows. Her black eyes blaze, and she is smiling at him with her whole face.

Julian can't help it. *Literally* can't help it. His face loosens from its stone mask, and he smiles back.

"Where did *you* come from? Never seen you around these parts before. I would've noticed, believe me."

"Another country," Julian says.

Agnes is much less friendly. "Julian, this is Huhana. She is the granddaughter of the oldest Maori chief over in Bluff. But, girl, don't interrupt us, we were talking."

"I thought you came to watch us rehearse?" Huhana comes around and kneels on the seats in front of them. She is covered in skins of outerwear, elk fur, sheepskin, leather. For some reason, Julian suspects she's got some body under those furs. One by one, the outer skins are discarded. Julian is proven correct. She is large and voluptuous. Her skirt and blouse barely contain her. The front buttons are popping off her shirt; her substantial breasts, tired of being cooped up, demand to be liberated. The smile doesn't leave the girl's face. "You're in our country now," she says. "How about a *hongi*?" Her smile is so flirtatious, Julian balks slightly, gets uncomfortable under Agnes's glare.

"Leave him alone, Huhana," Agnes says.

"Don't look so afraid, it's nothing untoward," the girl says to Julian. "You have to greet us as one of us. Lean in for a *hongi*." Huhana brings her face to Julian's face and presses her forehead to his forehead and her nose to his nose. "Julian, charmed, I'm sure," she says, barely pulling away and affecting a posh accent.

"Um, nice to meet you, Huhana," Julian says, himself barely pulling away.

"Why so formal? My friends call me Hula-Hoop. Or just Hula. Whatever you want." She smiles. "What*ever* you want."

Julian clears his throat and affects a poker face.

"Come on, say Hula-Hoop," she says, purring. "Or don't you want to be my friend?"

"Huhana, I'm serious," Agnes says. "First of all, Julian is Shae's friend, not yours. So behave yourself. And second, he and I are discussing matters of great importance. Now go. They've been calling your name for twenty minutes. Huhana is playing the self-absorbed, vicious Natasha," Agnes informs Julian. "Isn't it time you got going on that?"

Hula manages to simultaneously roll her eyes at Agnes and bat her lashes at Julian. "I'll be back, I promise." She winks and thunders down the aisle to the front of the theatre. "All's well, creatures, I'm here!" she shouts to the other women.

"I can't *stand* that girl," Agnes says.

"Oh? She seems all right to me." Julian squints toward the stage.

"No, she is a terrible influence on Shae. She's always dragging her to Bluff or worse to Dunedin, to all them bars and taverns and parties. I don't think she's ever met a man with her legs crossed."

What a gal, thinks Julian.

"Anyway, where were we?" says Agnes.

"You were telling me something about me and your daughter being four months at sea. Are you coming, too?"

Agnes shakes her head. "I can't leave Kiritopa. And he won't leave New Zealand. My life is with him. But Shae's can be anywhere."

Julian finally speaks truth to power he knows the mother doesn't want to hear. "You want my advice, Agnes?"

"No."

"Keep her with you. You'll be happier. She'll be happier." She can't be any *less* happy, that's for sure.

"Absolutely not. Fulani said. She goes with you."

"The witch knows nothing," says Julian. "There is nowhere to go."

"That's not true!"

"Trust me, it is. Keep her with you."

"Absolutely not."

"I'll stay with her," Julian says. "I won't leave." I have nowhere to go either.

"She's not safe here."

"Agnes, she is not safe anywhere."

Agnes sucks in her stunned breath. "Wow. Just wow. You better get yourself together, boy. Don't let me hear you talking like that again."

"Or what?" Julian says with great indifference.

"She can't stay here! Lately we've all been feeling nothing but foreboding. Even Kiritopa agrees with me, and Shae, too, though she won't admit it. Now that you've finally shown up, at least she's got a chance. In New York, she can be in a Ziegfeld folly. It's what she dreams about. Ziegfeld has been producing shows renowned for their style and beauty and humor for over a decade."

"That is true," Julian draws out, unsure whether to say the next thing. "Humor being one of the three."

Agnes squares her shoulders. "Shae can be funny. At the very least, she can *act* funny."

"At the very least."

"She can dance, she can sing. In New York, she'll be under true bright lights. She has many gifts. You'll see."

Many gifts—except the gift of life. He turns his eyes to the stage, where the director is still shouting orders and Shae stands with a copy of the play in her hands.

"It's what she wants," Agnes adds, "even if she pretends she wants other things."

"Like what?"

"Fishermen. Moonshiners. What else is there for her to do around here? Her latest conquest is a polar explorer. Can you imagine? I keep telling her those men are any port in a storm, but does she listen? She says she is one of those ports. She's got such a fresh mouth; Huhana has ruined her. But it's just Shae's way of escaping. She's suffocating in Invercargill."

"She seems to be doing all right," Julian says. "She helps you at the Yarrow, she's part of the local theatre. She's got friends, a big city to go to if she gets bored. It's not a bad wicket."

"Are you deaf and dumb or are you deliberately misunderstanding me?"

Julian turns to Agnes. "You think you know things? You know *nothing*. Once I thought I knew things, too. And I knew nothing. But I still know more than you."

"She can't stay here, I told you."

"And I'm telling *you* that on the other side of this life is a mother who *begged* to come with me so she could see her kid again—alive—even though the trip would most certainly kill her.

But you're already here. You don't have to walk barefoot down a river of ice when you're seventy-five. Your daughter is with you. Stop spinning and toiling. Give yourself what you want most."

"You know squat about what I want most."

"Do you think so?" says Julian. "If I am who you say I am, then I know all about your prophecy. Better than you."

Agnes clenches and unclenches her fists. "I want her to live. That's all."

Julian stares at the stage where Shae stands. "She'll live as long as she's supposed to. No less." He blinks. "And no more."

"The gypsy was clear."

"The gypsy can't help you. Hers is not the hand that guides you. She is not the one who sent you here."

"She is," Agnes says stubbornly, her body in a tremor.

"Well, she is certainly not the one who sent *me* here."

"She is…" Agnes whispers.

Julian can't make even Agnes understand. He knows both he and the mother must seem crazy to an outsider like Kiritopa and even to Shae herself, scarred as they are with the burns from a half-life of grief that sustains itself and regenerates and never fades.

Fed up with Agnes's hand-wringing, Julian moves by himself to the front, where he can sit in third row center and watch Shae become Masha in *Three Sisters*.

Chekhov died recently. In Invercargill, they're honoring him by performing his bleakest play. Shae has changed herself for the rehearsal. As Julian suspected, her drab tavern outfit is a costume. Here she wears eye makeup and lurid lipstick that makes her plump mouth look indelicate and suggestive. She has put on a fitted skirt, so he can see the outline of her hips, and a cream linen blouse, so he can see the outline of her breasts. She has let down her long dark hair, braiding it into a thick side plait. Her kohl-rimmed eyes are black fire. When she sees him sitting by himself in front of her, she scowls but doesn't waver. The entire time she speaks, she focuses defiantly on his face.

"Oh, I am *wretched*," Shae yells to Julian in the darkened theatre. "I'm almost twenty-seven. I've worked for years, and my mind is dried up. I've lost weight, lost my breasts"—she cups her breasts—"lost my youth. I've never gotten any joy, yet time keeps flying by, and I'm getting farther away from my actual beautiful life, slipping into some kind of an abyss. I'm in *despair*! How am I still alive, how have I not killed myself, to this day I don't understand. I thought all I wanted was an adventure, it's what I dreamed of, but now I know the awful truth. All I ever wanted was to be somebody else's adventure! I don't want money, or even fame. I just want to be the kind of somebody for whom another somebody would sail into the Southern Sea, someone who would search behind the sun for me, and who'd say when he found me, you are the one. Masha, Mashenka, my heart, my dearest one, *you* are the one."

How does she do it? Julian wipes his eyes. No matter what the life, or how thick the carapace, she manages to find a way to penetrate everything until a harpoon from her soul pierces through his.

∞

After rehearsal, Agnes leaves, and Julian waits for Shae outside in the cold. The Waihopai tributary by the Civic Centre is shallow and narrow, the tide deeply rolled away from the banks. On the exposed silt and sand, squawking white seagulls forage for food on their spindly legs. The wind remains fierce over the gray and sturdy Invercargill, a fishing town which the pragmatic Scots designed and arranged into orderly symmetrical grids. They organized the town and built low-to-the-ground houses out of wood and brick. Most of the streets in Invercargill have either Maori names or bear the names of Scottish rivers.

Shae comes out by herself, covered in fur. Under the elk hood, her hair is still in a braid and kohl remains around her eyes. But the red lipstick has been hastily wiped off, as if the young woman has no interest in subjugating Julian by her most enthralling feature.

"Your mother asked me to escort you back," he says, staring at the ground. He doesn't want to be subjugated either.

As they walk, he tries to make conversation, ask some questions. Tersely Shae responds, telling him about Invercargill, a little bit about Bluff, even less about Dunedin. "People travel to the other side of the world to start a new colony," she says with derision, "and then lack all imagination. Look at the names of the streets. Clyde Dee Tweed Tyne."

Careful not to ask about Hula-Hoop by name, Julian asks Shae about her friends in Bluff, where Bluff is, and how long it takes a train to get there (thirty minutes). He asks about her mother and about Kiritopa, who has been in their lives since mother and daughter first arrived in Dunedin, when Shae was two. Side by side Agnes and Kiritopa have worked at the Yarrow for almost twenty-five years. They've owned it for the last ten. Shae replies to Julian in monosyllables and asks him no questions. He gives up. These days, it's impossible for him to make small talk.

They walk the rest of the way in silence. It's not quite spring in Invercargill. It's just past the dead of winter. At the Yarrow, Agnes has prepared them some food and forces Shae to have her meal at his table. Lunch is a brief and wordless affair, like their two-mile promenade.

Thus begins the inauspicious courtship of Shae and Julian. It doesn't get better after the first day. In many ways it gets worse. Because eventually Shae speaks. Julian concludes that truculent brusqueness is infinitely preferable. Shae does not use her erotic mouth for good.

If Julian thinks *he* is reluctant to entertain Agnes's idea of sailing to the new world as husband and wife, he's got nothing on Shae. No woman could be less willing to go anywhere with a man than Shae is to go with him, even to walk to the Civic

Theatre to rehearse, even to take a train to Bluff to meet her fishermen friends, much less to board a ship to sail ten thousand miles to live with him in New York.

As far as marriage?

"Look, I know Mother told you what she wants," Shae says to him after a few days pass like this. They're walking to rehearsal. "Now I'm going to tell you what *I* want. I'm well aware of the things she's put into your head. She's put them into my head, too, and for a lot longer. But I'm not going. Most certainly not with you. She can't make me. And *you* can't make me." She leaves him with this salvo before she disappears inside the theatre: "She says that if I don't go with you, I will die. Let me tell you something—I'd rather die."

She says it as if it's even a choice.

"Oh, and unless I'm carried into the church in a casket," she adds, "you can forget about marriage."

Look at that. Julian has become Lord Falk. *I will give my body away to all men, including Lord Falk's swine herder, if it will stop that wretched man from marrying me.*

She turns back to him as she's about to enter the building. "It's a long rehearsal today, four hours," she says gruffly. "Come inside and wait, like she told you. I don't want to get hit again because you can't be bothered to stay put."

He comes inside, he waits. On the way back, before they reach the Yarrow, Shae initiates a conversation of her own. This is what dating sounds like in Invercargill: "You're silent, ice man, and I'm not a mind-reader so I can't tell what you're thinking. I don't even know if you heard me."

"Oh, I heard you, all right," says Julian. "I can hardly help that part, can I?"

"Great. As long as we understand each other, you and I will have no problems."

"Did I ask you to marry me?" he says.

"Don't even *think* of asking me."

"Did I even *think* of asking you?"

She's friends with people who are trained from birth to be warriors, and it shows. Shae puts up with nothing. Except her mother.

∞

"Has my daughter delighted you yet with the story of her *love* for the polar explorer?" Agnes says. She doesn't look impressed with Shae's romantic escapades.

"I haven't had the good fortune to be delighted with it, no," says Julian.

"He's a good man, likes to drink, likes a jolly crowd, likes women. *All* women. Besides his wife, that is, who's back in Britain minding his three children. Shae says he told her he will leave his wife for her. He *promised* her! Isn't that bloody hilarious. He was so drunk last year, he nearly missed the *Terra Nova*'s departure when they were leaving Port Chalmers for the Antarctic. Does that sound to you like he's a man of his word? The whole region turned out to see them off, and he was under the bed somewhere. And then he was running and fell off the docks into the water! They had to fish him out. Rumors were Robert Scott was so angry, he seriously considered leaving him behind."

Julian comes out of his apathetic trance. Shae is involved with a man in *Robert Scott*'s expedition? "What's his name?" Julian knows a few things about the *Terra Nova* voyage, unfortunately.

Agnes doesn't know or doesn't want to say. "I ask you, will a man like that leave his wife for her after he returns from Antarctica? Have you heard of anything so crazy?"

"I've heard a lot of crazy things lately, Agnes," Julian says. "And it depends what his name is."

∞

"I overheard Mother talking to you last night," Shae says to him in the windy morning as they walk to the Civic Theatre. "She doesn't think he will stay with me, but she doesn't know him and doesn't know us. I saw him a few weeks ago. And he promised me he would. Don't look so shocked."

"This is not my shocked face," Julian says. "This is my *frankly my dear, I don't give a damn* face."

"A few weeks ago he returned to Dunedin for *me*! He sneaked back onto the *Terra Nova* after wintering at Cape Evans. He wasn't supposed to do that, he was supposed to stay with his expedition. No one would risk so much unless they were serious about another person. No one could know he was here, and he only did it so we could have a few days together."

"Yes, it sounds as if it was quite a risk, lying in a berth on a ship, all for a few days together," Julian says, eyes straight ahead. "What a guy. What's his name?"

"What do you care what his name is?"

"Tell me or don't tell me. I'm just making conversation." He pulls the hat lower over his forehead. Kiritopa has found Julian an old sheepskin coat and an elk fur hat, so he's warmer, though the side flaps on the hat make it hard for him to see out of his periphery and sometimes to hear Shae. The flaps make it more difficult to watch over her, though to not hear her is a blessing.

"Edgar Evans, if you must know," Shae says.

Julian stops walking. He peers at her through the blowing wind. The gusts of salt water attack his face. His expression sets into hardness. "Where is Edgar Evans now?"

"Sailing back to Antarctica, I told you."

Julian resumes walking. "Edgar Evans is not coming back for you," he says.

"How do you know?" When Julian doesn't reply, Shae gets fed up. "Like I'm going to listen to *you*. I barely listen to my mother. And who the fuck are you? Oh, yeah. The fucking *one*."

Julian stops speaking to her.

Edgar Evans is a Welsh Navy officer, for over a decade one of Robert Falcon Scott's most trusted companions, first on the *Discovery*, and then on the *Terra Nova*. Edgar Evans sneaking onto a ship he wasn't supposed to be on would've been the best thing that could've happened to him, but only if he'd gotten so drunk again that the *Terra Nova* returned to Antarctica without him, and he was left behind. Because in just over two months, in November 1911, Edgar Evans will embark with Scott and three others on an ill-fated 1800-mile journey to the South Pole from which they will never return.

∞

There's a lot of work around the Yarrow. Julian is glad there is something for him to do other than trail a hostile chick around Southland. He likes Kiritopa. For years, the man has been doing everything himself, but he's getting old and can no longer manage the heavy stuff. The bricks in the perimeter fence have crumbled, some doors are off their hinges, the window frames are rotted. Julian welcomes the physical labor. It's harder to wallow when you're lifting heavy stones, and at the end of a long day, having hauled sand bags, and mixed cement, and spackled, and walked for miles through Invercargill by her side, sometimes Julian is too exhausted even for nightmares. He makes an effort not to fall asleep in the waters of the hot spring, into which he lowers himself every night to wash his body of the dirt that covers him.

Julian hasn't seen the sun once, and the wind is relentless. A week could've gone by, or three. The days of marking his arm with useless *dots* are long behind him. Kiritopa calls this Invercargill's dry season. It rains every other day. Only where one of the Waihopai estuaries flows into the Southern Ocean near Bluff are there ragged cliffs, high embankments, a severe vertical coast. The rest of the city is sea-level flat, roller-rink flat. And two thousand miles south across the ocean is Antarctica. Sometimes, when he is with Shae in Bluff, Julian wonders what it would be like to sail to the land of always winter, and not just sail, but sail away. Not to New York on a liner or to London on a whaleship, but in a rowboat to the end of the known world where no one and nothing would ever find them, but where they might be able to find each other. They certainly can't find each other in Invercargill.

Yes, Antarctica might be better. *Antarctica, the place where dreams come true,* Julian remembers Ashton calling it once, as he hauls the bricks into a pile, getting ready to rebuild part of the fallen wall surrounding the tavern.

# 43

# What Will They Care

I DON'T *CARE* THAT YOU'VE DONE THIS BEFORE, AND IT DIDN'T work.

That's Agnes.

Don't tell me your stories, she says. I *don't* care. This time will be different. Have you ever been to Invercargill before? Has she ever been named Shae before? I changed her *name*. Doesn't that mean anything? Have you married her before?

He wasn't marrying her now.

Marriage! Even simple human interaction is an ordeal. She has never been this hard. No one has been like her. Something has gotten corrupted in his doomed angel Mirabelle, and Julian doesn't know why. For whatever reason, Shae is a block of ice through and through, her yearning Masha in *Three Sisters* notwithstanding. Her yearning is an act, and in any case, she is not yearning for Julian.

Why can't he accept the possibility, Agnes keeps asking, that this time will not be like the others, because so much has changed—geographically, emotionally, physically—and because this time the mother and Julian are working together to protect Shae—and *most important* because this time Shae herself knows what's at stake.

"Has she ever known before how numbered her days are?" Agnes asks.

"No."

"There you go." To bolster her argument, Agnes drags Kiritopa forward.

Kiritopa tells Julian about an old Polynesian legend. In the Tasman Sea, there is a fathomless trench that opens up during a storm when all the Southern Cross stars are lined up in the sky, when Jupiter is either visible or under an occultation, like when Venus passed in front of it a hundred years ago, and generations of Maoris still tell the story of Jupiter and Venus to their children. Venus was seen with a naked eye, gliding and occluding the giant Jupiter. The southern sky lit up with an eerie fire glow that was as rare as it was sinister. The seas broke apart. "The bottomless place in the sea will swallow you, the legend goes," Kiritopa says, "but you don't vanish. You fly through a screaming warp like a newborn, and on the other side you live again."

"Yes," Julian says. "Cleon said this, too. Also the ancient Africans. Groaning you fly over the emptiness into the abyss of your death."

Agnes throws up her hands. "How is she going to fall in love with you when you're like this?"

"You're right," Julian says. "I can't make anyone fall in love with me. She has to come to me freely. Love compelled is not love. It's slavery."

"How can she come to you at all when you're like this?"

How can Julian come to her when she is like she is.

"Listen, Julian," Agnes says, "I don't know what part of the world you come from and I don't *care* to know. Maybe where you live, mothers don't *care* about their young. But we share this small corner of the world with the emperor penguin. The emperor can't fly and never sets one foot on land even to breed. The mother lays her eggs right on the sea ice. She lays them on the ice in the dead of the Antarctic winter, in sightless darkness, amid the most pitiless wind, during the harshest weather. She risks the blight of winter to save her chicks from leopard seals. Barely a quarter of her eggs survive. The mother penguin is willing to take that chance. Well, I don't have four children. I have just the one. And I have kept her hidden in the frightful dark for *you*. So don't tell me you're not going to step up. That you refuse to struggle against her odds. Four hundred adult birds in the penguin rookery sometimes produce as few as thirty chicks. Invercargill is my rookery, Julian Cruz. And your one willful but worthy chick awaits."

∞

Julian and Shae are not the only ones ambivalent about marriage and a sea voyage. Kiritopa says no one is safe with Julian, especially Shae. "Mother, can't you see? His insides have been taken out."

"Hogwash."

"Look at him, Mother," Kiritopa says. "He can't go out into the ocean. He can barely stand outside in the wind without keeling over. He needs more time in the hot spring. Only when he heals himself might he be able to help your daughter."

"I see nothing wrong with him," Agnes says. "And Godward has the safest ship. If she's going to be all right on any ship, it's his."

"I'm not going on Godward's ship, Mother," Shae says.

"Be quiet, Shayma. I'm talking to Kiritopa now." Agnes turns to her partner. "Julian's all I got," she says. "He's the only one who can protect her."

"He can't stand aright," Kiritopa says. "The sea will kill him."

"No, it won't, old man. What are you talking about?" Agnes is strident.

Kiritopa points to Julian, who tries to stand aright to prove Kiritopa wrong. "You don't have to be a gypsy to see his body is bent in half, overcome by the affliction inside him. He is sick."

"If he needs to act, he will act. I'm certain of it."

"Act? He can't even *stand*! He is crippled. He's been sliced through the core. A man like that can't go out into the open sea.

Keep him here. When he's better, six months, a year, maybe then they can go."

"No, Kiritopa," Agnes says.

"No, Kiritopa. She doesn't have six months, a year," Julian says, inaudibly, as he walks away. But he walks away bent through the middle.

A day later while cleaning the tavern tables and watching two young men talking over a cider, Julian breaks down. It's inexplicable and mortifying. Sinking into a chair, he sobs as if he will never stop. He doubles over his knees. He can't bear to see their casual laughing faces.

Neither Agnes nor Kiritopa know what to do. Grimly they stand nearby.

"What did I tell you?" Kiritopa says.

"I didn't want to hear it then, old man," Agnes exclaims, "and I don't want to hear it now." She thrusts a handkerchief at Julian. "What's the matter with you?"

Julian grows even more mute. He will never explain himself. And what is there to say. These people are not his confessors.

They are not his friends.

What will they care, Julian thinks as he lowers himself into the ground filled with steaming water and lies motionless, his head thrown back, a hot rag over his face, over his eyes so he doesn't see his life.

Everything that could be lost was lost.

What will they care.

Julian saw a star fall from heaven to earth into a bottomless pit. The pit was burned out wormwood, bitter with the bitterest smoke. The star fell like a lamp and was snuffed out, dying in the blackest black, in the coldest grass. Some men sought death and did not find it. And some men sought life and did not find it either.

What will they care.

Nothing remained in the whiteout desert that was Julian's life, across every icy plane, across every dimension. Everything was leveled.

Four men went out on a stag night in York the day before a wedding, pub crawling through every historic watering hole in the ancient town. Nigel, his brother Simon, a guy named Byron.

And Ashton.

What will they care.

Their guesthouse was twenty miles north of the city, near the Yorkshire dales. Late Friday night coming back, they decided to pop into one more pub, two miles from their inn. The pub was called the Three Horseshoes and it summoned their lives for last call.

They took a wrong turn and wound up in the hills above the dales, on a country road called Crag Lane. The road was blind and lined with trees. It was almost too narrow for one Mini-Cooper, much less for a Mini and a Fiesta to pass side by side. Drunk Nigel was speeding, and the raucous drunks in the car were singing. Nigel said later they'd been singing "The Wild Rover."

An impaired Nigel couldn't gauge the width of the road and no one else in the car was sober enough to see or care. Nigel thought he had plenty of room. When he saw that he didn't, he panicked and stepped on the gas. Oaks fenced the narrow way, oaks and gulleys. There was nowhere to turn, though the Fiesta driver desperately tried, a sixty-year-old man returning home with his wife after an anniversary dinner. Nigel's Mini crashed into the Fiesta, flipped on impact, and smashed into a tree.

The Mini wasn't a Volvo, it wasn't the safest car on the road. But even the vertical steel pillars of a Volvo would have had a hard time withstanding a high-speed collision with another car and a 400-year-old oak. Ashton managed to crawl away from the devastation into a ditch, which is where they found him at dawn the next morning.

Except for Nigel, everyone in both cars was dead, five people, including Nigel's brother, the groom-to-be, on the day of his wedding.

Including Ashton.

What will they care.

Julian, Devi, and Ava drove to Yorkshire to bring Ashton's body back to London.

But first, Julian had to identify him.

The priest at St. Monica's made a special dispensation for Devi, who'd been a parishioner for many years, and commenced a man Devi called his friend, a man who had not shown his face inside a church except on the day he was baptized and the day he was buried.

Julian never heard a man cry as Ashton's father had cried the day they buried his son. An old man overnight, Michael Bennett had to be held up to stand, supported by two of his five wives, four of them in attendance, Ashton's mother long gone.

Julian stood flanked by Ava and Devi. After the service, still in his funeral suit, he took a train to Greenwich, foregoing the interment, barely making it to the Observatory in time for noon. Julian and Ashton went into the ground together. Julian threw himself into the blue hole at the Transit Circle, resolved never to come back.

He had begged Ashton, implored him not to trust Nigel with anything important, like his life. Yet Ashton had begged Julian for many things, like to come with him to York. Julian could've. But he did not. The equinox was coming. He had a lot to do to get ready. Would've, could've, should've. *Run along, my friend.*

The unendurable sound of the head-on collision is what Julian heard through his silent hours. Ashton crawling away into the icy trenches is what he saw when he closed his eyes. His forehead pressed into the cold metal is where Julian was every minute of every day, sunk to his knees in the morgue, in front of the slab where Ashton lay.

*I've been a wild rover for many a year, and I've spent all my money on whiskey and beer, and now I'm returning with gold in great store, and I never will play the wild rover no more. And it's no, nay, never, no nay never no more, and I'll play the wild rover no never no more.*

What will they care.

# 44

# Termagant

OUTSIDE THE YARROW, THE COLD WIND BLOWS AND INSIDE there is also no peace. They fight about him constantly, and this afternoon they're fighting again. Julian can hear them as he chops wood, even over the sound of the axe, even with the flaps of his fur hat pulled down. Agnes storms outside and hooks her finger at him. In the kitchen under a bright light, the mother demands he roll up his sleeve and show Shae his arm. At first, Julian refuses. He's caused enough strife between mother and daughter. But after a few minutes he gets tired of the shouting and rolls up his sleeve.

Shae's wrath is a storm. "Mother, you want me to leave my life, leave my friends, leave you and sail to the other side of the globe because a limp stranger in a suit has the name *Mary* inked on his arm?"

"Ask him what the dots are for, Shayma!"

"I don't care!"

Julian rolls down his sleeve, throws on his coat and goes back outside, where the bitter wind howls. Like the mother, the daughter follows nothing but her fear.

And everything she does with the fear at her back, she makes worse.

"Tama, guess what—our new friend's got tattoos, *too*!" Shae says in a mocking voice later that evening to her young Maori friend Tama Kahurangi the son of the man who makes the strongest moonshine in Southland. She and Julian are in Bluff again, hanging out with her friends at the Noisy Orchard, one of the taverns that line the docks at the inlet. The whaleships come and go, and the fishermen and sailors and the itinerants arrive at Bluff from the sea, to get on another boat, to seek another life. People come to Invercargill and Bluff to vanish, and the Noisy Orchard is doing booming business before they do. No liquor served means the Kahurangis, selling raspberry hooch on the down low, are the wealthiest traders in Southland. Tama's uncle owns the Noisy Orchard.

"Show him," Shae says to Julian.

"No," Julian says to Shae.

"They're on his arm, Tama," Shae says with a baleful gleam. "Tiny dots."

"Ah, look at you and your baby tattoos," Tama says to Julian. Tama is a wiry, strapping kid, maybe twenty, his long hair braided and tied back, swirls of prominent black ridges covering most of his lower face. On top of his head, Tama's hair is cut in a spike. It makes him look dangerous even though the friendly smile doesn't leave his face. He gives Julian a once-over, the way a young man who fancies himself a fighter gives another man, to determine what he's facing. After a brief but intense scrutiny, Tama decides he's facing nothing, and the smile reappears in full. "You want to see real tattoos, whiteman?"

"No," says Julian.

Tama is not listening. "*These* are tattoos." The guy pulls open his shirt to show Julian his ripped pecs, covered with intricate tribal designs.

"You win."

Tama laughs. "I do win. But is that the best you can come up with?"

Julian glances coldly at Shae, who started this nonsense, glances warmer at the smiling Hula, at Tama's best friend Rangi, an easygoing, cheerful young man, always by Tama's side. "*Kia ora,*" Julian says and sits. *Have life. Be well.* He's not here to make trouble. He's come in peace. For now. "Anything for a man to drink? Or is it all baby cider?"

"I'll give you a man's drink," Tama says, "and if you can handle it, then how about I give you a real *moko*, the Maori way. It will be my gift to you." Smiling wickedly, Tama touches his ridged face. "You need a *moko*, whiteman. *Moko* tell your life story. And I'm just the guy to give it to you. I'm a trained *tohunga*, a tattoo specialist, the youngest *tohunga* in Southland. We don't usually give *moko* to whiteman because *moko* are *tapu*, they're sacred. But I'll make an exception in your case because you're a guest of Kiritopa, who is respected and beloved, and his guest at the Yarrow is our guest at the Orchard. What do you say? Can you take it?"

"How hard can it be?" Julian says. "*You* had them done. Sure. Let's do it the Maori way."

Even his quarrelsome, full-lipped Termagant reconsiders. "Tama, no," Shae says. "It was a joke. You don't need to do that."

"We don't need to do anything, except hunt and fight and drink, Shayma-Shayna. But the man said he wanted a *moko*," Tama says. "Is a woman going to stand between a man and his desire? What say you, son of Cruz?"

"No," Julian says, taking off his outer layers. "Nothing is going to stand between a man and his desire."

In a special *moko* room, in the corner of a glowing tavern by the ocean inlet, with half a dozen people surrounding them and the kerosene lamps burning, Julian removes his shirt in the warmth, removes his quartz necklace before Tama can comment on it, and sets his forearm face up on a flat wood surface. Tama sits quietly in a lotus position, appraising Julian's upper body. The daily sparring, the bag pummeling, the extreme Krav Maga self-defense training, and the recent masonry work have packed new mass on Julian's chest and shoulders.

"Not bad, whiteman," Tama says. "But no real tattoos."

"Well, you're going to fix that, right?"

"First you drink the shine," Tama says, banging the tall pewter goblet on the table. "If you can't hold your drink, I can't ink you." It looks like a *pint* of alcohol. Julian raises the mug in a salute to Shae, to Hula, to Rangi, to Tama and swallows it down.

Except for Shae, they applaud, Hula loudest of all. "Hey, you're all right," Tama says, pouring alcohol over Julian's arm to clean it. "Shae, I don't know what you're on about. This man's all right."

Shae says nothing. Julian says nothing. Hula and Rangi and Tama's young sister Tia begin a low humming chant. Tama takes off his own shirt. It's warm in the room. Tama is conspicuously tattooed on his chest and on both his arms.

"It took many years for me to get like this," Tama says, setting his instruments on the table. "With you, we start small, see how you do."

*Mia, Mary, Mallory, Miri, MIRABELLE* in capital letters in the middle of his forearm, and two sets of *dots* next to Mallory's and Miri's names, and an unfinished set next to MIRABELLE, 33 *dots*, and then he stopped marking the days, too busy drinking heroin and plotting murder.

"What are those?" Tama asks, pointing to the dotted black columns.

"Timekeepers," Julian replies, knowing that Shae is looking over his shoulder, wondering about the *dots*, perhaps trying to count them as her mother had suggested. He scrutinizes Tama's tools: a thin chisel made of white bone, a mallet, and a jar of black wood ash. "What's the bone from?" he asks the Maori. "Tiger?"

Tama roars with laughter. "What if I told you it was *human* bone," he says. "Would it make a difference?"

Julian's and Tama's gazes lock. "No," says Julian.

"I'm just joking with you. I don't know where the bone's from. Probably from a little lamb." Tama grins. "A little newborn lamb."

"Tama, don't do it," Shae says. "What if you hammer too hard and it goes through a vein? Kiritopa will kill you."

"That kind old man. He won't kill me." Tama flashes his white teeth. "I'm a *tohunga*. I know what I'm doing. Tia, are you watching, sister?" Tia, Hula, and Rangi chant louder. "Son of Cruz, are you ready?"

"I've been ready for half an hour while you've been yakking," Julian says.

"What name will continue the story of your life, whiteman? Shae?" Tama grins. "Or Hula?"

Hula runs up, throwing her arms around Julian. "Hula, Hula!" she says. "Ink Hula-Hoop, Tama."

"Get back, Hula. We start now. No more disruption."

"Mark me with *ASH*," Julian says.

Julian doesn't know why he agreed to this pissing contest. He must be trying to impress the impregnable fortress that is Shae. He must be drunk. He must be an idiot. It's astonishingly painful. Needle tattoos are not a walk in the park either, especially on the inside of the arm. But it doesn't compare to this. In a warm room, where no conversation is allowed, amid the Maori ritualized chanting, Tama literally *hammers* a white-bone spike dipped in soot into Julian's skin. He carves the ash into Julian's flesh with a chisel and a mallet. It's slow and painstaking and terrible. Three measly letters take hours to tap. Julian bleeds, Tama pours moonshine over him to wash off the blood, pours moonshine into Julian's throat, Tia, Rangi, and Hula dance and chant, Shae stands watching, and Tama, steady as he goes, continues to pound into the open wounds in Julian's arm.

Besides Hula-Hoop, Rangi is the most impressed with Julian. "You did well, whiteman," he keeps saying, slapping Julian's back. "Didn't he do well, Tama? He didn't even flinch."

∞

"You think that's going to sway me?" Shae says after they've left the train and are walking back to the Yarrow.

His arm bandaged, Julian is swooning from the drink and the pain. "Wasn't thinking of you."

"Yeah, sure. Maybe it'll get infected and you'll die, and all my problems will be solved."

"Sounds like a win-win to me," Julian says. "Why did you tell him about the tattoos on my arm? Were you trying to provoke me?"

"Wasn't thinking of you," Shae says, mocking him.

"Do you want me and Tama to fight?"

She shrugs. "Maybe you need to be put in your place."

"Woman, you have no idea what you're playing with." Julian tries to stop swerving and increase his pace.

"You have no idea what *you're* playing with," Shae says darkly. "Bad things happen to people all the time. Even without you being their prophecy. Hula's father cracked his head open two years ago. Three crayfishermen died last week when they got tangled up in their nets. One old man got hooked as he was strolling down the dock and bled to death. People die all the time."

"What's your point? Yes, people die. Gunshot wounds. Fires. Disease. Their cars flip over on black roads. So what?" Julian's bandaged arm presses against his stomach.

"What fucking cars? I'm saying we should *all* be a little more careful, frankly."

Julian wishes he could leave her on the street. He walks ahead of her. Now she has to hurry to catch up with him. Good.

"From now on," Julian says when she is by his side again, "I'm going to call you Termagant, not Shae."

"You call me that, I'll punch you."

"Do you want to know what it means?"

"Do I look like I want to know what it means?"

"It means a violent, overbearing, turbulent, brawling woman."

Her fist flies out. He jerks his head away.

"Fuck you for saying I'm violent."

"Termagant," Julian repeats. "A shrew, a virago—"

The fist flies out again, but this time, Julian grabs it. "Don't touch me," he says, sounding pretty dark himself, squeezing her balled-up hand harder than he has ever allowed himself to grip a woman. After a few moments of her ineffectual struggle, he lets her go. Something red churns inside him. Is that what he wants, too? A *fight* with her? He's had too much to drink, he's not thinking clearly. He's not feeling clearly. How far they have come from Grey Gardens, from the serene lake at Vine Cottage.

They continue walking.

Suddenly Julian draws to attention. He stops swerving. Behind Shae, on a wide empty street, he senses a moving shadow.

*Shae*, he whispers, but before he can say another word, a twisted-up guy jumps in front of her and gets in her face. She doesn't recognize him, though it's a small town and she knows almost everyone, both here and in Bluff. He's half-Maori, half-something else.

"Look at you," the guy says, licking his lips, his tongue darting in and out. "Aren't you a sight for sore eyes."

"Get away from her," Julian says, his right arm out, in front of Shae.

The guy, still lewdly clucking, doesn't glance at Julian. "Or what, whiteman? What are *you* gonna do?"

Julian sweeps her behind him and steps between her and the man. The assailant, wielding a strange short paddle, swings at Julian who normally would bob out of the way except he is the only thing standing between the attacker and Shae. So he can't bob out of the way. Instead Julian blocks the blow with his bandaged left forearm, takes another hard knock as the guy backhands him with the paddle, and as he's taking it, he lunges, catching and wrenching the guy's arm with his right, and hammerfists him in the ear with his left. Julian is ready for more, despite his bleeding gash. He is in a stance; all his nerves are live-wire. But the fellow drops to the ground and passes out.

Julian picks up the man's blade. It's green, shaped like a teardrop, and made of some kind of hard smooth well-polished stone. Jade, maybe?

"Are you okay?" he says to Shae.

"Fine, but you can't take his club," Shae says. Her gaze zooms in on Julian, pierces, understands, hardens, frightens.

"Watch me. Let's go. Before he comes to."

"It's an heirloom."

"Is it a weapon?"

"Yes, it's a *mere* club, but—"

"Then let's go. The weapons of the vanquished go with the victor. If he wants it, he can come and get it."

"He won't stop until he has it."

"How does he know who I am, or where I'm staying?" Taking her by the arm, Julian peers into her face. "Did you put him up to this?"

"Did I put up a freak to assault me on the street? Let go. There are migrant lunatics all over. You should know. You're one of them. We were in the wrong place at the wrong time. Let go, I said."

"You mean, walking back from the Bluff train, like we do three times a week?"

"Yes, like that." Shae stares at the fallen man, but mostly she stares at Julian. "How did you hit him like that?"

"Like what? I swatted him on the ear." He has not let go of her yet.

"What if he's dead? Look, his ear is bleeding. And his nose, and you didn't even hit him in the nose."

"He has a burst ear drum. He's not dead."

"His arm looks broken."

"Yes, his arm may be broken."

"If he's not dead, he'll come for you. Leave the *mere.*"

"If he's dead, he won't need it," Julian says, pulling Shae down the road. "And if he's alive, *I'll* need it."

In full awareness, despite being drunk, Julian had clocked the guy on the ear. Three inches forward on his temple, and Julian would have killed him.

∞

At the Yarrow, Julian and Shae confront Agnes. It takes two questions for the mother to confess that she was the one who had paid the indigent to attack them. She found him wandering the streets, looking for work. So she gave him work. But before their two questions for her, she has two questions for them. "What happened to your arm, why are you bleeding?" she says to Julian and then gives Shae the coldest of glares. "Did you have Tama brand him? Are you stupid?" She throws a dishtowel to Julian to press against his wound.

"She had nothing to do with it, Agnes," says Julian, wrapping the towel around his forearm. "I asked for it to be done." He doesn't want the mother to slap her again, even if she deserves it.

"Mother, don't change the subject," Shae says. "Did you pay a man to attack me?"

Julian thought Agnes would be sheepish or remorseful, but no, the woman blazes with self-righteous elation. All her features soften and glow. "I did," she says proudly. "I did it to prove to all you naysayers that I am right and you are wrong, each and every one of you. Kiritopa, come here. Did you hear what happened?" she says to the Maori. "You told me Julian couldn't protect a fish. Yet he nearly killed a man with one blow. What do you have to say about that, wise man? Maybe he won't protect a fish. But he'll protect *her*." Agnes looks so smug, so satisfied. She is beaming.

No one is happy with Agnes, least of all Shae.

"I did it for you, child," Agnes says, "to show you that you are safest when you are with him. No evil can come to you as long as he's by your side. He only seems spineless, my darling. It's his disguise. You should feel strengthened, not offended. As long as he's with you, you'll be all right." The mother looks so relieved.

"But, Mother," Shae says, "if you didn't force him to be by my side all the damn time, you wouldn't have needed to pay a man to assault me, and then I'd also be all right, the way I have been for twenty-six years."

"That's unassailable logic there, Agnes," Julian says. Kiritopa agrees. Everyone is against Agnes this evening. She doesn't care. Whistling, she saunters off to fill the lamps.

"The man could've killed us both, Mother," Shae calls after her. "He was carrying a *mere*." She gestures to Julian without addressing him by name. "Show Kiritopa. The club is dangerous, like an ice axe."

"Oh, you shouldn't have taken that," Kiritopa says, taking one glance at the *mere*.

"The vagrant hit him with it," Shae says. *"Twice."*

"And Julian is still standing?" says Kiritopa.

"He didn't budge, as if the guy barely tapped him," Shae says.

"I don't know what she's talking about," says Julian. "He did barely tap me."

Agnes returns. "I've set the table for you two. You must be hungry. In Bluff, all you do is drink. Sit. Eat. Break bread. There's a lot to celebrate. Now you two can finally get married. I will let Godward know we will need just one berth on his ship."

"Mother, I told *you*, and I told *him*"—Shae flings her hand in Julian's direction—"I'm not going with Godward. Or him. I'm not getting married. I love someone else."

"Phooey. You're not marrying Julian for love. That will come. Or not come, what do I care. You're marrying him to save your life. And don't mouth off to me, young lady. Even when I'm in a good mood, I won't stand for it. Let's see how well Julian tolerates you mouthing off to him when he is your husband. He is tough. I bet he won't be as easygoing as me."

Shae glares at Julian, who says nothing. He can make a joke, say the mother is right, he won't be as easygoing. He can be earnest, say the mother is wrong, he will be. He can be suggestive and ask if Shae would like for him to be easygoing. He can be naughty and ask if she'd like for him *not* to be easygoing. He has many options. He chooses to say *nothing*.

As soon as Agnes leaves, Shae leans over Julian sitting at the table, waiting for his food. "It will *never* happen," she says through clenched teeth. "Get it out of your head."

"It's out."

"I'll throw myself off the bluffs before I marry you."

"When?" says Julian.

∞

Tama eyes Julian with renewed interest after he learns about the fight in the street.

"Oh, looky who's here."

Julian's *moko* hasn't healed yet. He can't immerse his arm in water, can't go down into the grottos. It's sore, and he's sore, and is in no mood to be baited.

"Hello to you, too. *Kia ora.* Get me a drink, will you?"

Julian was going to sit down but Tama won't stop circling him. "So you think you're Mr. Tough Guy?"

Julian's hands remain in his pockets. Shae is off talking to Hula and Tia.

"What's this I hear about you knocking out a native with one punch and taking his *mere* for yourself?" Tama says. "Is that true?"

"It was a sucker punch. News travels fast around here."

"We only got four hundred people in Bluff. You give a shout; everyone hears. Sucker punch, huh? So he was distracted? He was unprepared? That doesn't sound to me like the guy who confronted you on the street, coming at you and your girl with his *mere*."

"I'm not his girl, Tama," Shae says loudly from the next table.

"She just gave a shout, did you hear?" Julian says. "She's not my girl. And yesterday I got lucky. The guy fell."

"He fell, did he?" Tama considers Julian. "So if he fell and you got lucky, how come you took your hands out of your pockets just now?"

"Well, you got so close to me, Tama, I thought you wanted to shake my hand." Julian takes a step toward the Maori. He needs to keep silent, but he's in ill humor. "I didn't know if you wanted to shake my hand," Julian says, "or kiss me."

After a beat, Tama laughs. His handshake is strong. Julian is not surprised by this. Tama looks strong.

"Let's have a drink, Tough Guy," Tama says. "I got some blackcurrant moonshine for you. We have a smaller crop than usual this year, but it's still our best and strongest."

Tama pours. He and Julian drink.

"Good?"

"Very good."

"You're quiet. Not a lot to say?"

"Sometimes better to listen," Julian replies. "What about you, you got anything to say?"

Tama gets up. For some reason, the kid decides instead of passing in front of Julian to pass behind him. Julian doesn't enjoy unfamiliar Maori boys who fancy themselves warriors stalking him from behind. As he's passing Julian's chair, Tama raises his hand and makes a circle with his index finger and thumb, as if he's about to flick Julian in the head—not to hurt him but to assert dominance. Before the Maori's fingers can touch his temple, Julian jacks up his right arm, knocks the hand away, twists his body while rising from the chair, and rams into Tama with his left shoulder. The shove is unexpected, and Tama is unprepared for it. He is knocked down, straight on his ass.

The Noisy Orchard goes mute.

Julian thinks about giving Tama an arm to help him up but decides against it.

"Sorry, dude, what were you doing?" Julian says. "For a second, it looked as if you were about to flick me in the head."

Tama jumps to his feet in one motion, like an acrobat. "I was passing by, minding my own business," he says lethally quietly.

"Oh. Because your hand was at my head."

Tama says nothing. He dusts himself off. There's a hush in the tavern.

"Was *that* a lucky punch, too?" Tama says.

"You thought that was a punch?" Julian smirks. "No, Tama, that wasn't a punch."

Tama laughs.

Everyone else laughs, too. The tension in the pub abates.

But now Julian knows—his hands must always be out of his pockets when he is in Tama's presence.

∞

A few nights later, when his arm feels better, though the tattoo still looks like a raw and nasty mess, Julian finally returns to the hot spring in the Yarrow's cellar. After an hour in the blistering water, he is calmed and tired. Maybe Kiritopa is right. Maybe a year of this and he'd be as good as new. Yeah, sure, he thinks, as he gets out and turns toward his towel.

Between him and the towel stands Shae, lit by a lonely candle. She wears her night clothes, as if she's about to turn in, a robe loosely held together by sashes. Her shoulder-length hair is down in a coming-apart braid. There is red paint on her lips, as if she's decided to subjugate him.

A dripping and naked Julian stands across from her. He's hot after being in the water so long. Steam rises from his skin into the cooler air. He pulls his wet hair back from his face and squeezes out the water. They stand for a few moments without speaking. He can't tell what's in her dilated eyes. She's looking at his body, he knows that.

Another moment goes by.

He speaks first. "Can you get me my towel," he says. "It's behind you."

Not taking her eyes off him, Shae hands it to him.

He presses the towel against his face, against his wet neck. He dries himself thoroughly before he wraps the towel around his waist. All the while she stands and watches.

"Did you come just to look," Julian says, "or is there another reason?"

She blinks. "I didn't come to look."

"So there's another reason?"

"I have a proposition for you."

"I'm listening." He sits on the edge of the grotto. She continues to stand.

"If you want it, you can have it," she says.

Julian rocks his head from side to side. "Well, well, that is quite an offer."

"Do you want to see what you're getting?" She goes to untie her robe.

He stops her with a hand gesture. "I know what I'm getting," he says. "How many times?"

"Once," she replies. "Twice, if you really want. But my condition is, after you have it, you leave. You take your things, you don't say a word to anyone, not Mother, not Kiritopa, you don't say goodbye, you go away, and you never return. So you'll have what you want. And then I will have what I want. Which is to stay here and be left alone by Mother and by you."

Julian is quiet, pretending to think.

*Oh, Shae. Don't you remember how you once loved me. And how I once loved you.*

He lowers his head.

*Yeah. Me neither.*

"Is that the bargain basement deal of the week you offered the other schmuck who came your way last year?" he asks. "Is that why he vanished, never to be seen again?"

"What if it was? What's it to you?"

Julian shrugs. "Isn't there a word for women who barter their sexual services to men they don't like? I know it, wait a sec, it'll come to me."

"What do I care what you call me? I do what I have to do. If it gets you out of my life, so be it."

"And what if it won't?" Julian stands up. "What if once I take what I want, I'll want more? What if I refuse to leave once I've had my fill of you?"

Shae backs away toward the door.

Julian steps closer. "And horror of horrors, what if," he says, flinging the towel off his waist, "once I've had my fill of you, *you'll* only want more? Did you think of that? That *you'll* want more and more?" Blood rushes to his extremities.

"Get away from me."

"I thought you wanted me close, Shae." Julian grabs her hand. "I thought you wanted me *real* close."

She gasps. There's nowhere for her to go. She is pinned between his inflamed naked body and the door.

"Get away from me," she breathes, trying to free her hand.

"As I suspected," says Julian. "So what's the point of us talking about what *if*, when you and I can't even agree on what *is*?"

"Get away! *That's* what is. That's all I want—you to get away from me."

"Come to me, get away from me. I'm getting mixed signals from you, Shae. Make up your mind." Julian steps away. "Oh, and tempting though your offer is, my answer is no. I mean—no, thank you."

"You'll be sorry," Shae says in a trembling voice as she opens the door. "Mark my words. You'll be gone from me for good, one way or another."

"Clearly," says Julian, "it will have to be another."

∞

And then the *Terra Nova* gets stuck in the polar ice.

He and Shae learn this the next time they are in Bluff. They've been spending a lot of time in Bluff lately because the

Civic Theatre got flooded when the normally shallow Waihopai inexplicably overflowed, and they had to shut down the rehearsals of *Three Sisters* until a new stage could be built. They hear that one of the local whaleships saw the *Terra Nova* boxed in about five hundred miles south, below Campbell Island, heaving and hissing, her engines on, attempting to power through the floes. She is still a long way from her destination in the Antarctic Great Barrier ice shelf, where she absolutely must be by the middle of October, because Robert Scott's polar teams are departing for the South Pole November 1, and Edgar Evans, who's not supposed to be on the *Terra Nova* at all but at Cape Evans with the rest of the group, must be with them.

Since Julian knows Edgar Evans does indeed depart with Scott on their historic voyage, he is only superficially interested in the fate of the *Terra Nova* and is not sure why Shae gets so animated when she hears the news. He watches her from a distance having energetic but hush-hush conversations with her fishermen friends, gesticulating to the roiling ocean.

On the train back to Invercargill, Shae explains things without Julian even having to ask. They're almost having a conversation. One of the Bluff whaleships is considering sailing out to the pack ice to sell the *Terra Nova* some coal, some blubber and some moonshine. It's a way to make quick money without doing very much. Julian listens but doesn't understand why Shae should be excited about what some whaleship may or may not do.

He understands better when they return to the Yarrow and Shae speaks to her mother. Shae has gotten an idea. She won't be outdone. Her mother has plans? Well, now Shae's got some, too. "I want to sail out with Tama and Niko to meet the *Terra Nova*," Shae says to her mother. "I want to say goodbye to Edgar Evans."

Agnes says no, as any sensible mother would, and Kiritopa also thinks it's a bad idea, but Shae proceeds to enthusiastically yet dispassionately argue her case. If she is going to New York with *him* (to whom she does not refer by name), then she's not going to see Edgar again.

"You're not going to see him again no matter what, Shae," Kiritopa says. "How close do you think Niko can get to the *Terra Nova*? What are you going to do, walk across the ice to him?"

Shae says she will if she has to. "Niko will sell them fifty casks of blubber and twenty barrels of moonshine. We'll bring them sleeping bags, skins. Kiritopa, you will give me a bottle of whisky to give to Edgar as a gift. I'll say my goodbyes, and after we return, I will do as you wish, Mother. No more arguments, no more tears. I promise. I will even travel to New York on Godward's ship, if you want."

"Not if I want. It's for you. It's for your life."

"If that's what you want," Shae stubbornly repeats. "I'll go. With him. I'll even marry him, if I have to."

Julian rolls his eyes. A gem of a woman.

Agnes exchanges a glance with Julian, a glance with Kiritopa.

"Don't look at me," Kiritopa says.

"Don't look at me," Julian says.

Traveling a 100 to a 150 nautical miles a day, it will take the whaleship four to five days to reach the *Terra Nova*. "Niko says he can get us close," Shae says. "A day to walk our supplies to them across the ice, and five days to return. Two weeks tops. We'll be back before the end of September, in plenty of time before Godward sails."

They look to Julian. He shrugs. He's got no opinion. He doesn't know what day he came, what day it is, what day it ends. He thinks he came around mid-August because Kiritopa told him it was nearing the end of a very cold winter. Black is white, day is night, summer is winter, love is hate, and his woman is not his.

"He is not ready to go out to sea, Mother," Kiritopa says.

Agnes turns to Julian. "Have you ever been out to sea?"

That perks Julian up. "What does this have to do with me? I'm not going, am I?"

"Of course you are," says Agnes.

"Of course you are," says *Shae*!

It's astonishing how little Julian is concerned with these days. Going out on a whaleship for a thousand-mile voyage into the Southern Ocean? It gets barely a shrug from the man who used to worry about riding horses in the glen with his beloved.

*You love taking the scenic route and ending up where you're not supposed to be, Ashton said.*

*I wind up on Antrobus Street not Antarctica! said Julian.*

And yet here Julian is, winding up in Antarctica, not Antrobus Street. He can't wait to tell Ashton all about it someday.

Kiritopa shakes his head.

"What are *you* shaking your head for, old man?" Agnes says. "You're going, too."

Kiritopa hates the open sea. He says he's not going.

"You must," Agnes says to her Maori partner. "He must go to protect her, but who's going to protect him? You *have* to go, Kiritopa."

For some reason, Shae is adamant that this doesn't happen. She cajoles and wheedles. She brings up Kiritopa's sea sickness, his age, his work around the Yarrow, his shopping, his cooking. Mother can't be without him. "Please, Mama," Shae says lovingly, putting her arms around her mother's and Kiritopa's shoulders. "Kiritopa should stay with you. There's absolutely no need for him to go. The whiteman will be fine. He'll be with me. He'll be among my friends."

It's the first time anyone has heard Shae call Agnes anything but *Mother*. It's like a fire alarm. They all sit up, take notice. Kiritopa's shoulders turn in. "Fine," he says to Agnes. "Your daughter's made it clear—I must go." He studies Shae's impassive face. "Who else is going?"

"Niko's crew. Tama's crew. Tia, of course. Hula says she wants to come, too, on a sea adventure."

Agnes groans.

Julian manages to keep from smiling.

Kiritopa presses further. "I understand Niko is letting you and his granddaughter on the boat. But is he letting *him* on his boat?"

"Of course. Tama vouched for him." She pats Kiritopa to reassure him. "He got inked the Maori way and he drank Tama's moonshine and didn't pass out. Plus he's got a *mere*. He's one of us." Shae smiles a dazzling Ziegfeld girl smile.

It's the first time Julian has seen her smile.

Why does it unsettle him so much?

# 45

## *Hinewai*

"THINK OF ALL THE WAYS ONE CAN DIE ON A SHIP. THERE'S scurvy or fever. There's fire at sea. A collision with another ship. A shipwreck. A drowning. A tidal wave. The ship can be struck by lightning, or just you. You could fall from a masthead. Your monkey belt can break. You could be hanged after a mutiny or thrown out on a floe, without a spear to catch your food. You could starve to death. You could be crushed by ice. There could be a storm. Or an angry whale. You could encounter hostile natives who nurse malice toward you and decide to slaughter you as part of their tribal rituals."

"The death sermon is over, Tama," says Kiritopa. "You've had enough moonshine for one night."

"Do you think so? Because I feel as if I haven't had enough." A dozen men and three women sit around the fire on the deck of the *Hinewai* after the sun has gone down.

"Pace yourself, son of Kahurangi," Kiritopa says. "This is only the beginning. We got two more weeks at sea. If you start here, where will you end?"

"Tell me, O son of Cruz," Tama says, addressing Julian, who sits close to the fire, hugging his knees, trying to stay warm, "where will this end?"

"What?" Julian says. "Sorry, Tama, repeat what you just said. Start from the top. I wasn't listening."

∞

*Hinewai* means fair maiden. Like a Valkyrie, a siren, a chooser of the slain.

The *Hinewai* is a 100-foot three-mast whaleship with a 350-horsepower steam engine. She's reinforced from bow to stern with five feet of oak and steel to protect her from the Antarctic ice. "She can crush and grind her way through some mighty glaciers, which is how we'll get close to the *Terra Nova*," says Niko Hunapo, the captain, a curt and mirthless man. He's not afraid of a little ice. He is over eighty; he's seen it all. He is tall and skeletal, wrinkled like a famished mastiff, and his skin is blistered by continual exposure to the wind and sun. The ridged intricate tattoos on his jaw have faded.

"Grandfather only looks mean," Hula tells Julian. "On the inside, he's a gentle soul. Like Kiritopa."

Kiritopa, Julian wants to say, doesn't look quite so mean.

There's room on the ship for 24 men, with a minimum crew of 16, but only 14 men and three women sail to bring fuel and light to the ice-locked *Terra Nova*.

The women: Shae, Hula, and Tama's 16-year-old sister Tia.

The men: Niko; Tama, the first mate; Rangi, the second mate; Aata, the third mate; the cook; seven forehands; Kiritopa.

And Julian.

Niko sleeps in the captain's quarters and gives the second-best cabin to his guest Kiritopa as a sign of respect, and Kiritopa gives it to Julian, himself taking the third best. The three girls, Shae, Hula, and Tia, bunk together in the steerage mid-ship, next to the cook, and the rest of the crew are in the forecastle, the triangle in the bow, sleeping in the bunks that line the walls.

Niko often takes his meals alone, but everyone else, the girls, the crew, the mates, and Julian, eat communally on deck, near the two-cauldron furnace called the tryworks where the seal and whale blubber is cooked, if a seal or a whale were to be caught.

But this isn't a hunting trip, it's a merchant trip, which is why there are relatively few men and why the cauldrons called the trypots boil water only, and sometimes fish soup. All the men double up on their duties. Everyone pitches in with everything. The men shovel coal into the furnace and unfurl the sails and polish the metal. Shae, Hula, and Tia are the stewards, the half-deck girls, and the deck cleaners. Kiritopa is the cook's helper.

There is no cooper, the guy who makes and maintains the wooden barrels, no blacksmith, the guy who cleans and sharpens the steel—and no doctor.

"Why do we need a doctor, it's ten days," Niko says. "If you can't stay healthy for ten days, you deserve to die."

∞

The weather on the ocean is unpredictable. It behaves like weather. One day the wind blows hard, and the sails are up, and they need no coal as the *Hinewai* leaves a formidable wake racing through the sea at ten knots. The next day, the men sweat soot as they shovel coal bricks into the furnace, and she barely moves at three knots. In the early mornings, before the women are up, the men dive naked into the subarctic water to wash themselves with cold-soap, though no matter how hard Julian scrubs, he can't seem to get the soot out of his pores. Blubber grease works better than cold-soap, though it smells much worse.

In the early mornings, it's below freezing. It warms up when the sun is out; the temperature rises into the fifties and dips again at sunset. Julian's cabin is close to the furnace, and when there's no wind and the furnace has been on all day, his room is so oppressively hot that one night, he sleeps out on deck near one of the masts, rolled up in an elk bag, until Kiritopa finds him and shakes him awake. "Are you feeble-minded? Do you have no memory of the things I told you? I don't care if you cook to death from the heat. You sleep behind locked doors. Say you understand. Sometimes I think I'm not speaking English."

∞

Hula Hunapo is a naked sorceress. Technically, she's not naked, but she might as well be. She acts naked. Some people act fully clothed even when naked. Hula has the opposite problem, and therefore the opposite effect on men. All men, including Julian.

Hula's father was a great warrior, but since he died two years ago in a boating accident (there seem to be a lot of those, as Tama has helpfully pointed out), Hula has been in a bit of a struggle to find herself a husband. Apparently, the Maoris have no problem with their unmarried daughters making themselves available during their search. It is only after marriage that fidelity is strictly enforced. Before the nuptials, open sexuality is not only allowed but encouraged, though to be fair, Hula Hoop needs little encouragement in that department. Sometimes Julian thinks that Hula and Tama might have a thing, but it's hard to tell because she's a temptress with everyone. Hula is a flirtatious igniter of men.

You know who is *not* a sorceress?

You know who does *not* act naked?

You know who is *not* a flirtatious igniter of men?

Julian's moody and irritable Valkyrie.

Only Hula says to him, "I'm *really* glad you're here."

Hula is a sexy girl.

But Hula is not the one.

The ocean was clear aqua when they left the wharfs near Bluff, but ten miles out the water turned a foreboding dark jade and ten miles after that, the color of bark. The farther out they sail, the more the world begins to look black and white, except for the china blue of the sky, like the eye color of someone Julian once knew.

Every night the aurora australis lights up the world in a phantasmagoria of intense pink and brightest green. Julian has never seen anything like it, except that once, in the mountains with Josephine. The lights flutter, flare, float. They look like windswept lilac bands. They never disappear, not after a minute, not after an hour. Even the Maori, accustomed to the southern light shows, tell Julian they've never seen the aurora so sustained, so vivid, so massive across the sky.

They ride south on their ocean horse in high spirits and with high hopes, but on their sixth morning, having effortlessly covered over five hundred miles, having sailed eight degrees of latitude straight south, having passed the uninhabited high-cliffed Campbell Island and encountered no trouble except for occasionally rough seas, the *Hinewai* awakens to find itself adrift in ship-sized fragments of ice. She pushes through, hoping for the sun to melt the rest. That day, they travel barely thirty miles. And the next morning, the ice gets thicker. The floes stretch for miles in every direction, including the one they came from, and the one they're going to.

It rains, which is a blessing, for not only does it melt the ice slightly, but they catch the rain in barrels and now have drinking water. Fresh water on a ship is like painite, the world's rarest mineral. The ship sails another sixty miles, and by sunset, Niko finally spots the three tall masts of the *Terra Nova*, matchsticks on the horizon, still at least ten miles away. The crew gets loudly excited. The end of their mission is literally in sight.

But at night, there's a blizzard and the next day an opal thunderstorm, and the night after that, the rainwater freezes over the ice, and the sea becomes like the surface of the moon, rock solid and ragged with peaks and glaciers. They have been boxed in by the floes, and the ship can't move in any direction. And ten miles away, like a mirage, a tiny dot of ink with three thin mast lines, stands the *Terra Nova*.

There's nothing to do but wait for the pack to break. This sets the entire crew on edge, except for Niko. He rations the food and water, orders Rangi to spot for seals, and remains on deck, silent and stoic, staring at the horizon through his field glasses. To conserve coal, he stops firing up the furnace, and Julian's cabin goes from sauna to *The Shining* overnight. He sleeps in all his clothes, in all his skins, under an elk sleeping bag and sheep fur. He hangs blankets over his bed and sleeps underneath them as in a tent. He is still cold.

The Antarctic ice is in the air, and there is frost on every breath. As far as the eye can see there is nothing but white sky and white land. The clouds descend and pour into every ice sculpture. In the mornings, petrels and fulmars squawk and fly over the ship through the fog that rolls in all the way down to the hard surface of the sea.

Julian's eyelashes freeze in the ferocious wind. Often it feels as if he can't breathe. Yet it's so beautiful out, and at dawn, before the rest of the ship awakens, Julian climbs on deck despite the cold, and in deepest solitude stands witness to the heavens and the moon and the stars and the paths of all the seas. There is nothing subtle about his pain. He is at the bottom of the earth, heading toward the ice continent where the world stops spinning. Above him, the planet still turns, turns someone else's years, turns someone else's life. Above his black head whirls the infinite before and the infinite after. Inside him everything stands still.

If only you could see this, Ashton, my friend.

What's the point of mourning *what if* when Julian can't stop mourning what is.

∞

Mercifully, a sunrise later it gets warmer, and the ice melts from Julian's beard, though not from the ocean, and the wind dies down at night. But when the wind subsides, other things rise up at night by the fire.

Unmindful of the cold, the men build a blaze in the tryworks out of blubber and wood. After supper and a substantial amount of moonshine, there is music and dance, and even cosplay, some of it sourced from local tribes, some of it from tribal practices of other South Pacific islands like Fiji and New Guinea. The young men, some Maori, some not, led by Tama, strip naked and strap on three-foot-long *kotekas* to their loins. *Kotekas* are penis sheaths, made of dried-out gourds, and are kept in place by a thin piece of string looped around the scrotum. For hours a dozen tattooed naked men outfitted with gourds boisterously perform the *haka*, a war dance that must scare the shit out of all the whales and seals in the sea, what with the rhythmic feet banging in marching unison, with the chants and songs, with the long bone spears in their hands pounding the deck. They bulge their eyes and stick out their tongues, and other things. It's quite a sight.

Rangi helpfully explains to Julian that the size of the *koteka* has nothing to do with the size of the man, "otherwise I'd be wearing the longest *koteka* here, all the way to the stern," the grinning Rangi says. "No, the *koteka* is short for work and long for festive occasions."

"Festive occasions like when your ship is icebound?" says Julian.

"Yes!" Rangi is good-humored and nice. Rangi is like a male Hula.

"Yes!" Aata agrees. Aata is a slow, round man who never leaves Rangi's side and who repeats everything Rangi says, including, "No, I'd be wearing the longest *koteka* here."

"There's only one way to determine that for sure, Aata," Rangi says. "Bring Hula-Hoop here and let her hand be our judge."

"Bring Hula-Hoop here and let her hand be our judge!" Aata repeats.

Hula, being one hell of a woman, instead of slapping Rangi upside the head, smiles and says she will do it only if Julian enters the fray. She actually makes him laugh. He politely declines, making an effort not to substitute *politely* with *unfortunately*.

The twelve days allotted to the entire trip come and go, and there is no release from the ice. Early one morning, Niko commands Rangi and Aata to go out to hunt for seals because he doesn't want to open any more barrels of blubber designated for sale to the *Terra Nova*. Rangi asks if Julian wants to come along, and Julian gladly accepts. It's been a long week without motion.

Rangi gives Julian a pair of fur-lined sea boots to use on the ice. He gives him an axe, a pick and hammer, a pocket knife, snow goggles, a whistle, and a water bottle. He gives him a harpoon and a mincing knife.

It takes four long hours, to spot a leopard seal sunning on one of the floes, a mile away from the ship.

Rangi has been hunting seals since he was a small boy. He is the most experienced and accurate hunter on the *Hinewai*. But, as he's about to throw the harpoon, he reconsiders and hands the weapon to Julian. "You might as well learn, whiteman," Rangi says. "I'm not always going to be by your side."

"You might as well learn, whiteman," Aata repeats.

"Make sure the rope at the end of the spear is not tangled or the harpoon won't fly," Rangi says. "Aim for its head, or if that's too small a target for you, for the fleshiest part of its back. Steady as she goes and don't twitch. Focus, then fire."

Without a preamble, Julian winds and throws the harpoon as he would a football or a fastball. The spear sails through the air and pierces the seal's head.

Rangi and Aata cheer quietly while yanking on the rope to get the seal to stop thrashing. After they get close to the animal, Rangi barely needs to stick in a long blade to bleed the seal out. Julian's well-aimed harpoon has already done most of the work.

It takes three men two hooks, thirty yards of rope, and two more hours to drag the heavy carcass back to the ship over the uneven surface of the ice. The ten-foot seal must weigh four hundred pounds.

They're greeted like conquering heroes.

The crew lowers the winch, attaching it to the seal's tail, and they hoist the carcass up to deck level, leaving it hanging upside down.

"Who killed the seal?" Tama asks.

"Julian!" Rangi says proudly. "He's a good student, Tama. He would make a fine fisherman. He's taken to the sea as if he was born to it."

"Yes, he does work hard," Tama says. "And so silently."

Julian throws off his bloodied outer skin and wipes the blade against his trouser leg. "What's there to say, Tama? I let my actions speak for me."

The entire crew—everyone but Niko—gets their hands dirty in flensing the seal, or removing its blubber. Rangi lends Julian one of the monkey belts and Julian attaches himself to the ballast at the back of the ship and uses his super sharp knife to slice the seal open from stem to stern. They're in luck because in the belly of the seal they find nearly two dozen undigested fish, whole and perfectly edible.

The cook grabs a net full of them and vanishes into the galley with Kiritopa, while Julian and Rangi, hanging off the ballast, use spades to slice off the seal blubber and throw the long strips onto the deck.

The brick tryworks has been fired up, the huge cast-iron trypots are ready to melt the blubber, or to render it. Julian's heart thumps a heavy beat when he hears Rangi use the word *render*. He doesn't look up on deck to seek out Shae, her face, her cold yet achingly familiar eyes, doesn't seek out the soul from hundreds of years of travels past, Shae who once stood next to him as Mary, while he rendered the suet for the candles, saying to him *do not address me, do not look at me*, yet who so wanted to be addressed, so wanted to be looked at. Who so wanted to be loved.

Not this soul.

The women use their own knives, shaped like push daggers—the blade perpendicular to the handle—to separate the blubber from the skin by slicing it off in thin layers called *bible leaves*. The thinner the layer of blubber, the faster it renders inside the trypot and the better the quality of the oil. They all work ceaselessly before the sun sets. It takes ten men and three women all the hours until dark to cut the blubber into layers and then into chunks, to boil the chunks in the trypots, and to pour out the oil into the lined-up casks.

When they're finally done, and it's dark, the deck, the pots, the knives, the spades, the boots, the clothes, everyone's faces, hands, hair, and mouths are slippery in dripping, reeking blubber grease. And there was wet-behind-the-ears Julian, thinking that making candles from suet was the worst thing he ever had to do and smell. Two crewmen slip and fall on the deck, afterward enduring some lengthy mocking.

There is no *haka* that night because the deck is too slick. It will be cleaned tomorrow morning, but for now, the crew eats, drinks, and sits on skins around the fire pit, having wiped the blubber off themselves as best they could.

Even Niko joins them this evening for the fish feast.

After hours of bonhomie, Niko loosens up and attempts to make Julian understand the circle of life. As if Julian's silence somehow means he doesn't understand it.

"The fish of the sea eat one another, whiteman," Niko says. "You understand that, don't you? The large fish eat the small, and the small eat the insects, the wolves eat men, and the men eat the dogs, and the dogs eat one another, and the gods devour other gods. So tell me, why should we not eat our enemies?"

They laugh. Everyone laughs, even Niko.

Everyone but Julian.

"Pardon him, Lord," Julian says, quoting Shaw, "who thinks the customs of his tribe are the laws of nature."

Kiritopa shoves him, whispering, "*Now* is the time you decide to speak? Silence!"

"Are you saying they are not the laws of nature, whiteman?" Tama says.

Kiritopa's elbow at his ribs keeps Julian from replying.

"Oh, but they are," Niko says. "In some cultures, death by eating is still law. Not ours, of course, but other cultures. As punishment for adultery, for robbery, for treacherous attacks—death by eating is still law."

"Many things were once law, so what?" Julian says. "Blood sacrifice of children was once law."

"I asked you a question, son of Cruz, a guest on my boat," Niko says. "Answer me. What is the harm of killing and eating your enemy? Would they not do the same to you if they could?"

Is that a rhetorical question? It is not an easy thing, to wean a warrior nation of its ancient rites. "I suppose they might," Julian says, to be agreeable, to end the conversation.

"There are worse things than being eaten," Niko says pleasantly. "Living as a slave, for one. And like I said, we wouldn't eat *all* men. Only our enemies."

"And you're not our enemy, are you, son of Cruz?" says Tama.

"I am not."

"So why do you look so worried, all of a sudden?"

Everyone laughs. Julian, sitting on the deck with his knees drawn up, fiddling with a short piece of rope, making and remaking it into knots, does not look up. The whaleship is a theatre for mortal combat because everything on the ship can be turned into a deadly weapon. There is ready access to spades with short handles and razor-sharp blades, access to spades with long heavy handles and heavy steel blades. There are hooks of infinite variety, attached to wooden handles that are built to fit perfectly into the human hand. There are pitchforks.

There are metal chains, steel cables, iron winches.

There is blubber oil, usually hot, often boiling.

There are bone spears of all sizes.

There's the harpoon.

There's the hand-held chopper the women carry, used mainly for flensing. If that blade is brought down, it's like the guillotine. Anything it touches will be amputated.

There is the ice axe.

You go out on a whaleboat with men, you better make sure you're going with men who have your back. Because one place you don't want to be on is a boat in the middle of the sea with men who harbor you ill-will.

"I'm not worried, nor do I look worried," Julian replies to Tama. "Tell me, Niko, would you eat the heads, too?"

Niko laughs, and the men laugh with him. "Of the head, we would eat only the brain," Niko replies with a warm smile. "To make us smarter."

But Tama has stopped smiling. "Son of Cruz," he says, "we sit around the fire at night, we tell stories, we sing, we dance, we pass the time. Yet you sit, you listen, and you say nothing."

"I just said a whole mess of things."

"You eat when we eat," Tama says. "You drink when we drink. You answer questions, yes. But you offer us nothing of your own. Why?"

"Where I come from, we have a saying," Julian says. "Only speak when it's time to say checkmate."

"What's checkmate?"

Julian takes a breath. "Sometimes a man must know when he is the main act or the audience," he says. "I'm happy to sit and listen. You are excellent entertainment, Tama."

"My question remains," Tama says. "Either you got no stories, or you have too many. Which is it? Shae, what do you think? Does son of Cruz have any stories he'd like to tell?"

"No," Shae says. "He's got nothing."

Julian stares into the knots in his hands.

"By the grim look on the whiteman's face, I'd say he disagrees with you, Shae," Tama says. "Don't you, son of Cruz?"

"No," Julian says. "The woman is right. I've got nothing." He doesn't so much as glance at her. He makes an effort not to clench his jaw.

"Kiritopa disagrees," Tama says. "I can see he thinks you are full of stories."

"I think no such thing," Kiritopa says.

"Next to Niko, Kiritopa is the hardest man on this boat to impress," Tama says. "Yet he is always by your side as if he is quite impressed by you."

"I think you're reading too much into it, Tama," Julian says. "The man just sits by my side."

"He is right, Tama," Kiritopa says. "I'm not that impressed by him. He doesn't know how to listen, for one." Kiritopa elbows Julian again.

"Kiritopa hates the boat," Tama continues. "Yet he's come on Niko's boat with you and Shae—who, by the way is not that impressed with you, it's true, but she is a woman, so it doesn't count. A man can always make a woman impressed with him if he really wants to, if you know what I mean, and clearly, you do not want to. Or can't." Tama smiles. "But my point is, Shae's been on this boat before, but Kiritopa never. Yet you are here and suddenly he is here."

"Yes," Julian says. "That is quite observant of you, Tama. We are all here."

"Come on, son of Cruz. I'm tired of listening to the sound of my own voice."

"You know what I do when I'm tired of listening to the sound of my voice?" Julian says. "I stop talking."

Tama laughs, though not easily.

"You heard our stories. Our *moko* tell the rest. Now you tell us something, for a change."

"What do you want to know?"

"There you go again, answering my questions with nothing. You have the body of a fighter, yet you carry almost no marks on you except for the two knife scars on your arm, your tiny dots, and your girl names. Shae's mother has been waiting for you for years. Isn't that right, Shae? So you must be somebody. You certainly carry yourself as if you think you are somebody. I'll tell you the truth, whiteman, your silence unsettles me. Friendly people talk to each other to pass the time, especially on ships when they're out at sea. Only animals lie mutely." Tama pauses. "Animals or enemies. Not friends. Your choice, whiteman. Are you a friend, or an enemy? Are you a human being, or are you an elk whose skin you wear? What are you?"

Julian glances at the stoic Kiritopa, sitting between him and the unreceptive Shae. He glances at the impassive Niko, at Rangi and Aata's friendly faces, at Hula and Tia's smiling, captivated faces. Tama's forbidding expression flickers in the high-contrast light of the blubber oil poured out onto the logs in the fire pit.

"You have your ancestors, Tama," Julian says. "And I have mine. My father's people were the Aztecs. Have you heard of them? A tribe of nomadic warriors who wandered for two hundred years in search of a home and fought everything that stood between them and their destination. While your family was settling in Southland and growing berries, my family was settling in Tenochtitlan, which became Mexico. They also had tattoos. They also had weapons. They also had blood sacrifice. They believed nothing was better than the tears of dying babies to bring about the rains and the harvests. And what about my mother's ancestors, you ask? They were from Norway. They were Vikings. My mother is a Norse woman. Her people were seafarers, warriors, and pirates. They built longships and traversed the globe. The Vikings were the first to make ships, and they showed everyone else how to survive at sea. The ship you are on is only as good as it is because my ancestors taught the world how to build it. The Norse men have a few tales of their own they tell around the fire. Have you heard the one about Volund? No? Let me tell it to you now. Volund falls in love with a fair maiden who one day vanishes from him. While he is turning the world upside down searching for her, he is taken prisoner by an enemy king who is angry with him for refusing to marry his daughter. In revenge, Volund murders all the king's sons and makes their body parts into jewelry which he presents to the king as a grisly gift. He escapes by forging a pair of golden wings, on which he flies away and continues searching for his lost *Hinewai*."

There's silence around the crackling fire. The aurora blazes in the sky.

"That's some story, son of Cruz," Tama says.

Julian rocks back, and resumes playing with his rope.

"I've never heard of these Norse men, these Aztecs. Are you making them up? It all sounds made up. Doesn't it, Tia?"

"Yes," his 16-year-old sister replies. "It sounds made up. But it's *wonderful*!"

"It *is* wonderful!" a smiling Hula agrees.

Shae says nothing.

Julian smiles. "Tama, you didn't say tell me a true story."

"So it's not true?"

"Do you want me to *tell* you it's true? Or do you want me to prove to you it's true?"

"Whatever you want, whiteman," Tama says. "Since I don't believe you, you might as well prove it to me."

Julian rises to his feet and stands with his hands at his sides, his unflinching gaze on Tama. "You want to know who I am, where I come from?" Julian says. There is no trace of a smile on his face or in his voice. "You think my body doesn't tell a story? It's because you haven't looked at me closely enough." He walks toward the young man. Tama jumps up. Everyone around the circle tenses, a natural reaction to seeing one man stride toward another in the night ring.

"Relax, Maori boy," Julian says. "I'm not going to hurt you." He grabs Tama's hand—making sure to reach with his right, to establish his handedness—bows his head and presses Tama's fingers hard into his skull, into the long, raised scar that runs from his crown nearly to his forehead.

"The scar is my *moko*," Julian says, straightening out and staring coldly into Tama's face. "And I didn't get it in the comfort of a warm room with song in my ears and moonshine in my throat. I bought it with my life. You want to know who I am? I am an Aztec and a Viking. *That* is my story."

# 46

# Hula-Hoop

SOME DAYS ARE LIKE THAT, FULL OF HUNTING SEALS AND convivial conversations about ancient civilizations and flensing men, and other days are quiet and the wind is light, and the sun shines, and they are still stuck in the ice, and the *Terra Nova* is still an ocean away, and nothing happens.

Almost nothing.

The ration gets smaller: a piece of salt horse, a biscuit, some molasses. Sometimes the cook prepares a careless petrel that has landed on the deck and is instantly harpooned. They stay in one place, chafing, waiting for something to happen so they can move forward or backward, impatient for movement, for action, for time to start ticking again so they can move to their future, whatever it may be.

The days are filled with routine ship chores like coiling and disentangling ropes and cleaning and sharpening and polishing the butchering instruments. Julian takes it upon himself to take care of that task, to wear the duties of a blacksmith.

Motion. Movement. Action. The future. Sometimes the bright days on the open deck are filled not with sharpening steel but with Hula.

∞

"Julian, I have some stories too about the old days," Hula says, inching toward him as they languish on the port side near the mizzenmast while the afternoon wanes. She hops onto a step by the furled-down sail. Julian's head is near her breasts. She has unbuttoned her sheepskin coat so he can fully partake of her copious cleavage inside the half-open tunic. "Do you want to hear a story?"

"From you, Hula? Always."

She undulates. "The Maoris and Europeans bartered things, like fish and weapons, in exchange for clothes and beads." She leans forward. "And sometimes, they bartered women."

"You don't *say*."

"Yes. *Sometimes*, as a sign of hospitality, the Maori chief offered one of his girls to his important guests as a sign of welcome and good graces."

"Hula, clearly the Maori are a *very* hospitable people."

She leans forward some more. "We really are. We truly are. I am especially hospitable."

One more inch and her bountiful breasts will be at Julian's mouth.

"One could never accuse you of being inhospitable, Hula."

"By the way," Hula says, batting her eyes and shaking her body, "just so you know, the chiefs *never* offer skinny pale crabby white women to their guests."

"No?" Where *is* the pale crabby white woman? Julian can't take his eyes off Hula's smiling face, and other things.

"No," Hula confirms. "It's supposed to be a *gift*, not a burden."

Julian laughs. Hula is so vivacious, so utterly unafraid, so sexually frank, that in this dark hard life with the wind blowing sideways, Julian finds himself unsurprisingly eager for some of her hospitality. She leans into him, her breasts pressing against his bearded face, their ample softness hardening him.

The girl arouses him. Her smile arouses him. Her breasts arouse him. It's not just Hula's visually exciting body. It's her openness. She is a toothy, voluptuous girl who giggles at his every word.

Recently Julian has been noticing that every time Hula is near him, he gets excited. He feels slightly guilty about it, but is no less excited. He wants his hands on her. He wants the relief that will follow. The ache for the relief heats up the blood in his veins. He wants her body to quench the abject thirst in his.

It's a cold late sunny afternoon, and he and Hula are passing the time, playing, keeping warm, his lust running hot. The boat sways, and she sways into him. He rights her and leaves his arm on her, just in case the boat lurches again. Better safe than sorry is Julian's motto.

I like the way you grab me, Hula purrs.

Just to make sure you don't fall, Hula-Hoop. We don't want you hurt.

Are you always so strong with your hands, she murmurs.

Possibly.

Would you always grab me like that...grab me to hold me steady?

If you like.

I'd *like*.

A beat.

I'd like that *very* much.

Another beat.

The girl clears her throat. Did you say there was something in your cabin you wanted to show me?

Julian doesn't speak.

I think there is, Hula says. Didn't you say you wanted to show it to me *real* bad?

Julian can't hide what's in his eyes, what's inside him and outside him. He glances around to see if anyone has spotted them talking like this, so close, so throatily, so shallow of breath. He looks around because he's praying there is no one around— not Niko, not Tia, not Tama, not Rangi—so he can take Hula to his cabin and jump through her fire hoops.

And who should Julian see *glaring* at him from across the deck but Shae.

She stands against the starboard bulwark, her arms crossed on her chest. And in *her* dark eyes, because it's also hard to hide, is fury, and disbelief, and jealousy—and *hurt*. In other words, there's a pottage of emotion burning inside Shae.

*Shae.*

She is the absolute last person on the ship that Julian wants to notice him and Hula, and he is bitterly disappointed. He is also enraged and deflated. Quite a trick to pull that off all at once. He backs away from Hula, lets go of the mast, gives the girl's fur a regretful platonic pat, says maybe another time, excuses himself, and vanishes down into the hatch, to his cabin below.

∞

A few minutes later, there's a sharp tap on his door.

Welcome to hell, Julian mutters. "Come in, I guess."

Shae opens the door, but doesn't come in. "We're preparing supper. Are you coming?"

"I'm not hungry."

He is on his bed, pretending to read. He doesn't look up at her. She steps in, slamming the door behind her. His cabin is tiny, and unfortunately the fight that's looming needs space, needs geographical distance, like a continent or two with maybe a black hole in between, three oceans, and a hundred years.

Julian knows this because of the anger broiling inside him, like an opal thunderstorm. He shouldn't be anywhere near her when he feels like this. She doesn't want to be near him when he feels like this.

How dare she. How *dare* she, of all people, wantonly thwart his plans for some delicious time-wasting.

Shae speaks first. "You got nothing to say?"

"Nope."

"Yes, you never do. Well, let's have at it. What's wrong with you?"

"I am literally, alone in my cabin, minding my own business."

"Why are you sore?"

"Who's sore."

"Look, don't misunderstand me," Shae says. "I don't give a shit what you do."

Julian bolts into a sitting position; the book falls to the floor. "Sure didn't look like it out there when you were stabbing me with your eyeballs."

"You didn't let me finish."

"Nor you me."

"I don't care *what* you do," Shae repeats, spitting words out, "but what *does* get my blood up is you pretending to Mother and Kiritopa you're some kind of fucking saint when all you want to do is fuck the first floozy who throws herself at you. You got some gall. She throws herself at everybody, you know."

"Lucky everybody."

"So? Go fuck her. Who's stopping you?"

"Somebody is stopping me—clearly."

"Oh, please. I'm not *stopping* you. I'm disgusted, is what I am."

"*You're* disgusted."

"Yes."

"Hey, black pot," Julian says, "why do you think I talk to *her*, not you, why do I *want* to talk to her, not you, why do I want to *look* at her, not you?"

"Like I care—and that's not all you want."

"Yes—that too!" Julian jumps up. "Because she's *nice*! She doesn't act like the creature from the fucking Black Lagoon. Or is it not an act, Shae?"

"She doesn't know how awful you are," Shae says. "She has no taste. Any man is good enough for her, even you."

"If only I could be worthy of her bad taste. When was the last time you smiled at me? Oh, that's right—never."

"Who'd want to smile at *you*."

They need more space. They are too close, yelling in a hiss through their grit teeth, flushed and fuming.

"When was the last time you talked nicely to me," he says, "or even the first time? When did you not roll your eyes every time I spoke? When did you flirt with me? Or shove your boobs in my face? Oh, that's right—fucking never."

"I'd sooner hang."

"Yes, you've made that clear. But when was the last time you smiled at *anybody*?"

"When I was with Edgar, if you really must know."

"I don't believe you!" Julian says, all clenched up, taking a threatening step to her. "I don't believe that man wants anything to do with you. Or that he would leave his wife for you—unless his wife is Medusa."

"Fuck you."

"You know how I know he wants nothing to do with you?" Julian says. "Because what *man* would?" All the oxygen in the cabin is being sucked up into his anger. "Do you have *any* idea what men even want? Have you *listened* to yourself? Have you *heard* yourself? Everything that comes out of your mouth is *dirt*! I haven't heard you speak a kind word to anybody or about anybody in all the time I've been with you." Julian's heart falls when he says those words. How long has it been? Five weeks? Six? Oh, God. But that's on the inside. On the outside he remains verbal and livid.

"Edgar," she says.

"Edgar *what*? You're nice to a man who's conveniently not here?" Julian sneers. "Tell me, is this charm offensive of yours the New Zealand way? Because you're going to die out as a civilization if all the women here are like you. What do you think you're offering this Edgar? And don't give me that knowing look. A million women can give him that and not beat him down while they do it."

"Why are you here with me, if that's how you feel?"

"You think I would've come here if I thought for a second this is how you'd be? You think I would've ever fallen in love with you in the first place if this is how you were to me? Fair fucking maiden indeed."

The pin falls. Julian loses his temper. It doesn't happen often. But it happens now. He yanks her to him, squeezing the flesh of her arms between his furious fingers. "If you only knew what I dragged my faith through, what I dragged my life through. I can't believe I nailed myself to your cross for *this.*" Convulsing, he rattles her. "You think I would've risked my *life* for you, ruined my body for you, sacrificed *every fucking thing* for you?" Groaning, he clamps her so hard he thinks he might break her arm. His voice sounds like it's been run over by a cement spreader. "To think what I lost while I was trying to make myself a better man for you. What a fucking joke. You're hateful. You're jealous I *flirt* with Hula? I'd fuck Niko's grandmother before I'd lay a hand on you. Hula doesn't make me feel every second like I want to rip my eyes out so I wouldn't have to look at her."

"What a bastard you are! You think you're getting on Godward's boat with me *now?*"

"Fuck you. No one is getting on Godward's boat. I know that better than *you*, hell's princess." Julian shoves her away, seeing red, feeling red, no longer in control of anything. "So do whatever you want. Yes, your Edgar Evans doesn't have much time, but you know what, he still has an eternity compared to what you've got, which is *nothing*. So smile, don't smile. By all means, spend your precious minutes like this. Soon none of it will matter. But hey, look on the bright side, at least you won't have to be chained to your miserable fucking self forever."

Gasping, she lunges for him. He grabs her hands. They struggle. She tries to hit him, to kick him, to head-butt him. He holds her away from him, watching her pant in breathless rage.

"You're a *fine* one to speak," Shae says, her voice breaking. "You think *you're* a ball of joy?" Tears run down her red face. "I don't think I've seen you smile *once* except when you're talking to *Hula*. What have *you* done to make me want you? What have you done to make me love you? You're the sourest pill on this ship, you never speak to anyone, you're a deaf-mute, you don't sing or dance or joke or do anything but stare at the sea and dream of fucking her!"

"Not her!"

"Let go of me!"

"Stop hitting me," Julian says, blocking her, slapping her fists away.

"Or *what*?"

"Stop hitting me and get the hell out of my cabin."

"No!"

"No?"

"You want to hit me back?" she says in a rasping voice. "Go ahead. I know you want to. You want to hurt me? So *hurt* me."

"If I hurt you, you won't get up."

"I'd like to see you try." Shae lunges for him again, her head like a ram, and Julian staggers back, but instead of head-butting him, she grabs him by his overshirt and kisses him. She kisses him so hard, her lips jam against his teeth. Her fists pounding his shoulders, then going around his back, still lashing at him, she kisses him in open-mouthed wrath like an untamed thing.

Julian doesn't know whether to shove her away or embrace her. The havoc between his body and soul is surreal.

"Either hurt me or fuck me," Shae says. "*That's* your choice."

"Why choose," he says, ripping her shirt, tearing it open, baring her breasts. Before he can touch her, she whirls around and bends over the bed, hiking up her skirt.

"Fuck me," she says, "until I can't stand up."

"This is how you want it?"

"This is how I want it."

Here is the next stage.

It's either love or violence.

Still trying to subdue his panting anger, Julian grips her hips. She balls up the blanket into her fists. She cries out when he enters her. He tries not to move to the rhythm of his fury. She buries her face in the blanket to muffle her moans.

*Hurry,* Shae says to him. *Hurry.*

Julian doesn't understand this command. Does she mean quicker? Or does she mean quickly? There is a world of difference.

She keeps repeating it. *Hurry,* I said. *Hurry.*

Not until *you* hurry. They're both gasping.

*Hurry,* Julian, *hurry,* God, *hurry, hurry, hurry...*

Oh, *now* she calls him by his name. He clasps her buttocks, squeezing her tighter over himself, adjusts his tempo, lowers himself a notch. He comes when she comes. But she comes in surprise, as if she wasn't expecting it. She forgets to stifle her turmoil.

Julian doesn't let go. Still pulsing, his hands relaxing on her, he bends forward. *Shae,* he whispers. She shoves him away with her hips, straightens out, pulls down her skirt, holds her torn shirt closed, and rushes out of the cabin without glancing back at him.

She doesn't meet his eye during supper, or afterward around the fire. She behaves toward him as she has been behaving. Like they're strangers. But when he gets up to go get himself some shine, he pours a little into a cup for her, and when he sits back down on the elk skin, he sidles up next to her.

Here, he says, handing her the drink.

She takes it from him without catching his eye. Kiritopa is coming back, she says.

He can sit on the other side of me. *Shae,* Julian whispers, and it sounds like *shh.* Knocking into her lightly, he stares into her face until she blinks and returns his gaze. Her lip quivers like she's about to cry. Kiritopa comes back. Julian faces forward.

It's not as if Kiritopa doesn't notice the titanic change in Julian's geography. He gives a measured look at Julian, staring ahead into the fire, at Shae, staring ahead into the fire, considers the situation for a moment, and then slowly lowers himself to the deck, taking his place by Julian's right side. Here, he says, I brought her a fur. Cover her shoulders. It's cold out.

Late that night after the lights are off, and everyone's asleep, everyone but Julian, there's a rapping at his cabin door.

She is outside. Wordlessly they stare at each other.

Julian pulls her in, presses her against the wood, kisses her deeply. Her arms dangle at her sides. One of her hands rises to grip his elbow. She's got such a full beautiful mouth. God, what a waste it has been.

Outside, the Southern Cross stars shine dim cold light down on the *Hinewai*, but below deck there's only the inky depths of the ocean. Julian and Shae bob and sway in the near darkness, anchored by the ice. He enfolds her in his arms, embracing her like a papa bear who's found his mama bear.

He wishes he didn't have to say anything, but he knows something is required of him. She is so sad and trembling. I'm sorry, Shae, Julian whispers, caressing her face, her hair. I'm so sorry. You're right. It's true, I haven't been at my best. Forgive me. He looks away. *My grief has broken me.*

She says nothing, exhaling, holding on to his arms. He latches the door. Mutely she stands, her fire eyes lowered. In a fever he kisses her soft lips. A small blubber candle burns a flickering yellow light through his cabin. Blow it out, she says.

You don't want me to look at you?

No!

You don't want to look at me?

A soft inhale. Just blow it out.

He blows it out. He brings her to the bed and sits, holding her hands while she stands in front of him. He looks up into her face.

Take off your clothes and come lie with me, Mary-Margaret Patmore.

What do you mean, take off my clothes?

Take off everything. Be naked.

Completely naked? No! Who does that? You're not naked.

I will be. In the dark Julian takes off his layers. The cabin is warm. Thank God, Niko relented and fired up the furnace a day ago, to rev the engine to help the pack ice break up.

How do I know you're naked? Shae says.

Standing up, Julian takes her hand and places it on himself. She groans. Her hand clasps him.

He kisses her. Go on, take off your clothes, Shae.

It doesn't seem as if she's been naked often during intimacy, she is so slow and reluctant to get undressed. She may have given her body to men, but she has kept a layer of fabric over herself, a cloak for her protection.

He stands waiting in the darkness, listening to her rustling noises. The ship bobs silently.

Are you naked?

I suppose, she says timidly. His hands reach for her. She is barely breathing. I'm sorry, too, she mutters into his shoulder. You have no idea what it's like to live as I've lived.

Julian has some idea, unfortunately. Look how beautiful you are. He cups her breasts, kisses them softly, kisses her nipples. Look what you've been hiding from me. He runs his hands down her back, over her buttocks, fondling her.

I tried to show you. You turned up your nose like you were too good for me.

That's not why. I just didn't want you to sell yourself short. Lie down.

Why?

I'll show you. Lie down. He sets her down on his narrow cot. Open your legs.

But Shae is not used to being on her back. It must feel too vulnerable to her, like an animal in surrender. She can't relax— and she most certainly can't open her legs. Julian lies on his side and for a long time caresses her with the tips of his fingers, from her face to her ankles. Almost like they're Mary and Julian in the tiny room off the chandlery. He touches her gently. She barely responds. He circles her more insistently. She responds a little more. He presses harder on her skin with his fingers. She responds some more. He balls his hand into a fist and kneads her with his prominent knuckles.

And to that Shae responds most strongly. To that, she curves and arches, she buckles and softens, she finally opens.

He kneels between her legs and kisses her stomach.

What are you doing?

What does it look like I'm doing? He caresses her hips.

I have no idea.

Instead of telling you, why don't I show you, he says, pressing his palms against her downy triangle, opening her with his thumbs.

Motionless she lies while he gives her his mouth. She is rigid as a board, her hands not touching his head but clenching the sheet underneath her. It is only when the lunar crescent appears briefly in the sky through the cabin's tiny window that Julian glimpses Shae's illuminated face, her head tipped back, eyes closed, the mouth open in a breathless O.

Oh, Shae, he whispers, soothing her, kissing her, caressing her with his words and his lips and his fingers. I really am sorry. Sometimes love looks like this, too, he murmurs between her legs. Not just you bending over the bed, counting the minutes until somebody knocks. He says it to comfort her, but he knows all too well this is how they live, this is how they've always lived. Counting the minutes until somebody knocks. His heart is filled to the brim with sorrow even when he brings joy to the one he loves, and finally even some comfort to himself.

Only afterward, do her hands take hold of his head. Come to me, she whispers.

Her legs quiver uncontrollably as he fits between them.

Shh, shh, he murmurs, kissing her while he makes love to her. She won't let him lift himself off her, two bears flattened against each other. When it's over, she doesn't shove him away. She doesn't release him. In the dark, Julian hears her crying.

What have I done, Shae whispers wrenchingly between her sobs.

*Shh.* Everything's going to be all right, Julian says. Those things I said to you, I didn't mean them. I was very upset. He wishes he had kept his temper.

Remember I asked you to forgive me if ever we came to combat and I said cruel things to you I did not mean?

You meant them.

No. If I'm angry, it's only because I want real life to live up to my dream of your perfection. Remember I told you that?

Not really, she says. But it's all right. I understand. I'm not angry. Not anymore. They don't matter, the words. They're just words. I know you didn't mean them. It's this you mean. Right here, giving me your body, giving me your mouth.

*You say to her be my goddess, and she agrees and opens her legs. What a burden you've put on her—and yourself. She must be what she is not. You must be what you are not. She is not a goddess.*

*Goddesses don't die.*

When night becomes day, Shae does not become a different woman to Julian. She remains quiet like him, not demonstrative or loud. But on deck, she allows him to stand by her side, and together they gaze at the ice over the sea, to the horizon where Edgar's ship is a gray smudge. When he brings her drink, her eyes stare into his and sometimes her hand rests on his. At night her warm body lies on top of him and underneath him. At night she speaks words to him, fragile words full of wounded pride and longing and tenderness.

Words like: The things you do to me, you were going to do it to Hula, too?

Not all of it.

Were you flirting with her just to make me mad, to make me jealous?

Sure, Julian says. Let's go with that.

Words like: Your eyes confound me. Your lips confound me. Your cock confounds me. I don't know who you are, why you look at me the way you do. Why you fuck me the way you do, why you kiss me the way you do. Everything about you bewilders me. For years, Mother told me you'd be coming. She didn't tell me you'd be like this.

Like what, Shae?

She moans.

And later: You were so silent, she says. You could've given me a sign about who you were, what I meant to you, so I would know how to act.

Sometimes, Julian says, you need to be nice to people even when you don't know of what use they may be to you. Because most of the time, you don't know. But you are *Mirabelle*, Julian wants to say. She was nothing but goodness and kindness walking on this earth. How she was all the time, to everyone, you can also be. You have it in you. I've seen it. I've known it.

Shae's fingers caress his body exceedingly tenderly, as if he's a newborn. As if both she and the human being she touches are touching and being touched for the first time. Julian has never been caressed more gently by anyone than he is by the calloused fingers of a roughened woman with the softest lips who herself prefers knuckles to fingertips.

"Look, I understand," Julian says, kissing her. "All human beings need someone to contend with. The contention strengthens us. To argue, to battle strengthens us."

"That's true," Shae says, not taking her hands off him. "We don't come to our belief limply." She squeezes him. "We come to it by combat."

"Yes." Julian closes his eyes. "And it's through this combat that we even find God sometimes. We hope this wins favor with Him, because God knows that we are contentious creatures who don't like to follow blindly, but instead wish to come to Him by the virtue of our hard-fought choice."

"I've come to you."

"And I to you."

"I wish I could explain how much I didn't want Mother to be right."

"You don't have to. I know."

"I wish she had never told me the prophecy. I wish I never knew."

"She should have never told you."

"It's blackened me."

"It's just crust, Shae. Wipe it away from your soul."

"I wasn't going to get together with Edgar, you know," she says. "I was trying to push you away with my words."

"I'm sorry I wasn't present enough to see it." Julian closes his eyes.

"I was so afraid of you," she says. "I didn't want to believe Mother. But after your fight with the Maori, I knew she was right."

"Hardly a fight."

"It wasn't what you did to him that did it. It was what you did to me."

"Um…"

"You and I were having the ugliest words. A second earlier, you were ready to knock me down, you looked so mad. And yet, the second you thought I might be in danger, your arm flew out in front of me. It was the first thing you did before you even took a breath. You put yourself between me and the world, Julian," says Shae. "That's how I knew Mother was telling the truth. I was even more scared of you then. I've been afraid and angry for years. You don't know how hard it is to live under the weight of your own death lurking around every corner."

Julian knows.

"I swear, I wasn't always like this," Shae says, her hands on his face, stroking his stubble. "Mother has ruined me."

"I swear, I wasn't always like this either," Julian says. He won't say what ruined him.

As soon as they deliver the blubber to the *Terra Nova*, Shae says she wants to sail back to Bluff and leave with Julian. "I don't care where. New York if you want. Or if you think it's too dangerous to spend all those months at sea, we can stay in New Zealand. I'd prefer that, no matter what Mother thinks. We can go hide in the deep mountain, near Queenstown. Maybe it'll be safer there? Or we can move with Mother and Kiritopa to Fjordland, to Lake Hauroko. We call it Mary Lake. He has been waiting for you to come so he and Mother could retire to a cabin he built there for the two of them. Mother has been working all her life in Southland, saving her money to buy the Yarrow because it was the first tavern into town. She didn't want to miss you when you walked into Invercargill. But Kiritopa is done. He can't wait to sell it and leave. Mary Lake is beautiful. We can get married, if you want. We can have a baby, if you want. Kiritopa and you can build us a cabin, near them. I'd be all right with that. I would prefer not to leave Mother and go to New York, but I'll go if you want. I know she is insane. But she's my mother. And Kiritopa has been a father to me all these years."

"Yes, he loves you very much. And I agree," Julian says. "Better not to leave your parents."

"Julian," Shae whispers, "have you found me before?"

He keeps his neutral face. He blinks away the faces of the one he loved. "Not you, no."

"But someone like me?"

"Yes. Someone like you."

"Tell me she is wrong. Or do you not know?"

"Wrong about what?"

"Fulani's prophecy."

Julian won't look at her. "Which part?"

"All of it."

Now he looks at her. "Don't you want some of it to be true?" Julian smiles as he holds her in his arms. "Don't you want a man to search behind the sun for you?" The tips of his fingers touch her face. "And when he finally found you, to say, Masha, my Mashenka, my heart, my dearest one. *You* are the one." Masha is Russian for *Mary*.

Yes, Shae whispers, tears trickling out. But only that part. I want to be your someone, Julian.

You are my someone, Shae. You've always been my someone.

For as long as I live, I will beg for your forgiveness, she says. But what do I possibly have to offer the one from whom I seek mercy?

Just your heart, he whispers back.

She talks and talks, nestled in his chest, stroking his stomach, and Julian lies and listens to the murmurs of her wind-beaten voice as it carries him away.

Sometimes the beast needs to be loved before it can be lovable.

Love her in her sin, that's what divine love means. Love her with the highest form of love on earth. Love everything. Then you will see mystery in everything.

# 47

# The Igloo

LITTLE BY LITTLE THE ICE BREAKS UP, ENOUGH FOR THE *Hinewai* to forge forward in spurts. The floes are heavy. With the engine fired up, the ship grinds through the bergs. It takes almost a week to move within half a mile of the *Terra Nova*.

Niko decides that half a mile is as close as they're going to get. Coal and supplies and tempers are running short. He orders his men to use ropes and sledges to drag the fifty casks of blubber and twenty barrels of moonshine across the wobbly ice floes.

Shae prepares to walk across the ice to greet Edgar. She will present him with Kiritopa's bottle of whisky and a new elk skin for his polar journey. Julian prepares to go with her. Kiritopa says he will go with Julian. The morning of the day they're about to set out, there's some back and forth about this fairly straightforward matter, an argument Julian doesn't understand. Neither Niko nor Tama want Kiritopa to go out on the ice. They cite safety and old age, both of which Kiritopa dismisses, but the captain and first mate are equally firm that Kiritopa remain behind.

Shae stays out of the squabbling except once when she says, "Come on, Tama, don't make a thing out of it. Let him come if he wants."

"No, Shae. You can go. Your whiteman can go. But Kiritopa stays with me."

"I am charged with his safety," Kiritopa says, pointing to Julian. "I go with him."

"Rangi will go with them," Tama says. "If something goes wrong, he'll be able to help Julian better than you."

"What could go wrong?" Kiritopa asks quietly.

"Well, you're clearly worried about something, old man. Whatever it is you're worried about, Rangi will handle it."

Because Rangi is by their side over the uneven, fluctuating, slippery ice floes, Julian can't ask Shae about the disagreement. And she doesn't volunteer.

It takes them over an hour on foot to navigate the distance from the *Hinewai* to the *Terra Nova*.

The crew members of the *Terra Nova* are down on the ice, receiving the barrels from Niko's men and hoisting them into the open hold. They express surprise that Julian and Shae have walked out onto the pack and warn them to return to their ship. "Once the ice starts to crack, the sea will open within minutes," one crew member says. "You don't want to get stuck here with us. Trust me, you don't want to sail to Antarctica." Neither Julian nor Shae responds. Rangi doesn't respond because it's not his place.

Shae puts her hands together and yells up to the deck for Edgar.

"Who's calling for me?" says a deep gruff voice. A man peers over the bulwark and smiles happily. Shae waves but doesn't smile.

A bundled-up sailor climbs down the rope ladder onto the ice and takes off his flap hat as he approaches Shae. Edgar Evans is a tall, broad man, good-looking and easygoing but clearly anxious about being icebound so long.

He embraces Shae and shakes hands with Julian but doesn't touch Rangi. "Why is he standing around?" Edgar says, pointing to the Maori. "Shae, tell him to go help the others. They have plenty of work to do. You see how the sun's been beating down today. And it's warmer. The floes can break any minute. Which is good for me, but not so good for you. You really shouldn't be here. Go," he says to Rangi. "Is he deaf? Why isn't he moving?"

"My captain told me to watch over them, so that's what I'm doing," the Maori says.

For some reason this makes Edgar more anxious. He glances at Shae, who doesn't catch his eye, and at the barrels the *Terra Nova* men are loading into the ship.

"How many more?" he calls out.

Another seventeen. Another round trip for seven men.

Edgar admits to fearing grave repercussions all around—if the ice doesn't break soon and he can't get free, or if the ice breaks too soon and kills Niko's men and half of his. Sometimes the ice cracks for no reason and is gone, going from frozen solid to floating free in less than an hour. Sometimes the actions of men can loosen it, destabilize it. "My worry is compounded," Edgar says, "because I cannot see the future."

Julian listens to Edgar with a small skeptical shrug. He wants to say that worry doesn't abate when you know the future.

Ask him.

Ask Shae.

"In the last four weeks, we've already used forty tons of coal to keep this ship going," Edgar says. "The ice had better break soon or we'll be out of coal. Even the additional fuel you've brought won't help us. Oh, well, we'll freeze to death drunk." He smiles. "No whisky for me, Shae?" Above them, on deck, the men are singing wildly. "Is it any wonder there's not a single sober man on this ship," Edgar says good-naturedly, "including me. We're preparing for a drunk death. But at least we'll go out singing, right?"

Julian shudders, looks around in vain for something to hold on to. Innocent words are lethal weapons in the mouths of unknowing men.

Extending her arms, Shae offers Edgar an elk fur and a bottle of Dunedin's homemade finest. "Both are from Kiritopa," she says. "He couldn't come. He told me to tell you *bon voyage*."

Edgar smiles. "Shae, you are a peach, you really are." Gratefully, he takes the bottle and the fur from her hands.

"Edgar, Julian is from Wales, like you," Shae says.

"Oh, yeah?" Edgar assesses Julian with friendly curiosity. "What part?"

"Bangor," Julian says, praying please be far from there.

God hears his prayers.

"I'm from Rhossili myself," Edgar says, "tiny place all the way south, near Swansea. So what's a white man from Wales doing on Niko's boat?"

"Sailing out to meet you," Shae answers for Julian.

Edgar casts Shae a long indeterminate look. "What are you playing at, girl?" he says quietly.

"Nothing, Edgar. We sailed for you. Honest. To bring you the shine."

"That's not what I'm asking."

"Blubber, liquor, fur," Shae says speedily. "We would've been here sooner, but we got trapped ourselves. Did you see us? For two weeks we've been stuck. We walked across to give you the gift and to say goodbye. To wish you luck."

"Why is *he* here with you?" Edgar points to Julian.

"He's a friend of my mother's and Kiritopa's," Shae says, blushing. She stands between the two men, jittery and twitching.

Edgar nods to Shae. "I'm going to take our new friend to that dinghy over there," he says, "and have a drink with him, Welshman to Welshman. It's not every day I meet a kindred spirit out here. You go on now. Go back to the *Hinewai*. Julian will return shortly. I'll have one of my men walk him back. Let's hope the ice holds."

"Edgar, there's nothing to worry about," Shae says. "Everything's okay."

"Who's worried?" Edgar says. "But I'm going to have a drink with him anyway. Go. Thanks for the hooch. I'll see you next autumn."

Julian steadies his blinkless gaze on Edgar Evans. Oh, the promises men make. "Here's the thing," Julian says, laying a hand on Shae's fur coat to keep her from walking away. "I promised her mother I'd look after her, and I don't want her walking on the ice without me. She stays with me. You said yourself the ice could crack any time."

"And *I* promised the captain I'd have them both back shortly," Rangi says. "So maybe we can hurry up with that drink."

"I wasn't talking to you," Edgar says. "I'm a naval officer and you're a mast hand. You don't address me."

"I'm not a mast hand," Rangi says. "I'm second mate."

"Edgar, it's fine," Julian says. "They'll wait for me. Let's have our drink. Go nowhere," he says to Shae.

"Don't you worry," Rangi answers for her. "We're not leaving without you."

Shae watches him with an intense, desperate look Julian can't decipher as he and Edgar start toward the boat. What is she concerned about? Does she think they're going to talk about her? That's not what men do. They don't talk about the women they're with.

Julian and Edgar climb into one of the tied-up boats with harpoons and fishing lines strewn on the bottom. "We've been hunting for our dinner to save on supplies," Edgar says, opening the bottle of liquor. They swig from the neck. The whisky is strong. "The Kiwis sure know how to make whisky, don't they? It's the volcanic ash in the soil and the silver spring water. Makes everything taste amazing." They drink again. "I have neither the time nor the sobriety to beat around the bush," the explorer says. "Leave them. Leave the Maori, leave the girl. You'll find another. Especially where you are."

"Where I am is in the middle of the subarctic ice," Julian says, "and there is only one woman here." He doesn't add that there is only one woman everywhere.

"I meant, it rains women in Southland. The wind blows them in from all over." Edgar is speaking light-hearted words, but he's not smiling. "Climb the ladder with me."

"Our ship is solid," Julian says, misunderstanding. "The ice is not very thick. We're stuck, but as you said yourself, not for long."

"It's not the ice I'm worried about, my friend," Edgar says. "It's the Maoris."

"No, they're good people. They didn't come here to fight you. They're unarmed." Julian drinks. "Rangi is young but he's a fine fellow. So is Kiritopa."

"It's not Kiritopa that worries me."

"Who, then, the helmsman? Niko is as decent as they come."

"Niko's a good fisherman. A good boatman." Edgar leans forward. "But here's what I know. No white man without a connection to Southland has ever set foot on Niko's boat. If they let you on their boat, it's to make trouble."

Julian shakes his head. "You're wrong."

"You sure about that?"

Julian is amused in a doleful way. It's not that he thinks there couldn't be trouble. But look at Edgar Evans concerned about Julian when his own life hangs in the balance.

"I've been around the Dunedin area many years," Edgar says. "I've lived here and drunk here, I've fixed my ships and bought provisions. I've had hospitality of all kinds, if you know what I mean. I've had good times and bad. I've done it all. I'm not proud of some of the things I've done, but I know a few things. And I know that no whiteman from out of town comes on a Maori boat. Especially not a ship owned by the Kahurangis."

"The ship isn't owned by the Kahurangis," Julian says. "It's Niko's boat."

Edgar shakes his head. "Niko may helm the boat, but Tama's family owns it. Since the prohibition, they bought out most of the whaleships in Bluff with their moonshine profits." He points up to the *Terra Nova*. "Come with me," he says. "We could use another hand on deck, and you look strong. The ship will drop me off and return to Dunedin to resupply. You'll return with her. Summer's just around the corner. November, December is nice around Dunedin. There's work, drink, food, plenty of women, like I said. The albatross come to mate on the Otago Peninsula in November. Besides being an apt metaphor, it's an unforgettable sight. You'll be fine. You'll live. Because I'm going to tell you something." Edgar lowers his voice so Rangi doesn't accidentally overhear. "If you go back with them, you're not getting off that boat. Not in one piece anyway." Edgar pauses. "They've been known to practice tribal justice out at sea."

"Do I need justice?" Julian asks, a chill running down his spine.

"They'll say you fell over drunk and drowned. They'll say a million things. Who's going to find you?" Edgar lowers his voice until he is whispering. "If they're against you, they will kill you. They will pierce your throat and drink your blood, and cut you up. The deck will run with your blood, and they'll say it was the blood of seals. They'll suck the brains out of your skull. Your bones they'll leave out in the sun to dry and hone them into hooks and spears. The Maoris use every part of the human carcass. They'll use your skull to carry water if it's not too leaky."

"My skull *is* leaky," Julian says, "so there's that."

"They are warriors, each and every one. The more tattoos, the more fierce the fighter."

Julian's heart beats faster. "Be honest, what part of what you just told me is hyperbole," he asks, "and what part is whisky?"

Edgar doesn't answer. "They would behead and disembowel the whiteman's women."

"Is *that* hyperbole? That was a long time ago, right? Hundreds of years ago?"

"Fifty years ago. As they say nowadays, flesh-eating is *mostly* not practiced in New Zealand anymore. Or, let's say, *rarely* practiced."

"Edgar," Julian says, "if what you're saying is right, how can I leave *her* with them?"

"Then bring her on my ship. It's safer than the *Hinewai*."

Julian shakes his head. "Edgar."

"Or let her return with them," Edgar says. "If they don't know she's with you, she might be all right. She's grown up with them. They trust her, more or less, as much as they can trust anyone outside their tribe." The man pauses. "Do *you* trust her?"

"Yes." But Julian's voice shakes. "She is my tribe."

"Whose idea was it to sail out in the first place? Tell me it wasn't hers."

A numbness creeps around Julian's edges, as if Shae is already dying.

"Why are you causing trouble?" Julian says. "She came here for you."

"I'm not causing trouble, mate. Trouble is here. I'm just pointing it out to you." Edgar talks quietly. "I mention this about her because of what she told me last year. She said a man had come to see her mother, a man who wanted to take her home with him to Ireland or the Isle of Man or something. She had to bargain with him to make him leave. He saw sense in the end, and left peacefully—or so she said. But she told me that if he hadn't vanished on his own, she would've vanished him."

Julian stares inside the boat. At the bottom, the ice has melted in the sun and water is seeping into his fur-lined boots. A false syllogism runs through his mind in a baffling refrain. Other men are betrayed. But I am not other men. Therefore, I am not betrayed. Did the beast, before it was loved, set things in motion that cannot be reversed?

"She told me about the man," Edgar says, "to please me, not scare me. She said she wanted to be with me so much she would do anything not to leave Southland. I said to her, Shae, leave if you want, I'm never here. I'm never staying. And I'm married. But she wouldn't listen."

"She sailed out here for you," Julian repeats dully. "That's what she told me, and I believe her."

Edgar shakes his head. "I'm an excuse, Welshman. I'm not the truth."

Julian can't lift his gaze. Is there something he has been missing? He's been missing a lot, chunks of his own life, fragments of others. Kiritopa wanting to walk across the ice with them and being nearly forcibly kept behind on the *Hinewai*. Rangi like a barnacle on their side.

Is Kiritopa insurance? To make sure Shae and Julian return?

Is Rangi security? To make sure they return?

"Rangi is not going to walk away from me in peace," Julian says. "And while I may be able to take care of one Maori, what are you going to do when all the others run down the ice to your ship with their harpoons and clubs and tomahawks looking for her and me?"

"Not her. Just you. Let her go back with them."

Julian shakes his head. "I can't." He looks steadily at Edgar. "You know I can't."

There is sadness in Edgar's smile. He doesn't speak for a moment or two. Then he lifts the bottle of whisky to the sky. "Let's raise a glass to you and me," Edgar says. "We're out of time. We don't know what awaits us. But you and I know where we've been. I've met a lot of men in my life. I can tell things about them. You've endured things. You've lost much. Yet you won't be deterred. You would've made a fine polar explorer. I've never met tougher men than polar men. Not soldiers at war, not naval officers, no one. Let me tell you a quick story of where *I've* just been this past winter before I sneaked off on this ship for an ill-considered jaunt that's turning into purgatory. Have you ever heard of a place called Inexpressible Island?"

Julian shakes his head.

"Yeah, no one in the world has," says Edgar. "Except us who were there. My friend Murray Levick said that the road to hell might be paved with good intentions, but hell itself was paved after the style of Inexpressible Island. Me and four other blokes, a scientist, a surgeon, a naval officer, and a cook— sounds like a joke, doesn't it?—got trapped by a blizzard on the Antarctic ice shelf. This island, if you could call it that, is a barren nothing, just rock covered by ice, and when we were there, we couldn't find even the rock. We'd been walking around, exploring, looking for the Adélie penguin, and maybe to get some emperor eggs to bring home for study. We thought we had plenty of time to get back to our main party, but the storm came sudden, and the snow drifts piled up high on top of the ice. We were separated from the rest of our team by hundreds of miles of drift and couldn't go anywhere. We couldn't go anywhere for *80 days*. At night the temperature dipped into minus 70°F. For ten weeks straight, it never got above *minus* 40°F. We built an igloo on the ice shelf and spent 80 days inside, staving off death. Weather permitting, we'd crawl out, kill a seal or a penguin, and crawl back in. When we couldn't catch or hunt, we'd eat the blubber we had, we burned it and greased our bodies with it to keep warm. We were all sick with scurvy and dysentery and stomach poisoning from eating raw and infected meat. For six of the eleven weeks we spent together, there was no light in the sky. The only light was from our blubber lamp. How it stank! And yet every night when we made it through another day alive, we felt so happy. We drank, and read aloud, we mocked each other, told jokes, sang songs. We talked about our families, our wives, our children, our mistresses. I got closer to those four men than I ever got to anyone. Because we weren't alone. We were in it together." Edgar smiles. "Two together? They're always going somewhere. Two together is always an adventure."

Julian bows his head. His fists are in his stomach.

"And that's what we were," Edgar says. "Adventurers. Nobody cares how we suffered. Nobody cares if man has made the worst journey before he died, or the easiest."

"What matters," Julian says, quoting Bukowski from long ago, *"is how you walk through the fire."* He doubles over.

"Yes!" says Edgar. "What matters is that we, who lived through it, know what we lived through. We want to let others know that we had been on a great quest together. We were gallant, and steadfast, and we didn't waver." Edgar points to Shae standing off in the distance, anxiously watching them. "She is in your igloo on Inexpressible Island, waiting for you."

Julian's head remains lowered. She's the only one left in it.

"I understand," Edgar says. "I never would've abandoned my men either." Reaching into his boot he passes something to Julian under the elk fur. "Take it, don't say no," Edgar says. "You might need it."

Julian peeks under the blanket. It's a six-inch Bowie knife, with a razor-sharp double-edged blade and a pin-point tip. "I can't take your knife, Edgar."

"You can and you will. I'll get another. I've had this one since the *Discovery*. It's my gift to you, fellow countryman."

They have one more swig of the nearly empty bottle, then get up unsteadily and shake hands. Julian has hidden the knife in his boot. "Take care not to cut yourself, Edgar," Julian says. "And take care not to fall. There's a hundred-mile glacier you must climb to get to the South Pole. You don't want an unhealed cut and a head injury out there in the drifts and the winds."

"How do you know about the Beardmore Glacier? You've been to the South Pole?"

Julian shakes his head. As Edgar has warned him, so Julian has returned the favor. Out here on the Antarctic ice, by the hull of the *Terra Nova*, a historic, legendary ship, Julian feels close to a break in the lining of the universe, to the fracture in the order of all things. Before he lets go of Edgar's hand, he says, "Know this—after your trip to the South Pole, no one will attempt the journey again. *Ever*. So rest easy. The world will know how you walked through the fire."

Edgar smiles, his powers of comprehension occluded by whisky.

"Thanks, Julian, my Welsh compatriot," he says. "*Kia ora*. Have life. Be well."

Edgar Evans will die. A fall down the Beardmore Glacier, a head wound, an unhealed cut, frostbite, fever. No one will know what happened to his body. It will never be found.

# 48

## Door Number Two

JULIAN PEERS INTO SHAE'S CLOSED FACE BEFORE THEY START back with Rangi, trying to catch her eye, searching for the truth of what awaits him upon their return. She won't meet his gaze. Won't or can't?

They do not speak as they walk back. The floes slide about, watered down by the sun and iced by the wind.

It's a treacherous journey.

And the sun is going down.

Other men are betrayed.

But I am not other men.

Therefore, I am not betrayed.

Back on the *Hinewai*, the crew celebrates the success of their mission. They delivered the load, lightened their ship, and got paid without losing a man. Everyone's optimistic the ice will melt soon and they will be able to return home. The *haka* chanting and stomping is remarkably loud that evening, the stories boisterous and the moonshine free-flowing.

Tama asks Julian for another story. "We like your odd little tales, whiteman. Tell us one more for the road."

Julian takes a swill of his drink, glances at Kiritopa on one side of him, Shae on the other. The old Maori shakes his head and shrugs. "You want to provoke him some more?" Kiritopa says. "Be my guest."

Shae doesn't raise her eyes. She hasn't raised her eyes since they've returned from the *Terra Nova*. She acts as if she wants to become invisible.

"Have you heard the one about the lady, or the tiger, Tama?" says Julian.

"Can't say that I have."

"It's a good story. It was written thirty years ago. It's about an ordinary man who is taken prisoner by a king."

"You sure like these stories about kings and ordinary men."

"I seem to, don't I? Well, in this particular kingdom, the sovereign dispenses justice in his own way."

"As is his right," Tama says. "He is the king."

"Yes," Julian says. "He places the men accused of wrongdoing in front of two closed doors. Behind one is a beautiful woman. Behind the other is a ravenous tiger. The king asks the man to choose which door to open. If he opens door number one, he will be married to the fair maiden, and all will be well. If he chooses door number two, a vicious tiger will end his life."

Tama smiles. "I like this story, son of Cruz. I like it more than your last one."

"I thought you might," says Julian. "But it's never wise to judge a story until you see it through to the end. Only when it's all told, can you truly know what it's about. Where was I? Oh, yes. The hero in our story is brought before the court for justice. But this man—unlike the one in my earlier story about the Valkyrie—has actually been having an affair with the king's daughter. Before the trial, the princess, apparently to help save her lover, learns behind which door waits the tiger. Before the man makes his selection, she nods to him in the direction of the door he should choose. But here's the thing," Julian says, "the princess knows that one way he will meet his death, and the other way, he will be married to another woman. Either way, he will be lost to her." Julian pauses. "And she to him. She nods toward *a* door. The man points to the door, and it opens."

Everyone in the circle, even Shae, leans toward Julian to hear how it ends. Falling quiet, Julian swallows some shine. "That's it, ladies and gentlemen," he says. "There is no more. That's how the story ends. You don't find out which door he opens. You never learn the fate the princess has chosen for her lover. Is death by tiger preferable to marriage to someone else? Only the writer knows. And he is mum."

The men and women groan in frustration and disbelief. They express loud dissatisfaction with such an ambiguous end. Tama in particular is deeply disappointed. He urges Julian to provide an end for them. "I pity you if where you come from, these are the kind of stories you tell," Tama says. "In this part of the world, we like real endings. Bad or good. One way or another."

"So make an ending for the story, Tama," Julian says. "It's up to you. What do you think?"

For another hour, the group debates the proper end to the story of the lady, or the tiger. Hula and Tia don't believe the princess would let her beloved be killed. The men declare that death is preferable to willingly giving away your lover to someone else. Kiritopa refrains. Shae refrains.

"Shae, why so silent all of a sudden?" Tama asks. "*You* of all people have no opinion?" His black eyes gleam in the firelight.

"Shut up, Tama."

"Come on, girl, don't be shy. You have an opinion on everything. Write an end to that story." The young Maori laughs. Shae doesn't speak. Even when Julian nudges her lightly to prod her to answer, she refuses.

"In a surprise twist, the woman is silent on the matter. But what about you, whiteman?" Tama asks. "How do you think the story ends?"

"The story never ends," Julian says. "But the man is doomed either way. He opens the door and finds both—the lady, *and* the tiger." He doesn't look at Shae, or Tama, or anyone, only at the fire, and at his hands knotted into fists. "Love and death are both behind door number two. Behind door number one, there is nothing."

# 49

# Heart of Darkness

THAT NIGHT SHAE DOESN'T COME TO HIS BED UNTIL LATE. There's a heaviness inside Julian he can't shake, a magnet on his heart from the cold dread of Edgar's words, from Shae's terrified face as they walked back to the *Hinewai*.

It's also not quiet. The ice must already be breaking, for there's a din against the hull of the ship that rattles the lamps and Julian's teeth. He can't sleep. He goes up on deck, looks around, walks around under the cold, clear, starlit sky. There is no aurora in the heavens tonight. A few minutes after he returns to his cabin, he hears her familiar scratching.

He pulls her inside, barricades the door behind her. They climb clothed into the elk sleeping bag and lie together breathing heavily, first face to face and then, when neither of them can bear it, her back to his front. Julian is so full of emotion, for many minutes he can't speak. It's the dead of night.

Is it true what Edgar told me.

I don't know what he told you.

They're barely whispering. They're communicating almost telepathically.

How did you get me on this boat?

I asked Niko, and he said yes.

Edgar told me it's not Niko's boat.

I asked Tama, and he said yes, she whispers.

Shae...did you bring me out into the open sea because you wanted Tama and me to fight? Because you wanted Tama to kill me?

Of course not. It's barely a breath.

Is that why you didn't want Kiritopa to come? Because you didn't want him to stand witness to it? You didn't want to endanger *him*?

Of course not.

Shae, what have you *done*?

*Julian, forgive me!* she cries, spinning around to him. I've lived the last ten years of my life, knowing that when you came, my death wouldn't be far behind, that I would have to leave with you or *die*!

Fulani didn't say you had to leave with *me,* Julian says. She said I had to leave with *you*. Is this where you brought me, Shae, to my death? *And to yours.*

Think about my life, Julian! When I was twelve, I might have found it romantic, a knight dressed in black coming to rescue his princess. But I'm twenty-six. I didn't want to go anywhere. I didn't want to be rescued! For many years I refused to believe Mother. I thought she was irrational, she, who didn't like me going to Dunedin by myself, wanted to send me away ten thousand miles to New York! I was her child, and yet she wanted to never see me again! Every good thing in my life has been poisoned by knowing the hour of my death.

So you brought me out to sea to be killed? You thought you could barter Mephisto for your life with my life?

She sobs.

Don't you know how much I loved you, Julian says brokenly. You condemned me to die.

I'm sorry, Julian. It was before I knew you.

You knew me, Shae. You knew who I was. And when you met me, you finally knew who you were. *Masha, Mashenka, my dearest one.*

The unspeakable betrayal strangles his heart.

∞

They exchange more whispers before dawn.

Julian, I'm going to take care of it.

Julian hasn't slept. Can Hula or Tia help you? he asks.

Shae shakes her head. Tribe will out. Rangi won't help you either. But I will talk to Tama when he wakes up.

Julian can't look at her. It's as if she doesn't know who Tama is. You can't ask him, he says. You can never speak to him of this. You know that better than me.

They sit on the bed, side by side, without touching.

What did you give him for my life? asks Julian.

Oil. Moonshine, she says, gray with shame.

They breathe heavily.

I'm sorry, Julian. I promise you, I will make it right—one way or another.

Clearly, Julian says, it will have to be another.

She shakes.

Once I'm dead, do you think you'll be safe? He gets up to go.

Jumping up, she grabs onto his coat. Julian, wait, don't go yet, don't leave me.

Don't talk to him. There is nothing you can do now. The bell has rung.

Her face is distorted, her lip twisted. You promised Mother no matter where I go, you would follow me. Did you mean it?

It wasn't your mother I promised this, he says. It was you.

She looks him full in the face. *You are the only one who can lead me out.* That's what the gypsy said. That means you can't be left in their hands. They will show you no mercy. She doesn't say what she is clearly thinking. *They will show me no mercy, too.*

Say nothing to him, Julian says. Do you promise me?

No. She wipes the tears from her eyes. I'm sorry, my love.

Don't be sorry. Do whatever you have to do to save yourself. You know it's what I came here for.

I know.

When you're on deck or down below, remember to stand so no one can come up behind you. And be on the opposite side of the ship from me. No matter where I am, stay away from me.

Why?

He is quiet. Stand back from the line of fire, Shae, he whispers, gliding his heavy hand across her faithless heart.

When Julian climbs out to the still empty deck and looks onto the sea, the ice is gone, and the *Terra Nova* is gone. It's as if there had never been a ship, or ice, or barrels rolled on the floes, or the grease, or the blood of leopard seals dragged back to be flensed, or Edgar and his whisky and his devastating words, followed by Shae's devastating words. All of it has vanished. Only the spring October sun is bursting blue on the black and white horizon. The ocean is motionless like glass. It's like a painting.

*It was before I knew you.*

Can it be true? Was it all a dream?

Below deck, through the wood boards of the stern, Julian hears rising voices. As soon as he hears, he knows it wasn't a dream.

"Leave him alone, Tama."

*Don't, Shae!* Julian wants to yell. *Don't! Please...*

"We made a bargain, Shae. Why are we still discussing it?"

"So what? You got your money. Let it go. *Kia ora.*"

"We made an iron-clad bargain. And money was not the only thing I wanted."

"Please, Tama."

"I thought you wanted him out of your life? I'm going to give you what we both want, Shae."

"I don't want it anymore."

"Why?"

"Come on, Tama. We've been friends our whole lives."

"Yes, we've been friends. But he is nothing to you. Right, Shae? He is nothing to you?"

"Don't do this, Tama. I beg you…"

"Don't do what?" It's Kiritopa, who has opened the door to his cabin.

"Stay out of it, old man. This doesn't concern you."

"He's right, Kiritopa, stay out of it!" That's Shae. "Go back inside. Everything's fine. I'll handle it."

"There is nothing to handle," Tama says. "Shae and I made a little deal, and she's trying to go back on her word."

"What kind of deal?"

"It's nothing, Kiritopa."

"Why don't you want to tell him, Shae?"

"Shut up, Tama!"

"Don't shout at me, woman. Kiritopa, your adopted daughter and I had agreed, among other things, that I would take her to see her former lover before he broke through the ice, and in return she would let me have a minute on deck with the whiteman."

Julian, listening in, is bent over the open hatch in a deepest bow.

"The man insulted me," Tama continues. "He insulted me in my own place of business. I didn't touch him, and he knocked me down in front of my people. That kind of slight cannot go unanswered. You know that as well as I do."

"Why didn't you try harder to remain on your feet, Tama?" Kiritopa says. "It's not his fault you can't stand straight."

"Don't provoke me, old man. Shae and I agreed. Everyone gets what they want."

"It's not what I want!" says Shae.

"You mean, it's not what you want anymore. What changed your mind, princess, his exceptional *koteka*? That's not how a bargain works. A promise is a promise."

"Tama, stop it," Kiritopa says. "The man is a guest aboard Niko's ship."

"It's not Niko's ship," says Tama. "It's my ship."

"Your father's, you mean."

"So mine," says Tama.

"Let's get Niko out here and see what he says about it."

"Did you not hear me when I said Niko has no say in this?"

"Niko is the captain of this ship!" Kiritopa thunders. "He has final say in everything."

"I have relieved him of his command, old man. *I* am now in charge of this ship."

"Tama, please!" Shae cries.

"I don't know what you're both so upset about. All I want is a fight—fair and square. If son of Cruz beats me, he lives."

"Absolutely not, Tama," says Kiritopa. "I won't allow it."

"Back away, old man." There is a sound of a scuffle, of shoving. "You don't want to threaten me. It would not end well. He is my enemy. And a friend of my enemy is my enemy, too. After he dies, there will be no protection for you, and especially you, whitewoman, if you have switched your allegiance. I show no mercy to those who are against me."

Julian has no time to waste. He can't go below deck. Kiritopa, Tama, and Shae are arguing in a corridor that's barely a foot wide. It's a death trap. Julian won't be able to get Shae out of the tube-like cage. Yet in a moment neither Shae nor Kiritopa are going to get out of that cage on their own.

Julian walks quickly across mid-ship, almost running, to the large steel trunk, where the butchering tools are stowed. He has stowed some things there himself over the past few days, in preparation for all contingencies. He flings open the trunk, searching for his dirty towel.

Close behind him he hears Rangi's voice.

"Are we going hunting? Is that why you're looking for weapons?" Rangi says. "Because I don't see any seals out there."

"Yeah, we don't see any seals out there," says Aata.

Julian slams the trunk closed, and slowly turns around. Rangi and Aata face him. Rangi's face has lost its friendliness. Something else has overtaken it, a deep malevolence. "I dropped my rope and my grease rags in here the other day when I was cleaning the blades," Julian says, showing the men the rope and the towel. "I didn't want to leave filth behind. Back off, will you? You're crowding me."

"Maybe we want to crowd you," Rangi says.

"Maybe we want to crowd you," Aata says.

Julian takes a breath. He needed a few more minutes to get ready. He didn't realize the point of no return would come so soon. The point when he must act or die. And if he dies, Shae will be left in their hands. *The friend of my enemy is my enemy.*

The time has come for you to act, the Lord says.

A strike to the bicep with a *mere* is not only painful, it renders the arm useless. A strike to the forearm, a strike to the back of the hand. It's extremely painful and the bones are easily broken. That's what Julian wants to do, hit Rangi with the *mere* to incapacitate him, but the two men are standing too close for Julian to get the *mere* out of his pocket. If he had the club in hand, he could dispatch them ruthlessly but most important, quietly. He doesn't want to alarm Tama with unnecessary noise. Tama has Shae and Kiritopa in his grasp.

Julian opens his hands to let the rope and the rags fall to the deck. "Oops," he says, raising his left fist. Rangi blocks it with his right. Which is what Julian wants, since Rangi is right-handed and has now been neutralized. Pushing Rangi's right hand away, Julian grabs Aata by the hair and smashes the man's head into Rangi's turned and unprotected face. He bangs the men's heads together one more time, to knock them out. Noiselessly he lowers them to the deck and then spends a minute in frenetic but controlled activity.

The last thing he does is pop down into the steerage and wake up Tia. Hula doesn't even stir when he brings the young girl, half-awake and frightened, onto the deck, nearly carrying her because her legs won't hold her. "Don't be afraid," he says, shielding her eyes. "I won't hurt you." Patting her down, he removes the chopper knife from the pocket of her nightdress. The young girl sleeps with a blade on her. "But you might hurt me, eh?" He chucks the knife into the sea. "Now, here's what I need you to do. Call for your brother, Tia. Lift the hatch and ask him to come up on deck, and as soon as he's here, run back to your bed and don't come out for anything, got it?"

She shakes. "And if I don't call my brother?"

"You want to help him, don't you?"

"What are you going to do if I don't, hurt me?"

"I'm not going to hurt you," Julian says. "But I will throw you overboard. And that water is cold. Your brother will have to jump in to save you, and then he really won't stand a chance. And how will you feel if he doesn't jump in to save you? So if you really want to help him, you will call his name, and you will run and hide. Believe me, he doesn't want to worry about you being on deck." He drags her to the hatch that leads to the main cabins and pops the lid. "Kiritopa, Shae, can you come out here, please," Julian calls down. "I want to show you something." He nudges the girl. "Go on, Tia. Help your brother live."

"Back away from the hatch, son of Cruz," Tama calls from down below. "Your woman is here with me."

"And your sister is here with me."

"Tama," says Tia in a small voice. "Come up. I need you."

There is a foreboding silence, and then movement. Kiritopa climbs out first. Shae is second, with Tama holding her ankle. When he sees Tia by Julian's side, he lets go of Shae, who runs to Kiritopa. "Let her go," Tama says. "This is between you and me, whiteman."

"So why are you clutching Shae's skirts, then, if it's between you and me?" says Julian, pushing Tia away.

"He took my *blade*, Tama, I'm sorry!" cries Tia.

"Get out of here, Tia," says Julian.

"Yes, Tia, go on," Tama says. "Let me take care of it. In a few minutes, it will all be over, and then you can come out. Stay below until I call you."

Giving Tama a long, fearful glance, Tia disappears down into the steerage.

Tama stands on deck assessing the situation.

Julian has bound Rangi's and Aata's ankles and wrists together in handcuff knots. He has slipped a noose knot around their necks and holds the ends of the twine in his hand. He has dragged both men to the middle of the deck and left them lying by the cast-iron cauldrons.

Tama considers his mates—Aata passed out, Rangi bleeding from his broken nose, rope around their necks.

Julian is evaluating some things himself: who's on deck, where they stand, what they are doing, what's in their hands. How far they are from him, how far they are from Shae.

Wearing no overcoat, only a tunic with pockets and a skin vest over it, Julian backs up all the way to the port bulwark, so no one can get behind him. He positions himself next to the trunk with the butchering weapons. The trunk no longer holds any interest for him, but it does sit directly in the path between midship and bow, so no crewman can attack Julian from the side without either going around the trunk or jumping and running across it. The sails are not up yet. *Hinewai*'s entire deck is laid out in front of Julian, to his left and his right. Across from him on the starboard side, Shae stands with terror in her eyes, bundled up in what looks like a half-dozen furs. Julian wishes he could tell her it's going to be all right. But they've run out of time for last words. They've run out of time for a lot of things. *Stand back from the line of fire*. There are no more second chances. There are no rules, no ref, no right, no wrong. There is no closing bell. The last man standing lives.

"What's going on here?" Tama says in a casual voice, as if he's chanced upon his mates playing cards when they should be furling sail.

"What's going on here," Julian says, "is a small medical emergency. This is why it's important to have a doctor on board. Because every once in a while, your men fall out of line. And suddenly they get a noose around their necks." Julian yanks on the rope and the men choke.

"I asked them to keep an eye on you," Tama says.

"That's your first mistake," Julian says. "You didn't send your A team. Unless that was your A team. In which case—that's your second mistake. Look what you've done, you've immobilized your crew when you should've been making peace and getting us home. What happened to *kia ora*?"

Tama struts out onto center deck, his back to the stern, and shifts in place from foot to foot. Neither he nor Julian take a blink away from each other. Julian can judge other fighters. Tama is a real fighter.

"So here's what occurs to me," Tama says. "It's a funny thing, and it takes a while to put together in your head."

"Especially *your* head."

"Words aren't going to bother me, *whiteman*. But ever since you've come into our lives, bad things started happening."

Julian glances across deck to Shae and Kiritopa, who are pressed into each other against the bulwark, the Maori's arm around Shae. Niko is nowhere to be seen; but the crew has climbed up from the forecastle and spread out at the bow of the ship.

Julian watches Tama eyeball his Maori men. Defuse the opponent by any means necessary. The only rule is that there are no rules. *Whatever it takes.* He doesn't blame Tama for his tactics, though he holds him in contempt for them.

Julian hears it before he sees it. It's in the periphery of his left eye and unfortunately he can't see well out of the periphery of his left eye. He especially can't see out of the periphery of his *left* eye when the mortal danger that is Tama is in the periphery of his *right*. But Julian has been on the alert for the slightest sound, the barest movement, and he hears the air change shape. Without turning his head, he ducks, and the tomahawk whistles over him and lodges in the wood deck a few feet away. The crewman who'd just been wielding the axe jumps onto the steel trunk, and heads for Julian.

He jumps onto the trunk unwisely, for Julian has thickly greased the surface of it with a towel full of blubber. The man's legs go out from under him. He slides across and falls clumsily by the axe he's just thrown. Instead of jumping to his feet and pulling up the axe, the crewman compounds his errors by trying to pull it up from a sitting position.

"Get up, Matu!" Tama yells, not moving from where he stands.

Julian strides over to Matu and kicks him in the face, sending him sprawling. He jumps on the man's arm, breaking his elbow, and pulling the axe out of Matu's limp hand swings it cheekside at Matu's head.

Never balance your power against your opponent's power. Defeat him by any means necessary. This isn't the ring. This is the ultimate self-defense—kill or die.

Julian is about to hurl the tomahawk overboard because he doesn't want deadly weapons around that he can't control, but two more men come at him from the bow. Like a bull, one heads for Julian; again unwisely, since Julian is holding an axe. The time for cheekside has passed. With both hands, Julian swings the axe like a bat, driving the blade into the man's abdomen. He strides to the second man who has flung open the trunk and stands over it panting in confusion, as if he wanted to find a mincing blade to stick into Julian and can't seem to locate it. Before the guy has a chance to turn, Julian grabs him by the scruff of the neck, smashes his face down into the steel-reinforced bulwark and throws him overboard.

"You're not going to miss him, Tama," Julian says. "He was a bleeder with a glass jaw."

In the bow, there are four crewmen left, but for some reason they seem less eager to run aft and attack Julian.

Yanking the axe out of the sailor's gut, Julian throws the man into the sea, and Matu after him. "You're a child playing captain," he says to Tama, who still hasn't moved, except in place, as if waiting for the starting gun to go off. "Are you going to have all your men fight your fights for you? You're nothing but a little boy. Do you ever plan to fight me like you were just bragging to Kiritopa?"

"Oh, I'm planning to fight you, whiteman," Tama says.

"Are you planning to surprise me with it? I agree, the element of surprise *is* important in combat," Julian says, walking over to the steel trunk. He has decided to keep the axe. Tama doesn't seem as eager to attack Julian either while he holds a bloodied and dripping tomahawk in his hands. "Here's my surprise for *you*." Julian flips the trunk on its side to show Tama it's empty. "All your flensing knives are at the bottom of the ocean with three of your men," Julian says. "If you want the rest of your crew to fight me, they're going to have to take their chances with what they've got."

"I don't need them," Tama says. "I'll fight you on my own. But a man must know why he's dying before he dies."

"Well, before you tell me why I must die," says Julian, pulling out the jade *mere* club, "why don't you first tell your men to get the fuck away from mid-ship. I don't like them crawling like roaches and upsetting me. My hands sometimes jerk when I'm upset." With his right hand, he smashes the eye of the axe down on Aata's ankle. Aata screams. "Like that."

Tama gives a signal. The men pull back.

"Are you the captain or aren't you?" Julian says. "I heard you tell Kiritopa you're the captain now. What's the captain's first order of duty? To protect his ship. And the second is to protect his men. You're really crap at both. If you keep this up, soon you'll have no men left to raise your sails. Tell the rest of them to stand down."

"I did."

"Farther, Tama. Send them below deck."

"You don't give me orders."

Julian slams the *mere* club into Rangi's mouth. "Below fucking deck, Tama. This is between you and me."

Tama waves off his crew. They drop below Julian's sightline. Julian would like to say they drop below his sightline enthusiastically.

"Now—continue," Julian says. "You were saying? I must die because…"

"The *Terra Nova* got stuck in the ice when it shouldn't have," Tama says in a crippled-by-fury voice.

"That's *my* fault?"

"The Waihopai overflowed, its banks eroded, and the Civic Centre flooded."

"*That's* my fault?"

"Shae's play got closed down."

"Wait a minute," Julian says, "that *can't* be my fault."

"The blackberry crop was drowned out by historic rains and we couldn't make our moonshine. And this is our dry season."

"The *rains* are my fault?"

"There have been fewer whales and seals because of all the drama in the skies, drama such as we've never seen."

"Okay," Julian says. "That one I'll give you. The aurora is my fault."

"Where does it come from, this new force pressing down on the earth, lighting everything up?" says Tama, pacing like a caged animal. "You came from nowhere, whiteman, you appeared in our midst as if summoned by dark powers. On your arms you carry symbols of things you refuse to explain."

"I'm like Mary Poppins," Julian says. "I never explain anything."

"You reject a woman like our Hula."

Julian narrows his eyes at Tama. "Is the enemy king angry that I rejected his daughter?" he says ominously.

"I'm not the enemy," Tama says. He is so enraged he is growling. "*You* are the enemy. Very soon, your story will end. There is one of you and twelve of us."

"You might want to check your math. Also," Julian says, hearing Rangi choke under the noose, gurgling blood from his broken mouth, "you might want to wrap up the life lessons because your best friend here is on his last breath."

"*You* are going to stop breathing," Tama says. He smiles. It is a brutal smile. "Tell me this, whiteman—when *you* die, what do you think is going to happen to your woman?"

*Oh, Shae. Why did you speak to him about me? Didn't you know who he was?* Julian won't allow himself even a glance in her direction.

"Tama! Don't you *dare* kill him." It's Niko, who has climbed out on deck.

"Niko, go back downstairs!" Tama yells. "Stay out of this! This is between him and me."

As soon as Kiritopa sees Niko, he pushes Shae toward the bow, away from himself, and reaches into his coat. "That is not how we do things," Niko says, striding to the center and facing Tama. "You do not kill your enemy until he sees with his own two eyes what happens to his woman." Old Niko looms on deck as if he's still the commander. "That is how *victors* do things," he says. "First they enjoy the feast of victory. Tama, you will manacle him, and he will watch as we tie her to the mast and rip out her still beating heart, and then we—"

Niko's mistake is that he says these words facing Tama instead of Kiritopa.

Julian hurls the axe at Niko's head. He misses. He misses because Niko jerks. He jerks because Kiritopa doesn't miss. He has pitched a barbed harpoon he has pulled from his coat.

The spear enters Niko's neck, and the barb exits his throat. Niko collapses, blood spurting out over Rangi and Aata. Kiritopa steps forward, pulls the axe out of the deck and returns to Shae's side, holding the axe in his hands.

The deck is slick with the blood of men.

Julian pulls the Bowie knife from his boot. In one hand he wields the knife, in the other, the *mere* club.

Screaming a war cry, Tama charges at Julian. In one hand, he holds his own knife, in the other a *mere* club.

Julian advances on the rushing Tama but feints to the right. Tama pitches his blade at Julian's face. But Julian only feints to the right. He sidesteps left, and the knife flies past. As Tama hurtles past him, having lost his footing and his balance in the blood on deck, Julian thrusts the Bowie up into Tama's tricep. It doesn't penetrate as fully as Julian would like. Tama is wearing layers to protect him, almost like chain mail. The Maori lands on top of his dead captain and his dying men, but now he's armed only with the *mere*. Julian grabs Tama's fallen blade and pitches it into the sea. Everything is in the sea, and still the sea is not full.

For a suspended moment, Tama is motionless. Then he springs to his feet, from lying to standing in one practiced motion. He leaps into the air, twisting and extending his body and kicks Julian in the chest, knocking him to the ground and the Bowie knife out of his hand. The knife slides away. They scramble to their feet and ram against each other.

They brawl. Bare-fisted they punch each other and block the punches with their short flat paddles. Julian doesn't allow a gap between himself and the Maori. Any space or time he leaves is space or time for Tama to get away or to run and grab the Bowie knife. They punch-block-hold, kick-punch-kick. Julian's every punch is on the half-beat. In three seconds, he lands six blows against Tama. Every time Julian punches, it's to the center of Tama's head. Tama's nose gets broken. Julian's nose gets broken. It doesn't stop either man. Tama has many strengths as a fighter, but he does not do what Julian does, which is block and strike in the same move. Tama blocks, and then punches, and because of that he often misses. Though not often enough.

Tama is dangerous because he is impervious to secondary injury and immune to sharp pain, even extreme pain, so no kick in the shin or a penetrating knife wound in his tricep deters him. No fracture or disability halts his attack. Julian breaks Tama's rib with a palm strike and kicks his knee—twice—yet Tama is not stopped. Tama has been trained to fight through fractures and beatings. He will not fall into shock from blows to his ribs or collarbone. Even a nasty jab with the *mere*, knocking out one of his teeth doesn't stop him.

The only thing that will stop him is a fatal blow. But Tama protects himself as Julian protects himself. He dodges and weaves as Julian dodges and weaves. They both guard their heads with their arms. They cover their temples, their ears, their necks, their points of ultimate weakness. They go at each other like they're taking a bow, chin to chest. They protect their throats. Both men know a strike to the throat means death. No one can recover from a crushed windpipe, not a Maori, not a Viking.

Tama is a vicious fighter. He is more proficient with his *mere* than Julian, and he wields it like a shield and a kettlebell. He gets Julian off balance and smashes him on the head with the club. It feels as if half of Julian's head has blown off, like a fucking electric bulb exploded in his skull. He loses his balance and his own *mere*. Julian grapples with Tama. He knows he can't let Tama hit him again. One more strike to the head, and Julian will be down for good. Krav Maga has trained Julian not to stop fighting until the enemy is motionless or dead. The trouble is, he can't get Tama motionless. He has pitted his power against the Maori but can't finish him off. And now he is without his *mere*, while Tama still has his.

Julian pivots, sidesteps, ducks Tama's blows. He shoulder rolls. Tama keeps swinging the *mere* over and over. The adrenaline masks the pain, but Julian's left forearm is pulp from blocking that fucking club. He and Tama are about the same height, but Julian has twenty pounds of muscle on the kid. Tama is younger but Julian's reflexes are quicker. They have to be, or he'd get beaten to death with the *mere*. It's those reflexes that allow Julian to slip under an overhand *mere* blow, grab Tama's right wrist from the side and wrench it. The wrist snaps. Finally—the *mere* falls from Tama's hand.

The Maori is wobbly for half a second, but that half-second is enough for Julian. He hammerfists Tama, aiming for the temple, trying to end Tama's life, but the Maori jerks his head. Julian must have burst his drum because Tama bleeds from his ear, but he still lowers his chin and barrels forward. Julian barely manages to avoid a side jab into his Adam's apple. But this time he doesn't let a slightly off-balance Tama take a step back and regroup, not even for a half-second. Julian punches him with a brutal left, left, left, right and left again. He lets a dazed Tama grab his right arm, while he hits him again and again with his left, aiming for the throat and breaking the man's jaw instead.

But despite the broken jaw, despite the pummeling, Tama doesn't fall. Julian hits him with the meaty part of the palm directly into his sternum, hits him so hard that Tama drops to his knees as if he's just had a heart attack. Julian steps away, no longer facing Tama but coming at him from the side. He drives his palm flat up into Tama's already broken nose, and snaps Tama's head back. Tama sways, lists, but doesn't fall.

One of his eyes swollen shut, Tama smiles, spitting blood and a tooth out of his mouth.

"Julian!" Shae screams. It's a piercing, gut-wrenching wail. "Watch out!"

Julian's Bowie knife is clutched in Tama's left fist.

Shae's scream gives Julian a blink to jerk his wrist away from the flashing blade and step behind the Maori. Julian grabs him in a choke hold to snap his neck and nearly screams himself. There is searing pain in his right hand. Tama has sliced through Julian's hand to free himself. Julian can no longer get a firm enough grip on Tama's neck to break it. Tama's jaw and throat are slippery with Julian's blood. Tama wrestles free and turns to Julian, who has sunk to his knees, trying to hide his devastating injury.

"You're going to die, whiteman," Tama says. Both men are on their knees.

"Julian!" Shae screams again. She wrestles away from Kiritopa.

"Shae, no!" Julian yells.

Before the crying-out Maori can grab her coats to stop her, Shae throws herself over the side of the ship into the freezing water.

Julian is out of time. He makes a supernatural effort to get to his feet. With his remaining strength, he kicks Tama in the face, pitching him back. The knife slips out of Tama's grasp. Tama crawls toward it and Julian hobbles toward it, hooking his crippled hand to his body. Grabbing at Julian's tunic, Tama tries to get off his knees, to stand up. Julian seizes the knife with his barely closing, swollen left fist, because his other hand, pouring blood, is useless. He lifts his arm in the air, spins around, and thrusts the Bowie blade straight down into Tama's raised face, driving it to the hilt into Tama's eye.

Kiritopa cries, pointing to the water.

Julian limps to the bulwark and falls into the ocean after Shae.

He opens his eyes under water to see where she is and shuts them quickly before he is blinded by salt freeze. She is sinking into the watery darkness. As hard as he can, he paddles down to her. The furs have made her heavy, her boots and cardigans and skins have doubled her weight.

It's almost as if she has deliberately weighted herself down.

But she is alive!

Shae, Shae. Why did you do that? He is dead, we'll be okay, we just have to swim to the surface. Julian tries to unbutton her coats with his one working hand. Hold on to me. I'll pull us out. Briefly he opens his eyes again. The water around them is darkened with his blood.

Her arms reach out to him, grab him around the neck. She pulls him to her, holds him to herself.

Julian stops fighting, stops feeling the piercing cold. His legs stop treading water. He stops pumping with his free arm. Stops or can't?

Stops.

She is barely holding on to him. But he doesn't let go of her.

Wrapping his arms around her, he presses his face to her freezing face.

Shae, I beg you, don't leave me behind. Take me with you. I can't go back. Don't leave me behind, Shae, Julian pleads as their entwined bodies sink into the black abyss of the Southern Sea.

If I die, I will never know how my story ends.

Please, Shae.

I don't want to go back to the world I made with my own two hands.

Paullina Simons is the author of *Tully, The Bronze Horseman*, and other beloved novels. Born and raised in the Soviet Union, she immigrated to the United States in the mid-seventies. She has lived in Rome, London, and Dallas, and now lives in New York with her husband and a dwindling number of her four children.

### Lone Star
Buried in the treasures of the fledgling post-Communist world, Chloe finds a charming American vagabond named Johnny, who carries a guitar, an easy smile - and a lifetime of secrets.

### Bellagrand
A sweeping love story a historical veracity rarely seen in romantic fiction. You'll be turning pages into the wee hours of the night to find out their fate as you find out the fate of Alexander's family before *The Bronze Horseman*.

### Children of Liberty
Deeply emotional and satisfying. Features a cast of characters you'll root for as they fight against their feelings, but discover that true love can never be denied.

### The Summer Garden
A novel of the enduring power of love and commitment The magnificent conclusion to the trilogy, considered to be the Russian *Thorn Birds*.

### Tatiana and Alexander
A novel of the enduring power of love and commitment — against the forces of war and the equally dangerous forces of keeping the peace. The second book in the trilogy that was set in motion when Tatiana fell in love with her Red Army officer, Alexander Belov, in wartime Leningrad in 1941.

### Bronze Horseman
A sweeping love story set in Leningrad at the height of the German blockade of the Russian city during World War II.